217

THE WARDEN

Oxford University Press, Amen House, London E.C.4

GLASGOW NEW YORK TORONTO MELBOURNE WELLINGTON
BOMBAY CALCUTTA MADRAS KARACHI LAHORE DACCA
CAPE TOWN SALISBURY NAIROBI IBADAN ACCRA
KUALA LUMPUR HONG KONG

THE WARDEN

BY

ANTHONY TROLLOPE

WITH

AN INTRODUCTION BY

RICHARD CHURCH

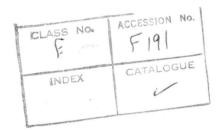

LONDON

OXFORD UNIVERSITY PRESS

ANTHONY TROLLOPE

Born, Keppel Street, Russell Square, London,
24 April 1815
Died, 34 Welbeck Street, Cavendish Square,
London, 6 December 1882

The Warden *was first published in* 1855. *In* The
World's Classics *it was first published in* 1918, *and
reprinted in* 1928, 1932, 1939, 1942, 1949, 1950,
1955, *and* 1958. *Re-set, with an introduction by
Richard Church,* 1961, *and reprinted* 1963

Introduction © *Oxford University Press 1961*

PRINTED IN GREAT BRITAIN

CONTENTS

THE BARSETSHIRE NOVELS

appeared in this order

The Warden (1855)
Barchester Towers (1857)
Doctor Thorne (1858)
Framley Parsonage (1861)
The Small House at Allington (1864)
The Last Chronicle of Barset (1867)

INTRODUCTION

WHEN an author's early work is belatedly praised, he is apt to be somewhat chagrined, and to fear that his powers are in decline. Even Trollope might have had misgivings of this kind, could he observe today how his first essay in the Barchester Novels endears itself more and more to the rising generations of his devotees. But he was not a character to worry fretfully about his standing. He was practical enough to want a substantial and intelligent public, but the niceties of the higher criticism left him unmoved in his own day, and it is safely to be presumed that his ghost, revisiting the Athenaeum coffee-room today and overhearing the enthusiastic conversation of members in reference to his second great burst of popularity, would be equally content to accept praise and appraisal with a degree of good-humoured brusquerie.

As for this second fame which has come to Trollope's novels after some half-century of obscuration, his biographer, Michael Sadleir, had something to say fifteen years ago.

Though period prejudice destroyed him, the prejudice of another period must not be allowed to overstress his resurrection. It is true that his flavour is as agreeable to contemporary mentality as it was repellent to the eighteen-eighties; that his candour and his lack of affectation are grateful to an epoch which inevitably is an epoch of reaction from elaborate trifling. It is true that the last thirty years of declared and undeclared war have given a sudden lustre to such normal peaceful things as form the theme of his many novels. But Trollope deserves greater consideration than as a mere escapist author, and at the same time a judgment more stringent than would be passed by a new-found enthusiasm for his Victorianism.

That extract is from Sadleir's biography of Trollope, a piece of work that would have pleased its subject because of its steady balance, its dignity of tone, its sane judgement. Toward the end of the book, Sadleir sums up with an examination of the qualities which Trollope did not possess; but this negative analysis was in order to distil the following passage, which may be accepted as a final word about so openly elusive an author.

Wherein lies that strange potency, which renders work so featureless, so sober and so undemonstrative an entertainment than which few are more enthralling? It lies surely in his acceptance and his profound understanding of ordinary daily life. In the tale of English literature he is— to put the matter in a phrase—the supreme novelist of acquiescence.

That is a true estimate of this enduring novelist. But the acquiescence, usually taking the form of a patient stoicism in his characters (at least those who survive the storms of daily life) is broken from time to time by an outburst of what may be called heroism, if not romantic gesture. The first volume of the Barchester Novels, *The Warden*, is an example of such an outbreak. Its plot, if it may be said to possess a plot, consists entirely of a statement of the conditions that impose this outbreak, of its form and the family and social conflict it causes (with almost a national relevance), and its tea-cup triumph. As a piece of structure in fiction, with parallel symbolism, it is to be compared with the story of *The Vicar of Wakefield*, another masterpiece in simplicity. Trollope and Goldsmith had a quality in common which they shared with Balzac. This suggestion may sound wholly extravagant when one considers the utter disparity in all other characteristics between these authors: but all three were moved, in their attitude toward their fellow creatures, by a kind of pragmatic optimism. It made them tolerant of individuals, and rebellious toward society as it functions in all the pretences of ambition, fear, and greed. There was a touch of the zany in Goldsmith, and of the monster in Balzac, quite foreign to Trollope's equable nature: but in all his books this close and sympathetic understanding of the men and women who fill the scene is unremitting in its charity, just as his suspicions and even hostility never relaxes toward the representatives of 'society', the crowd, the general opinion, the law, newspapers, ecclesiastics (as distinct from Christians).

The Warden is representative of both these attitudes. The dear old fellow, who is the hero of the tale, and the most loved of all Trollope's characters, stands out so distinctly because he is placed as it were between these two major impulses or passions by which Trollope functioned as a novelist, if not as a Civil Servant. In this book the whole situation, the relationship between the individual and the expectations and claims of society and of *caste*, is brought to a crisis at the beginning, and is disposed of through the Christlike nature of the Warden himself; meek, gentle Mr. Harding, with his younger daughter behind him as a miniature Madonna to give him the confidence to pursue his own revolt against self-interest and the arrogant paternalism of his profession in the Church, as expressed by the formidable Archdeacon, Dr. Grantly, who is to play so firm-footed a part in the later Barchester Novels.

The movement of the tale is thus as simple as the mood in which it is engendered. There is the Warden, living outside the harsh world, among his dozen eremites, in the comfort of the ancient almshouse which he administers, with £800 a year (a nice income at that time). He has been placed in this sinecure by his old friend the Bishop, the father of the Archdeacon. Then a young newcomer to the cloisters, a liberal-minded doctor, who is in love with the younger daughter of the Warden, pokes his nose into the affairs of the almshouse, and begins to act on high principle.

The storm in the tea-cup threatens to slop over into the national saucer, and the belligerent Archdeacon goes to war against the leading newspaper of the land, and the radical fellow who started the trouble. He is about to win, when suddenly quiet little Mr. Harding, who throughout the book has been fretting under the inflammation of his conscience, goes behind the back of his son-in-law the Archdeacon, and resigns!

That is really all the story. But Trollope fills out this almost naïve plot with all the wisdom and experience gathered during his early struggles against poverty, and his close acquaintance with officialdom as a Civil Servant. He knows intimately how things work in Whitehall and Fleet Street, to say nothing of Dean's Yard. So persuasive, indeed, is he in the detail of this the first of the Barchester Novels that posterity has almost been convinced that he must have lived most of his life in Salisbury Cathedral Close. But that is not the fact. He says, in the Autobiography whose candour broke on the world just at the height of the Oscar Wilde period of 'art for art's sake', and ruined his reputation overnight:

In the course of my job with the General Post Office I visited Salisbury, and whilst wandering there one midsummer evening round the purlieus of the cathedral I conceived the story of *The Warden*,—from whence came that series of novels of which Barchester, with its bishops, deans and archdeacon, was the central site. I may as well declare at once that no one at their commencement could have had less reason than myself to presume himself to be able to write about clergymen. I have often been asked in what period of my early life I have lived so long in a cathedral city as to have become intimate with the ways of a Close. I have never lived in any cathedral city,—except London, never knew anything of any Close, and at that time had enjoyed no peculiar intimacy with any clergyman. My archdeacon, who has been said to be lifelike, and for whom I confess that I have all a parent's fond affection, was, I think, the simple result of an effort of my moral consciousness.

So he goes on to explain how all these figures, now so solidly placed in the history of English provincial society, are figments of his imagination. So solid, indeed, that many readers are ready to deny the faculty of imagination to Trollope, and to regard him rather as a stolid and untemperamental reporter.

Trollope had abundance of temperament. There is a Celtic strain in his blood. He could induce thunder, though in daily life it was confined more to echoing round the drawing-room of the Athenaeum than in the open welkin of the outside world. Its outbursts, Jovian as well as jovial, in the books gave them that freshness of atmosphere without which they might, by now, have become stuffy. That may be why Max Beerbohm always said of *The Warden* that it 'was a perfect novel'. He was comparing it, as I have heard him say, with the Turgeniev canon, for its precision and compression, the wisdom in the throw-away gesture, the authoritativeness in the aside.

These stronger effects come out sometimes as professional criticism, as where, in *The Warden*, he suddenly turns on his contemporary Thomas Carlyle:

Dr. Pessimist Anticant was a Scotchman, who had passed a great portion of his early days in Germany; he had studied there with much effect, and had learnt to look with German subtilty into the root of things, and to examine for himself their intrinsic worth and worthlessness. No man ever resolved more bravely than he to accept as good nothing that was evil; to banish from him as evil nothing that was good. 'Tis a pity that he should not have recognised the fact, that in this world no good is unalloyed, and that there is but little evil that has not in it some seed of what is wholly good.

That ironical attitude toward all pronouncers of ukase, all authoritarians, whether in Church or State, breaks out again and again. It makes the relationship between Archdeacon Grantly and his quiet wife, Mr. Harding's elder daughter, 'during the colloquies in the sanctum of their dressing-rooms':

Strangers at Plumstead Episcopi, when they saw the imperious brow with which he commanded silence from the large circle of visitors, children, and servants who came together in the morning to hear him read the word of God, and watched how meekly that wife seated herself behind her basket of keys with a little girl on each side, as she caught that commanding glance; strangers, I say, seeing this, could little guess that some fifteen minutes since she had stoutly held her ground against him, hardly allowing him to open his mouth in his own defence.

Is it surprising that Max Beerbohm loved this book so filially?

Then another aspect of this ironic vein outcrops in a Dickensian form, more outrageous and inclined to vulgarity, as it were with a hearty slap on the back that almost breaks the sober mesh of the story as a whole. Its instance here is in the character of Sir Abraham Haphazard, the Attorney-General, who has been extravagantly briefed by Grantly as a big gun to blow to smithereens the pretensions of this intruding Radical backed by the *Jupiter* (the great daily newspaper whose identity everybody knows). The very phrasing becomes Dickensian in its rhythm:

> Sir Abraham was a tall thin man, with hair prematurely grey, but bearing no other sign of age; he had a slight stoop, in his neck rather than his back, acquired by his constant habit of leaning forward as he addressed his various audiences. He might be fifty years old, and would have looked young for his age, had not constant work hardened his features, and given him the appearance of a machine with a mind. His face was full of intellect, but devoid of natural expression. You would say he was a man to use, and then have done with; a man to be sought for on great emergencies, but ill adapted for ordinary services; a man whom you would ask to defend your property, but to whom you would be sorry to confide your love.

So it works up, in an outburst of exfoliating rhetoric which we would expect to emanate rather from John Street in Bloomsbury than from the sober quarter of Montague Square.

But all this external consideration of *The Warden* does not explain the deepest quality of all, on which Trollope's work is founded; the rock of the very man himself. In this respect, we may apply to him his own words, written of Mr. Harding. 'He had very often been moved to pity—to that inward weeping of the heart for others' woes.' There is the secret of this novelist's survival. He learned in a hard school during his impressionable years. He never forgot the price of suffering, and its reward.

1960   RICHARD CHURCH

1

HIRAM'S HOSPITAL

THE Rev. Septimus Harding was, a few years since, a beneficed clergyman residing in the cathedral town of ——; let us call it Barchester. Were we to name Wells or Salisbury, Exeter, Hereford, or Gloucester, it might be presumed that something personal was intended; and as this tale will refer mainly to the cathedral dignitaries of the town in question, we are anxious that no personality may be suspected. Let us presume that Barchester is a quiet town in the West of England, more remarkable for the beauty of its cathedral and the antiquity of its monuments, than for any commercial prosperity; that the west end of Barchester is the cathedral close, and that the aristocracy of Barchester are the bishop, dean, and canons, with their respective wives and daughters.

Early in life Mr. Harding found himself located at Barchester. A fine voice and a taste for sacred music had decided the position in which he was to exercise his calling, and for many years he performed the easy but not highly paid duties of a minor canon. At the age of forty a small living in the close vicinity of the town increased both his work and his income, and at the age of fifty he became precentor of the cathedral.

Mr. Harding had married early in life, and was the father of two daughters. The eldest, Susan, was born soon after his marriage; the other, Eleanor, not till ten years later. At the time at which we introduce him to our readers he was living as precentor at Barchester with his youngest daughter, then twenty-four years of age; having been many years a widower, and having married his eldest daughter to a son of the bishop, a very short time before his installation to the office of precentor.

Scandal at Barchester affirmed that had it not been for the beauty of his daughter, Mr. Harding would have remained a minor canon; but here probably Scandal lied, as she so often does; for even as a minor canon no one had been more popular among his reverend brethren in the close, than Mr. Harding; and Scandal, before she had reprobated Mr. Harding for being made precentor by his friend the bishop, had loudly blamed the bishop for having so long omitted to do something for his friend Mr. Harding. Be this as it may, Susan Harding, some twelve years since, had married the Rev. Dr. Theophilus Grantly, son of the bishop, archdeacon of Barchester, and rector of Plumstead Episcopi, and her father became, a few months later, precentor of Barchester Cathedral, that office being, as is not usual, in the bishop's gift.

Now there are peculiar circumstances connected with the precentorship which must be explained. In the year 1434 there died at Barchester one John Hiram, who had made money in the town as a wool-stapler, and in his will he left the house in which he died and certain meadows and closes near the town, still called Hiram's Butts, and Hiram's Patch, for the support of twelve superannuated wool-carders, all of whom should have been born and bred and spent their days in Barchester; he also appointed that an almshouse should be built for their abode, with a fitting residence for a warden, which warden was also to receive a certain sum annually out of the rents of the said butts and patches. He, moreover, willed, having had a soul alive to harmony, that the precentor of the cathedral should have the option of being also warden of the almshouses, if the bishop in each case approved.

From that day to this the charity had gone on and prospered—at least, the charity had gone on, and the estates had prospered. Wool-carding in Barchester there was no longer any; so the bishop, dean, and warden, who took it in turn to put in the old men, generally appointed some hangers-on of their own; worn-out gardeners, decrepit grave-diggers, or octogenarian sextons, who thankfully received a comfortable lodging and one shilling and fourpence a day, such being the stipend to which, under the will of John Hiram, they were declared to be entitled. Formerly, indeed—that is, till within some fifty years of the present time—they received but sixpence a day, and their breakfast and dinner was found them at a common table by the warden, such an arrangement being in stricter conformity with the absolute wording of old Hiram's will: but this was thought to be inconvenient, and to suit the tastes of neither warden nor bedesmen, and the daily one shilling and fourpence was substituted with the common consent of all parties, including the bishop and the corporation of Barchester.

Such was the condition of Hiram's twelve old men

when Mr. Harding was appointed warden; but if they may be considered as well-to-do in the world according to their condition, the happy warden was much more so. The patches and butts which, in John Hiram's time, produced hay or fed cows, were now covered with rows of houses; the value of the property had gradually increased from year to year and century to century, and was now presumed by those who knew anything about it, to bring in a very nice income; and by some who knew nothing about it, to have increased to an almost fabulous extent.

The property was farmed by a gentleman in Barchester, who also acted as the bishop's steward—a man whose father and grandfather had been stewards to the bishops of Barchester, and farmers of John Hiram's estate. The Chadwicks had earned a good name in Barchester; they had lived respected by bishops, deans, canons, and precentors; they had been buried in the precincts of the cathedral; they had never been known as griping, hard men, but had always lived comfortably, maintained a good house, and held a high position in Barchester society. The present Mr. Chadwick was a worthy scion of a worthy stock, and the tenants living on the butts and patches, as well as those on the wide episcopal domains of the see, were well pleased to have to do with so worthy and liberal a steward.

For many, many years—records hardly tell how many, probably from the time when Hiram's wishes had been first fully carried out—the proceeds of the estate had been paid by the steward or farmer to the warden, and by him divided among the bedesmen; after which division he paid himself such sums

as became his due. Times had been when the poor
warden got nothing but his bare house, for the patches
had been subject to floods, and the land of Barchester
butts was said to be unproductive; and in these
hard times the warden was hardly able to make out
the daily dole for his twelve dependents. But by
degrees things mended; the patches were drained,
and cottages began to rise upon the butts, and the
wardens, with fairness enough, repaid themselves
for the evil days gone by. In bad times the poor men
had had their due, and therefore in good times they
could expect no more. In this manner the income of
the warden had increased; the picturesque house attached to the hospital had been enlarged and adorned,
and the office had become one of the most coveted of
the snug clerical sinecures attached to our church. It
was now wholly in the bishop's gift, and though the
dean and chapter, in former days, made a stand on the
subject, they had thought it more conducive to their
honour to have a rich precentor appointed by the
bishop, than a poor one appointed by themselves.
The stipend of the precentor of Barchester was eighty
pounds a year. The income arising from the wardenship of the hospital was eight hundred, besides the
value of the house.

Murmurs, very slight murmurs, had been heard in
Barchester—few indeed, and far between—that the
proceeds of John Hiram's property had not been fairly
divided: but they can hardly be said to have been of
such a nature as to have caused uneasiness to any
one: still the thing had been whispered, and Mr.
Harding had heard it. Such was his character in Barchester, so univeral was his popularity, that the very

fact of his appointment would have quieted louder whispers than those which had been heard; but Mr. Harding was an open-handed, just-minded man, and feeling that there might be truth in what had been said, he had, on his instalment, declared his intention of adding twopence a day to each man's pittance, making a sum of sixty-two pounds eleven shillings and fourpence, which he was to pay out of his own pocket. In doing so, however, he distinctly and repeatedly observed to the men, that though he promised for himself, he could not promise for his successors, and that the extra twopence could only be looked on as a gift from himself, and not from the trust. The bedesmen, however, were most of them older than Mr. Harding, and were quite satisfied with the security on which their extra income was based.

This munificence on the part of Mr. Harding had not been unopposed. Mr. Chadwick had mildly but seriously dissuaded him from it; and his strong-minded son-in-law, the archdeacon, the man of whom alone Mr. Harding stood in awe, had urgently, nay, vehemently, opposed so impolitic a concession: but the warden had made known his intention to the hospital before the archdeacon had been able to interfere, and the deed was done.

Hiram's Hospital, as the retreat is called, is a picturesque building enough, and shows the correct taste with which the ecclesiastical architects of those days were imbued. It stands on the banks of the little river, which flows nearly round the cathedral close, being on the side furthest from the town. The London road crosses the river by a pretty one-arched bridge, and, looking from this bridge, the stranger will see the windows of the old men's rooms, each pair of windows separated by a small buttress. A broad gravel walk runs between the building and the river, which is always trim and cared for; and at the end of the walk, under the parapet of the approach to the bridge, is a large and well-worn seat, on which, in mild weather, three or four of Hiram's bedesmen are sure to be seen seated. Beyond this row of buttresses, and further from the bridge, and also further from the water which here suddenly bends, are the pretty oriel windows of Mr. Harding's house, and his well-mown lawn. The entrance to the hospital is from the London road, and is made through a ponderous gateway under a heavy stone arch, unnecessary, one would suppose, at any time, for the protection of twelve old men, but greatly conducive to the good appearance of Hiram's charity. On passing through this portal, never closed to any one from 6 a.m. till 10 p.m., and never open afterwards, except on application to a huge, intricately hung mediæval bell, the handle of which no uninitiated intruder can possibly find, the six doors of the old men's abodes are seen, and beyond them is a slight iron screen, through which the more happy portion of the Barchester élite pass into the Elysium of Mr. Harding's dwelling.

Mr. Harding is a small man, now verging on sixty years, but bearing few of the signs of age; his hair is rather grizzled, though not grey; his eye is very mild, but clear and bright, though the double glasses which are held swinging from his hand, unless when fixed upon his nose, show that time has told upon his sight; his hands are delicately white, and both hands and feet are small; he always wears a black frock coat, black knee-breeches, and black gaiters, and somewhat scandalises some of his more hyper-clerical brethren by a black neck-handkerchief.

Mr. Harding's warmest admirers cannot say that he was ever an industrious man; the circumstances of his life have not called on him to be so; and yet he can hardly be called an idler. Since his appointment to his precentorship, he has published, with all possible additions of vellum, typography, and gilding, a collection of our ancient church music, with some correct dissertations on Purcell, Crotch, and Nares. He has greatly improved the choir of Barchester, which, under his dominion, now rivals that of any cathedral in England. He has taken something more than his fair share in the cathedral services, and has played the violoncello daily to such audiences as he could collect, or, *faute de mieux*, to no audience at all.

We must mention one other peculiarity of Mr. Harding. As we have before stated, he has an income of eight hundred a year, and has no family but his one daughter; and yet he is never quite at ease in money matters. The vellum and gilding of 'Harding's Church Music' cost more than any one knows, except the author, the publisher, and the Rev. Theophilus Grantly, who allows none of his father-in-law's extravagances to escape him. Then he is generous to his daughter, for whose service he keeps a small carriage and pair of ponies. He is, indeed, generous to all, but especially to the twelve old men who are in a peculiar manner under his care. No doubt with such an income Mr. Harding should be above the world,

as the saying is; but, at any rate, he is not above
Archdeacon Theophilus Grantly, for he is always
more or less in debt to his son-in-law, who has, to
a certain extent, assumed the arrangement of the
precentor's pecuniary affairs.

2

THE BARCHESTER REFORMER

Mr. Harding has been now precentor of Barchester for ten years; and, alas, the murmurs respecting the proceeds of Hiram's estate are again becoming audible. It is not that any one begrudges to Mr. Harding the income which he enjoys, and the comfortable place which so well becomes him; but such matters have begun to be talked of in various parts of England. Eager pushing politicians have asserted in the House of Commons, with very telling indignation, that the grasping priests of the Church of England are gorged with the wealth which the charity of former times has left for the solace of the aged, or the education of the young. The well-known case of the Hospital of St. Cross has even come before the law courts of the country, and the struggles of Mr. Whiston, at Rochester, have met with sympathy and support. Men are beginning to say that these things must be looked into.

Mr. Harding, whose conscience in the matter is clear, and who has never felt that he had received a pound from Hiram's will to which he was not entitled, has naturally taken the part of the church in talking over these matters with his friend, the bishop, and his son-in-law, the archdeacon. The archdeacon, indeed, Dr. Grantly, has been somewhat loud in the matter. He is a personal friend of the dignitaries of the Rochester

Chapter, and has written letters in the public press on the subject of that turbulent Dr. Whiston, which, his admirers think, must well nigh set the question at rest. It is also known at Oxford that he is the author of the pamphlet signed 'Sacerdos' on the subject of the Earl of Guildford and St. Cross, in which it is so clearly argued that the manners of the present times do not admit of a literal adhesion to the very words of the founder's will, but that the interests of the church for which the founder was so deeply concerned are best consulted in enabling its bishops to reward those shining lights whose services have been most signally serviceable to Christianity. In answer to this, it is asserted that Henry de Blois, founder of St. Cross, was not greatly interested in the welfare of the reformed church, and that the masters of St. Cross, for many years past, cannot be called shining lights in the service of Christianity; it is, however, stoutly maintained, and no doubt felt, by all the archdeacon's friends, that his logic is conclusive, and has not, in fact, been answered.

With such a tower of strength to back both his arguments and his conscience, it may be imagined that Mr. Harding has never felt any compunction as to receiving his quarterly sum of two hundred pounds. Indeed, the subject has never presented itself to his mind in that shape. He has talked not unfrequently, and heard very much about the wills of old founders and the incomes arising from their estates, during the last year or two; he did even, at one moment, feel a doubt (since expelled by his son-in-law's logic) as to whether Lord Guildford was clearly entitled to receive so enormous an income as he does from the revenues of St. Cross; but that he himself was overpaid with his modest eight hundred pounds;—he who, out of that, voluntarily gave up sixty-two pounds eleven shillings and fourpence a year to his twelve old neighbours;—he who, for the money, does his precentor's work as no precentor has done it before, since Barchester Cathedral was built;—such an idea has never sullied his quiet, or disturbed his conscience.

Nevertheless, Mr. Harding is becoming uneasy at the rumour which he knows to prevail in Barchester on the subject. He is aware that, at any rate, two of his old men have been heard to say, that if every one had his own, they might each have their hundred pounds a year, and live like gentlemen, instead of a beggarly one shilling and sixpence a day; and that they had slender cause to be thankful for a miserable dole of twopence, when Mr. Harding and Mr. Chadwick, between them, ran away with thousands of pounds which good old John Hiram never intended for the like of them. It is the ingratitude of this which stings Mr. Harding. One of this discontented pair, Abel Handy, was put into the hospital by himself; he had been a stone-mason in Barchester, and had broken his thigh by a fall from a scaffolding, while employed about the cathedral; and Mr. Harding had given him the first vacancy in the hospital after the occurrence, although Dr. Grantly had been very anxious to put into it an insufferable clerk of his at Plumstead Episcopi, who had lost all his teeth, and whom the archdeacon hardly knew how to get rid of by other means. Dr. Grantly has not forgotten to remind Mr. Harding how well satisfied with his one and sixpence a day old Joe Mutters would have been, and how injudicious it was on the part of Mr. Harding to allow a radical from the town to get into the concern. Probably Dr. Grantly forgot, at the moment, that the charity was intended for broken-down journeymen of Barchester.

There is living at Barchester a young man, a surgeon, named John Bold, and both Mr. Harding and Dr. Grantly are well aware that to him is owing the pestilent rebellious feeling which has shown itself in the hospital; yes, and the renewal, too, of that disagreeable talk about Hiram's estates which is now again prevalent in Barchester. Nevertheless, Mr. Harding and Mr. Bold are acquainted with each other; we may say, are friends, considering the great disparity in their years. Dr. Grantly, however, has a holy horror of the impious demagogue, as on one occasion he called Bold, when speaking of him to the precentor; and being a more prudent far-seeing man than Mr. Harding, and possessed of a stronger head, he already perceives that this John Bold will work great trouble in Barchester. He considers that he is to be regarded as an enemy, and thinks that he should not be admitted into the camp on anything like friendly terms. As John Bold will occupy much of our attention, we must endeavour to explain who he is, and why he takes the part of John Hiram's bedesmen.

John Bold is a young surgeon, who passed many of his boyish years at Barchester. His father was a physician in the city of London, where he made a moderate fortune, which he invested in houses in that city. The Dragon of Wantly inn and posting-house belonged to him, also four shops in the High Street, and a moiety of the new row of genteel villas (so called in the advertisements), built outside the town just beyond Hiram's Hospital. To one of these Dr. Bold retired to spend the evening of his life, and to die; and here his son John spent his holidays, and afterwards his Christmas vacation when he went from school to study surgery in the London hospitals. Just as John Bold was entitled to write himself surgeon and apothecary, old Dr. Bold died, leaving his Barchester property to his son, and a certain sum in the three per cents. to his daughter Mary, who is some four or five years older than her brother.

John Bold determined to settle himself at Barchester, and look after his own property, as well as the bones and bodies of such of his neighbours as would call upon him for assistance in their troubles. He therefore put up a large brass plate with 'John Bold, Surgeon,' on it, to the great disgust of the nine practitioners who were already trying to get a living out of the bishop, dean, and canons; and began housekeeping with the aid of his sister. At this time he was not more than twenty-four years old; and though he has now been three years in Barchester, we have not heard that he has done much harm to the nine worthy practitioners. Indeed, their dread of him has died away; for in three years he has not taken three fees.

Nevertheless, John Bold is a clever man, and would, with practice, be a clever surgeon; but he has got quite into another line of life. Having enough to live on, he has not been forced to work for bread; he has declined to subject himself to what he calls the drudgery of the profession, by which, I believe, he means the general work of a practising surgeon; and has found other employment. He frequently binds up the bruises and sets the limbs of such of the poorer classes as profess his way of thinking—but this he does for love. Now I will not say that the archdeacon is strictly correct in stigmatising John Bold as a demagogue, for I hardly know how extreme must be a man's opinions before he can be justly so called; but Bold is a strong reformer. His passion is the reform of all abuses; state abuses, church abuses, corporation abuses (he has got himself elected a town councillor of Barchester, and has so worried three consecutive mayors, that it became somewhat difficult to find a fourth), abuses in medical practice, and general abuses in the world at large. Bold is thoroughly sincere in his patriotic endeavours to mend mankind, and there is something to be admired in the energy with which he devotes himself to remedying evil and stopping injustice; but I fear that he is too much imbued with the idea that he has a special mission for reforming. It would be well if one so young had a little more diffidence himself, and more trust in the honest purposes of others—if he could be brought to believe that old customs need not necessarily be evil, and that changes may possibly be dangerous; but no, Bold has all the ardour and all the self-assurance of a Danton, and hurls his anathemas against time-honoured practices with the violence of a French Jacobin.

No wonder that Dr. Grantly should regard Bold as a firebrand, falling, as he has done, almost in the centre of the quiet ancient close of Barchester Cathedral. Dr. Grantly would have him avoided as the plague; but the old Doctor and Mr. Harding were fast friends. Young Johnny Bold used to play as a boy on Mr. Harding's lawn; he has many a time won the precentor's heart by listening with rapt attention to his sacred strains; and since those days, to tell the truth at once, he has nearly won another heart within the same walls.

Eleanor Harding has not plighted her troth to John Bold, nor has she, perhaps, owned to herself how dear to her the young reformer is; but she cannot endure that any one should speak harshly of him. She does not dare to defend him when her brother-in-law is so loud against him; for she, like her father, is somewhat afraid of Dr. Grantly; but she is beginning greatly to dislike the archdeacon. She persuades her father that it would be both unjust and injudicious to banish his young friend because of his politics; she cares little to go to houses where she will not meet him, and, in fact, she is in love.

Nor is there any good reason why Eleanor Harding should not love John Bold. He has all those qualities which are likely to touch a girl's heart. He is brave, eager, and amusing; well-made and good-looking; young and enterprising; his character is in all respects good; he has sufficient income to support a wife; he is her father's friend; and, above all, he is in love with her: then why should not Eleanor Harding be attached to John Bold?

Dr. Grantly, who has as many eyes as Argus, and has long seen how the wind blows in that direction, thinks there are various strong reasons why this should not be so. He has not thought it wise as yet to speak to his father-in-law on the subject, for he knows how foolishly indulgent is Mr. Harding in everything that concerns his daughter; but he has discussed the matter with his all-trusted helpmate, within that sacred recess formed by the clerical bed-curtains at Plumstead Episcopi.

How much sweet solace, how much valued counsel has our archdeacon received within that sainted enclosure! 'Tis there alone that he unbends, and comes down from his high church pedestal to the level of a mortal man. In the world Dr. Grantly never lays aside that demeanour which so well becomes him. He has all the dignity of an ancient saint with the sleekness of a modern bishop; he is always the same; he is always the archdeacon; unlike Homer, he never nods. Even with his father-in-law, even with the bishop and dean, he maintains that sonorous tone and lofty deportment which strikes awe into the young hearts of Barchester, and absolutely cows the whole parish of Plumstead Episcopi. 'Tis only when he has exchanged that ever-new shovel hat for a tasselled nightcap, and those shining black habiliments for his accustomed *robe de nuit*, that Dr. Grantly talks, and looks, and thinks like an ordinary man.

Many of us have often thought how severe a trial of faith must this be to the wives of our great church dignitaries. To us these men are personifications of St. Paul; their very gait is a speaking sermon; their clean and sombre apparel exacts from us faith and submission, and the cardinal virtues seem to hover round their sacred hats. A dean or archbishop, in the garb of his order, is sure of our reverence, and a well-got-up bishop fills our very souls with awe. But how can this feeling be perpetuated in the bosoms of those who see the bishops without their aprons, and the archdeacons even in a lower state of dishabille?

Do we not all know some reverend, all but sacred, personage before whom our tongue ceases to be loud and our step to be elastic? But were we once to see him stretch himself beneath the bed-clothes, yawn widely, and bury his face upon his pillow, we could chatter before him as glibly as before a doctor or a lawyer. From some such cause, doubtless, it arose that our archdeacon listened to the counsels of his wife, though he considered himself entitled to give counsel to every other being whom he met.

'My dear,' he said, as he adjusted the copious folds of his nightcap, 'there was that John Bold at your father's again to-day. I must say your father is very imprudent.'

'He is imprudent—he always was,' replied Mrs. Grantly, speaking from under the comfortable bed-clothes. 'There's nothing new in that.'

'No, my dear, there's nothing new—I know that; but, at the present juncture of affairs, such imprudence is—is—I'll tell you what, my dear, if he does not take care what he's about, John Bold will be off with Eleanor.'

'I think he will, whether papa takes care or no; and why not?'

'Why not!' almost screamed the archdeacon, giving so rough a pull at his nightcap as almost to bring it over his nose; 'why not!—that pestilent, interfering upstart, John Bold—the most vulgar young person I ever met! Do you know that he is

18

meddling with your father's affairs in a most uncalled-for—most——' And being at a loss for an epithet sufficiently injurious, he finished his expressions of horror by muttering, 'Good heavens!' in a manner that had been found very efficacious in clerical meetings of the diocese. He must for the moment have forgotten where he was.

'As to his vulgarity, archdeacon' (Mrs. Grantly had never assumed a more familiar term than this in addressing her husband), 'I don't agree with you. Not that I like Mr. Bold—he is a great deal too conceited for me; but then Eleanor does, and it would be the best thing in the world for papa if they were to marry. Bold would never trouble himself about Hiram's Hospital if he were papa's son-in-law.' And the lady turned herself round under the bed-clothes, in a manner to which the doctor was well accustomed, and which told him, as plainly as words, that as far as she was concerned the subject was over for that night.

'Good heavens!' murmured the doctor again—he was evidently much put beside himself.

Dr. Grantly is by no means a bad man; he is exactly the man which such an education as his was most likely to form; his intellect being sufficient for such a place in the world, but not sufficient to put him in advance of it. He performs with a rigid constancy such of the duties of a parish clergyman as are, to his thinking, above the sphere of his curate, but it is as an archdeacon that he shines.

We believe, as a general rule, that either a bishop or his archdeacons have sinecures: where a bishop works, archdeacons have but little to do, and *vice versa.* In the diocese of Barchester the Archdeacon of Barchester does the work. In that capacity he is diligent, authoritative, and, as his friends particularly boast, judicious. His great fault is an overbearing assurance of the virtues and claims of his order, and his great foible is an equally strong confidence in the dignity of his own manner and the eloquence of his own words. He is a moral man, believing the precepts which he teaches, and believing also that he acts up to them; though we cannot say that he would give his coat to the man who took his cloak, or that he is prepared to forgive his brother even seven times. He is severe enough in exacting his dues, considering that any laxity in this respect would endanger the security of the church; and, could he have his way, he would consign to darkness and perdition, not only every individual reformer, but every committee and every commission that would even dare to ask a question respecting the appropriation of church revenues.

'They are church revenues: the laity admit it. Surely the church is able to administer her own revenues.' 'Twas thus he was accustomed to argue, when the sacrilegious doings of Lord John Russell and others were discussed either at Barchester or at Oxford.

It was no wonder that Dr. Grantly did not like John Bold, and that his wife's suggestion that he should become closely connected with such a man dismayed him. To give him his due, the archdeacon never wanted courage; he was quite willing to meet his enemy on any field and with any weapon. He had that belief in his own arguments that he felt sure of success, could he only be sure of a fair fight on the part of his adversary. He had no idea that John Bold could really prove that the income of the hospital was malappropriated; why then, should peace be sought for on such base terms? What! bribe an unbelieving enemy of the church with the sister-in-law of one dignitary and the daughter of another—with a young lady whose connections with the diocese and chapter of Barchester were so close as to give her an undeniable claim to a husband endowed with some of its sacred wealth! When Dr. Grantly talks of unbelieving enemies, he does not mean to imply want of belief in the doctrines of the church, but an equally dangerous scepticism as to its purity in money matters.

Mrs. Grantly is not usually deaf to the claims of the high order to which she belongs. She and her husband rarely disagree as to the tone with which the church should be defended; how singular, then, that in such a case as this she should be willing to succumb! The archdeacon again murmurs 'Good heavens!' as he lays himself beside her, but he does so in a voice audible only to himself, and he repeats it till sleep relieves him from deep thought.

Mr. Harding himself has seen no reason why his daughter should not love John Bold. He has not been unobservant of her feelings, and perhaps his deepest regret at the part which he fears Bold is about to take regarding the hospital arises from the dread that he may be separated from his daughter, or that she may be separated from the man she loves. He has never spoken to Eleanor about her lover; he is the last man in the world to allude to such a subject unconsulted, even with his own daughter; and had he considered that he had ground to disapprove of Bold, he would have removed her, or forbidden him his house; but he saw no such ground. He would probably have preferred a second clerical son-in-law, for Mr. Harding, also, is attached to his order; and, failing in that, he would at any rate have wished that so near a connection should have thought alike with him on church matters. He would not, however, reject the man his daughter loved because he differed on such subjects with himself.

Hitherto Bold had taken no steps in the matter in any way annoying to Mr. Harding personally. Some months since, after a severe battle, which cost him not a little money, he gained a victory over a certain old turnpike woman in the neighbourhood, of whose charges another old woman had complained to him. He got the act of Parliament relating to the trust, found that his protégée had been wrongly taxed, rode through the gate himself, paying the toll, then brought an action against the gate-keeper, and proved that all people coming up a certain by-lane, and going down a certain other by-lane, were toll-free. The fame of his success spread widely abroad, and he began to be looked on as the upholder of the rights of the poor of Barchester. Not long after this success, he heard from different quarters that Hiram's bedesmen were treated as paupers, whereas the property to which they were, in effect, heirs was very large; and he was instigated by the lawyer whom he had employed in the case of the turnpike to call upon Mr. Chadwick for a statement as to the funds of the estate.

Bold had often expressed his indignation at the malappropriation of church funds in general, in the hearing of his friend the precentor; but the conversation had never referred to anything at Barchester; and when Finney, the attorney, induced him to interfere with the affairs of the hospital, it was against Mr. Chadwick that his efforts were to be directed. Bold soon found that if he interfered with Mr. Chadwick as steward, he must also interfere with Mr. Harding as warden; and though he regretted the situation in which this would place him, he was not the man to flinch from his undertaking from personal motives.

As soon as he had determined to take the matter in hand, he set about his work with his usual energy. He got a copy of John Hiram's will, of the wording of which he made himself perfectly master. He ascertained the extent of the property, and as nearly as he could the value of it; and made out a schedule of what he was informed was the present distribution of its income. Armed with these particulars, he called on Mr. Chadwick, having given that gentleman notice of his visit; and asked him for a statement of the income and expenditure of the hospital for the last twenty-five years.

This was of course refused, Mr. Chadwick alleging that he had no authority for making public the concerns of a property in managing which he was only a paid servant.

'And who is competent to give you that authority, Mr. Chadwick?' asked Bold.

'Only those who employ me, Mr. Bold,' said the steward.

'And who are those, Mr. Chadwick?' demanded Bold.

Mr. Chadwick begged to say that if these inquiries were made merely out of curiosity, he must decline answering them: if Mr. Bold had any ulterior proceeding in view, perhaps it would be desirable that any necessary information should be sought for in a professional way by a professional man. Mr. Chadwick's attorneys were Messrs. Cox and Cummins, of Lincoln's Inn. Mr. Bold took down the address of Cox and Cummins, remarked that the weather was cold for the time of the year, and wished Mr. Chadwick good-morning. Mr. Chadwick said it was cold for June, and bowed him out.

He at once went to his lawyer, Finney. Now, Bold was not very fond of his attorney, but, as he said, he merely wanted a man who knew the forms of law, and who would do what he was told for his money. He had no idea of putting himself in the hands of a lawyer. He wanted law from a lawyer as he did a coat from a tailor, because he could not make it so well himself; and he thought Finney the fittest man in Barchester for his purpose. In one respect, at any rate, he was right; Finney was humility itself.

Finney advised an instant letter to Cox and Cummins, mindful of his six-and-eightpence. 'Slap at them at once, Mr. Bold. Demand categorically and explicitly a full statement of the affairs of the hospital.'

'Suppose I were to see Mr. Harding first,' suggested Bold.

'Yes, yes, by all means,' said the acquiescing Finney; 'though, perhaps, as Mr. Harding is no man

of business, it may lead—lead to some little difficulties; but perhaps you're right. Mr. Bold, I don't
think seeing Mr. Harding can do any harm.' Finney
saw from the expression of his client's face that he
intended to have his own way.

3

THE BISHOP OF BARCHESTER

BOLD at once repaired to the hospital. The day was now far advanced, but he knew that Mr. Harding dined in the summer at four, that Eleanor was accustomed to drive in the evening, and that he might therefore probably find Mr. Harding alone. It was between seven and eight when he reached the slight iron gate leading into the precentor's garden, and though, as Mr. Chadwick observed, the day had been cold for June, the evening was mild, and soft, and sweet. The little gate was open. As he raised the latch he heard the notes of Mr. Harding's violoncello from the far end of the garden, and, advancing before the house and across the lawn, he found him playing: and not without an audience. The musician was seated in a garden-chair just within the summer house, so as to allow the violoncello which he held between his knees to rest upon the dry stone flooring; before him stood a rough music desk, on which was open a page of that dear sacred book, that much-laboured and much-loved volume of church music, which had cost so many guineas; and around sat, and lay, and stood, and leaned, ten of the twelve old men who dwelt with him beneath old John Hiram's roof. The two reformers were not there. I will not say that in their hearts they were conscious of any wrong done or to be done to their mild warden, but latterly they had kept aloof from him, and his music was no longer to their taste.

It was amusing to see the positions, and eager listening faces of these well-to-do old men. I will not say that they all appreciated the music which they heard, but they were intent on appearing to do so; pleased at being where they were, they were determined, as far as in them lay, to give pleasure in return; and they were not unsuccessful. It gladdened the precentor's heart to think that the old bedesmen whom he loved so well admired the strains which were to him so full of almost ecstatic joy; and he used to boast that such was the air of the hospital, as to make it a precinct specially fit for the worship of St. Cecilia.

Immediately before him, on the extreme corner of the bench which ran round the summer-house, sat one old man, with his handkerchief smoothly lain upon his knees, who did enjoy the moment, or acted enjoyment well. He was one on whose large frame many years, for he was over eighty, had made small havoc, —he was still an upright, burly, handsome figure, —with an open, ponderous brow, round which clung a few, though very few, thin grey locks. The coarse black gown of the hospital, the breeches, and buckled shoes became him well; and as he sat with his hands folded on his staff, and his chin resting on his hands, he was such a listener as most musicians would be glad to welcome.

This man was certainly the pride of the hospital. It had always been the custom that one should be selected as being to some extent in authority over the others; and though Mr. Bunce, for such was his

The Warden

name, and so he was always designated by his inferior brethren, had no greater emoluments than they, he had assumed, and well knew how to maintain, the dignity of his elevation. The precentor delighted to call him his sub-warden, and was not ashamed, occasionally, when no other guest was there, to bid him sit down by the same parlour fire, and drink the full glass of port which was placed near him. Bunce never went without the second glass, but no entreaty ever made him take a third.

'Well, well, Mr. Harding; you're too good, much too good,' he'd always say, as the second glass was filled; but when that was drunk, and the half hour over, Bunce stood erect, and with a benediction which his patron valued, retired to his own abode. He knew the world too well to risk the comfort of such halcyon moments, by prolonging them till they were disagreeable.

Mr. Bunce, as may be imagined, was most strongly opposed to innovation. Not even Dr. Grantly had a more holy horror of those who would interfere in the affairs of the hospital; he was every inch a churchman, and though he was not very fond of Dr. Grantly personally, that arose from there not being room in the hospital for two people so much alike as the doctor and himself, rather than from any dissimilarity in feeling. Mr. Bunce was inclined to think that the warden and himself could manage the hospital without further assistance; and that, though the bishop was the constitutional visitor, and as such entitled to special reverence from all connected with John Hiram's will, John Hiram never intended that his affairs should be interfered with by an archdeacon.

84

At the present moment, however, these cares were off his mind, and he was looking at his warden, as though he thought the music heavenly, and the musician hardly less so.

As Bold walked silently over the lawn, Mr. Harding did not at first perceive him, and continued to draw his bow slowly across the plaintive wires; but he soon found from his audience that some stranger was there, and looking up, began to welcome his young friend with frank hospitality.

'Pray, Mr. Harding; pray don't let me disturb you,' said Bold; 'you know how fond I am of sacred music.'

'Oh! it's nothing,' said the precentor, shutting up the book and then opening it again as he saw the delightfully imploring look of his old friend Bunce. 'Oh, Bunce, Bunce, Bunce, I fear that after all thou art but a flatterer. Well, I'll just finish it then; it's a favourite little bit of Bishop's; and then, Mr. Bold, we'll have a stroll and a chat till Eleanor comes in and gives us tea.' And so Bold sat down on the soft turf to listen, or rather to think how, after such sweet harmony, he might best introduce a theme of so much discord, to disturb the peace of him who was so ready to welcome him kindly.

Bold thought that the performance was soon over, for he felt that he had a somewhat difficult task, and he almost regretted the final leave-taking of the last of the old men, slow as they were in going through their adieus.

Bold's heart was in his mouth, as the precentor made some ordinary but kind remark as to the friendliness of the visit.

'One evening call,' said he, 'is worth ten in the morning. It's all formality in the morning; real social talk never begins till after dinner. That's why I dine early, so as to get as much as I can of it.'

'Quite true, Mr. Harding,' said the other; 'but I fear I've reversed the order of things, and I owe you much apology for troubling you on business at such an hour; but it is on business that I have called just now.'

Mr. Harding looked blank and annoyed; there was something in the tone of the young man's voice which told him that the interview was intended to be disagreeable, and he shrank back at finding his kindly greeting so repulsed.

'I wish to speak to you about the hospital,' continued Bold.

'Well, well, anything I can tell you I shall be most happy——'

'It's about the accounts.'

'Then, my dear fellow, I can tell you nothing, for I'm as ignorant as a child. All I know is, that they pay me £800 a year. Go to Chadwick, he knows all about the accounts; and now tell me, will poor Mary Jones ever get the use of her limb again?'

'Well, I think she will, if she's careful; but, Mr. Harding, I hope you won't object to discuss with me what I have to say about the hospital.'

Mr. Harding gave a deep, long-drawn sigh. He did object, very strongly object, to discuss any such subject with John Bold; but he had not the business tact of Mr. Chadwick, and did not know how to relieve himself from the coming evil; he sighed sadly, but made no answer.

'I have the greatest regard for you, Mr. Harding,' continued Bold; 'the truest respect, the most sincere——'

'Thank ye, thank ye, Mr. Bold,' interjaculated the precentor somewhat impatiently; 'I'm much obliged, but never mind that; I'm as likely to be in the wrong as another man—quite as likely.'

'But, Mr. Harding, I must express what I feel, lest you should think there is personal enmity in what I'm going to do.'

'Personal enmity! Going to do! Why, you're not going to cut my throat, nor put me into the Ecclesiastical Court——'

Bold tried to laugh, but he couldn't. He was quite in earnest, and determined in his course, and couldn't make a joke of it. He walked on awhile in silence before he recommenced his attack, during which Mr. Harding, who had still the bow in his hand, played rapidly on an imaginary violoncello. 'I fear there is reason to think that John Hiram's will is not carried out to the letter, Mr. Harding,' said the young man at last; 'and I have been asked to see into it.'

'Very well, I've no objection on earth; and now we need not say another word about it.'

'Only one word more, Mr. Harding. Chadwick has referred me to Cox and Cummins, and I think it my duty to apply to them for some statement about the hospital. In what I do I may appear to be interfering with you, and I hope you will forgive me for doing so.'

'Mr. Bold,' said the other, stopping, and speaking with some solemnity, 'if you act justly, say nothing in this matter but the truth, and use no unfair weapons

31

in carrying out your purposes, I shall have nothing to forgive. I presume you think I am not entitled to the income I receive from the hospital, and that others are entitled to it. Whatever some may do, I shall never attribute to you base motives because you hold an opinion opposed to my own and adverse to my interests: pray do what you consider to be your duty; I can give you no assistance, neither will I offer you any obstacle. Let me, however, suggest to you, that you can in no wise forward your views nor I mine, by any discussion between us. Here comes Eleanor and the ponies, and we'll go in to tea.'

Bold, however, felt that he could not sit down at ease with Mr. Harding and his daughter after what had passed, and therefore excused himself with much awkward apology; and merely raising his hat and bowing as he passed Eleanor and the pony chair, left her in disappointed amazement at his departure.

Mr. Harding's demeanour certainly impressed Bold with a full conviction that the warden felt that he stood on strong grounds, and almost made him think that he was about to interfere without due warrant in the private affairs of a just and honourable man; but Mr. Harding himself was anything but satisfied with his own view of the case.

In the first place, he wished for Eleanor's sake to think well of Bold and to like him, and yet he could not but feel disgusted at the arrogance of his conduct. What right had he to say that John Hiram's will was not fairly carried out? But then the question would arise within his heart, Was that will fairly acted on? Did John Hiram mean that the warden of his hospital should receive considerably more out of the legacy

than all the twelve old men together for whose behoof
the hospital was built? Could it be possible that John
Bold was right, and that the reverend warden of the
hospital had been for the last ten years and more the
unjust recipient of an income legally and equitably
belonging to others? What if it should be proved
before the light of day that he, whose life had been so
happy, so quiet, so respected, had absorbed £800 to
which he had no title, and which he could never repay?
I do not say that he feared that such was really the
case; but the first shade of doubt now fell across his
mind, and from this evening, for many a long, long
day, our good, kind loving warden was neither happy
nor at ease.

Thoughts of this kind, these first moments of
much misery, oppressed Mr. Harding as he sat
sipping his tea, absent and ill at ease. Poor Eleanor
felt that all was not right, but her ideas as to the cause
of the evening's discomfort did not go beyond her
lover, and his sudden and uncivil departure. She
thought there must have been some quarrel between
Bold and her father, and she was half angry with both,
though she did not attempt to explain to herself why
she was so.

Mr. Harding thought long and deeply over these
things, both before he went to bed and after it, as he
lay awake, questioning within himself the validity of
his claim to the income which he enjoyed. It seemed
clear at any rate that, however unfortunate he might
be at having been placed in such a position, no one
could say that he ought either to have refused the
appointment first, or to have rejected the income
afterwards. All the world—meaning the ecclesiastical

world as confined to the English church—knew that the wardenship of the Barchester Hospital was a snug sinecure, but no one had ever been blamed for accepting it. To how much blame, however, would he have been open had he rejected it! How mad would he have been thought had he declared, when the situation was vacant and offered to him, that he had scruples as to receiving £800 a year from John Hiram's property, and that he had rather some stranger should possess it! How would Dr. Grantly have shaken his wise head, and have consulted with his friends in the close as to some decent retreat for the coming insanity of the poor minor canon! If he was right in accepting the place, it was clear to him also that he would be wrong in rejecting any part of the income attached to it. The patronage was a valuable appanage of the bishopric; and surely it would not be his duty to lessen the value of that preferment which had been bestowed on himself; surely he was bound to stand by his order.

But somehow these arguments, though they seemed logical, were not satisfactory. Was John Hiram's will fairly carried out? that was the true question: and if not, was it not his especial duty to see that this was done—his especial duty, whatever injury it might do to his order—however ill such duty might be received by his patron and his friends? At the idea of his friends, his mind turned unhappily to his son-in-law. He knew well how strongly he would be supported by Dr. Grantly, if he could bring himself to put his case into the archdeacon's hands and to allow him to fight the battle; but he knew also that he would find no sympathy there for his doubts, no friendly feeling, no inward comfort. Dr. Grantly would be ready enough to take up his cudgel against all comers on behalf of the church militant, but he would do so on the distasteful ground of the church's infallibility. Such a contest would give no comfort to Mr. Harding's doubts. He was not so anxious to prove himself right, as to be so.

I have said before that Dr. Grantly was the working man of the diocese, and that his father the bishop was somewhat inclined to an idle life. So it was; but the bishop, though he had never been an active man, was one whose qualities had rendered him dear to all who knew him. He was the very opposite to his son; he was a bland and a kind old man, opposed by every feeling to authoritative demonstrations and episcopal ostentation. It was perhaps well for him, in his situation, that his son had early in life been able to do that which he could not well do when he was younger, and which he could not have done at all now that he was over seventy. The bishop knew how to entertain the clergy of his diocese, to talk easy small-talk with the rectors' wives, and put curates at their ease; but it required the strong hand of the archdeacon to deal with such as were refractory either in their doctrines or their lives.

The bishop and Mr. Harding loved each other warmly. They had grown old together, and had together spent many, many years in clerical pursuits and clerical conversation. When one of them was a bishop and the other only a minor canon they were even then much together; but since their children had married, and Mr. Harding had become warden and precentor, they were all in all to each other. I will not say that they managed the diocese between them, but they spent much time in discussing the man who did, and in forming little plans to mitigate his wrath against church delinquents, and soften his aspirations for church dominion.

Mr. Harding determined to open his mind, and confess his doubts to his old friend; and to him he went on the morning after John Bold's uncourteous visit.

Up to this period no rumour of these cruel proceedings against the hospital had reached the bishop's ears. He had doubtless heard that men existed who questioned his right to present to a sinecure of £800 a year, as he had heard from time to time of some special immorality or disgraceful disturbance in the usually decent and quiet city of Barchester: but all he did, and all he was called on to do, on such occasions, was to shake his head, and to beg his son, the great dictator, to see that no harm happened to the church.

It was a long story that Mr. Harding had to tell before he made the bishop comprehend his own view of the case; but we need not follow him through the tale. At first the bishop counselled but one step, recommended but one remedy, had but one medicine in his whole pharmacopœia strong enough to touch so grave a disorder—he prescribed the archdeacon. 'Refer him to the archdeacon,' he repeated, as Mr. Harding spoke of Bold and his visit. 'The archdeacon will set you quite right about that,' he kindly said, when his friend spoke with hesitation of the justness of his cause. 'No man has got up all that so well as the archdeacon;' but the dose, though large, failed to quiet the patient; indeed it almost produced nausea.

'But, bishop,' said he, 'did you ever read John Hiram's will?'

The bishop thought probably he had, thirty-five years ago, when first instituted to his see, but could not state positively: however, he very well knew that he had the absolute right to present to the wardenship, and that the income of the warden had been regularly settled.

'But, bishop, the question is, who has the power to settle it? If, as this young man says, the will provides that the proceeds of the property are to be divided into shares, who has the power to alter these provisions?' The bishop had an indistinct idea that they altered themselves by the lapse of years; that a kind of ecclesiastical statute of limitation barred the rights of the twelve bedesmen to any increase of income arising from the increased value of property. He said something about tradition; more of the many learned men who by their practice had confirmed the present arrangement; then went at some length into the propriety of maintaining the due difference in rank and income between a beneficed clergyman and certain poor old men who were dependent on charity; and concluded his argument by another reference to the archdeacon.

The precentor sat thoughtfully gazing at the fire, and listening to the good-natured reasoning of his friend. What the bishop said had a sort of comfort in it, but it was not a sustaining comfort. It made Mr. Harding feel that many others—indeed, all others of his own order—would think him right; but it failed to prove to him that he truly was so.

'Bishop,' said he, at last, after both had sat silent

for a while, 'I should deceive you and myself too, if I did not tell you that I am very unhappy about this. Suppose that I cannot bring myself to agree with Dr. Grantly!—that I find, after inquiry, that the young man is right, and that I am wrong—what then?'

The two old men were sitting near each other— so near that the bishop was able to lay his hand upon the other's knee, and he did so with a gentle pressure. Mr. Harding well knew what that pressure meant. The bishop had no further argument to adduce; he could not fight for the cause as his son would do; he could not prove all the precentor's doubts to be groundless; but he could sympathise with his friend, and he did so; and Mr. Harding felt that he had received that for which he came. There was another period of silence, after which the bishop asked, with a degree of irritable energy very unusual with him, whether this 'pestilent intruder' (meaning John Bold) had any friends in Barchester.

Mr. Harding had fully made up his mind to tell the bishop everything; to speak of his daughter's love, as well as his own troubles; to talk of John Bold in his double capacity of future son-in-law and present enemy; and though he felt it to be sufficiently disagreeable, now was his time to do it.

'He is very intimate at my own house, bishop.' The bishop stared. He was not so far gone in orthodoxy and church militancy as his son, but still he could not bring himself to understand how so declared an enemy of the establishment could be admitted on terms of intimacy into the house, not only of so firm a pillar as Mr. Harding, but one so much injured as the warden of the hospital.

'Indeed, I like Mr. Bold much, personally,' continued the disinterested victim; 'and to tell you the "truth" '—he hesitated as he brought out the dreadful tidings—'I have sometimes thought it not improbable that he would be my second son-in-law.' The bishop did not whistle: we believe that they lose the power of doing so on being consecrated; and that in these days one might as easily meet a corrupt judge as a whistling bishop; but he looked as though he would have done so, but for his apron.

What a brother-in-law for the archdeacon! what an alliance for Barchester close! what a connection for even the episcopal palace! The bishop, in his simple mind, felt no doubt that John Bold, had he so much power, would shut up all cathedrals, and probably all parish churches; distribute all tithes among Methodists, Baptists, and other savage tribes; utterly annihilate the sacred bench, and make shovel hats and lawn sleeves as illegal as cowls, sandals, and sackcloth! Here was a nice man to be initiated into the comfortable arcana of ecclesiastical snuggeries; one who doubted the integrity of parsons, and probably disbelieved the Trinity!

Mr. Harding saw what an effect his communication had made, and almost repented the openness of his disclosure; he, however, did what he could to moderate the grief of his friend and patron. 'I do not say that there is any engagement between them. Had there been, Eleanor would have told me; I know her well enough to be assured that she would have done so; but I see that they are fond of each other; and as a man and a father, I have had no objection to urge against their intimacy.'

'But, Mr. Harding,' said the bishop, 'how are you to oppose him, if he is your son-in-law?'

'I don't mean to oppose him; it is he who opposes me; if anything is to be done in defence, I suppose Chadwick will do it. I suppose——'

'Oh, the archdeacon will see to that: were the young man twice his brother-in-law, the archdeacon will never be deterred from doing what he feels to be right.'

Mr. Harding reminded the bishop that the archdeacon and the reformer were not yet brothers, and very probably never would be; exacted from him a promise that Eleanor's name should not be mentioned in any discussion between the father bishop and son archdeacon respecting the hospital; and then took his departure, leaving his poor old friend bewildered, amazed, and confounded.

4

HIRAM'S BEDESMEN

THE parties most interested in the movement which is about to set Barchester by the ears were not the foremost to discuss the merit of the question, as is often the case; but when the bishop, the archdeacon, the warden, the steward, and Messrs. Cox and Cummins, were all busy with the matter, each in his own way, it is not to be supposed that Hiram's bedesmen themselves were altogether passive spectators. Finney, the attorney, had been among them, asking sly questions, and raising immoderate hopes, creating a party hostile to the warden, and establishing a corps in the enemy's camp, as he figuratively calls it to himself. Poor old men; whoever may be righted or wronged by this inquiry, they at any rate will assuredly be only injured: to them it can only be an unmixed evil. How can their lot be improved? all their wants are supplied; every comfort is administered; they have warm houses, good clothes, plentiful diet, and rest after a life of labour; and above all, that treasure so inestimable in declining years, a true and kind friend to listen to their sorrows, watch over their sickness, and administer comfort as regards this world, and the world to come!

John Bold sometimes thinks of this, when he is talking loudly of the rights of the bedesmen, whom he has taken under his protection; but he quiets the suggestion within his breast with the high-sounding name of justice: 'Fiat justitia ruat cœlum.' These old men should, by rights, have one hundred pounds a year instead of one shilling and sixpence a day, and the warden should have two hundred or three hundred pounds instead of eight hundred pounds. What is unjust must be wrong; what is wrong should be righted; and if he declined the task, who else would do it?

'Each one of you is clearly entitled to one hundred pounds a year by common law:' such had been the important whisper made by Finney into the ears of Abel Handy, and by him retailed to his eleven brethren.

Too much must not be expected from the flesh and blood even of John Hiram's bedesmen, and the positive promise of one hundred a year to each of the twelve old men had its way with most of them. The great Bunce was not to be wiled away, and was upheld in his orthodoxy by two adherents. Abel Handy, who was the leader of the aspirants after wealth, had, alas, a stronger following. No less than five of the twelve soon believed that his views were just, making with their leader a moiety of the hospital. The other three, volatile unstable minds, vacillated between the two chieftains, now led away by the hope of gold, now anxious to propitiate the powers that still existed.

It had been proposed to address a petition to the bishop as visitor, praying his lordship to see justice done to the legal recipients of John Hiram's Charity, and to send copies of this petition and of the reply it would elicit to all the leading London papers, and thereby to obtain notoriety for the subject. This it was thought would pave the way for ulterior legal proceedings. It would have been a great thing to have had the signatures and marks of all the twelve injured legatees; but this was impossible: Bunce would have cut his hand off sooner than have signed it. It was then suggested by Finney that if even eleven could be induced to sanction the document, the one obstinate recusant might have been represented as unfit to judge on such a question—in fact, as being *non compos mentis*—and the petition would have been taken as representing the feeling of the men. But this could not be done: Bunce's friends were as firm as himself, and as yet only six crosses adorned the document. It was the more provoking, as Bunce himself could write his name legibly, and one of those three doubting souls had for years boasted of like power, and possessed, indeed, a Bible, in which he was proud to show his name written by himself some thirty years ago—'Job Skulpit'; but it was thought that Job Skulpit, having forgotten his scholarship, on that account recoiled from the petition, and that the other doubters would follow as he led them. A petition signed by half the hospital would have but a poor effect.

It was in Skulpit's room that the petition was now lying, waiting such additional signatures as Abel Handy, by his eloquence, could obtain for it. The six marks it bore were duly attested, thus:

his	his	his
Abel + Handy,	Greg^y + Moody,	Mathew + Spriggs,
mark	mark	mark

etc., and places were duly designated in pencil for those brethren who were now expected to join: for

43

Skulpit alone was left a spot on which his genuine signature might be written in fair clerk-like style. Handy had brought in the document, and spread it out on the small deal table, and was now standing by it persuasive and eager. Moody had followed with an inkhorn, carefully left behind by Finney; and Spriggs bore aloft, as though it were a sword, a well-worn ink-black pen, which from time to time he endeavoured to thrust into Skulpit's unwilling hand.

With the learned man were his two abettors in indecision, William Gazy and Jonathan Crumple. If ever the petition were to be forwarded, now was the time, so said Mr. Finney; and great was the anxiety on the part of those whose one hundred pounds a year, as they believed, mainly depended on the document in question.

'To be kept out of all that money,' as the avaricious Moody had muttered to his friend Handy, 'by an old fool saying that he can write his own name like his betters!'

'Well, Job,' said Handy, trying to impart to his own sour, ill-omened visage a smile of approbation, in which he greatly failed; 'so you're ready now, Mr. Finney says; here's the place, d'ye see,'—and he put his huge brown finger down on the dirty paper,—'name or mark, it's all one. Come along, old boy; if so be we're to have the spending of this money, why the sooner the better—that's my maxim.'

'To be sure,' said Moody. 'We a'n't none of us so young; we can't stay waiting for old Catgut no longer.'

It was thus these miscreants named our excellent friend. The nickname he could easily have forgiven, but the allusion to the divine source of all his melodious joy would have irritated even him. Let us hope he never knew the insult.

'Only think, old Billy Gazy,' said Spriggs, who rejoiced in greater youth than his brethren, but having fallen into a fire when drunk, had had one eye burnt out, one cheek burnt through, and one arm nearly burnt off, and who, therefore, in regard to personal appearance, was not the most prepossessing of men, 'a hundred a year, and all to spend; only think, old Billy Gazy;' and he gave a hideous grin that showed off his misfortunes to their full extent.

Old Billy Gazy was not alive to much enthusiasm. Even these golden prospects did not arouse him to do more than rub his poor old bleared eyes with the cuff of his bedesman's gown, and gently mutter; 'he didn't know, not he; he didn't know.'

'But you'd know, Jonathan,' continued Spriggs, turning to the other friend of Skulpit's, who was sitting on a stool by the table, gazing vacantly at the petition. Jonathan Crumple was a meek, mild man, who had known better days; his means had been wasted by bad children, who had made his life wretched till he had been received into the hospital, of which he had not long been a member. Since that day he had known neither sorrow nor trouble, and this attempt to fill him with new hopes was, indeed, a cruelty.

'A hundred a year's a nice thing, for sartain, neighbour Spriggs,' said he. 'I once had nigh to that myself, but it didn't do me no good.' And he gave a low sigh, as he thought of the children of his own loins who had robbed him.

'And shall have again, Joe,' said Handy; 'and will have some one to keep it right and tight for you this time.'

Crumple sighed again—he had learned the impotency of worldly wealth, and would have been satisfied, if left untempted, to have remained happy with one and sixpence a day.

'Come, Skulpit,' repeated Handy, getting impatient, 'you're not going to go along with old Bunce in helping that parson to rob us all. Take the pen, man, and right yourself. Well,' he added, seeing that Skulpit still doubted, 'to see a man as is afraid to stand by hisself is, to my thinking, the meanest thing as is.'

'Sink them all for parsons, says I,' growled Moody; 'hungry beggars, as never thinks their bellies full till they have robbed all and everything!'

'Who's to harm you, man?' argued Spriggs. 'Let them look never so black at you, they can't get you put out when you're once in—no, not old Catgut, with Calves to help him!' I am sorry to say the archdeacon himself was designated by this scurrilous allusion to his nether person.

'A hundred a year to win, and nothing to lose,' continued Handy. 'My eyes! Well, how a man's to doubt about sich a bit of cheese as that passes me— but some men is timorous—some men is born with no pluck in them—some men is cowed at the very first sight of a gentleman's coat and waistcoat.'

Oh, Mr. Harding, if you had but taken the archdeacon's advice in that disputed case, when Joe Mutters was this ungrateful demagogue's rival candidate!

'Afraid of a parson,' growled Moody, with a look of ineffable scorn. 'I tell ye what I'd be afraid of—I'd

46

be afraid of not getting nothing from 'em but just
what I could take by might and right—that's the most
I'd be afraid on of any parson of 'em all.'

'But,' said Skulpit, apologetically, 'Mr. Harding's
not so bad—he did give us twopence a day, didn't
he now?'

'Twopence a day!' exclaimed Spriggs with scorn,
opening awfully the red cavern of his lost eye.

'Twopence a day!' muttered Moody with a curse;
'sink his twopence!'

'Twopence a day!' exclaimed Handy; 'and I'm
to go, hat in hand, and thank a chap for twopence a
day, when he owes me a hundred pounds a year; no,
thank ye; that may do for you, but it won't for me.
Come, I say, Skulpit, are you a going to put your
mark to this here paper, or are you not?'

Skulpit looked round in wretched indecision
to his two friends. 'What d'ye think, Bill Gazy?'
said he.

But Bill Gazy couldn't think. He made a noise like
the bleating of an old sheep, which was intended to
express the agony of his doubt, and again muttered
that 'he didn't know.'

'Take hold, you old cripple,' said Handy, thrusting
the pen into poor Billy's hand: 'there, so—ugh! you
old fool, you've been and smeared it all—there—
that'll do for you—that's as good as the best name as
ever was written:' and a big blotch of ink was presumed to represent Billy Gazy's acquiescence.

'Now, Jonathan,' said Handy, turning to Crumple.

'A hundred a year's a nice thing, for sartain,' again
argued Crumple. 'Well, neighbour Skulpit, how's it
to be?'

The Warden

'Oh, please yourself,' said Skulpit: 'please yourself, and you'll please me.'

The pen was thrust into Crumple's hand, and a faint, wandering, meaningless sign was made, betokening such sanction and authority as Jonathan Crumple was able to convey.

'Come, Job,' said Handy, softened by success, 'don't let' em have to say that old Bunce has a man like you under his thumb—a man that always holds his head in the hospital as high as Bunce himself, though you're never axed to drink wine, and sneak, and tell lies about your betters as he does.'

Skulpit held the pen, and made little flourishes with it in the air, but still hesitated.

'And if you'll be said by me,' continued Handy, 'you'll not write your name to it at all, but just put your mark like the others,'—the cloud began to clear from Skulpit's brow:—'we all know you can do it if you like, but maybe you wouldn't like to seem uppish, you know.'

'Well, the mark would be best,' said Skulpit: 'One name and the rest marks wouldn't look well, would it?'

'The worst in the world,' said Handy; 'there—there:' and stooping over the petition, the learned clerk made a huge cross on the place left for his signature.

'That's the game,' said Handy, triumphantly pocketing the petition; 'we're all in a boat now, that is, the nine of us; and as for old Bunce, and his cronies, they may——' But as he was hobbling off to the door, with a crutch on one side and a stick on the other, he was met by Bunce himself.

48

'Well, Handy, and what may old Bunce do?' said the grey-haired, upright senior.

Handy muttered something, and was departing; but he was stopped in the doorway by the huge frame of the new comer.

'You've been doing no good here, Abel Handy,' said he, ''tis plain to see that; and 'tisn't much good, I'm thinking, you ever do.'

'I mind my own business, Master Bunce,' muttered the other, 'and do you do the same. It ain't nothing to you what I does—and your spying and poking here won't do no good nor yet no harm.'

'I suppose then, Job,' continued Bunce, not noticing his opponent, 'if the truth must out, you've stuck your name to that petition of theirs at last.'

Skulpit looked as though he were about to sink into the ground with shame.

'What is it to you what he signs?' said Handy. 'I suppose if we all wants to ax for our own, we needn't ax leave of you first, Mr. Bunce, big a man as you are; and as to your sneaking in here, into Job's room when he's busy, and where you're not wanted——'

'I've knowed Job Skulpit, man and boy, sixty years,' said Bunce, looking at the man of whom he spoke, 'and that's ever since the day he was born. I knowed the mother that bore him, when she and I were little wee things, picking daisies together in the close yonder; and I've lived under the same roof with him more nor ten years; and after that I may come into his room without axing leave, and yet no sneaking neither.'

'So you can, Mr. Bunce,' said Skulpit; 'so you can, any hour, day or night.'

49

'And I'm free also to tell him my mind,' continued
Bunce, looking at the one man and addressing the
other; 'and I tell him now that he's done a foolish
and a wrong thing. He's turned his back upon one
who is his best friend; and is playing the game of
others, who care nothing for him, whether he be poor
or rich, well or ill, alive or dead. A hundred a year?
Are the lot of you soft enough to think that if a
hundred a year be to be given, it's the likes of you
that will get it?'—and he pointed to Billy Gazy,
Spriggs, and Crumple. 'Did any of us ever do anything worth half the money? Was it to make gentlemen of us we were brought in here, when all the
world turned against us, and we couldn't longer earn
our daily bread? A'n't you all as rich in your ways as
he in his?'—and the orator pointed to the side on
which the warden lived. 'A'n't you getting all you
hoped for, ay, and more than you hoped for? Wouldn't
each of you have given the dearest limb of his body
to secure that which now makes you so unthankful?'

'We wants what John Hiram left us,' said Handy.
'We wants what's ourn by law; it don't matter what
we expected. What's ourn by law should be ourn,
and by goles we'll have it.'

'Law!' said Bunce, with all the scorn he knew how
to command—'law! Did ye ever know a poor man
yet was the better for law, or for a lawyer? Will Mr.
Finney ever be as good to you, Job, as that man has
been? Will he see to you when you're sick, and comfort you when you're wretched? Will he——'

'No, nor give you port wine, old boy, on cold
winter nights! he won't do that, will he?' asked
Handy; and laughing at the severity of his own wit,

he and his colleagues retired, carrying with them, however, the now powerful petition.

There is no help for spilt milk; and Mr. Bunce could only retire to his own room, disgusted at the frailty of human nature—Job Skulpit scratched his head—Jonathan Crumple again remarked that, 'for sartain sure a hundred a year was very nice'—and Billy Gazy again rubbed his eyes, and lowly muttered that 'he didn't know.'

5

DR. GRANTLY VISITS THE HOSPITAL

THOUGH doubt and hesitation disturbed the rest of our poor warden, no such weakness perplexed the nobler breast of his son-in-law. As the indomitable cock preparing for the combat sharpens his spurs, shakes his feathers, and erects his comb, so did the archdeacon arrange his weapons for the coming war, without misgiving and without fear. That he was fully confident of the justice of his cause let no one doubt. Many a man can fight his battle with good courage, but with a doubting conscience. Such was not the case with Dr. Grantly. He did not believe in the Gospel with more assurance than he did in the sacred justice of all ecclesiastical revenues. When he put his shoulder to the wheel to defend the income of the present and future precentors of Barchester, he was animated by as strong a sense of a holy cause, as that which gives courage to a missionary in Africa, or enables a sister of mercy to give up the pleasures of the world for the wards of a hospital. He was about to defend the holy of holies from the touch of the profane; to guard the citadel of his church from the most rampant of its enemies; to put on his good armour in the best of fights; and secure, if possible, the comforts of his creed for coming

generations of ecclesiastical dignitaries. Such a work
required no ordinary vigour; and the archdeacon
was, therefore, extraordinarily vigorous. It demanded
a buoyant courage, and a heart happy in its toil; and
the archdeacon's heart was happy, and his courage
was buoyant.

He knew that he would not be able to animate his
father-in-law with feelings like his own, but this did
not much disturb him. He preferred to bear the brunt
of the battle alone, and did not doubt that the warden
would resign himself into his hands with passive submission.

'Well, Mr. Chadwick,' he said, walking into the
steward's office a day or two after the signing of the
petition as commemorated in the last chapter: 'anything from Cox and Cummins this morning?' Mr.
Chadwick handed him a letter; which he read, strok-
ing the tight-gaitered calf of his right leg as he did
so. Messrs. Cox and Cummins merely said that they
had as yet received no notice from their adversaries;
that they could recommend no preliminary steps; but
that should any proceeding really be taken by the
bedesmen, it would be expedient to consult that very
eminent Queen's Counsel, Sir Abraham Haphazard.

'I quite agree with them,' said Dr. Grantly, re-
folding the letter. 'I perfectly agree with them.
Haphazard is no doubt the best man; a thorough
churchman, a sound conservative, and in every respect the best man we could get—he's in the house,
too, which is a great thing.'

Mr. Chadwick quite agreed.

'You remember how completely he put down that
scoundrel Horseman about the Bishop of Beverley's

income; how completely he set them all adrift in the earl's case.' Since the question of St. Cross had been mooted by the public, one noble lord had become *'the earl,' par excellence*, in the doctor's estimation. 'How he silenced that fellow at Rochester. Of course we must have Haphazard; and I'll tell you what, Mr. Chadwick, we must take care to be in time, or the other party will forestall us.'

With all his admiration for Sir Abraham, the doctor seemed to think it not impossible that that great man might be induced to lend his gigantic powers to the side of the church's enemies.

Having settled this point to his satisfaction, the doctor stepped down to the hospital, to learn how matters were going on there; and as he walked across the hallowed close, and looked up at the ravens who cawed with a peculiar reverence as he wended his way, he thought with increased acerbity of those whose impiety would venture to disturb the goodly grace of cathedral institutions.

And who has not felt the same? We believe that Mr. Horseman himself would relent, and the spirit of Sir Benjamin Hall give way, were those great reformers to allow themselves to stroll by moonlight round the towers of some of our ancient churches. Who would not feel charity for a prebendary, when walking the quiet length of that long aisle at Winchester, looking at those decent houses, that trim grassplat, and feeling, as one must, the solemn, orderly comfort of the spot! Who could be hard upon a dean while wandering round the sweet close of Hereford, and owning that in that precinct, tone and colour, design and form, solemn tower and storied window, are all in unison, and all perfect! Who could lie basking in the cloisters of Salisbury, and gaze on Jewel's library and that unequalled spire, without feeling that bishops should sometimes be rich!

The tone of our archdeacon's mind must not astonish us; it has been the growth of centuries of church ascendancy; and though some fungi now disfigure the tree, though there be much dead wood, for how much good fruit have not we to be thankful? Who, without remorse, can batter down the dead branches of an old oak, now useless, but, ah! still so beautiful, or drag out the fragments of the ancient forest, without feeling that they sheltered the younger plants, to which they are now summoned to give way in a tone so peremptory and so harsh?

The archdeacon, with all his virtues, was not a man of delicate feeling; and after having made his morning salutations in the warden's drawing-room, he did not scruple to commence an attack on 'pestilent' John Bold in the presence of Miss Harding, though he rightly guessed that that lady was not indifferent to the name of her enemy.

'Nelly, my dear, fetch me my spectacles from the back room,' said her father, anxious to save both her blushes and her feelings.

Eleanor brought the spectacles, while her father was trying, in ambiguous phrases, to explain to her too-practical brother-in-law that it might be as well not to say anything about Bold before her, and then retreated. Nothing had been explained to her about Bold and the hospital; but, with a woman's instinct, she knew that things were going wrong.

'We must soon be doing something,' commenced

the archdeacon, wiping his brows with a large, bright-coloured handkerchief, for he had felt busy, and had walked quick, and it was a broiling summer's day. 'Of course you have heard of the petition?'

Mr. Harding owned, somewhat unwillingly, that he had heard of it.

'Well,'—the archdeacon looked for some expressions of opinion, but none coming, he continued—'We must be doing something, you know; we mustn't allow these people to cut the ground from under us while we sit looking on.' The archdeacon, who was a practical man, allowed himself the use of every-day expressive modes of speech when among his closest intimates, though no one could soar into a more intricate labyrinth of refined phraseology when the church was the subject, and his lower brethren were his auditors.

The warden still looked mutely in his face, making the slightest possible passes with an imaginary fiddle bow, and stopping, as he did so, sundry imaginary strings with the fingers of his other hand. 'Twas his constant consolation in conversational troubles. While these vexed him sorely, the passes would be short and slow, and the upper hand would not be seen to work; nay the strings on which it operated would sometimes lie concealed in the musician's pocket, and the instrument on which he played would be beneath his chair; but as his spirit warmed to the subject— as his trusting heart, looking to the bottom of that which vexed him, would see its clear way out, —he would rise to a higher melody, sweep the unseen strings with a bolder hand, and swiftly fingering the cords from his neck, down along his waistcoat, and up again to his very ear, create an ecstatic strain of perfect music, audible to himself and to St. Cecilia, and not without effect.

'I quite agree with Cox and Cummins,' continued the archdeacon. 'They say we must secure Sir Abraham Haphazard. I shall not have the slightest fear in leaving the case in Sir Abraham's hands.'

The warden played the slowest and saddest of tunes. It was but a dirge on one string.

'I think Sir Abraham will not be long in letting Master Bold know what he's about. I fancy I hear Sir Abraham cross-questioning him at the Common Pleas.'

The warden thought of his income being thus discussed, his modest life, his daily habits, and his easy work; and nothing issued from that single cord, but a low wail of sorrow. 'I suppose they've sent this petition up to my father.' The warden didn't know; he imagined they would do so this very day.

'What I can't understand is, how you let them do it, with such a command as you have in the place, or should have with such a man as Bunce. I cannot understand why you let them do it.'

'Do what?' asked the warden.

'Why, listen to this fellow Bold, and that other low pettifogger, Finney—and get up this petition too. Why didn't you tell Bunce to destroy the petition?'

'That would have been hardly wise,' said the warden.

'Wise—yes, it would have been very wise if they'd done it among themselves. I must go up to the palace and answer it now, I suppose. It's a very short answer they'll get, I can tell you.'

'But why shouldn't they petition, doctor?'

'Why shouldn't they!' responded the archdeacon, in a loud brazen voice, as though all the men in the hospital were expected to hear him through the walls; 'why shouldn't they? I'll let them know why they shouldn't: by-the-by, warden, I'd like to say a few words to them all together.'

The warden's mind misgave him, and even for a moment he forgot to play. He by no means wished to delegate to his son-in-law his place and authority of warden; he had expressly determined not to interfere in any step which the men might wish to take in the matter under dispute; he was most anxious neither to accuse them nor to defend himself. All these things he was aware the archdeacon would do in his behalf, and that not in the mildest manner; and yet he knew not how to refuse the permission requested.

'I'd so much sooner remain quiet in the matter,' said he, in an apologetic voice.

'Quiet!' said the archdeacon, still speaking with his brazen trumpet; 'do you wish to be ruined in quiet?'

'Why, if I am to be ruined, certainly.'

'Nonsense, warden; I tell you something must be done—we must act; just let me ring the bell, and send the men word that I'll speak to them in the quad.'

Mr. Harding knew not how to resist, and the disagreeable order was given. The quad, as it was familiarly called, was a small quadrangle, open on one side to the river, and surrounded on the others by the high wall of Mr. Harding's garden, by one gable end of Mr. Harding's house, and by the end of the row of buildings which formed the residences of the bedesmen. It was flagged all round, and the centre was stoned; small stone gutters ran from the four corners of the square to a grating in the centre; and attached to the end of Mr. Harding's house was a conduit with four cocks covered over from the weather, at which the old men got their water, and very generally performed their morning toilet. It was a quiet, sombre place, shaded over by the trees of the warden's garden. On the side towards the river, there stood a row of stone seats, on which the old men would sit and gaze at the little fish, as they flitted by in the running stream. On the other side of the river was a rich, green meadow, running up to and joining the deanery, and as little open to the public as the garden of the dean itself. Nothing, therefore, could be more private than the quad of the hospital; and it was there that the archdeacon determined to convey to them his sense of their refractory proceedings.

The servant soon brought in word that the men were assembled in the quad, and the archdeacon, big with his purpose, rose to address them.

'Well, warden, of course you're coming,' said he, seeing that Mr. Harding did not prepare to follow him.

'I wish you'd excuse me,' said Mr. Harding.

'For heaven's sake, don't let us have division in the camp,' replied the archdeacon: 'let us have a long pull and a strong pull, but above all a pull all together; come, warden, come; don't be afraid of your duty.'

Mr. Harding was afraid; he was afraid that he was being led to do that which was not his duty: he was not, however, strong enough to resist, so he got up and followed his son-in-law.

The old men were assembled in groups in the quadrangle—eleven of them at least, for poor old Johnny Bell was bed-ridden, and couldn't come; he had, however, put his mark to the petition, as one of Handy's earliest followers. 'Tis true he could not move from the bed where he lay; 'tis true he had no friend on earth, but those whom the hospital contained; and of those the warden and his daughter were the most constant and most appreciated; 'tis true that every thing was administered to him which his failing body could require, or which his faint appetite could enjoy; but still his dull eye had glistened for a moment at the idea of possessing a hundred pounds a year 'to his own cheek,' as Abel Handy had eloquently expressed it; and poor old Johnny Bell had greedily put his mark to the petition.

When the two clergymen appeared, they all uncovered their heads. Handy was slow to do it, and hesitated; but the black coat and waistcoat, of which he had spoken so irreverently in Skulpit's room, had its effect even on him, and he too doffed his hat. Bunce, advancing before the others, bowed lowly to the archdeacon, and with affectionate reverence expressed his wish, that the warden and Miss Eleanor were quite well; 'and the doctor's lady,' he added, turning to the archdeacon, 'and the children at Plumstead, and my lord;' and having made his speech, he also retired among the others, and took his place with the rest upon the stone benches.

As the archdeacon stood up to make his speech, erect in the middle of that little square, he looked like an ecclesiastical statue placed there, as a fitting impersonation of the church militant here on earth;

60

his shovel hat, large, new, and well-pronounced, a churchman's hat in every inch, declared the profession as plainly as does the Quaker's broad brim; his heavy eyebrows, large open eyes, and full mouth and chin expressed the solidity of his order; the broad chest, amply covered with fine cloth, told how well to do was its estate; one hand ensconced within his pocket, evinced the practical hold which our mother church keeps on her temporal possessions; and the other, loose for action, was ready to fight if need be in her defence; and, below these, the decorous breeches, and neat black gaiters showing so admirably that well-turned leg, betokened the decency, the outward beauty and grace of our church establishment.

'Now, my men,' he began, when he had settled himself well in his position; 'I want to say a few words to you. Your good friend, the warden here, and myself, and my lord the bishop, on whose behalf I wish to speak to you, would all be very sorry, very sorry indeed, that you should have any just ground of complaint. Any just ground of complaint on your part would be removed at once by the warden, or by his lordship, or by me on his behalf, without the necessity of any petition on your part.' Here the orator stopped for a moment, expecting that some little murmurs of applause would show that the weakest of the men were beginning to give way; but no such murmurs came. Bunce, himself, even sat with closed lips, mute and unsatisfactory. 'Without the necessity of any petition at all,' he repeated. 'I'm told you have addressed a petition to my lord.' He paused for a reply from the men, and after a while, Handy plucked up courage and said, 'Yes, we has.'

'You have addressed a petition to my lord, in which, as I am informed, you express an opinion that you do not receive from Hiram's estate all that is your due.' Here most of the men expressed their assent. 'Now what is it you ask for? What is it you want that you haven't got here? What is it——'

'A hundred a year,' muttered old Moody, with a voice as if it came out of the ground.

'A hundred a year!' ejaculated the archdeacon militant, defying the impudence of these claimants with one hand stretched out and closed, while with the other he tightly grasped, and secured within his breeches pocket, that symbol of the church's wealth which his own loose half-crowns not unaptly represented. 'A hundred a year! Why, my men, you must be mad; and you talk about John Hiram's will! When John Hiram built a hospital for worn-out old men, worn-out old labouring men, infirm old men past their work, cripples, blind, bed-ridden, and such like, do you think he meant to make gentlemen of them? Do you think John Hiram intended to give a hundred a year to old single men, who earned perhaps two shillings or half-a-crown a day for themselves and families in the best of their time? No, my men, I'll tell you what John Hiram meant; he meant that twelve poor old worn-out labourers, men who could no longer support themselves, who had no friends to support them, who must starve and perish miserably if not protected by the hand of charity; he meant that twelve such men as these should come in here in their poverty and wretchedness, and find within these walls shelter and food before their death, and a little leisure to make their peace with God. That was what John

Dr. Grantly Visits the Hospital

Hiram meant: you have not read John Hiram's will, and I doubt whether those wicked men who are advising you have done so. I have; I know what his will was; and I tell you that that was his will, and that that was his intention.'

Not a sound came from the eleven bedesmen, as they sat listening to what, according to the archdeacon, was their intended estate. They grimly stared upon his burly figure, but did not then express, by word or sign, the anger and disgust to which such language was sure to give rise.

'Now let me ask you,' he continued: 'do you think you are worse off than John Hiram intended to make you? Have you not shelter, and food, and leisure? Have you not much more? Have you not every indulgence which you are capable of enjoying? Have you not twice better food, twice a better bed, ten times more money in your pocket than you were ever able to earn for yourselves before you were lucky enough to get into this place? And now you send a petition to the bishop, asking for a hundred pounds a year! I tell you what, my friends; you are deluded, and made fools of by wicked men who are acting for their own ends. You will never get a hundred pence a year more than what you have now: it is very possible that you may get less; it is very possible that my lord the bishop, and your warden, may make changes——'

'No, no, no,' interrupted Mr. Harding, who had been listening with indescribable misery to the tirade of his son-in-law; 'no, my friends. I want no changes —at least no changes that shall make you worse off than you now are, as long as you and I live together.'

'God bless you, Mr. Harding,' said Bunce; and 'God bless you, Mr. Harding, God bless you, sir: we know you was always our friend,' was exclaimed by enough of the men to make it appear that the sentiment was general.

The archdeacon had been interrupted in his speech before he had quite finished it; but he felt that he could not recommence with dignity after this little ebullition, and he led the way back into the garden, followed by his father-in-law.

'Well,' said he, as soon as he found himself within the cool retreat of the warden's garden; 'I think I spoke to them plainly.' And he wiped the perspiration from his brow; for making a speech under a broiling midday sun in summer, in a full suit of thick black cloth, is warm work.

'Yes, you were plain enough,' replied the warden, in a tone which did not express approbation.

'And that's everything,' said the other, who was clearly well satisfied with himself; 'that's everything: with those sort of people one must be plain, or one will not be understood. Now, I think they did understand me—I think they knew what I meant.'

The warden agreed. He certainly thought they had understood to the full what had been said to them.

'They know pretty well what they have to expect from us; they know how we shall meet any refractory spirit on their part; they know that we are not afraid of them. And now I'll just step into Chadwick's, and tell him what I've done; and then I'll go up to the palace, and answer this petition of theirs.'

The warden's mind was very full—full nearly to overcharging itself; and had it done so—had he allowed himself to speak the thoughts which were working within him, he would indeed have astonished the archdeacon by the reprobation he would have expressed as to the proceeding of which he had been so unwilling a witness. But different feelings kept him silent; he was as yet afraid of differing from his son-in-law—he was anxious beyond measure to avoid even a semblance of rupture with any of his order, and was painfully fearful of having to come to an open quarrel with any person on any subject. His life had hitherto been so quiet, so free from strife; his little early troubles had required nothing but passive fortitude; his subsequent prosperity had never forced upon him any active cares—had never brought him into disagreeable contact with any one. He felt that he would give almost anything—much more than he knew he ought to do—to relieve himself from the storm which he feared was coming. It was so hard that the pleasant waters of his little stream should be disturbed and muddied by rough hands; that his quiet paths should be made a battlefield; that the unobtrusive corner of the world which had been allotted to him, as though by Providence, should be invaded and desecrated, and all within it made miserable and unsound.

Money he had none to give; the knack of putting guineas together had never belonged to him; but how willingly, with what a foolish easiness, with what happy alacrity, would he have abandoned the half of his income for all time to come, could he by so doing have quietly dispelled the clouds that were gathering over him—could he have thus compromised the matter between the reformer and the conservative, between his possible son-in-law, Bold, and his positive son-in-law, the archdeacon.

And this compromise would not have been made from any prudential motive of saving what would yet remain, for Mr. Harding still felt little doubt but he should be left for life in quiet possession of the good things he had, if he chose to retain them. No; he would have done so from the sheer love of quiet, and from a horror of being made the subject of public talk. He had very often been moved to pity—to that inward weeping of the heart for others' woes; but none had he ever pitied more than that old lord, whose almost fabulous wealth, drawn from his church preferments, had become the subject of so much opprobrium, of such public scorn; that wretched clerical octogenarian Crœsus, whom men would not allow to die in peace—whom all the world united to decry and to abhor.

Was he to suffer such a fate? Was his humble name to be bandied in men's mouths, as the gormandiser of the resources of the poor, as of one who had filched from the charity of other ages wealth which had been intended to relieve the old and the infirm? Was he to be gibbeted in the press, to become a byword for oppression, to be named as an example of the greed of the English church? Should it ever be said that he had robbed those old men, whom he so truly and so tenderly loved in his heart of hearts? As he slowly paced, hour after hour, under those noble lime-trees, turning these sad thoughts within him, he became all but fixed in his resolve that some great step must be taken to relieve him from the risk of so terrible a fate.

Dr. Grantly Visits the Hospital

In the meanwhile, the archdeacon, with contented mind and unruffled spirit, went about his business. He said a word or two to Mr. Chadwick, and then finding, as he expected, the petition lying in his father's library, he wrote a short answer to the men, in which he told them that they had no evils to redress, but rather great mercies for which to be thankful; and having seen the bishop sign it, he got into his brougham and returned home to Mrs. Grantly, and Plumstead Episcopi.

6

THE WARDEN'S TEA PARTY

AFTER much painful doubting, on one thing only could Mr. Harding resolve. He determined that at any rate he would take no offence, and that he would make this question no cause of quarrel either with Bold or with the bedesmen. In furtherance of this resolution, he himself wrote a note to Mr. Bold, the same afternoon, inviting him to meet a few friends and hear some music on an evening named in the next week. Had not this little party been promised to Eleanor, in his present state of mind he would probably have avoided such gaiety; but the promise had been given, the invitations were to be written, and when Eleanor consulted her father on the subject, she was not ill pleased to hear him say, 'Oh, I was thinking of Bold, so I took it into my head to write to him myself, but you must write to his sister.'

Mary Bold was older than her brother, and, at the time of our story, was just over thirty. She was not an unattractive young woman, though by no means beautiful. Her great merit was the kindliness of her disposition. She was not very clever, nor very animated, nor had she apparently the energy of her brother; but she was guided by a high principle of right and wrong; her temper was sweet, and her faults were fewer in number than her virtues. Those who casually met Mary Bold thought little of her; but those who knew her well loved her well, and the longer they knew her the more they loved her. Among those who were fondest of her was Eleanor Harding; and though Eleanor had never openly talked to her of her brother, each understood the other's feelings about him. The brother and sister were sitting together when the two notes were brought in.

'How odd,' said Mary, 'that they should send two notes. Well, if Mr. Harding becomes fashionable, the world is going to change.'

Her brother understood immediately the nature and intention of the peace-offering; but it was not so easy for him to behave well in the matter, as it was for Mr. Harding. It is much less difficult for the sufferer to be generous than for the oppressor. John Bold felt that he could not go to the warden's party; he never loved Eleanor better than he did now; he had never so strongly felt how anxious he was to make her his wife as now, when so many obstacles to his doing so appeared in view. Yet here was her father himself, as it were, clearing away those very obstacles, and still he felt that he could not go to the house any more as an open friend.

As he sat thinking of these things with the note in his hand, his sister was waiting for his decision.

'Well,' said she, 'I suppose we must write separate answers, and both say we shall be very happy.'

'You'll go, of course, Mary,' said he; to which she readily assented. 'I cannot,' he continued, looking serious and gloomy. 'I wish I could, with all my heart.'

'And why not John?' said she. She had as yet heard

nothing of the new-found abuse which her brother was about to reform—at least nothing which connected it with her brother's name.

He sat thinking for a while till he determined that it would be best to tell her at once what it was that he was about: it must be done sooner or later.

'I fear I cannot go to Mr. Harding's house any more as a friend, just at present.'

'Oh, John! Why not? Ah, you've quarrelled with Eleanor!'

'No, indeed,' said he; 'I've no quarrel with her as yet.'

'What is it, John?' said she, looking at him with an anxious, loving face, for she knew well how much of his heart was there in that house which he said he could no longer enter.

'Why,' said he at last, 'I've taken up the case of these twelve old men of Hiram's Hospital, and of course that brings me into contact with Mr. Harding. I may have to oppose him, interfere with him, perhaps injure him.'

Mary looked at him steadily for some time before she committed herself to reply, and then merely asked him what he meant to do for the old men.

'Why, it's a long story, and I don't know that I can make you understand it. John Hiram made a will, and left his property in charity for certain poor old men, and the proceeds, instead of going to the benefit of these men, goes chiefly into the pocket of the warden and the bishop's steward.'

'And you mean to take away from Mr. Harding his share of it?'

'I don't know what I mean yet. I mean to inquire

about it. I mean to see who is entitled to this property. I mean to see, if I can, that justice be done to the poor of the city of Barchester generally, who are, in fact, the legatees under the will. I mean, in short, to put the matter right, if I can.'

'And why are you to do this, John?'

'You might ask the same question of anybody else,' said he; 'and according to that the duty of righting these poor men would belong to nobody. If we are to act on that principle, the weak are never to be protected, injustice is never to be opposed, and no one is to struggle for the poor!' And Bold began to comfort himself in the warmth of his own virtue.

'But is there no one to do this but you, who have known Mr. Harding so long? Surely, John, as a friend, as a young friend, so much younger than Mr. Harding——'

'That's woman's logic, all over, Mary. What has age to do with it? Another man might plead that he was too old; and as to his friendship, if the thing itself be right, private motives should never be allowed to interfere. Because I esteem Mr. Harding, is that a reason that I should neglect a duty which I owe to these old men? or should I give up a work which my conscience tells me is a good one, because I regret the loss of his society?'

'And Eleanor, John?' said the sister, looking timidly into her brother's face.

'Eleanor, that is, Miss Harding, if she thinks fit —that is, if her father—or, rather, if she—or, indeed, he—if they find it necessary——but there is no necessity now to talk about Eleanor Harding; but

71

this I will say, that if she has the kind of spirit for which I give her credit, she will not condemn me for doing what I think to be a duty.' And Bold consoled himself with the consolation of a Roman.

Mary sat silent for a while, till at last her brother reminded her that the notes must be answered, and she got up, and placed her desk before her, took out her pen and paper, wrote on it slowly—

'PAKENHAM VILLAS,
'*Tuesday Morning.*

'MY DEAR ELEANOR,
    'I——'

and then stopped, and looked at her brother.

'Well, Mary, why don't you write it?'

'Oh, John,' said she, 'dear John, pray think better of this.'

'Think better of what?' said he.

'Of this about the hospital—of all this about Mr. Harding—of what you say about those old men. Nothing can call upon you—no duty can require you to set yourself against your oldest, your best friend. Oh, John, think of Eleanor. You'll break her heart and your own.'

'Nonsense, Mary; Miss Harding's heart is as safe as yours.'

'Pray, pray, for my sake, John, give it up. You know how dearly you love her.' And she came and knelt before him on the rug. 'Pray give it up. You are going to make yourself, and her, and her father miserable: you are going to make us all miserable. And for what? For a dream of justice. You will never make those twelve men happier than they now are.'

72

'You don't understand it, my dear girl,' said he, smoothing her hair with his hand.

'I do understand it, John. I understand that this is a chimera—a dream that you have got. I know well that no duty can require you to do this mad—this suicidal thing. I know you love Eleanor Harding with all your heart, and I tell you now that she loves you as well. If there was a plain, a positive duty before you, I would be the last to bid you neglect it for any woman's love; but this——oh, think again, before you do anything to make it necessary that you and Mr. Harding should be at variance.' He did not answer, as she knelt there, leaning on his knees, but by his face she thought that he was inclined to yield. 'At any rate let me say that you will go to this party. At any rate do not break with them while your mind is in doubt.' And she got up, hoping to conclude her note in the way she desired.

'My mind is not in doubt,' at last he said, rising. 'I could never respect myself again were I to give way now, because Eleanor Harding is beautiful. I do love her: I would give a hand to hear her tell me what you have said, speaking on her behalf; but I cannot for her sake go back from the task which I have commenced. I hope she may hereafter acknowledge and respect my motives, but I cannot now go as a guest to her father's house.' And the Barchester Brutus went out to fortify his own resolution by meditations on his own virtue.

Poor Mary Bold sat down, and sadly finished her note, saying that she would herself attend the party, but that her brother was unavoidably prevented from doing so. I fear that she did not admire as she should have done the self-devotion of his singular virtue.

The party went off as such parties do. There were fat old ladies, in fine silk dresses, and slim young ladies, in gauzy muslin frocks; old gentlemen stood up with their backs to the empty fireplace, looking by no means so comfortable as they would have done in their own armchairs at home; and young gentlemen, rather stiff about the neck, clustered near the door, not as yet sufficiently in courage to attack the muslin frocks, who awaited the battle, drawn up in a semicircular array. The warden endeavoured to induce a charge, but failed signally, not having the tact of a general; his daughter did what she could to comfort the forces under her command, who took in refreshing rations of cake and tea, and patiently looked for the coming engagement: but she herself, Eleanor, had no spirit for the work; the only enemy whose lance she cared to encounter was not there, and she and others were somewhat dull.

Loud above all voices was heard the clear sonorous tones of the archdeacon as he dilated to brother parsons of the danger of the church, of the fearful rumours of mad reforms even at Oxford, and of the damnable heresies of Dr. Whiston.

Soon, however, sweeter sounds began timidly to make themselves audible. Little movements were made in a quarter notable for round stools and music stands. Wax candles were arranged in sconces, big books were brought from hidden recesses, and the work of the evening commenced.

How often were those pegs twisted and retwisted before our friend found that he had twisted them

enough; how many discordant scrapes gave promise
of the coming harmony. How much the muslin fluttered and crumpled before Eleanor and another nymph
were duly seated at the piano; how closely did that
tall Apollo pack himself against the wall, with his
flute, long as himself, extending high over the heads
of his pretty neighbours; into how small a corner
crept that round and florid little minor canon, and
there with skill amazing found room to tune his accustomed fiddle!

And now the crash begins: away they go in full
flow of harmony together—up hill and down dale—
now louder and louder, then lower and lower; now
loud, as though stirring the battle; then low, as
though mourning the slain. In all, through all, and
above all, is heard the violoncello. Ah, not for nothing were those pegs so twisted and retwisted—listen,
listen! Now alone that saddest of instruments tells its
touching tale. Silent, and in awe, stand fiddle, flute,
and piano, to hear the sorrows of their wailing
brother. 'Tis but for a moment: before the melancholy of those low notes has been fully realised, again
comes the full force of all the band—down go the
pedals, away rush twenty fingers scouring over the
bass notes with all the impetus of passion. Apollo
blows till his stiff neckcloth is no better than a rope,
and the minor canon works with both arms till he
falls in a syncope of exhaustion against the wall.

How comes it that now, when all should be silent,
when courtesy, if not taste, should make men listen
—how is it at this moment the black-coated corps
leave their retreat and begin skirmishing? One by
one they creep forth, and fire off little guns timidly,

and without precision. Ah, my men, efforts such as
these will take no cities, even though the enemy
should be never so open to assault. At length a more
deadly artillery is brought to bear; slowly, but with
effect, the advance is made; the muslin ranks are
broken, and fall into confusion; the formidable array
of chairs gives way; the battle is no longer between
opposing regiments, but hand to hand, and foot to
foot with single combatants, as in the glorious days
of old, when fighting was really noble. In corners,
and under the shadow of curtains, behind sofas and
half hidden by doors, in retiring windows, and sheltered by hanging tapestry, are blows given and returned, fatal, incurable, dealing death.

Apart from this another combat arises, more sober
and more serious. The archdeacon is engaged against
two prebendaries, a pursy full-blown rector assisting
him, in all the perils and all the enjoyments of short
whist. With solemn energy do they watch the shuffled
pack, and, all-expectant, eye the coming trump. With
what anxious nicety do they arrange their cards,
jealous of each other's eyes! Why is that lean doctor
so slow—cadaverous man with hollow jaw and sunken
eye, ill beseeming the richness of his mother church!
Ah, why so slow, thou meagre doctor? See how the
archdeacon, speechless in his agony, deposits on the
board his cards, and looks to heaven or to the ceiling
for support. Hark, how he sighs, as with thumbs in
his waistcoat pocket he seems to signify that the end
of such torment is not yet even nigh at hand! Vain is
the hope, if hope there be, to disturb that meagre
doctor. With care precise he places every card,
weighs well the value of each mighty ace, each

guarded king, and comfort-giving queen; speculates on knave and ten, counts all his suits, and sets his price upon the whole. At length a card is led, and quick three others fall upon the board. The little doctor leads again, while with lustrous eye his partner absorbs the trick. Now thrice has this been done —thrice has constant fortune favoured the brace of prebendaries, ere the archdeacon rouses himself to the battle; but at the fourth assault he pins to the earth a prostrate king, laying low his crown and sceptre, bushy beard, and lowering brow, with a poor deuce.

'As David did Goliath,' says the archdeacon, pushing over the four cards to his partner. And then a trump is led, then another trump; then a king—and then an ace—and then a long ten, which brings down from the meagre doctor his only remaining tower of strength—his cherished queen of trumps.

'What, no second club?' says the archdeacon to his partner.

'Only one club,' mutters from his inmost stomach the pursy rector, who sits there redfaced, silent, impervious, careful, a safe but not a brilliant ally.

But the archdeacon cares not for many clubs, or for none. He dashes out his remaining cards with a speed most annoying to his antagonists, pushes over to them some four cards as their allotted portion, shoves the remainder across the table to the redfaced rector; calls out 'two by cards and two by honours, and the odd trick last time,' marks a treble under the candle-stick, and has dealt round the second pack before the meagre doctor has calculated his losses.

And so went off the warden's party, and men and women arranging shawls and shoes declared how pleasant it had been; and Mrs. Goodenough, the red-faced rector's wife, pressing the warden's hand, declared she had never enjoyed herself better; which showed how little pleasure she allowed herself in this world, as she had sat the whole evening through in the same chair without occupation, not speaking, and unspoken to. And Matilda Johnson, when she allowed young Dickson of the bank to fasten her cloak round her neck, thought that two hundred pounds a year and a little cottage would really do for happiness; besides, he was sure to be manager some day. And Apollo, folding his flute into his pocket, felt that he had acquitted himself with honour; and the arch-deacon pleasantly jingled his gains; but the meagre doctor went off without much audible speech, muttering ever and anon as he went, 'three and thirty points!' 'three and thirty points!'

And so they all were gone, and Mr. Harding was left alone with his daughter.

What had passed between Eleanor Harding and Mary Bold need not be told. It is indeed a matter of thankfulness that neither the historian nor the novelist hears all that is said by their heroes or heroines, or how would three volumes or twenty suffice! In the present case so little of this sort have I overheard, that I live in hopes of finishing my work within 300 pages, and of completing that pleasant task—a novel in one volume; but something had passed between them, and as the warden blew out the wax candles, and put his instrument into its case, his daughter stood sad and thoughtful by the empty fireplace,

78

determined to speak to her father, but irresolute as to what she would say.

'Well, Eleanor,' said he, 'are you for bed?'

'Yes,' said she, moving, 'I suppose so; but papa—Mr. Bold was not here to-night; do you know why not?'

'He was asked; I wrote to him myself,' said the warden.

'But do you know why he did not come, papa?'

'Well, Eleanor, I could guess; but it's no use guessing at such things, my dear. What makes you look so earnest about it?'

'Oh, papa, do tell me,' she exclaimed, throwing her arms round him, and looking into his face; 'what is it he is going to do? What is it all about? Is there any—any—any—' she didn't well know what word to use—'any danger?'

'Danger, my dear, what sort of danger?'

'Danger to you, danger of trouble, and of loss, and of——. Oh, papa, why hav'n't you told me of all this before?'

Mr. Harding was not the man to judge harshly of any one, much less of the daughter whom he now loved better than any living creature; but still he did judge her wrongly at this moment. He knew that she loved John Bold; he fully sympathised in her affecttion; day after day he thought more of the matter, and, with the tender care of a loving father, tried to arrange in his own mind how matters might be so managed that his daughter's heart should not be made the sacrifice to the dispute which was likely to exist between him and Bold. Now, when she spoke to him for the first time on the subject, it was natural that he should think more of her than of himself, and that he should imagine that her own cares, and not his, were troubling her.

He stood silent before her awhile, as she gazed up into his face, and then kissing her forehead he placed her on the sofa.

'Tell me, Nelly,' he said (he only called her Nelly in his kindest, softest, sweetest moods, and yet all his moods were kind and sweet), 'tell me, Nelly, do you like Mr. Bold—much?'

She was quite taken aback by the question. I will not say that she had forgotten herself, and her own love in thinking about John Bold, and while conversing with Mary: she certainly had not done so. She had been sick at heart to think that a man of whom she could not but own to herself that she loved him, of whose regard she had been so proud, that such a man should turn against her father to ruin him. She had felt her vanity hurt, that his affection for her had not kept him from such a course; had he really cared for her, he would not have risked her love by such an outrage. But her main fear had been for her father, and when she spoke of danger, it was of danger to him and not to herself.

She was taken aback by the question altogether: 'Do I like him, papa?'

'Yes, Nelly, do you like him? Why shouldn't you like him? but that's a poor word—do you love him?' She sat still in his arms without answering him. She certainly had not prepared herself for an avowal of affection, intending, as she had done, to abuse John Bold herself, and to hear her father do so also. 'Come, my love,' said he, 'let us make a clean breast of it: do you tell me what concerns yourself, and I will tell you what concerns me and the hospital.'

And then, without waiting for an answer, he described to her, as he best could, the accusation that was made about Hiram's will; the claims which the old men put forward; what he considered the strength and what the weakness of his own position; the course which Bold had taken, and that which he presumed he was about to take; and then by degrees, without further question, he presumed on the fact of Eleanor's love, and spoke of that love as a feeling which he could in no way disapprove: he apologised for Bold, excused what he was doing; nay, praised him for his energy and intentions; made much of his good qualities, and harped on none of his foibles; then, reminding his daughter how late it was, and comforting her with much assurance which he hardly felt himself, he sent her to her room, with flowing eyes and a full heart.

When Mr. Harding met his daughter at breakfast the next morning, there was no further discussion on the matter, nor was the subject mentioned between them for some days. Soon after the party Mary Bold called at the hospital, but there were various persons in the drawing-room at the time, and she therefore said nothing about her brother. On the day following, John Bold met Miss Harding in one of the quiet, sombre, shaded walks of the close. He was most anxious to see her, but unwilling to call at the warden's house, and had in truth waylaid her in her private haunts.

'My sister tells me,' said he, abruptly hurrying on with his premeditated speech, 'my sister tells me that you had a delightful party the other evening. I was so sorry I could not be there.'

'We were all sorry,' said Eleanor, with dignified composure.

'I believe, Miss Harding, you understood why, at this moment——' And Bold hesitated, muttered, stopped, commenced his explanation again, and again broke down.

Eleanor would not help him in the least.

'I think my sister explained to you, Miss Harding?'

'Pray don't apologise, Mr. Bold; my father will, I am sure, always be glad to see you, if you like to come to the house now as formerly; nothing has occurred to alter his feelings: of your own views you are, of course, the best judge.'

'Your father is all that is kind and generous; he always was so; but you, Miss Harding, yourself—— I hope you will not judge me harshly, because——'

'Mr. Bold,' said she, 'you may be sure of one thing; I shall always judge my father to be right, and those who oppose him I shall judge to be wrong. If those who do not know him oppose him, I shall have charity enough to believe that they are wrong, through error of judgment; but should I see him attacked by those who ought to know him, and to love him, and revere him, of such I shall be constrained to form a different opinion.' And then curtseying low she sailed on, leaving her lover in anything but a happy state of mind.

7

THE *JUPITER*

Though Eleanor Harding rode off from John Bold on a high horse, it must not be supposed that her heart was so elate as her demeanour. In the first place, she had a natural repugnance to losing her lover; and in the next, she was not quite so sure that she was in the right as she pretended to be. Her father had told her, and that now repeatedly, that Bold was doing nothing unjust or ungenerous; and why then should she rebuke him, and throw him off, when she felt herself so ill able to bear his loss?— but such is human nature, and young-lady-nature especially. As she walked off from him beneath the shady elms of the close, her look, her tone, every motion and gesture of her body, belied her heart; she would have given the world to have taken him by the hand, to have reasoned with him, persuaded him, cajoled him, coaxed him out of his project; to have overcome him with all her female artillery, and to have redeemed her father at the cost of herself; but pride would not let her do this, and she left him without a look of love or a word of kindness.

Had Bold been judging of another lover and of another lady, he might have understood all this as well as we do; but in matters of love men do not see clearly in their own affairs. They say that faint heart never won fair lady; and it is amazing to me how fair ladies are won, so faint are often men's hearts! Were it not for the kindness of their nature, that seeing the weakness of our courage they will occasionally descend from their impregnable fortresses, and themselves aid us in effecting their own defeat, too often would they escape unconquered if not unscathed, and free of body if not of heart.

Poor Bold crept off quite crestfallen; he felt that as regarded Eleanor Harding his fate was sealed, unless he could consent to give up a task to which he had pledged himself, and which indeed it would not be easy for him to give up. Lawyers were engaged, and the question had to a certain extent been taken up by the public; besides, how could a high-spirited girl like Eleanor Harding really learn to love a man for neglecting a duty which he assumed! Could she allow her affection to be purchased at the cost of his own self-respect?

As regarded the issue of his attempt at reformation in the hospital, Bold had no reason hitherto to be discontented with his success. All Barchester was by the ears about it. The bishop, the archdeacon, the warden, the steward, and several other clerical allies, had daily meetings, discussing their tactics, and preparing for the great attack. Sir Abraham Haphazard had been consulted, but his opinion was not yet received: copies of Hiram's will, copies of warden's journals, copies of leases, copies of accounts, copies of everything that could be copied, and of some that could not, had been sent to him; and the case was assuming most creditable dimensions. But, above all, it had been mentioned in the daily *Jupiter*. That all-powerful organ of the press in one of its leading

thunderbolts launched at St. Cross, had thus remarked: 'Another case, of smaller dimensions indeed,
but of similar import, is now likely to come under
public notice. We are informed that the warden or
master of an old almshouse attached to Barchester
Cathedral is in receipt of twenty-five times the annual
income appointed for him by the will of the founder,
while the sum yearly expended on the absolute purposes of the charity has always remained fixed. In
other words, the legatees under the founder's will
have received no advantage from the increase in the
value of the property during the last four centuries,
such increase having been absorbed by the so-called
warden. It is impossible to conceive a case of greater
injustice. It is no answer to say that some six or nine
or twelve old men receive as much of the goods of
this world as such old men require. On what founda-
tion, moral or divine, traditional or legal, is grounded
the warden's claim to the large income he receives
for doing nothing? The contentment of these almsmen, if content they be, can give him no title to this
wealth! Does he ever ask himself, when he stretches
wide his clerical palm to receive the pay of some
dozen of the working clergy, for what service he is
so remunerated? Does his conscience ever entertain
the question of his right to such subsidies? Or is it
possible that the subject never so presents itself to
his mind; that he has received for many years, and
intends, should God spare him, to receive for years
to come these fruits of the industrious piety of past
ages, indifferent as to any right on his own part, or
of any injustice to others! We must express an opinion
that nowhere but in the Church of England, and only

there among its priests, could such a state of moral indifference be found.'

I must for the present leave my readers to imagine the state of Mr. Harding's mind after reading the above article. They say that forty thousand copies of the *Jupiter* are daily sold, and that each copy is read by five persons at the least. Two hundred thousand readers then would hear this accusation against him; two hundred thousand hearts would swell with indignation at the griping injustice, the barefaced robbery of the warden of Barchester Hospital! And how was he to answer this? How was he to open his inmost heart to this multitude, to these thousands, the educated, the polished, the picked men of his own country; how show them that he was no robber, no avaricious lazy priest scrambling for gold, but a retiring, humble-spirited man, who had innocently taken what had innocently been offered to him?

'Write to the *Jupiter*,' suggested the bishop.

'Yes,' said the archdeacon, more worldly wise than his father, 'yes, and be smothered with ridicule; tossed over and over again with scorn; shaken this way and that, as a rat in the mouth of a practised terrier. You will leave out some word or letter in your answer, and the ignorance of the cathedral clergy will be harped upon; you will make some small mistake, which will be a falsehood, or some admission, which will be self-condemnation; you will find yourself to have been vulgar, ill-tempered, irreverent, and illiterate, and the chances are ten to one, but that being a clergyman, you will have been guilty of blasphemy! A man may have the best of causes, the best of talents, and the best of tempers;

he may write as well as Addison, or as strongly as Junius; but even with all this he cannot successfully answer, when attacked by the *Jupiter*. In such matters it is omnipotent. What the Czar is in Russia, or the mob in America, that the *Jupiter* is in England. Answer such an article! No warden; whatever you do, don't do that. We were to look for this sort of thing, you know; but we need not draw down on our heads more of it than is necessary.'

The article in the *Jupiter*, while it so greatly harassed our poor warden, was an immense triumph to some of the opposite party. Sorry as Bold was to see Mr. Harding attacked so personally, it still gave him a feeling of elation to find his cause taken up by so powerful an advocate: and as to Finney, the attorney, he was beside himself. What! to be engaged in the same cause and on the same side with the *Jupiter*; to have the views he had recommended seconded, and furthered, and battled for by the *Jupiter*! Perhaps to have his own name mentioned as that of the learned gentleman whose efforts had been so successful on behalf of the poor of Barchester! He might be examined before committees of the House of Commons, with heaven knows how much a day for his personal expenses—he might be engaged for years on such a suit! There was no end to the glorious golden dreams which this leader in the *Jupiter* produced in the soaring mind of Finney.

And the old bedesmen, they also heard of this article, and had a glimmering, indistinct idea of the marvellous advocate which had now taken up their cause. Abel Handy limped hither and thither through the rooms, repeating all that he understood to have been printed, with some additions of his own which he thought should have been added. He told them how the *Jupiter* had declared that their warden was no better than a robber, and that what the *Jupiter* said was acknowledged by the world to be true. How the *Jupiter* had affirmed that each one of them—'each one of us, Jonathan Crumple, think of that!'—had a clear right to a hundred a year; and that if the *Jupiter* had said so, it was better than a decision of the Lord Chancellor: and then he carried about the paper, supplied by Mr. Finney, which, though none of them could read it, still afforded in its very touch and aspect positive corroboration of what was told them; and Jonathan Crumple pondered deeply over his returning wealth; and Job Skulpit saw how right he had been in signing the petition, and said so many scores of times; and Spriggs leered fearfully with his one eye; and Moody, as he more nearly approached the coming golden age, hated more deeply than ever those who still kept possession of what he so coveted. Even Billy Gazy and poor bed-ridden Bell became active and uneasy, and the great Bunce stood apart with lowering brow, with deep grief seated in his heart, for he perceived that evil days were coming.

It had been decided, the archdeacon advising, that no remonstrance, explanation, or defence should be addressed from the Barchester conclave to the editor of the *Jupiter;* but hitherto that was the only decision to which they had come.

Sir Abraham Haphazard was deeply engaged in preparing a bill for the mortification of papists, to be called the 'Convent Custody Bill,' the purport of which was to enable any Protestant clergyman over fifty years of age to search any nun whom he suspected of being in possession of treasonable papers or jesuitical symbols: and as there were to be a hundred and thirty-seven clauses in the bill, each clause containing a separate thorn for the side of the papist, and as it was known the bill would be fought inch by inch, by fifty maddened Irishmen, the due construction and adequate dove-tailing of it did consume much of Sir Abraham's time. The bill had all its desired effect. Of course it never passed into law; but it so completely divided the ranks of the Irish members, who had bound themselves together to force on the ministry a bill for compelling all men to drink Irish whisky, and all women to wear Irish poplins, that for the remainder of the session the Great Poplin and Whisky League was utterly harmless.

Thus it happened that Sir Abraham's opinion was not at once forthcoming, and the uncertainty, the expectation, and suffering of the folk of Barchester was maintained at a high pitch.

8

PLUMSTEAD EPISCOPI

T H E reader must now be requested to visit the rectory of Plumstead Episcopi; and as it is as yet still early morning, to ascend again with us into the bedroom of the archdeacon. The mistress of the mansion was at her toilet; on which we will not dwell with profane eyes, but proceed into a small inner room, where the doctor dressed and kept his boots and sermons; and here we will take our stand, premising that the door of the room was so open as to admit of a conversation between our reverend Adam and his valued Eve.

'It's all your own fault, archdeacon,' said the latter. 'I told you from the beginning how it would end, and papa has no one to thank but you.'

'Good gracious, my dear,' said the doctor, appearing at the door of his dressing-room, with his face and head enveloped in the rough towel which he was violently using; 'how can you say so? I am doing my very best.'

'I wish you had never done so much,' said the lady, interrupting him. 'If you'd just have let John Bold come and go there, as he and papa liked, he and Eleanor would have been married by this time, and we should not have heard one word about all this affair.'

'But, my dear——'

'Oh, it's all very well, archdeacon; and of course you're right; I don't for a moment think you'll ever admit that you could be wrong; but the fact is, you've brought this young man down upon papa by huffing him as you have done.'

'But, my love——'

'And all because you didn't like John Bold for a brother-in-law. How is she ever to do better? papa hasn't got a shilling; and though Eleanor is well enough, she has not at all a taking style of beauty. I'm sure I don't know how she's to do better than marry John Bold; or as well indeed,' added the anxious sister, giving the last twist to her last shoe-string.

Dr. Grantly felt keenly the injustice of this attack; but what could he say? He certainly had huffed John Bold; he certainly had objected to him as a brother-in-law, and a very few months ago the very idea had excited his wrath: but now matters were changed; John Bold had shown his power, and, though he was as odious as ever to the archdeacon, power is always respected, and the reverend dignitary began to think that such an alliance might not have been imprudent. Nevertheless, his motto was still 'no surrender'; he would still fight it out; he believed confidently in Oxford, in the bench of bishops, in Sir Abraham Haphazard, and in himself; and it was only when alone with his wife that doubts of defeat ever beset him. He once more tried to communicate this confidence to Mrs. Grantly, and for the twentieth time began to tell her of Sir Abraham.

'Oh, Sir Abraham!' said she, collecting all her house keys into her basket before she descended;

'Sir Abraham won't get Eleanor a husband; Sir Abraham won't get papa another income when he has been worreted out of the hospital. Mark what I tell you, archdeacon: while you and Sir Abraham are fighting, papa will lose his preferment; and what will you do then with him and Eleanor on your hands? besides, who's to pay Sir Abraham? I suppose he won't take the case up for nothing?' And so the lady descended to family worship among her children and servants, the pattern of a good and prudent wife.

Dr. Grantly was blessed with a happy, thriving family. There were, first, three boys, now at home from school for the holidays. They were called, respectively, Charles James, Henry, and Samuel. The two younger (there were five in all) were girls; the elder, Florinda, bore the name of the Archbishop of York's wife, whose godchild she was: and the younger had been christened Grizzel, after a sister of the Archbishop of Canterbury. The boys were all clever, and gave good promise of being well able to meet the cares and trials of the world; and yet they were not alike in their dispositions, and each had his individual character, and each his separate admirers among the doctor's friends.

Charles James was an exact and careful boy; he never committed himself; he well knew how much was expected from the eldest son of the Archdeacon of Barchester, and was therefore mindful not to mix too freely with other boys. He had not the great talents of his younger brothers, but he exceeded them in judgment and propriety of demeanour; his fault, if he had one, was an over-attention to words instead of things; there was a thought too much *finesse* about him, and, as even his father sometimes told him, he was too fond of a compromise.

The second was the archdeacon's favourite son, and Henry was indeed a brilliant boy. The versatility of his genius was surprising, and the visitors at Plumstead Episcopi were often amazed at the marvellous manner in which he would, when called on, adapt his capacity to apparently most uncongenial pursuits. He appeared once before a large circle as Luther the reformer, and delighted them with the perfect manner in which he assumed the character; and within three days he again astonished them by acting the part of a Capuchin friar to the very life. For this last exploit his father gave him a golden guinea, and his brothers said the reward had been promised beforehand in the event of the performance being successful. He was also sent on a tour into Devonshire; a treat which the lad was most anxious of enjoying. His father's friends there, however, did not appreciate his talents, and sad accounts were sent home of the perversity of his nature. He was a most courageous lad, game to the backbone.

It was soon known, both at home, where he lived, and within some miles of Barchester Cathedral, and also at Westminster, where he was at school, that young Henry could box well and would never own himself beat; other boys would fight while they had a leg to stand on, but he would fight with no leg at all. Those backing him would sometimes think him crushed by the weight of blows and faint with loss of blood, and his friends would endeavour to withdraw him from the contest; but no, Henry never gave in, was never weary of the battle. The ring was the only

element in which he seemed to enjoy himself; and
while other boys were happy in the number of their
friends, he rejoiced most in the multitude of his foes.

His relations could not but admire his pluck, but
they sometimes were forced to regret that he was
inclined to be a bully; and those not so partial to him
as his father was, observed with pain that, though he
could fawn to the masters and the archdeacon's friends,
he was imperious and masterful to the servants and
the poor.

But perhaps Samuel was the general favourite;
and dear little Soapy, as he was familiarly called, was
as engaging a child as ever fond mother petted. He
was soft and gentle in his manners, and attractive in
his speech; the tone of his voice was melody, and
every action was a grace; unlike his brothers, he was
courteous to all, he was affable to the lowly, and
meek even to the very scullery maid. He was a boy
of great promise, minding his books and delighting
the hearts of his masters. His brothers, however,
were not particularly fond of him; they would complain to their mother that Soapy's civility all meant
something; they thought that his voice was too often
listened to at Plumstead Episcopi, and evidently
feared that, as he grew up, he would have more
weight in the house than either of them; there was,
therefore, a sort of agreement among them to put
young Soapy down. This, however, was not so easy
to be done; Samuel, though young, was sharp; he
could not assume the stiff decorum of Charles James,
nor could he fight like Henry; but he was a perfect
master of his own weapons, and contrived, in the
teeth of both of them, to hold the place which he had

assumed. Henry declared that he was a false, cunning creature; and Charles James, though he always spoke of him as his dear brother Samuel, was not slow to say a word against him when opportunity offered. To speak the truth, Samuel was a cunning boy, and those even who loved him best could not but own that for one so young he was too adroit in choosing his words, and too skilled in modulating his voice.

The two little girls Florinda and Grizzel were nice little girls enough, but they did not possess the strong sterling qualities of their brothers; their voices were not often heard at Plumstead Episcopi; they were bashful and timid by nature, slow to speak before company even when asked to do so; and though they looked very nice in their clean white muslin frocks and pink sashes, they were but little noticed by the archdeacon's visitors.

Whatever of submissive humility may have appeared in the gait and visage of the archdeacon during his colloquy with his wife in the sanctum of their dressing-rooms was dispelled as he entered his breakfast-parlour with erect head and powerful step. In the presence of a third person he assumed the lord and master; and that wise and talented lady too well knew the man to whom her lot for life was bound, to stretch her authority beyond the point at which it would be borne. Strangers at Plumstead Episcopi, when they saw the imperious brow with which he commanded silence from the large circle of visitors, children, and servants who came together in the morning to hear him read the word of God, and watched how meekly that wife seated herself behind her basket of keys with a little girl on each side,

as she caught that commanding glance; strangers, I
say, seeing this, could little guess that some fifteen
minutes since she had stoutly held her ground against
him, hardly allowing him to open his mouth in his
own defence. But such is the tact and talent of women!

And now let us observe the well-furnished breakfast-
parlour at Plumstead Episcopi, and the comfortable
air of all the belongings of the rectory. Comfortable they certainly were, but neither gorgeous
nor even grand; indeed, considering the money that
had been spent there, the eye and taste might have
been better served; there was an air of heaviness
about the rooms which might have been avoided
without any sacrifice of propriety; colours might have
been better chosen and lights more perfectly diffused;
but perhaps in doing so the thorough clerical aspect
of the whole might have been somewhat marred; at
any rate, it was not without ample consideration that
those thick, dark, costly carpets were put down;
those embossed, but sombre papers hung up; those
heavy curtains draped so as to half exclude the light
of the sun: nor were these old-fashioned chairs
bought at a price far exceeding that now given for
more modern goods, without a purpose. The break-
fast-service on the table was equally costly and equally
plain; the apparent object had been to spend money
without obtaining brilliancy or splendour. The urn
was of thick and solid silver, as were also the tea-pot,
coffee-pot, cream-ewer, and sugar-bowl; the cups
were old, dim dragon china, worth about a pound a
piece, but very despicable in the eyes of the uninitiated. The silver forks were so heavy as to be
disagreeable to the hand, and the bread-basket was of

a weight really formidable to any but robust persons. The tea consumed was the very best, the coffee the very blackest, the cream the very thickest; there was dry toast and buttered toast, muffins and crumpets; hot bread and cold bread, white bread and brown bread, home-made bread and bakers' bread, wheaten bread and oaten bread; and if there be other breads than these, they were there; there were eggs in napkins, and crispy bits of bacon under silver covers; and there were little fishes in a little box, and devilled kidneys frizzling on a hot-water dish; which, by-the-by, were placed closely contiguous to the plate of the worthy archdeacon himself. Over and above this, on a snow-white napkin, spread upon the sideboard, was a huge ham and a huge sirloin; the latter having laden the dinner table on the previous evening. Such was the ordinary fare at Plumstead Episcopi.

And yet I have never found the rectory a pleasant house. The fact that man shall not live by bread alone seemed to be somewhat forgotten; and noble as was the appearance of the host, and sweet and good-natured as was the face of the hostess, talented as were the children, and excellent as were the viands and the wines, in spite of these attractions, I generally found the rectory somewhat dull. After breakfast the archdeacon would retire, of course to his clerical pursuits. Mrs. Grantly, I presume, inspected her kitchen, though she had a first-rate housekeeper, with sixty pounds a year; and attended to the lessons of Florinda and Grizzel, though she had an excellent governess with thirty pounds a year: but at any rate she disappeared: and I never could make companions of the boys. Charles James, though he always looked as though there was something in him, never seemed to have much to say; and what he did say he would always unsay the next minute. He told me once that he considered cricket, on the whole, to be a gentleman-like game for boys, provided they would play without running about; and that fives, also, was a seemly game, so that those who played it never heated themselves. Henry once quarrelled with me for taking his sister Grizzel's part in a contest between them as to the best mode of using a watering-pot for the garden flowers; and from that day to this he has not spoken to me, though he speaks at me often enough. For half an hour or so I certainly did like Sammy's gentle speeches; but one gets tired of honey, and I found that he preferred the more admiring listeners whom he met in the kitchen-garden and back precincts of the establishment; besides, I think I once caught Sammy fibbing.

On the whole, therefore, I found the rectory a dull house, though it must be admitted that everything there was of the very best.

After breakfast, on the morning of which we are writing, the archdeacon, as usual, retired to his study, intimating that he was going to be very busy, but that he would see Mr. Chadwick if he called. On entering this sacred room he carefully opened the paper case on which he was wont to compose his favourite sermons, and spread on it a fair sheet of paper and one partly written on; he then placed his inkstand, looked at his pen, and folded his blotting paper; having done so, he got up again from his seat, stood with his back to the fireplace, and yawned comfortably, stretching out vastly his huge arms and opening his burly chest. He then walked across the room and locked the door; and having so prepared himself, he threw himself into his easy chair, took from a secret drawer beneath his table a volume of Rabelais, and began to amuse himself with the witty mischief of Panurge; and so passed the archdeacon's morning on that day.

He was left undisturbed at his studies for an hour or two, when a knock came to the door, and Mr. Chadwick was announced. Rabelais retired into the secret drawer, the easy chair seemed knowingly to betake itself off, and when the archdeacon quickly undid his bolt, he was discovered by the steward working, as usual, for that church of which he was so useful a pillar. Mr. Chadwick had just come from London, and was, therefore, known to be the bearer of important news.

'We've got Sir Abraham's opinion at last,' said Mr. Chadwick, as he seated himself.

'Well, well, well!' exclaimed the archdeacon impatiently.

'Oh, it's as long as my arm,' said the other; 'it can't be told in a word, but you can read it;' and he handed him a copy, in heaven knows how many spun-out folios, of the opinion which the attorney-general had managed to cram on the back and sides of the case as originally submitted to him.

'The upshot is,' said Chadwick, 'that there's a screw loose in their case, and we had better do nothing. They are proceeding against Mr. Harding and myself, and Sir Abraham holds that, under the wording of the will, and subsequent arrangements legally sanctioned, Mr. Harding and I are only paid servants.

The defendants should have been either the Corporation of Barchester, or possibly the chapter or your father.'

'W—hoo!' said the archdeacon; 'so Master Bold is on the wrong scent, is he?'

'That's Sir Abraham's opinion; but any scent almost would be a wrong scent. Sir Abraham thinks that if they'd taken the corporation, or the chapter, we could have baffled them. The bishop, he thinks, would be the surest shot; but even there we could plead that the bishop is only visitor, and that he has never made himself a consenting party to the performance of other duties.'

'That's quite clear,' said the archdeacon.

'Not quite so clear,' said the other. 'You see the will says, "My lord, the bishop, being graciously pleased to see that due justice be done." Now, it may be a question whether, in accepting and administering the patronage, your father has not accepted also the other duties assigned. It is doubtful, however; but even if they hit that nail—and they are far off from that yet—the point is so nice, as Sir Abraham says, that you would force them into fifteen thousand pounds' cost before they could bring it to an issue! and where's that sum of money to come from?'

The archdeacon rubbed his hands with delight; he had never doubted the justice of his case, but he had begun to have some dread of unjust success on the part of his enemies. It was delightful to him thus to hear that their cause was surrounded with such rocks and shoals; such causes of shipwreck unseen by the landsman's eye, but visible enough to the keen eyes of practical law mariners. How wrong his wife was to wish that Bold should marry Eleanor! Bold! why if he should be ass enough to persevere, he would be a beggar before he knew whom he was at law with!

'That's excellent, Chadwick—that's excellent! I told you Sir Abraham was the man for us;' and he put down on the table the copy of the opinion, and patted it fondly.

'Don't you let that be seen, though, archdeacon.'

'Who?—I!—not for worlds,' said the doctor.

'People will talk, you know, archdeacon.'

'Of course, of course,' said the doctor.

'Because, if that gets abroad, it would teach them how to fight their own battle.'

'Quite true,' said the doctor.

'No one here in Barchester ought to see that but you and I, archdeacon.'

'No, no, certainly no one else,' said the archdeacon, pleased with the closeness of the confidence; 'no one else shall.'

'Mrs. Grantly is very interested in the matter, I know,' said Mr. Chadwick.

Did the archdeacon wink, or did he not? I am inclined to think he did not quite wink; but that without such, perhaps, unseemly gesture he communicated to Mr. Chadwick, with the corner of his eye, intimation that, deep as was Mrs. Grantly's interest in the matter, it should not procure for her a perusal of that document; and at the same time he partly opened the small drawer, above spoken of, deposited the paper on the volume of Rabelais, and showed to Mr. Chadwick the nature of the key which guarded these hidden treasures. The careful steward then expressed himself contented. Ah! vain man! he could fasten up his Rabelais, and other things secret, with all the skill of Bramah or of Chubb; but where could he fasten up the key which solved these mechanical mysteries? It is probable to us that the contents of no drawer in that house were unknown to its mistress, and we think, moreover, that she was entitled to all such knowledge.

'But,' said Mr. Chadwick, 'we must, of course, tell your father and Mr. Harding so much of Sir Abraham's opinion as will satisfy them that the matter is doing well.'

'Oh, certainly—yes, of course,' said the doctor.

'You had better let them know that Sir Abraham is of opinion that there is no case at any rate against Mr. Harding; and that as the action is worded at present, it must fall to the ground; they must be non-suited if they carry it on; you had better tell Mr. Harding, that Sir Abraham is clearly of opinion that he is only a servant, and as such not liable—or if you like it, I'll see Mr. Harding myself.'

'Oh, I must see him to-morrow, and my father too, and I'll explain to them exactly so much,—you won't go before lunch, Mr. Chadwick: well, if you will, you must, for I know your time is precious;' and he shook hands with the diocesan steward, and bowed him out.

The archdeacon had again recourse to his drawer, and twice read through the essence of Sir Abraham Haphazard's law-enlightened and law-bewildered brains. It was very clear that to Sir Abraham, the justice of the old men's claim or the justice of Mr. Harding's defence were ideas that had never presented themselves. A legal victory over an opposing party was the service for which Sir Abraham was, as he imagined, to be paid; and that he, according to his lights, had diligently laboured to achieve, and with probable hope of success. Of the intense desire which Mr. Harding felt to be assured on fit authority that he was wronging no man, that he was entitled in true equity to his income, that he might sleep at night without pangs of conscience, that he was no robber, no spoiler of the poor; that he and all the world might be openly convinced that he was not the man which the *Jupiter* had described him to be; of such longings on the part of Mr. Harding, Sir Abraham was entirely ignorant; nor, indeed, could it be looked on as part of his business to gratify such desires. Such was not the system on which his battles were fought, and victories gained. Success was his object, and he was generally successful. He conquered his enemies by their weakness rather than by his own strength, and it had been found almost impossible to make up a case in which Sir Abraham, as an antagonist, would not find a flaw.

The archdeacon was delighted with the closeness of the reasoning. To do him justice, it was not a selfish triumph that he desired; he would personally lose nothing by defeat, or at least what he might lose did not actuate him; but neither was it love of justice which made him so anxious, nor even mainly solicitude for his father-in-law. He was fighting a part of a never-ending battle against a never-conquered foe—that of the church against its enemies.

He knew Mr. Harding could not pay all the expense of these doings; for these long opinions of Sir Abraham's, these causes to be pleaded, these speeches to be made, these various courts through which the case was, he presumed, to be dragged. He knew that he and his father must at least bear the heavier portion of this tremendous cost; but to do the archdeacon justice, he did not recoil from this. He was a man fond of obtaining money, greedy of a large income, but open-handed enough in expending it, and it was a triumph to him to foresee the success of this measure, although he might be called on to pay so dearly for it himself.

9

THE CONFERENCE

ON the following morning the archdeacon was with
his father betimes, and a note was sent down to the
warden begging his attendance at the palace. Dr.
Grantly, as he cogitated on the matter, leaning back
in his brougham as he journeyed into Barchester,
felt that it would be difficult to communicate his own
satisfaction either to his father or to his father-in-law.
He wanted success on his own side and discomfiture
on that of his enemies. The bishop wanted peace on
the subject; a settled peace if possible, but peace at
any rate till the short remainder of his own days had
spun itself out. Mr. Harding required, not only success and peace, but he also demanded that he might
stand justified before the world.

The bishop, however, was comparatively easy to
deal with; and before the arrival of the other, the
dutiful son had persuaded his father that all was
going on well, and then the warden arrived.

It was Mr. Harding's wont, whenever he spent a
morning at the palace, to seat himself immediately
at the bishop's elbow, the bishop occupying a huge
armchair fitted up with candlesticks, a reading table,
a drawer, and other paraphernalia, the position of
which chair was never moved, summer or winter;
and when, as was usual, the archdeacon was there
also, he confronted the two elders, who thus were

enabled to fight the battle against him together; and together submit to defeat, for such was their constant fate.

Our warden now took his accustomed place, having greeted his son-in-law as he entered, and then affectionately inquired after his friend's health. There was a gentleness about the bishop to which the soft womanly affection of Mr. Harding particularly endeared itself, and it was quaint to see how the two mild old priests pressed each other's hands, and smiled and made little signs of love.

'Sir Abraham's opinion has come at last,' began the archdeacon. Mr. Harding had heard so much, and was most anxious to know the result.

'It is quite favourable,' said the bishop, pressing his friend's arm. 'I am so glad.'

Mr. Harding looked at the mighty bearer of the important news for confirmation of these glad tidings.

'Yes,' said the archdeacon; 'Sir Abraham has given most minute attention to the case; indeed, I knew he would—most minute attention; and his opinion is— and as to his opinion on such a subject being correct, no one who knows Sir Abraham's character can doubt—his opinion is, that they hav'n't got a leg to stand on.'

'But as how, archdeacon?'

'Why, in the first place:—but you're no lawyer, warden, and I doubt you won't understand it; the gist of the matter is this:—under Hiram's will two paid guardians have been selected for the hospital; the law will say two paid servants, and you and I won't quarrel with the name.'

'At any rate I will not if I am one of the servants,' said Mr. Harding. 'A rose, you know——'

'Yes, yes,' said the archdeacon, impatient of poetry at such a time. 'Well, two paid servants, we'll say; one to look after the men, and the other to look after the money. You and Chadwick are these two servants, and whether either of you be paid too much, or too little, more or less in fact than the founder willed, it's as clear as daylight that no one can fall foul of either of you for receiving an allotted stipend.'

'That does seem clear,' said the bishop, who had winced visibly at the words servants and stipend, which, however, appeared to have caused no uneasiness to the archdeacon.

'Quite clear,' said he, 'and very satisfactory. In point of fact, it being necessary to select such servants for the use of the hospital, the pay to be given to them must depend on the rate of pay for such services, according to their market value at the period in question; and those who manage the hospital must be the only judges of this.'

'And who does manage the hospital?' asked the warden.

'Oh, let them find that out; that's another question: the action is brought against you and Chadwick; that's your defence, and a perfect and full defence it is. Now that I think very satisfactory.'

'Well,' said the bishop, looking inquiringly up into his friend's face, who sat silent awhile, and apparently not so well satisfied.

'And conclusive,' continued the archdeacon; 'if they press it to a jury, which they won't do, no twelve men in England will take five minutes to decide against them.'

'But according to that,' said Mr. Harding, 'I might as well have sixteen hundred a year as eight, if the managers choose to allot it to me; and as I am one of the managers, if not the chief manager, myself, that can hardly be a just arrangement.'

'Oh, well; all that's nothing to the question. The question is, whether this intruding fellow, and a lot of cheating attorneys and pestilent dissenters, are to interfere with an arrangement which every one knows is essentially just and serviceable to the church. Pray don't let us be splitting hairs, and that amongst ourselves, or there'll never be an end of the cause or the cost.'

Mr. Harding again sat silent for a while, during which the bishop once and again pressed his arm, and looked in his face to see if he could catch a gleam of a contented and eased mind; but there was no such gleam, and the poor warden continued playing sad dirges on invisible stringed instruments in all manner of positions: he was ruminating in his mind on this opinion of Sir Abraham, looking to it wearily and earnestly for satisfaction, but finding none. At last he said, 'Did you see the opinion, archdeacon?'

The archdeacon said he had not—that was to say, he had—that was, he had not seen the opinion itself; he had seen what had been called a copy, but he could not say whether of a whole or part; nor could he say that what he had seen were the *ipsissima verba* of the great man himself; but what he had seen contained exactly the decision which he had announced,

and which he again declared to be to his mind extremely satisfactory.

'I should like to see the opinion,' said the warden;
'that is, a copy of it.'

'Well, I suppose you can if you make a point of it;
but I don't see the use myself; of course it is essential
that the purport of it should not be known, and it is
therefore unadvisable to multiply copies.'

'Why should it not be known?' asked the warden.

'What a question for a man to ask!' said the archdeacon, throwing up his hands in token of his surprise; 'but it is like you—a child is not more innocent
than you are in matters of business. Can't you see
that if we tell them that no action will lie against
you, but that one may possibly lie against some
other person or persons, that we shall be putting
weapons into their hands, and be teaching them how
to cut our own throats?'

The warden again sat silent, and the bishop again
looked at him wistfully: 'The only thing we have now
to do,' continued the archdeacon, 'is to remain quiet,
hold our peace, and let them play their own game as
they please.'

'We are not to make known then,' said the warden,
'that we have consulted the attorney-general, and
that we are advised by him that the founder's will is
fully and fairly carried out.'

'God bless my soul!' said the archdeacon, 'how
odd it is that you will not see that all we are to do is
to do nothing: why should we say anything about the
founder's will? We are in possession; and we know
that they are not in a position to put us out; surely
that is enough for the present.'

Mr. Harding rose from his seat and paced thoughtfully up and down the library, the bishop the while watching him painfully at every turn, and the archdeacon continuing to pour forth his convictions that the affair was in a state to satisfy any prudent mind.

'And the *Jupiter*?' said the warden, stopping suddenly.

'Oh! the *Jupiter*,' answered the other. 'The *Jupiter* can break no bones. You must bear with that; there is much, of course, which it is our bounden duty to bear; it cannot be all roses for us here,' and the archdeacon looked exceedingly moral; 'besides, the matter is too trivial, of too little general interest to be mentioned again in the *Jupiter*, unless we stir up the subject.' And the archdeacon again looked exceedingly knowing and worldly wise.

The warden continued his walk; the hard and stinging words of that newspaper article, each one of which had thrust a thorn as it were into his inmost soul, were fresh in his memory; he had read it more than once, word by word, and what was worse, he fancied it was as well known to every one as to himself. Was he to be looked on as the unjust griping priest he had been there described? Was he to be pointed at as the consumer of the bread of the poor, and to be allowed no means of refuting such charges, of clearing his begrimed name, of standing innocent in the world, as hitherto he had stood? Was he to bear all this, to receive as usual his now hated income, and be known as one of those greedy priests who by their rapacity have brought disgrace on their church? and why? Why should he bear all this? why should he die, for he felt that he could not live, under such a weight of obloquy? As he paced up and down the room he resolved in his misery and enthusiasm that he could with pleasure, if he were allowed, give up his place, abandon his pleasant home, leave the hospital, and live poorly, happily, and with an unsullied name, on the small remainder of his means.

He was a man somewhat shy of speaking of himself, even before those who knew him best, and whom he loved the most; but at last it burst forth from him, and with a somewhat jerking eloquence he declared that he could not, would not, bear this misery any longer.

'If it can be proved,' said he at last, 'that I have a just and honest right to this, as God well knows I always deemed I had; if this salary or stipend be really my due, I am not less anxious than another to retain it. I have the well-being of my child to look to. I am too old to miss without some pain the comforts to which I have been used; and I am, as others are, anxious to prove to the world that I have been right, and to uphold the place I have held; but I cannot do it at such a cost as this. I cannot bear this. Could you tell me to do so?' And he appealed, almost in tears, to the bishop, who had left his chair, and was now leaning on the warden's arm as he stood on the further side of the table facing the archdeacon. 'Could you tell me to sit there at ease, indifferent, and satisfied, while such things as these are said loudly of me in the world?'

The bishop could feel for him and sympathise with him, but he could not advise him, he could only say,

'No, no, you shall be asked to do nothing that is painful; you shall do just what your heart tells you to be right; you shall do whatever you think best yourself. Theophilus, don't advise him, pray don't advise the warden to do anything which is painful.'

But the archdeacon, though he could not sympathise, could advise; and he saw that the time had come when it behoved him to do so in a somewhat peremptory manner.

'Why, my lord,' he said, speaking to his father: and when he called his father 'my lord,' the good old bishop shook in his shoes, for he knew that an evil time was coming. 'Why, my lord, there are two ways of giving advice: there is advice that may be good for the present day; and there is advice that may be good for days to come: now I cannot bring myself to give the former, if it be incompatible with the other.'

'No, no, no, I suppose not,' said the bishop, re-seating himself, and shading his face with his hands. Mr. Harding sat down with his back to the further wall, playing to himself some air fitted for so calamitous an occasion, and the archdeacon said out his say standing, with his back to the empty fireplace.

'It is not to be supposed but that much pain will spring out of this unnecessarily raised question. We must all have foreseen that, and the matter has in no wise gone on worse than we expected; but it will be weak, yes, and wicked also, to abandon the cause and own ourselves wrong, because the inquiry is painful. It is not only ourselves we have to look to; to a certain extent the interest of the church is in our keeping. Should it be found that one after another of those who hold preferment abandoned it whenever it might be attacked, is it not plain that such attacks would be renewed till nothing was left us? and, that if so deserted, the Church of England must fall to the ground altogether? If this be true of many, it is true of one. Were you, accused as you now are, to throw up the wardenship, and to relinquish the preferment which is your property, with the vain object of proving yourself disinterested, you would fail in that object, you would inflict a desperate blow on your brother clergymen, you would encourage every cantankerous dissenter in England to make a similar charge against some source of clerical revenue, and you would do your best to dishearten those who are most anxious to defend you and uphold your position. I can fancy nothing more weak, or more wrong. It is not that you think that there is any justice in these charges, or that you doubt your own right to the wardenship: you are convinced of your own honesty, and yet would yield to them through cowardice.'

'Cowardice!' said the bishop, expostulating. Mr. Harding sat unmoved, gazing on his son-in-law.

'Well; would it not be cowardice? would he not do so because he is afraid to endure the evil things which will be falsely spoken of him? Would that not be cowardice? And now let us see the extent of the evil which you dread. The *Jupiter* publishes an article which a great many, no doubt, will read; but of those who understand the subject how many will believe the *Jupiter*? Every one knows what its object is: it has taken up the case against Lord Guildford and against the Dean of Rochester, and that against half a dozen bishops; and does not every one know that it would take up any case of the kind, right or wrong, false or true, with known justice or known injustice, if by doing so it could further its own views? Does not all the world know this of the *Jupiter*? Who that really knows you will think the worse of you for what the *Jupiter* says? And why care for those who do not know you? I will say nothing of your own comfort, but I do say that you could not be justified in throwing up, in a fit of passion, for such it would be, the only maintenance that Eleanor has; and if you did so, if you really did vacate the wardenship, and submit to ruin, what would that profit you? If you have no future right to the income, you have had no past right to it; and the very fact of your abandoning your position would create a demand for repayment of that which you have already received and spent.'

The poor warden groaned as he sat perfectly still, looking up at the hard-hearted orator who thus tormented him, and the bishop echoed the sound faintly from behind his hands; but the archdeacon cared little for such signs of weakness, and completed his exhortation.

'But let us suppose the office to be left vacant, and that your own troubles concerning it were over; would that satisfy you? Are your only aspirations in the matter confined to yourself and family? I know they are not. I know you are as anxious as any of us for the church to which we belong; and what a grievous blow would such an act of apostasy give her? You owe it to the church of which you are a member and a minister, to bear with this affliction, however

severe it may be: you owe it to my father, who instituted you, to support his rights: you owe it to those
who preceded you to assert the legality of their position: you owe it to those who are to come after you, to
maintain uninjured for them that which you received
uninjured from others; and you owe to us all the
unflinching assistance of perfect brotherhood in this
matter, so that upholding one another we may support our great cause without blushing and without
disgrace.'

And so the archdeacon ceased, and stood self-
satisfied, watching the effect of his spoken wisdom.

The warden felt himself, to a certain extent, stifled;
he would have given the world to get himself out
into the open air without speaking to, or noticing
those who were in the room with him; but this was
impossible. He could not leave without saying something, and he felt himself confounded by the archdeacon's eloquence. There was a heavy, unfeeling,
unanswerable truth in what he had said; there was
so much practical, but odious common sense in it,
that he neither knew how to assent or to differ. If it
were necessary for him to suffer, he felt that he could
endure without complaint and without cowardice,
providing that he was self-satisfied of the justice of
his own cause. What he could not endure was, that
he should be accused by others, and not acquitted by
himself. Doubting, as he had begun to doubt, the
justice of his own position in the hospital, he knew
that his own self-confidence would not be restored
because Mr. Bold had been in error as to some legal
form; nor could he be satisfied to escape, because,
through some legal fiction, he who received the

greatest benefit from the hospital might be considered only as one of its servants.

The archdeacon's speech had silenced him—stupefied him—annihilated him; anything but satisfied him. With the bishop it fared not much better. He did not discern clearly how things were, but he saw enough to know that a battle was to be prepared for; a battle that would destroy his few remaining comforts, and bring him with sorrow to the grave.

The warden still sat, and still looked at the archdeacon, till his thoughts fixed themselves wholly on the means of escape from his present position, and he felt like a bird fascinated by gazing on a snake.

'I hope you agree with me,' said the archdeacon at last, breaking the dread silence; 'my lord, I hope you agree with me.'

Oh, what a sigh the bishop gave! 'My lord, I hope you agree with me,' again repeated the merciless tyrant.

'Yes, I suppose so,' groaned the poor old man, slowly.

'And you, warden?'

Mr. Harding was now stirred to action—he must speak and move, so he got up and took one turn before he answered.

'Do not press me for an answer just at present; I will do nothing lightly in the matter, and of whatever I do I will give you and the bishop notice.' And so without another word he took his leave, escaping quickly through the palace hall, and down the lofty steps, nor did he breathe freely till he found himself alone under the huge elms of the silent close. Here he walked long and slowly, thinking on his case

116

with a troubled air, and trying in vain to confute the archdeacon's argument. He then went home, resolved to bear it all—ignominy, suspense, disgrace, self-doubt, and heart-burning—and to do as those would have him, who he still believed were most fit and most able to counsel him aright.

10

TRIBULATION

MR. HARDING was a sadder man than he had ever
yet been when he returned to his own house. He
had been wretched enough on that well-remembered
morning when he was forced to expose before his
son-in-law the publisher's account for ushering into
the world his dear book of sacred music; when after
making such payments as he could do unassisted, he
found that he was a debtor of more than three hundred
pounds; but his sufferings then were as nothing to
his present misery;—then he had done wrong, and
he knew it, and was able to resolve that he would not
sin in like manner again; but now he could make no
resolution, and comfort himself by no promises of
firmness. He had been forced to think that his lot had
placed him in a false position, and he was about to
maintain that position against the opinion of the
world and against his own convictions.

He had read with pity, amounting almost to
horror, the strictures which had appeared from time
to time against the Earl of Guildford as master of
St. Cross, and the invectives that had been heaped
on rich diocesan dignitaries and overgrown sinecure
pluralists. In judging of them, he judged leniently;
the whole bias of his profession had taught him to
think that they were more sinned against than sin-
ning, and that the animosity with which they had

been pursued was venomous and unjust; but he had not the less regarded their plight as most miserable. His hair had stood on end and his flesh had crept as he read the things which had been written; he had wondered how men could live under such a load of disgrace; how they could face their fellow-creatures while their names were bandied about so injuriously and so publicly—and now this lot was to be his—he, that shy, retiring man, who had so comforted himself in the hidden obscurity of his lot, who had so enjoyed the unassuming warmth of his own little corner, he was now to be dragged forth into the glaring day, and gibbeted before ferocious multitudes. He entered his own house a crestfallen, humiliated man, without a hope of overcoming the wretchedness which affected him.

He wandered into the drawing-room where was his daughter; but he could not speak to her now, so he left it, and went into the book-room. He was not quick enough to escape Eleanor's glance, or to prevent her from seeing that he was disturbed; and in a little while she followed him. She found him seated in his accustomed chair with no book open before him, no pen ready in his hand, no ill-shapen notes of blotted music lying before him as was usual, none of those hospital accounts with which he was so precise and yet so unmethodical: he was doing nothing, thinking of nothing, looking at nothing; he was merely suffering.

'Leave me, Eleanor, my dear,' he said; 'leave me, my darling, for a few minutes, for I am busy.'

Eleanor saw well how it was, but she did leave him, and glided silently back to her drawing-room.

When he had sat a while, thus alone and unoccupied, he got up to walk again—he could make more of his thoughts walking than sitting, and was creeping out into his garden, when he met Bunce on the threshold.

'Well, Bunce,' said he, in a tone that for him was sharp, 'what is it? do you want me?'

'I was only coming to ask after your reverence,' said the old bedesman, touching his hat; 'and to inquire about the news from London,' he added after a pause.

The warden winced, and put his hand to his forehead and felt bewildered.

'Attorney Finney has been there this morning,' continued Bunce, 'and by his looks I guess he is not so well pleased as he once was, and it has got abroad somehow that the archdeacon has had down great news from London, and Handy and Moody are both as black as devils. And I hope,' said the man, trying to assume a cheery tone, 'that things are looking up, and that there'll be an end soon to all this stuff which bothers your reverence so sorely.'

'Well, I wish there may be, Bunce.'

'But about the news, your reverence?' said the old man, almost whispering.

Mr. Harding walked on, and shook his head impatiently. Poor Bunce little knew how he was tormenting his patron.

'If there was anything to cheer you, I should be so glad to know it,' said he, with a tone of affection which the warden in all his misery could not resist.

He stopped, and took both the old man's hands in his. 'My friend,' said he, 'my dear old friend, there is nothing; there is no news to cheer me—God's will be done:' and two small hot tears broke away from his eyes and stole down his furrowed cheeks.

'Then God's will be done,' said the other solemnly; 'but they told me that there was good news from London, and I came to wish your reverence joy; but God's will be done,' and so the warden again walked on, and the bedesman, looking wistfully after him and receiving no encouragement to follow, returned sadly to his own abode.

For a couple of hours the warden remained thus in the garden, now walking, now standing motionless on the turf, and then, as his legs got weary, sitting unconsciously on the garden seats, and then walking again. And Eleanor, hidden behind the muslin curtains of the window, watched him through the trees as he now came in sight, and then again was concealed by the turnings of the walk; and thus the time passed away till five, when the warden crept back to the house and prepared for dinner.

It was but a sorry meal. The demure parlourmaid, as she handed the dishes and changed the plates, saw that all was not right, and was more demure than ever: neither father nor daughter could eat, and the hateful food was soon cleared away, and the bottle of port placed upon the table.

'Would you like Bunce to come in, papa?' said Eleanor, thinking that the company of the old man might lighten his sorrow.

'No, my dear, thank you, not to-day; but are not you going out, Eleanor, this lovely afternoon? don't stay in for me, my dear.'

'I thought you seemed so sad, papa.'

'Sad,' said he, irritated; 'well, people must all

have their share of sadness here; I am not more exempt than another: but kiss me, dearest, and go now; I will, if possible, be more sociable when you return.'

And Eleanor was again banished from her father's sorrow. Ah! her desire now was not to find him happy, but to be allowed to share his sorrows; not to force him to be sociable, but to persuade him to be trustful.

She put on her bonnet as desired, and went up to Mary Bold; this was now her daily haunt, for John Bold was up in London among lawyers and church reformers, diving deep into other questions than that of the wardenship of Barchester; supplying information to one member of Parliament, and dining with another; subscribing to funds for the abolition of clerical incomes, and seconding at that great national meeting at the Crown and Anchor a resolution to the effect, that no clergyman of the Church of England, be he who he might, should have more than a thousand a year, and none less than two hundred and fifty. His speech on this occasion was short, for fifteen had to speak, and the room was hired for two hours only, at the expiration of which the Quakers and Mr. Cobden were to make use of it for an appeal to the public in aid of the Emperor of Russia; but it was sharp and effective; at least he was told so by a companion with whom he now lived much, and on whom he greatly depended—one Tom Towers, a very leading genius, and supposed to have high employment on the staff of the *Jupiter*.

So Eleanor, as was now her wont, went up to Mary Bold, and Mary listened kindly, while the daughter spoke much of her father, and, perhaps kinder still, found a listener in Eleanor, while she spoke about her brother. In the meantime the warden sat alone, leaning on the arm of his chair; he had poured out a glass of wine, but had done so merely from habit, for he left it untouched; there he sat gazing at the open window, and thinking, if he can be said to have thought, of the happiness of his past life. All manner of past delights came before his mind, which at the time he had enjoyed without considering them; his easy days, his absence of all kind of hard work, his pleasant shady home, those twelve old neighbours whose welfare till now had been the source of so much pleasant care, the excellence of his children, the friendship of the dear old bishop, the solemn grandeur of those vaulted aisles, through which he loved to hear his own voice pealing; and then that friend of friends, that choice ally that had never deserted him, that eloquent companion that would always, when asked, discourse such pleasant music, that violoncello of his—ah, how happy he had been! but it was over now; his easy days and absence of work had been the crime which brought on him his tribulation; his shady home was pleasant no longer; maybe it was no longer his; the old neighbours, whose welfare had been so desired by him, were his enemies; his daughter was as wretched as himself; and even the bishop was made miserable by his position. He could never again lift up his voice boldly as he had hitherto done among his brethren, for he felt that he was disgraced; and he feared even to touch his bow, for he knew how grievous a sound of wailing, how piteous a lamentation, it would produce.

He was still sitting in the same chair and the same posture, having hardly moved a limb for two hours, when Eleanor came back to tea, and succeeded in bringing him with her into the drawing-room.

The tea seemed as comfortless as the dinner, though the warden, who had hitherto eaten nothing all day, devoured the plateful of bread and butter, unconscious of what he was doing.

Eleanor had made up her mind to force him to talk to her, but she hardly knew how to commence: she must wait till the urn was gone, till the servant would no longer be coming in and out.

At last everything was gone, and the drawing-room door was permanently closed; then Eleanor, getting up and going round to her father, put her arm round his neck, and said, 'Papa, won't you tell me what it is?'

'What what is, my dear?'

'This new sorrow that torments you; I know you are unhappy, papa.'

'New sorrow! it's no new sorrow, my dear; we have all our cares sometimes;' and he tried to smile, but it was a ghastly failure; 'but I shouldn't be so dull a companion; come, we'll have some music.'

'No, papa, not to-night—it would only trouble you to-night;' and she sat upon his knee, as she sometimes would in their gayest moods, and with her arm round his neck, she said: 'Papa, I will not leave you till you talk to me; oh, if you only knew how much good it would do to you, to tell me of it all.'

The father kissed his daughter, and pressed her to his heart; but still he said nothing: it was so hard to him to speak of his own sorrows; he was so shy a man even with his own child!

'Oh, papa, do tell me what it is; I know it is about the hospital, and what they are doing up in London, and what that cruel newspaper has said; but if there be such cause for sorrow, let us be sorrowful together; we are all in all to each other now: dear, dear papa, do speak to me.'

Mr. Harding could not well speak now, for the warm tears were running down his cheeks like rain in May, but he held his child close to his heart, and squeezed her hand as a lover might, and she kissed his forehead and his wet cheeks, and lay upon his bosom, and comforted him as a woman only can do.

'My own child,' he said, as soon as his tears would let him speak, 'my own, own child, why should you too be unhappy before it is necessary? It may come to that, that we must leave this place, but till that time comes, why should your young days be clouded?'

'And is that all, papa? If that be all, let us leave it, and have light hearts elsewhere: if that be all, let us go. Oh, papa, you and I could be happy if we had only bread to eat, so long as our hearts were light.'

And Eleanor's face was lighted up with enthusiasm as she told her father how he might banish all his care; and a gleam of joy shot across his brow as this idea of escape again presented itself, and he again fancied for a moment that he could spurn away from him the income which the world envied him; that he could give the lie to that wielder of the tomahawk who had dared to write such things of him in the *Jupiter;* that he could leave Sir Abraham, and the archdeacon, and Bold, and the rest of them with their lawsuit among them, and wipe his hands altogether of so sorrow-stirring a concern. Ah, what happiness might there be in the distance, with Eleanor and him in some small cottage, and nothing left of their former grandeur but their music! Yes, they would walk forth with their music books, and their instruments, and shaking the dust from off their feet as they went, leave the ungrateful place. Never did a poor clergyman sigh for a warm benefice more anxiously than our warden did now to be rid of his.

'Give it up, papa,' she said again, jumping from his knees and standing on her feet before him, looking boldly into his face; 'give it up, papa.'

Oh, it was sad to see how that momentary gleam of joy passed away; how the look of hope was dispersed from that sorrowful face, as the remembrance of the archdeacon came back upon our poor warden, and he reflected that he could not stir from his now hated post. He was as a man bound with iron, fettered with adamant: he was in no respect a free agent; he had no choice. 'Give it up!' Oh, if he only could: what an easy way that were out of all his troubles!

'Papa, don't doubt about it,' she continued, thinking that his hesitation arose from his unwillingness to abandon so comfortable a home; 'is it on my account that you would stay here? Do you think that I cannot be happy without a pony-carriage and a fine drawing-room? Papa, I never can be happy here, as long as there is a question as to your honour in staying here; but I could be gay as the day is long in the smallest tiny little cottage, if I could see you come in and go out with a light heart. Oh! papa, your face tells so much; though you won't speak to me with your voice, I know how it is with you every time I look at you.'

How he pressed her to his heart again with almost a spasmodic pressure! How he kissed her as the tears fell like rain from his old eyes! How he blessed her, and called her by a hundred soft sweet names which now came new to his lips! How he chid himself for ever having been unhappy with such a treasure in his house, such a jewel on his bosom, with so sweet a flower in the choice garden of his heart! And then the flood-gates of his tongue were loosed, and, at length, with unsparing detail of circumstances, he told her all that he wished, and all that he could not do. He repeated those arguments of the archdeacon, not agreeing in their truth, but explaining his inability to escape from them—how it had been declared to him that he was bound to remain where he was by the interests of his order, by gratitude to the bishop, by the wishes of his friends, by a sense of duty, which, though he could not understand it, he was fain to acknowledge. He told her how he had been accused of cowardice, and though he was not a man to make much of such a charge before the world, now in the full candour of his heart he explained to her that such an accusation was grievous to him; that he did think it would be unmanly to desert his post, merely to escape his present sufferings, and that, therefore, he must bear as best he might the misery which was prepared for him.

And did she find these details tedious? Oh, no; she encouraged him to dilate on every feeling he expressed, till he laid bare the inmost corners of his heart to her. They spoke together of the archdeacon, as two children might of a stern, unpopular, but still respected schoolmaster, and of the bishop as a parent

kind as kind could be, but powerless against an omnipotent pedagogue.

And then, when they had discussed all this, when
the father had told all to the child, she could not be
less confiding than he had been; and as John Bold's
name was mentioned between them, she owned how
well she had learned to love him—'had loved him
once,' she said. 'but she would not, could not do so
now—no, even had her troth been plighted to him,
she would have taken it back again—had she sworn
to love him as his wife, she would have discarded
him, and not felt herself forsworn, when he proved
himself the enemy of her father.'

But the warden declared that Bold was no enemy
of his, and encouraged her love; and gently rebuked,
as he kissed her, the stern resolve she had made to
cast him off; and then he spoke to her of happier days
when their trials would all be over; and declared that
her young heart should not be torn asunder to please
either priest or prelate, dean or archdeacon. No, not
if all Oxford were to convocate together, and agree
as to the necessity of the sacrifice.

And so they greatly comforted each other—and in
what sorrow will not such mutual confidence give
consolation!—and with a last expression of tender
love they parted, and went comparatively happy to
their rooms.

11

IPHIGENIA

WHEN Eleanor laid her head on her pillow that night, her mind was anxiously intent on some plan by which she might extricate her father from his misery; and, in her warm-hearted enthusiasm, self-sacrifice was decided on as the means to be adopted. Was not so good an Agamemnon worthy of an Iphigenia? She would herself personally implore John Bold to desist from his undertaking; she would explain to him her father's sorrows, the cruel misery of his position; she would tell him how her father would die if he were thus dragged before the public and exposed to such unmerited ignominy; she would appeal to his old friendship, to his generosity, to his manliness, to his mercy; if need were, she would kneel to him for the favour she would ask; but before she did this, the idea of love must be banished. There must be no bargain in the matter. To his mercy, to his generosity, she could appeal; but as a pure maiden, hitherto even unsolicited, she could not appeal to his love, nor under such circumstances could she allow him to do so. Of course, when so provoked he would declare his passion; that was to be expected; there had been enough between them to make such a fact sure; but it was equally certain that he must be rejected. She could not be understood as saying, Make my father free and I am the reward. There would be no sacrifice in that—not so had Jephthah's daughter saved her father—not so could she show to that kindest, dearest of parents how much she was able to bear for his good. No; to one resolve must her whole soul be bound; and so resolving, she felt that she could make her great request to Bold with as much self-assured confidence as she could have done to his grandfather.

And now I own I have fears for my heroine; not as to the upshot of her mission—not in the least as to that; as to the full success of her generous scheme, and the ultimate result of such a project, no one conversant with human nature and novels can have a doubt; but as to the amount of sympathy she may receive from those of her own sex. Girls below twenty and old ladies above sixty will do her justice; for in the female heart the soft springs of sweet romance reopen after many years, and again gush out with waters pure as in earlier days, and greatly refresh the path that leads downwards to the grave. But I fear that the majority of those between these two eras will not approve of Eleanor's plan. I fear that unmarried ladies of thirty-five will declare that there can be no probability of so absurd a project being carried through; that young women cn their knees before their lovers are sure to get kissed, and that they would not put themselves in such a position did they not expect it; that Eleanor is going to Bold only because circumstances prevent Bold from coming to her; that she is certainly a little fool, or a little schemer, but that in all probability she is thinking a good deal more about herself than her father.

Dear ladies, you are right as to your appreciation

of the circumstances, but very wrong as to Miss
Harding's character. Miss Harding was much younger
than you are, and could not, therefore, know, as you
may do, to what dangers such an encounter might
expose her. She may get kissed; I think it very
probable that she will; but I give my solemn word
and positive assurance, that the remotest idea of such
a catastrophe never occurred to her as she made the
great resolve now alluded to.

And then she slept; and then she rose refreshed;
and met her father with her kindest embrace and most
loving smiles; and on the whole their breakfast was
by no means so triste as had been their dinner the day
before; and then, making some excuse to her father
for so soon leaving him, she started on the commencement of her operations.

She knew that John Bold was in London, and that,
therefore, the scene itself could not be enacted to-day;
but she also knew that he was soon to be home,
probably on the next day, and it was necessary that
some little plan for meeting him should be concerted
with his sister Mary. When she got up to the house,
she went, as usual, into the morning sitting-room,
and was startled by perceiving, by a stick, a great
coat, and sundry parcels which were lying about, that
Bold must already have returned.

'John has come back so suddenly,' said Mary,
coming into the room; 'he has been travelling all
night.'

'Then I'll come up again some other time,' said
Eleanor, about to beat a retreat in her sudden dismay.

'He's out now, and will be for the next two hours,'

said the other; 'he's with that horrid Finney; he only came to see him, and he returns by the mail-train to-night.'

Returns by the mail-train to-night, thought Eleanor to herself, as she strove to screw up her courage—away again to-night—then it must be now or never; and she again sat down, having risen to go.

She wished the ordeal could have been postponed: she had fully made up her mind to do the deed, but she had not made up her mind to do it this very day; and now she felt ill at ease, astray, and in difficulty.

'Mary,' she began, 'I must see your brother before he goes back.'

'Oh yes, of course,' said the other; 'I know he'll be delighted to see you;' and she tried to treat it as a matter of course, but she was not the less surprised; for Mary and Eleanor had daily talked over John Bold and his conduct, and his love, and Mary would insist on calling Eleanor her sister, and would scold her for not calling Bold by his Christian name; and Eleanor would half confess her love, but like a modest maiden would protest against such familiarities even with the name of her lover; and so they talked hour after hour, and Mary Bold, who was much the elder, looked forward with happy confidence to the day when Eleanor would not be ashamed to call her her sister. She was, however, fully sure that just at present Eleanor would be much more likely to avoid her brother than to seek him.

'Mary, I must see your brother, now, to-day, and beg from him a great favour;' and she spoke with a

solemn air, not at all usual to her; and then she went
on, and opened to her friend all her plan, her well-
weighed scheme for saving her father from a sorrow
which would, she said, if it lasted, bring him to his
grave. 'But, Mary,' she continued, 'you must now,
you know, cease any joking about me and Mr. Bold;
you must now say no more about that; I am not
ashamed to beg this favour from your brother, but
when I have done so, there can never be anything
further between us;' and this she said with a staid
and solemn air, quite worthy of Jephthah's daughter
or of Iphigenia either.

It was quite clear that Mary Bold did not follow
the argument. That Eleanor Harding should appeal,
on behalf of her father, to Bold's better feelings
seemed to Mary quite natural; it seemed quite natural
that he should relent, overcome by such filial tears,
and by so much beauty; but, to her thinking, it was
at any rate equally natural, that having relented,
John should put his arm round his mistress's waist,
and say: 'Now having settled that, let us be man and
wife, and all will end happily!' Why his good nature
should not be rewarded, when such reward would
operate to the disadvantage of none, Mary, who had
more sense than romance, could not understand; and
she said as much.

Eleanor, however, was firm, and made quite an
eloquent speech to support her own view of the question: she could not condescend, she said, to ask such a
favour on any other terms than those proposed. Mary
might, perhaps, think her high-flown, but she had her
own ideas, and she could not submit to sacrifice her
self-respect.

'But I am sure you love him—don't you?' pleaded Mary; 'and I am sure he loves you better than anything in the world.'

Eleanor was going to make another speech, but a tear came to each eye, and she could not; so she pretended to blow her nose, and walked to the window, and made a little inward call on her own courage, and finding herself somewhat sustained, said sententiously: 'Mary, this is nonsense.'

'But you do love him,' said Mary, who had followed her friend to the window, and now spoke with her arms close wound round the other's waist. 'You do love him with all your heart—you know you do; I defy you to deny it.'

'I—' commenced Eleanor, turning sharply round to refute the charge; but the intended falsehood stuck in her throat, and never came to utterance. She could not deny her love, so she took plentifully to tears, and leant upon her friend's bosom and sobbed there, and protested that, love or no love, it would make no difference in her resolve, and called Mary, a thousand times, the most cruel of girls, and swore her to secrecy by a hundred oaths, and ended by declaring that the girl who could betray her friend's love, even to a brother, would be as black a traitor as a soldier in a garrison who should open the city gates to the enemy. While they were yet discussing the matter, Bold returned, and Eleanor was forced into sudden action: she had either to accomplish or abandon her plan; and having slipped into her friend's bedroom, as the gentleman closed the hall door, she washed the marks of tears from her eyes, and resolved within herself to go through with it. 'Tell him I am here, said she, 'and coming in; and mind, whatever you do, don't leave us.' So Mary informed her brother, with a somewhat sombre air, that Miss Harding was in the next room, and was coming to speak to him.

Eleanor was certainly thinking more of her father than herself, as she arranged her hair before the glass, and removed the traces of sorrow from her face; and yet I should be untrue if I said that she was not anxious to appear well before her lover: why else was she so sedulous with that stubborn curl that would rebel against her hand, and smooth so eagerly her ruffled ribands? why else did she damp her eyes to dispel the redness, and bite her pretty lips to bring back the colour? Of course she was anxious to look her best, for she was but a mortal angel after all. But had she been immortal, had she flitted back to the sitting-room on a cherub's wings, she could not have had a more faithful heart, or a truer wish to save her father at any cost to herself.

John Bold had not met her since the day when she left him in dudgeon in the cathedral close. Since that his whole time had been occupied in promoting the cause against her father, and not unsuccessfully. He had often thought of her, and turned over in his mind a hundred schemes for showing her how disinterested was his love. He would write to her and beseech her not to allow the performance of a public duty to injure him in her estimation; he would write to Mr. Harding, explain all his views, and boldly claim the warden's daughter, urging that the untoward circumstances between them need be no bar to their ancient friendship, or to a closer tie; he would throw

135

himself on his knees before his mistress; he would
wait and marry the daughter when the father had
lost his home and his income; he would give up
the lawsuit and go to Australia, with her of course,
leaving the *Jupiter* and Mr. Finney to complete the
case between them. Sometimes as he woke in the
morning fevered and impatient, he would blow out
his brains and have done with all his cares—but this
idea was generally consequent on an imprudent supper enjoyed in company with Tom Towers.

How beautiful Eleanor appeared to him as she
slowly walked into the room! Not for nothing had
all those little cares been taken. Though her sister,
the archdeacon's wife, had spoken slightingly of her
charms, Eleanor was very beautiful when seen aright.
Hers was not of those impassive faces, which have the
beauty of a marble bust; finely chiselled features,
perfect in every line, true to the rules of symmetry, as
lovely to a stranger as to a friend, unvarying unless
in sickness, or as age affects them. She had no startling
brilliancy of beauty, no pearly whiteness, no radiant
carnation. She had not the majestic contour that rivets
attention, demands instant wonder and then disap-
points by the coldness of its charms. You might pass
Eleanor Harding in the street without notice, but you
could hardly pass an evening with her and not lose
your heart.

She had never appeared more lovely to her lover
than she now did. Her face was animated though it
was serious, and her full dark lustrous eyes shone
with anxious energy; her hand trembled as she took
his, and she could hardly pronounce his name, when
she addressed him. Bold wished with all his heart

that the Australian scheme was in the act of realisa-
tion, and that he and Eleanor were away together,
never to hear further of the lawsuit.

He began to talk, asked after her health—said
something about London being very stupid, and
more about Barchester being very pleasant; declared
the weather to be very hot, and then inquired after
Mr. Harding.

'My father is not very well,' said Eleanor.

John Bold was very sorry, so sorry: he hoped it
was nothing serious, and put on the unmeaningly
solemn face which people usually use on such occasions.

'I especially want to speak to you about my father,
Mr. Bold; indeed, I am now here on purpose to do so.
Papa is very unhappy, very unhappy indeed, about
this affair of the hospital: you would pity him, Mr.
Bold, if you could see how wretched it has made
him.'

'Oh, Miss Harding!'

'Indeed you would—any one would pity him; but
a friend, an old friend as you are—indeed you would.
He is an altered man; his cheerfulness has all gone,
and his sweet temper, and his kind happy tone of
voice; you would hardly know him if you saw him,
Mr. Bold, he is so much altered; and—and—if this
goes on, he will die.' Here Eleanor had recourse to
her handkerchief, and so also had her auditors; but she
plucked up her courage, and went on with her tale.
'He will break his heart, and die. I am sure, Mr. Bold,
it was not you who wrote those cruel things in the
newspaper——'

John Bold eagerly protested that it was not, but

his heart smote him as to his intimate alliance with Tom Towers.

'No, I am sure it was not; and papa has not for a moment thought so; you would not be so cruel—but it has nearly killed him. Papa cannot bear to think that people should so speak of him, and that every body should hear him so spoken of:—they have called him avaricious, and dishonest, and they say he is robbing the old men, and taking the money of the hospital for nothing.'

'I have never said so, Miss Harding. I——'

'No,' continued Eleanor, interrupting him, for she was now in the full flood tide of her eloquence; 'no, I am sure you have not; but others have said so; and if this goes on, if such things are written again, it will kill papa. Oh! Mr. Bold, if you only knew the state he is in! Now papa does not care much about money.'

Both her auditors, brother and sister, assented to this, and declared on their own knowledge that no man lived less addicted to filthy lucre than the warden.

'Oh! it's so kind of you to say so, Mary, and of you too, Mr. Bold. I couldn't bear that people should think unjustly of papa. Do you know he would give up the hospital altogether, only he cannot. The archdeacon says it would be cowardly, and that he would be deserting his order, and injuring the church. Whatever may happen, papa will not do that: he would leave the place to-morrow willingly, and give up his house, and the income and all if the archdeacon ——' Eleanor was going to say 'would let him,' but she stopped herself before she had compromised her father's dignity; and giving a long sigh, she added —'Oh, I do so wish he would.'

'No one who knows Mr. Harding personally accuses him for a moment,' said Bold.

'It is he that has to bear the punishment; it is he that suffers,' said Eleanor; 'and what for? what has he done wrong? how has he deserved this persecution? he that never had an unkind thought in his life, he that never said an unkind word!' and here she broke down, and the violence of her sobs stopped her utterance.

Bold, for the fifth or sixth time, declared that neither he nor any of his friends imputed any blame personally to Mr. Harding.

'Then why should he be persecuted?' ejaculated Eleanor through her tears, forgetting in her eagerness that her intention had been to humble herself as a suppliant before John Bold—'why should he be singled out for scorn and disgrace? why should he be made so wretched? Oh! Mr. Bold'—and she turned towards him as though the kneeling scene were about to be commenced—'oh! Mr. Bold, why did you begin all this? You, whom we all so—so—valued!'

To speak the truth, the reformer's punishment was certainly come upon him, for his present plight was not enviable; he had nothing for it but to excuse himself by platitudes about public duty, which it is by no means worth while to repeat, and to reiterate his eulogy on Mr. Harding's character. His position was certainly a cruel one: had any gentleman called upon him on behalf of Mr. Harding he could of course have declined to enter upon the subject; but how could he do so with a beautiful girl, with the daughter of the man whom he had injured, with his own love?

In the meantime Eleanor recollected herself, and

again summoned up her energies. 'Mr. Bold,' said she, 'I have come here to implore you to abandon this proceeding.' He stood up from his seat, and looked beyond measure distressed. 'To implore you to abandon it, to implore you to spare my father, to spare either his life or his reason, for one or the other will pay the forfeit if this goes on. I know how much I am asking, and how little right I have to ask anything; but I think you will listen to me as it is for my father. Oh, Mr. Bold, pray, pray do this for us—pray do not drive to distraction a man who has loved you so well.'

She did not absolutely kneel to him, but she followed him as he moved from his chair, and laid her soft hands imploringly upon his arm. Ah! at any other time how exquisitely valuable would have been that touch! but now he was distraught, dumbfounded, and unmanned. What could he say to that sweet suppliant; how explain to her that the matter now was probably beyond his control; how tell her that he could not quell the storm which he had raised?

'Surely, surely, John, you cannot refuse her,' said his sister.

'I would give her my soul,' said he, 'if it would serve her.'

'Oh, Mr. Bold,' said Eleanor, 'do not speak so; I ask nothing for myself; and what I ask for my father, it cannot harm you to grant.'

'I would give her my soul, if it would serve her,' said Bold, still addressing his sister; 'everything I have is hers, if she will accept it; my house, my heart, my all; every hope of my breast is centred in her;

her smiles are sweeter to me than the sun, and when I see her in sorrow as she now is, every nerve in my body suffers. No man can love better than I love her.'

'No, no, no,' ejaculated Eleanor; 'there can be no talk of love between us. Will you protect my father from the evil you have brought upon him?'

'Oh, Eleanor, I will do anything; let me tell you how I love you!'

'No, no, no!' she almost screamed. 'This is unmanly of you, Mr. Bold. Will you, will you, will you leave my father to die in peace in his quiet home?' and seizing him by his arm and hand, she followed him across the room towards the door. 'I will not leave you till you promise me; I'll cling to you in the street; I'll kneel to you before all the people. You shall promise me this, you shall promise me this, you shall——' And she clung to him with fixed tenacity, and reiterated her resolve with hysterical passion.

'Speak to her, John; answer her,' said Mary, bewildered by the unexpected vehemence of Eleanor's manner; 'you cannot have the cruelty to refuse her.'

'Promise me, promise me,' said Eleanor; 'say that my father is safe—one word will do. I know how true you are; say one word, and I will let you go.'

She still held him, and looked eagerly into his face, with her hair dishevelled and her eyes all bloodshot. She had no thought now of herself, no care now for her appearance; and yet he thought he had never seen her half so lovely; he was amazed at the intensity of her beauty, and could hardly believe that it was she whom he had dared to love. 'Promise me,' said she; 'I will not leave you till you have promised me.'

141

'I will,' said he at length; 'I do—all I can do, I will do.'

'Then may God Almighty bless you for ever and ever!' said Eleanor; and falling on her knees with her face on Mary's lap, she wept and sobbed like a child: her strength had carried her through her allotted task, but now it was wellnigh exhausted.

In a while she was partly recovered, and got up to go, and would have gone, had not Bold made her understand that it was necessary for him to explain to her how far it was in his power to put an end to the proceedings which had been taken against Mr. Harding. Had he spoken on any other subject, she would have vanished, but on that she was bound to hear him; and now the danger of her position commenced. While she had an active part to play, while she clung to him as a suppliant, it was easy enough for her to reject his proffered love, and cast from her his caressing words; but now—now that he had yielded, and was talking to her calmly and kindly as to her father's welfare, it was hard enough for her to do so. Then Mary Bold assisted her; but now she was quite on her brother's side. Mary said but little, but every word she did say gave some direct and deadly blow. The first thing she did was to make room for her brother between herself and Eleanor on the sofa: as the sofa was full large for three, Eleanor could not resent this, nor could she show suspicion by taking another seat; but she felt it to be a most unkind proceeding. And then Mary would talk as though they three were joined in some close peculiar bond together; as though they were in future always to wish together, contrive together, and act together;

and Eleanor could not gainsay this; she could not make another speech, and say, 'Mr. Bold and I are strangers, Mary, and are always to remain so!'

He explained to her that, though undoubtedly the proceeding against the hospital had commenced solely with himself, many others were now interested in the matter, some of whom were much more influential than himself; that it was to him alone, however, that the lawyers looked for instruction as to their doings, and, more important still, for the payment of their bills; and he promised that he would at once give them notice that it was his intention to abandon the cause. He thought, he said, that it was not probable that any active steps would be taken after he had seceded from the matter, though it was possible that some passing allusion might still be made to the hospital in the daily *Jupiter*. He promised, however, that he would use his best influence to prevent any further personal allusion being made to Mr. Harding. He then suggested that he would on that afternoon ride over himself to Dr. Grantly, and inform him of his altered intentions on the subject, and with this view, he postponed his immediate return to London.

This was all very pleasant, and Eleanor did enjoy a sort of triumph in the feeling that she had attained the object for which she had sought this interview; but still the part of Iphigenia was to be played out. The gods had heard her prayer, granted her request, and were they not to have their promised sacrifice? Eleanor was not a girl to defraud them wilfully; so, as soon as she decently could, she got up for her bonnet.

'Are you going so soon?' said Bold, who half an hour since would have given a hundred pounds that he was in London, and she still at Barchester.

'Oh yes!' said she. 'I am so much obliged to you; papa will feel this to be so kind.' She did not quite appreciate all her father's feelings. 'Of course I must tell him, and I will say that you will see the arch-deacon.'

'But may I not say one word for myself?' said Bold.

'I'll fetch you your bonnet, Eleanor,' said Mary, in the act of leaving the room.

'Mary, Mary,' said she, getting up and catching her by her dress; 'don't go, I'll get my bonnet myself.' But Mary, the traitress, stood fast by the door, and permitted no such retreat. Poor Iphigenia!

And with a volley of impassioned love, John Bold poured forth the feelings of his heart, swearing, as men do, some truths and many falsehoods; and Eleanor repeated with every shade of vehemence the 'No, no, no,' which had had a short time since so much effect; but now, alas! its strength was gone. Let her be never so vehement, her vehemence was not respected; all her 'No, no, no's' were met with counter asseverations, and at last were overpowered. The ground was cut from under her on every side. She was pressed to say whether her father would object; whether she herself had any aversion (aversion! God help her, poor girl! the word nearly made her jump into his arms); any other preference (this she loudly disclaimed); whether it was impossible that she should love him (Eleanor could not say that it was impossible): and so at last, all her defences demolished, all her maiden barriers swept away, she capitulated, or rather marched out with the honours of war, vanquished evidently, palpably vanquished, but still not reduced to the necessity of confessing it.

And so the altar on the shore of the modern Aulis reeked with no sacrifice.

12

MR. BOLD'S VISIT TO PLUMSTEAD

WHETHER or no the ill-natured prediction made by
certain ladies in the beginning of the last chapter
was or was not carried out to the letter, I am not in
a position to state. Eleanor, however, certainly did
feel herself to have been baffled as she returned home
with all her news to her father. Certainly she had been
victorious, certainly she had achieved her object, certainly she was not unhappy, and yet she did not feel
herself triumphant. Everything would run smooth
now. Eleanor was not at all addicted to the Lydian
school of romance; she by no means objected to her
lover because he came in at the door under the name
of Absolute, instead of pulling her out of a window
under the name of Beverley; and yet she felt that she
had been imposed upon, and could hardly think of
Mary Bold with sisterly charity. 'I did think I could
have trusted Mary,' she said to herself over and over
again. 'Oh that she should have dared to keep me in
the room when I tried to get out!' Eleanor, however,
felt that the game was up, and that she had now nothing further to do but to add to the budget of news
which was prepared for her father, that John Bold
was her accepted lover.

We will, however, now leave her on her way, and
go with John Bold to Plumstead Episcopi, merely
premising that Eleanor on reaching home will not

find things so smooth as she fondly expected; two messengers had come, one to her father and the other to the archdeacon, and each of them much opposed to her quiet mode of solving all their difficulties; the one in the shape of a number of the *Jupiter*, and the other in that of a further opinion from Sir Abraham Haphazard.

John Bold got on his horse and rode off to Plumstead Episcopi; not briskly and with eager spur, as men do ride when self-satisfied with their own intentions; but slowly, modestly, thoughtfully, and somewhat in dread of the coming interview. Now and again he would recur to the scene which was just over, support himself by the remembrance of the silence that gives consent, and exult as a happy lover. But even this feeling was not without a shade of remorse. Had he not shown himself childishly weak thus to yield up the resolve of many hours of thought to the tears of a pretty girl? How was he to meet his lawyer? How was he to back out of a matter in which his name was already so publicly concerned? What, oh, what! was he to say to Tom Towers? While meditating these painful things he reached the lodge leading up to the archdeacon's glebe, and for the first time in his life found himself within the sacred precincts.

All the doctor's children were together on the slope of the lawn close to the road, as Bold rode up to the hall door. They were there holding high debate on matters evidently of deep interest at Plumstead Episcopi, and the voices of the boys had been heard before the lodge gate was closed.

Florinda and Grizzel, frightened at the sight of

so well-known an enemy to the family, fled on the first appearance of the horseman, and ran in terror to their mother's arms; not for them was it, tender branches, to resent injuries, or as members of a church militant to put on armour against its enemies. But the boys stood their ground like heroes, and boldly demanded the business of the intruder.

'Do you want to see anybody here, sir?' said Henry, with a defiant eye and a hostile tone, which plainly said that at any rate no one there wanted to see the person so addressed; and as he spoke he brandished aloft his garden water-pot, holding it by the spout, ready for the braining of any one.

'Henry,' said Charles James slowly, and with a certain dignity of diction, 'Mr. Bold of course would not have come without wanting to see some one; if Mr. Bold has a proper ground for wanting to see some person here, of course he has a right to come.'

But Samuel stepped lightly up to the horse's head, and offered his services. 'Oh, Mr. Bold,' said he, 'papa, I'm sure, will be glad to see you; I suppose you want to see papa. Shall I hold your horse for you? Oh what a very pretty horse!' and he turned his head and winked funnily at his brothers. 'Papa has heard such good news about the old hospital to-day. We know you'll be glad to hear it, because you're such a friend of grandpapa Harding, and so much in love with Aunt Nelly!'

'How d'ye do, lads?' said Bold, dismounting. 'I want to see your father if he's at home.'

'Lads!' said Henry, turning on his heel and addressing himself to his brother, but loud enough to be heard by Bold; 'lads, indeed! if we're lads, what does he call himself?'

Charles James condescended to say nothing further, but cocked his hat with much precision, and left the visitor to the care of his youngest brother.

Samuel stayed till the servant came, chatting and patting the horse; but as soon as Bold had disappeared through the front door, he stuck a switch under the animal's tail to make him kick if possible.

The church reformer soon found himself tête-à-tête with the archdeacon in that same room, in that sanctum sanctorum of the rectory, to which we have already been introduced. As he entered he heard the click of a certain patent lock, but it struck him with no surprise; the worthy clergyman was no doubt hiding from eyes profane his last much-studied sermon; for the archdeacon, though he preached but seldom, was famous for his sermons. No room, Bold thought, could have been more becoming for a dignitary of the church; each wall was loaded with theology; over each separate bookcase was printed in small gold letters the names of those great divines whose works were ranged beneath; beginning from the early fathers in due chronological order, there were to be found the precious labours of the chosen servants of the church down to the last pamphlet written in opposition to the consecration of Dr. Hampden; and raised above this were to be seen the busts of the greatest among the great: Chrysostom, St. Augustine, Thomas à Becket, Cardinal Wolsey, Archbishop Laud, and Dr. Philpotts.

Every appliance that could make study pleasant and give ease to the overtoiled brain was there;

chairs made to relieve each limb and muscle; reading-desks and writing-desks to suit every attitude; lamps and candles mechanically contrived to throw their light on any favoured spot, as the student might desire; a shoal of newspapers to amuse the few leisure moments which might be stolen from the labours of the day; and then from the window a view right through a bosky vista along which ran a broad green path from the rectory to the church—at the end of which the tawny-tinted fine old tower was seen with all its variegated pinnacles and parapets. Few parish churches in England are in better repair, or better worth keeping so, than that at Plumstead Episcopi; and yet it is built in a faulty style: the body of the church is low—so low, that the nearly flat leaden roof would be visible from the churchyard, were it not for the carved parapet with which it is surrounded. It is cruciform, though the transepts are irregular, one being larger than the other; and the tower is much too high in proportion to the church. But the colour of the building is perfect; it is that rich yellow grey which one finds nowhere but in the south and west of England, and which is so strong a characteristic of most of our old houses of Tudor architecture. The stone work also is beautiful; the mullions of the windows and the thick tracery of the Gothic work-manship is as rich as fancy can desire; and though in gazing on such a structure one knows by rule that the old priests who built it, built it wrong, one cannot bring oneself to wish that they should have made it other than it is.

When Bold was ushered into the book-room, he found its owner standing with his back to the empty fireplace ready to receive him, and he could not but perceive that that expansive brow was elated with triumph, and that those full heavy lips bore more prominently than usual an appearance of arrogant success.

'Well, Mr. Bold,' said he—'well, what can I do for you? Very happy, I can assure you, to do anything for such a friend of my father-in-law.'

'I hope you'll excuse my calling, Dr. Grantly.'

'Certainly, certainly' said the archdeacon; 'I can assure you, no apology is necessary from Mr. Bold; only let me know what I can do for him.'

Dr. Grantly was standing himself, and he did not ask Bold to sit, and therefore he had to tell his tale standing, leaning on the table, with his hat in his hand. He did, however, manage to tell it; and as the archdeacon never once interrupted him, or even encouraged him by a single word, he was not long in coming to the end of it.

'And so, Mr. Bold, I'm to understand, I believe, that you are desirous of abandoning this attack upon Mr. Harding.'

'Oh, Dr. Grantly, there has been no attack, I can assure you——'

'Well, well, we won't quarrel about words; I should call it an attack—most men would so call an endeavour to take away from a man every shilling of income that he has to live upon; but it shan't be an attack, if you don't like it; you wish to abandon this —this little game of backgammon you've begun to play.'

'I intend to put an end to the legal proceedings which I have commenced.'

'I understand,' said the archdeacon. 'You've already had enough of it; well, I can't say that I am surprised; carrying on a losing lawsuit where one has nothing to gain, but everything to pay, is not pleasant.'

Bold turned very red in the face. 'You misinterpret my motives,' said he; 'but, however, that is of little consequence. I did not come to trouble you with my motives, but to tell you a matter of fact. Good-morning, Dr. Grantly.'

'One moment—one moment,' said the other. 'I don't exactly appreciate the taste which induced you to make any personal communication to me on the subject; but I dare say I'm wrong, I dare say your judgment is the better of the two; but as you have done me the honour—as you have, as it were, forced me into a certain amount of conversation on a subject which had better, perhaps, have been left to our lawyers, you will excuse me if I ask you to hear my reply to your communication.'

'I am in no hurry, Dr. Grantly.'

'Well, I am, Mr. Bold; my time is not exactly leisure time, and, therefore, if you please, we'll go to the point at once—you're going to abandon this lawsuit?'—and he paused for a reply.

'Yes, Dr. Grantly, I am.'

'Having exposed a gentleman who was one of your father's warmest friends to all the ignominy and insolence which the press could heap upon his name, having somewhat ostentatiously declared that it was your duty as a man of high public virtue to protect those poor old fools whom you have humbugged there at the hospital, you now find that the game costs more than it's worth, and so you make up your mind to have done with it. A prudent resolution, Mr. Bold; but it is a pity you should have been so long coming to it. Has it struck you that we may not now choose to give over? that we may find it necessary to punish the injury you have done to us? Are you aware, sir, that we have gone to enormous expense to resist this iniquitous attempt of yours?'

Bold's face was now furiously red, and he nearly crushed his hat between his hands; but he said nothing.

'We have found it necessary to employ the best advice that money could procure. Are you aware, sir, what may be the probable cost of securing the services of the attorney-general?'

'Not in the least, Dr. Grantly.'

'I dare say not, sir. When you recklessly put this affair into the hands of your friend Mr. Finney, whose six and eightpences and thirteen and fourpences may, probably, not amount to a large sum, you were indifferent as to the cost and suffering which such a proceeding might entail on others; but are you aware, sir, that these crushing costs must now come out of your own pocket?'

'Any demand of such a nature which Mr. Harding's lawyer may have to make will doubtless be made to my lawyer.'

' "Mr. Harding's lawyer and my lawyer!" Did you come here merely to refer me to the lawyers? Upon my word I think the honour of your visit might have been spared! And now, sir, I'll tell you what my opinion is—my opinion is, that we shall not allow you to withdraw this matter from the courts.'

'You can do as you please, Dr. Grantly; good-morning.'

'Hear me out, sir,' said the archdeacon; 'I have here in my hands the last opinion given in this matter by Sir Abraham Haphazard. I dare say you have already heard of this—I dare say it has had something to do with your visit here to-day.'

'I know nothing whatever of Sir Abraham Haphazard or his opinion.'

'Be that as it may, here it is; he declares most explicitly that under no phasis of the affair whatever have you a leg to stand upon; that Mr. Harding is as safe in his hospital as I am here in my rectory; that a more futile attempt to destroy a man was never made, than this which you have made to ruin Mr. Harding. Here,' and he slapped the paper on the table, 'I have this opinion from the very first lawyer in the land; and under these circumstances you expect me to make you a low bow for your kind offer to release Mr. Harding from the toils of your net! Sir, your net is not strong enough to hold him; sir, your net has fallen to pieces, and you knew that well enough before I told you—and now, sir, I'll wish you good-morning, for I'm busy.'

Bold was now choking with passion. He had let the archdeacon run on because he knew not with what words to interrupt him; but now that he had been so defied and insulted, he could not leave the room without some reply.

'Dr. Grantly,' he commenced.

'I have nothing further to say or to hear,' said the archdeacon. 'I'll do myself the honour to order your horse.' And he rang the bell.

'I came here, Dr. Grantly, with the warmest, kindest feelings——'

'Oh, of course you did; nobody doubts it.'

'With the kindest feelings—and they have been most grossly outraged by your treatment.'

'Of course they have—I have not chosen to see my father-in-law ruined; what an outrage that has been to your feelings!'

'The time will come, Dr. Grantly, when you will understand why I called upon you to-day.'

'No doubt, no doubt. Is Mr. Bold's horse there? That's right; open the front door. Good-morning, Mr. Bold;' and the doctor stalked into his own drawing-room, closing the door behind him, and making it quite impossible that John Bold should speak another word.

As he got on his horse, which he was fain to do feeling like a dog turned out of a kitchen, he was again greeted by little Sammy.

'Good-bye, Mr. Bold; I hope we may have the pleasure of seeing you again before long; I am sure papa will always be glad to see you.'

That was certainly the bitterest moment in John Bold's life. Not even the remembrance of his successful love could comfort him; nay, when he thought of Eleanor he felt that it was that very love which had brought him to such a pass. That he should have been so insulted, and be unable to reply! That he should have given up so much to the request of a girl, and then have had his motives so misunderstood! That he should have made so gross a mistake as this visit of his to the archdeacon's! He bit the top of his whip, till he penetrated the horn of which it was made:

he struck the poor animal in his anger, and then was doubly angry with himself at his futile passion. He had been so completely checkmated, so palpably overcome! and what was he to do? He could not continue his action after pledging himself to abandon it; nor was there any revenge in that—it was the very step to which his enemy had endeavoured to goad him!

He threw the reins to the servant who came to take his horse, and rushed upstairs into his drawing-room, where his sister Mary was sitting.

'If there be a devil,' said he, 'a real devil here on earth, it is Dr. Grantly.' He vouchsafed her no further intelligence, but again seizing his hat, he rushed out, and took his departure for London without another word to any one.

13

THE WARDEN'S DECISION

THE meeting between Eleanor and her father was
not so stormy as that described in the last chapter,
but it was hardly more successful. On her return from
Bold's house she found her father in a strange state.
He was not sorrowful and silent as he had been on
that memorable day when his son-in-law lectured
him as to all that he owed to his order; nor was he in
his usual quiet mood. When Eleanor reached the
hospital, he was walking to and fro upon the lawn,
and she soon saw that he was much excited.

'I am going to London, my dear.' he said as
soon as he saw her.

'London, papa!'

'Yes, my dear, to London; I will have this matter
settled some way; there are some things, Eleanor,
which I cannot bear.'

'Oh, papa, what is it?' said she, leading him by the
arm into the house. 'I had such good news for you,
and now you make me fear I am too late.' And then,
before he could let her know what had caused this
sudden resolve, or could point to the fatal paper
which lay on the table, she told him that the lawsuit
was over, that Bold had commissioned her to assure
her father in his name that it would be abandoned, that
there was no further cause for misery, that the whole
matter might be looked on as though it had never been

discussed. She did not tell him with what determined vehemence she had obtained this concession in his favour, nor did she mention the price she was to pay for it.

The warden did not express himself peculiarly gratified at this intelligence, and Eleanor, though she had not worked for thanks, and was by no means disposed to magnify her own good offices, felt hurt at the manner in which her news was received. 'Mr. Bold can act as he thinks proper, my love,' said he; 'if Mr. Bold thinks he has been wrong, of course he will discontinue what he is doing; but that cannot change my purpose.'

'Oh, papa!' she exclaimed, all but crying with vexation; 'I thought you would have been so happy —I thought all would have been right now.'

'Mr. Bold,' continued he, 'has set great people to work—so great that I doubt they are now beyond his control. Read that, my dear.' The warden, doubling up a number of the *Jupiter*, pointed to the peculiar article which she was to read. It was to the last of the three leaders, which are generally furnished daily for the support of the nation, that Mr. Harding directed her attention. It dealt some heavy blows on various clerical delinquents; on families who received their tens of thousands yearly for doing nothing; on men who, as the article stated, rolled in wealth which they had neither earned nor inherited, and which was in fact stolen from the poorer clergy. It named some sons of bishops, and grandsons of archbishops; men great in their way, who had redeemed their disgrace in the eyes of many by the enormity of their plunder; and then, having disposed of these levia-thans, it descended to Mr. Harding.

'We alluded some weeks since to an instance of similar injustice, though in a more humble scale, in which the warden of an almshouse at Barchester has become possessed of the income of the greater part of the whole institution. Why an almshouse should have a warden we cannot pretend to explain, nor can we say what special need twelve old men can have for the services of a separate clergyman, seeing that they have twelve reserved seats for themselves in Barchester Cathedral. But be this as it may, let the gentleman call himself warden or precentor, or what he will, let him be never so scrupulous in exacting religious duties from his twelve dependants, or never so negligent as regards the services of the cathedral, it appears palpably clear that he can be entitled to no portion of the revenue of the hospital, excepting that which the founder set apart for him; and it is equally clear that the founder did not intend that three-fifths of his charity should be so consumed.

'The case is certainly a paltry one after the tens of thousands with which we have been dealing, for the warden's income is after all but a poor eight hundred a year: eight hundred a year is not magnificent preferment of itself, and the warden may, for anything we know, be worth much more to the church; but if so, let the church pay him out of funds justly at its own disposal.

'We allude to the question of the Barchester almshouse at the present moment, because we understand that a plea has been set up which will be peculiarly revolting to the minds of English churchmen. An action has been taken against Mr. Warden Harding, on behalf of the almsmen, by a gentleman acting

159

solely on public grounds, and it is to be argued that Mr. Harding takes nothing but what he receives as a servant of the hospital, and that he is not himself responsible for the amount of stipend given to him for his work. Such a plea would doubtless be fair, if any one questioned the daily wages of a bricklayer employed on the building, or the fee of the charwoman who cleans it; but we cannot envy the feeling of a clergyman of the Church of England who could allow such an argument to be put in his mouth.

'If this plea be put forward we trust Mr. Harding will be forced as a witness to state the nature of his employment; the amount of work that he does; the income which he receives; and the source from whence he obtained his appointment. We do not think he will receive much public sympathy to atone for the annoyance of such an examination.'

As Eleanor read the article her face flushed with indignation, and when she had finished it, she almost feared to look up at her father.

'Well, my dear,' said he, 'what do you think of that—is it worth while to be a warden at that price?'

'Oh, papa;—dear papa!'

'Mr. Bold can't unwrite that, my dear—Mr. Bold can't say that that shan't be read by every clergyman at Oxford; nay, by every gentleman in the land:' and then he walked up and down the room, while Eleanor in mute despair followed him with her eyes. 'And I'll tell you what, my dear,' he continued, speaking now very calmly, and in a forced manner very unlike himself; 'Mr. Bold can't dispute the truth of every word in that article you have just read—nor can I.' Eleanor stared at him, as though she scarcely understood the words he was speaking. 'Nor can I, Eleanor: that's the worst of all, or would be so if there were no remedy. I have thought much of all this since we were together last night;' and he came and sat beside her, and put his arm round her waist as he had done then. 'I have thought much of what the archdeacon has said, and of what this paper says; and I do believe I have no right to be here.'

'No right to be warden of the hospital, papa?'

'No right to be warden with eight hundred a year; no right to be warden with such a house as this; no right to spend in luxury money that was intended for charity. Mr. Bold may do as he pleases about his suit, but I hope he will not abandon it for my sake.'

Poor Eleanor! this was hard upon her. Was it for this she had made her great resolve! For this that she had laid aside her quiet demeanour, and taken upon her the rants of a tragedy heroine! One may work and not for thanks, but yet feel hurt at not receiving them; and so it was with Eleanor: one may be disinterested in one's good actions, and yet feel discontented that they are not recognised. Charity may be given with the left hand so privily that the right hand does not know it, and yet the left hand may regret to feel that it has no immediate reward. Eleanor had had no wish to burden her father with a weight of obligation, and yet she had looked forward to much delight from the knowledge that she had freed him from his sorrows: now such hopes were entirely over: all that she had done was of no avail; she had humbled herself to Bold in vain; the evil was utterly beyond her power to cure!

She had thought also how gently she would whisper

to her father all that her lover had said to her about herself, and how impossible she had found it to reject him: and then she had anticipated her father's kindly kiss and close embrace as he gave his sanction to her love. Alas! she could say nothing of this now. In speaking of Mr. Bold, her father put him aside as one whose thoughts and sayings and acts could be of no moment. Gentle reader, did you ever feel yourself snubbed? Did you ever, when thinking much of your own importance, find yourself suddenly reduced to a nonentity? Such was Eleanor's feeling now.

'They shall not put forward this plea on my behalf,' continued the warden. 'Whatever may be the truth of the matter, that at any rate is not true; and the man who wrote that article is right in saying that such a plea is revolting to an honest mind. I will go up to London, my dear, and see these lawyers myself, and if no better excuse can be made for me than that, I and the hospital will part.'

'But the archdeacon, papa?'

'I can't help it, my dear; there are some things which a man cannot bear,—I cannot bear that'—and he put his hand upon the newspaper.

'But will the archdeacon go with you?'

To tell the truth, Mr. Harding had made up his mind to steal a march upon the archdeacon. He was aware that he could take no steps without informing his dread son-in-law, but he had resolved that he would send out a note to Plumstead Episcopi detailing his plans, but that the messenger should not leave Barchester till he himself had started for London; so that he might be a day before the doctor, who, he had no doubt, would follow him. In that

162

day, if he had luck, he might arrange it all; he might explain to Sir Abraham that he, as warden, would have nothing further to do with the defence about to be set up; he might send in his official resignation to his friend the bishop, and so make public the whole transaction, that even the doctor would not be able to undo what he had done. He knew too well the doctor's strength and his own weakness to suppose he could do this, if they both reached London together; indeed, he would never be able to get to London, if the doctor knew of his intended journey in time to prevent it.

'No, I think not,' said he. 'I think I shall start before the archdeacon could be ready—I shall go early to-morrow morning.'

'That will be best, papa,' said Eleanor, showing that her father's ruse was appreciated.

'Why yes, my love. The fact is, I wish to do all this before the archdeacon can—can interfere. There is a great deal of truth in all he says—he argues very well, and I can't always answer him; but there is an old saying, Nelly: "Every one knows where his own shoe pinches!" He'll say that I want moral courage, and strength of character, and power of endurance, and it's all true; but I'm sure I ought not to remain here, if I have nothing better to put forward than a quibble: so, Nelly we shall have to leave this pretty place.'

Eleanor's face brightened up, as she assured her father how cordially she agreed with him.

'True, my love,' said he, now again quite happy and at ease in his manner. 'What good to us is this place or all the money, if we are to be ill-spoken of?'

'Oh, papa, I am so glad!'

'My darling child! It did cost me a pang at first, Nelly, to think that you should lose your pretty drawing-room, and your ponies, and your garden: the garden will be the worst of all—but there is a garden at Crabtree, a very pretty garden.'

Crabtree Parva was the name of the small living which Mr. Harding had held as a minor canon, and which still belonged to him. It was only worth some eighty pounds a year, and a small house and glebe, all of which were now handed over to Mr. Harding's curate; but it was to Crabtree glebe that Mr. Harding thought of retiring. This parish must not be mistaken for that other living, Crabtree Canonicorum, as it is called. Crabtree Canonicorum is a very nice thing; there are only two hundred parishioners; there are four hundred acres of glebe; and the great and small tithes, which both go to the rector, are worth four hundred pounds a year more. Crabtree Canonicorum is in the gift of the dean and chapter, and is at this time possessed by the Honourable and Reverend Dr. Vesey Stanhope, who also fills the prebendal stall of Goosegorge in Barchester Chapter, and holds the united rectory of Eiderdown and Stogpingum, or Stoke Pinquium, as it should be written. This is the same Dr. Vesey Stanhope whose hospitable villa on the Lake of Como is so well known to the élite of English travellers, and whose collection of Lombard butterflies is supposed to be unique.

'Yes,' said the warden, musing, 'there is a very pretty garden at Crabtree; but I shall be sorry to disturb poor Smith.' Smith was the curate of Crabtree, a gentleman who was maintaining a wife and half a dozen children on the income arising from his profession.

Eleanor assured her father that, as far as she was concerned, she could leave her house and her ponies without a single regret. She was only so happy that he was going—going where he would escape all this dreadful turmoil.

'But we will take the music, my dear.'

And so they went on planning their future happiness, and plotting how they would arrange it all without the interposition of the archdeacon, and at last they again became confidential, and then the warden did thank her for what she had done, and Eleanor, lying on her father's shoulder, did find an opportunity to tell her secret: and the father gave his blessing to his child, and said that the man whom she loved was honest, good, and kind-hearted, and right-thinking in the main—one who wanted only a good wife to put him quite upright—'a man, my love,' he ended by saying, 'to whom I firmly believe that I can trust my treasure with safety.'

'But what will Dr. Grantly say?'

'Well, my dear, it can't be helped—we shall be out at Crabtree then.'

And Eleanor ran upstairs to prepare her father's clothes for his journey; and the warden returned to his garden to make his last adieus to every tree, and shrub, and shady nook that he knew so well.

14

MOUNT OLYMPUS

WRETCHED in spirit, groaning under the feeling of insult, self-condemning, and ill-satisfied in every way, Bold returned to his London lodgings. Ill as he had fared in his interview with the archdeacon, he was not the less under the necessity of carrying out his pledge to Eleanor; and he went about his ungracious task with a heavy heart.

The attorneys whom he had employed in London received his instructions with surprise and evident misgiving; however, they could only obey, and mutter something of their sorrow that such heavy costs should only fall upon their own employer,—especially as nothing was wanting but perseverance to throw them on the opposite party. Bold left the office which he had latterly so much frequented, shaking the dust from off his feet; and before he was down the stairs, an edict had already gone forth for the preparation of the bill.

He next thought of the newspapers. The case had been taken up by more than one; and he was well aware that the keynote had been sounded by the *Jupiter*. He had been very intimate with Tom Towers, and had often discussed with him the affairs of the hospital. Bold could not say that the articles in that paper had been written at his own instigation. He did not even know, as a fact, that they had been written

166

by his friend. Tom Towers had never said that such a view of the case, or such a side in the dispute, would be taken by the paper with which he was connected. Very discreet in such matters was Tom Towers, and altogether indisposed to talk loosely of the concerns of that mighty engine of which it was his high privilege to move in secret some portion. Nevertheless Bold believed that to him were owing those dreadful words which had caused such panic at Barchester,—and he conceived himself bound to prevent their repetition. With this view he betook himself from the attorneys' to that laboratory where, with amazing chemistry, Tom Towers compounded thunderbolts for the destruction of all that is evil and for the furtherance of all that is good, in this and other hemispheres.

Who has not heard of Mount Olympus,—that high abode of all the powers of type, that favoured seat of the great goddess Pica, that wondrous habitation of gods and devils, from whence, with ceaseless hum of steam and never-ending flow of Castalian ink, issue forth fifty thousand nightly edicts for the governance of a subject nation?

Velvet and gilding do not make a throne, nor gold and jewels a sceptre. It is a throne because the most exalted one sits there;—and a sceptre because the most mighty one wields it. So it is with Mount Olympus. Should a stranger make his way thither at dull noonday, or during the sleepy hours of the silent afternoon, he would find no acknowledged temple of power and beauty, no fitting fane for the great Thunderer, no proud façades and pillared roofs to support the dignity of this greatest of earthly potentates. To the outward and uninitiated eye, Mount

167

Olympus is a somewhat humble spot, undistinguished, unadorned—nay, almost mean. It stands alone, as it were, in a mighty city, close to the densest throng of men, but partaking neither of the noise nor the crowd; a small secluded, dreary spot, tenanted, one would say, by quite unambitious people at the easiest rents. 'Is this Mount Olympus?' asks the unbelieving stranger. 'Is it from these small, dark, dingy buildings that those infallible laws proceed which cabinets are called upon to obey; by which bishops are to be guided, lords and commons controlled, judges instructed in law, generals in strategy, admirals in naval tactics, and orange-women in the management of their barrows?' 'Yes, my friend—from these walls. From here issue the only known infallible bulls for the guidance of British souls and bodies. This little court is the Vatican of England. Here reigns a pope, self-nominated, self-consecrated—ay, and much stranger too—self-believing!—a pope whom, if you cannot obey him, I would advise you to disobey as silently as possible; a pope hitherto afraid of no Luther; a pope who manages his own inquisition, who punishes unbelievers as no most skilful inquisitor of Spain ever dreamt of doing—one who can excommunicate thoroughly, fearfully, radically; put you beyond the pale of men's charity; make you odious to your dearest friends, and turn you into a monster to be pointed at by the finger!'

Oh heavens! and this is Mount Olympus!

It is a fact amazing to ordinary mortals that the *Jupiter* is never wrong. With what endless care, with what unsparing labour, do we not strive to get together for our great national council the men most fitting to compose it. And how we fail! Parliament is always wrong: look at the *Jupiter*, and see how futile are their meetings, how vain their council, how needless all their trouble! With what pride do we regard our chief ministers, the great servants of state, the oligarchs of the nation on whose wisdom we lean, to whom we look for guidance in our difficulties! But what are they to the writers of the *Jupiter*? They hold council together and with anxious thought painfully elaborate their country's good; but when all is done, the *Jupiter* declares that all is nought. Why should we look to Lord John Russell— why should we regard Palmerston and Gladstone, when Tom Towers without a struggle can put us right? Look at our generals, what faults they make; at our admirals, how inactive they are. What money, honesty, and science can do, is done; and yet how badly are our troops brought together, fed, conveyed, clothed, armed, and managed. The most excellent of our good men do their best to man our ships, with the assistance of all possible external appliances; but in vain. All, all is wrong—alas! alas! Tom Towers, and he alone, knows all about it. Why, oh why, ye earthly ministers, why have ye not followed more closely this heaven-sent messenger that is among us?

Were it not well for us in our ignorance that we confided all things to the *Jupiter*? Would it not be wise in us to abandon useless talking, idle thinking, and profitless labour? Away with majorities in the House of Commons, with verdicts from judicial bench given after much delay, with doubtful laws, and the fallible attempts of humanity! Does not the *Jupiter*, coming forth daily with fifty thousand impressions full of unerring decision on every mortal subject, set all matters sufficiently at rest? Is not Tom Towers here, able to guide us and willing?

Yes indeed, able and willing to guide all men in all things, so long as he is obeyed as autocrat should be obeyed—with undoubting submission: only let not ungrateful ministers seek other colleagues than those whom Tom Towers may approve; let church and state, law and physic, commerce and agriculture, the arts of war, and the arts of peace, all listen and obey, and all will be made perfect. Has not Tom Towers an all-seeing eye? From the diggings of Australia to those of California, right round the habitable globe, does he not know, watch, and chronicle the doings of every one? From a bishopric in New Zealand to an unfortunate director of a North-west passage, is he not the only fit judge of capability? From the sewers of London to the Central Railway of India,—from the palaces of St. Petersburg to the cabins of Connaught, nothing can escape him. Britons have but to read, to obey, and be blessed. None but the fools doubt the wisdom of the *Jupiter*; none but the mad dispute its facts.

No established religion has ever been without its unbelievers, even in the country where it is the most firmly fixed; no creed has been without scoffers; no church has so prospered as to free itself entirely from dissent. There are those who doubt the *Jupiter*! They live and breathe the upper air, walking here unscathed, though scorned—men, born of British mothers and nursed on English milk, who scruple not to say that Mount Olympus has its price, that Tom Towers can be bought for gold!

Mount Olympus

Such is Mount Olympus, the mouthpiece of all the wisdom of this great country. It may probably be said that no place in this 19th century is more worthy of notice. No treasury mandate armed with the signatures of all the government has half the power of one of those broad sheets, which fly forth from hence so abundantly, armed with no signature at all.

Some great man, some mighty peer—we'll say a noble duke—retires to rest feared and honoured by all his countrymen—fearless himself; if not a good man, at any rate a mighty man—too mighty to care much what men may say about his want of virtue. He rises in the morning degraded, mean, and miserable; an object of men's scorn, anxious only to retire as quickly as may be to some German obscurity, some unseen Italian privacy, or, indeed, anywhere out of sight. What has made this awful change? what has so afflicted him? An article has appeared in the *Jupiter*; some fifty lines of a narrow column have destroyed all his grace's equanimity, and banished him for ever from the world. No man knows who wrote the bitter words; the clubs talk confusedly of the matter, whispering to each other this and that name; while Tom Towers walks quietly along Pall Mall, with his coat buttoned close against the east wind, as though he were a mortal man, and not a god dispensing thunderbolts from Mount Olympus.

It was not to Mount Olympus that our friend Bold betook himself. He had before now wandered round that lonely spot, thinking how grand a thing it was to write articles for the *Jupiter*; considering within himself whether by any stretch of the powers within him he could ever come to such distinction; wondering

171

how Tom Towers would take any little humble
offering of his talents; calculating that Tom Towers
himself must have once had a beginning, have once
doubted as to his own success. Towers could not
have been born a writer in the *Jupiter*. With such
ideas, half ambitious and half awe-struck, had Bold
regarded the silent-looking workshop of the gods; but
he had never yet by word or sign attempted to influence the slightest word of his unerring friend. On
such a course was he now intent; and not without
much inward palpitation did he betake himself to the
quiet abode of wisdom, where Tom Towers was to
be found o' mornings inhaling ambrosia and sipping
nectar in the shape of toast and tea.

Not far removed from Mount Olympus, but somewhat nearer to the blessed regions of the West, is
the most favoured abode of Themis. Washed by the
rich tide which now passes from the towers of Cæsar
to Barry's halls of eloquence; and again back, with new
offerings of a city's tribute, from the palaces of peers
to the mart of merchants, stand those quiet walls
which Law has delighted to honour by its presence.
What a world within a world is the Temple! how
quiet are its 'entangled walks,' as some one lately
has called them, and yet how close to the densest
concourse of humanity! how gravely respectable its
sober alleys, though removed but by a single step
from the profanity of the Strand and the low iniquity
of Fleet Street! Old St. Dunstan, with its bell-smiting
bludgeoners, has been removed; the ancient shops
with their faces full of pleasant history are passing
away one by one; the bar itself is to go—its doom
has been pronounced by the *Jupiter*; rumour tells

us of some huge building that is to appear in these latitudes dedicated to law, subversive of the courts of Westminster, and antagonistic to the Rolls and Lincoln's Inn; but nothing yet threatens the silent beauty of the Temple: it is the mediæval court of the metropolis.

Here, on the choicest spot of this choice ground, stands a lofty row of chambers, looking obliquely upon the sullied Thames; before the windows, the lawn of the Temple Gardens stretches with that dim yet delicious verdure so refreshing to the eyes of Londoners. If doomed to live within the thickest of London smoke you would surely say that that would be your chosen spot. Yes, you, you whom I now address, my dear, middle-aged bachelor friend, can nowhere be so well domiciled as here. No one here will ask whether you are out or at home; alone or with friends; here no Sabbatarian will investigate your Sundays, no censorious landlady will scrutinize your empty bottle, no valetudinarian neighbour will complain of late hours. If you love books, to what place are books so suitable? The whole spot is redolent of typography. Would you worship the Paphian goddess, the groves of Cyprus are not more taciturn than those of the Temple. Wit and wine are always here, and always together; the revels of the Temple are as those of polished Greece, where the wildest worshipper of Bacchus never forgot the dignity of the god whom he adored. Where can retirement be so complete as here? where can you be so sure of all the pleasures of society?

It was here that Tom Towers lived, and cultivated with eminent success the tenth Muse who now governs the periodical press. But let it not be supposed that his chambers were such, or so comfortless, as are frequently the gaunt abodes of legal aspirants. Four chairs, a half-filled deal book-case with hangings of dingy green baize, an old office table covered with dusty papers, which are not moved once in six months, and an older Pembroke brother with rickety legs, for all daily uses; a despatcher for the preparation of lobsters and coffee, and an apparatus for the cooking of toast and mutton chops; such utensils and luxuries as these did not suffice for the well-being of Tom Towers. He indulged in four rooms on the first floor, each of which was furnished, if not with the splendour, with probably more than the comfort of Stafford House. Every addition that science and art have lately made to the luxuries of modern life was to be found there. The room in which he usually sat was surrounded by book-shelves carefully filled; nor was there a volume there which was not entitled to its place in such a collection, both by its intrinsic worth and exterior splendour: a pretty portable set of steps in one corner of the room showed that those even on the higher shelves were intended for use. The chamber contained but two works of art—the one, an admirable bust of Sir Robert Peel, by Power, declared the individual politics of our friend; and the other, a singularly long figure of a female devotee, by Millais, told equally plainly the school of art to which he was addicted. This picture was not hung, as pictures usually are, against the wall; there was no inch of wall vacant for such a purpose: it had a stand or desk erected for its own accommodation; and there on her pedestal, framed and glazed, stood the devotional lady looking intently at a lily as no lady ever looked before.

Our modern artists, whom we style Pre-Raphaelites, have delighted to go back, not only to the finish and peculiar manner, but also to the subjects of the early painters. It is impossible to give them too much praise for the elaborate perseverance with which they have equalled the minute perfections of the masters from whom they take their inspiration: nothing probably can exceed the painting of some of these latter-day pictures. It is, however, singular into what faults they fall as regards their subjects: they are not quite content to take the old stock groups—a Sebastian with his arrows, a Lucia with her eyes in a dish, a Lorenzo with a gridiron, or the Virgin with two children. But they are anything but happy in their change. As a rule, no figure should be drawn in a position which it is impossible to suppose any figure should maintain. The patient endurance of St. Sebastian, the wild ecstasy of St. John in the Wilderness, the maternal love of the Virgin, are feelings naturally portrayed by a fixed posture; but the lady with the stiff back and bent neck, who looks at her flower, and is still looking from hour to hour, gives us an idea of pain without grace, and abstraction without a cause.

It was easy, from his rooms, to see that Tom Towers was a Sybarite, though by no means an idle one. He was lingering over his last cup of tea, surrounded by an ocean of newspapers, through which he had been swimming, when John Bold's card was brought in by his tiger. This tiger never knew that his master was at home, though he often knew that he was not, and thus Tom Towers was never invaded but by his own consent. On this occasion, after twisting the card twice in his fingers, he signified to his attendant imp that he was visible; and the inner door was unbolted, and our friend announced.

I have before said that he of the *Jupiter* and John Bold were intimate. There was no very great difference in their ages, for Towers was still considerably under forty; and when Bold had been attending the London hospitals, Towers, who was not then the great man that he has since become, had been much with him. Then they had often discussed together the objects of their ambition and future prospects; then Tom Towers was struggling hard to maintain himself, as a briefless barrister, by short-hand reporting for any of the papers that would engage him; then he had not dared to dream of writing leaders for the *Jupiter*, or canvassing the conduct of Cabinet ministers. Things had altered since that time: the briefless barrister was still briefless, but he now despised briefs: could he have been sure of a judge's seat, he would hardly have left his present career. It is true he wore no ermine, bore no outward marks of a world's respect; but with what a load of inward importance was he charged! It is true his name appeared in no large capitals; on no wall was chalked up 'Tom Towers for ever'—'Freedom of the Press and Tom Towers;' but what member of Parliament had half his power? It is true that in far-off provinces men did not talk daily of Tom Towers but they read the *Jupiter*, and acknowledged that without the *Jupiter* life was not worth having. This kind of hidden but still conscious glory suited the nature of the man.

He loved to sit silent in a corner of his club and listen to the loud chattering of politicians, and to think how they all were in his power—how he could smite the loudest of them, were it worth his while to raise his pen for such a purpose. He loved to watch the great men of whom he daily wrote, and flatter himself that he was greater than any of them. Each of them was responsible to his country, each of them must answer if inquired into, each of them must endure abuse with good humour, and insolence without anger. But to whom was he, Tom Towers, responsible? No one could insult him; no one could inquire into him. He could speak out withering words, and no one could answer him: ministers courted him, though perhaps they knew not his name; bishops feared him; judges doubted their own verdicts unless he confirmed them; and generals, in their councils of war, did not consider more deeply what the enemy would do, than what the *Jupiter* would say. Tom Towers never boasted of the *Jupiter*; he scarcely ever named the paper even to the most intimate of his friends; he did not even wish to be spoken of as connected with it; but he did not the less value his privileges, or think the less of his own importance. It is probable that Tom Towers considered himself the most powerful man in Europe; and so he walked on from day to day, studiously striving to look a man, but knowing within his breast that he was a god.

15

TOM TOWERS, DR. ANTICANT,
AND MR. SENTIMENT

'Ah, Bold! how are you? You haven't breakfasted?'

'Oh yes, hours ago. And how are you?'

When one Esquimau meets another, do the two, as an invariable rule, ask after each other's health? is it inherent in all human nature to make this obliging inquiry? Did any reader of this tale ever meet any friend or acquaintance without asking some such question, and did any one ever listen to the reply? Sometimes a studiously courteous questioner will show so much thought in the matter as to answer it himself, by declaring that had he looked at you he needn't have asked; meaning thereby to signify that you are an absolute personification of health: but such persons are only those who premeditate small effects.

'I suppose you're busy?' inquired Bold.

'Why, yes, rather; or I should say rather not. I have a leisure hour in the day, this is it.'

'I want to ask you if you can oblige me in a certain matter.'

Towers understood in a moment, from the tone of his friend's voice, that the certain matter referred to the newspaper. He smiled, and nodded his head, but made no promise.

'You know this lawsuit that I've been engaged in,' said Bold.

Tom Towers intimated that he was aware of the action which was pending about the hospital.

'Well, I've abandoned it.'

Tom Towers merely raised his eyebrows, thrust his hands into his trousers' pockets, and waited for his friend to proceed.

'Yes, I've given it up. I needn't trouble you with all the history; but the fact is that the conduct of Mr. Harding—— Mr. Harding is the——'

'Oh yes, the master of the place; the man who takes all the money and does nothing,' said Tom Towers, interrupting him.

'Well, I don't know about that; but his conduct in the matter has been so excellent, so little selfish, so open, that I cannot proceed in the matter to his detriment.' Bold's heart misgave him as to Eleanor as he said this; and yet he felt that what he said was not untrue. 'I think nothing should now be done till the wardenship be vacant.'

'And be again filled,' said Towers, 'as it certainly would, before any one heard of the vacancy; and the same objection would again exist. It's an old story that of the vested rights of the incumbent; but suppose the incumbent has only a vested wrong, and that the poor of the town have a vested right, if they only knew how to get at it: is not that something the case here?'

Bold couldn't deny it, but thought it was one of those cases which required a good deal of management before any real good could be done. It was a pity that he had not considered this before he crept into the lion's mouth, in the shape of an attorney's office.

'It will cost you a good deal, I fear,' said Towers.

'A few hundreds,' said Bold—'perhaps three hundred; I can't help that, and am prepared for it.'

'That's philosophical. It's quite refreshing to hear a man talking of his hundreds in so purely indifferent a manner. But I'm sorry you are giving the matter up. It injures a man to commence a thing of this kind, and not carry it through. Have you seen that?' and he threw a small pamphlet across the table, which was all but damp from the press.

Bold had not seen it nor heard of it; but he was well acquainted with the author of it—a gentleman whose pamphlets, condemnatory of all things in these modern days, had been a good deal talked about of late.

Dr. Pessimist Anticant was a Scotchman, who had passed a great portion of his early days in Germany; he had studied there with much effect, and had learnt to look with German subtilty into the root of things, and to examine for himself their intrinsic worth and worthlessness. No man ever resolved more bravely than he to accept as good nothing that was evil; to banish from him as evil nothing that was good. 'Tis a pity that he should not have recognised the fact, that in this world no good is unalloyed, and that there is but little evil that has not in it some seed of what is goodly.

Returning from Germany, he had astonished the reading public by the vigour of his thoughts, put forth in the quaintest language. He cannot write English, said the critics. No matter, said the public;

we can read what he does write, and that without
yawning. And so Dr. Pessimist Anticant became
popular. Popularity spoilt him for all further real use,
as it has done many another. While, with some diffidence, he confined his objurgations to the occasional
follies or shortcomings of mankind; while he
ridiculed the energy of the squire devoted to the
slaughter of partridges, or the mistake of some
noble patron who turned a poet into a gauger of beer-
barrels, it was all well; we were glad to be told our
faults and to look forward to the coming millennium,
when all men, having sufficiently studied the works
of Dr. Anticant, would become truthful and energetic.
But the doctor mistook the signs of the times and the
minds of men, instituted himself censor of things in
general, and began the great task of reprobating
everything and everybody, without further promise
of any millenium at all. This was not so well; and, to
tell the truth, our author did not succeed in his undertaking. His theories were all beautiful, and the code
of morals that he taught us certainly an improvement
on the practices of the age. We all of us could, and
many of us did, learn much from the doctor while he
chose to remain vague, mysterious, and cloudy: but
when he became practical, the charm was gone.

His allusion to the poet and the partridges was
received very well. 'Oh, my poor brother,' said he,
'slaughtered partridges a score of brace to each gun,
and poets gauging ale-barrels, with sixty pounds a
year, at Dumfries, are not the signs of a great era!—
perhaps of the smallest possible era yet written of.
Whatever economies we pursue, political or other,
let us see at once that this is the maddest of the

181

uneconomic: partridges killed by our land magnates at, shall we say, a guinea a head, to be retailed in Leadenhall at one shilling and ninepence, with one poacher in limbo for every fifty birds! our poet, maker, creator, gauging ale, and that badly, with no leisure for making or creating, only a little leisure for drinking, and such like beer-barrel avocations! Truly, a cutting of blocks with fine razors while we scrape our chins so uncomfortably with rusty knives! Oh, my political economist, master of supply and demand, division of labour and high pressure—oh, my loud-speaking friend, tell me, if so much be in you, what is the demand for poets in these kingdoms of Queen Victoria, and what the vouchsafed supply?'

This was all very well: this gave us some hope. We might do better with our next poet, when we got one; and though the partridges might not be abandoned, something could perhaps be done as to the poachers. We were unwilling, however, to take lessons in politics from so misty a professor; and when he came to tell us that the heroes of Westminster were naught, we began to think that he had written enough. His attack upon despatch boxes was not thought to have much in it; but as it is short, the doctor shall again be allowed to speak his sentiments.

'Could utmost ingenuity in the management of red tape avail anything to men lying gasping—we may say, all but dead; could despatch boxes with never-so-much velvet lining and Chubb's patent, be of comfort to a people *in extremis*, I also, with so many others, would, with parched tongue, call on the name of Lord John Russell; or, my brother, at your advice, on Lord Aberdeen; or, my cousin, on Lord Derby, at yours; being, with my parched tongue, indifferent to such matters. 'Tis all one. Oh, Derby! Oh, Gladstone! Oh, Palmerston! Oh, Lord John! Each comes running with serene face and despatch box. Vain physicians! though there were hosts of such, no despatch box will cure this disorder! What! are there other doctors' new names, disciples who have not burdened their souls with tape? Well, let us call again. Oh, Disraeli, great oppositionist, man of the bitter brow! or, Oh, Molesworth, great reformer, thou who promisest Utopia. They come; each with that serene face, and each—alas, me! alas, my country!—each with a despatch box!

'Oh, the serenity of Downing Street!

'My brothers, when hope was over on the battlefield, when no dimmest chance of victory remained, the ancient Roman could hide his face within his toga, and die gracefully. Can you and I do so now? If so, 'twere best for us; if not, oh my brothers, we must die disgracefully, for hope of life and victory I see none left to us in this world below. I for one cannot trust much to serene face and despatch box!'

There might be truth in this, there might be depth of reasoning; but Englishmen did not see enough in the argument to induce them to withdraw their confidence from the present arrangement of the government, and Dr. Anticant's monthly pamphlet on the decay of the world did not receive so much attention as his earlier works. He did not confine himself to politics in these publications, but roamed at large over all matters of public interest, and found everything bad. According to him nobody was true, and not only nobody, but nothing; a man could not

take off his hat to a lady without telling a lie—the
lady would lie again in smiling. The ruffles of the
gentleman's shirt would be fraught with deceit, and
the lady's flounces full of falsehood. Was ever anything more severe than that attack of his on chip
bonnets, or the anathemas with which he endeavoured
to dust the powder out of the bishops' wigs?

The pamphlet which Tom Towers now pushed
across the table was entitled *Modern Charity*, and
was written with the view of proving how much in
the way of charity was done by our predecessors—
how little by the present age; and it ended by a comparison between ancient and modern times, very
little to the credit of the latter.

'Look at this,' said Towers, getting up and turning over the pages of the pamphlet, and pointing to a
passage near the end. 'Your friend the warden, who
is so little selfish, won't like that, I fear.' Bold read
as follows—

'Heavens, what a sight! Let us with eyes wide
open see the godly man of four centuries since, the
man of the dark ages; let us see how he does his godlike work, and, again how the godly man of these
latter days does his.

'Shall we say that the former is one walking painfully through the world, regarding, as a prudent man,
his worldly work, prospering in it as a diligent man
will prosper, but always with an eye to that better
treasure to which thieves do not creep in? Is there
not much nobility in that old man, as, leaning on his
oaken staff, he walks down the high street of his
native town, and receives from all courteous saluta-
tion and acknowledgment of his worth? A noble old

man, my august inhabitants of Belgrave Square and such like vicinity—a very noble old man, though employed no better than in the wholesale carding of wool.

'This carding of wool, however, did in those days bring with it much profit, so that our ancient friend, when dying, was declared, in whatever slang then prevailed, to cut up exceeding well. For sons and daughters there was ample sustenance with assistance of due industry; for friends and relatives some relief for grief at this great loss; for aged dependants comfort in declining years. This was much for one old man to get done in that dark fifteenth century. But this was not all: coming generations of poor woolcarders should bless the name of this rich one; and a hospital should be founded and endowed with his wealth for the feeding of such of the trade as could not, by diligent carding, any longer duly feed themselves.

''Twas thus that an old man in the fifteenth century did his godlike work to the best of his power, and not ignobly, as appears to me.

'We will now take our godly man of latter days. He shall no longer be a woolcarder, for such are not now men of mark. We will suppose him to be one of the best of the good, one who has lacked no opportunities. Our old friend was, after all, but illiterate; our modern friend shall be a man educated in all seemly knowledge; he shall, in short, be that blessed being—a clergyman of the Church of England!

'And now, in what perfectest manner does he in this lower world get his godlike work done and put out of hand? Heavens! in the strangest of manners.

Oh, my brother! in a manner not at all to be believed but by the most minute testimony of eyesight. He does it by the magnitude of his appetite—by the power of his gorge; his only occupation is to swallow the bread prepared with so much anxious care for these impoverished carders of wool—that, and to sing indifferently through his nose once in the week some psalm more or less long—the shorter the better, we should be inclined to say.

'Oh, my civilised friends!—great Britons that never will be slaves, men advanced to infinite state of freedom and knowledge of good and evil—tell me, will you, what becoming monument you will erect to an highly-educated clergyman of the Church of England?'

Bold certainly thought that his friend would not like that: he could not conceive anything that he would like less than this. To what a world of toil and trouble had he, Bold, given rise by his indiscreet attack upon the hospital!

'You see,' said Towers, 'that this affair has been much talked of, and the public are with you. I am sorry you should give the matter up. Have you seen the first number of the *Almshouse*?'

No; Bold had not seen the *Almshouse*. He had seen advertisements of Mr. Popular Sentiment's new novel of that name, but had in no way connected it with Barchester Hospital, and had never thought a moment on the subject.

'It's a direct attack on the whole system,' said Towers. 'It'll go a long way to put down Rochester, and Barchester, and Dulwich, and St. Cross, and all such hotbeds of peculation. It's very clear that

Sentiment has been down to Barchester, and got up the whole story there; indeed, I thought he must have had it all from you, it's very well done, as you'll see: his first numbers always are.'

Bold declared that Mr. Sentiment had got nothing from him, and that he was deeply grieved to find that the case had become so notorious.

'The fire has gone too far to be quenched,' said Towers; 'the building must go now; and as the timbers are all rotten, why, I should be inclined to say, the sooner the better. I expected to see you get some éclat in the matter.'

This was all wormwood to Bold. He had done enough to make his friend the warden miserable for life, and had then backed out just when the success of his project was sufficient to make the question one of real interest. How weakly he had managed his business! he had already done the harm, and then stayed his hand when the good which he had in view was to be commenced. How delightful would it have been to have employed all his energy in such a cause —to have been backed by the *Jupiter*, and written up to by two of the most popular authors of the day! The idea opened a view into the very world in which he wished to live. To what might it not have given rise? what delightful intimacies—what public praise—to what Athenian banquets and rich flavour of Attic salt?

This, however, was now past hope. He had pledged himself to abandon the cause; and could he have forgotten the pledge, he had gone too far to retreat. He was now, this moment, sitting in Tom Towers' room with the object of deprecating any further articles in the *Jupiter*, and, greatly as he disliked the job, his petition to that effect must be made.

'I couldn't continue it,' said he, 'because I found I was in the wrong.'

Tom Towers shrugged his shoulders. How could a successful man be in the wrong! 'In that case,' said he, 'of course you must abandon it.'

'And I called this morning to ask you also to abandon it,' said Bold.

'To ask me,' said Tom Towers, with the most placid of smiles, and a consummate look of gentle surprise, as though Tom Towers was well aware that he of all men was the last to meddle in such matters.

'Yes,' said Bold, almost trembling with hesitation. 'The *Jupiter*, you know, has taken the matter up very strongly. Mr. Harding has felt what it has said deeply; and I thought that if I could explain to you that he personally has not been to blame, these articles might be discontinued.'

How calmly impassive was Tom Towers' face, as this innocent little proposition was made! Had Bold addressed himself to the doorposts in Mount Olympus, they would have shown as much outward sign of assent or dissent. His quiescence was quite admirable; his discretion certainly more than human.

'My dear fellow,' said he, when Bold had quite done speaking, 'I really cannot answer for the *Jupiter*.'

'But if you saw that these articles were unjust, I think that you would endeavour to put a stop to them. Of course nobody doubts that you could, if you chose.'

'Nobody and everybody are always very kind, but unfortunately are generally very wrong.'

'Come, come, Towers,' said Bold, plucking up his courage, and remembering that for Eleanor's sake he was bound to make his best exertion; 'I have no doubt in my own mind but that you wrote the articles yourself, and very well written they were: it will be a great favour if you will in future abstain from any personal allusion to poor Harding.'

'My dear Bold,' said Tom Towers, 'I have a sincere regard for you. I have known you for many years, and value your friendship; I hope you will let me explain to you, without offence, that none who are connected with the public press can with propriety listen to interference.'

'Interference!' said Bold, 'I don't want to interfere.'

'Ah, but, my dear fellow, you do; what else is it? You think that I am able to keep certain remarks out of a newspaper. Your information is probably incorrect, as most public gossip on such subjects is; but, at any rate, you think I have such power, and you ask me to use it: now that is interference.'

'Well, if you choose to call it so.'

'And now suppose for a moment that I had this power, and used it as you wish; isn't it clear that it would be a great abuse? Certain men are employed in writing for the public press; and if they are induced either to write or to abstain from writing by private motives, surely the public press would soon be of little value. Look at the recognised worth of different newspapers, and see if it does not mainly depend on the assurance which the public feel that such a paper is, or is not, independent. You alluded to the *Jupiter*: surely you cannot but see that the weight of the *Jupiter* is too great to be moved by any private request, even though it should be made to a much more influential person than myself: you've only to think of this, and you'll see that I am right.'

The discretion of Tom Towers was boundless: there was no contradicting what he said, no arguing against such propositions. He took such high ground that there was no getting on it. 'The public is defrauded,' said he, 'whenever private considerations are allowed to have weight.' Quite true, thou greatest oracle of the middle of the nineteenth century, thou sententious proclaimer of the purity of the press— the public is defrauded when it is purposely misled. Poor public! how often is it misled! against what a world of fraud has it to contend!

Bold took his leave, and got out of the room as quickly as he could, inwardly denouncing his friend Tom Towers as a prig and a humbug. 'I know he wrote those articles,' said Bold to himself. 'I know he got his information from me. He was ready enough to take my word for gospel when it suited his own views, and to set Mr. Harding up before the public as an imposter on no other testimony than my chance conversation; but when I offer him real evidence opposed to his own views, he tells me that private motives are detrimental to public justice! Confound his arrogance! What is any public question but a conglomeration of private interests? What is any newspaper article but an expression of the views taken by one side? Truth! it takes an age to ascertain the truth of any question! The idea of Tom Towers talking of public motives and purity of purpose! Why, it wouldn't give him a moment's uneasiness to change his politics to-morrow, if the paper required it.'

Tom Towers, Dr. Anticant, and Mr. Sentiment

Such were John Bold's inward exclamations as he made his way out of the quiet labyrinth of the Temple; and yet there was no position of worldly power so coveted in Bold's ambition as that held by the man of whom he was thinking. It was the impregnability of the place which made Bold so angry with the possessor of it, and it was the same quality which made it appear so desirable.

Passing into the Strand, he saw in a bookseller's window an announcement of the first number of the *Almshouse*; so he purchased a copy, and hurrying back to his lodgings, proceeded to ascertain what Mr. Popular Sentiment had to say to the public on the subject which had lately occupied so much of his own attention.

In former times great objects were attained by great work. When evils were to be reformed, reformers set about their heavy task with grave decorum and laborious argument. An age was occupied in proving a grievance, and philosophical researches were printed in folio pages, which it took a life to write, and an eternity to read. We get on now with a lighter step, and quicker: ridicule is found to be more convincing than argument, imaginary agonies touch more than true sorrows, and monthly novels convince, when learned quartos fail to do so. If the world is to be set right, the work will be done by shilling numbers.

Of all such reformers Mr. Sentiment is the most powerful. It is incredible the number of evil practices he has put down: it is to be feared he will soon lack subjects, and that when he has made the working classes comfortable, and got bitter beer put into proper-sized pint bottles, there will be nothing further for him left to do. Mr. Sentiment is certainly a very powerful man, and perhaps not the less so that his good poor people are so very good; his hard rich people so very hard; and the genuinely honest so very honest. Namby-pamby in these days is not thrown away if it be introduced in the proper quarters. Divine peeresses are no longer interesting, though possessed of every virtue; but a pattern peasant or an immaculate manufacturing hero may talk as much twaddle as one of Mrs. Ratcliffe's heroines, and still be listened to. Perhaps, however, Mr. Sentiment's great attraction is in his second-rate characters. If his heroes and heroines walk upon stilts, as heroes and heroines, I fear, ever must, their attendant satellites are as natural as though one met them in the street: they walk and talk like men and women, and live among our friends a rattling, lively life; yes, live, and will live till the names of their calling shall be forgotten in their own, and Buckett and Mrs. Gamp will be the only words left to us to signify a detective police officer or a monthly nurse.

The *Almshouse* opened with a scene in a clergyman's house. Every luxury to be purchased by wealth was described as being there: all the appearances of household indulgence generally found amongst the most self-indulgent of the rich were crowded into this abode. Here the reader was introduced to the demon of the book, the Mephistopheles of the drama. What story was ever written without a demon? What novel, what history, what work of any sort, what world, would be perfect without existing principles both of good and evil? The demon of the

Almshouse was the clerical owner of this comfortable abode. He was a man well stricken in years, but still strong to do evil: he was one who looked cruelly out of a hot, passionate, bloodshot eye; who had a huge red nose with a carbuncle, thick lips, and a great double, flabby chin, which swelled out into solid substance, like a turkey cock's comb, when sudden anger inspired him: he had a hot, furrowed, low brow, from which a few grizzled hairs were not yet rubbed off by the friction of his handkerchief: he wore a loose unstarched white handkerchief, black loose ill-made clothes, and huge loose shoes, adapted to many corns and various bunions: his husky voice told tales of much daily port wine, and his language was not so decorous as became a clergyman. Such was the master of Mr. Sentiment's *Almshouse*. He was a widower, but at present accompanied by two daughters, and a thin and somewhat insipid curate. One of the young ladies was devoted to her father and the fashionable world, and she of course was the favourite; the other was equally addicted to Puseyism and the curate.

The second chapter of course introduced the reader to the more especial inmates of the hospital. Here were discovered eight old men; and it was given to be understood that four vacancies remained unfilled, through the perverse ill-nature of the clerical gentleman with the double chin. The state of these eight paupers was touchingly dreadful: sixpence-farthing a day had been sufficient for their diet when the almshouse was founded; and on sixpence-farthing a day were they still doomed to starve, though food was four times as dear, and money four times as plentiful. It was shocking to find how the conversation of these eight starved old men in their dormitory shamed that of the clergyman's family in his rich drawing-room. The absolute words they uttered were not perhaps spoken in the purest English, and it might be difficult to distinguish from their dialect to what part of the country they belonged; the beauty of the sentiment, however, amply atoned for the imperfection of the language; and it was really a pity that these eight old men could not be sent through the country as moral missionaries, instead of being immured and starved in that wretched almshouse.

Bold finished the number; and as he threw it aside, he thought that that at least had no direct appliance to Mr. Harding, and that the absurdly strong colouring of the picture would disenable the work from doing either good or harm. He was wrong. The artist who paints for the million must use glaring colours, as no one knew better than Mr. Sentiment when he described the inhabitants of his almshouse; and the radical reform which has now swept over such establishments has owed more to the twenty numbers of Mr. Sentiment's novel, than to all the true complaints which have escaped from the public for the last half century.

16

A LONG DAY IN LONDON

THE warden had to make use of all his very moderate powers of intrigue to give his son-in-law the slip, and get out of Barchester without being stopped on his road. No schoolboy ever ran away from school with more precaution and more dread of detection; no convict, slipping down from a prison wall, ever feared to see the gaoler more entirely than Mr. Harding did to see his son-in-law as he drove up in the pony carriage to the railway station, on the morning of his escape to London.

The evening before he went he wrote a note to the archdeacon, explaining that he should start on the morrow on his journey; that it was his intention to see the attorney-general if possible, and to decide on his future plans in accordance with what he heard from that gentleman; he excused himself for giving Dr. Grantly no earlier notice, by stating that his resolve was very sudden; and having entrusted this note to Eleanor, with the perfect, though not expressed, understanding that it was to be sent over to Plumstead Episcopi without haste, he took his departure.

He also prepared and carried with him a note for Sir Abraham Haphazard, in which he stated his name, explaining that he was the defendant in the case of 'The Queen on behalf of the Wool-carders of

Barchester *v.* Trustees under the will of the late John Hiram,' for so was the suit denominated, and begged the illustrious and learned gentleman to vouchsafe to him ten minutes' audience at any hour on the next day. Mr. Harding calculated that for that one day he was safe; his son-in-law, he had no doubt, would arrive in town by an early train, but not early enough to reach the truant till he should have escaped from his hotel after breakfast; and could he thus manage to see the lawyer on that very day, the deed might be done before the archdeacon could interfere.

On his arrival in town the warden drove, as was his wont, to the Chapter Hotel and Coffee House, near St. Paul's. His visits to London of late had not been frequent; but in those happy days when Harding's *Church Music* was going through the press, he had been often there; and as the publisher's house was in Paternoster Row, and the printer's press in Fleet Street, the Chapter Hotel and Coffee House had been convenient. It was a quiet, sombre, clerical house, beseeming such a man as the warden, and thus he afterwards frequented it. Had he dared, he would on this occasion have gone elsewhere to throw the archdeacon further off the scent; but he did not know what violent steps his son-in-law might take for his recovery if he were not found at his usual haunt, and he deemed it not prudent to make himself the object of a hunt through London.

Arrived at his inn, he ordered dinner, and went forth to the attorney-general's chambers. There he learnt that Sir Abraham was in Court, and would not probably return that day. He would go direct from Court to the House; all appointments were, as a

rule, made at the chambers; the clerk could by no
means promise an interview for the next day; was
able, on the other hand, to say that such interview
was, he thought, impossible; but that Sir Abraham
would certainly be at the House in the course of the
night, where an answer from himself might possibly
be elicited.

To the House Mr. Harding went, and left his
note, not finding Sir Abraham there. He added a most
piteous entreaty that he might be favoured with an
answer that evening, for which he would return. He
then journeyed back sadly to the Chapter Coffee
House, digesting his great thoughts, as best he
might, in a clattering omnibus, wedged in between a
wet old lady and a journeyman glazier returning
from his work with his tools in his lap. In melancholy
solitude he discussed his mutton chop and pint of
port. What is there in this world more melancholy
than such a dinner? A dinner, though eaten alone, in
a country hotel may be worthy of some energy; the
waiter, if you are known, will make much of you;
the landlord will make you a bow and perhaps put
the fish on the table; if you ring you are attended to,
and there is some life about it. A dinner at a London
eating-house is also lively enough, if it have no other
attraction. There is plenty of noise and stir about it,
and the rapid whirl of voices and rattle of dishes dis-
perses sadness. But a solitary dinner in an old, respectable, sombre, solid London inn, where nothing
makes any noise but the old waiter's creaking shoes;
where one plate slowly goes and another slowly
comes without a sound; where the two or three
guests would as soon think of knocking each other

down as of speaking; where the servants whisper, and the whole household is disturbed if an order be given above the voice—what can be more melancholy than a mutton chop and a pint of port in such a place?

Having gone through this Mr. Harding got into another omnibus, and again returned to the House. Yes, Sir Abraham was there, and was that moment on his legs, fighting eagerly for the hundred and seventh clause of the Convent Custody Bill. Mr. Harding's note had been delivered to him; and if Mr. Harding would wait some two or three hours, Sir Abraham could be asked whether there was any answer. The House was not full, and perhaps Mr. Harding might get admittance into the Strangers' Gallery, which admission, with the help of five shillings, Mr. Harding was able to effect.

This bill of Sir Abraham's had been read a second time and passed into committee. A hundred and six clauses had already been discussed and had occupied only four mornings and five evening sittings: nine of the hundred and six clauses were passed, fifty-five were withdrawn by consent, fourteen had been altered so as to mean the reverse of the original proposition, eleven had been postponed for further consideration, and seventeen had been directly negatived. The hundred and seventh ordered the bodily searching of nuns for Jesuitical symbols by aged clergymen, and was considered to be the real mainstay of the whole bill. No intention had ever existed to pass such a law as that proposed, but the government did not intend to abandon it till their object was fully attained by the discussion of this clause. It was known that it would be insisted on with terrible vehemence by Protestant Irish members, and as vehemently denounced by the Roman Catholic; and it was justly considered that no further union between the parties would be possible after such a battle. The innocent Irish fell into the trap as they always do, and whisky and poplins became a drug in the market.

A florid-faced gentleman with a nice head of hair, from the south of Ireland, had succeeded in catching the speaker's eye by the time that Mr. Harding had got into the gallery, and was denouncing the proposed sacrilege, his whole face glowing with a fine theatrical frenzy.

'And this is a Christian country?' said he. (Loud cheers; counter cheers from the ministerial benches. 'Some doubt as to that,' from a voice below the gangway.) 'No, it can be no Christian country, in which the head of the bar, the lagal adviser (loud laughter and cheers)—yes, I say the legal adviser of the crown (great cheers and laughter)—can stand up in his seat in this house (prolonged cheers and laughter), and attempt to lagalise indacent assaults on the bodies of religious ladies.' (Deafening cheers and laughter, which were prolonged till the honourable member resumed his seat.)

When Mr. Harding had listened to this and much more of the same kind for about three hours, he returned to the door of the House, and received back from the messenger his own note, with the following words scrawled in pencil on the back of it: 'To-morrow, 10 p.m.—my chambers.—A. H.'

He was so far successful,—but 10 p.m.: what an hour Sir Abraham had named for a legal interview!

Mr. Harding felt perfectly sure that long before that Dr. Grantly would be in London. Dr. Grantly could not, however, know that this interview had been arranged, nor could he learn it unless he managed to get hold of Sir Abraham before that hour; and as this was very improbable, Mr. Harding determined to start from his hotel early, merely leaving word that he should dine out, and unless luck were much against him, he might still escape the archdeacon till his return from the attorney-general's chambers.

He was at breakfast at nine, and for the twentieth time consulted his Bradshaw, to see at what earliest hour Dr. Grantly could arrive from Barchester. As he examined the columns, he was nearly petrified by the reflection that perhaps the archdeacon might come up by the night mail-train! His heart sank within him at the horrid idea, and for a moment he felt himself dragged back to Barchester without accomplishing any portion of his object. Then he remembered that had Dr. Grantly done so, he would have been in the hotel, looking for him long since.

'Waiter,' said he, timidly.

The waiter approached, creaking in his shoes, but voiceless.

'Did any gentleman—a clergyman, arrive here by the night mail-train?'

'No, sir, not one,' whispered the waiter, putting his mouth nearly close to the warden's ear.

Mr. Harding was reassured.

'Waiter,' said he again, and the waiter again creaked up. 'If any one calls for me, I am going to dine out, and shall return about eleven o'clock.'

A Long Day in London

The waiter nodded, but did not this time vouchsafe any reply; and Mr. Harding, taking up his hat, proceeded out to pass a long day in the best way he could, somewhere out of sight of the archdeacon.

Bradshaw had told him twenty times that Dr. Grantly could not be at Paddington station till 2 p.m., and our poor friend might therefore have trusted to the shelter of the hotel for some hours longer with perfect safety; but he was nervous. There was no knowing what steps the archdeacon might take for his apprehension: a message by electric telegraph might desire the landlord of the hotel to set a watch upon him; some letter might come which he might find himself unable to disobey; at any rate, he could not feel himself secure in any place at which the archdeacon could expect to find him; and at 10 a.m. he started forth to spend twelve hours in London.

Mr. Harding had friends in town had he chosen to seek them; but he felt that he was in no humour for ordinary calls, and he did not now wish to consult with any one as to the great step which he had determined to take. As he had said to his daughter, no one knows where the shoe pinches but the wearer. There are some points on which no man can be contented to follow the advice of another—some subjects on which a man can consult his own conscience only. Our warden had made up his mind that it was good for him at any cost to get rid of this grievance; his daughter was the only person whose concurrence appeared necessary to him, and she did concur with him most heartily. Under such circumstances he would not, if he could help it, consult any one further, till advice would be useless. Should the archdeacon catch him, indeed, there would be much advice, and much consultation of a kind not to be avoided; but he hoped letter things; and as he felt that he could not now converse on indifferent subjects, he resolved to see no one till after his interview with the attorney-general.

He determined to take sanctuary in Westminster Abbey, so he again went thither in an omnibus, and finding that the doors were not open for morning service, he paid his twopence, and went in as a sightseer. It occurred to him that he had no definite place of rest for the day, and that he should be absolutely worn out before his interview if he attempted to walk about from 10 a.m. to 10 p.m., so he sat himself down on a stone step, and gazed up at the figure of William Pitt, who looks as though he had just entered the church for the first time in his life and was anything but pleased at finding himself there.

He had been sitting unmolested about twenty minutes when the verger asked him whether he wouldn't like to walk round. Mr. Harding didn't want to walk anywhere, and declined, merely observing that he was waiting for the morning service. The verger seeing that he was a clergyman, told him that the doors of the choir were now open, and showed him into a seat. This was a great point gained; the archdeacon would certainly not come to morning service at Westminster Abbey, even though he were in London; and here the warden could rest quietly, and, when the time came, duly say his prayers.

He longed to get up from his seat, and examine the

music-books of the choristers, and the copy of the litany from which the service was chanted, to see how far the little details at Westminster corresponded with those at Barchester, and whether he thought his own voice would fill the church well from the Westminster precentor's seat. There would, however, be impropriety in such meddling, and he sat perfectly still, looking up at the noble roof, and guarding against the coming fatigues of the day.

By degrees two or three people entered; the very same damp old woman who had nearly obliterated him in the omnibus, or some other just like her; a couple of young ladies with their veils down, and gilt crosses conspicuous on their prayer-books; an old man on crutches; a party who were seeing the abbey, and thought they might as well hear the service for their twopence, as opportunity served; and a young woman with her prayer-book done up in her handkerchief, who rushed in late, and, in her hurried entry, tumbled over one of the forms, and made such a noise that every one, even the officiating minor canon, was startled, and she herself was so frightened by the echo of her own catastrophe that she was nearly thrown into fits by the panic.

Mr. Harding was not much edified by the manner of the service. The minor canon in question hurried in, somewhat late, in a surplice not in the neatest order, and was followed by a dozen choristers, who were also not as trim as they might have been: they all jostled into their places with a quick hurried step, and the service was soon commenced. Soon commenced and soon over—for there was no music, and time was not unnecessarily lost in the chanting. On the whole Mr. Harding was of opinion that things were managed better at Barchester, though even there he knew that there was room for improvement.

It appears to us a question whether any clergyman can go through our church service with decorum, morning after morning, in an immense building, surrounded by not more than a dozen listeners. The best actors cannot act well before empty benches, and though there is, of course, a higher motive in one case than the other, still even the best of clergymen cannot but be influenced by their audience; and to expect that a duty should be well done under such circumstances, would be to require from human nature more than human power.

When the two ladies with the gilt crosses, the old man with his crutch, and the still palpitating housemaid were going, Mr. Harding found himself obliged to go too. The verger stood in his way, and looked at him and looked at the door, and so he went. But he returned again in a few minutes, and re-entered with another twopence. There was no other sanctuary so good for him.

As he walked slowly down the nave, and then up one aisle, and then again down the nave and up the other aisle, he tried to think gravely of the step he was about to take. He was going to give up eight hundred a year voluntarily; and doom himself to live for the rest of his life on about a hundred and fifty. He knew that he had hitherto failed to realise this fact as he ought to do. Could he maintain his own independence and support his daughter on a hundred and fifty pounds a year without being a burden on any one? His son-in-law was rich, but nothing could induce him to lean on his son-in-law after acting, as he intended to do, in direct opposition to his son-in-law's counsel. The bishop was rich, but he was about to throw away the bishop's best gift, and that in a manner to injure materially the patronage of the giver: he could neither expect nor accept anything further from the bishop. There would be not only no merit, but positive disgrace, in giving up his wardenship, if he were not prepared to meet the world without it. Yes, he must from this time forward bound all his human wishes for himself and his daughter to the poor extent of so limited an income. He knew he had not thought sufficiently of this, that he had been carried away by enthusiasm, and had hitherto not brought home to himself the full reality of his position.

He thought most about his daughter, naturally. It was true that she was engaged, and he knew enough of his proposed son-in-law to be sure that his own altered circumstances would make no obstacle to such a marriage; nay, he was sure that the very fact of his poverty would induce Bold more anxiously to press the matter; but he disliked counting on Bold in this emergency, brought on, as it had been, by his doing. He did not like saying to himself—Bold has turned me out of my house and income, and, therefore, he must relieve me of my daughter; he preferred reckoning on Eleanor as the companion of his poverty and exile—as the sharer of his small income.

Some modest provision for his daughter had been long since made. His life was insured for three thousand pounds, and this sum was to go to Eleanor. The archdeacon, for some years past, had paid the premium, and had secured himself by the immediate possession of a small property which was to have gone to Mrs. Grantly after her father's death. This matter, therefore, had been taken out of the warden's hands long since, as, indeed, had all the business transactions of his family, and his anxiety was, therefore, confined to his own life income.

Yes. A hundred and fifty per annum was very small, but still it might suffice; but how was he to chant the litany at the cathedral on Sunday mornings, and get the service done at Crabtree Parva? True, Crabtree Church was not quite a mile and a half from the cathedral; but he could not be in two places at once? Crabtree was a small village, and afternoon service might suffice, but still this went against his conscience; it was not right that his parishioners should be robbed of any of their privileges on account of his poverty. He might, to be sure, make some arrangements for doing weekday service at the cathedral; but he had chanted the litany at Barchester so long, and had a conscious feeling that he did it so well, that he was unwilling to give up the duty.

Thinking of such things, turning over in his own mind together small desires and grave duties, but never hesitating for a moment as to the necessity of leaving the hospital, Mr. Harding walked up and down the abbey, or sat still meditating on the same stone step, hour after hour. One verger went and another came, but they did not disturb him; every now and then they crept up and looked at him, but they did so with a reverential stare, and, on the whole, Mr. Harding found his retreat well chosen. About

four o'clock his comfort was disturbed by an enemy
in the shape of hunger. It was necessary that he should
dine, and it was clear that he could not dine in the
abbey: so he left his sanctuary not willingly, and
betook himself to the neighbourhood of the Strand to
look for food.

His eyes had become so accustomed to the gloom
of the church, that they were dazed when he got out
into the full light of day, and he felt confused and
ashamed of himself, as though people were staring
at him. He hurried along, still in dread of the archdeacon, till he came to Charing Cross, and then
remembered that in one of his passages through the
Strand he had seen the words 'Chops and Steaks' on
a placard in a shop window. He remembered the
shop distinctly; it was next door to a trunk-seller's,
and there was a cigar shop on the other side. He
couldn't go to his hotel for dinner, which to him
hitherto was the only known mode of dining in London at his own expense; and, therefore, he would get
a steak at the shop in the Strand. Archdeacon Grantly
would certainly not come to such a place for his dinner.

He found the house easily—just as he had observed
it, between the trunks and the cigars. He was rather
daunted by the huge quantity of fish which he saw
in the window. There were barrels of oysters, heca-
tombs of lobsters, a few tremendous-looking crabs,
and a tub full of pickled salmon; not, however, being aware of any connection between shell-fish and
iniquity, he entered, and modestly asked a slatternly
woman, who was picking oysters out of a great
watery reservoir, whether he could have a mutton
chop and a potato.

The woman looked somewhat surprised, but answered in the affirmative, and a slipshod girl ushered him into a long back room, filled with boxes for the accommodation of parties, in one of which he took his seat. In a more miserably forlorn place he could not have found himself: the room smelt of fish, and sawdust, and stale tobacco smoke, with a slight taint of escaped gas; everything was rough, and dirty, and disreputable; the cloth which they put before him was abominable; the knives and forks were bruised, and hacked, and filthy; and everything was impregnated with fish. He had one comfort, however: he was quite alone; there was no one there to look on his dismay; nor was it probable that any one would come to do so. It was a London supper-house. About one o'clock at night the place would be lively enough, but at the present time his seclusion was as deep as it had been in the abbey.

In about half an hour the untidy girl, not yet dressed for her evening labours, brought him his chop and potatoes, and Mr. Harding begged for a pint of sherry. He was impressed with an idea, which was generally prevalent a few years since, and is not yet wholly removed from the minds of men, that to order a dinner at any kind of inn, without also ordering a pint of wine for the benefit of the landlord, was a kind of fraud—not punishable, indeed, by law, but not the less abominable on that account. Mr. Harding remembered his coming poverty, and would willingly have saved his half-crown, but he thought he had no alternative; and he was soon put in possession of some horrid mixture procured from the neighbouring public-house.

His chop and potatoes, however, were eatable, and having got over as best he might the disgust created by the knives and forks, he contrived to swallow his dinner. He was not much disturbed: one young man, with pale face and watery fish-like eyes, wearing his hat ominously on one side, did come in and stare at him, and ask the girl, audibly enough, 'Who that old cock was;' but the annoyance went no further, and the warden was left seated on his wooden bench in peace, endeavouring to distinguish the different scents arising from lobsters, oysters, and salmon.

Unknowing as Mr. Harding was in the ways of London, he felt that he had somehow selected an ineligible dining-house, and that he had better leave it. It was hardly five o'clock—how was he to pass the time till ten? Five miserable hours! He was already tired, and it was impossible that he should continue walking so long. He thought of getting into an omnibus, and going out to Fulham for the sake of coming back in another: this, however, would be weary work, and as he paid his bill to the woman in the shop, he asked her if there were any place near where he could get a cup of coffee. Though she did keep a shell-fish supper-house, she was very civil, and directed him to the cigar divan on the other side of the street.

Mr. Harding had not a much correcter notion of a cigar divan than he had of a London dinner-house, but he was desperately in want of rest, and went as he was directed. He thought he must have made some mistake when he found himself in a cigar shop, but the man behind the counter saw immediately that he was a stranger, and understood what he wanted. 'One shilling, sir—thank ye, sir—cigar, sir?—ticket for coffee, sir— you'll only have to call the waiter. Up those stairs, if you please, sir. Better take the cigar, sir—you can always give it to a friend you know. Well, sir, thank ye, sir—as you are so good, I'll smoke it myself.' And so Mr. Harding ascended to the divan, with his ticket for coffee, but minus the cigar.

The place seemed much more suitable to his requirements than the room in which he had dined: there was, to be sure, a strong smell of tobacco, to which he was not accustomed; but after the shell-fish, the tobacco did not seem disagreeable. There were quantities of books, and long rows of sofas. What on earth could be more luxurious than a sofa, a book, and a cup of coffee? An old waiter came up to him, with a couple of magazines and an evening paper. Was ever anything so civil? Would he have a cup of coffee, or would he prefer sherbet? Sherbet! Was he absolutely in an Eastern divan, with the slight addition of all the London periodicals? He had, however, an idea that sherbet should be drunk sitting cross-legged, and as he was not quite up to this, he ordered the coffee.

The coffee came, and was unexceptionable. Why, this divan was a paradise! The civil old waiter suggested to him a game of chess: though a chess player he was not equal to this, so he declined, and, putting up his weary legs on the sofa, leisurely sipped his coffee, and turned over the pages of his Blackwood. He might have been so engaged for about an hour, for the old waiter enticed him to a second cup of coffee, when a musical clock began to play. Mr. Harding then closed his magazine, keeping his place with his finger, and lay, listening with closed eyes to the clock. Soon the clock seemed to turn into a violoncello, with piano accompaniments, and Mr. Harding began to fancy the old waiter was the Bishop of Barchester; he was inexpressibly shocked that the bishop should have brought him his coffee with his own hands; then Dr. Grantly came in, with a basket full of lobsters, which he would not be induced to leave downstairs in the kitchen; and then the warden couldn't quite understand why so many people would smoke in the bishop's drawing-room; and so he fell fast asleep, and his dreams wandered away to his accustomed stall in Barchester Cathedral, and the twelve old men he was so soon about to leave for ever.

He was fatigued, and slept soundly for some time. Some sudden stop in the musical clock woke him at length, and he jumped up with a start, surprised to find the room quite full: it had been nearly empty when his nap began. With nervous anxiety he pulled out his watch, and found that it was half-past nine. He seized his hat, and, hurrying downstairs, started at a rapid pace for Lincoln's Inn.

It still wanted twenty minutes to ten when the warden found himself at the bottom of Sir Abraham's stairs, so he walked leisurely up and down the quiet inn to cool himself. It was a beautiful evening at the end of August. He had recovered from his fatigue; his sleep and the coffee had refreshed him, and he was surprised to find that he was absolutely enjoying himself, when the inn clock struck ten. The sound was hardly over before he knocked at Sir Abraham's door, and was informed by the clerk who received him that the great man would be with him immediately.

17

SIR ABRAHAM HAPHAZARD

Mr. HARDING was shown into a comfortable inner sitting-room, looking more like a gentleman's book-room than a lawyer's chambers, and there waited for Sir Abraham. Nor was he kept waiting long: in ten or fifteen minutes he heard a clatter of voices speaking quickly in the passage, and then the attorney-general entered.

'Very sorry to keep you waiting, Mr. Warden,' said Sir Abraham, shaking hands with him; 'and sorry, too, to name so disagreeable an hour; but your notice was short, and as you said to-day, I named the very earliest hour that was not disposed of.'

Mr. Harding assured him that he was aware that it was he that should apologise.

Sir Abraham was a tall thin man, with hair prematurely grey, but bearing no other sign of age; he had a slight stoop, in his neck rather than his back, acquired by his constant habit of leaning forward as he addressed his various audiences. He might be fifty years old, and would have looked young for his age, had not constant work hardened his features, and given him the appearance of a machine with a mind. His face was full of intellect, but devoid of natural expression. You would say he was a man to use, and then have done with; a man to be sought for on great emergencies, but ill adapted for ordinary services; a man whom you would ask to defend your property, but to whom you would be sorry to confide your love. He was bright as a diamond, and as cutting, and also as unimpressionable. He knew every one whom to know was an honour, but he was without a friend; he wanted none, however, and knew not the meaning of the word in other than its parliamentary sense. A friend! Had he not always been sufficient to himself, and now, at fifty, was it likely that he should trust another? He was married, indeed, and had children, but what time had he for the soft idleness of conjugal felicity? His working days or term times were occupied from his time of rising to the late hour at which he went to rest, and even his vacations were more full of labour than the busiest days of other men. He never quarrelled with his wife, but he never talked to her,—he never had time to talk, he was so taken up with speaking. She, poor lady, was not unhappy; she had all that money could give her, she would probably live to be a peeress, and she really thought Sir Abraham the best of husbands.

Sir Abraham was a man of wit, and sparkled among the brightest at the dinner-tables of political grandees: indeed, he always sparkled; whether in society, in the House of Commons, or the courts of law, coruscations flew from him; glittering sparkles, as from hot steel, but no heat; no cold heart was ever cheered by warmth from him, no unhappy soul ever dropped a portion of its burden at his door.

With him success alone was praiseworthy, and he knew none so successful as himself. No one had thrust him forward; no powerful friends had pushed him along on his road to power. No; he was attorney-general, and would, in all human probability, be lord chancellor by sheer dint of his own industry and his own talent. Who else in all the world rose so high with so little help? A premier, indeed! Who had ever been premier without mighty friends? An archbishop! Yes, the son or grandson of a great noble, or else, probably, his tutor. But he, Sir Abraham, had had no mighty lord at his back; his father had been a country apothecary, his mother a farmer's daughter. Why should he respect any but himself? And so he glitters along through the world, the brightest among the bright; and when his glitter is gone, and he is gathered to his fathers, no eye will be dim with a tear, no heart will mourn for its lost friend.

'And so, Mr. Warden,' said Sir Abraham, 'all our trouble about this lawsuit is at an end.'

Mr. Harding said he hoped so, but he didn't at all understand what Sir Abraham meant. Sir Abraham, with all his sharpness, could not have looked into his heart and read his intentions.

'All over. You need trouble yourself no further about it; of course they must pay the costs, and the absolute expense to you and Dr. Grantly will be trifling—that is, compared with what it might have been if it had been continued.'

'I fear I don't quite understand you, Sir Abraham.'

'Don't you know that their attorneys have noticed us that they have withdrawn the suit?'

Mr. Harding explained to the lawyer that he knew nothing of this, although he had heard in a round-about way that such an intention had been talked of; and he also at length succeeded in making Sir Abraham understand that even this did not satisfy him. The attorney-general stood up, put his hands into his breeches' pockets, and raised his eye-brows, as Mr. Harding proceeded to detail the grievance from which he now wished to rid himself.

'I know I have no right to trouble you personally with this matter, but as it is of most vital importance to me, as all my happiness is concerned in it, I thought I might venture to seek your advice.'

Sir Abraham bowed, and declared his clients were entitled to the best advice he could give them; particularly a client so respectable in every way as the Warden of Barchester Hospital.

'A spoken word, Sir Abraham, is often of more value than volumes of written advice. The truth is, I am ill-satisfied with this matter as it stands at present. I do see—I cannot help seeing, that the affairs of the hospital are not arranged according to the will of the founder.'

'None of such institutions are, Mr. Harding, nor can they be; the altered circumstances in which we live do not admit of it.'

'Quite true—that is quite true; but I can't see that those altered circumstances give me a right to eight hundred a year. I don't know whether I ever read John Hiram's will, but were I to read it now I could not understand it. What I want you, Sir Abraham, to tell me, is this—am I, as warden, legally and distinctly entitled to the proceeds of the property, after the due maintenance of the twelve bedesmen?'

Sir Abraham declared that he couldn't exactly say in so many words that Mr. Harding was legally entitled to, etc., etc., etc., and ended in expressing a strong opinion that it would be madness to raise any

further question on the matter, as the suit was to be
—nay, was, abandoned.

Mr. Harding, seated in his chair, began to play a
slow tune on an imaginary violoncello.

'Nay, my dear sir,' continued the attorney-general,
'there is no further ground for any question; I don't
see that you have the power of raising it.'

'I can resign,' said Mr. Harding, slowly playing
away with his right hand, as though the bow were
beneath the chair in which he was sitting.

'What! throw it up altogether?' said the attorney-
general, gazing with utter astonishment at his client.

'Did you see those articles in the *Jupiter*?' said
Mr. Harding, piteously, appealing to the sympathy
of the lawyer.

Sir Abraham said he had seen them. This poor
little clergyman, cowed into such an act of extreme
weakness by a newspaper article, was to Sir Abraham so contemptible an object, that he hardly knew
how to talk to him as to a rational being.

'Hadn't you better wait,' said he, 'till Dr. Grantly
is in town with you? Wouldn't it be better to postpone any serious step till you can consult with him?'

Mr. Harding declared vehemently that he could
not wait, and Sir Abraham began seriously to doubt
his sanity.

'Of course,' said the latter, 'if you have private
means sufficient for your wants, and if this——'

'I haven't a sixpence, Sir Abraham,' said the warden.

'God bless me! Why, Mr. Harding, how do you
mean to live?'

Mr. Harding proceeded to explain to the man of
law that he meant to keep his precentorship—that

was eighty pounds a year; and, also, that he meant to fall back upon his own little living of Crabtree, which was another eighty pounds. That, to be sure, the duties of the two were hardly compatible; but perhaps he might effect an exchange. And then, recollecting that the attorney-general would hardly care to hear how the service of a cathedral church is divided among the minor canons, stopped short in his explanations.

Sir Abraham listened in pitying wonder. 'I really think, Mr. Harding, you had better wait for the archdeacon. This is a most serious step—one for which, in my opinion, there is not the slightest necessity; and, as you have done me the honour of asking my advice, I must implore you to do nothing without the approval of your friends. A man is never the best judge of his own position.'

'A man is the best judge of what he feels himself. I'd sooner beg my bread till my death than read such another article as those two that have appeared, and feel, as I do, that the writer has truth on his side.'

'Have you not a daughter, Mr. Harding—an unmarried daughter?'

'I have,' said he, now standing also, but still playing away on his fiddle with his hand behind his back. 'I have, Sir Abraham; and she and I are completely agreed on this subject.'

'Pray excuse me, Mr. Harding, if what I say seems impertinent; but surely it is you that should be prudent on her behalf. She is young, and does not know the meaning of living on an income of a hundred and fifty pounds a year. On her account give up this idea. Believe me, it is sheer Quixotism.'

218

Sir Abraham Haphazard

The warden walked away to the window, and then back to his chair; and then, irresolute what to say, took another turn to the window. The attorney-general was really extremely patient, but he was beginning to think that the interview had been long enough.

'But if this income be not justly mine, what if she and I have both to beg?' said the warden at last, sharply, and in a voice so different from that he had hitherto used, that Sir Abraham was startled. 'If so, it would be better to beg.'

'My dear sir, nobody now questions its justness.'

'Yes, Sir Abraham, one does question it—the most important of all witnesses against me—I question it myself. My God knows whether or no I love my daughter; but I would sooner that she and I should both beg, than that she should live in comfort on money which is truly the property of the poor. It may seem strange to you, Sir Abraham, it is strange to myself, that I should have been ten years in that happy home, and not have thought of these things till they were so roughly dinned into my ears. I cannot boast of my conscience, when it required the violence of a public newspaper to awaken it; but, now that it is awake, I must obey it. When I came here I did not know that the suit was withdrawn by Mr. Bold, and my object was to beg you to abandon my defence. As there is no action, there can be no defence; but it is, at any rate, as well that you should know that from to-morrow I shall cease to be the warden of the hospital. My friends and I differ on this subject, Sir Abraham, and that adds much to my sorrow; but it cannot be helped.' And, as he finished what he had to

219

say, he played up such a tune as never before had graced the chambers of any attorney-general. He was standing up, gallantly fronting Sir Abraham, and his right arm passed with bold and rapid sweeps before him, as though he were embracing some huge instrument, which allowed him to stand thus erect; and with the fingers of his left hand he stopped, with preternatural velocity, a multitude of strings, which ranged from the top of his collar to the bottom of the lappet of his coat. Sir Abraham listened and looked in wonder. As he had never before seen Mr. Harding, the meaning of these wild gesticulations was lost upon him; but he perceived that the gentleman who had a few minutes since been so subdued as to be unable to speak without hesitation, was now impassioned —nay, almost violent.

'You'll sleep on this, Mr. Harding, and to-morrow——'

'I have done more than sleep upon it,' said the warden; 'I have laid awake upon it, and that night after night. I found I could not sleep upon it: now I hope to do so.'

The attorney-general had no answer to make to this; so he expressed a quiet hope that whatever settlement was finally made would be satisfactory; and Mr. Harding withdrew, thanking the great man for his kind attention.

Mr. Harding was sufficiently satisfied with the interview to feel a glow of comfort as he descended into the small old square of Lincoln's Inn. It was a calm, bright, beautiful night, and by the light of the moon, even the chapel of Lincoln's Inn, and the sombre row of chambers, which surround the quadrangle, looked well. He stood still a moment to collect his thoughts, and reflect on what he had done, and was about to do. He knew that the attorney-general regarded him as little better than a fool, but that he did not mind; he and the attorney-general had not much in common between them; he knew also that others, whom he did care about, would think so too; but Eleanor, he was sure, would exult in what he had done, and the bishop, he trusted, would sympathise with him.

In the meantime he had to meet the archdeacon, and so he walked slowly down Chancery Lane and along Fleet Street, feeling sure that his work for the night was not yet over. When he reached the hotel he rang the bell quietly, and with a palpitating heart; he almost longed to escape round the corner, and delay the coming storm by a further walk round St. Paul's Churchyard, but he heard the slow creaking shoes of the old waiter approaching, and he stood his ground manfully.

18

THE WARDEN IS VERY OBSTINATE

'Dr. Grantly is here, sir,' greeted his ears before the door was well open, 'and Mrs. Grantly. They have a sitting-room above, and are waiting up for you.'

There was something in the tone of the man's voice which seemed to indicate that even he looked upon the warden as a runaway school-boy, just recaptured by his guardian, and that he pitied the culprit, though he could not but be horrified at the crime.

The warden endeavoured to appear unconcerned, as he said, 'Oh, indeed! I'll go upstairs at once;' but he failed signally. There was, perhaps, a ray of comfort in the presence of his married daughter; that is to say, of comparative comfort, seeing that his son-in-law was there; but how much would he have preferred that they should both have been safe at Plumstead Episcopi! However, upstairs he went, the waiter slowly preceding him; and on the door being opened the archdeacon was discovered standing in the middle of the room, erect, indeed, as usual, but oh! how sorrowful! and on the dingy sofa behind him reclined his patient wife.

'Papa, I thought you were never coming back,' said the lady; 'it's twelve o'clock.'

'Yes, my dear,' said the warden. 'The attorney-general named ten for my meeting; to be sure ten is late, but what could I do, you know? Great men will have their own way.'

And he gave his daughter a kiss, and shook hands with the doctor, and again tried to look unconcerned.

'And you have absolutely been with the attorney-general?' asked the archdeacon.

Mr. Harding signified that he had.

'Good heavens, how unfortunate!' And the archdeacon raised his huge hands in the manner in which his friends are so accustomed to see him express disapprobation and astonishment. 'What will Sir Abraham think of it? Did you not know that it is not customary for clients to go direct to their counsel?'

'Isn't it?' asked the warden, innocently. 'Well, at any rate, I've done it now. Sir Abraham didn't seem to think it so very strange.'

The archdeacon gave a sigh that would have moved a man-of-war.

'But, papa, what did you say to Sir Abraham?' asked the lady.

'I asked him, my dear, to explain John Hiram's will to me. He couldn't explain it in the only way which would have satisfied me, and so I resigned the wardenship.'

'Resigned it!' said the archdeacon, in a solemn voice, sad and low, but yet sufficiently audible—a sort of whisper that Macready would have envied, and the galleries have applauded with a couple of rounds. 'Resigned it! Good heavens!' And the dignitary of the church sank back horrified into a horse-hair armchair.

'At least I told Sir Abraham that I would resign; and of course I must now do so.'

'Not at all,' said the archdeacon, catching a ray of hope. 'Nothing that you say in such a way to your own counsel can be in any way binding on you; of course you were there to ask his advice. I'm sure Sir Abraham did not advise any such step.'

Mr. Harding could not say that he had.

'I am sure he disadvised you from it,' continued the reverend cross-examiner.

Mr. Harding could not deny this.

'I'm sure Sir Abraham must have advised you to consult your friends.'

To this proposition also Mr. Harding was obliged to assent.

'Then your threat of resignation amounts to nothing, and we are just where we were before.'

Mr. Harding was now standing on the rug, moving uneasily from one foot to the other. He made no distinct answer to the archdeacon's last proposition, for his mind was chiefly engaged on thinking how he could escape to bed. That his resignation was a thing finally fixed on, a fact all but completed, was not in his mind a matter of any doubt; he knew his own weakness; he knew how prone he was to be led; but he was not weak enough to give way now, to go back from the position to which his conscience had driven him, after having purposely come to London to declare his determination: he did not in the least doubt his resolution, but he greatly doubted his power of defending it against his son-in-law.

'You must be very tired, Susan,' said he: 'wouldn't you like to go to bed?'

But Susan didn't want to go till her husband went.
—She had an idea that her papa might be bullied if
she were away: she wasn't tired at all, or at least she
said so.

The archdeacon was pacing the room, expressing,
by certain noddles of his head, his opinion of the
utter fatuity of his father-in-law.

'Why,' at last he said—and angels might have
blushed at the rebuke expressed in his tone and emphasis—'Why did you go off from Barchester so
suddenly? Why did you take such a step without
giving us notice, after what had passed at the palace?'

The warden hung his head, and made no reply: he
could not condescend to say that he had not intended
to give his son-in-law the slip; and as he had not the
courage to avow it, he said nothing.

'Papa has been too much for you,' said the lady.

The archdeacon took another turn, and again
ejaculated, 'Good heavens!', this time in a very
low whisper, but still audible.

'I think I'll go to bed,' said the warden, taking up
a side candle.

'At any rate, you'll promise me to take no further
step without consultation,' said the archdeacon. Mr.
Harding made no answer, but slowly proceeded to
light his candle. 'Of course,' continued the other,
'such a declaration as that you made to Sir Abraham
means nothing. Come, warden, promise me this. The
whole affair, you see, is already settled, and that with
very little trouble or expense. Bold has been com-
pelled to abandon his action, and all you have to do is
to remain quiet at the hospital.' Mr. Harding still
made no reply, but looked meekly into his son-in-law's

face. The archdeacon thought he knew his father-in-law, but he was mistaken; he thought that he had already talked over a vacillating man to resign his promise. 'Come,' said he, 'promise Susan to give up this idea of resigning the wardenship.'

The warden looked at his daughter, thinking probably at the moment that if Eleanor were contented with him, he need not so much regard his other child, and said, 'I am sure Susan will not ask me to break my word, or to do what I know to be wrong.'

'Papa,' said she, 'it would be madness in you to throw up your preferment. What are you to live on?'

'God, that feeds the young ravens, will take care of me also,' said Mr. Harding, with a smile, as though afraid of giving offence by making his reference to scripture too solemn.

'Pish!' said the archdeacon, turning away rapidly. 'If the ravens persisted in refusing the food prepared for them, they wouldn't be fed.' A clergyman generally dislikes to be met in argument by any scriptural quotation; he feels as affronted as a doctor does, when recommended by an old woman to take some favourite dose, or as a lawyer when an unprofessional man attempts to put him down by a quibble.

'I shall have the living of Crabtree,' modestly suggested the warden.

'Eighty pounds a year!' sneered the archdeacon.

'And the precentorship,' said the father-in-law.

'It goes with the wardenship,' said the son-in-law. Mr. Harding was prepared to argue this point, and began to do so, but Dr. Grantly stopped him. 'My dear warden,' said he, 'this is all nonsense. Eighty pounds or a hundred and sixty makes very little difference. You can't live on it—you can't ruin Eleanor's prospects for ever. In point of fact, you can't resign; the bishop wouldn't accept it; the whole thing is settled. What I now want to do is to prevent any inconvenient tittle-tattle—any more newspaper articles.'

'That's what I want, too,' said the warden.

'And to prevent that,' continued the other, 'we mustn't let any talk of resignation get abroad.'

'But I shall resign,' said the warden, very, very meekly.

'Good heavens! Susan, my dear, what can I say to him?'

'But, papa,' said Mrs. Grantly, getting up, and putting her arm through that of her father, 'what is Eleanor to do if you throw away your income?'

A hot tear stood in each of the warden's eyes as he looked round upon his married daughter. Why should one sister who was so rich predict poverty for another? Some such idea as this was on his mind, but he gave no utterance to it. Then he thought of the pelican feeding its young with blood from its own breast, but he gave no utterance to that either; and then of Eleanor waiting for him at home, waiting to congratulate him on the end of all his trouble.

'Think of Eleanor, papa,' said Mrs. Grantly.

'I do think of her,' said her father.

'And you will not do this rash thing?' The lady was really moved beyond her usual calm composure.

'It can never be rash to do right,' said he. 'I shall certainly resign this wardenship.'

227

'Then, Mr. Harding, there is nothing before you but ruin,' said the archdeacon, now moved beyond all endurance. 'Ruin both for you and Eleanor. How do you mean to pay the monstrous expenses of this action?'

Mrs. Grantly suggested that, as the action was abandoned, the costs would not be heavy.

'Indeed they will, my dear,' continued he. 'One cannot have the attorney-general up at twelve o'clock at night for nothing;—but of course your father has not thought of this.'

'I will sell my furniture,' said the warden.

'Furniture!' ejaculated the other, with a most powerful sneer.

'Come, archdeacon,' said the lady, 'we needn't mind that at present. You know you never expected papa to pay the costs.'

'Such absurdity is enough to provoke Job,' said the archdeacon, marching quickly up and down the room. 'Your father is like a child. Eight hundred pounds a year!—eight hundred and eighty with the house—with nothing to do. The very place for him. And to throw that up because some scoundrel writes an article in a newspaper! Well—I have done my duty. If he chooses to ruin his child I cannot help it;' and he stood still at the fire-place, and looked at himself in a dingy mirror which stood on the chimney-piece.

There was a pause for about a minute, and then the warden, finding that nothing else was coming, lighted his candle, and quietly said, 'Good-night.'

'Good-night, papa,' said the lady.

And so the warden retired; but, as he closed the door behind him, he heard the well-known ejaculation,—slower, lower, more solemn, more ponderous than ever—'Good heavens!'

19

THE WARDEN RESIGNS

THE party met the next morning at breakfast; and a very sombre affair it was—very unlike the breakfasts at Plumstead Episcopi.

There were three thin, small, dry bits of bacon, each an inch long, served up under a huge old plated cover; there were four three-cornered bits of dry toast, and four square bits of buttered toast; there was a loaf of bread, and some oily-looking butter; and on the sideboard there were the remains of a cold shoulder of mutton. The archdeacon, however, had not come up from his rectory to St. Paul's Churchyard to enjoy himself and therefore nothing was said of the scanty fare.

The guests were as sorry as the viands—hardly anything was said over the breakfast-table. The archdeacon munched his toast in ominous silence, turning over bitter thoughts in his deep mind. The warden tried to talk to his daughter, and she tried to answer him; but they both failed. There were no feelings at present in common between them. The warden was thinking only of getting back to Barchester, and calculating whether the archdeacon would expect him to wait for him; and Mrs. Grantly was preparing herself for a grand attack which she was to make on her father, as agreed upon between herself and her husband during their curtain confabulation of that morning.

The Warden Resigns

When the waiter had creaked out of the room with the last of the teacups, the archdeacon got up and went to the window, as though to admire the view. The room looked out on a narrow passage which runs from St. Paul's Churchyard to Paternoster Row; and Dr. Grantly patiently perused the names of the three shopkeepers whose doors were in view. The warden still kept his seat at the table, and examined the pattern of the table-cloth; and Mrs. Grantly, seating herself on the sofa, began to knit.

After a while the warden pulled his Bradshaw out of his pocket, and began laboriously to consult it. There was a train for Barchester at 10 a.m. That was out of the question, for it was nearly ten already. Another at 3 p.m.; another, the night mail-train, at 9 p.m. The three o'clock train would take him home to tea, and would suit him very well.

'My dear,' said he, 'I think I shall go back home at three o'clock to-day. I shall get home at half-past eight. I don't think there's anything to keep me in London.'

'The archdeacon and I return by the early train to-morrow, papa; won't you wait and go back with us?'

'Why, Eleanor will expect me to-night; and I've so much to do; and——'

'Much to do!' said the archdeacon *sotto voce*; but the warden heard him.

'You'd better wait for us, papa.'

'Thank ye, my dear! I think I'll go this afternoon.' The tamest animal will turn when driven too hard, and even Mr. Harding was beginning to fight for his own way.

'I suppose you won't be back before three?' said the lady, addressing her husband.

'I must leave this at two,' said the warden.

'Quite out of the question,' said the archdeacon, answering his wife, and still reading the shop-keepers' names; 'I don't suppose I shall be back till five.'

There was another long pause, during which Mr. Harding continued to study his Bradshaw.

'I must go to Cox and Cumming,' said the arch-deacon at last.

'Oh, to Cox and Cumming,' said the warden. It was quite a matter of indifference to him where his son-in-law went.

The names of Cox and Cumming had now no interest in his ears. What had he to do with Cox and Cumming further, having already had his suit finally adjudicated upon in a court of conscience, a judg-ment without power of appeal fully registered, and the matter settled so that all the lawyers in London could not disturb it. The archdeacon could go to Cox and Cumming, could remain there all day in anxious discussion; but what might be said there was no longer matter of interest to him, who was so soon to lay aside the name of warden of Barchester Hospital.

The archdeacon took up his shining new clerical hat, and put on his black new clerical gloves, and looked heavy, respectable, decorous, and opulent, a decided clergyman of the Church of England, every inch of him. 'I suppose I shall see you at Barchester the day after to-morrow,' said he.

The warden supposed he would.

'I must once more beseech you to take no further

steps till you see my father; if you owe me nothing,' and the archdeacon looked as though he thought a great deal were due to him, 'at least you owe so much to my father;' and, without waiting for a reply, Dr. Grantly wended his way to Cox and Cumming.

Mrs. Grantly waited till the last fall of her husband's foot was heard, as he turned out of the court into St. Paul's Churchyard, and then commenced her task of talking her father over.

'Papa,' she began, 'this is a most serious business.'

'Indeed it is,' said the warden, ringing the bell.

'I greatly feel the distress of mind you must have endured.'

'I am sure you do, my dear'; and he ordered the waiter to bring him pen, ink, and paper.

'Are you going to write, papa?'

'Yes, my dear—I am going to write my resignation to the bishop.'

'Pray, pray, papa, put it off till our return,—pray put it off till you have seen the bishop,—dear papa! for my sake, for Eleanor's!——'

'It is for your sake and Eleanor's that I do this. I hope, at least, that my children may never have to be ashamed of their father.'

'How can you talk about shame, papa?' and she stopped while the waiter creaked in with the paper, and then slowly creaked out again; 'how can you talk about shame? you know what all your friends think about this question.'

The warden spread his paper on the table, placing it on the meagre blotting-book which the hotel afforded, and sat himself down to write.

'You won't refuse me one request, papa?' continued

his daughter; 'you won't refuse to delay your letter for two short days? Two days can make no possible difference.'

'My dear,' said he naïvely, 'if I waited till I got to Barchester, I might, perhaps, be prevented.'

'But surely you would not wish to offend the bishop?' said she.

'God forbid! The bishop is not apt to take offence, and knows me too well to take in bad part anything that I may be called on to do.'

'But, papa——'

'Susan,' said he, 'my mind on this subject is made up; it is not without much repugnance that I act in opposition to the advice of such men as Sir Abraham Haphazard and the archdeacon; but in this matter I can take no advice, I cannot alter the resolution to which I have come.'

'But two days, papa——'

'No—nor can I delay it. You may add to my present unhappiness by pressing me, but you cannot change my purpose; it will be a comfort to me if you will let the matter rest:' and, dipping his pen into the inkstand, he fixed his eyes intently on the paper.

There was something in his manner which taught his daughter to perceive that he was in earnest: she had at one time ruled supreme in her father's house, but she knew that there were moments when, mild and meek as he was, he would have his way, and the present was an occasion of the sort. She returned, therefore, to her knitting, and very shortly after left the room.

The warden was now at liberty to compose his letter, and, as it was characteristic of the man, it shall be given at full length. The official letter, which, when written, seemed to him to be too formally cold to be sent alone to so dear a friend, was accompanied by a private note; and both are here inserted.

The letter of resignation ran as follows:

'CHAPTER HOTEL, ST. PAUL'S,
'LONDON,
'*August*, 18—.

'MY LORD BISHOP,

'It is with the greatest pain that I feel myself constrained to resign into your Lordship's hands the wardenship of the hospital at Barchester, which you so kindly conferred upon me, now nearly twelve years since.

'I need not explain the circumstances which have made this step appear necessary to me. You are aware that a question has arisen as to the right of the warden to the income which has been allotted to the wardenship; it has seemed to me that this right is not well made out, and I hesitate to incur the risk of taking an income to which my legal claim appears doubtful.

'The office of precentor of the cathedral is, as your Lordship is aware, joined to that of the warden; that is to say, the precentor has for many years been the warden of the hospital; there is, however, nothing to make the junction of the two offices necessary, and, unless you or the dean and chapter object to such an arrangement, I would wish to keep the precentorship. The income of this office will now be necessary to me; indeed, I do not know why I should be ashamed to say that I should have difficulty in supporting myself without it.

'Your Lordship, and such others as you may please to consult on the matter, will at once see that my resignation of the wardenship need offer not the slightest bar to its occupation by another person. I am thought in the wrong by all those whom I have consulted in the matter; I have very little but an inward and an unguided conviction of my own to bring me to this step, and I shall, indeed, be hurt to find that any slur is thrown on the preferment which your kindness bestowed on me, by my resignation of it. I, at any rate for one, shall look on any successor whom you may appoint as enjoying a clerical situation of the highest respectability, and one to which your Lordship's nomination gives an indefeasible right.

'I cannot finish this official letter without again thanking your Lordship for all your great kindness, and I beg to subscribe myself

'Your Lordship's most obedient servant,

'SEPTIMUS HARDING,
*'Warden of Barchester Hospital, and
Precentor of the Cathedral.'*

He then wrote the following private note:

'MY DEAR BISHOP,

'I cannot send you the accompanying official letter without a warmer expression of thanks for all your kindness than would befit a document which may to a certain degree be made public. You, I know, will understand the feeling, and, perhaps, pity the weakness which makes me resign the hospital. I am not made of calibre strong enough to withstand public attack. Were I convinced that I stood on ground perfectly firm, that I was certainly justified in taking eight hundred a year under Hiram's will, I should feel bound by duty to retain the position, however unendurable might be the nature of the assault; but, as I do not feel this conviction, I cannot believe that you will think me wrong in what I am doing.

'I had at one time an idea of keeping only some moderate portion of the income; perhaps three hundred a year, and of remitting the remainder to the trustees; but it occurred to me, and I think with reason, that by so doing I should place my successors in an invidious position, and greatly damage your patronage.

'My dear friend, let me have a line from you to say that you do not blame me for what I am doing, and that the officiating vicar of Crabtree Parva will be the same to you as the warden of the hospital.

'I am very anxious about the precentorship: the archdeacon thinks it must go with the wardenship; I think not, and, that, having it, I cannot be ousted. I will, however, be guided by you and the dean. No other duty will suit me so well, or come so much within my power of adequate performance.

'I thank you from my heart for the preferment which I am now giving up, and for all your kindness, and am, dear bishop, now as always,

'Yours most sincerely
'SEPTIMUS HARDING.

'LONDON,
'—*August*, 18—.

Having written these letters and made a copy of the former one for the benefit of the archdeacon, Mr. Harding, whom we must now cease to call the warden, he having designated himself so for the last time, found that it was nearly two o'clock, and that he must prepare for his journey. Yes, from this time he never again admitted the name by which he had been so familiarly known, and in which, to tell the truth, he had rejoiced. The love of titles is common to all men, and a vicar or fellow is as pleased at becoming Mr. Archdeacon or Mr. Provost, as a lieutenant at getting his captaincy, or a city tallow-chandler in becoming Sir John on the occasion of a Queen's visit to a new bridge. But warden he was no longer, and the name of precentor, though the office was to him so dear, confers in itself no sufficient distinction; our friend, therefore, again became Mr. Harding.

Mrs. Grantly had gone out; he had, therefore, no one to delay him by further entreaties to postpone his journey; he had soon arranged his bag, and paid his bill, and, leaving a note for his daughter, in which he put the copy of his official letter, he got into a cab and drove away to the station with something of triumph in his heart.

Had he not cause for triumph? Had he not been supremely successful? Had he not for the first time in his life held his own purpose against that of his son-in-law, and manfully combated against great odds—against the archdeacon's wife as well as the archdeacon? Had he not gained a great victory, and was it not fit that he should step into his cab with triumph?

He had not told Eleanor when he would return, but she was on the look out for him by every train by which he could arrive, and the pony-carriage was at the Barchester station when the train drew up at the platform.

'My dear,' said he, sitting beside her, as she steered her little vessel to one side of the road to make room for the clattering omnibus as they passed from the station into the town; 'I hope you'll be able to feel a proper degree of respect for the vicar of Crabtree.'

'Dear papa,' said she, 'I am so glad.'

There was great comfort in returning home to that pleasant house, though he was to leave it so soon, and in discussing with his daughter all that he had done, and all that he had to do. It must take some time to get out of one house into another; the curate at Crabtree could not be abolished under six months, that is, unless other provision could be made for him; and then the furniture—the most of that must be sold to pay Sir Abraham Haphazard for sitting up till twelve at night. Mr. Harding was strangely ignorant as to lawyers' bills; he had no idea, from twenty pounds to two thousand, as to the sum in which he was indebted for legal assistance. True, he had called in no lawyer himself; true, he had been no consenting party to the employment of either Cox and Cumming, or Sir Abraham; he had never been consulted on such matters;—the archdeacon had managed all this himself, never for a moment suspecting that Mr. Harding would take upon him to end the matter in a way of his own. Had the lawyers' bills been ten thousand pounds, Mr. Harding could not have helped it; but he was not on that account disposed to dispute his own liability. The question never occurred to him; but it did occur to him that he had very little money at his banker's, that he could receive nothing further from the hospital, and that the sale of the furniture was his only resource.

'Not all, papa,' said Eleanor pleadingly.

'Not quite all, my dear,' said he; 'that is, if we can help it. We must have a little at Crabtree—but it can only be a little; we must put a bold front on it, Nelly; it isn't easy to come down from affluence to poverty.'

And so they planned their future mode of life; the father taking comfort from the reflection that his daughter would soon be freed from it, and she resolving that her father would soon have in her own house a ready means of escape from the solitude of the Crabtree vicarage.

When the archdeacon left his wife and father-in-law at the Chapter Coffee House to go to Messrs. Cox and Cumming, he had no very defined idea of what he had to do when he got there. Gentlemen when at law, or in any way engaged in matters requiring legal assistance, are very apt to go to their lawyers without much absolute necessity;—gentlemen when doing so, are apt to describe such attendance as quite compulsory, and very disagreeable. The lawyers, on the other hand, do not at all see the necessity, though they quite agree as to the disagreeable nature of the visit;—gentlemen when so engaged are usually somewhat gravelled at finding nothing to say to their learned friends; they generally talk a little politics, a little weather, ask some few foolish questions about their suit, and then withdraw, having passed half an hour in a small dingy waiting-room, in company with some junior assistant-clerk, and ten minutes with the members of the firm; the business is then over for which the gentleman has come up to London, probably a distance of a hundred and fifty miles. To be sure he goes to the play, and dines at his friend's club, and has a bachelor's liberty and bachelor's recreation for three or four days; and he could not probably plead the desire of such gratifications as a reason to his wife for a trip to London.

Married ladies, when your husbands find they are positively obliged to attend their legal advisers, the nature of the duty to be performed is generally of this description.

The archdeacon would not have dreamt of leaving London without going to Cox and Cumming; and yet he had nothing to say to them. The game was up; he plainly saw that Mr. Harding in this matter was not to be moved; his only remaining business on this head was to pay the bill and have done with it: and I think it may be taken for granted, that whatever the cause may be that takes a gentleman to a lawyer's chambers, he never goes there to pay his bill.

Dr. Grantly, however, in the eyes of Messrs. Cox and Cumming, represented the spiritualities of the diocese of Barchester, as Mr. Chadwick did the temporalities, and was, therefore, too great a man to undergo the half-hour in the clerk's room. It will not be necessary that we should listen to the notes of sorrow in which the archdeacon bewailed to Mr. Cox the weakness of his father-in-law, and the end of all their hopes of triumph; nor need we repeat the various exclamations of surprise with which the mournful intelligence was received. No tragedy occurred, though Mr. Cox, a short and somewhat bull-necked man, was very near a fit of apoplexy when he first attempted to ejaculate that fatal word—resign!

Over and over again did Mr. Cox attempt to enforce on the archdeacon the propriety of urging on Mr. Warden the madness of the deed he was about to do.

'Eight hundred a year!' said Mr. Cox.

'And nothing whatever to do!' said Mr. Cumming, who had joined the conference.

'No private fortune, I believe,' said Mr. Cox.

'Not a shilling,' said Mr. Cumming, in a very low voice, shaking his head.

'I never heard of such a case in all my experience,' said Mr. Cox.

'Eight hundred a year, and as nice a house as any gentleman could wish to hang up his hat in,' said Mr. Cumming.

'And an unmarried daughter, I believe,' said Mr. Cox, with much moral seriousness in his tone. The archdeacon only sighed as each separate wail was uttered, and shook his head, signifying that the fatuity of some people was past belief.

'I'll tell you what he might do,' said Mr. Cumming, brightening up. 'I'll tell you how you might save it—let him exchange.'

'Exchange where?' said the archdeacon.

'Exchange for a living. There's Quiverful, of Puddingdale—he has twelve children, and would be delighted to get the hospital. To be sure Puddingdale is only four hundred, but that would be saving something out of the fire: Mr. Harding would have a curate, and still keep three hundred or three hundred and fifty.'

The archdeacon opened his ears and listened; he really thought the scheme might do.

'The newspapers,' continued Mr. Cumming, 'might hammer away at Quiverful every day for the next six months without his minding them.'

The archdeacon took up his hat, and returned to his hotel, thinking the matter over deeply. At any rate he would sound Quiverful. A man with twelve children would do much to double his income.

20

FAREWELL

O N the morning after Mr. Harding's return home he received a note from the bishop full of affection, condolence, and praise. 'Pray come to me at once,' wrote the bishop, 'that we may see what had better be done; as to the hospital, I will not say a word to dissuade you: but I don't like your going to Crabtree: at any rate, come to me at once.'

Mr. Harding did go to him at once; and long and confidential was the consultation between the two old friends. There they sat together the whole long day, plotting to get the better of the archdeacon, and to carry out little schemes of their own, which they knew would be opposed by the whole weight of his authority.

The bishop's first idea was, that Mr. Harding, if left to himself, would certainly starve—not in the figurative sense in which so many of our ladies and gentlemen do starve on incomes from one to five hundred a year; not that he would be starved as regarded dress coats, port wine, and pocket-money; but that he would positively perish of inanition for want of bread.

'How is a man to live, when he gives up all his income?' said the bishop to himself. And then the good-natured little man began to consider how his friend might be best rescued from a death so horrid and painful.

Farewell

His first proposition to Mr. Harding was, that they should live together at the palace. He, the bishop, positively assured Mr. Harding that he wanted another resident chaplain—not a young, working chaplain, but a steady, middle-aged chaplain; one who would dine and drink a glass of wine with him, talk about the archdeacon, and poke the fire. The bishop did not positively name all these duties, but he gave Mr. Harding to understand that such would be the nature of the service required.

It was not without much difficulty that Mr. Harding made his friend see that this would not suit him; that he could not throw up the bishop's preferment, and then come and hang on at the bishop's table; that he could not allow people to say of him that it was an easy matter to abandon his own income, as he was able to sponge on that of another person. He succeeded, however, in explaining that the plan would not do, and then the bishop brought forward another which he had in his sleeve. He, the bishop, had in his will left certain moneys to Mr. Harding's two daughters, imagining that Mr. Harding would himself want no such assistance during his own lifetime. This legacy amounted to three thousand pounds each, duty free; and he now pressed it as a gift on his friend.

'The girls, you know,' said he, 'will have it just the same when you're gone—and they won't want it sooner—and as for the interest during my lifetime, it isn't worth talking about. I have more than enough.'

With much difficulty and heartfelt sorrow, Mr. Harding refused also this offer. No; his wish was to support himself, however poorly—not to be supported on the charity of anyone. It was hard to make the bishop understand this; it was hard to make him comprehend that the only real favour he could confer was the continuation of his independent friendship; but at last even this was done. At any rate, thought the bishop, he will come and dine with me from time to time, and if he be absolutely starving I shall see it.

Touching the precentorship, the bishop was clearly of opinion that it could be held without the other situation—an opinion from which no one differed; and it was therefore soon settled among all the parties concerned, that Mr. Harding should still be the precentor of the cathedral.

On the day following Mr. Harding's return, the archdeacon reached Plumstead full of Mr. Cumming's scheme regarding Puddingdale and Mr. Quiverful. On the very next morning he drove over to Puddingdale, and obtained the full consent of the wretched clerical Priam, who was endeavouring to feed his poor Hecuba and a dozen of Hectors on the small proceeds of his ecclesiastical kingdom. Mr. Quiverful had no doubts as to the legal rights of the warden; his conscience would be quite clear as to accepting the income; and as to the *Jupiter*, he begged to assure the archdeacon that he was quite indifferent to any emanations from the profane portion of the periodical press.

Having so far succeeded, he next sounded the bishop; but here he was astonished by most unexpected resistance. The bishop did not think it would do. 'Not do, why not?' and seeing that his father was not shaken, he repeated the question in a severer form: 'Why not do, my lord?'

His lordship looked very unhappy, and shuffled about in his chair, but still didn't give way; he thought Puddingdale wouldn't do for Mr. Harding; it was too far from Barchester.

'Oh! of course he'll have a curate.'

The bishop also thought that Mr. Quiverful wouldn't do for the hospital; such an exchange wouldn't look well at such a time; and, when pressed harder, he declared he didn't think Mr. Harding would accept of Puddingdale under any circumstances.

'How is he to live?' demanded the archdeacon.

The bishop, with tears in his eyes, declared that he had not the slightest conception how life was to be sustained within him at all.

The archdeacon then left his father, and went down to the hospital; but Mr. Harding. wouldn't listen at all to the Puddingdale scheme. To his eyes it had no attraction; it savoured of simony, and was likely to bring down upon him harder and more deserved strictures than any he had yet received: he positively declined to become vicar of Puddingdale under any circumstances.

The archdeacon waxed wroth, talked big, and looked bigger; he said something about dependence and beggary, spoke of the duty every man was under to earn his .bread, made passing allusions to the follies of youth and waywardness of age, as though Mr. Harding were afflicted by both, and ended by declaring that he had done. He felt that he had left no stone unturned to arrange matters on the best and easiest footing; that he had, in fact, so arranged them, that he had so managed that there was no further need of any anxiety in the matter. And how had he been paid? His advice had been systematically rejected; he had been not only slighted, but distrusted and avoided; he and his measures had been utterly thrown over, as had been Sir Abraham, who, he had reason to know, was much pained at what had occurred. He now found it was useless to interfere any further, and he should retire. If any further assistance were required from him, he would probably be called on, and should be again happy to come forward. And so he left the hospital, and has not since entered it from that day to this.

And here we must take leave of Archdeacon Grantly. We fear that he is represented in these pages as being worse than he is; but we have had to do with his foibles, and not with his virtues. We have seen only the weak side of the man, and have lacked the opportunity of bringing him forward on his strong ground. That he is a man somewhat too fond of his own way, and not sufficiently scrupulous in his manner of achieving it, his best friends cannot deny. That he is bigoted in favour, not so much of his doctrines as of his cloth, is also true: and it is true that the possession of a large income is a desire that sits near his heart. Nevertheless, the archdeacon is a gentleman and a man of conscience; he spends his money liberally, and does the work he has to do with the best of his ability; he improves the tone of society of those among whom he lives. His aspirations are of a healthy, if not of the highest, kind. Though never an austere man, he upholds propriety of conduct both by example and precept. He is generous to the poor, and hospitable to the rich; in matters of religion he is sincere, and yet no Pharisee; he is in earnest, and yet no fanatic. On the whole, the Archdeacon of Barchester is a man doing more good than harm—a man to be furthered and supported, though perhaps also to be controlled; and it is matter of regret to us that the course of our narrative has required that we should see more of his weakness than his strength.

Mr. Harding allowed himself no rest till everything was prepared for his departure from the hospital. It may be as well to mention that he was not driven to the stern necessity of selling all his furniture: he had been quite in earnest in his intention to do so, but it was soon made known to him that the claims of Messrs. Cox and Cumming made no such step obligatory. The archdeacon had thought it wise to make use of the threat of the lawyer's bill, to frighten his father-in-law into compliance; but he had no intention to saddle Mr. Harding with costs, which had been incurred by no means exclusively for his benefit. The amount of the bill was added to the diocesan account, and was, in fact, paid out of the bishop's pocket, without any consciousness on the part of his lordship. A great part of his furniture he did resolve to sell, having no other means to dispose of it; and the ponies and carriage were transferred, by private contract, to the use of an old maiden lady in the city.

For his present use Mr. Harding took a lodging in Barchester, and thither were conveyed such articles as he wanted for daily use—his music, books, and instruments, his own arm-chair, and Eleanor's pet sofa; her teapoy and his cellaret, and also the slender

but still sufficient contents of his wine-cellar. Mrs.
Grantly had much wished that her sister would re-
side at Plumstead, till her father's house at Crabtree
should be ready for her; but Eleanor herself strongly
resisted this proposal. It was in vain urged upon her,
that a lady in lodgings cost more than a gentleman;
and that, under her father's present circumstances,
such an expense should be avoided. Eleanor had not
pressed her father to give up the hospital in order
that she might live at Plumstead Rectory and he alone
in his Barchester lodgings; nor did Eleanor think
that she would be treating a certain gentleman very
fairly, if she betook herself to the house which he
would be the least desirous of entering of any in the
county. So she got a little bedroom for herself behind
the sitting-room, and just over the little back parlour
of the chemist, with whom they were to lodge.
There was somewhat of a savour of senna softened
by peppermint about the place; but, on the whole,
the lodgings were clean and comfortable.

The day had been fixed for the migration of the
ex-warden, and all Barchester were in a state of
excitement on the subject. Opinion was much divided
as to the propriety of Mr. Harding's conduct. The
mercantile part of the community, the mayor and
corporation, and council, also most of the ladies,
were loud in his praise. Nothing could be more
noble, nothing more generous, nothing more upright. But the gentry were of a different way of
thinking—especially the lawyers and the clergymen.
They said such conduct was very weak and un-
dignified; that Mr. Harding evinced a lamentable
want of esprit de corps, as well as courage; and that

such an abdication must do much harm, and could
do but little good.

On the evening before he left, he summoned all the
bedesmen into his parlour to wish them good-bye.
With Bunce he had been in frequent communication
since his return from London, and had been at much
pains to explain to the old man the cause of his
resignation, without in any way prejudicing the position of his successor. The others, also, he had seen
more or less frequently; and had heard from most of
them separately some expression of regret at his
departure; but he had postponed his farewell till the
last evening.

He now bade the maid put wine and glasses on the
table; and had the chairs arranged around the room;
and sent Bunce to each of the men to request they
would come and say farewell to their late warden.
Soon the noise of aged scuffling feet was heard upon
the gravel and in the little hall, and the eleven men
who were enabled to leave their rooms were assembled.

'Come in, my friends, come in,' said the warden—
he was still warden then. 'Come in, and sit down;'
and he took the hand of Abel Handy, who was the
nearest to him, and led the limping grumbler to a
chair. The others followed slowly and bashfully; the
infirm, the lame, and the blind: poor wretches! who
had been so happy, had they but known it! Now their
aged faces were covered with shame, and every kind
word from their master was a coal of fire burning on
their heads.

When first the news had reached them that Mr.
Harding was going to leave the hospital, it had been

received with a kind of triumph—his departure was, as it were, a prelude to success. He had admitted his want of right to the money about which they were disputing; and as it did not belong to him, of course it did to them. The one hundred a year to each of them was actually becoming a reality; and Abel Handy was a hero, and Bunce a faint-hearted sycophant, worthy neither honour nor fellowship. But other tidings soon made their way into the old men's rooms. It was first notified to them that the income abandoned by Mr. Harding would not come to them; and these accounts were confirmed by attorney Finney. They were then informed that Mr. Harding's place would be at once filled by another. That the new warden could not be a kinder man they all knew; that he would be a less friendly one most suspected; and then came the bitter information that, from the moment of Mr. Harding's departure, the twopence a day, his own peculiar gift, must of necessity be withdrawn.

And this was to be the end of all their mighty struggle—of their fight for their rights—of their petition, and their debates, and their hopes! They were to change the best of masters for a possible bad one, and to lose twopence a day each man! No; unfortunate as this was, it was not the worst, or nearly the worst, as will just now be seen.

'Sit down, sit down, my friends,' said the warden; 'I want to say a word to you and to drink your healths, before I leave you. Come up here, Moody, here is a chair for you; come, Jonathan Crumple'—and by degrees he got the men to be seated. It was not surprising that they should hang back with faint hearts, having returned so much kindness with such deep ingratitude. Last of all of them came Bunce, and with sorrowful mien and slow step got into his accustomed seat near the fire-place.

When they were all in their places, Mr. Harding rose to address them; and then finding himself not quite at home on his legs, he sat down again. 'My dear old friends,' said he, 'you all know that I am going to leave you.'

There was a sort of murmur ran round the room, intended, perhaps, to express regret at his departure; but it was but a murmur, and might have meant that or anything else.

'There has been lately some misunderstanding between us. You have thought, I believe, that you did not get all that you were entitled to, and that the funds of the hospital have not been properly disposed of. As for me, I cannot say what should be the disposition of these moneys, or how they should be managed, and I have therefore thought it best to go.'

'We never wanted to drive your reverence out of it,' said Handy.

'No, indeed, your reverence,' said Skulpit. 'We never thought it would come to this. When I signed the petition—that is I didn't sign it, because——'

'Let his reverence speak, can't you?' said Moody.

'No,' continued Mr. Harding; 'I am sure you did not wish to turn me out; but I thought it best to leave you. I am not a very good hand at a lawsuit, as you may all guess; and when it seemed necessary that our ordinary quiet mode of living should be disturbed, I thought it better to go. I am neither angry nor offended with any man in the hospital.'

Here Bunce uttered a kind of groan, very clearly expressive of disagreement.

'I am neither angry nor displeased with any man in the hospital,' repeated Mr. Harding, emphatically. 'If any man has been wrong—and I don't say any man has—he has erred through wrong advice. In this country all are entitled to look for their own rights, and you have done no more. As long as your interests and my interests were at variance, I could give you no counsel on this subject; but the connection between us has ceased; my income can no longer depend on your doings, and therefore, as I leave you, I venture to offer to you my advice.'

The men all declared that they would from henceforth be entirely guided by Mr. Harding's opinion in their affairs.

'Some gentleman will probably take my place here very soon, and I strongly advise you to be prepared to receive him in a kindly spirit and to raise no further question among yourselves as to the amount of his income. Were you to succeed in lessening what he has to receive, you would not increase your own allowance. The surplus would not go to you; your wants are adequately provided for, and your position could hardly be improved.'

'God bless your reverence, we knows it,' said Spriggs.

'It's all true, your reverence,' said Skulpit. 'We sees it all now.'

'Yes, Mr. Harding,' said Bunce, opening his mouth for the first time; 'I believe they do understand it now, now that they've driven from under the same roof with them such a master as not one of them will ever know again—now that they're like to be in sore want of a friend.'

'Come, come, Bunce,' said Mr. Harding, blowing his nose and manœuvring to wipe his eyes at the same time.

'Oh, as to that,' said Handy, 'we none of us never wanted to do Mr. Harding no harm; if he's going now, it's not along of us; and I don't see for what Mr. Bunce speaks up agen us that way.'

'You've ruined yourselves, and you've ruined me too, and that's why,' said Bunce.

'Nonsense, Bunce,' said Mr. Harding; 'there's nobody ruined at all. I hope you'll let me leave you all friends, I hope you'll all drink a glass of wine in friendly feeling with me and with one another. You'll have a good friend, I don't doubt, in your new warden; and if ever you want any other, why after all I'm not going so far off but that I shall sometimes see you;' and then, having finished his speech, Mr. Harding filled all the glasses, and himself handed each a glass to the men round him, and raising his own said—

'God bless you all! you have my heartfelt wishes for your welfare. I hope you may live contented, and die trusting in the Lord Jesus Christ, and thankful to Almighty God for the good things He has given you. God bless you, my friends!' and Mr. Harding drank his wine.

Another murmur, somewhat more articulate than the first, passed round the circle, and this time it was intended to imply a blessing on Mr. Harding. It had, however, but little cordiality in it. Poor old men! how could they be cordial with their sore consciences

and shamed faces? how could they bid God bless him
with hearty voices and a true benison, knowing, as
they did, that their vile cabal had driven him from his
happy home, and sent him in his old age to seek
shelter under a strange roof-tree? They did their
best, however; they drank their wine, and withdrew.

As they left the hall-door, Mr. Harding shook
hands with each of the men, and spoke a kind word
to them about their individual cases and ailments;
and so they departed, answering his questions in the
fewest words, and retreated to their dens, a sorrowful repentant crew.

All but Bunce, who still remained to make his own
farewell. 'There's poor old Bell,' said Mr. Harding;
'I mustn't go without saying a word to him; come
through with me, Bunce, and bring the wine with
you;' and so they went through to the men's cottages,
and found the old man propped up as usual in his bed.

'I've come to say good-bye to you, Bell,' said Mr.
Harding, speaking loud, for the old man was deaf.

'And are you going away, then, really?' asked
Bell.

'Indeed I am, and I've brought you a glass of wine;
so that we may part friends, as we lived, you know.'

The old man took the proffered glass in his shaking hands, and drank it eagerly. 'God bless you,
Bell!' said Mr. Harding; 'good-bye, my old friend.'

'And so you're really going?' the man again asked.

'Indeed I am, Bell.'

The poor old bed-ridden creature still kept Mr.
Harding's hand in his own, and the warden thought
that he had met with something like warmth of feeling in the one of all his subjects from whom it was the

least likely to be expected; for poor old Bell had nearly outlived all human feelings. 'And your reverence,' said he, and then he paused, while his old palsied head shook horribly, and his shrivelled cheeks sank lower within his jaws, and his glazy eye gleamed with a momentary light; 'and your reverence, shall we get the hundred a year, then?'

How gently did Mr. Harding try to extinguish the false hope of money which had been so wretchedly raised to disturb the quiet of the dying man! One other week and his mortal coil would be shuffled off; in one short week would God resume his soul, and set it apart for its irrevocable doom; seven more tedious days and nights of senseless inactivity, and all would be over for poor Bell in this world; and yet, with his last audible words, he was demanding his moneyed rights, and asserting himself to be the proper heir of John Hiram's bounty! Not on him, poor sinner as he was, be the load of such sin!

Mr. Harding returned to his parlour, meditating with a sick heart on what he had seen, and Bunce with him. We will not describe the parting of these two good men, for good men they were. It was in vain that the late warden endeavoured to comfort the heart of the old bedesman; poor old Bunce felt that his days of comfort were gone. The hospital had to him been a happy home, but it could be so no longer. He had had honour there, and friendship; he had recognised his master, and been recognised; all his wants, both of soul and body, had been supplied, and he had been a happy man. He wept grievously as he parted from his friend, and the tears of an old man are bitter. 'It is all over for me in this world,' said he, as he gave the last squeeze to Mr. Harding's hand; 'I have now to forgive those who have injured me—and to die.'

And so the old man went out, and then Mr. Harding gave way to his grief and he too wept aloud.

2 1

CONCLUSION

OUR tale is now done, and it only remains to us to collect the scattered threads of our little story, and to tie them into a seemly knot. This will not be a work of labour, either to the author or to his readers; we have not to deal with many personages, or with stirring events, and were it not for the custom of the thing, we might leave it to the imagination of all concerned to conceive how affairs at Barchester arranged themselves.

On the morning after the day last alluded to, Mr. Harding, at an early hour, walked out of the hospital, with his daughter under his arm, and sat down quietly to breakfast at his lodgings over the chemist's shop. There was no parade about his departure; no one, not even Bunce, was there to witness it; had he walked to the apothecary's thus early to get a piece of court plaster, or a box of lozenges, he could not have done it with less appearance of an important movement. There was a tear in Eleanor's eye as she passed through the big gateway and over the bridge; but Mr. Harding walked with an elastic step, and entered his new abode with a pleasant face.

'Now, my dear,' said he, 'you have everything ready, and you can make tea here just as nicely as in the parlour at the hospital.' So Eleanor took off her bonnet and made the tea. After this manner did the late Warden of Barchester Hospital accomplish his flitting, and change his residence.

It was not long before the archdeacon brought his father to discuss the subject of a new warden. Of course he looked upon the nomination as his own, and he had in his eye three or four fitting candidates, seeing that Mr. Cumming's plan as to the living of Puddingdale could not be brought to bear. How can I describe the astonishment which confounded him, when his father declared that he would appoint no successor to Mr. Harding?

'If we can get the matter set to rights, Mr. Harding will return,' said the bishop; 'and if we cannot, it will be wrong to put any other gentleman into so cruel a position.'

It was in vain that the archdeacon argued and lectured, and even threatened; in vain he my-lorded his poor father in his sternest manner; in vain his 'good heavens!' were ejaculated in a tone that might have moved a whole synod, let alone one weak and aged bishop. Nothing could induce his father to fill up the vacancy caused by Mr. Harding's retirement.

Even John Bold would have pitied the feelings with which the archdeacon returned to Plumstead: the church was falling, nay, already in ruins; its dignitaries were yielding without a struggle before the blows of its antagonists; and one of its most respected bishops, his own father—the man considered by all the world as being in such matters under his, Dr. Grantly's control—had positively resolved to capitulate, and own himself vanquished!

And how fared the hospital under this resolve of its visitor? Badly indeed. It is now some years since

Conclusion

Mr. Harding left it, and the warden's house is still tenantless. Old Bell has died, and Billy Gazy; the one-eyed Spriggs has drunk himself to death, and three others of the twelve have been gathered into the churchyard mould. Six have gone, and the six vacancies remain unfilled! Yes, six have died, with no kind friend to solace their last moments, with no wealthy neighbour to administer comforts and ease the stings of death. Mr. Harding, indeed, did not desert them; from him they had such consolation as a dying man may receive from his Christian pastor; but it was the occasional kindness of a stranger which ministered to them, and not the constant presence of a master, a neighbour, and a friend.

Nor were those who remained better off than those who died. Dissensions rose among them, and contests for pre-eminence; and then they began to understand that soon one among them would be the last—some one wretched being would be alone there in that now comfortless hospital—the miserable relic of what had once been so good and so comfortable.

The building of the hospital itself has not been allowed to go to ruins. Mr. Chadwick, who still holds his stewardship, and pays the accruing rents into an account opened at a bank for the purpose, sees to that; but the whole place has become disordered and ugly. The warden's garden is a wretched wilderness, the drive and paths are covered with weeds, the flower-beds are bare, and the unshorn lawn is now a mass of long damp grass and unwholesome moss. The beauty of the place is gone; its attractions have withered. Alas! a very few years since it was the prettiest spot in Barchester, and now it is a disgrace to the city.

Mr. Harding did not go out to Crabtree Parva. An arrangement was made which respected the homestead of Mr. Smith and his happy family, and put Mr. Harding into possession of a small living within the walls of the city. It is the smallest possible parish, containing a part of the Cathedral Close and a few old houses adjoining. The church is a singular little Gothic building, perched over a gateway, through which the Close is entered, and is approached by a flight of stone steps which leads down under the archway of the gate. It is no bigger than an ordinary room—perhaps twenty-seven feet long by eighteen wide—but still it is a perfect church. It contains an old carved pulpit and reading-desk, a tiny altar under a window filled with dark old-coloured glass, a font, some half-dozen pews, and perhaps a dozen seats for the poor; and also a vestry. The roof is high pitched, and of black old oak, and the three large beams which support it run down to the side walls, and terminate in grotesquely carved faces—two devils and an angel on one side, two angels and a devil on the other. Such is the church of St. Cuthbert at Barchester, of which Mr. Harding became rector, with a clear income of seventy-five pounds a year.

Here he performs afternoon service every Sunday, and administers the Sacrament once in every three months. His audience is not large; and, had they been so, he could not have accommodated them: but enough come to fill his six pews, and on the front seat of those devoted to the poor is always to be seen our old friend Mr. Bunce, decently arrayed in his bedesman's gown.

Mr. Harding is still precentor of Barchester; and

it is very rarely the case that those who attend the Sunday morning service miss the gratification of hearing him chant the Litany, as no other man in England can do it. He is neither a discontented nor an unhappy man; he still inhabits the lodgings to which he went on leaving the hospital, but he now has them to himself. Three months after that time Eleanor became Mrs. Bold, and of course removed to her husband's house.

There were some difficulties to be got over on the occasion of the marriage. The archdeacon, who could not so soon overcome his grief, would not be persuaded to grace the ceremony with his presence, but he allowed his wife and children to be there. The marriage took place in the cathedral, and the bishop himself officiated. It was the last occasion on which he ever did so; and, though he still lives, it is not probable that he will ever do so again.

Not long after the marriage, perhaps six months, when Eleanor's bridal-honours were fading, and persons were beginning to call her Mrs. Bold without twittering, the archdeacon consented to meet John Bold at a dinner-party, and since that time they have become almost friends. The archdeacon firmly believes that his brother-in-law was, as a bachelor, an infidel, an unbeliever in the great truths of our religion; but that matrimony has opened his eyes, as it has those of others. And Bold is equally inclined to think that time has softened the asperities of the archdeacon's character. Friends though they are, they do not often revert to the feud of the hospital.

Mr. Harding, we say, is not an unhappy man: he keeps his lodgings, but they are of little use to him, except as being the one spot on earth which he calls his own. His time is spent chiefly at his daughter's or at the palace; he is never left alone, even should he wish to be so; and within a twelve-month of Eleanor's marriage his determination to live at his own lodging had been so far broken through and abandoned, that he consented to have his violoncello permanently removed to his daughter's house.

Every other day a message is brought to him from the bishop. 'The bishop's compliments, and his lordship is not very well to-day, and he hopes Mr. Harding will dine with him.' This bulletin as to the old man's health is a myth; for though he is over eighty he is never ill, and will probably die some day, as a spark goes out, gradually and without a struggle. Mr. Harding does dine with him very often, which means going to the palace at three and remaining till ten; and whenever he does not the bishop whines, and says that the port wine is corked, and complains that nobody attends to him, and frets himself off to bed an hour before his time.

It was long before the people of Barchester forgot to call Mr. Harding by his long well-known name of Warden. It had become so customary to say Mr. Warden, that it was not easily dropped. 'No, no,' he always says when so addressed, 'not warden now, only precentor.'

REPRINTED LITHOGRAPHICALLY IN GREAT BRITAIN
AT THE UNIVERSITY PRESS, OXFORD
BY VIVIAN RIDLER
PRINTER TO THE UNIVERSITY

AUTHOR A. TROLLOPE.

TITLE THE WARDEN

Date	Name
20/5/09	

Maggie Hope was born and raised in County Durham. She worked as a nurse for many years, before giving up her career to raise her family.

Also by Maggie Hope:

A Wartime Nurse
A Mother's Gift
A Nurse's Duty
A Daughter's Gift
Molly's War
The Servant Girl
A Daughter's Duty
Like Mother, Like Daughter
Orphan Girl
Eliza's Child
Workhouse Child
The Miner's Girl
An Orphan's Secret

Acknowledgements

My thanks are due to Mr and Mrs Walker, my aunt and uncle, who live in Cowley, and their friend and local historian, Mr Hope, of Cowley. Also, I owe a debt of gratitude to Durham Records Office and Bishop Auckland Town Hall Library.

Chapter One

Hannah crouched in the kitchen, her younger brother and sister clutched tightly to her.

'Aah, aah, aah, Nora, Nora – '

The tortured voice coming from the front room rose higher and higher and Jane and Harry buried their faces in Hannah's skirts, their hands covering their ears and their bodies racked with sobbing. Hannah stared unseeingly out of the window, desperate to get away from the sound of Da's pain. But Betty had told her to keep the young ones in the kitchen, 'out of the way', she had said. Betty was twelve and she was in the front room with Mam, in case she was needed for anything when the doctor came.

There was another voice in the front room now – the doctor, that was whose voice it was, Hannah realised, and she looked down at the heads in her lap.

'Whisht now,' she said softly. 'Whisht. The doctor's here, he'll make Da better, he will, you'll see.' But suddenly there was a scream from the front room worse than anything that had gone before and Harry wrenched himself away from Hannah's grasp and ran to the back door and out of the yard.

'Harry, Harry!' she called, releasing Jane and racing after him, and even though he was only four years old and she was ten, she didn't manage to catch him until he was halfway down the row.

'Harry! I told you you had to stay with me!' she cried, pulling him roughly to her and then Jane was there, hanging on to her skirt and shrieking with terror. 'You left me, you left me!' Jane cried and she and Harry set up such a bawling they could be heard all along the pit rows.

'Howay in along of me, hinnies.'

The calm, sympathetic voice caused all three children to look up. It was Mrs Holmes who lived in the end house, the official's house; she was picking Harry up in her arms and cuddling him into her, not caring that his tears were staining her white pinafore.

'That's right, Phoebe, take them in. Just until the ambulance goes, anyroad.'

Hannah looked round and saw that a cluster of women had gathered round them, all clucking in sympathy.

'Your da will be all right, you'll see,' said one. 'Go on along of Mrs Holmes now, Hannah, take the bairns inside, that'll be best.'

In the distance there was the clanging of a bell, getting nearer and nearer. Hannah knew what it was: the Union ambulance, coming to take Da. She watched the end of the back alley and sure enough the green-painted ambulance went by, slowing as it turned into the front row.

'Howay, pet,' she said to Jane, and, taking the smaller girl's hand, she followed Mrs Holmes and Harry into the kitchen of the end house.

Mr Holmes was sitting in front of the fire, still black from the pit. The sight of him made Hannah close her eyes tightly but she couldn't cut out the vivid picture she had of her da, lying on a board on a flat cart as his marras, as miners called their workmates, brought him home from the pit, with Mr Holmes, the shift overman, walking in front of the pony as he tried to pick out a path which avoided any potholes.

'Now then,' said Mrs Holmes, 'sit ye down. I'd wager you haven't had your dinners yet, have you? Now I have a nice pan of broth on the bar keeping hot, you shall have a bowlful each.'

The children looked at her with round eyes, even Hannah. The broth smelled really meaty and they hadn't had anything to eat since breakfast. Harry's stomach rumbled; he glanced up at Hannah anxiously and Mrs Holmes noticed it.

'Howay, Harry, your mam won't mind you having something to eat in our house,' she encouraged him. 'I'll

3

put a cushion on this chair so you can reach the table comfortably. Now, lasses, sit on the form at that side. Don't worry, I tell you, your mam won't mind. And after, I'll give you a can of broth to take home for the others. That'll help your mam out, like.'

The children sat round the table, Harry balanced on a fat, round cushion filched from Mr Holmes's chair, and soon they were tucking into bowls of Mrs Holmes's broth. At least, Harry and Jane were tucking in; Hannah's throat had closed in, she found she couldn't swallow after the first mouthful. She stared at the yellow globules of fat floating on the top but she wasn't really seeing them. Instead she was listening for the ambulance bell starting up again, taking Da away.

'It looks badly,' Mr Holmes said quietly to his wife but not so quietly that Hannah's sharp ears didn't hear. 'Poor lad's back's broke, I doubt.'

'A fall of stone, was it?' asked Mrs Holmes.

'Aye. The deputy had fired the shot all right, none could fault him; he'd got the men back out of the road first and the coalface came down. It was after the black dust thinned and settled and the men were returning to the face that it happened. Jake was the first back. He was always the first, always eager to get back to work. You know the name he had for hard work. Well, the shot must have disturbed a fault in the roof, loosened the stone, for suddenly there was a rumble and the men jumped back, away from the

4

danger, they all knew what it meant, but Jake was caught
when the stone came down. There wasn't a lot, the others
soon got it off him, but the damage was done.'

Hannah stared at her broth, feeling sick. She looked
up at the wooden beams of the kitchen ceiling, imagining them falling on her and Jane and Harry, and
shuddered. Suddenly, she knew she was definitely going
to be sick and she mumbled something to Mrs Holmes,
and rushed out to the drain in the yard and retched
and retched.

Mrs Holmes glanced at her husband, biting her lip.
'There, now, we shouldn't have said anything in front
of the bairns,' she said. 'That Hannah's a sensitive lass.'

Jane and Harry had stopped eating and were gazing
through the window at their sister who was crouched
over the drain.

'Don't worry, now, she'll be all right,' Mrs Holmes
reassured them. 'I'll fetch her back, poor lass.'

Hannah's eyes were watering and she was trembling
violently when Mrs Holmes took hold of her shoulders
and drew her back to the kitchen door.

'Howay, lass,' Mrs Holmes said, 'it's the shock, that's
what. You have to be strong now, you big ones, for the
sake of little Jane and Harry.' She offered Hannah a large
handkerchief, a real one, not a piece of rag, which was
what the Armstrong children usually used for a hanky,
and Hannah wiped her face. They paused in the doorway

as they heard a motor starting up, followed by the loud clanging of the bell on top of the union ambulance and Hannah's trembling increased until she was shaking uncontrollably.

'They'll be taking him to the County Hospital,' said Mr Holmes. 'Eeh, lass, you're shivering, come away in by the fire and have a warm.'

'Thank you, Mr Holmes,' Hannah said, surprising herself at how normal her voice sounded, 'but we'll have to get back. Betty said we had to stay in the kitchen, she'll be mad if she can't find us.'

'All right, lass, if you want to,' said Mrs Holmes. 'Wait on a minute, though, I'll give you that broth. It'll likely do for your mam and Alfred.'

Hannah stood quietly, with Jane and Harry hanging on to her skirt, as Mrs Holmes went into the pantry and brought out a large tin can with a lid in the form of a cup. Picking up the pan, she filled the can with what was left of the broth.

'Poor bairns,' Mrs Holmes said to her husband as she watched the children go down the yard and out into the back lane. 'Whatever's going to happen to them now?'

'Jake'll get compensation,' said Mr Holmes.

'Hmm!' His wife's expression showed plainly what she thought of the compensation rates for hewers who were injured in the mine.

*

'Where've you been?' demanded Betty as the children trooped into the kitchen of the Armstrong house. 'Mam's gone in the ambulance with me da and I have to get some dinner ready for Alf when he comes in from work. An' you let the fire get down, it'll be ages before it's hot enough to cook anything.'

Betty had one of her mother's aprons tied round her thin twelve-year-old body and drooping almost to her ankles. She was a tall girl, with fair hair and brown eyes, now red and strained-looking.

'Mrs Holmes took us in her house,' volunteered Jane. 'She gave us some grand broth, Betty, we've brought you some an' all.'

'You shouldn't take food off folk!' snapped Betty. 'You know Mam says we haven't to.'

Jane looked crestfallen and Hannah put the can of steaming broth on the table. 'Mrs Holmes said Mam wouldn't mind, not when we've trouble in the house,' she said. 'Didn't we take some to Mrs Gittens when Mr Gittens was hurt in the pit? Anyroad, it'll do nicely for Alf's dinner. Mam just made the bread this morning, it'll be grand and fresh for him with the broth.'

Betty looked undecided, she was very conscious of the fact that she was in charge of the household, if only temporarily, but she glanced at the smouldering fire and back at the can of broth on the table and made up her mind.

'Don't leave it on the table to get cold, our Hannah,' she said. 'Get the pan from the pantry and put it on the bar to keep warm. Alf won't eat it if it's cold, will he?'

Hannah rushed to do Betty's bidding.

It seemed to Hannah in the next few weeks that she was always rushing to do Betty's bidding. The moment she came in from school, even as she walked down the yard, Betty was issuing her instructions. 'Fetch a bucket of coal in', 'Peel the taties', 'Go to the shop' – even little Jane had to do her share. For Mam was busy with Da, who had been sent home from the hospital in a boxlike bed on wheels, unable to sit up or move his body from the chest down. He lived in the front room now and it was Alf who came in black from his work on the screens where he cleaned the coal of stone. Alf sat in Da's chair by the fire though he was only fourteen years old, and waited for Hannah to fill the tin bath with hot water from the boiler by the fire and demanded his dinner on time. For Alf was the only one bringing in a wage now, even if it was only four shillings a week.

'Seventeen and tuppence,' said Mam the first time Alf brought home Da's weekly compensation. 'It'll be four-teen and ninepence when they take off the war money an' they'll be doing that, sure as shot, now the war's over and done with. An' we can't live on that, there's only one thing for it, we need another wage coming in.'

'Mam! I can't go to work, I'm not thirteen yet,' said Betty, suddenly looking very young and vulnerable.

'Not you, pet,' answered her mother. 'Our Robert'll have to come home.'

Hannah sat beside Jane and Harry on the horse-hair sofa and all three gazed at Mam. What was she talking about? thought Hannah. Robert wouldn't want to come home, he didn't like it in Winton. Why, the last time he'd come he'd told her that he was going to work on the carriers with his uncle Billy when he left school. Robert lived with Grandma Armstrong, miles away in Consett; they hadn't even seen him for almost a year.

'Robert's only thirteen, Mam,' said Betty.

'Aye. Well, he can take the leaving exam like Alf did. If he knows his letters and his figuring, the gaffer will take him on, he's sure to when his father broke his back in the pit. You and Alf will have to look to your da on Saturday, Betty, while I go to Consett and tell your grandma. Best not put it in a letter. I'll away up to see the manager now, see about getting him a job.'

Nora Armstrong looked the three younger children over critically.

'Hannah, wash Harry's face, you three are coming along of me. It won't hurt to show the manager I've got bairns to feed an' all,' she said as she looked in the mahogany-framed mirror which hung over the high mantelpiece. She smoothed her dark hair away from her forehead, then, satisfied with her appearance, went to the middle door which led into the front room.

'I'm going up to the colliery office, Jake,' she said. 'You'll be all right for a while, will you?'

'Aye, I'm fine. I'm enjoying the rest, lying here,' came the sardonic reply.

'I'll only be half an hour,' Nora said. 'I'm taking the little ones; Betty will be here, though, if you want her.'

'Well, get away, woman, if you're going,' Jake answered irritably.

Nora took her shawl from the hook on the back door and wrapped it round her.

'Are you not going to wear your Sunday coat?' asked Betty, sounding surprised.

'No. It's better not to let them think I'm well off, a shawl's the best thing,' said Nora.

They walked up the row, Nora holding Harry's hand and Hannah behind with Jane. The children were quiet; even Hannah was nervous of meeting the colliery manager, while Jane and Harry looked white and strained. It wasn't far to the pit yard and the colliery office was just inside the gates, a red brick building with steps leading up to the entrance. Parked beside the steps was a motorcar and sitting in the passenger seat was a boy of about fifteen, a boy in a suit with a Norfolk jacket and a proper collar and tie and his dark hair slicked back over his ears.

'Look, Hannah, a motorcar,' cried Harry, grinning with delight. 'By; isn't it grand? What does it say, Hannah? Those letters on the front, I mean.' Harry was fairly dancing round the car; he touched the gleaming coachwork and the bright silver of the headlights. 'When I grow up I'm going to have a motorcar just like this,' he declared.

'Sunbeam, that's what it says,' said Hannah. She was almost as entranced by the machine as Harry was.

'Sunbeam coupé,' said the boy and he climbed out of the car. All three children quietened and Harry drew close to his mother.

'He talks funny,' Harry said in a whisper which nevertheless was heard by them all. The boy smiled.

'Would you like to sit in my seat for a minute?' he asked Harry.

'Eeh, no,' said Mrs Armstrong, pulling the child to her.

'Mam!' said Harry, his eyes bright with hope, and she gave in.

'All right, but just for a minute. We have to see the manager before he goes home,' she decreed.

'Oh, my father's with him now, he won't be going home yet,' said the boy. He held the door open for Harry, who clambered on to the padded leather seat and sat quietly, gazing at the dashboard with its knobs and dials, happiness oozing out of him.

The boy looked down at Hannah, smiling, and she smiled back shyly. By, he was a grand lad, she thought, letting Harry have a go in his car. She reckoned he was about the same age as Alf, but he was so tall and good-looking and his clothes were so clean. Even his hands were clean, she saw, there were no scars or black bits under the skin, his hands were soft and white. He didn't work on the screens, she decided. He had kind eyes, though. Was he a prince? A prince like in Cinderella?

Hannah looked up, startled, as the office window opened and a man stuck his head out.

'Timothy! Get that boy out of there at once. At once, do you hear? God knows what dirt and disease he might be carrying, not to mention fleas. I told you to sit in the car until I was ready, did I not, sir?'.

'Come on, Harry, we have to go in now,' said Nora. She had turned a fiery red and kept her head bent as she lifted Harry out of the car. Hannah was mortified, she burned with the shame of it. Her family didn't have fleas, nor nits either. Everybody in the rows knew Mam was spitting clean – why, didn't she rake their heads every night with the small-tooth comb? Just in case they picked anything up at school, that was.

'We haven't got fleas, Mam, have we not?' she said as Jane and Harry began to whimper.

'No, we have not!' snapped Nora. 'We're as clean as anybody, we are.'

12

Hannah stoke a glance at the boy, who was sheepishly climbing into the car.

'Dust the seat before you sit down, Timothy,' roared the man at the window.

'Yes, Father,' the boy mumbled. He took a blue duster from the tray under the dashboard and rubbed it over the seat.

'There'll be no dirt on it,' hissed Hannah and Timothy looked at her, his eyes shamed.

'Howay, Hannah,' snapped her mother and Hannah followed her up the steps and into the office.

There was a desk just inside with a clerk sitting behind it. Through the partition window behind him, Hannah could see the man, Timothy's father, talking to the manager.

'Yes, what do you want?' demanded the clerk. 'It's almost closing time, you've left it a bit late, whatever it is.'

'I'm Mrs Armstrong,' said Nora, holding her head high. Two bright spots of colour still burned in her cheeks. 'I've come to see the manager.'

'Oh, yes, it was your man who was hurt by that last fall of stone, wasn't it? Well, you can't see the manager now, he has Lord Akers's agent, Mr Durkin, with him. You'll have to come back tomorrow.'

The clerk gave a dismissive nod and shuffled the papers together on his desk, but Nora was not about to go.

'I'll wait until I can see him,' she insisted, her voice rising. 'Surely he'll see me, when my Jake's had his back broke in the pit?' The incident with Harry and the car had filled her with resentment, stiffening her resolve.

'My good woman – ' the clerk began, but he was interrupted by the manager, who opened the door to the inner office and poked his head out.

'What's the commotion, Robinson?' he asked testily.

'It's Mrs Armstrong, sir, the wife of the hewer who was injured in that last roof fall. I told her you were busy.'

'Get her to come in, Hudson, I might as well hear what she has to say while I'm here,' a voice called from behind the manager. Harry shrank into Hannah's skirt, whimpering once more.

Hannah patted his head. 'It's all right, Harry,' she whispered.

'Yes, of course, Mr Durkin,' said the manager and held the door open for Nora and her children.

They stood before the desk, Nora, Hannah and the two little ones between them. They were not offered seats though there were a couple of chairs by the wall besides the comfortable armchair occupied by Timothy's father.

Hannah gazed at him in awe. It was bad enough having to come to see the manager, but Mr Durkin was like no one she had ever seen before. She looked at the smooth black cloth of his suit, his highly polished shoes and white spats. He held a shiny walking stick with a silver top in one hand and was tapping it idly against one leg of his chair. He was tall and elegant and his shirt collar was snowy white against the pale skin of his neck. She watched him as he looked the children over, his face expressionless.

'Well, what is it, Mrs Armstrong?' asked Mr Hudson, who had returned to his chair behind the desk.

'Well . . . '

Nora was suddenly tongue-tied.

'Come along now, Mrs Armstrong, we haven't got all day,' Mr Hudson said briskly.

'She's been getting weekly compensation, hasn't she, Mr Hudson?' Mr Durkin put in.

'Yes, sir, seventeen shillings and twopence,' answered the manager.

'Well, then, that's all right.'

'I was wanting to ask you if you'll set our Robert on, on the screens, I mean,' Nora said, finding her tongue at last.

'Robert? Is that your son? We already have one son of yours working on the screens, haven't we?'

'Yes, sir. Alf. But Robert's turned thirteen and he'll sit the test to leave school. We need the money, sir, seventeen shillings doesn't keep a family, sir.'

Mr Durkin stopped playing with his stick and stared at her, frowning. 'What do you mean, it's not enough? I'd have you know, it's all you're going to get.

The trouble with you people is you don't know how to handle money correctly. Remember, the Compensation Committee haven't decided on your husband's case yet. There's some question as to whether it was his own fault, and if that is the decision they come to, you are not entitled to anything. We are paying you now and we don't have to, you know. And we're allowing you to stay in the colliery house when we could put another workman in.'

Nora gasped. Her face whitened and she leaned forwards, putting her hands on the desk to prop herself up. She closed her eyes for a moment.

'Are you feeling faint, Mrs Armstrong?' Mr Hudson got to his feet hurriedly and brought Nora a chair. 'Would you like a glass of water?' He poured some water into a glass from the carafe on the desk and offered it to her and she took a sip.

The agent watched the little drama curiously but with little obvious concern. When Nora sat back, the colour returning to her cheeks, he spoke again.

'Come now, Mrs Armstrong, I only said the committee hasn't decided yet. There's no need to take on.'

'I don't know what we'll do without compensation,' said Nora. 'We can't hardly manage as it is.'

'I did not say there would be no compensation, I simply said we as a company may not be liable. But Lord Akers is a benevolent employer, I think you'll find. Now,

16

come, we have work to do here. I think we have allowed
you enough time.'

Nora got to her feet, looking and feeling defeated.
Hannah looked up into her mother's face and saw the
misery there; then she looked at Mr Durkin and she
hated him. She hated the way he talked to her mother
and most of all she hated the way he spoke, fancy like
but frightening, like the wicked man in the pantomime
she'd seen at chapel last Christmas. She took hold of her
mother's hand and squeezed it in an effort to comfort her
as they turned for the door.

They were in the outer office, almost outside altogether
when Mr Hudson followed them and spoke to the clerk.

'Robert Armstrong. Put his name down to start on the
screens next week,' he said. Without looking at Nora, he
turned on his heel and went back into his office.

Chapter Two

Hannah was playing house in the yard with Jane when Robert came home. The two girls had their mother's wooden clothes horse open in a V and an old blanket thrown over it to make a tent. Inside the tent was an old clippie mat and Harry lying down on it pretending to be a baby. Harry didn't want to be the baby, he wanted to be the father, but he gave in when the girls insisted.

All three children abandoned the game and scrambled out of the tent when they heard their mother's voice at the gate.

'Now then, Robert,' Nora was saying, 'you're a big lad now, it's time you went out to work. Anyroad, we need the money so that's the end of that. Now stop making a fuss, there's a good lad.'

'Gran calls me Bob,' muttered Robert, 'and so does Uncle Billy.'

Hannah stood in a row with Harry and Jane, watching her mother and Robert curiously.

'Righto, then, we'll call you Bob if that's what you want,' said Nora as she led the way up the yard. 'Now, come and say hallo to your sisters and brother.'

Three pairs of dark eyes looked solemnly at Bob as he stood awkwardly before them. He was a tall, ungainly boy with the same shock of dark hair as they all had. It was almost two years since they had last seen him, and only Hannah had any remembrance of him at all. The little ones were shy of him and huddled in Hannah's skirts.

'Hallo,' said Bob, looking down at the brick-paved yard. He scuffed the hobnails of one boot back and forth over the bricks.

Hannah suddenly felt sorry for Bob. His face was flushed and his eyes full of unshed tears. She smiled at him, while Jane and Harry hung their heads, overcome with shyness.

'Clear that mess up, our Hannah, and mind, don't forget to fold that blanket up properly and put it away. Right then, Bob, let's away in. Betty will have the tea ready,' Nora said briskly. She went inside, followed after a second or two by Bob and the two younger children. Hannah was left to dismantle the tent.

The family were already sitting round the table when she got in after putting the clothes horse back in the wash house in the yard.

'You bide with me, our Bob,' Alf was saying in his 'big brother' voice which Hannah knew so well and resented almost as much. 'You'll get on all right on the screens tomorrow if you do what I say.'

Bob looked down at the meat-paste sandwich on his plate. Hannah could see that his fists were clenched so hard the knuckles were white. She took a bite out of her own sandwich and chewed it carefully. He looks so unhappy, she thought.

'Did you not want to come back home to live, Bob?' she asked. 'It's nice here, you know, there's the bunny banks and sometimes there's the magic lantern at chapel. And – ' Hannah meant to make Bob feel at home and tell him of all the nice things about Winton. But all she did was to cause his pent-up feelings to burst out. He stood up from the table and glared at her so hard she dropped her sandwich.

'This isn't my home!' he shouted. 'I live at Consett, that's my home, with Gran and Uncle Billy. I'm going back an' all, I'm going back to school and then I'm going to help Uncle Billy in his carrier business, that's what I'm going to do. I'm not going down the pit, I'm not. I don't care about your stupid bunny banks – what sort of a name is that for a rabbit warren, anyway?'

'Robert! Sit down!'

The roar came from the open door of the front room where Da was lying in his box bed. All the children gazed at him in shock. It was the first time they had heard Da shout since the accident. Robert subsided into his seat and there was a moment's silence.

'Bob,' Nora said. 'Bob, you have to stay here, pet. I know you love your gran, but you're needed here.'

'I don't care,' answered Bob, though this time he kept his voice low. 'I'm going back. You didn't want me when I was little, why should I come back now? Gran's been my mam.'

Hannah stared at him, wide-eyed. She tried to imagine what it would be like if she had to go and live in another place and go out to work doing something she didn't want to do, but it was hard to imagine such a thing.

'Bob, Bob, it wasn't like that. We did want you, son, but Betty came along and you were nought but a babby yourself. Times were bad, pet, your father was on short time. Your gran could look after you and feed you better, your grandda was an overman and they only had Billy left at home. Try to understand, Bob, there's a good lad.'

Hannah watched her mother as she talked. Mam looked as distressed as Bob was himself. A lump formed in Hannah's own throat. She looked down at the sandwich on her plate; suddenly she didn't feel hungry any more and the sandwich looked enormous. If she didn't eat it now, she would get it for her supper, she knew that well enough.

She'd been looking forward to seeing Bob again. It had not occurred to her that he wouldn't want to come. Everything had changed since Da hurt his back in the pit, she thought. If only they could go back to the way it was before.

It was Christmas before Jake's claim for permanent disability compensation was allowed by the committee. Hannah came running in from school on the day before the Christmas holiday, clutching the green paper Christmas tree she had cut out in class together with a multicoloured paper chain and a hat made out of newspaper.

'Look, Mam, look,' she said, 'we made them in school. Can we put them on the wall?' She was excited and didn't at first notice that Mam was smiling for the first time in months and Da's 'chariot', as he had begun to call his wheeled bed, had been brought out of the front room and was by the settee.

'Why, they're grand, pet,' declared Mam. 'We'll hang the paper chain round the mirror, what do you think, Jake? And the tree, why, it's almost like a real one, isn't it? We'll stick it on the wall, eh?'

'Aye,' said Da. Hannah looked at him, he too was smiling.

Forgetting about the paper tree and the chain for a minute, Hannah looked from one to the other. Her mother was relaxed and happy-looking, and so was Da. For a minute she had a wild hope that Da was going to get better and everything would soon be back to normal.

'Are you a bit better, Da?' she asked anxiously, fearful of his answer.

'A bit, pet, a bit,' he said. 'All the better for getting my compensation through, I am.'

Hannah smiled. The tiny hope that her father was going to get back to his normal health died, but the money made her mother and father happy and that was good. The atmosphere in the house had changed and she responded to it eagerly. 'Can Bob go back to Consett now?' she asked and her mother's smile faded. 'No, no, pet, he'll have to stay here and work. He'll be all right, you'll see, he'll get used to it. All the lads have to go to work.' She looked down at Jake and bit her lip. Bob wasn't settling down as they had hoped; he still hankered after going back to live in Consett.

Hannah felt a twinge of sadness for Bob but it was soon forgotten in the excitement of decorating the kitchen for Christmas. Jane had a paper chain from school too, and there was some holly which Alf had garnered from the hedge by the bunny banks and with bits stuck on the frame of Jake and Nora's wedding picture which hung on one wall, and the red paper bell which came out every year hanging from the gas light, the kitchen soon began to look quite festive.

Hannah had made a star from silver paper culled from Da's cigarette packet, and was pinning it to the top of the paper Christmas tree when Robert and Alf came in from work.

'Hurry up, Hannah, and get the bath in for the lads,' said Betty. 'I'm busy tonight.' She had been ironing a great pile of clothes on the table and now she rushed to get the ironing out of the way so that the table could be laid for the meal.

Obediently, Hannah went out into the yard and reached up to take the bath down from where it hung on a nail.

'Do you see my Christmas tree, Bob?' she asked brightly as she lugged the bath in and put it down before the fire. She smiled as she ladled hot water out of the boiler into the bath ready for Alf, who always insisted on being the first to wash as he was the oldest. She was thinking the Christmas tree was just the thing to cheer Bob up, he was always so glum.

Bob looked at the cut-out tree stuck on the wall with its star slightly lopsided on the top of it.

'Uncle Billy bought a real one from the market last year,' he said. 'That's just a bit of paper.'

Hannah was crestfallen. Suddenly the tree didn't seem quite so festive as she had thought it did.

'Eeh, a real tree?' Harry asked Bob, round-eyed. 'A big one, like at the Sunday school party?'

'Of course, a real tree,' snapped Bob, 'a big one an' all.'

Harry was snubbed; the light faded from his eyes and he looked down at his boots. He was still a little in awe of his new-found brother and easily put down by him.

24

'Bob, what's the matter with your face?' Da asked all of a sudden, and everyone turned to look at Bob.

'Nothing,' said Bob.

'Oh!' cried Hannah, distressed, 'you've hurt your eye, I didn't see it at first.' Bob's left eye was swollen and bruised purple and there was a small cut and a streak of dried blood along the cheekbone underneath.

'Who did that to you, Bob?' asked Mam quietly. She had come out of the pantry carrying a tureen for the potatoes which were simmering on the bar. Putting the dish down on the table, she put her finger under Bob's chin and lifted it so that she could look at the bruise in the gas light. Even though his face was covered in black smears from the coal dust, the black eye was becoming more obvious all the time.

'Nobody,' said Bob, twisting his face away.

'It was Ralph Cornish, Mam,' said Alf. Alf was already kneeling before the tin bath, stripped to the waist and lathering himself with a bar of carbolic soap.

'Ralph Cornish? But he's a full-grown man!' exclaimed Mam. 'Whatever did he do that for?'

'He said our Bob was cheeky,' said Alf. He bent over the bath and dipped his head under the water, rinsing off the lather before reaching for the towel which Hannah was automatically holding out to him.

'An' were you, Bob?' Mam asked quietly.

There was a low growl from Jake. 'If he was, do you think that gives a ruffian like Ralph Cornish the right to hit a bit lad like Bob? What are you thinking about, woman?'

'I didn't say anything, Mother,' said Bob. He was the only one to call Nora Mother. 'We were just coming out of the pit-yard gate and he pushed me out of the way and I asked him who he thought he was pushing, that's all.'

'I told you to keep out of his way,' said Alf. 'He takes after his da, that one, they're both of them bullies.'

Jake swore. 'By God,' he said, 'if I only had the use of my legs I'd go up there now and show him what for. Like his da, do you say? He hasn't got a da, that one, or if he has, nobody knows who it is. Wesley Cornish took up with his mother when Ralph was a bairn. Aye, and left his own wife and bairns to God and Providence an' all, he did. That Ralph's a bas –'

'Jake!' Nora cut him off sharply. 'The children are listening. Don't use bad language in my house.'

Hannah and Jane were indeed listening, wide-eyed. Their father's head was moving restlessly from side to side in agitation on the pillow of the 'chariot'. Harry got under the table and stuck his thumb in his mouth.

Hannah's brow creased in puzzlement. What did Da mean, Ralph Cornish hadn't got a da? She couldn't understand that at all.

'Why, man, it's enough to make a saint swear,' said Jake, but his voice was quieter though still bitter. Nora shook her head at him and turned back to Bob.

'Let's get that face washed, lad,' she said. 'Betty, come on, we'll empty the bath and fill it with some fresh water.'

'It's cold water that eye needs,' counselled Jake. Before his accident he had started a first-aid course as part of his training to become a deputy. An ambition which was lost now, 'like snow on the oven top', as Nora had commented sadly.

'You'll have to wash up the dishes tonight, Hannah,' said Betty. 'I've got enough to do with the mending and darning.'

'But we have to go to the choir practice, it's the last one before the carol singing,' said Hannah, dismayed. Hannah loved the chapel choir. She had a fine voice, pure and strong for her age and already showing signs of deepening to mezzo-soprano.

'If you hurry you can still go, it's not until six o'clock, is it? I can see to your da after that,' said her mother, and Hannah relaxed.

'We're going carol singing all round the village on Sunday night,' she announced happily. 'Mr Hodgson says we're even going up to the manager's house, even to Mr Durkin's house an' all. We're taking the little harmonium too, if it doesn't snow, like.' She was torn between wanting it to snow for Christmas and wanting to sing with the accompaniment of the harmonium.

Nora's face hardened at the mention of Mr Durkin. She had not forgotten the humiliation she had had to endure from him at the colliery office.

'You'll not get much out of the agent,' she observed tartly. 'And his house is a mile and a half away from the village an' all, it'll be a long way to walk for nowt. Still, I dare say Mr Hodgson reckons he knows best, he's the choirmaster, after all.'

The snow came during the night, but left only a thin covering, which crisped into ice crystals soon after it fell. There was a little more on Sunday morning, as the children sat in Sunday school, and Mr Hodgson, who was a Sunday school superintendent as well as choirmaster, had a harder time than usual keeping order. The children were excited to see the soft flakes falling past the high windows. They sang 'In the Deep Mid-Winter', and Hannah threw herself into it heart and soul, imagining to herself the Baby in a cold, draughty stable with snow falling outside just as it was falling in Winton now.

By the time the Sunday school was out, the snow had stopped and a strong, freezing wind was blowing down on them from the fells to the west.

'I'm cold,' whined Harry. Hannah tied his muffler in a cross over his chest and fastened it at the back.

'We'll have a race home,' she said. She and Harry went whooping along the row and into the house, with Jane trailing behind them looking white and cold.

'Does Father Christmas come tonight?' Harry asked his mother as he'd asked her every day for a week.

'Only to good boys and girls,' said Nora.

'Father Christmas!' said Bob scornfully, but his mother quelled him with a look.

At seven o'clock, the choir assembled outside the chapel. Hannah stamped her boots on the frozen ground and tucked her chin in her mother's shawl which was tied over her coat, but she was so excited she didn't really feel the cold. This was the first year she had been allowed to sing with the grown-up choir, not just with the Sunday school singers, and she held her candle carefully even though it was not yet lit, not here under the street lights lit by gas from the colliery. The candle was for when they walked out to the manager's house in Old Winton and then on up to Durham Road, where Lord Akers's agent, Mr Durkin, lived.

'You stick close to me, mind,' Betty admonished. 'I don't want you dancing off on your own like you do.'

Betty was more bossy every day, Hannah reflected as she moved her fingers about inside her mitts in an attempt to warm them up. The mitts were really a pair of Da's socks but they were nice and warm, each sock folded over on itself to make a double layer of wool. There was a burst of male laughter and she looked over to where Alf was standing with a group of men and boys. He was holding his hand in a funny way, she thought; staring hard, she saw the tiny red glow and realised he was holding a cigarette, turned back into his cupped hand to hide it. Quickly, she moved to stand between him and Betty. If Betty saw Alf smoking she would be sure to tell Da.

When Mr Hodgson came out with Laurie, his son, who was the organ player, they were carrying the tiny harmonium between them. At last the singers were off.

'By, it's grand, isn't it, Betty?' Hannah cried as they trudged away from the rows of miners' cottages to the village. They had sung two carols at each end of each row. Alf and his friends had rattled their collecting boxes labelled 'METHODIST MISSION TO THE POOR' and almost every household in the rows had contributed a penny; Mr Holmes had put in sixpence. Hannah crunched the thin, icy layer of snow beneath her boots, fairly dancing along as she wondered what it would be like to be 'the Poor' and not have any money at all, not even the compensation, nor a house to live in. She gazed up at the clear starry sky and wondered which one was the Star of Bethlehem.

'It'll be grand when we get back home,' said Betty dourly. Hannah's excitement dimmed a little, but only for a minute. They had just reached old Winton and Mr Hodgson halted before the Black Boy. The choir gathered round the harmonium under the swinging sign with its picture of a little pit lad with a candle in his hat.

'Once in Royal David's City' rang through the air and men tumbled out of the inn, some with tankards of beer in their hands. Hannah knew a lot of them, for they were neighbours and friends of her father's. There were some disapproving looks among the choir but the collecting boxes were satisfactorily heavier by the time Alf and his friends had done the rounds of the drinkers and she was glad for the sake of the Poor.

However, farther along the street the choir met with the opposition. The vicar and his party of waits from St Martin's, the village church, were out carol singing too. After the first clash of hymns, Mr Hodgson decided the best thing to do was take his choir elsewhere.

'We only show them up with our singing, anyroad,' he said. 'Howay, lads and lasses, we'll away up to Durham Road to the agent's place.'

'Mebbe you'd better go home, our Hannah, it's a long way to Durham Road,' said Betty.

Hannah gasped with dismay. 'I want to come,' she cried. 'I can walk, I'm not tired.'

'Let her come, Betty,' said Alf, 'lest we never hear the last of it.'

'Well, all right,' Betty conceded, 'but you'd better keep up, mind.'

Durham Road was really nearer to Bishop Auckland than Winton and the party set off on the short cut across the fields. It was quite a climb in places but Hannah forced herself to keep well to the front of the party, just to show Betty she could manage.

At last they reached the house and trooped up the drive. The laughing and talking quietened as they approached the house, most of them walking more slowly as they got near to the imposing stone pillars before the front door.

'Now then,' said Mr Hodgson, 'light your candles now. Don't step on the grass, mind, keep to the gravel.'

Guilty feet shuffled off the grass and the choir clustered round the harmonium, their uplifted faces lit by the glow of the candles. Hannah gazed at the light shining through a chink in the curtains and her heart began to beat rapidly. She was frightened of Mr Durkin – would he chase them away? Mr Durkin didn't like pit folk, he'd said so that day at the colliery office.

The harmonium started up and the choir sang 'Oh Come All Ye Faithful'. Suddenly they were bathed in a light which put the candles to shame as the curtains were drawn back.

'Electric,' breathed Hannah. She'd seen electric light before, but only in the shops in Newgate Street. She forgot to sing as she gazed into the room, at the red plush armchairs and the huge Christmas tree in the corner, twinkling with gold and silver ornaments and topped by a big fairy with shining silver wings. And then she forgot about the Christmas tree as she saw Timothy, the boy who had been in the car, standing by the window, smiling straight at her.

The choir finished their carol and the door opened. Hannah shrank back against her sister but it was not Mr Durkin who came to the door, it was a stranger, tall and haughty, dressed in a funny sort of black jacket and striped trousers.

'The master says you're to come into the hall, and mind you wipe your feet,' he announced grandly, looking over the heads of the choir as though he was speaking to the trees at the end of the drive. Hannah looked uncertainly at Mr Hodgson but he was moving forwards quite unperturbed and the choir was following him.

They were ushered into a large hall, all gleaming, polished wood and with a red carpet in the middle. At one end there was a wide staircase and there was even carpet going up the stairs, not a strip of linoleum like they had at home.

Mr Durkin and Timothy came through a door at the side and Hannah was thankful to see that the agent was smiling.

'Good evening to you all,' he said and they all mumbled a reply. Hannah smiled shyly at Timothy and he smiled back.

'Can you sing "Still the Night", do you think?' asked Mr Durkin.

'Yes, sir, of course.' The choirmaster beamed. He glanced down at Hannah and hesitated. 'I wonder, sir . . . our little Hannah here, she has a lovely voice and she's been rehearsing it for the Sunday-school party. Would you like to hear her sing the first verse, sir? Then we'll all join in the second.'

Hannah's throat closed up and she stared up at Mr Hodgson, her dark eyes filled with fright. Surely he wasn't going to make her sing for Mr Durkin! But Mr Hodgson chose not to see the appeal on her face; instead, he took hold of her shoulder and drew her to the front of the choir.

'Now then, pet,' he encouraged her, 'just pretend you're singing in the chapel. Sing it just like we practised.' Drawing a tuning fork from his waistcoat pocket, he struck the note, and Hannah opened her mouth obediently, though she was sure she wasn't going to be able to sing at all.

But sing she did, faltering a little over the first few notes but then losing herself in the lovely old carol. Her pure tones gained strength and rang out over the choir and the well of the staircase lent resonance to the music. The choir joined in the second verse and after a while Hannah was conscious of a new voice. Looking across at Timothy, she realised it was his baritone she could hear.

34

There was a moment's silence after the hymn before Mr Durkin finally broke it. 'Very nice,' he said. 'Timothy, fetch some mince pies from the kitchen.' He took a gold watch out of his waistcoat pocket and peered at the dial pointedly. 'Well, good night to you all and a merry Christmas.' He turned and went back through a door at the side of the hall, not even noticing the collection box held up by Alf. Mr Hodgson sighed.

Timothy came back and handed round a plate of mince pies and the choir ate them quietly. Seeing the collection box, he fumbled in his pocket and put in a sixpence.

'You have a lovely voice,' he said to Hannah, and she smiled shyly.

'You an' all,' she answered.

'Well, we'd better be going, we still have to go to the manager's house,' said Mr Hodgson and he ushered the choir out of the hall and down the drive.

Hannah looked round just before they got to the gates and saw Timothy standing at the window, watching them. On impulse, she gave a little wave and he must have seen her for he lifted his arm and waved back. Hannah felt a tiny glow of happiness. Was he lonely in that big house with his father and the snooty man, she wondered.

Chapter Three

The Christmas of 1920 was the best one Hannah could remember. 'Like magic,' she breathed to Jane when Grandma came with Uncle Billy on Christmas morning and Bob's face lit up at the sight of them. That was the second good thing to happen. The first had been coming downstairs that morning to find that the stockings they had pinned to the mantelpiece valance were bulging.

'Father Christmas came!' Harry shouted. Betty reached up, unpinned the stockings and handed them round. Besides the usual apple, orange and handful of hazelnuts, each stocking held a bag of sweets: black bullets and humbugs. For Harry there was a hand-carved wooden truck and Jane had a wooden doll with real clothes.

'Father Christmas brought it because I've been good,' said Harry thickly, through a mouth bulging with humbug. He clutched his truck to his chest as though someone were going to snatch it from him.

'They had a gathering for Da in the pit,' said Alf prosaically. Luckily, the two youngest children didn't hear this.

Grandma had brought a chicken to go with the piece of belly pork Mam had in the oven. She put it down on the table, kissed Bob and asked him how he was getting on and then went into the front room to see her injured son. After about ten minutes she came out again.

'Howay, Hannah,' she said and her voice was so trembly that Hannah looked up at her with quick sympathy. 'We'll start the dinner, eh? Let Betty have an easy morning for a change.' Grandma's eyes were wet and her hands were trembling as she took the chicken out of her basket and got it ready for the oven.

'You can chop the sage with the onion, Hannah,' she went on. 'Now mind, breathe through your mouth so the onions don't make you cry.'

Hannah kept chopping away at the onions and mixing the dried sage and breadcrumbs in with them, but she remembered to breathe through her mouth so they didn't make her cry and it was Grandma who had to keep taking out her handkerchief to wipe her eyes, not Hannah.

'I forgot to breathe properly,' said Grandma once. She blew her nose and smiled tightly at Hannah.

The dinner was grand. Mam brought Da out of the front room and they were all together for the meal.

Hannah beamed as she looked round at them all; even Da was smiling.

After dinner, Uncle Billy took all the children for a ride in his cart. They went round the rows and up into the old village, doing a circuit which led back to the house, with the children waving to all their friends. Harry wanted to go again but Uncle Billy explained that the pony would have to have a rest before taking them back to Consett after tea. Reluctantly, Harry allowed himself to be lifted down. Uncle Billy let him help unharness the pony and showed him how to fit on his nosebag, and then Bob went off for a walk up the bunny banks with his uncle. And later there was spice cake for tea, and a glass of ginger wine for everyone.

'Tomorrow will be even better,' breathed Hannah as she settled down in the iron-framed bed she shared with Jane. 'Tomorrow is my birthday and the Sunday school party and there's to be a magic lantern.'

The house was quiet. Grandma and Uncle Billy had left soon after tea, and the family had watched the lantern bobbing on the side of the cart until it disappeared. Hannah had gazed anxiously at Bob, standing beside her watching the cart. She had caught hold of his hand and squeezed it.

'They'll be back, Bob,' she had said softly.

Bob had shaken off her hand. 'Aw, leave me alone, Hannah,' he had said. 'I'm all right, man.' And he had stumped off up the yard to the back door.

Hannah put her arm round the thin body of her little sister and snuggled into her. Eleven! I'm eleven tomorrow, she thought as she drifted near to sleep. And, unexpectedly, into her mind popped the image of the boy, Timothy Durkin, so lonely he had looked in that great house in Durham Road. 'I hope he had a lovely Christmas too,' she whispered to herself and snuggled into her pillow.

'The demand for coal is slackening,' said Daniel Durkin moodily. Timothy, sitting opposite him at the dinner table, watched his father as he played with his wine glass, twirling it round and round in his fingers.

'It is?' asked Mr Abbot, the vicar. Mr Abbot had only recently been appointed to the living of St Martin's; he was a bachelor not yet thirty years old and knew nothing whatsoever of the coal trade, coming as he did from a farming community in Yorkshire.

Timothy sat quietly, wishing the interminable dinner were over so that he could excuse himself and go up to his room. Maude, the housemaid, brought in the steaming Christmas pudding and the men were quiet as she placed it before Daniel along with a dish of brandy butter.

'That will be all, thank you, Maude,' said Daniel. 'I can manage.'

'Thank you, sir,' said Maude and went out.

Timothy gazed at the enormous fruit-filled pudding and felt slightly sick. He remembered the Christmas pudding his mother had made four years before.

'Have a stir, Timothy,' she had cried to him. 'Make a wish, Timothy.'

And he'd taken the wooden spoon in his hand and stirred and knocked the bag of flour over with his elbow and the table and floor had been covered in the fine white dust.

'We'd better clean it up or Mrs Bates will be cross with us for making a mess of her kitchen,' his mother had said, but she was smiling as she said it, not angry at all. But when Christmas came and the pudding was placed on the dining table, his mother was dead. Timothy forced his mind away from the memory of it and looked up at his father.

'None for me, thank you,' he said as Daniel took up the serving spoon.

'Don't be silly, Timothy,' his father said sharply. 'You don't want to hurt Mrs Bates's feelings, do you?'

'No, of course not, Father,' said Timothy and accepted the plate the vicar passed him.

'You were saying, the coal trade was slackening,' said Mr Abbot. 'I'm afraid I know very little about it, myself.'

Daniel ate a spoonful of pudding before replying. 'Very good,' he pronounced. 'I must congratulate Mrs Bates.'

'Oh yes, indeed,' said Mr Abbot.

'Hmm. Well, perhaps I should not have mentioned business on a festive day like this,' said Daniel. 'But I do have it on my mind, I'm afraid. Demand was bound to slacken some time now the war is over, but try telling the men that.' He shook his head and took another spoonful of pudding before putting down his spoon and wiping his mouth with his napkin. 'It's the wages bill, you see.' He sighed. 'Between you and me, it will have to be cut.' He looked across at Mr Abbot earnestly. 'Miners are well paid, you know, compared with, say, agricultural labourers. Most farmworkers only get forty-six shillings a week. Some of our hewers can earn four pounds a week.'

'The men should be thankful they have work,' said the vicar. 'After all, they have their coal allowance, too. Some of the labouring population in the south are hard put to pay for coal. And there are ex-servicemen still out of work, or so I understand. After all, the miners didn't have to fight, or most of them didn't.'

Timothy looked surprised. He remembered the victory parade when the soldiers had come back from France and marched through Winton. Surely they were miners? But the vicar was talking of parish matters now, and he could not interrupt to ask about it. Instead Timothy turned his attention to his food, looking down at the lump of pudding on his plate. He took his spoon and stirred it around, trying to make it look as though he had eaten some of it. A coal fire blazed in the grate of the ornate marble fireplace and he felt uncomfortably hot. Mr Abbot did not like the miners, he thought, remembering how the vicar had replied when Daniel had asked him how he liked living in Winton.

'To tell you the truth, Mr Durkin,' Mr Abbot had said, 'I would never have come had I known there were two flourishing Methodist churches here, besides the Congregationalists and the Roman Catholics. We are outnumbered, I fear. And as for the miners, either they waste their wages on drink or they are ranting teetotallers and I find it hard put to tell which is worst.'

The door opened and Mr Bates came in with the decanter of port. Timothy breathed a sigh of relief.

'May I be excused, Father?' he asked and at his father's nod he escaped to his room and took off his jacket. Thank goodness another Christmas was almost over, he thought as he stood by the window, gazing out over the trees to where the winding wheel and chimney stacks of the colliery towered over the colliery rows. Another two weeks and he would be back at school in Barnard Castle. At least he had friends at school, there was no one here.

Looking down on the village reminded him of the chapel choir, and in particular of the little girl wrapped in a shawl which reached down to her knees and up over her head so that only her small face peeped out, pink with cold. He remembered her from the time she had come to the colliery office with her mother and little brother, and he still felt hot with embarrassment at the way his father had spoken to them.

When she had come with the choir she had stood beside what was obviously her older sister, for they both had dimples in their chins and dark eyes fringed with black lashes. It must be nice to be part of a big family, Timothy mused. And then, when she sang, such a large, pure voice had emerged from such a little girl that he had been enchanted and drawn to sing along with her.

A germ of an idea was forming in Timothy's mind. There were some days left before he had to go back to school. Tomorrow he would go down into Winton and find the chapel, maybe he could make some friends and even join the choir. He always enjoyed singing at school, though when he had asked to take singing lessons his father had stated that they were a waste of time and money and so he had given up the idea.

Next evening Timothy told his father he was going for a pre-dinner stroll and set off through the fields to Winton Colliery. As he approached the small, cramped houses, the rows practically on top of one another, he almost turned back at the smell; he had forgotten about the smell. The air was laden with sulphurous fumes from the cokeworks and ashes and coal dust from the colliery waste heap mingled with the stink from the ash closets in the narrow back alleys. He wrinkled his nose, breathed through his mouth and went on to the tall stone building which was the Methodist chapel and schoolroom, standing alone on a patch of waste ground midway between the village and the pit.

The windows of the schoolroom were ablaze with light and he could hear children laughing and shouting. Timothy hesitated for a few minutes, fearing they would think he was intruding. In the end he walked in through the open side door into a hall strung with paper chains and a platform at one end with a woman sitting at an old upright piano. Over the platform was a huge painted sign, 'SUFFER THE CHILDREN TO COME UNTO ME.'

The children were sitting in a large ring on the floor and playing 'pass the parcel'. There was a great deal of noise and confusion as the parcel went round the circle, being dropped by hands too eager to pass it on and picked up hurriedly, while the lady on the platform banged out a tune he couldn't recognise. No one saw him at first, not until the music stopped suddenly and it was Hannah holding the parcel. Her face registered her disappointment but she handed over the parcel to her neighbour and left the circle. As all eyes followed her, they caught sight of Timothy inside the doorway and suddenly there was a hush. Mr Hodgson, from his position as referee in the middle of the circle, gazed blankly at the intruder before remembering his manners and rushing to greet him.

'Master Durkin! How nice of you to come,' he cried.

'I . . . I heard the merriment and wondered . . . I hope I don't intrude,' Timothy faltered.

'Indeed no, everyone is welcome in the Lord's house,' said Mr Hodgson grandly. 'The children have had their tea but I'm sure there will be some Christmas cake left for you. Will you stay? There's to be a magic-lantern show and then Father Christmas is coming with gifts for the children. This is their day, you know.'

'Thank you, I will,' said Timothy and he looked down at Hannah, and smiled and she forgot her disappointment at not winning the parcel and smiled back into his deep-blue eyes. Mrs Roberts brought Timothy a slice of cake and he and Hannah sat at the side of the hall and watched as the game continued, the circle dwindling until at last there was a winner and it was Harry. Timothy shared in Hannah's delight as Harry brought his prize to be admired: a colouring book and a packet of crayons. All the children crowded round to see, forgetting their shyness of Timothy. Then it was time for the magic lantern and the flickering pictures of black children in Africa with the Methodist missionaries their collected pennies had helped to send out to teach the heathen. Father Christmas came after that and Hannah had a pretty, lace-embroidered handkerchief, delicate and white.

'It's my birthday today,' she confided to Timothy and blushed in embarrassment when he fished in his pocket and brought out a shilling.

'I didn't mean . . . ' she said unhappily.

'No, of course you didn't, I never thought that,' he assured her. 'But please take it, I want you to have it.' And Hannah stowed the shilling along with her lace handkerchief in the pocket of her dress.

'I just meant that it always feels like the Sunday school party is my birthday party too,' she explained earnestly.

The party finished with the children singing carols. Timothy joined in unselfconsciously, his baritone ringing out over the voices of the rest. He was enjoying himself hugely.

As they all filed out of the schoolroom, Mr Hodgson stopped him.

'Come back any time you like, lad,' he said. 'The choir could just do with a singer like you.'

'Thank you, I will,' answered Timothy. He waved to them all and in particular to Hannah before striding off over the fields to Durham Road.

'You're late, sir,' snapped Daniel as his son let himself into the house. Daniel was standing in the doorway of the dining room, frowning heavily.

'Sorry, Father,' said Timothy. 'I won't be a moment changing.' As he washed his hands and face and combed his hair ready to go down to dinner, he found himself smiling into the mirror; he felt happier than he had done during the whole of the holiday and not the least bit sorry.

Chapter Four

'Hannah! Hannah, get up out of bed now, will you?'

Something in Betty's voice made Hannah jump up immediately, her feet landing on the icy cold linoleum, at which her toes curled up in protest. She hurriedly found her boots and crammed her bare feet into them, then pulled her dress on over her nightie and raced downstairs.

Betty was standing by the fire with the heavy kettle in her hand, pouring water into the teapot. Hannah blinked. It was only six o'clock, she could see by the wall clock, yet the kitchen was already warmed up as though the fire had been on for hours.

'What's the matter, Betty?' Hannah asked as she went up to the fire and held her hands out to the blaze.

'The baby's come,' said Betty.

'The baby? What baby?' Hannah had been bending down to tie her bootlaces but she straightened up and stared at her sister.

'What baby do you think?' Betty snapped, but Hannah could see she was not really cross for she was smiling. 'We've a new baby brother,' she added, her tone softening. As though to verify her words, the sound of a baby crying came from the front room, and Mam's voice hushing it.

Betty laughed at Hannah's astonishment. 'You mean you didn't know Mam was having a bairn?' she asked, using that superior tone of voice which Hannah hated. 'Why did you think she was getting so fat, then?'

Hannah blushed; she hadn't even noticed Mam was fat. She bent her head and finished tying her boots.

'Hurry up, you'll have to stay off school and see to the breakfast and everything. I'll have enough to do, seeing to Da and helping Mam with the baby,' said Betty. 'Now, take some tea in for Mam, she could do with a cup now it's over.'

Obediently, Hannah took the cup of tea and pushed open the door to the front room. The room was warm in spite of the snow falling outside, for the fire was lit in the black-leaded grate and the old wooden cradle was drawn up beside it. Da's box bed was pulled up by one side of the double bed and in the bed there was Mam, sitting up with a bundle in her arms and smiling at Hannah.

'Eeh, thanks, pet, I could just do with that,' said Mam softly. 'Howay, come and see your new baby brother. Quiet now, your father's just got back to sleep.'

Hannah stared down at the tiny, red-faced mite wrapped in the faded crochet shawl she could dimly remember from when Harry was a baby, and she fell instantly in love.

'By, he's bonny,' she whispered. 'What's his name, Mam?'

'We think we'll call him Walton, after your grandfather. Now, will you put him in his cradle for me? Careful, now.'

Hannah took the baby in her arms and carried him to the cradle, laying him down and covering him with the tiny flannelette sheet she remembered Mam making from the corner of an old, torn, full-size one. She gazed down at the sleeping baby, reluctant to leave him.

'Go on now, pet, go and help Betty,' said Mam. 'Be a good lass and do what she says. I think I'll have a rest now, while the bairn's asleep.'

For the next few weeks, while the wintry weather turned to spring, Hannah's days were filled with peeling vegetables and boiling puddings, possing clothes in the wooden wash tub and helping Betty to iron them with the flat irons heated on the bar of the kitchen fire. And helping with baby Walton. That was what she liked to do, she would change his nappies and cheerfully wash them out and hang them on the line in the yard. She hovered anxiously over him whenever Jane asked to hold him. And when Hannah managed to catch threepence in a wedding 'hoy-out', when the groom throws a handful of copper into the street for good luck, she bought a hank of white wool and laboriously knitted him a tiny cap. But then the kiddy-catcher came and Hannah had to go back to school.

At first, she worried about Walton and would hurry home from school to make sure he was all right. But Mam was stronger now and could see to both Da and the baby herself. In April there was something else to worry about: the owners locked the men out of the pits until such time as they should see sense and agree to new terms.

'At least we have your father's compensation money coming in,' said Nora. 'Now the pit's idle some folk'll have nothing.'

'Nay, lass,' said Jake, 'there's the relief, if anyone's starving.'

Nora snorted. 'Not for a man on his own, there's not. The board reckons too much has been paid out to them as isn't in proper distress. And anyway, those who do get it have to pay it back when the pit starts up again. I read it in the *Chronicle*.'

'The *Chronicle* said Peter Lee's petitioning Parliament,' Alf volunteered. 'He says some of the men won't have much more than two pound a week if they go back on the new terms.'

'Aye. Well, we've got fourteen shillings and ninepence, now the war rating has been taken off us and you and our Bob's laid idle.'

'The union's giving out credit notes for the Co-op store,' said Betty. 'To be paid back after, like.'

'Aye, that's the nub of it,' said Nora. 'How would we pay anything back? Your da's not going back to work. And the lads don't get that much on the screens.'

No matter how they talked round it, Hannah thought as she trudged to school with Jane, they didn't have enough even though they had the compensation. She looked up at the colliery winding wheel, so still and quiet. The gates of the pit yard were closed and locked and the yard itself was deserted. It began to rain, the water coming down in hard sheets which soon had tiny rivulets of water black with coal dust running under the gates and out over the pavement to the gutter.

'Mind you don't step in the water,' she said sharply to Jane. 'You know you haven't to get your feet wet, it makes you cough.'

Jane sniffled miserably, hunched her chin down between her shoulders and dragged her feet. 'I want to go home, I feel bad,' she whimpered.

'Well, you can't,' said Hannah. She put an arm round Jane's shoulders and hurried her on. 'Come on, it's not so far now and maybe the teacher will have some cocoa for us.'

That was something else Mam had seen in the *Chronicle*. The teachers had recommended that breakfast and dinner should be provided for the children. And as the two girls came to the gates of the schoolyard they both began to quicken their steps, for there, drawn up to the main door, was the motor van belonging to the Co-op store. A man was lifting out boxes and carrying them into the school.

'Now then, girls.' Miss High, the headmistress, stood on the top step of the girls' entrance. 'Form your lines now. We're going into school early today, there's cocoa and bread for everyone.'

The children were not to tell twice. In record time they had formed lines according to which class they were in and stood patiently waiting for the order to march forwards. The only sound was that of the man from the store whistling as he went backwards and forwards to the van; the children knew better than to talk in line.

'We've had our dinners, Mam,' cried Hannah when she got home after school. 'We had bread and scrape and cocoa for breakfast before we started our lessons. And then we had soup at dinnertime. And Miss High says we're to have our breakfast and dinner every day, even Saturday and Sunday.'

'That's grand pet,' said Nora absently and Hannah's face fell.

'I . . . I thought you would be pleased,' she said.

'Eeh, I am, I am,' said her mother. 'It's Jane, though, she's come home poorly.' Jane was still in the junior section at school and got out half an hour earlier than Hannah. She was lying on the settee wrapped up in Nora's shawl.

Hannah hadn't thought anything of it when she came in, for Jane often had a rest when she came in from school. Now she looked at her little sister properly and felt a sick alarm at what she saw. Jane had a high colour in her cheeks and her eyes were wide open and shining brightly but she didn't seem to be seeing anything.

'Jane?' Hannah whispered, but Jane didn't appear to know her or even see her.

'Come away, Hannah, she can't hear you. Now, I want you to run down to the doctor's with this note. I'm feared for the bairn,' said Nora, handing over a folded piece of cheap writing paper.

Nodding dumbly, Hannah turned and ran through the rows and on up the road to the doctor's house in Old Winton. By the time she reached the large stone-built house she was panting heavily and a stitch in her side caused her to double up, but she followed the instructions on the notice by the gate, 'Patients and messages through the yard at the back'. At the sight of her white, anxious face, the men squatting on their haunches around the door, in the way of all pitmen used to working in cramped seams, moved quickly to allow her passage through. Inside, the wall benches were full of women gossiping in hushed voices as they waited their turn to see the doctor, but Hannah went straight to the hatch in the far wall where the dispenser stood before his rows of medicine bottles and handed him her note.

He peered at it, then looked over his half-spectacles at her.

'The doctor's busy just now, don't you know it's surgery time?' he said.

'Our Jane's very bad,' Hannah persisted. He frowned before deciding. 'Well, I'll have a word with him when he has a minute.'

Hannah licked her dry lips and cast a desperate glance around at the women watching her. 'Can you not have a word with him now?' she asked, fear for Jane making her bold.

'No, I cannot,' said the dispenser, who was also the man who came round on Friday evenings to collect the 'panel' money, the fourpence a week Mam paid for the doctor's services.

'Why, man, can you not see how worried the bairn is?' a voice said from the benches. Hannah looked round and saw it was Mrs Holmes, the overman's wife. The dispenser transferred his attention from the girl to the woman.

'Everybody in their turn, Mrs Holmes,' he pronounced. 'Why didn't they send for the doctor before the surgery started, anyway?'

'Likely there was no one to send, you barmy sod,' said Mrs Holmes. She looked away from him dismissively and spoke to Hannah. 'Go on, pet, you can ask the doctor yourself if *he* won't. It's my turn next and you can go in along of me.'

'No need for that, Mrs Holmes,' said the dispenser huffily. 'If it's urgent I'll go in to him now.' After a deferential knock he went through the door which connected the dispensary with the surgery.

By, she was a nice woman, Mrs Holmes, Hannah thought as she sped home. A grand woman. But as she ran up the yard she forgot about Mrs Holmes, for through the lighted window she could see Mam bending over the settee while Harry was standing crying and sucking his thumb by the table.

'He's coming, Mam, the doctor's coming – ' Hannah stopped short as Nora stood up and Hannah saw the towel she was holding was covered in blood, bright-red blood. Jane was lying still and white and quiet, and dread rose up in Hannah's throat.

'What is it? For God's sake, Nora, what's the matter?'

Da, shouting from his box bed in the front room, could hardly be heard for the noise of Harry's sobs and the baby Walton woke and added his terrified screams.

'Whist, Harry, whisht,' said Hannah, moving to her little brother and putting her arm around him. 'Howay, now, come into the front room, I have to see to the bairn.'

'Oh, God,' Nora was moaning as she snatched the clean tea cloth from the brass line under the mantel shelf and used it to wipe the beads of sweat from Jane's face and neck. 'Oh, God, oh, God, where's our Betty? Where's the flaming doctor?'

'If by the flaming doctor you mean me, I'm here,' said Dr Short as he came in and, taking in the situation at a glance, strode over to the settee. 'Now, send the children out of the room, this is no place for them. And pull yourself together, Mrs Armstrong, I need your help while I examine the lassie.'

Hannah dragged Harry into the front room and closed the door before taking Walton from his cradle and cuddling the wet bundle into her chest. Harry went to his father's bedside and, leaning over, buried his head in the pillow.

'Now then, stop blubbing, Harry, you're a big lad now,' said Jake and patted his son's head. 'What happened with Jane?' he asked Hannah. 'I thought she just had a bad cough or maybe the influenza.'

Hannah couldn't bear the anxiety and frustration in his face and she looked quickly down at the baby in her arms. 'Our Jane's spitting blood,' she mumbled as she sat down and began to unpin Walton's sopping nappy.

Jake looked relieved for a minute but then his eyes narrowed. 'How much blood?'

A vivid picture of Mam holding the blood-sodden towel came to Hannah and she bent to her work of changing the baby, unable to answer at first. Walton was still crying and she desperately wanted him to stop so that she could hear what the doctor was saying in the kitchen.

The Coal Miner's Daughter

'How much blood, Hannah?' Jake raised his voice.

'A lot, Da.'

'Oh, my God!'

Hannah lifted the clean and dry baby and leaned him against her shoulder, rocking him gently. After a few moments, his sobs subsided. She stole a glance at her father, who was lying with a curiously blank expression on his face as he absently patted Harry's head.

'I'll ring for the ambulance as soon as I get back to the surgery,' she heard the doctor say. 'In the meanwhile, keep her quiet and don't give her anything to eat or drink.'

'Maybe Jane has scarlet fever,' whispered Hannah. She remembered the time the year before when May Martin in the next row had scarlet fever and she and Jane had watched as the ambulance came to take May to the fever hospital. 'Touch collar, never follow, don't come to our door,' they had chanted, fingering their collars, but the charm hadn't worked, for now the ambulance was coming for Jane.

'I doubt it's scarlet fever, pet,' said Da. 'Put the baby in the cradle now and go and help your mam, our Betty's not back from work yet.'

Hannah did as he bid her, fetching in a pail of cold water from the pump on the end of the row to soak the bloodied clothes in, fetching a clean nightie for Jane from the chest of drawers upstairs. All the time, Jane lay still and quiet and Hannah could not bear to look at her.

When Betty came home from her work at Mr Hudson's house, she and Mam stood huddled together whispering. Hannah couldn't hear properly but she did catch the word 'consumption' and her eyes widened anxiously. 'Consumption' was a word to be whispered, never spoken aloud.

Jane didn't go to the fever hospital, she went to the sanatorium, which was high in Weardale where the wind was fresh and bracing and would blow the germs away in no time, or so her father told Hannah. But the days and weeks dragged on and Jane didn't come home. Mam went to visit her once during the lockout, walking into Bishop Auckland and catching the train from there. She took six large oranges given to her by Mr Nelson, who was a greengrocer and a chapel man, and a little purse with a string to hang round her neck which Hannah had made for Jane out of a piece of bombazine left over from two years ago when Nora had made her good dress. But it was becoming more difficult every day to find money to live and the fare to Weardale was just too much.

Hannah had an idea. The school hall was so crowded at dinnertime, surely no one would notice Harry? Anyway, he was almost five and would be starting school in a few weeks. So why couldn't he have his dinner with the other children? After all, it was Sunday and after dinner they all went home again, they didn't have to stand in line and go back into their classrooms.

'It'll be all right if you stand close to me and keep on the side away from Mr Carney,' Hannah warned Harry as they waited in the queue by the school gates. Harry nodded and moved in closer to his sister among the crowd of children. His mouth watered; he could smell the beef even at this distance from the school hall.

'Will there be meat, Hannah?' he whispered, his eyes shining. Yesterday he had had a bowl of soup from the soup kitchen, broth thick with vegetables but with little trace of the ham which was said to be in it.

'Whisht!' Hannah hissed, glancing quickly at the gate which Mr Carney, the school caretaker, was unlocking to allow the children in. Mr Carney knew the Armstrong family too well, he was aware that Harry was not yet at school. The children surged forwards as the gates opened, heading for the hall.

'Walk, don't run!' shouted Mr Carney. 'Anyone who runs will go to the back of the queue.' He lifted his chin and glared officiously at a small girl who was doing a little skip of delight in her anticipation of the food. She dropped her head and blushed scarlet.

Hannah managed to get Harry past Mr Carney and into the hall without the caretaker seeing him. She hustled him to a seat beside her on the long forms by the trestle table. Harry's eyes shone, for not only were there boiled potatoes on the plate in front of him but also a slice of meat – not pressed brawn or cow heel either, but proper boiled beef. He picked up his knife and fork at once, took a bite and chewed blissfully.

'Wait, Harry!' Hannah whispered urgently. 'Miss Dunne has to say grace.' Luckily, Miss Dunne, the duty teacher this Sunday, was not taking too much notice of what the children were doing. She was resentful of having to come in to work on a Sunday and wanted to get the meal over with so that she could go home.

'For what we are about to receive, may the Lord make us truly thankful,' she intoned rapidly.

'Amen,' said the children, and there was a clatter of tin cutlery on pottery plates as they dived into the meal. There was no chattering among them, no laughing, no mischief; simply a steady concentration on eating the food on their plates. Within ten minutes all eyes were turned to the server at the head of the table, for sometimes on a Sunday some children had gone to grandparents, there might therefore be some food left. This time they were lucky, for at a nod from Miss Dunne the server began to dole out an extra potato each.

'Harry Armstrong, what are you doing here?'

Both Hannah and Harry jumped in their seats and looked round in horror. They had been watching the server, the caretaker's assistant, coming nearer and nearer and hadn't realised that Mr Carney was also approaching from the other end of the hall. He grabbed hold of Harry, tucked him under his arm, kicking and screaming, and dumped him in front of Miss Dunne.

'Leave him alone!' shrieked Hannah, practically falling over the form as she rushed to follow her brother. She put her arms around him and he buried his face in her skirt, his screams fading to a thin, hiccuping wail.

'This lad isn't five yet, he's not a scholar here,' said Mr Carney, his mouth pulled down in frowning outrage.

'He's five next month,' Hannah asserted. 'He's nearly old enough.'

'Hannah Armstrong,' snapped Miss Dunne, 'don't you dare speak until you're spoken to. You know the rules: the meal is for the schoolchildren and the boy isn't at school yet. Did you bring him in here?'

'He was hungry!' Hannah cried. 'What difference did it make anyroad? There was dinner left over today, I knew there would be on a Sunday.'

'That's as may be, my girl,' said Miss Dunne, 'but now I'll have to go and see your mother, she will have to pay for what the boy ate. That will be threepence.' The teacher was very angry for it meant that she was going to be late home if she had to go down into the miners' hovels. Besides, she had her new dress on, ready for her afternoon walk with her intended, and she would likely get it marked.

'Threepence!' Hannah gasped. By, she would catch it from Mam now and Betty an' all. And what would Da say if they didn't have threepence left from the compensation money and they had to admit it to snooty Miss Dunne?

'Can . . . Can I bring it tomorrow, miss?' she asked desperately, trying to put off the time when the money would have to be forthcoming.

'No, you can't,' snapped Miss Dunne. 'The rules are quite clear: if a child not on the school register manages to get a free meal, then the parents must be charged. I have to collect it immediately.'

Harry felt his sister trembling and his wails grew louder, punctuated by enormous, gulping hiccups.

'Stop that bellowing boy,' shouted Miss Dunne, losing her patience altogether. She grabbed hold of his shoulder and pulled him round to face her. 'You are a very naughty boy, do you hear me? What you did was stealing. Perhaps it will be a good thing when you do start school, it's very obvious that you need discipline. Now, come with – Oh!' Miss Dunne released her hold on Harry and jumped back in horror for suddenly the boy vomited beef and potatoes and gravy all over her new dress. As the teacher stood frozen for a moment, watching his heaving shoulders, Hannah took her chance. She grasped Harry's arm and raced from the hall, his feet barely touching the ground as she flew along, to a chorus of giggles and chatter from the rest of the children.

Chapter Five

'*The Beggar Prince* is on at the Hippodrome in Auckland, Mam,' said Hannah. She was reading from a copy of the *Auckland Chronicle* which Mrs Holmes had given her to light the fire; the Armstrongs could no longer afford a newspaper. She was silent for a moment as she tried to picture a beggar prince in her mind – someone like Timothy Durkin, she thought, tall with blue eyes and black hair. Except that Timothy Durkin was no beggar, being the agent's son, she reminded herself.

'Hurry up with that fire, I want to melt some soap to wash the woollens through,' Mam interrupted her thoughts.

'It says here that you should buy Rinso, it's a soap powder, then you won't have to boil soap,' said Hannah. '"Rinso, the cold water washer, less waste, more comfort,"' she quoted.

'Oh aye, does it tell you what to use for money to buy it? Will they take fresh air?' Nora smiled grimly and carried on grating the bar of hard brown soap. Hurriedly, Hannah crumpled the paper, laid it in the grate and criss-crossed it with sticks garnered from the bunny banks. There were no pit-prop offcuts for the lads to bring home while the pit was still idle, they were Norwegian pine and made the best fire sticks. She piled cinders and a few lumps of coal on top of the sticks and lit the paper with a match before standing well back from it. The day was uncomfortably warm and the fire added to the discomfort immediately, but it was the only means they had of boiling water or cooking. A flame curled lazily upwards and the sticks settled, causing a charred piece of paper to fall on the hearth.

"'Considerable damage to the denes by miners seeking fuel,'" she read aloud as she picked it up. 'We could do with some of that, the coalhouse is almost empty.'

'Aye,' said Nora, sighing heavily. 'What we'll do then I don't know.'

'It's not fair, Mam, is it?'

Nora knew what Hannah meant; even if they were not locked out of the pit, Alf and Robert were too young to get a coal allowance so the Armstrongs, along with the widows in the village, were dependent on their neighbours, most of whom gave them a couple of buckets of coal when their own allowance came. But now the neighbours were short themselves.

'Nowt's fair in this world,' she said wearily. 'Now go on up to the allotment and see if Alf has any vegetables ready for the pot. I could make a dinner if I had some vegetables. You can take Walton, he could do with some fresh air.'

Hannah put Walton in the black pram which had served all the Armstrong children when they were babies, though it had been second-hand when it was bought for Alf. One of the wheels was a bit rickety but it still could be pushed along fairly easily. The hood had broken off years ago but that didn't matter either unless it rained. Today was a lovely June day and there was no chance of rain. Her heart lifted as she walked along the row to the path leading to the allotment gardens, daydreaming as she went. Walton lay on his back gurgling peacefully. He was late in trying to sit up but Mam said he would do it in his own good time.

Hannah watched him, fantasizing that he was her very own baby and she was pushing him along with her husband by her side. She soon became engrossed in the fantasy, holding an imaginary conversation with the shadowy man by her side, discussing the pros and cons of lace curtains for the parlour window and whether to paint the bathroom pale green or cream. 'We must be sure which we would like best,' she said under her breath, 'for it may have to last a long time.' Hannah had borrowed a book from the school library only last week, full of helpful hints on how to be a good housewife and mother. She tried to follow its advice with regard to Walton. 'Babies need plenty of fresh air,' the book had said, and Hannah felt virtuous as she remembered it. Walton looked up at her and smiled. Suddenly her attention was caught by loud voices coming from the allotment gardens.

'It was you. You've pinched the last of my spring cabbage!' shouted Alf.

'Aye, and what are you going to do about it?' a jeering voice answered.

Hannah rose up on her toes to peer over the hedge. It was Lancelot Cornish, standing with his hands on his hips and grinning at Alf. Hannah bit her lip. Lancelot was the same age and build as Alf, but she could see his older brother Ralph lounging on the path, holding Bob easily with one hand and carrying a stick in the other.

Enraged, Alf flung himself at Lancelot with his fists flailing and Lancelot fell back for a moment, his grin fading. But Ralph had thrown Bob aside and in two strides he reached Alf and pulled him off Lancelot. Holding him off with one hand, he felled him with a blow from his fist. Alf lay dazed as Ralph turned to Bob and instead found Hannah. She rushed at him, kicking him on the shins and pummelling him with her small fists.

'Leave my brothers alone, you great bully!' she screamed at him. Luckily for her, miners working at the other end of the allotments had heard the commotion and came running up to separate the two families. 'What's going on here?' shouted a burly hewer at Ralph. 'You fighting with bairns and lasses now, Ralph Cornish?'

'It's her went for me,' Ralph said, the bullying tone gone from his voice all of a sudden. 'And anyroad, Alf hit my little brother.'

Alf was picking himself up and fingering his jaw, which was swelling up alarmingly. 'They took my cabbage,' he mumbled thickly.

The hewer became even angrier and the other miners muttered among themselves. Stealing food was a serious offence at any time but stealing food during a lockout was heinous.

'I have a good mind to tell the polis!' one of them shouted. 'I will if you don't give the lad his cabbage back. Howay then, where have you got it hid?' The miners advanced on the Cornish brothers purposefully.

'Aw, I only meant to have a bit of a laugh with him,' said Lancelot. 'I'll get the bloody cabbage.' He walked over to the Cornish allotment, a patch of ground which was as untidy and full of rubbish as the Cornish house. He picked up the cabbage from behind a stand of stinging nettles and thrust it in Alf's face.

'Try that again and you'll have us all to answer to,' said the burly hewer. 'An' them wi' their da with a broken back an' all.' He spat on the ground at Ralph's feet to show his disgust and, satisfied, began to walk back to his own allotment. Lancelot shot a murderous look at Bob and Alf but in the end decided it was best to leave matters as they were, at least until he could catch one of them on his own. He contented himself with a snarled, 'I'll fettle you later!' and sloped off after his half-brother Ralph.

Hannah felt herself shaking with the reaction, and she grasped the handle of Walton's pram as hard as she could and gritted her teeth so that her brothers wouldn't see how upset she was. But if she had looked up she would have seen that neither of them was watching her, they were grim-faced as they gazed at each other.

'Best not let yourself be caught on your own, lad,' Alf advised Bob, and Bob nodded. 'Howay then, let's be off home,' Alf went on. 'Hannah, put the cabbage in the bottom of the pram.' So the Armstrongs made their way back down the path and cut on to the road for the village.

'You're just going to have to keep out of the way of those Cornishes,' Jake said heavily when told the story. From his bed in the chariot, he gazed keenly at the side of Alf's face, which was swelling up and turning purple. 'You'll be all right if you keep with the other men and don't let them catch you on your own.'

'That's what I told our Bob,' agreed Alf.

'There's a band concert on in the bishop's park this afternoon,' Nora put in. 'Why don't you all go together? You an' all, Betty, I can manage myself this afternoon.'

'Eeh, I don't know,' Betty started to object but Hannah could see by her face that she would really like to go. The concert was a big one, all the colliery bands for miles around were playing, for it was in aid of the locked-out miners and their families. And Betty loved to hear a brass band.

'Go on. It's Saturday, after all, there's not a lot to do, I can manage. And if you all stick together, those Cornish lads will leave you alone,' Nora urged her.

Hannah looked up anxiously at her mother, 'Can we go, Mam, me and Harry?'

'I don't know, I haven't forgotten the time you sneaked him in to school dinner and it cost me threepence I couldn't afford,' Nora said sternly and Hannah hung her head.

'Let them go, Nora, they get little enough enjoyment,' said Jake. Hannah flashed him a grateful glance.

'I'll give you a piggyback,' Alf offered Harry, and the little boy beamed. 'Mind, you'd best not be a nuisance or we'll leave you to find your own way home,' Alf threatened.

'I won't, Alf, honest,' Harry said earnestly.

They set off along the road to the footpath which led into the town of Bishop Auckland. Betty and Hannah walked together in front, laughing and talking, and Bob and Alf, with Harry on his shoulders, followed. They were not alone on the path. Quite a number of miners and their families were making their way to the bishop's park and for once the lockout seemed to be forgotten: there was a great deal of light-hearted banter as groups came together for the walk. By the time the children reached the town and turned into the straight length of Newgate Street which led down to the marketplace, the pavement was fairly taken up with miners and their families, good-naturedly jostling each other.

Hannah gazed around her, her eyes shining. It was a long time since she had been in this main shopping street and she loved it. She stopped to read one of the bills posted up on the walls between the shops:

CANADA WANTS

Men for farmers

Women for domestic work

Boys and youths to train as farmers

Apply Canada Chambers.

There was an address in London but she didn't have time to read that for Betty was looking back and calling her.

'Come on, Hannah! Don't dawdle, you know Mam said we had to stick together.'

Hannah hurried after them, her thoughts filled with what it would be like to go to Canada to work, to leave her family and friends and maybe never see them again. But then her attention was diverted by a handbill for the Hippodrome picture house. It was a cowboy film, *A Fighting Fool,* with Tom Mix, plus the story of Shackleton's expedition to the Antarctic – 'British pluck and endurance,' it said, and Hannah's heart swelled with pride. But then they saw a board outside a newsagent's which told them of Sinn Féin causing great havoc on the Durham coast with incendiary devices and explosives, and she shivered as though a cloud had passed over the sun.

The marketplace was full of stalls selling all kinds of goods; there were even some fishwives from Shields, selling cod, caller herrings, shrimps and mussels. She listened to them calling, 'Caller herring! Caller herring! Kippers, twopence a pair!' in their sing-song accent, which showed they were from farther north. They saw her interest and one called over to her encouragingly, 'Come buy, hinny, twopence a pair kippers, ha'penny, a bag of shrimps.'

But Hannah shook her head and hurried after Alf, who was striding towards the castle gates with Harry on his shoulders, the little boy wriggling with excitement until Alf lost patience and put him down on the ground to walk. Hannah had only a halfpenny and much as she liked shrimps she had to keep her money to put into one of the collecting boxes in the park.

The crowd of miners walked under the stone arches of the castle gates on to the broad gravelled path which led past the castle walls to the entrance of the park. The gate in the inner castle wall was open and the people from the pit villages looked in on this other world, the green lawns and carriageway which led to the ancient castle with its mullioned windows and stone portico. But they didn't stop to gape. In the distance they could hear the sound of a band playing, too far away to recognise the tune but close enough to make Harry skip along beside his big brothers. For, of course, on a family outing like this, Harry would stay with the lads; Hannah was abandoned to walk with Betty.

There was something of a bottleneck at the old iron kissing gate which led into the park proper, but at last they were in and free to run down the grassy banks to where the bands were playing.

'By, it's grand, Hannah, isn't it?' said Harry, his eyes bright with excitement so that he forgot for a moment that he was with the lads.

'It is, pet,' Hannah agreed. She wandered over to where the Dean and Chapter colliery band from Ferryhill were playing. A small, thin young man, smart in the navy blue and red of the band uniform, was playing a trumpet solo, pure and sweet with the deeper tones of the larger horns coming in to harmonise. She was soon lost in the music. The solo was followed by brisk Souza marches and then more local tunes, 'Bobby Shafto' and 'Blaydon Races'.

The afternoon was warm and soon Harry had joined a crowd of children paddling in the stream which ran along the bottom of the little valley on its way to join the river Wear. Hannah watched, thinking it would be nice to feel the cool water over her feet herself, but Betty vetoed it.

'You're too big now to be plodging with the bairns, our Hannah,' she said sternly, so Hannah contented herself with sitting, by the side of the stream and dangling her hand in the cool water, and Betty sat beside her.

'Well, will you just look at the snooty Armstrong lasses, playing with the bairns,' a voice said behind them. Hannah's heart sank. Not another confrontation with the Cornish family, she thought, not twice in one day. This was Kathleen Cornish sneering at her and Betty, she knew that even before she looked round.

Kathleen Cornish was standing, legs apart, hands on hips and grinning from ear to ear. She had her mother's bold good looks though her hair, a brassy red, was only slightly darker than that of her father, Wesley Cornish. She was wearing a short red dress which clashed oddly with her hair and when Hannah looked closer she realised that Kathleen was wearing rouge on her cheeks and her lips were smeared unevenly with lipstick.

'Get away from us, Kathleen Cornish,' said Betty harshly.

Hannah looked up at her sister in surprise; she had never heard Betty speak so rudely to anyone. Betty's lips were compressed in a straight line and her eyes were flashing. Hannah jumped up to range herself beside Betty, though she wasn't at all sure why she was doing it.

'Ooh, think you're better than I am, do you, Betty Armstrong?' Kathleen had lost her bantering tone and she thrust her head forwards as she spoke to Betty.

'I wouldn't have to be much to be better than you,' Betty said evenly and Hannah gasped. Though she hadn't a notion what this was all about, she bunched her fists, thinking that this was fighting talk and the taller, stronger Kathleen would go for Betty so she'd better be ready to help her sister. But Kathleen looked away from the two Armstrong girls to where Alf and Bob were standing with a few of their friends on the top of a nearby knoll.

'I'm not going to belt you, I've got better things to do,' she smirked, changing her attitude completely. 'Anyroad, your Alf doesn't think he's too good for me; he likes me, he does.'

'An' you're a big liar, Kathleen Cornish,' snapped Betty. 'Alf wouldn't touch you with a bargepole, he wouldn't.'

Kathleen only smiled knowingly and minced off up the hill to where the boys were gathered, her hips swaying scandalously from side to side.

'She's a disgrace to Winton, that one, her and her mother, both,' said a woman who was sitting on the grass watching her two toddlers playing in the water. 'Eeh, it's a good job they live in Winton village, if they were still in the colliery rows the men would run them out.'

Hannah turned startled eyes on the woman and recognised her as Mrs Hutchinson, who lived a couple of streets away from them.

'Our Alf wouldn't have anything to do with her,' Betty said again, speaking for Mrs Hutchinson's benefit, Hannah could tell. From the top of the knoll came the sound of male voices laughing and mixed in with it was the high giggling of a girl.

'Alf! Bob! Howay now, we have to be going if we want to get home. Harry's tired, he'll be asleep before we get there if we don't get a move on.' She walked to the water's edge and dragged a reluctant Harry out of the water.

'I don't want to go home,' wailed the boy but it was no use, Betty was drying his feet with the large piece of rag which was her handkerchief and forcing them into his boots.

'We have to go,' she repeated. 'Now come on, be a good lad.'

Alf and Bob were walking slowly down the bank to them. 'I don't know what the hurry is,' Bob grumbled.

'It's time Harry was back,' repeated Betty. 'You know we said we'd all stick together so you'll have to come with us.'

The bands were still playing as the Armstrongs straggled up the bankside to the path.

'Piggyback, Alf,' cried Harry, 'piggyback.'

'It's our Bob's turn,' Alf replied surlily. Bob knelt down on the ground so that Harry could climb on to his back.

'I'm not carrying you all the way, mind,' he warned, but he set off jauntily enough.

Hannah and Betty were left bringing up the rear. As they emerged through the castle gates into the marketplace, they could see that some of the market traders were packing up for the day. The fishwives from Shields had already gone to catch the train, leaving a strong smell of rotting fish around the stall.

'What did you mean about Kathleen Cornish?' Hannah asked Betty as they walked along Newgate Street. They were a few feet behind the boys and unlikely to be overheard. 'Did she do something bad?'

Betty laughed shortly. 'Oh, never mind, you're too young to know,' she said, infuriating her sister.

'I'm nearly thirteen,' said Hannah, lifting her chin and sticking out her chest. 'I will be left school altogether a year come Christmas, won't I?'

Betty glanced at her brothers, who were striding out, lengthening the distance between them. She came closer to Hannah and lowered her tone.

'Her and her mother have been working in the marketplace, earning a bit extra, like.'

Hannah gazed at Betty in bewilderment. 'Well, they're lucky to get work, aren't they? What's wrong with that?'

Betty sighed and leaned even closer to Hannah's ear. 'Dafty, I mean they've been going with men for money!'

Hannah blushed scarlet, as much with embarrassment at showing her ignorance as anything else. She quickened her step to catch up with the boys for she didn't want to hear any more. She knew what it meant: it meant Kathleen and her mother were whores and harlots. And she knew because the minister had read a lesson from the Old Testament about whores and harlots and she had looked the words up in the dictionary at school and it said a harlot was a woman who hired herself for sexual intercourse, so she had looked up 'sexual intercourse' and Miss High had caught her at it and rapped her knuckles with the ruler. Hannah pushed the thought of that day from her mind. Miss High had made her feel dirty, somehow.

The family trudged home, taking much longer than they had to come into the town earlier in the day. Bob got tired of carrying Harry and made him walk once they got to the footpath through the fields, but Harry went to sleep on his feet and had to be carried anyway, Bob and Alf taking turns. When they got to the gate of their house at last, Alf didn't come in.

'I'm going out,' he said and disappeared up the row.

Chapter Six

Hannah woke up in the early dawn bathed in sweat. The wall clock in the kitchen below chiming four o'clock had brought her out of her dreams. She remembered she was in her own bed at home, and not standing in the station at Bishop Auckland waving a tearful goodbye to Alf, who was going away to Canada to be a farmer. She turned over on to her back and flung the sheet from her body and lay allowing the slight draught from the open window to cool her through her nightie. Gradually, the feeling of loss left her and her heartbeat returned to normal. Alf wouldn't go to Canada, of course he wouldn't, she told herself, it was just that advertisement in Newgate Street which had preyed on her mind.

Downstairs in the front room the baby began to cry hungrily and through the thin boards which served both as bedroom floor and kitchen ceiling, she heard her mother moving quietly about, the murmur of Da's voice and Mam's soft answer. Beside her in the bed, Betty turned over in her sleep. No one was going anywhere, Hannah told herself sleepily, there was no reason to. The lockout would be over soon and the lads would go back to work and everything would be all right again.

She began to think of the choir practice to be held in the evening and the concert next week in the big chapel in Bishop Auckland. Maybe Timothy Durkin would be there, she thought. The last time he was home from school he had come to the meeting at Chapel and he had come to choir practice too.

She liked Timothy, she mused, he always spoke to her as though she was a person and not a tiresome little girl, as Alf so often did. Though Mr Hodgson insisted on calling him Master Durkin and the rest of the choir fought shy of calling him anything at all, Hannah thought of him as Timothy, in her mind at least.

She dropped into a doze and her dreams were brighter now; she was singing with Timothy before a huge audience, a duet she'd never heard before yet was singing in perfect harmony with him and he was looking down into her eyes and smiling and he looked as grand in his fine suit, tall and dark and broad-shouldered—

'Hannah? Hannah, will you wake up now? Come down and see to Walton. I'm busy with your da.'

It was her mother's voice cutting into her dream. Hannah opened her eyes and found it was broad daylight already. Betty was gone from the bed, she had to be at work in Mr Hudson's house by eight o'clock, and Hannah could smell the smoke from the kitchen fire, lit to boil the kettle for breakfast.

Jumping up, she tossed off her nightie and pulled on her shift, stiff drawers and cotton dress. The day was going to be another warm one, from the bedroom window she could see the sun shining on the field which lay by the end of the rows and the slight haze on the higher pasture. She paused for only a second and gazed out at the pit ponies grazing there, moving slowly along with their heads down and their tails swishing rhythmically against the flies. They were having a fine holiday, she thought, now they had got accustomed to the sunlight. Picking up her boots, she ran down the cool linoleum which covered the stairs and into the hot kitchen.

'The bairn's just woken up, I let him lie because he had such a bad night. I think he's cutting a tooth, poor babby,' Mam greeted her. She had filled a bowl of water from the set pot in the range and was taking it into the front room to give Jake a bed bath.

'I'll see to him then,' Hannah answered. She bent over the pram where Walton was struggling against the belt which they used to tie him in now he was getting big enough to move about; any time now he would be sitting up by himself. The baby was soaked, not just his nappy and nightgown but the blanket and sheets down to the waterproof jaconet sheet which protected his mattress, but he smiled angelically when he saw Hannah and, as usual, a wave of love washed over her.

'Come on, pet, let's have you comfortable,' she said softly as she lifted him up, and he crowed with delight. She soon had him lying naked on a towel on the rag rug where he kicked his tiny legs and watched her preparing the tin bath for him. By the time she had him washed, dressed and sitting on her knee as she fed him arrowroot mixed with a little diluted condensed milk, Nora had finished getting Jake ready for the day and she came into the kitchen to share a cup of tea with Hannah.

'I wish we could afford to buy proper milk for the bairn, he needs it,' she said wistfully. Her tone caused Hannah to look critically at the baby. He seemed fine to her, maybe a little pale but she put that down to the heat.

'He's all right, isn't he, Mam?' she asked.

'He'd be better if I could feed him myself or if I could buy fresh milk for him,' answered her mother. 'I wouldn't like him to get rickets.'

Alarm rose in Hannah. Anxiously she stared at Walton's legs lying on her lap; they seemed like any other baby's legs to her, a little bit bent, but so had Harry's legs been and they were straight enough now. But Harry had been breastfed for his first year, whereas Mam's milk had failed when Walton was only two months old. She thought of the children she knew at school, whose legs were bowed or knock-kneed with the rickets, and she definitely didn't want it to happen to Walton. One way or another they would have to get fresh milk from the farm if that was what he needed.

'Eeh, don't look so worried, Hannah,' said her mother. 'This lockout can't go on for ever. When the lads go back to work we'll be better able to afford things.'

When the lockout's over, thought Hannah as she poured fresh water into the tin bath and grated Sunlight soap into it to make a lather. She remembered when she was small and grown-ups were always saying, 'When the war is over, this or that would be better,' but somehow it never was. She rubbed vigorously at the baby's clothes before flinging them into a bowl of blue rinsing water and wringing them out. Though the day was warm and dry, it was Sunday and no one hung washing out on a Sunday, so she draped them over the brass line under the mantelpiece instead.

Afterwards she wheeled Walton's pram up the track to the high pasture so that he could watch the pit ponies in the field. She had no sugar to coax them to her but she pulled a few choice dandelions from the trackside and a sturdy Shetland pony of no more than ten hands came to her and delicately took the juicy stems from her hand. Below her in the village she could see children wending their way to chapel for Sunday school. Momentarily she felt guilty, she would go to chapel and choir practice in the evening, and she couldn't leave the baby for Mam to see to in the morning as well as the evening, not when she had Da to see to. And Betty had to work at the manager's house on Sunday mornings.

Hannah looked across the field to the farmhouse and buildings, idly wondering what it would be like to belong to a farmer's family and have lots of fresh milk and eggs. The thought put an idea into her head. She would ask Farmer Burton if he had any odd jobs she could do in exchange for milk for Walton, or maybe Mrs Burton would let her help in the house or with the children. After school, of course, or maybe on a Saturday. And when she wasn't needed to see to Walton.

'Nay, lass, we have no jobs going for girls,' said Mr Burton when she reached the farmyard. A big man with a red, weather-beaten face and kindly eyes, he paused in his work of sluicing down the milking shed to look at Hannah and Walton in his decrepit pram. 'Anyroad, aren't you still at school?' he went on.

'It's nearly the summer holidays,' Hannah pointed out. 'And I meant odd jobs, something I could do after school or maybe on Saturdays,' said Hannah.

'Nay, I'm sorry, lass,' the farmer repeated. He turned off the water hose, and took a large broom and began to sweep the water from the flags with the long, slow movements of the countryman. Hannah watched him for a moment and then tried again.

'Mr Burton, do you think Mrs Burton might have some odd jobs I can do? I don't need pay, just a can of milk two or three times a week for the bairn.'

The farmer paused again. 'I don't think so, lass,' he said, but then he saw Hannah's disappointed expression and added, 'Look, lass, this farm belongs to Lord Akers, same as the mine. While your da's on strike, I'd be in trouble if I gave you work, do you see?'

'My da's not on strike,' said Hannah.

'Well, locked out then. When he goes back to work it will be different.'

'He's not locked out, his back's broken,' said Hannah.

The farmer stopped what he was doing and walked over to where she was standing holding Walton's pram.

'Are you Jake Armstrong's lass?' he asked, and Hannah nodded. Mr Burton shook his head sympathetically, tut-tutting aloud. 'I was right sorry when I heard about your da's accident,' he said. Hesitating for only a moment, he went on, 'Just you go on up to the dairy and tell the wife I say to give you a can of milk for the bairn.'

'I'll have to work for it, though, we're not to take charity, Da says.'

'Aye, well, I'm sure Mrs Burton will think of something you can do. Now go on, like I tell you.'

Hannah turned the pram round in the dusty yard, which smelled so strongly of manure it was almost as hard on the nostrils as the coke ovens, and pushed the uncomplaining Walton over to the dairy on the side of the house. She didn't have to ask, for Mrs Burton had heard her voice and had come to the door of the dairy to see who it was.

'Give the lass a can of milk, Dot,' called Mr Burton.

'But –'

'Go on, give her a can of milk,' he repeated when his wife hesitated. 'It's Jake Armstrong's bairn, you know, the one what had his back broke in the pit.'

'I'll do some odd jobs for you, Mrs Burton, I'll do anything,' Hannah said eagerly. She stood at the door of the dairy, hesitating to go in on the clean floor with her dirty boots.

'No need,' said the farmer's wife as she dipped a shining steel measure into a bucket of milk.

'I have to, Mrs Burton, or I can't take the milk,' Hannah insisted.

The woman folded her arms across her ample chest and pursed her lips as she looked down at her. 'Well, I suppose you can turn the butter churn while I scald out the milk cans,' she decided. 'Mind you clean your boots before you come in, there's a scraper by the wall if you look. Will the bairn be all right if you leave him outside?'

'Oh yes, he's asleep, Mrs Burton,' Hannah said happily and hurried to do what she was told.

'Did you go asking Fanner Burton for milk?' demanded Nora when Hannah came home and triumphantly put the can of fresh milk on the kitchen table. 'Haven't I told you we take no charity here?'

'It's not charity, Mam, I helped Mrs Burton with the churning and she gave me the milk in payment. And she says I can go up three times a week after school and I can take the baby an' all, if I like.'

'Well, I don't know . . . ' Nora was doubtful at first. 'It doesn't seem much to do in return for two gills of milk.'

'It is, Mam,' Hannah reassured her. 'It's quite hard work, really. And it means we have milk for Walton and maybe some to spare to make a barley pudding or maybe even rice pudding, doesn't it?'

Nora nodded her head. It was true, fresh milk would allay her fears for Walton and a milk pudding might even stimulate Jake's appetite. He was taking less and less nourishment these days, sometimes he wouldn't eat anything at all and he was becoming thinner every day, his skin taking on a translucent, bluish hue which frightened her. She had asked Dr Short if there was nothing more he could do, or if Jake should go back into the county hospital for tests, but the dour Scottish doctor only shook his head gravely. Still, she hoped against hope that one day Jake's shattered back would begin to heal and the nerves knit together. The thought was the only thing which saved her from complete despair.

*

Timothy Durkin was already in chapel when Hannah took her place beside Betty. She returned his quick smile of greeting shyly, suddenly conscious of the fact that her Sunday dress of faded blue cotton was a hand-me-down from Betty and was beginning to be tight round her chest. It didn't matter, she told herself, that the skirt was short too, short skirts were fashionable. Wasn't Amy, the doctor's daughter, wearing a skirt which barely covered her knees?

'Stop looking over at the lads,' Betty whispered fiercely. 'You'll catch it from Alf if he sees you making a show of yourself.'

Hannah blushed and looked down at her hymn book as the preacher announced the first hymn. They were soon standing to sing 'Summer suns are glowing', but she could hear Timothy's baritone above the rest, and she was conscious of him all through the prayers and sermon.

Betty went home after the service while Hannah stayed behind for choir practice. She stood quietly in her place, waiting for Mr Hodgson to call the choir to order, but Mr Hodgson seemed in no hurry tonight. He and the other men were discussing the lockout. Prayers had been said during the service for an early end to the dispute.

'The labourer is worthy of his hire,' said one man, 'doesn't it say so right here in the Bible? We're only asking to keep what we've got; why, man, if they get their way we won't have a living wage.'

'I doubt some of the men cannot last out,' said another. 'There is a great deal of distress in the whole coalfield. It's not for ourselves – we could manage, I think – but it's the women and the bairns.'

The men were nodding their heads in agreement when Mr Hodgson noticed Timothy standing nearby, well within earshot. 'Now then,' he said, 'this is not the time to be discussing politics. We're here to practise for the concert next Saturday night in Bishop Auckland.' He nodded meaningfully in the direction of the agent's son and Timothy lifted his chin and stared right back at him, a challenge in his eyes. 'I am not a spy, I would not tell anyone of anything I heard in chapel,' he said.

'No, no, of course not, Master Durkin,' Mr Hodgson replied. 'Now, come along, choir, get into your places, we have a full programme to go through tonight. There is only one more rehearsal, that's on Tuesday evening at six o'clock, and I expect everyone to be on time.'

Soon they were deep into rehearsing the hymns and songs which formed the programme for the concert. Mostly hymns, of course, but one or two sacred songs and even a couple of local songs, for the concert was expected to draw in the townsfolk, not just their own people. They practised for an hour and a half until at last Mr Hodgson called a halt.

'That's enough for now, then,' he said. 'Master Durkin, perhaps you'd be so kind as to stay behind with Hannah and we'll go through your duet. It won't take long, I'm sure Hannah knows it well by now and you'll pick it up quickly, you always do.'

They were to sing 'Count Your Blessings' and Hannah did indeed know it well; she had been singing it at least once a day since it was given to her by the choirmaster. But she found it sounded altogether different when Timothy's voice was joined to hers, and soon forgot her shyness of him as she lost herself in the music. All too soon Mr Hodgson pronounced himself satisfied and they were free to go home.

'If you wait a moment while I lock up, I'll walk you home, Hannah,' said Mr Hodgson. 'It's a mite late for a young lass to be out on her own.'

'I'll see Hannah safely back to her house,' Timothy offered.

Mr Hodgson hesitated for only a moment before agreeing. 'Very well, Master Durkin. It's very good of you, I'm sure. Well, goodnight, then. Goodnight, Hannah.'

Once outside, Hannah's shyness overcame her and she walked along by Timothy's side, desperately trying to think of something to say, anything.

'You don't have to come all the way to the door,' she ventured at last. 'It's just along the road here.'

'It's no bother,' said Timothy. He drew a paper packet out of his pocket and offered it to her. 'Won't you have a caramel?'

'Thank you,' said Hannah, awkwardly taking one of the sweets. She unwrapped it, put it in her mouth and then wished she hadn't, for how was she going to be able to talk to him with her mouth full of toffee?

Timothy was asking about the chapel in Bishop Auckland. 'Is it a large place? Will there be a big congregation?' he wanted to know.

They had arrived at the gate of the yard and Hannah paused, swallowing hastily. The sticky toffee seemed to clog her throat so that when she tried to speak her voice came out huskily.

'It's . . . ' She coughed and tried again. 'It is big,' she began, but then she caught sight of Mam looking out at her from the kitchen window.

'Is that you, Hannah? Who's that with you, is it Mr Hodgson? Bring him in, do, don't keep him standing at the gate.'

'No, Mam, it's Timothy Durkin.'

'Who? Bring him in, whoever it is. If he's been good enough to walk home with you, he's good enough to bring in and thank properly.'

'I don't think–' Timothy began, but Hannah was already walking up the yard and, after a moment's hesitation, he followed.

'Timothy is in the choir, Mam,' said Hannah as they went inside. She looked around the kitchen, seeing it with new eyes as she remembered the hallway of the Durkin house where the choir had sung carols last Christmas. The old wooden table had a worn cover of American oilcloth and behind it was a mahogany press which had belonged to Nora's mother and had seen better days. The black-leaded range shone brightly enough but now that the dinner was over the fire had been allowed to go out; there was coal only for cooking during the lockout so the iron kettle was not in its usual place, singing on the bar.

She saw her mother's face was a fierce red and suddenly Hannah remembered that the last time Mam had seen Timothy was in the pit yard when his father had so humiliated her.

'Timothy brought me home from the choir practice, Mam,' she said lamely.

'I'm sure it was very good of Master Durkin,' Mam said, not looking at Hannah but staring hard at Timothy. 'I'm sorry we can't offer you a cup of tea, Master Durkin. As you can see, we have no coal for the fire.'

Timothy looked as embarrassed as Nora. 'No, no, don't think of it, I must be on my way home. I have to be . . . I must get back . . . Goodbye, Hannah, Mrs Armstrong.' He turned and almost ran down the yard to the gate.

'Why did you bring a lad like that in here?' Nora demanded.

'But you said to bring him in, Mam,' Hannah answered. She was mortified, for she had seen the shabby kitchen as Timothy saw it, poverty-stricken, and she had seen the shock in his eyes. Miserably she stared up at her mother. 'He was just helping Mr Hodgson, bringing me home.'

'You could have come home yourself, it's nobbut a stride,' snapped Nora. 'Now get away up to bed, Betty's been there this last half-hour. What the agent's son wants coming to our chapel I don't know. Why doesn't he stick to his own kind?'

'He likes to sing in the choir, Mam, he's a good singer,' said Hannah.

'Aye, well, do they not sing in their church, like?' retorted her mother. 'Now go on, away to bed with you.'

Timothy was walking through the fields to Durham Road, his mind full of conflicting images. In all his seventeen years he had never been inside one of the miners' cottages until now, even though he had lived on the outskirts of Winton all his life. He was shaken by the poverty he had seen. To be unable to boil a kettle because there was no coal in the coalhouse? A miner's coalhouse? Of course, he knew by what his father had said almost every day since he came home from school for the holidays that it was their own fault, the men were on strike, even though they themselves disputed the fact, saying they were locked out. But how could Hannah's father be on strike? Wasn't he disabled, injured in the pit? Surely he should have a coal allowance?

Timothy left the fields behind him and walked up the metalled road which led to Durham Road and his home. For the first time he was beginning to question his father's views.

Chapter Seven

The evening of the concert was fine and dry so the choir could walk into Bishop Auckland from Winton without fear of getting their feet wet, an important thing from Hannah's point of view because her boots had got too tight and she had to walk in sandshoes. The chapel in Cockton Hill was thronged with people for all the seats had been sold. She had been worried that Timothy wouldn't come and she would have to sing the duet with Hodgson, but as she walked up the path with the other girls of the choir she saw his tall figure standing in the porch waiting for them. There was not much time for greetings; the stewards were hurrying them into position along with the other choirs. There was to be an address by the minister before the concert and it was almost time to begin.

'Hallo, Hannah,' Timothy found time to say. 'You were right, it is a big chapel, almost as big as St Andrew's.'

Hannah smiled at him in relief, not only because he had actually turned up but also because he seemed the same as ever. But she couldn't say anything for Mr Hodgson was hushing them into silence and in the main body of the church the murmuring of voices had stopped as the audience looked to the front expectantly.

Mr Hughes, the minister, began with a short prayer and thanked everyone for coming before getting to the main business of the evening.

'As you know, this evening's proceeds are for the relief of the distress in the town and surrounding villages. Consequently, if anyone finds it in their hearts to add a little extra to their ticket money, there will be a retiring collection plate by the door as you leave after the concert. As the good Lord has blessed you, so we ask for your donations to this worthy cause. Now, with no more ado, we will do our best to entertain you and earn your contributions.'

Hannah's heart fluttered with nervousness as the organist began to play the grand organ with its silver pipes reaching to the roof. But somehow she forgot her misgivings as the choirs went from hymns to sacred songs interspersed by soloists. The choir from Winton sang 'Bobby Shafto', the lament of a young girl of long ago who lost her lover when he sailed away to London to become the Member of Parliament for Durham. And then it was time for her duet with Timothy.

There was a rustle of surprise when they went to the front, the girl in her shabby blue dress and the tall boy in his fine broadcloth suit. Quite a few people recognised him and there were some raised eyebrows in the pews. They sang 'Count Your Blessings' and, for an encore, an old miner's song, 'The Caller', their voices ringing out clear and true, each the perfect complement for the other. The song was about a knocker-up man who went round the miners' houses, calling weary men who were due to go on shift from their beds.

'Ho, marras, 'tis the Caller cries,
And his voice in the gloom of the night mist dies.'

It was the third and fourth verses that affected the audience, as Mr Hodgson had thought they would when he included them in the programme. The clear young voices filled the crowded chapel.

'The collier sleeps e'en now he's dreaming
of a pure bright world, and loved ones there.
He basks in the rays of fortune beaming
In some far land full and fair.

Dream on, thou poor and ill-used collier,
slaves may have visions bright.
There's one above who deems thee holier
than the wealthiest in His sight.'

As Mr Hodgson had hoped, the song was a great success and the collecting plate was full when the crowd left the chapel.

Hannah was only thankful she hadn't forgotten her lines. Afterwards, when the choirs were invited into the schoolroom to partake of the supper laid on for them, she found herself overwhelmed by the number of people who wished to congratulate her and Timothy. There was only one thing which marred the occasion for her. Timothy suddenly decided he had to go home early.

It was just after a distinguished-looking gentleman came up to them. 'Well, Timothy,' he said, a rather puzzled expression on his face. 'I didn't expect to see a Durkin here, let alone one taking part in the concert. Though you sang very well, my boy, very well indeed.'

'Thank you, sir,' Timothy answered, and after a moment the gentleman moved on.

'I have to go, I'm sorry,' Timothy blurted and hurried out before Hannah could even say goodnight to him.

'Well, sir, what do you think you are about?'

It was a few days after the concert and as Timothy came down to breakfast he found his father waiting for him, in such an angry mood that he didn't even bother to greet his son, merely barking the question at him.

'Good morning, Father,' Timothy said. He helped himself to bacon and eggs from the hotplate on the sideboard, more for something to do than because he felt hungry. In fact, his appetite had left him as he realised that Mr Hall, the gentleman who had greeted him on the evening of the concert, must have spoken to his father, as he had dreaded he would do.

'Well, damn you, what have you to say for yourself?' demanded his father. Timothy was granted a few minutes' grace to gather his thoughts as the housemaid brought in a fresh pot of coffee.

'Thank you, May,' he said to her as she picked up the empty pot and took it out of the room.

'I'm waiting,' said Mr Durkin, once she had closed the door behind her.

'I'm not sure what you mean, Father.'

'You know what I'm talking about all right. What sort of a fool do you think I looked when old Hall told me my own son was taking part in a concert at the Primitive Methodists' and not only that, he actually sang some damn fool song about the poor miners?'

Mr Durkin's face had been getting redder and redder and his voice rose angrily until he was almost shouting.

Timothy looked down at his plate but he hardly saw the congealing food there. Mr Hall hadn't taken long to rush to his father with the story, he thought bitterly. A businessman in the town, Timothy had been surprised to see him at the concert; he had thought none of his father's friends would be there.

'You'd better answer me, my lad, or by God I'll take a strap to you, big as you are!'

Timothy put down his unused knife and fork and stared his father straight in the eye. 'I joined the choir at Winton Chapel,' he said. 'You know I enjoy singing and they have a good choir for a mining village. I'm not hurting anything by going there.'

'Not hurting anything? Why, you've made me the laughing stock of the club! My son going to a Methodist chapel, I'll not have it, do you hear? Church of England, that's the only church for gentlemen of our class and don't you forget it. How dare you shame me by going to that bloody place?'

'It's perfectly respectable, Father, else why was Mr Hall there?' Timothy was stung into replying, rashly, as he saw by his father's face, which was turning from red to purple.

'Where Mr Hall goes is his business! But you will not go there again, do you hear me? And of all things, you not only go to a concert in aid of the wretched miners, you have to take part in it! When you know of this dispute? How on earth do you expect us to get the stubborn fools to be reasonable and go back to work at a realistic wage if people are for ever giving them handouts? The wages bill was crippling the industry, haven't I said it time and time again? These people don't seem to realise how well off they are, nothing to worry about but putting in a fair week's work and getting paid for it.'

'They don't seem to be very well off to me,' Timothy muttered.

Mr Durkin practically exploded. 'No, of course they're not now, but whose fault is that? All they have to do is go back to work and earn their pay, haven't I just told you?' He stood up from the table, upsetting his coffee cup over the damask tablecloth. Striding over to the fireplace, he turned with his back to it, the better to be able to glare down at his son.

Unhappily, Timothy watched the brown stain spread on the cloth. He thought of the poverty he had seen in the village, especially in Hannah's house, where her father lay, injured in one of the pits his father was responsible for. He remembered the shock he had been hard put to hide when he entered the kitchen of the house, a house without even the means to boil a kettle now the mine was laid idle. But his father was talking again.

'We could handle the miners, even the leaders and troublemakers. Or I could, at least, and most of the other agents and owners too. All you have to do for some of them is give them free beer. Aye, we could handle them all right if it wasn't for these damn left-wing, teetotalling Methodists.'

'Father, a labourer is worthy of his hire.' Timothy quoted a saying which he'd heard often in the chapel

the last few times he had been there. This only enraged
Mr Durkin further.

'Get out of my sight!' he yelled, causing Mary, who
was just coming in to clear the breakfast table, to drop
the tray with a tremendous clatter, which served to
emphasise his words. 'Go to your room, sir, how dare
you presume to judge me? Get out this minute! You won't
get another chance to defy me, you'll go to my brother's
house in Yorkshire until it's time for you to go back to
school. And think yourself lucky I don't throw you out
of the house now, without a penny to bless yourself with!
Get out!'

It was hard to tell whether the last 'Get out!' was
directed at Mary or Timothy; the poor girl turned and
ran for the kitchen in a flood of tears and Timothy had
no option but to retire to his room.

He was not allowed to stay there long. Mr Durkin lost
no time in getting in touch with his brother by telephone,
and Timothy was packed off on the afternoon train for
York, there to spend the rest of his summer holiday in
the gloomy house of his father's elder brother.

Hannah never knew why Timothy stopped coming to
chapel or choir practice. She was unhappy about it at first,
but she was so busy during the summer, what with seeing to baby Walton and doing odd jobs for Mrs Burton,
the farmer's wife, that she had little time to think about

anything else. By reading snippets from the old *Auckland Chronicles* which Mrs Holmes gave the Armstrongs, she knew that the miners wanted a National Wages Board but the owners would not agree to it. The owners insisted that the men give in and agree to their terms before they would be allowed back to work. Peter Lee, the Durham miners' leader, told a *Chronicle* reporter, 'Some of our men, if they went back at the price offered, would have very little over two pounds a week.'

But the men knew they had little chance of holding out and despair hung like a cloud over the pit rows, lightened only by the pit-pony Derby which was held one hot afternoon, in aid of the miners' families. Mr Hodgson and the other Methodists frowned on such a way of making money but there was no doubt it was a great success, with the ponies being ridden by their drivers. The mine managers turned a blind eye to the proceedings for, after all, the ponies were getting fat and needed exercising and, in any case, they knew that they were winning the dispute.

Alf and Bob came home full of excitement about the races.

'There was a Lockout Handicap and a Workingman's Club Stakes,' Bob told his mother and Hannah. 'And I had a threepenny bet in the Aged Miners' Cup and I won at three to one so I had a shilling back.'

Hannah was slightly scandalised that her brother should have had a bet on a horse, even though it was only a pit pony, but she smiled delightedly at him nevertheless. 'That's grand, Bob,' she said, and meant it. At least, she thought, Bob seemed to be settling down with the family now and there had been no more trouble with the Cornish brothers, thank goodness.

The following week, the miners had to give in to the owners' demands and go back to work on reduced wages. The dispute was over and everyone felt that it would be a good job when 1921 was over, it had not been a good year. There had not even been a Miners' Gala in Durham city that July, for the pit folk had nothing to celebrate.

'Kathleen Cornish and her mother are coming down the row,' reported Harry as he came in from playing cricket in the back lane with his friends. He carried the fire shovel with him, for it had been the bat, and the stumps were chalked on the wall of the coalhouse.

His mother looked startled. 'Sally Cornish? I didn't think she had the brass to show her face in the rows after the way those two carried on during the lockout.'

It was Harry's turn to look surprised. 'What did they do, Mam?' he asked.

'Never you mind,' was all Nora had time to say before she saw Sally and her daughter Kathleen turn into the backyard and walk up to the door.

'Are you there, Mrs Armstrong?'

Sally didn't wait for an answer before marching into the kitchen. The family were all home except for Alf, who was on shift at the pit, and Betty, who was at her work at the Hudson house. Alf had graduated from the coal screens and now worked as a putter underground on the adult shift system. Mrs Cornish looked round the room and nodded at Jake in his chariot in the corner.

'How are you, Jake? I was meaning to come and see you but you know how it is when there's a family to see to,' she said, her tone full of solicitude. Nora gasped at it. It was almost a year since Jake had been injured and none of the Cornish family had even enquired after him. And they would not have been welcome in the rows if they had.

Hannah, who was sitting with Walton on her knee while she fed him mashed potatoes and gravy, paused with the spoon halfway to his mouth and stared at Kathleen. The older girl looked different from the last time she had seen her; her face was devoid of make-up and her carroty hair hung lank and dull. Baby Walton lifted his hand to the spoon and cried at this sudden cessation of his feeding and Hannah hastily put the spoon to his mouth.

'What do you want, Sally?' asked Nora, her voice grim.

'It's not me, it's our Kathleen, poor lass. She's fallen wrong with a bairn and I want your Alf to do the right thing by her.'

Hannah stared at her. What on earth had it to do with Alf? She'd known other girls in the rows to be expecting a baby before they were married, but usually all it meant was that they married their sweethearts a bit earlier than intended. But Alf was not Kathleen's sweetheart, of course he wasn't. Alf was only just sixteen and Kathleen was almost twenty.

'Alf? It has nothing to do with our Alf!' said Jake, echoing Hannah's thoughts.

'Aye but it has!'

Mrs Cornish put her hands on her hips and glared determinedly from him to Nora. Beside her, Kathleen nodded her head vigorously to support her mother's assertion.

'Don't you come here with your tales about my lad,' Nora warned them, her cheeks turning pink and her eyes flashing. 'Hannah, take Harry and the babby into the front room out of the way. Whatever lies these two are saying are not for young ears.'

'Aw, Mam, I'm hungry, I want my tea,' Harry wailed, but his mother cut him off short.

'Do as you're told, go on with Hannah,' she snapped. 'Take a piece of bread and dripping if you're hungry.' Hannah picked a slice of bread from the plate on the table and smeared beef dripping on it for Harry. She closed the door to the front room behind her and sat down by the fireplace with the baby leaning on her shoulder sleepily. Even with the door closed her sharp ears could pick up everything that was said in the kitchen.

'Our Alf hasn't been with your lass,' Mam said flatly.

'Well, she says he has,' retorted Sally Cornish. 'An' I believe her an' all. If our Kathleen says the bairn's Alf's then that's whose it is. And I want to know what he's going to do about it.'

'Nothing, that's what he'll do,' said Mam, her voice rising. 'Why, by all reports she has been with all sorts down in the marketplace at Auckland. I dare say she could name any amount of lads as could be responsible for her condition, but Alf is not one of them, do you hear me?'

'Don't you shout at me. I'm as good as you are, I'm as good as any of the Armstrongs. I'll set our Wesley on to you, that I will do, and our Ralph an' all.'

'Oh, aye, like the big bully set on Bob, a lad half his size. If you think we're feared of you or your bullyboys, you're sadly mistaken. You're no better than you should be yourself. Don't think you weren't seen plying your mucky trade in the town, there's many a one from the rows saw you.'

Against Hannah's shoulder, the baby stirred restlessly, disturbed by the anger in his mother's voice, and Hannah cuddled him, rocking him in her arms. Harry came and stood close to her; the raised voices had upset him too.

'Well! You bloody evil-minded old – ' Sally began, but she was interrupted by Kathleen.

'Mam, don't, you know I need Alf,' she said.

'Aye, I bet you do,' Jake said grimly. 'Eeh, if I could only get up from this damn bed –'

'Whisht now, Jake, don't take on,' Nora put in swiftly. 'It's bad for you to get upset, you know it is. I won't let them get away with this, don't worry now.'

'We're not wanting to get away with anything,' said Sally, changing her tone altogether. 'But my lass has been taken down and your Alf is responsible. All we want is for him to face up to his responsibilities, own up and give the bairn a father. It's no more than anybody would expect, you can't always have your fun and get away scot free.'

'Get out of my house, the pair of you, and don't come near us again!' Jake suddenly roared. 'Whores, the pair of you, the lass as bad as her mother! What do you take us for, bloody fools? If the lass has no father for her bairn, that doesn't mean she can name the first lad she thinks of. Anyroad, she's no worse than her mother, is she? You came back here to Winton with Ralph a nameless babby and no sign of a father for him. An' worse, you took Meg Cornish's man away from her, leaving her to bring up her bairns on her own; don't think the folk round here have forgotten about that. Not that Wesley Cornish amounts to anything, big nowt that he is. Get out of my sight, I'm warning you, and if you send your lads round here I'll set the polis on them.'

Hannah was sitting with one arm round Harry by now and the other holding the baby. Her heart was beating painfully against her ribs. She was sure Ralph and Lancelot

Cornish, even Wesley, would be coming round and forcing Alf to marry Kathleen somehow, and if he wouldn't do it they would get their revenge on the Armstrongs.

'We're going, we're going,' she heard Sally say, sounding less sure of herself all of a sudden. 'But we're not beaten yet. You ask Alf if he's been with our Kathleen when he comes in. He'll be a bloody liar if he says he hasn't.'

It was very quiet after Kathleen Cornish and her mother had gone. Harry moved away from Hannah's protective arm, remembering that he was a big boy now and old enough to go to school. Hannah laid the sleeping baby in his cot and after hesitating for a short while, she opened the door which connected the front room with the kitchen.

Jake was lying, white and silent, his eyes closed. Her mother was in the act of lifting the iron pan on to the fire to warm up the boiled meat pudding which would be Alf's dinner when he came in from the pit.

'Is my dinner ready now, Mam?' Harry asked, his fears forgotten as his hunger returned.

'Yes, sit down at the table, it's waiting in the oven,' his mother said quietly. In the distance they heard the sound of the hooter at the pit, signalling the change of shifts. 'Hannah, bring in the bath tin, Alf will be here in a minute.'

'Yes, Mam.'

Hannah went into the backyard and took the bath down from where it was hanging on a nail on the wall.

She brought it in and placed it on the clippie mat before the fire and got the ladle tin, ready to ladle the water from the boiler as soon as Alf walked in the door. If his bath wasn't ready for him, Alf was usually so hungry he would eat his dinner in his pit dirt, which meant that Hannah had to wait until he had had his bath so that she could empty it and clear away any mess, and that made her late in going up to Burton's farm. But as it happened, she need not have bothered. As soon as Alf walked into the house, her mother turned to her.

'Go on, Hannah, get away up to the farm now. I can see to Alf's bath and put the little 'uns to bed. Anyroad, Betty will be coming in just now, she'll give me a hand.'

Hannah didn't argue, she knew her parents wanted her out of the way while they talked to Alf. 'Righto, I'll be as quick as I can,' she said. 'I think there'll just be the eggs to wash tonight, Mrs Burton might give me a few to bring home an' all.' She took her coat down from the hook on the back door and went out quickly without looking at Alf. But not too quickly to miss Harry's eager question to his brother.

'Alf, Mrs Cornish says you took their Kathleen down. Did you, Alf? What's taken down mean, Alf?'

Chapter Eight

'You've been a proper fool, Alf,' said Jake.

It was the week after Kathleen Cornish and her mother had visited the Armstrongs and by now the news was all over Winton, even the children in school were saying that Alf Armstrong would have to marry Kathleen Cornish. For the trouble was that Kathleen and her mother had retired from their trade when the pit was working again and, what was more, someone had seen Alf with her up among the bunny banks. So no one bothered any more about telling Hannah to leave the room when the subject was being discussed.

Alf hung his head, his face the colour of beetroot. 'Aye, I know, Da,' he muttered.

'Well, I still think she's blaming you for another lad's work,' said Nora. 'An' I don't see why you should marry that piece. So I've been thinking. You should go away to work; I hear there's work in the south, you can go there.

Why, if you look in the *Northern Echo* you can see loads of advertisements for strong working lads.'

Hannah felt a sudden tightening in her chest – was Alf going to have to leave Winton? Agitated, she turned to the baby in his pram so her back was to the others and they couldn't see how dismayed she was.

'What, leave the pit?' Alf was startled enough to raise his face and look his mother straight in the eye, something he hadn't wanted to do these last few days.

'What's wrong with that? The pit hasn't done this family any favours, has it? No, you'd be better off in a nice clean factory, I saw one on the news at the pictures the last time I was there.'

'But, Mam, what'll you do without my money?' asked Alf. 'We're hard put to manage as it is.'

'An' how much do you think I'd see of your money once that lass gets her claws into you?' demanded Nora. 'No, me and your da's been talking it over and we think that's the best thing for you to do.'

'I don't want to go away,' Alf said miserably.

'Aw, don't go like a soft bairn on us now, lad,' said Jake. 'If you were man enough to go with a woman you're man enough to go away to work. You'll be able to come home sometimes, the lasses do it all the time, go away to place and come home for a summer holiday every year.'

Which is true enough, thought Hannah. She was dreading the day when she might have to go away herself in search of work, for there was precious little in Winton or even in Bishop Auckland.

'It's not right,' said Bob hotly. 'If one of us can leave the pit and go away it should be me. You know I want to work with Uncle Billy on the carrier wagon, don't you?'

Nora looked at his flushed face sadly. 'I'm sorry lad, I am,' she said. 'It's just the way things have turned out, isn't it? It's nobody's fault but that lying Kathleen Cornish.'

Bob looked from his mother to Alf, a picture of frustration, then he muttered something which Hannah didn't catch and, picking up his cap from the side table, he planted it on his head and rushed out of the door.

'He'll get over it,' his mother commented as she watched him leave the yard.

Alf and his mother went into Bishop Auckland to the Labour Exchange to see what sort of jobs were available in the south of England, though Alf had to be persuaded into it. But the weeks were passing by and Kathleen's belly was getting bigger, perhaps bigger than it should have been if it was conceived when she said it was, Nora hinted darkly to anyone who would listen. Mrs Cornish lay in wait to catch Nora on her way to the store so she could demand to know when Alf was going to do right by her lass. And in the pit, Wesley Cornish was making sarcastic remarks, whenever Alf was near, about lads that wanted their fun but didn't want to pay for it. So far,

Nora had managed to be vague about setting a date for the wedding but she knew she couldn't keep it up for ever.

'You'll likely be able to make good money,' she encouraged him as they boarded the bus which nowadays went all the way into the marketplace in Auckland. 'You'll be able to get decent lodgings and still send us a bit home.'

He gazed at her, his normally open face full of trouble. But it was an altogether brighter Alf who came home a couple of hours later.

'We're to go to Oxford,' he said. 'There's a party of us going down to be apprenticed to the Morris Car Company. Just think, I'm going to make cars. And the pay is good when you've learned the job, and they find you lodgings an' all.'

Hannah beamed at him. Alf liked cars, he always watched them with great interest on the rare occasions when one came into the village, other than the bull-nosed Morris coupé which belonged to Dr Short. She could see her brother was thrilled to be actually going to work where cars were made.

'Aye, well, keep it to yourself for now,' warned Jake. 'You don't want it to be getting about that you're going, do you? Best if it doesn't get back to the Cornishes.'

Alf looked worried. 'But there's a group of us going, Da, about twenty, they might hear of it. Though luckily I'm the only one from Winton.'

'It'll be all right, you'll see,' said Nora. 'Everything will turn out champion.'

Bob muttered something which Hannah couldn't catch and she looked across the table at him enquiringly.

'What did you say, Bob?'

'I said I think I'll go over to Consett and see Grandma this weekend,' he replied, staring hard at his mother as if challenging her to say that they couldn't afford the fare. But Nora merely nodded in understanding.

'Aye, that's a good idea, Bob,' she said. 'It's a while since you went over to see her.' She would just have to put off her visit to Weardale to see Jane until she had saved the fare again, she thought. Maybe when she went to the Co-op store she would buy a pretty card and send it to her, the stamp would only cost a halfpenny.

Hannah went to bed that night sad that Alf was going away. 'At least he's not going to Canada,' she whispered to herself remembering the poster in Newgate Street. 'Not halfway across the world.' But what with Jane going away to the sanatorium and now Alf leaving home, she felt the family was breaking up, though she knew it was silly to think like that. Alf would come home some time and so would Jane as soon as she was better. And she *would* get better, Hannah told herself, the sanatorium would make her better, even if it did take a long time to do it.

*

So Alf went to Oxford, or rather to a place called Cowley, Oxon. Hannah puzzled about that until she could look it up in the atlas at school and found that Cowley was to Oxford rather as Winton was to Bishop Auckland, a separate place really but almost a suburb. And Oxon was to Oxford city as County Durham was to Durham city, it was just a different way of putting it.

He managed to get away without the Cornish family finding out until it was too late, and their fury was a sight to behold.

'Your Alf's done wrong by my lass,' screamed Sally. She had marched round to the Armstrong house as soon as she heard about Alf's going and now she stood at the back door, her hair falling over her red face and her once blue dress stained a patchy black. The floral-print apron tied round her waist was, if anything, even dirtier than her dress and her feet were thrust into an unlaced pair of men's boots. She bunched her hands into fists as Nora went to the door, and, seeing it, Hannah hastily put the baby in his cot pram and went to support her mother.

'I wasn't going to let you blame Alf for something he didn't do,' Nora said determinedly and she took hold of the door with one hand and pushed it shut so that Sally had to jump back hastily.

'Close the door on me, would you?' she bawled, spittle spouting from her mouth and dribbling down her chin. She took her fist and banged loudly on the door till Hannah thought she could see it shake.

'Hey, what's all this?'

Hannah looked out of the window and saw that the noise had brought their neighbours to the gate and Mr Holmes, the overman, was walking up the yard.

'These bloody Armstrongs think they're better than the rest of us,' shouted Sally. 'There's my Kathleen so badly she cannot get out of bed, all because that Alf Armstrong's deserted her.'

'You come away this instant, woman, or I'll call the polis,' said Mr Holmes and Hannah blessed the fact that he was the night-shift overman and so happened to be at home when the ruckus started.

Sally faltered for only a moment when he confronted her, then she appealed to the crowd at the gate. 'What about my lass, abandoned and with a bairn on the way? By, if she was one of yours, you would make sure right was done by her, I dare swear.' But she stopped when she realised that the onlookers were hostile to her, not to the Armstrongs.

'You should be ashamed of yourself, coming round here, Sally Cornish!' shouted Mrs Hardy from next door. 'I thought we'd chased you from the rows long since, you brazen-faced hussy! And now you come pestering a family where the man's lying with his back broke. Get away from here, or I'll send you on your way meself.'

'No need for that,' said Mr Holmes. 'Just go and get Mr Parry. I'll stay here and see she does no more harm.'

Sally gasped. 'Do you mean to say you'd set the polis on me? When you know it was Alf Armstrong?'

'Aw, you never fooled anybody,' jeered a voice from the back of the crowd. 'Why, man, the lad's only sixteen, good luck to him, I say, even if he did do it. I'm pleased he's got away from here. There's nowt for the young folk here and that's the truth.'

Sally suddenly stopped blustering and started to cry, great drunken sobs which made Hannah realise for the first time that she had been drinking, even though it was only the middle of the afternoon.

'Come on, Mrs Cornish,' said Mr Holmes, 'you'd best away home.' He spoke quietly now for he could see that she was defeated. Gulping, she wiped her eyes on her filthy pinafore and started down the yard without a backward glance at the house. Mr Holmes walked with her though with a couple of yards between them for the rank smell of her had been somehow intensified by the scene. The crowd at the gate parted silently to allow her through. Her unlaced boots flopped up and down on her ankles as she walked up the row. Cautiously, Hannah opened the door and went to peep round the gate. Sally was almost to the end of the row and when she got there she turned to face the crowd still lingering in case there was anything more to see.

'Right!' she bellowed. 'Right! I know none of you likes me and mine though what I ever did to you I don't know. But we'll get our own back, me and mine, just you wait till my Wesley finds out about this.'

Hannah's heart beat fearfully as Sally stumped off round the corner. Not that she was frightened for herself, but for Bob she was, he was on his own now without even Alf to stand by his side. What might Lancelot Cornish or Ralph do to him if they caught him on his own?

'Please watch out for yourself, Bob,' she pleaded with him when he came in.

'Aw, I'm not frightened of Lancelot Cornish,' he boasted. 'Anyroad, who could be frightened of a fellow with a cissy name like Lancelot?'

But Hannah wasn't taken in by her brother's bravado and she noticed that when he went backwards and forwards to the pit he always managed to be in among a crowd of others, mostly older men, and he rarely went out at night on his own.

The warm weather gave way to the sharp north-east winds of autumn and the days became steadily colder. In Winton the pit was working normally though not all the seams reopened. The winding wheel buzzed round busily and the smell from the cokeworks was as sulphurous as ever.

'Farmer Burton says I can begin potato picking for him on Monday, Mam,' Hannah said as she came in from the farm one Saturday evening.

'What about school?' asked Nora wearily.

'It'll be all right, there are always some people take the time off to go potato picking, Mam. And I can earn six shillings if I work the week.'

'Well, there's no doubt it will come in handy. I had a postal order for five shillings from Alf this morning; he's a good lad, he sends the money every fortnight, bless him. But it's not the same as having him at the pit.'

'Well, there's talk of some seam closure there,' Bob put in. He was sitting in the rocking chair before the fire, in the seat which had been his father's, then Alf's, and which Bob had now inherited. 'Some of the putters are expecting getting laid off.'

Nora sighed. 'Aye, these are bad times, Christmas coming on an' all. Everybody is hard up. It's paying back the five shillings a week to the Co-op store to pay for the groceries they had during the lockout that's the trouble. If things don't get any better they'll be paying till Kingdom come. Thank God we owe nobody anything.'

'Aye, but we have nothing, either,' grumbled Bob.

Hannah gazed sympathetically at him. He was fed up, she knew, because he hadn't the fare to go to Consett for the weekend. The last time he had been there he came home full of tales of how Uncle Billy had let him drive the wagon from the station with the parcels for Walter Willson's, the grocery store and the Meadow Dairy too.

'That's what I'll do one day, Hannah,' he said, determination making his boyish features seem older. 'When I'm twenty-one I'll be able to do what I want to do.'

Hannah knew what she wanted to do also, though she kept it to herself, fearing that if she told anyone it would never happen. She wanted to go to night school in Bishop Auckland as soon as she left school altogether; she wanted to better herself. 'I'll learn shorthand and typing,' she promised herself, 'as soon as I can save the money for the fees.' She felt sure that a bright girl with ambition and office skills could rise to great things in Auckland, maybe in a bank or the Co-op store. The only trouble would be finding the fees for night school but, one way or another, she would get the money. Hannah was determined she was not going to go into service, neither locally in Bishop Auckland nor away from home.

But 1921 was not yet finished with the Armstrongs. Before the year was out, tragedy struck.

It was in the cold hard days of December, when an icy wind whistled through the crack in the back door and played havoc with Nora's rheumatism, that Jake Armstrong died. Hannah was lying in bed, snuggled against her sister to preserve the warmth under the bed-clothes, when she heard her mother's terrible cry.

'Jake! Oh, my God, Jake!'

Both Betty and Hannah jumped out of bed and flung themselves down the stairs to the open door of the front room.

Their mother was leaning over the box on wheels which was Jake's 'chariot', her arm across his thin chest and her head buried in the pillow beside the still, gaunt face. The girls moved into the room, automatically going one to either side until they were standing close.

Hannah looked down at her father's face, and even in her grief she noticed that the lines of pain which she had become used to seeing in his face had smoothed out somehow, he was lying as though asleep. For a moment she thought her mother was mistaken, he seemed so peaceful, but then she realised how still he was, his mouth dropped slightly open in death, his eyes not properly closed. There was no breathing, none at all.

Nora's wild keening stopped and she got to her feet, only one convulsive sob racking her frame before she picked up a towel which she had brought in ready for Jake's morning wash and dried the tears from her face. 'What will we do, Jake, what will we do without you?' she asked softly now, and her daughters began to weep together quietly, tears running down their faces. In the corner, Walton awoke and for once Hannah did not run straight to him so that his cries became louder and louder and he struggled to a sitting position in his pram and glared at his mother and sisters in outrage.

'See to the bairn, Hannah,' his mother said quietly and Hannah dried her eyes and went over to the baby.

The rest of the day went in a blur for her, feeding and changing Walton and helping Betty clean and tidy the house in readiness for the visitors who would be coming to pay their respects. A telegram had to be sent to Consett to tell Jake's mother of his death, the doctor had to be fetched and Mr Hudson, the colliery manager, had to be informed; these were all tasks which Bob could do. The house was busy until the funeral, filled with visitors coming and going, and Hannah was expected to keep Harry and the baby out of the way for most of the time.

The funeral was held on the Wednesday before Christmas and it was on the morning of the funeral that the envelope came from Mr Hudson containing a voucher for six pounds to pay for the funeral expenses and a letter explaining that in accordance with the agreement reached by the Coal-Owners' Association, no more compensation was due, since Mr Armstrong was not deemed to have died from his injuries following the accident as he had lived more than one year after it had happened. Nora stared at it, her expression unreadable, then she put it away in the top drawer of the press.

It was a fine day, cold but sunny, when Jake Armstrong was buried in the churchyard of St Martin's. Mrs Holmes looked after the two youngest Armstrongs so that Hannah and Betty could follow their father's coffin to chapel and from there to the churchyard. Grandma was down from Consett and she walked dry-eyed with Nora, followed by Alf who came up from Oxford on the train. The houses in the rows drew their curtains as a mark of respect until the funeral party had passed, and most of the men off shift were waiting respectfully at the doors of the chapel to follow the family inside. Afterwards, the Co-op Funeral Service supplied a tea of ham sandwiches and cakes, all included in the six pounds.

What amazed Hannah, who was still a mass of pain and jangling nerve endings, was the hearty way the guests put away the feast, the plates being emptied so rapidly she began to fear there would not be enough. At last everyone appeared to have eaten their fill and drunk all the tea they needed. And they sat back and began to reminisce about her father, what a good man he had been, a good father to his bairns, a good and reliable worker for his marras in the pit, how he had borne his injuries with such fortitude. So gradually, as the afternoon wore on, the memory of Jake began to acquire a saintly overlay which Hannah couldn't recognise.

A great weariness was overtaking her and when she looked at her mother she could see that she too looked wearied to death. The guests seemed to have realised it too and, one by one, they began to leave until only the family were left and they could all relax around the kitchen fire.

'How are you off for money, Nora?' asked Grandma. 'I know it's not the day to be bringing it up, but I have to go back to Consett the morn. And it's something that has to be talked about. Now I can spare a bit if you're short. Was there any insurance on Jake?'

Nora shook her head. 'No, I couldn't manage to keep it up. But at least the funeral's paid for. I'll have my widow's pension and there was another gathering at the pit, twenty-three pounds that is, a fair bit. I know there are eight hundred men but times are hard, I could expect no more.'

Hannah, sitting in the corner with Walton on her lap, guzzling away at a bottle of milk dropped in by Farmer Burton, felt dimly outraged. How could they sit there, talking about money, when Da was dead? She rocked herself and the baby to and fro as he sucked steadily and gazed up at her with large, unblinking brown eyes. Misery rose in her like a tide, swamping her throat and choking her, swamping her eyes so that she could hardly see the baby on her lap.

Her mother's eyes were sharp and she saw Hannah's expression and understood. 'Life goes on, lass,' she said softly. 'We have to live and there's two little lads to feed and care for till they are old enough to see to themselves. Your da would understand, pet, and so will you when you're older.'

Chapter Nine

'Our Betty's got a lad,' Harry announced as he came in from school, late as usual, his seven-year-old face alive with mischief. 'Me and Billy seen them when we went up the lane looking for conkers.'

'So that's where you've been instead of coming home for your tea,' his mother observed wearily. She finished ironing Bob's best shirt and hung it on the clothes horse by the fire before taking another garment from the pile on the end of the table.

'Saw, not seen,' said Hannah. She was standing at the opposite end of the kitchen table, which had been covered by a folded flannelette sheet as a makeshift ironing pad, helping her mother with the ironing.

'Eh?' said Harry, looking from his mother to Hannah, disappointed that his news wasn't having much of an effect on them.

'Billy and I saw them,' said Hannah who was taking a course called English for Secretaries in Bishop Auckland twice a week. Next year she was going to take shorthand and typing and hoped to get a proper office job the year after that. She took her cooled flat iron back to the range and exchanged it for one of those heating on the bar. She picked up the hot iron with a folded rag to protect her hand and spat on it judiciously. It hissed satisfactorily and she took it back to the table and inserted it into the steel 'iron protector' and fastened the pin across it.

'Billy and I saw them,' said Harry in an affected voice. He put his hand on his hip and minced round the kitchen repeating it over and over.

'Harry, behave yourself or you'll get no tea at all,' Nora snapped. Hannah looked across the table to her, seeing how tired her mother's face looked, the droop to her shoulders.

'Mam, sit down and have a rest. I'll finish this lot off, I have plenty of time before I go back to the farm.'

'I think I will, pet, if you don't mind,' answered her mother. She finished the nightie she was ironing and returned her flat iron to the bar. Sighing, she sank down in her rocking chair and stretched her legs out on the steel fender.

Hannah watched her anxiously. It was almost three years since Jake's death and in that time, her mother had seemed to age ten years. She had hit on a scheme to supplement her widow's pension: she went into Auckland every Saturday, bought in a few groceries as cheaply as she could and sold them at a modest profit in a makeshift shop in the front room. Of course, her customers were mostly housewives who ran out of supplies and wanted just enough to last them until they could get to the Co-op store, maybe a quarter pound of sugar or two ounces of lard. Today it seemed that everyone in the rows had run out of something, usually when she was busy with something else. And she couldn't afford to turn away custom, no matter how small the purchase.

Hannah had now left school but there was no full-time work for her in the district, all she had was the small amount of money she earned by helping out at Farmer Burton's. And Bob, though he was almost a man now, could only get datal work in the pit and was on a bare subsistence wage, for day labouring paid poorly. Alf still sent money home but the intervals between the postal orders were becoming longer and longer and Hannah guessed that he was courting a lass.

'Where's my tea, Mam?' demanded Harry. 'I'm hungry.'

'Stay there, I'll get it, Mam,' Hannah said quickly. She used the rag she had wrapped round the handle of the iron to lift a plate of potatoes and cabbage doused in pork dripping she'd bought at Manner's butcher's shop in Newgate Street on her way to her class the evening before. She brought the wooden stool which had been

127

Da's cracket when he worked in the pit – the cracket which he used to sit on or lean against when hewing coal crouched in a low seam – and put it on the mat before the fire. Placing the dinner on the cracket, she brought him a knife and fork from the dresser.

'You'll have to kneel on the mat and eat it there,' she said. 'I need the table for the ironing. If you'd come straight home from school you could have eaten at the table like a Christian.'

Harry made no demur but fell to with a will. Walton, who had been playing under the table, came out and stood beside him, absorbed in watching him eat. At two and a half, Walton was tall and thin for his age and always hungry.

'Leave Harry alone, you've had your tea,' Nora said to him, and his face crumpled. Harry offered him a potato on the end of his fork and, after a quick glance at his mother, the toddler took it and crammed it into his mouth, chewing noisily. Nora leaned forwards and pulled him on to her lap, cuddling him in to her chest.

'Come on, my chick,' she said and began rocking gently, crooning a nameless tune to him.

Hannah had finished the ironing and was folding the flannelette sheet when Betty came in. The whole family gaped in astonishment as they saw the man who was with her. There was something familiar about his face, though Hannah couldn't think what it was, and he was so tall he had to stoop as he came in the door. Although it was the middle of the week, he was wearing a good suit and his reddish hair was slicked back smoothly from his forehead, not covered by a cloth cap such as everyone else in the rows wore.

'Mam,' Betty began, her voice sounding high and nervous. 'Mam, this is Thomas Cornish.' She flashed a brief smile at the man who was hovering in the doorway, unsure of his welcome. 'Everybody calls him Tucker.'

'Cornish? Did you say Cornish?' Nora sounded as though she couldn't believe what she was hearing and Hannah too stared at him, dumbfounded. Now she knew why he looked so familiar; he had the same colouring as the Cornish boys, the same fair, freckled skin and light reddish hair. But he was different from them at the same time, with his fresh, clean clothes and open, honest face. Was he a cousin?

'I telled you that our Betty had a lad,' observed Harry with a look of self-justification.

'Told,' Hannah whispered automatically, still watching the stranger. Betty's uncertain smile slipped and she glared at Harry for a quick second before turning back to her mother, but before she could speak Tucker himself intervened.

'Cornish, that's right, Mrs Armstrong,' he said, stepping forwards and extending his right hand to Nora. 'Though I'm sometimes called Grizedale after my step-father.' His hand was still outstretched, almost forcing

the issue with her, so that in the end her natural polite-
ness won through and she put down Walton and took
it, though she never had thought to shake hands with a
Cornish. Then light dawned.

'Eeh, Tucker Cornish! You're Meg Maddison's lad,
aren't you? By, the last time I saw you, you were a little
lad. There were two of you, weren't there? Now, were
you the oldest or was it – what's his name?'

'Christopher, though he gets Kit. No, I'm the second one.'

'Well, come in, lad, come in and I'll make a pot of tea.
How's your mother? Do you know, I always liked her, I
thought that Wesley Cornish treated her rotten.'

Nora, her tiredness forgotten, busied herself in filling
the kettle and making tea. Betty led Tucker to the horse-
hair settee, where they sat side by side as though both of
them were company.

Hastily, Hannah got the Sunday tablecloth out of the
dresser drawer and laid the table. Harry grinned with
delight as he was sent into the front room to fetch ginger
biscuits from the large, square tin in the 'shop'. It wasn't
very often that the Armstrongs got to eat any of the biscuits his mother sold.

'Now then,' said Nora, when they were all settled with
their tea and Harry and Walton were nibbling round the
edges of their ginger biscuits, seeing whose would last
the longest. 'Tell me how your mother and the others are
getting on now, and afterwards you can tell me about

you and our Betty. 'Cause I have to say that she's never even mentioned you to her family.'

Betty blushed. 'Oh, Mam,' she said, putting down her cup and staring at it as though it were responsible for her embarrassment, 'there wasn't anything to tell, really there wasn't.'

In front of them all, Tucker took her hand and squeezed it and Hannah gasped. Such an open display of sympathy and affection was practically a declaration of intent to marry. She looked at her sister with new eyes and realised Betty was attractive; the pink blush on her normally white skin looked very pretty against her dark hair. Hannah put up a hand to her own cloud of hair, the same colour as Betty's, just as their complexions were the same. Did that mean that she herself was as pretty as Betty was?

'Hannah, stop dreaming and get away out to your work. You're going to be late tonight as it is,' her mother said briskly.

Reluctantly, Hannah got to her feet and went to the door, looking back in astonishment when Tucker half rose and said goodbye.

'I'll see you again, Hannah,' he went on courteously.

She went up to the farm, hurrying now to make up time, but her thoughts were back in the kitchen with her family. She was desperate to know what was being said so she could find out more about Tucker and what he was doing in Winton.

*

'Eeh, I remember Meg Maddison well,' said Nora. It was the following morning and Hannah was tidying up after Bob's bath while her mother chopped up vegetables for soup. She had managed to get a ham bone from the butcher and had it simmering slowly on the bar. 'Poor motherless lass, she was, always working for her family, her brothers and sisters. Then she had to go and marry that Wesley Cornish and get two lads of her own. Though, you know, when he was younger he wasn't so bad as he is now, dirty drunken beast that he is, though he was spoiled rotten by his mam. But then Sally Hawkins got her claws into him and Meg and her bairns were left to God and providence. Not a penny piece could she get out of him. But still, she fell on her feet in the end, got on with Jonty Grizedale from up at the Hall. A proper gentleman he was – and still is, I should suppose. Of course, there was precious little money left, Jonty's da had run through that, but Tucker said they went away to the coast, Marsden, I think he said, Jonty has a farm there.'

The front door opened and Mrs Hutchinson from the next row called out, 'Are you there, Mrs Armstrong? I'm only wanting a fresh egg if you've got one, I thought I'd do some egg and cheese in the oven for the bairns' dinner. I haven't time to go to the store.'

Nora put down her vegetable knife and went through to serve her with the single egg. 'A penny, that'll be,' she said.

'They're only eightpence a dozen up at the store,' grumbled Mrs Hutchinson.

'Well, you're welcome to try to buy an odd one there, if you can make the time to go, that is,' said Nora evenly.

'Nay, nay, I'll take it, I didn't mean nothing.'

'Some folk think I should be doing this for nothing, just the good of my health,' Nora observed as she came back into the kitchen and picked up her knife to finish off a carrot. 'Now, what were we talking about?'

'Tucker Cornish and his family,' said Hannah, impatient to hear more about her sister's boyfriend. 'It must be grand to live on a farm beside the sea, don't you think so, Bob?'

'I like the moors better,' said Bob from his chair by the fire. Bob was seventeen now and his shoulders were beginning to broaden out with the hard muscles of a labourer in the pit. He shook his head in wonderment. 'Are you sure Tucker Cornish is serious about our Betty? I mean, all the lasses will be after him, him being an undermanager. An' then, he's getting old now, he must be nearly thirty. Nobody gets to be an undermanager lest they're getting on a bit, never mind how clever they are. And Betty is a daft bit of a lass, she's only sixteen.'

'Well, he is a clever lad, anybody can see that, an' a good worker too, I have no doubt. And if he suits our Betty, he suits me,' Nora said firmly.

'Aw, Mam, if our Betty's courting the undermanager I'll never hear the last of it. The lads'll say I've gone over to the bosses,' Bob protested.

'Don't talk barmy, Bob,' said Mam, quite unconcerned and Hannah noticed that as she tipped the vegetables into the pan on the bar and added salt and pepper, that she was smiling softly to herself. She's pleased that Betty's lad is an official, she thought, and guessed why. It would be a little bit of security, because officials don't get locked out of the mine ever, nor had she heard of them going on strike.

'Tucker wants to get married at Christmas,' Betty confided as she lay in bed beside Hannah a few weeks later.

'Christmas? But you've only been courting for a month or two,' said Hannah, surprised. 'What will folk say? They'll think you have to get married.'

'Well,' answered Betty with some spirit, 'if they can add up they'll find out they're wrong, won't they? Anyroad, he's got the undermanager's house to go into, you know the one that's on the road past Old Winton. And he wants me in it, he says now he's met me he wants a proper home with me in it, he's sick of living in lodgings. He had to live in lodgings when he first left home and went to Horden and now he's got this job he wants to settle down. With me,' she repeated, as though she had to remind herself it was all true.

Hannah could hardly imagine Betty living in the under-manager's house, it was so big, set in a garden with lawns and fully grown trees. But these last few weeks Betty had blossomed and as Hannah thought back she realised it had begun to happen ever since the day her sister had met Tucker at Mr Hudson's house. Now it was a seven-day wonder in the rows that a Cornish was the undermanager and, what was more, he wanted to marry Betty Armstrong. Betty had a diamond ring to prove it and that was another wonder, for in these hard times a girl was lucky to get a wedding ring, let alone an engagement ring.

Wesley Cornish was mad as all get-out to find him and his lads working under Tucker, the son he had abandoned all those years ago. Bob said Ralph and Lancelot were hard put to be civil to him but they had to be to keep their jobs. Hannah would have given a lot to be in the pit and see those two have to take orders from their half-brother. She smiled to herself in the dark as she thought of it.

She lay quietly, her thoughts returning to her sister and her lover, wondering what it was like to be in love as they were. She thought of the lads in the village, Bob's marras, some of them, and others she had been to school with. But none of them sparked any feelings at all in her, let alone love. She loved Bob and Harry and little Walton, and she couldn't imagine leaving them to go and live with someone else and what's more, do so blithely in the way Betty was obviously prepared to do. No, the sort of love that made Betty look so bright-eyed and gormless whenever she saw Tucker was a mystery to her. Though she had to admit that Tucker was special, so handsome and kind and rich an' all, she knew no one at all who could measure up to him.

Betty had fallen silent and Hannah guessed she was asleep by her deep and even breathing. Restlessly, she turned on her side and closed her own eyes, trying to will herself to sleep. And eventually, she slept and dreamed that a young and very rich businessman in Bishop Auckland came courting her and when she looked up into his face it was Timothy Durkin, the agent's son.

The dream came back to her as she scrubbed the kitchen floor the following day and she smiled wryly. Some chance of anyone coming courting her, she thought, let alone Timothy Durkin. It was two years since she had seen him in any case, and he had probably forgotten all about her. No doubt he had just taken the choir up to amuse himself that summer, he must have been bored. But he had dropped it soon enough when something better had come along, and he never came into the village now. Sighing, Hannah finished her scrubbing and took her pail of dirty water to the outside drain to empty. Well, anyone can dream, she told herself ruefully as she dried her hands on her sacking apron.

Chapter Ten

'Not a bad little motor, this, Tony, don't you think?' said Timothy, 'even if it is a pre-war model.'

The young man sitting in the passenger seat of the 1912 Austin tourer nodded his head in agreement. Indeed, as he was well aware that the car was his friend's pride and joy he had to agree, it was not in his nature to offend a friend.

They were just edging on to the Great North Road on the second lap of their journey home for Christmas. That is Timothy was going home; though Tony's family had an estate near Durham, his father being Lord Akers, their main residence was in London, Park Lane, to be exact. But his parents were spending the winter in Cannes and when Timothy asked him to accompany him home for Christmas, Tony accepted with alacrity.

The two young men had known each other slightly since they were boys, Lord Akers being the owner of the estate and its mining interests and Timothy's father his agent, though it was not until they bumped into each other at Oxford that their friendship had developed. Their two families were almost as far removed socially from each other as were the Durkins and Armstrongs, yet it didn't seem to matter in the enclosed world of the university, and they had discovered during their first year that they had many things in common. Both had had essentially lonely childhoods and both had hated boarding school, though Tony had gone to Eton and Timothy to a smaller school in Barnard Castle on Durham's border with Yorkshire.

'Where shall we stay tonight?' Timothy asked now. 'Or do you want to rush on to Bishop Auckland without stopping? We will if you like, I think the old bus is up to it. She ran pretty well yesterday.' They had set out the day before and done almost ninety miles before looking for somewhere to spend the night, finally deciding on a tiny country inn. They had been the only guests but their rooms were clean and adequate and the food good.

'Let's do that then,' said Tony. 'Though won't your father be expecting us tomorrow rather than today?'

'It won't matter,' Timothy answered, thinking to himself that his father would hardly notice what day he came home. The fact that the son of Lord Akers was coming with him would make a difference, Timothy had no illusions about that.

'There's a long, long trail awinding into the land of my dreams,' Tony carolled as they sped northwards, touching forty miles an hour in places, for Timothy wanted to show what the old car could do. He had bought it the week before and this was the first time he had had the chance to put it to a real test and in spite of his apparent confidence he was slightly anxious; after all, the journey was the best part of two hundred miles. But the engine was responding to him beautifully and he relaxed after a while and added his baritone to his friend's

By one o'clock they were on the outskirts of Doncaster and sitting in the Miner's Arms with a pie and a pint while the tourer had a rest. It was Tony who had caught sight of the shabby little pub and suggested they stop there.

'Most appropriate, my boy,' he said grandly to Timothy as he led the way in to the bar. 'Doesn't it remind you of home?'

Timothy had never been in a working-class pub in his life, let alone one at home in Auckland. In Oxford the pubs he and Tony frequented were all given over to students.

As they went into the bar, which was half filled with men, most of them miners and some still black from the pit, the buzz of conversation stilled. Timothy, sensitive to the atmosphere, hesitated, but Tony didn't appear to notice. He moved through them to the bar, nodding a greeting.

'Afternoon, landlord,' he said in his booming upper-class accent. 'Two pints of bitter, please, and a couple of those pies you have there. Pork pies, are they?'

'Lamb,' said the landlord, not bothering to return the greeting.

One of the men standing at the end of the bar hawked loudly and spat into the spittoon at his feet. Tony showed no sign of noticing anything, he was absorbed in watching the landlord drawing the foaming pints of beer.

'Come on, Tim, we'll sit over there,' he said, a pint in one hand and a plate with two pies on it in the other, and led the way to a table in a corner. Only when they were sitting down and tucking into their pies did the other men in the bar turn away and resume their conversations.

Timothy looked round the dingy bar with its walls and ceiling darkened to a deep brown with tobacco smoke. The floorboards were bare and pitted with tiny dents caused by the studs in pit boots, at least he thought it must be that for most of the men were wearing pit boots whether they were dirty from the pit or not.

There was the unmistakable smell which Timothy remembered from the times he had accompanied his father to the mine offices, the smell of coal and coke ovens mixed with strong tobacco. It brought to his memory the time he had seen the miners step out of the cage as they came to bank at the top of the shaft and immediately light up pipes and cigarettes and begin coughing and spitting to clear their tubes of the dreaded coal and stone dust. For, of course, smoking was strictly forbidden down the mines, the danger of explosions was ever present.

Timothy polished his pie off quickly, finding he was hungry. He drank some of the strong beer and looked over to a group of men talking by the bar, catching one man staring at him, his expression unreadable. Timothy acknowledged him with a slight nod of the head and the man immediately looked away and took a large swallow of beer. His clothes were stiff and black with coal dust and he was still wearing leather knee protectors.

'Have another, Tim?'

'No, I don't think so, thanks,' Timothy answered. He watched the miners, becoming aware that whenever he or Tony spoke they paused in their conversation and listened, making no effort to hide the fact. He began to feel uncomfortable, ready to go. But Tony was already on his feet and heading for the bar. Silently, the men made way for him.

'You men all work in the same mine?' Tony's ringing, aristocratic accent sounded loud and clear and utterly foreign to the thick South Yorkshire accents of the workmen. But he was bending benignly to the group nearest him, his face expressing a genuine interest.

'Aye, we do, those of us who haven't been laid off, that is,' replied one at last, the one who had been watching them earlier.

Tony nodded his head sympathetically. 'Trade's bad, I know,' he said sagely, delving into his pocket and pulling out a handful of coins to pay the landlord. The change jangled as he dropped it back in the pocket and the miners all looked towards the sound.

'Oh, aye? An' tha'll know all about it, would thaa?' said the miner, lifting his chin aggressively to Tony. He was a short man, barely five foot six, but his shoulders were broad and powerful even against Tony's rugby-playing bulk. Tony seemed oblivious to it and remained standing at the bar, smiling down at the men.

'I know a little,' he answered. 'After all, my father's in the mining business.'

Oh, Lord, thought Timothy helplessly, is he going to tell them his father's a mine owner? He knew from his own father how bitter the men were as their condition gradually worsened over the last few years; he had no reason to think that the miners here were any better off than those in Durham.

'Have you been on the dole, mister?' a man was asking, his voice flat and unemotional.

'Well, no, of course, I'm still a student,' admitted the Honourable Anthony Akers. 'I haven't actually – '

'Naa,' said the man, turning to the bar and picking up his pint. 'Naa, thaa hasn't.' He drained his pot, replaced it on the bar and wiped his mouth with the back of his hand.

'Well,' said Tony reasonably, 'I suppose it does give you a bit of a holiday, doesn't it? And times will get better, they always do, and in the meantime, you have the dole, haven't you? I mean, if you can afford to drink beer in the middle of the day – ' He faltered as he caught the expression on the faces of the miners. As a man they stepped forward, an angry growl coming from more than one throat.

'Coming into our alehouse . . . ' Timothy heard one say, while another butted in, 'An', "a twopenny pair of kippers is good enough for any working man's dinner", is that it?' he said, quoting from a well-known Tory minister's speech of the week before which had made all the papers.

'Now then, lads, I'll have no trouble here,' said the landlord, but before he had finished his warning Timothy was on his feet and had hold of Tony's arm and was drawing him outside.

'But I haven't finished my beer,' Tony protested, though he allowed himself to be drawn.

'Yes, you have,' said Timothy as he propelled his friend through the door to the kerb and the waiting car. 'That's if you don't want to be lynched.'

'But I said nothing to antagonise them,' Tony said indignantly as Timothy cranked the engine with the starting handle and, as it burst into life, jumped into the driving seat.

'No? Well, just look behind you then,' said Timothy, indicating the open door of the pub where miners were standing, staring after them.

Tony shook his head in wonderment as they drove through the quiet afternoon traffic of Doncaster. 'There was no arguing with them, in any case,' he said. 'How can you argue with a man who suddenly begins to talk about kippers?'

But by the time Timothy had explained the relevance of smoked herring to the argument, Tony's interest had waned. He was singing once again as they hit open road on the far side of the town and began to pick up speed.

'Let the whole wide world keep turning, just so long as I have you,' he sang, only slightly off key. Timothy was glad that the car was open-topped for all the cold day, at least most of the noise was carried away with the wind.

It was already dark by the time the car pulled up in Durham Road. Tony jumped out to open the gates so that they could drive up to the front of the house. As Timothy stopped the engine, he saw the portly figure of his father standing in the lighted window of the dining room and when they got out of the car and lifted their luggage from the dicky, he opened the door and came down to greet them.

'Timothy, my boy,' he cried, smiling broadly. 'I wasn't expecting you until tomorrow. And you, Anthony, let me welcome you. As I told your father on the telephone only the other day, we are delighted to have you with us for Christmas.' He held out his hand to Tony, who had perforce to put his suitcase down to shake hands with his host.

'Don't worry about the luggage, dear boy, the servants will bring it in,' Mr Durkin went on, sweeping Tony up the steps and into the house. Timothy smiled grimly to himself as he followed.

Arrangements for the wedding of Betty and Tucker were almost finished. The chapel had been booked for the Saturday before Christmas and Mr Hughes, the minister, had had his usual little talk with the happy pair. The reception, paid for by Tucker at his insistence, would be held in the chapel schoolroom. Alf was coming home from Oxford and Tucker's mother, Meg Grizedale, was coming with Hope, her young daughter, and Kit Cornish, her eldest son.

'I hope you don't mind that Tucker's father won't be able to come,' Meg wrote to Nora. 'I'm afraid he can't leave the farm for a whole day. However, we are both delighted for Tucker and Betty. He has worked so hard to get where he is and I know Betty is just the girl to help him.'

Tucker had taken Betty over to the coast to see his parents one weekend at the beginning of December. Afterwards, as she and Hannah lay in bed together, the place where all their confidences were shared, Betty had told her sister all about the farm by the sea and the family living there.

'Oh, it's lovely, Hannah,' she said. 'It's an old stone farmhouse and when you lie in bed at night you can hear the sea, it's like a lullaby. And Tucker's mam is lovely, she hasn't put on any airs, she talked about how it used to be in Winton and how sorry she was to hear about Da, she knew him, you know. And Mr Grizedale, you would never think he came from Grizedale Hall, he talked to me so ordinary somehow, yet he's a proper gent, so polite.

But Kit, now, oh, it's sad to see him, Hannah, it really is. He was hurt in the war, you know, left for dead in the trenches, Tucker says. He has a gammy leg now, though he manages to get about, help on the farm. But it's his mind that's funny, he's very quiet and seems to get on better with the dogs and other animals than with people. It was his experiences in the war, Tucker says, he was all right before.'

Hannah lay awake a long time after her sister fell asleep, trying to visualise the farm by the sea and the family that lived there. Poor Kit, she thought, what horrors he must have experienced to make him as he was.

Nora had baked the wedding cakes herself. There were three of them: a large one which was to be cut at the wedding feast, a smaller one which was for Mrs Grizedale to take home and give out to Tucker's friends and relations, and a small one which was to be saved for the christening of the first baby. When they were put together in tiers, supported by silver-coloured pillars and with a tiny bride and groom made of sugar, bought in Auckland for a scandalous five shillings and elevenpence halfpenny, little Walton couldn't take his eyes off them.

The wedding was at eleven o'clock and even though it was but a short walk to the chapel from the rows, Tucker had hired a grand, open-topped car with gleaming black paint, a Humber, with plush leather upholstery and floating white ribbons decorating the bonnet.

It made three journeys round the rows, going up and down every one before heading for the chapel. The first time it held Nora, resplendent in mauve crepe, and Bob, in a dark serge suit and stiff white collar which was obviously uncomfortable for he kept trying to insert a finger behind it to ease it from his neck. On the second journey there was Hannah, in a new dusty-pink satin dress with a low waist and hemline which dipped to a point on one side and a coronet of Christmas roses on her head, showing off the dark gloss of her hair. With her she had Harry and Walton, both unrecognisably clean and tidy in new suits. The people of the rows came out to watch the grand sight; Harry, from his seat beside Hannah, bowed, smiled and waved his hand as he had seen the Prince of Wales do on the newsreel at the pictures, and Walton imitated him until a bump in the unmade road caused him to fall off his seat and tears threatened. Hannah had to put down her posy and pick him up, promising him a piece of wedding cake if he didn't cry.

Nora had drawn all her dividend from the Co-op store to help pay for the new clothes, determined that Tucker should not have all the expense, even though it meant she had nothing to fall back on if things got worse. And as Hannah travelled along so grandly in the motorcar, she couldn't help thinking that she had to get some work soon, her mother couldn't afford to keep her with only the small amount she made at the farm coming in. But still, it was Betty's wedding day, not the time to worry about money, she told herself as the car drew up before the chapel and she helped her little brothers out.

It took only ten minutes for the car to return with Betty, even though it had gone round the rows. Hannah's heart swelled with pride as Betty got out with Alf, who was to give her away. Alf looked handsome and prosperous and so much like his father had been before the accident in the pit that she felt tears prick the back of her eyes. He was the only one of the Armstrongs to have been able to afford to buy his own suit for the wedding. But Betty, in her white satin gown with a lace veil over her dark hair, drew gasps of admiration from the group of onlookers round the chapel gates.

'By, you look grand, Betty,' Hannah whispered, as she hurried to arrange the satin train of the dress so that it would flow smoothly down the aisle after her sister. Then Betty took Alf's arm and the organ played 'Here Comes the Bride' as the bridal procession started down the aisle to where Tucker, flanked by Kit, his brother, was standing waiting.

It was afterwards, at the reception in the schoolroom, that Hannah met Tucker's family. As bridesmaid, she was sitting beside Kit who was best man, but apart from a brief hallo when Tucker introduced them properly, he hardly opened his mouth during the whole of the meal, either to eat or to talk. He sat there, staring at his plate for most of the time, answering in monosyllables when she tried to start a conversation until in the end, Hannah decided to give it up. And when the meal was ended and the blackcurrant cordial poured into the glasses for the toasts, it was his mother who rose to toast the bridal pair.

Hope, Tucker's half-sister, sat quietly beside her mother, watching everything with obvious interest. She was perhaps a little younger than herself, Hannah noted, yet looked quite self-possessed and smart in her cherry-red costume and cloche hat which fitted over her ears so that only wisps of her fashionably cut hair showed below it. She looked across and saw Hannah watching her, and smiled so that Hannah found herself smiling back.

Meg Grizedale was also dressed smartly yet simply in a similar costume to her daughter's, though the skirt was longer and the material was dark green edged with white. Once the meal was over and people began to move around, Meg went to sit beside Hannah's mother and the two women began to talk amicably. Beside Meg's costume, Nora's mauve crepe didn't look quite so smart as Hannah had thought when her mother first put it on. Suddenly it was obvious that the crepe was cheap, would probably shrink the first time it was washed, and there was something odd about the cut, it dragged slightly over her mother's thin hips.

'Hallo, may I sit beside you?' someone said in her ear.

Hannah turned to see Hope beside her, already sliding into the chair that had been Kit's. Hannah hadn't even noticed he had gone.

'I think we should be friends, don't you?' Hope went on, her warm smile lighting up her face. Before Hannah had time to reply they were interrupted by a commotion at the door of the schoolroom. Hannah heard Ralph and Wesley Cornish shouting belligerently.

'I've come to see my lad get wed,' said Wesley, his words slurring into one another.

Mr Hughes, who had been standing chatting to Meg and Nora, strode to the door. 'Now, come on, Mr Cornish,' he said reasonably. 'You've been drinking, don't you think you should go home and sleep it off?'

Wesley pushed past him roughly and took a few steps into the room, closely followed by Ralph. The guests looked at him, unsure what to do.

'Why wasn't I invited to my lad's wedding?' Wesley demanded and those closest to him moved back, away from the stench of beer and rum. 'Didn't I have a bloody right, me, his own father? Where's he at, Tucker, where the hell are you? Coming over here so that you can lord it over me down the pit and then not even asking me to your wedding?'

Tucker stepped forwards with Alf close by his side, ready to back him up if necessary. 'You weren't invited, so why don't you get out of here?' he asked quietly.

'I have a bloody right to be here, I have as much right as anybody else, I'm telling you. Don't you go telling me what to do, we're not down the pit now, you know,' shouted Wesley.

Tucker moved forward, grasped him by the lapels of his filthy suit and lifted him off his feet. 'You have no rights over me at all,' he said, his voice low and passionate. 'You did nothing for Kit and me when we were bairns, it was left to my mother to bring us up with no help from you at all. Don't talk to me about rights.' He dropped Wesley on his heels so that he stumbled slightly and had to struggle for a moment to regain his balance.

Ralph stepped forwards, waving his arms and shouting. 'Hey, leave him alone or you'll have me to deal – '

He got no further, for Mr Hughes and Mr Hodgson each took hold of him by the upper arms and dragged him backwards to the door and outside. But while everyone's gaze was diverted to his stepson, Wesley had got his eye on Meg and stepped towards where she stood, her face white and expressionless, her head held high.

'Well, see here if it isn't that frozen-faced bitch who took my lads away from me in the first place. Will you look at her? Butter wouldn't melt in her bloody mouth. Thought she was too good for me, did you know that? But not too good to play the whore with that Jonty Grizedale, was she?'

Meg stood still as he swayed close to her, spittle dribbling from his mouth, and Nora stepped forward and took her arm to draw her away. The next moment Alf and Tucker had hold of Wesley and were yanking him back, away from the women.

'Don't you ever speak to my mother again, do you hear?' yelled Tucker. 'If you do, so help me I'll – '

'Please, Mr Cornish, please, let's have an end to this unpleasantness,' said Mr Hughes, who was just coming back into the schoolroom. 'Remember where you are.'

'Sorry, minister,' Tucker muttered, relaxing his grip on Wesley. As he did so, Wesley stumbled over Alf's foot, falling heavily on his side on the floor. There was the ominous sound of breaking glass and a strong smell of rum filled the air of the room, which had never before smelled of strong liquor. Wesley squealed loudly and scrambled to his hands and knees. Beneath him the rum spread, staining the scrubbed white boards of the schoolroom floor.

'You've done for me, you bloody sods, I've been stabbed, I'm bleeding to death,' he cried, gingerly feeling down his side with one hand. 'Fetch the polis, somebody, will you? And the ambulance, I need the ambulance.'

Tucker bent down and hauled Wesley to his feet. Bits of broken glass dropped away from his trousers to the floor, where they glistened against the wood. Wesley howled at him to let him be, his face bright red with rage where it was not covered with greyish-black stubble.

'I'm only looking to see if you really are hurt,' said Tucker as he undid Wesley's belt and dragged his shirt up to expose the flesh, still black from the night before's pit dirt. As he did so, he released a strong stench of body odour combined with the peculiar smell of body lice and the men around, who were used to bathing every day when they came off shift, stepped back, making audible signs of disgust.

There was a tiny trickle of blood where a piece of bottle glass had scratched him, but otherwise Wesley looked unharmed.

'There's nothing the matter with you,' said Tucker, letting him go. 'Now, get out of here before I throw you out.'

But Wesley, once he was assured that he was unhurt, regained his aggressiveness. 'I'll go when I – ' he began, but the men around him had had enough. Three or four of them caught hold of him and carried him to the doorway and out into the unmade-up road, where they dropped him in the gutter. He lay there beside his step-son, who had collapsed into insensibility, a dark stain slowly creeping along his trouserleg where he was in the process of wetting himself.

Hannah and Hope, along with most of the rest of the wedding guests, had followed the men out to the door with Meg and Nora close behind.

Hope, catching sight of her mother, went to her and Meg put her arms around her. 'Can we go home now, Mam?' she asked, her voice that of a small girl and Hannah knew she had changed her mind about making friends now.

Hannah didn't hear Meg's reply, her gaze had been drawn to a motorcar which had stopped on the opposite side of the road. It was an Austin tourer and sitting in it were two young men surveying the scene, one of whom she recognised instantly.

'Well, my boy.' The ringing tones of the Honourable Anthony Akers sounded loud and clear to the cluster of wedding guests at the door of the chapel schoolroom. 'You said you would show me how pitmen lived but I think I've seen enough, don't you? Shall we be on our way to Durham now?'

Hannah and Timothy stared for a brief moment into each other's eyes and she shrank at the contempt she saw in his. Then he deliberately looked away to the road ahead without a flicker of acknowledgement.

'Certainly, Tony,' he said and the car glided on down the road.

Chapter Eleven

'You can please yourself which you do, Hannah,' said Nora. 'But you know yourself you cannot stay at home, not now. You've got to earn your own living, haven't you?'

Hannah looked down at her hands which were clenched in her lap, she knew that her mother was right, of course she did. If only she could get work in Bishop Auckland or even Shildon, she thought miserably. It was ironic that Bob, who still desperately wanted to go back to Grandma's in Consett and work with Uncle Billy, had to stay at home to help his mother financially while Hannah had to go away for the very same reason.

'There's only Harry and Walton needs seeing to now, Hannah, I can manage on my own,' her mother went on. 'And Betty will be living close anyroad. But we don't want to have to take money from Tucker, do we? Not when you're old enough to take a job.'

'No, Mam,' said Hannah, almost inaudibly.

'Well, I told you about the housemaid's job I saw advertised in the *Chronicle,*' Nora went on. 'Harrogate's not so far and it's thirty-six pounds a year, not too bad for a young lass.' Her heart ached as she looked at the bowed head of her daughter and she almost told her she didn't have to go, she could wait a little while longer to see if she could get anything nearer home. But Hannah had to start earning a living; she was almost sixteen and earning a few coppers at the Burtons' farm was not enough, even though she often brought home eggs and milk.

'I don't want to go as a housemaid, Mam,' said Hannah at last. 'If I can go back with Alf to Oxford, I'd rather do that.' At least there would be one other Armstrong near, she thought.

'You might still have to go into service,' warned Nora but Hannah didn't answer. I'm not, she vowed silently, I'm not going to be a housemaid, I don't care what. A place like Oxford, there's bound to be night schools I can go to, I'll ask Alf.'

Alf, when he came in from Bishop Auckland, where he had been to the pictures with Bob to see Tom Mix in the latest cowboy film, was a bit taken aback at first to think he was to have the job of taking Hannah back with him to Cowley and helping her to get lodgings and a job. But after a few minutes he agreed.

'There's plenty of work in Oxford,' he said, 'good paid work an' all, even for girls. Better than round here, at

157

any rate. I'll ask Ma if she has a spare room for her.' But then he remembered that Ma, which was the name given by all the lodgers in the house to the landlady, Mrs Prendergast, just took in boys. 'Girls cause trouble,' he had heard her say often enough. He looked at his sister but he really couldn't see that she would cause any trouble with his fellow lodgers, she was too skinny for a start and her unfashionably long hair hung down her back tied with a plain black ribbon. And then there was her dress, down over her skinny knees and with a little girl's round collar.

'I hope she has a better dress than that,' he said. 'I don't want her to show me up in front of my mates, do I?'

Hannah flushed with anger and indignation. 'If there's anyone showing anyone up it'll be you shaming me,' she burst out, her fists clenching by her sides.

'You needn't take it like that, I didn't mean anything,' said Alf calmly. 'It's just you don't know what it's like down there, man, it's a different world.'

Hannah remembered that expression as she sat on the bus which was taking them from Oxford railway station to Cowley, Alf by her side, and her basketwork box containing her clothes balanced on their knees. She gazed out of the window, fascinated by everything she saw. The busy streets were thronged with people, most of them well dressed and prosperous-looking; not a single corner with unemployed men sitting on their hunkers depressed and shabby as it was at home. The shops were filled with customers and they all seemed to be buying.

And the streets were filled with motorcars of all kinds, she even saw two or three like the one Timothy Durkin had been driving on the day of Betty's wedding.

'Usually the place is full of undergraduates,' Alf volunteered. 'Luckily they don't come back to pester everyone else for a week or two yet.'

Timothy is a student, thought Hannah, is that an undergraduate? But she didn't show her ignorance by asking Alf, she would find out in time. They passed high stone walls with entrances through which she glimpsed grass lawns and buildings similar to Auckland Castle, or perhaps Palace Green in Durham, where the castle was on one side and the cathedral on the other. Only here, they passed one after another.

'Queen's,' said Alf laconically, and a bit farther on, 'Magdalen, the choir boys sing on the roof there on the first of May.'

Hannah peered through the window, trying to see the roof. How did choir boys stay up on that sloping slate? But again, she didn't ask. Alf was sitting back looking out of the window with an expression of boredom on his face and she told herself this was an everyday experience for him and she didn't want to make a nuisance of herself by asking questions. She knew her brother, in the ordinary way of things he would never have had her trailing round after him.

'This is the Cowley Road,' said Alf, and Hannah watched eagerly as the buildings began to thin out, giving glimpses of marshy ground. There was a church with a cemetery attached and several scattered cottages; briefly, a stream not unlike the Gaunless which flowed by Winton Colliery on its way to the Wear; then more houses; and suddenly Alf was getting to his feet.

'Come on, look sharp,' he said, tugging the box from her lap so that a loose piece of basket weave snagged on her dress and he had to wait impatiently while she freed it and it left a tiny tear. They got off the bus and walked away from the main road. Despite the weight of the box on his shoulder, Alf strode on ahead so that she had to keep breaking into a little run to keep up with him.

'Rymers Lane,' she read out loud, delighted with such a whimsical name.

'What?' Alf looked back at her without slowing his stride. 'Come on, Hannah, it's getting late. If Ma won't take you we'll have to find somewhere else for you to stay before dark.'

Hannah hurried after him and they passed the steam-plough works and turned the corner into Hockmore Street, where there were a few shops and houses. Having rounded another corner, Alf stopped before the gate of a terraced house with a small front garden with bare rose bushes and shrubs giving it the forlorn air of a winter garden anywhere. But under the bushes, Hannah could see snowdrops and the green shoots of crocuses which surprised her for the new year was barely a week old. Alf had a key to the front door and he unlocked it and motioned Hannah inside, where she found herself in a small hall with a door to their right and a staircase with a carpet patterned in roses. At the farther end of the hall, by the well of the staircase, was an open door to the kitchen; she could see a white sink and painted cupboards.

'Ma, are you there?' he called and a plump, middle-aged woman came out of the door to their right.

'Oh, hallo, Mr Armstrong,' she said, though she was not looking at him but at Hannah. 'You're back then. Just in time for tea, too. And who's this then, your young lady? You know I don't allow young ladies in the house.'

Hannah looked down at the rose-patterned carpet which ran along the length of the hall, over a brown linoleum. She felt very embarrassed.

'This is my sister, Ma, she's come down to look for work.'

Mrs Prendergast regarded Hannah, her gaze unsmiling. 'Your sister, eh? Well, you know the rules, Mr Armstrong, you'll have to find somewhere else for her to stay.'

'But couldn't she stay here just for tonight, please? We've been travelling all day and she's tired.'

They were talking about her as though she wasn't there, thought Hannah. The landlady hadn't even said hallo to her yet. She drew herself up and stepped forwards, looking into Mrs Prendergast's face.

'Don't worry about me,' she said. 'I'll find somewhere. I'm sure I don't have to stay here.'

'She's only a slip of a girl,' Mrs Prendergast observed. 'Are you sure she's old enough to be seeking work? Looks more like she should be at school to me.' She was still addressing her remarks to Alf.

Hannah was furious. 'I am almost sixteen, Mrs Prendergast,' she snapped, stretching the truth a little for she was only just turned fifteen. 'I am quite capable of earning my own living. I'm a good worker, all I need is a start.' All the lessons in English grammar and pronunciation which she had learned at night school went into this speech; she even remembered to round off her vowels.

'Well,' said Mrs Prendergast, 'at least your accent is not so bad as your brother's was when he first came down. Couldn't understand a word he said, most of the time.'

Hannah picked up her box by the leather strap which held it closed. 'You have your tea, Alf,' she said. 'I'll just go down to that little shop we saw at the end of the road.

There were cards in the window, I'm sure some of them were wanting lodgers.'

'Don't be daft, Hannah,' said Alf. 'I'm not letting you look on your own, I'll come with you – '

'Never mind,' said Mrs Prendergast, suddenly changing her mind. 'She can stay here, for a short while at any rate. I've been thinking, I could do with some help in the house, my charlady is off nursing a sick husband and my back's not what it was – this damp, cold weather gives me gyp. If she helps me out with the scrubbing and such, she can stay for now. It will only be for a week or two, though.'

'I'm not looking to be a housemaid,' said Hannah.

'Oh, hoity-toity!' retorted Mrs Prendergast. 'Please yourself, I'm sure.'

'Hannah, don't be daft, it'll tide you over till you get something.' Alf turned his back on his landlady and whispered urgently to his sister. She looked up at him, her anger dying away. She hadn't much choice but to accept Mrs Prendergast's offer, she knew. She put the box down again on the floor.

'Thank your very much for your kind offer,' she said. 'So long as it is only a temporary arrangement I will be pleased to stay here and help you.'

Mrs Prendergast nodded, placated. 'So long as you understand I won't have you making eyes at the lodgers. This is a respectable house.'

'Hannah is a respectable girl, Ma,' said Alf in an offended tone of voice.

'Well, I didn't mean to imply she wasn't,' the land-lady answered him, relaxing into a smile. 'Come along now. Leave your luggage in the hall, Hannah. There's no room at the dining-room table for you but I will set you a place in the kitchen and when you've eaten I'll show you your room. It's only the attic but the bed is comfort-able enough.'

In the days that followed, Hannah's opinion of Mrs Prendergast softened until she came to like the older woman. She was strict with her, not allowing her to mix with her young men, as she called them, apart from Alf, but she was fair and only expected Hannah to work in the mornings so she had the rest of the day to look for work and a place of her own to live. Ma was a widow, her husband had worked at the John Allan Steam Plough and Engineering Company and when he died she had begun taking in lodgers to supplement her pension. She was a good cook and her house soon acquired such a good reputation that she rarely had a spare room to let. Hannah didn't mind the attic; it was somewhere clean and warm to sleep, and if she rose early enough she had the bathroom to herself before the lodgers wanted it.

Hannah revelled in the bathroom with its iron bath enamelled white and the white porcelain handbasin with a mirror above it. She revelled in the fact that the water from the hot-water tap ran truly hot, though the geyser had to be lit first. It was very like the bathroom in the undermanager's house where Betty and Tucker now lived, though the water there was heated from a coal-fired boiler in the scullery. This was the first time Hannah had lived in a house with a real bathroom and she was delighted with it. When she had said so to Alf he had told her not to be so obvious about it, she was showing him up, acting as though she had never seen a bathroom before. She tried to hide her feelings but she loved popping into the bathroom at every opportunity to wash her hands, and this was easy to do for it was downstairs, off the kitchen.

The water closet was built into the house though the door was outside, side by side with the back door. She loved that too, it was so different from the ash closet at the end of the yard at home, a place which was always smelly no matter how clean her mother tried to keep it.

'It's like living in paradise,' she said softly to herself one day shortly after she had arrived in Cowley. It was afternoon and she was walking along Rymers Lane to catch the bus into Oxford. It was a fairly warm, sunny day for January and the air was fresh and invigorating. She was going to see about a job she had seen advertised in the *Oxford Mail,* a job in a newsagent's shop near the railway station.

'Much better to wait till you get something in Cowley,' Ma had counselled, but Hannah didn't want to work in Cowley. She wanted to work in Oxford itself where life seemed so much more exciting, even if she had fares to pay for the bus into town.

The bus was coming up to the stop and she had to run the last few steps, but soon she was sitting in a window seat gazing out as it picked up speed along the Oxford Road. Paradise, she thought again dreamily, enchanted with the clean streets and made-up roads thronged with cars and people milling about, looking as if they had somewhere to go and something to do when they got there, not like at home. It was hard to believe they were in the same country as Winton Colliery, where dejection hung heavy in the air along with the coal dust and smells from the ash closets.

Paradise, except for the dull ache inside her for home, for the sight of little Walton running towards her with his thin little arms outstretched for her to lift him up and hug him, and Harry coming in late from school once again, and her mother standing at the kitchen table, washing up in the chipped enamel bowl and putting the pots to drain on the tin tray. Suddenly her eyes dimmed and a lump rose up in her throat. Fiercely, she clenched her hands in the lap of her good dress, the warm serge dress which her mother had found the money from somewhere to buy for her. The dress had seemed fine enough when she first put it on in Winton but in a place like Oxford it looked what it was, a dress bought for warmth and durability rather than style or fashion, and the material was rough and scratchy so that it irritated her skin and prickled between her shoulder blades. And the three-quarter coat she wore over it hung loosely for it had been one of Betty's and Betty was a bigger girl than she was altogether.

'Carfax,' shouted the conductor and Hannah stumbled from the bus, determined to walk the rest of the way to clear her head of silly low notions. Holding her head in the air, she walked along pretending to herself she was wearing a dress she had seen in the window of the shop opposite the bus stop, a dress of lime-green wool with a chic little jacket and a cloche hat of the same colour. After a moment or two her momentary bout of homesickness receded and her natural buoyant spirits returned.

She found the newsagent's shop without any trouble and went in, reminding herself to watch how she spoke, to keep her vowels nicely rounded and, above all, not to let a hint of North Country idiom creep into her speech.

'Mr Ridley?' she said primly to the man behind the counter, a man of about forty-five with a Kaiser Bill moustache and streaks of grey in his bushy hair. He looked at her enquiringly and she went on, 'I've come about the job as sales assistant.'

'Have you now,' came a woman's voice from the back of the shop. 'You've never come all the way from Durham today for a job in our shop, have you, pet?'

Hannah watched, startled, as a hand drew aside the curtain which screened the back shop from the customers and a stout little woman with a merry grin on her face stepped into the shop. Her accent was pure Geordie, with the sing-song tones of somewhere near Sunderland, or so Hannah guessed.

'No, no, just from Cowley, I came down last week. I'm staying in Cowley, my brother works there,' said Hannah, wondering how the woman had known she came from Durham when she had taken such pains to disguise her accent. Mr Ridley laughed heartily.

'Nay, lass, the wife didn't really think you'd come down specially for the job. She's one for a little joke, that's all.'

Mrs Ridley held the curtain up and beckoned to Hannah, her smile widening so that her eyes almost disappeared in the fold of flesh between her plump cheeks and brow.

'Howay through here, hinny,' she said. 'I'll put the kettle on and we'll have a nice cup of tea while we talk.'

It was a happy, triumphant Hannah who took the bus back to Cowley a couple of hours later. She fairly skipped down Rymers Lane in the gathering gloom of a wet winter evening and round the corner to Mrs Prendergast's boarding house, going up the path by the side of the house to the back door.

'I've got a job, Ma,' she cried as she went in. 'I start tomorrow.'

'Just as well,' said Mrs Prendergast. 'It's time you were moving out of here. I've noticed the way the boys look at you and I want no trouble in my house.' She closed the door of the gas oven where she had been basting a shoulder of lamb and straightened up to look at Hannah, who was opening her mouth to protest. 'Oh, I don't say it's your fault, I'm sure you don't encourage them, I will say that for you. But boys being what they are, it's best you go and the lady what does for me is coming back tomorrow in any case, I don't need you any more.'

'Ma!' cried Hannah, all her elation draining from her. Where was she to go? She hadn't looked for another place to live yet – what was the point until she was earning? She had banked on Ma letting her stay, at least for another week.

Chapter Twelve

'Well, don't look so worried,' said Ma, 'I'm not going to throw you out on the street. You'll just have to start looking for somewhere else, there are lots of people that take in boarders. You can have a couple of days to look around.'

When Alf came in from work he was quite philosophical about it. 'You'll get somewhere,' he said. 'Anyway, I haven't time to talk about it tonight, I'm going out.' Straight after tea he rushed upstairs to get ready, whistling as he went, and Hannah guessed he was seeing a girl again, the same girl he had already been out with twice since he came back only a week ago. No wonder he can't afford to send Mam much money home, she thought. Still, Mr Ridley had promised her twenty shillings a week and extra if she worked overtime; she should be able to spare some of that to send home, she told herself optimistically.

But there was the problem of how she was going to keep herself and pay fares into Oxford and pay for a room as well out of the tiny sum of money she had left. She had only brought two pounds with her and it was alarming how quickly the money had disappeared. She went up to her attic room and carefully counted out what she had left as she sat on the bed. Eleven shillings and threepence. She counted it again to make sure but the sum remained the same.

There was nothing else for it, she would have to ask Alf to help her out, and that meant that he would have even less to send home, or spend on his girlfriend. The homesickness which always lurked in the back of her mind, grew larger and larger, casting a dark shadow over her thoughts, and she lay down on the bed, for the first time allowing it to take over. Alf would help her, she knew that, he was her brother, wasn't he? If there had been some urgent need for money at home then everyone in the family was expected to help all they could but here there was only Alf. And Alf, she suspected, was courting and his thoughts fully occupied with the girl, whoever it was.

Well, she thought, sitting up on the bed, moping wasn't going to do any good. She had to get out and do something, look at the cards in the corner-shop window for a start.

But when she did, she found there were none at all advertising for a girl lodger.

*

Next morning, the sky held only a few red-streaked clouds, promising a bright day, though with a chill wind blowing along Oxford Road as she waited at the bus stop. It was only half past seven, for she was to begin work at eight o'clock, but there was a queue of people all going in to work. She caught the eye of the girl standing next to her and smiled, and the girl smiled back warmly. She looked only a little older than Hannah, a pretty girl with blonde curls and friendly blue eyes, wearing a bright-red hat with a feather in the brim. When the bus came along, Hannah found herself standing beside the girl, squashed up against her in fact, for the vehicle was crowded with people. She had to bend her head quickly to avoid getting the girl's feather in her eye, and the girl saw it and moved her head backwards out of Hannah's way.

'Murder, isn't it?' she said to Hannah, pulling the corner of her lips down in a mock grimace.

Hannah nodded.

'Going to work, are you? Do you live round here?'

Hannah admitted that yes, she was indeed on her way to work and she was living just off Hockmore Street.

'My name's Gloria, I work in Timothy White's,' the girl said and looked enquiringly at Hannah. She was so warm and friendly that Hannah quite forgot to try to hide her accent and answered her quite naturally.

'Hannah. Hannah Armstrong,' she said. 'I've just come here to live and I've got work in Ridley's newsagent's, that's near the station.'

'Oh yes, I think I know it,' cried Gloria, sounding as delighted as if she had found out they were long-lost cousins. By the time the journey was over and they were stepping off the bus, it felt to Hannah as though she had known Gloria for ages; they were chatting together like old friends.

'I'll see you on the bus tomorrow, Hannah,' Gloria called merrily as she went on her way, the feather in her red hat bouncing with her every step.

Hannah was still smiling as she approached the door of the newsagent's and went in, all her troubles forgotten, for she felt that she had found a friend.

'Good morning, Mr Ridley,' she cried cheerfully to the man behind the counter, who was busy stacking a shelf behind him with cigarettes.

'What cheor,' he answered and she grinned. Mrs Ridley had told her the day before that they had lived in Oxford since 1912, yet his Geordie accent and way of greeting had not altered one jot.

'Gan on through and put the kettle on, will you?' he asked. 'The missus will be coming in a minute with my breakfast and I'm fair clemmed for it. I've been here since five o'clock and mind, I've been right busy.'

'Yes, Mr Ridley,' said Hannah obediently and went through the curtain to the back shop, where there was a rickety table with a gas ring on it and some cups, saucers and cutlery. She hung her coat on a hook on the back door alongside Mr Ridley's, took down an overall and put it on as she had been told to do the day before when Mrs Ridley had issued her with instructions. It was evident that the overall belonged to the older woman, Hannah could easily have wound it twice round herself, but she bunched it at the back to make it look better from the front and tied the belt fairly tightly to keep it in position. She filled the tin kettle from the single cold tap over the sink in the corner and put it to boil on the gas ring. There was a cracked mirror hanging above the sink and she peered into it; seeing her hair was windblown, she tidied it up as best she could with her hands and was ready to go back into the shop. She must bring a comb tomorrow, she thought.

'The prices are on everything,' said Mr Ridley. 'An' if they're not, you just have to ask.'

The shop was filling up with people on their way to work and impatient for their morning newspaper; Hannah was soon working hard selling Woodbine and Park Drive cigarettes, matches, mints and magazines along with the papers. It wasn't difficult, she found; she had a good head for figures and soon was remembering prices without having to check all the time.

Mrs Ridley came in just as the kettle began to boil and fried bacon and eggs on the gas ring in the back shop for Mr Ridley's breakfast. The smell of the bacon hung about for a while but it was not unpleasant. So the morning went on, customers coming and going at intervals, mostly according to when the trains got in. Hannah had half an hour for lunch, which she ate in the back shop with Mrs Ridley, who had brought sandwiches enough for them all and to spare.

'I'd take you in myself, pet,' she said when Hannah, rather hesitantly for this was, after all, her first day at work, asked if she could go early to look for somewhere to live. 'But we only have a tiny flat. All our money went on the shop, d'you see, an' though we mebbe could manage to buy a house now as the business is a good little earner, we've settled where we are, it's nice and handy and big enough for the two of us. But you go off at half past four, we'll manage. Anyroad, you're not going to be any use to us if you haven't got a place to live, are you? But why don't you look in the *Oxford Times*? There'll likely be a place in there. Though the ones in the town will be too dear for you, you'd best try for a room in Cowley.'

At half past four, Hannah was standing on the bus stand waiting for the bus, the folded paper clutched in her hand, an address in the Accommodation to Let column underlined in pencil. And within half an hour she was ringing the bell of a house in Cruel Lane, only a short distance from Mrs Prendergast's. But there was no reply, though she rang the bell three times and she checked the address in her paper again, but it was right enough, 39, Cruel Lane.

Disconsolately, Hannah walked away and up the lane to Mrs Prendergast's. She let herself in the back door and went straight up to her room, hoping to avoid seeing Ma Prendergast, but the landlady had heard her come in and followed her up the stairs.

'Have you found a place to stay?' she asked, with no preamble at all. Hannah looked at her uncompromising face and wished Alf was back from work to stand beside her. She felt very young and alone and her longing for home was more intense than ever.

'Not yet,' she admitted. 'But I have picked a place out of the paper, only they were out when I called.'

'You'd best go back after tea, then,' said Mrs Prendergast. 'In the meantime, as you're home early you can help me with the vegetables. I'm a bit late with them, as it happens.'

Hannah sat down on the edge of the bed. 'By,' she said aloud to the empty attic, 'for two pins I would walk out of here and never come back, even if I had to sleep on the streets. That woman! I don't know where I am with her, I don't, one minute she's all right and the next minute she's . . . she's . . . ' Hannah couldn't think of the right adjective to describe what she thought of Ma Prendergast. Sighing, she got to her feet, went down the stairs to the kitchen and attacked a mound of carrots with the vegetable knife.

She managed to catch Alf on his own after tea and poured out all her worries to him. He stood leaning on the doorpost of his room, for Hannah wasn't allowed inside even though he was her brother, and gazed indulgently down at her.

'Oh, go on,' he said. 'Ma was just trying to get you to hurry up and find somewhere, she'd never put you out. Anyroad, if she did, she'd find she'd lost me an' all and she wouldn't want to do that, I've been with her since I came down to Oxford and she knows I'm a good payer.'

'But she doesn't like me,' said Hannah, her voice all forlorn.

'It's not that,' Alf reassured her. 'It's just that the last girl lodger she had got herself into trouble with one of the men and Ma was frightened she would get a reputation for a disorderly house. It's nothing to do with you.'

'A disorderly house?' said Hannah and her eyes flashed and two flags of colour stained her cheeks. How could Ma think she was that sort of a girl?

Alf saw her look of outrage and grinned. 'Oh, I told you, it's not you, it would be the same with any girl living in the house. But you're just a kid, I don't know why she should be worried about you.'

Hannah was about to retort when she remembered she needed Alf's help, so it was best not to get into an argument with him. He wasn't rushing out tonight, she observed, he seemed quite happy to stand about talking to her.

'I have an address in Cruel Lane, I got it from the *Oxford Times,*' she said to him. 'Will you come with me to see it? Only I'm a bit worried I won't have enough money to pay the first week's rent if I get the room, what with my fares into town too. Will you be able to help me out?'

Alf shrugged, resignedly. 'Oh, all right,' he said. 'Just wait a minute while I get ready.'

They walked up the road side by side to number 39 and Hannah was relieved to see that there was a light in the window. Alf rang the bell and after a moment the door opened and a middle-aged man stood there, dressed in his shirtsleeves and braces and holding a newspaper in his hand. He peered over a pair of glasses enquiringly.

'Good evening,' said Hannah. 'I've come about the room.'

'Gloria!'

The man stepped back and shouted in the direction of the kitchen and after a moment a girl came out, wiping her hands on a tea towel.

'There's no need to yell, Dad,' she said crossly, 'I can hear perfectly well – oh, hallo, you're the girl I met on the bus this morning, aren't you?'

'Yes, Hannah Armstrong, I've come about the room,' said Hannah, her strained features relaxing into a smile. 'And this is my brother, Alf,' she said as an afterthought.

'Do come in,' said Gloria. 'I'll just take this tea towel back to the kitchen, I'll be with you in a tick. This is my father, Dan Morgan. Take them into the sitting room, Dad.'

Obediently, Mr Morgan led the way into a pleasant front room with a square brown carpet on the floor surrounded by linoleum. He motioned them towards seats on the comfortable-looking chesterfield and Hannah sat down beside her brother. In a minute or two, Gloria came into the room with a tray of tea and biscuits.

'You'll have a cup of tea, won't you?' she said and handed round dainty china cups and saucers. Her father sat in a chair by the fire, watching her proudly, his forgotten newspaper still in his hand.

'You've come about the room?' said Gloria when they were settled.

Hannah looked at Alf nervously. She was beginning to think there was no way she could afford a room in this house, she could see that it was newly decorated and the furniture and curtains were of the best quality. But Alf was looking at Gloria as though he had never seen a girl before, he seemed to have forgotten why they had come.

'I can't afford to pay very much,' Hannah mumbled at last.

'Oh, we're not charging a lot,' Gloria exclaimed, 'are we, Dad?'

'Well . . . ' said Mr Morgan.

'No, we thought ten shillings a week, that's all, with breakfast and evening meal. That's not too much, is it? Oh, do say you'll take it, we'd love to have you.'

Hannah did a quick calculation in her head. If she paid ten shillings a week for her board and her fares to work were three shillings and sixpence a week, that left six shillings and sixpence. If she saved half-a-crown a week and sent home ten shillings every month, then she had four shillings for her clothes and everything else, including lunches – she couldn't expect Mrs Ridley to provide her lunch every day. Still, she could eat a good breakfast and maybe manage on a sandwich or an apple at lunchtime.

'I'll take it,' she said, glancing at Alf for approval, and he nodded enthusiastically. 'Er, do you need a week's money in advance?'

'Well,' said Gloria, looking doubtfully at her father. 'Can you manage it? I know you said you were only starting work.'

'Of course we can manage it,' said Alf grandly, speaking for the first time. He stood up and dug into his trouser pocket to bring out a small fold of ten-shilling notes, perhaps thirty shillings, Hannah guessed. He handed over a note to Gloria, who took it and held it in her hand, smiling happily.

'Oh, I'm so glad you're coming, I liked you as soon as I saw you this morning at the bus stop,' she said to Hannah. 'Now let me see, it's Wednesday tomorrow and my half-day, can you come tomorrow night? I'll have the room ready by then.'

So it was agreed. Mr Morgan had taken no part in it at all, he'd left everything to his young daughter. But Hannah, sipping her tea and watching Gloria over the rim of her cup, thought she understood why. Gloria was so self-assured, so businesslike and so pretty, all the qualities she felt she lacked herself. And now the business was over with, she chatted on composedly about this and that, how there were only three of them living in the house, there was an older brother who was working nights, and she wanted another girl to live with them to be company for her.

'My mother is dead, you see,' she said.

'Oh, I'm sorry,' said Hannah, and Alf tut-tutted his sympathy too.

'It was a long time ago, four years,' said Gloria, a shadow wiping out her smile for barely a moment before she shook her pretty curls and picked up the plate of biscuits to offer them round again.

'Thank you, but we'd better be going now,' said Hannah, rising to her feet, and a reluctant Alf put down his cup and rose also. Gloria saw them to the door.

'I'll see you tomorrow then,' she said, standing on the doorstep rubbing her arms against the cold winter's breeze. Nevertheless, she stayed on the step with the door open until brother and sister were rounding a bend in the lane.

'Mind, she's a bonny girl,' said Alf, and Hannah grinned.

'Yes. You looked a bit bedazzled,' she answered. 'Gormless an' all.'

'Why, you cheeky young imp, I'll knock your block off,' said Alf, lifting his hand to her in mock rage, and she ducked and danced on ahead of him. When they got back to Ma Prendergast's, she sought her out in the kitchen immediately and told her she had found a place and would be out of the house the next day.

'So you see, you need not have worried about me,' she said proudly. 'I am not the sort of girl to bring trouble to a house in any case.' She turned on her heel and went up to her attic room and wrote a long letter to her mother and Betty, telling them how well she was doing.

'I've got a job, Mam, working in a newsagent's, and the owners are from Shields and very nice. And I have a nice room just along the road from Alf and there's a very nice girl there, called Gloria.'

Hannah paused and chewed her pencil. It had just occurred to her that she hadn't even seen the room. But she shrugged the thought away; the room would be fine, she knew.

Chapter Thirteen

Hannah soon settled in to working in Ridley's, travelling with Gloria every morning on the bus into town and coming home every evening to the house in Cruel Lane where Gloria reigned supreme. Reggie, her easy-going brother, and Dan Morgan, her doting father, seemed unable or unwilling to cross her at all. Gloria was charming and sunny-tempered most of the time and Hannah loved having her for a friend, someone who knew her way around. Her first year in Oxford fairly flew past. And suddenly, Alf was paying his sister more attention than he had ever done, turning up most evenings, 'to see how she was getting on', he would explain, though when he got there he spent more time chatting with Gloria than with Hannah.

'Aren't you going out with your girlfriend tonight then?' Hannah asked him pointedly one evening, when she and Gloria were having a serious discussion about boys and their peculiarities and Alf turned up and spoiled it.

'What girlfriend?' he asked, frowning quickly at her before turning to Gloria and smiling. 'I haven't got a girlfriend, not at the moment.'

Then he became friendly with Reggie and they would discuss the relative merits of the cars they were going to buy as soon as they had a little more money saved. Alf was all for getting a bull-nosed Morris – after all, he could get one for less than a hundred pounds with his staff discount – whereas Reggie would have to pay a hundred and twenty for the Austin Seven he fancied.

It made Hannah unhappy to hear Alf talk so grandly of acquiring a car when things were so bad at home in Winton. But life was so different in Oxford, there was an air of prosperity about the place and it was seductive, anything was possible, all you had to do was work a little harder, do some overtime and there would be the money to buy what you fancied. Alf wasn't even in a union; the Morris workers got good money without a union, he explained to her, and in any case, to join a union was to court dismissal.

'Dad only gives me five pounds a week for the house-keeping, you know,' Gloria grumbled one day. She was looking longingly at a costume in a shop window, with a pearl-grey short skirt and long jacket with dusty pink collar and cuffs and piped round the edge of the jacket. 'Just the thing for the summer,' she said.

Hannah gazed at it. It certainly was smart and would look great on Gloria, but it cost six pounds. Six pounds might as well be sixty, she thought, it was a waste of time yearning for something so expensive. She herself had her eye on the pretty print dresses in a shop near Ridley's, twenty-nine and eleven they were and in the latest style, cut severely straight and without sleeves.

The girls separated and went to their work. Even though Hannah was used to Gloria's way of speaking now, she couldn't help a wry smile as she remembered the way she grumbled, about having only five pounds a week for the housekeeping. That was more than twice as much as Mam had at home in Winton.

The shop was full and Hannah hurried through to the back to change into the overall which Mrs Ridley had made for her. It was a good job she had made it a size too big, Hannah reflected, for she was putting on weight and her bosom was developing at last. A quick flick of the comb through her hair, cut in a bob by a hairdresser in Hockmore Street, and she was ready to take her place behind the counter with Mr Ridley. Trade was steady and she was kept pretty busy for most of the morning, but as usual there was a small hiatus round about half past eleven, just before the lunchtime rush. Hannah was replenishing the stocks of cigarettes on the shelf behind the counter while she had a spare minute or two when Mr Ridley nudged her.

'Do you see that chap over there? He's been looking at that magazine for ten minutes – what does he think this is, a reading room? I'll be having a word with him just now.'

Hannah looked over her shoulder at the man, obviously an undergraduate, and as she did so he looked up and caught her eye.

'Hallo, Hannah,' he said. 'I thought it was you.'

Hannah blushed a bright scarlet. All she could think of was the last time she had seen him, sitting in a car with his supercilious friend looking over the Cornish men drunk in the gutter outside the chapel at Winton on Betty and Tucker's wedding day. In her mind's eye she could still picture his expression of contempt and disgust as he had started the car and driven away.

'Oh, if he's a friend of yours,' said Mr Ridley. 'I didn't realise.' He nodded affably to Timothy, who stepped towards the counter. But Hannah had found her voice and her pride.

'No, no, not a friend,' she said calmly. 'I'm surprised he even remembers my name.'

Timothy halted abruptly, his smile of greeting fading. 'Well, of course – ' he began and then thought better of it. Fishing in his pocket, he pulled out some coins. 'Er, how much is this?' he asked.

'One shilling,' said Hannah and held out her hand for the money.

Timothy put the copy of the *Strand* down to sort two sixpenny pieces from the change in his hand and gave her them. He paused and glanced over at Mr Ridley, who was regarding him stolidly, then he spun round on his heel and walked to the door.

'Mr Durkin, Timothy!'

He turned back as Hannah called to him, but she was simply holding out his magazine. He took it and left the shop.

'What was that about, pet?' asked Mr Ridley. 'Who is the toff?'

'Oh, nobody. Well, he is, he comes from home, not Winton exactly, but outside. His father is the mine agent.'

'Oh aye, is he now,' commented Mr Ridley, lifting his eyebrows mockingly to show how impressed he wasn't. Coming from Shields, he was well aware of a mine agent's importance.

Hannah didn't see Timothy again that summer of 1925 and she told herself that she didn't want to either. But sometimes, when she walked past one of the colleges and peeped through the entrance to that other world, she fancied she did see his tall figure at the distant end of the quadrangle. Or sometimes, when there was a quiet moment in the shop and the doorbell tinkled, she looked up quickly, thinking it might be him. But it never was, yet she was always aware of the fact that he was in the city, somewhere close. Not that it mattered to her at all, she told herself.

In August, Hannah, Gloria and Alf travelled north on the train for a week's holiday. Gloria stood on the platform with her arm linked through Alf's, holding her hand so that the sun sparkled on the tiny diamond in the gold ring on her finger. She looked so pretty and smart in her grey and pink costume, for Mr Morgan had given her the whole of six pounds she needed to buy it. Hannah, in her print dress and plain cardigan, had a few misgivings about what Gloria would think of Winton, with its towering winding wheel, slag heap, narrow rows of colliery houses and no tarmac on the roads. But then she felt disloyal; Winton was a grand place, she told herself, the folk were grand and the countryside around the village was grand, much better than Oxfordshire.

But when they arrived at Bishop Auckland and had to walk down Newgate Street to catch the bus, Hannah was dismayed to see the air of decay and poverty which hung over everything like a grey fog. Even the bigger shops looked poor things to those she remembered from Oxford, and in Kingsway there was a great long queue at the Labour Exchange. Even though the weather was warm, the men all wore cloth caps pulled down over their heads and their hands in their pockets.

Hannah watched Gloria covertly as they descended from the bus and walked the last few yards to the colliery rows, past a group of unemployed miners sitting on their hunkers by the wall of the chapel. She was waiting to see the horrified reaction she was sure would come to Gloria's face, the girl from Oxford wouldn't be able to help it. But apart from a slight tightening of her nostrils as they passed by the ash closets, Gloria appeared to be delighted to be there and had eyes only for Alf.

'It's a bit different to Oxford,' Hannah ventured as she determinedly led the way to the front of the house as though they weren't family – family always went in by the backyard. But she had forgotten that Mam had the front room turned into a shop and when they opened the door a bell tinkled and her sister Jane came out from the kitchen, ready to serve a customer.

'Jane! You're home at last,' Hannah cried, forgetting all about Gloria and Alf in her delighted surprise. 'When did they let you out?'

Jane didn't reply for a moment, she was busy calling to the rest of the family in the kitchen. 'Mam! Bob, come and see, our Hannah's back an' Alf an' all.'

Suddenly they were all there, hugging and kissing each other and laughing and crying together and Hannah was exclaiming at how much Walton had grown, why, he must be almost ready for school. Harry, taller and thinner now, his pale face looking more and more like his brother's, was hanging back shyly, watching Gloria as though she had dropped in from Mars.

189

'This is Gloria, Mam,' said Alf proudly. 'Gloria, this is my mother, and my brother Bob and sister Jane, and the little 'uns are Harry and Walton.' And Gloria was charming and pleasant to everyone, even shaking hands with little Walton.

'There's parkin for tea,' he informed her solemnly, 'and stotty cake and best butter, not margarine or dripping.'

'How lovely!' said Gloria, though Hannah was quite sure she had never eaten margarine or dripping before in her life, and she silently blessed her future sister-in-law for being so nice. Now that Gloria had actually seen the worst, as it were, Hannah felt she could relax and enjoy her homecoming.

They sat round the kitchen table and ate bread in the form of stotty cakes hot from the oven with butter melting over it and followed up with ginger parkin. Gloria swore that it was the best tea she had ever tasted.

'You are a wonderful cook, Mrs Armstrong,' she said, full of admiration. Nora blushed and mumbled something about it being easy to be a good cook if you had plenty of the right ingredients.

'Oh, I'm sure I'll never be able to cook like you,' said Gloria. 'What a comedown it will be for poor Alf.' Alf smiled fondly at her and everyone knew he didn't believe that at all.

'Well, Bob,' Alf said at last, man to man, like, for Bob had taken no part in the conversation so far. 'How's things at the pit?'

'Badly,' Bob said shortly. 'It's a three-day week we're on now. And expecting to be laid idle altogether by the autumn.'

'It's going back to the gold standard that's made it worse,' said Alf sagely. 'I was reading about it in the *Oxford Times*. But I thought with the government subsidy the pits would keep on working.'

'Aye. Well, Mr Durkin is playing it canny, he reckons Lord Akers can only keep half the pits open, there's no demand, he says. If there's no demand, why does he want us to work an extra hour every day and for no more pay? Tell me that. Anyroad, Lord Akers can afford to go gallivanting all over the world an' all, he shows no signs of going bust. An' this government's on the side of the owners, if it hadn't been for the unions there would have been no subsidy neither.'

Bob was in full flow, his bitter voice went on and on and Hannah could see that Gloria's smile was slipping.

'Alf says they have no need for a union at the car works,' she intervened. 'Isn't that right, dear?'

'Well,' said Alf, glancing at Bob, 'it's different at Morris's.'

Bob shot him a look of contempt. 'Aye, different,' he snapped. 'But what happens when everyone has a car as wants one? Will it be different then?' His voice rose passionately and he stuck his head forward so that the frayed edge of his collar became all the more noticeable, a collar which Hannah could see had already been turned once.

'Now, lads, let's not have any arguments today. I've been looking forward to seeing the family all together again, don't spoil it,' said Mam, and a fraught silence fell.

'Come on, Gloria, we'll walk up to the bunny banks,' Alf said at last, jumping up and holding his hand out to her. 'It's nice up there, you'll like it.' With an air of relief, Gloria went with him to the door and paused before going out, flashing a hesitant smile at the family grouped round the table.

The bell tinkled from the front room and Hannah started to her feet. 'I'll go, Mam,' she said, 'you have a rest.' She went into the 'shop' and weighed out a penny-worth of yeast for a tired-looking woman with a mewling child hanging on to her skirt.

'Hallo, Hannah,' the woman said and Hannah, who hadn't recognised her when she first came in, looked more closely and was surprised to see it was Mrs Hutchinson, looking at least fifteen years older than when she had last seen her. They chatted for a minute or two and then Mrs Hutchinson went on her way, saying she had to get the bread laid down to rise or there would be none for the morning.

Back in the kitchen, there was only Jane and her mother. Bob had gone out and Harry and Walton were playing in the back lane.

'It's lovely to be back,' Hannah said, 'really great to see you home as well, Jane. Are you home for good, now?'

'Oh yes, I'm cured, they say,' Jane answered. At fourteen, Jane was a quiet, reserved girl and acted almost like a guest in the house, Hannah noticed, thinking sadly that it must have been the years in the sanatorium that did it. The old, close relationship they once had was completely gone.

When Hannah suggested that the three of them should call in the boys and walk up to see Betty and Tucker, Jane demurred, saying she would rather stay in by herself and read, 'while I have the house quiet and to myself,' she said. So Hannah, her mother and the two children walked up the row and out of the village to the undermanager's house.

Looking at the house as they went through the flower garden, full of the scent of roses and phlox, Hannah was surprised at how different it was from her memory of it. Oh, it was still grand next to the cottages in the miners' rows, but in comparison with the new houses being built in Cowley it wasn't so grand at all. But she forgot all that in the delight of greeting Betty, seven months pregnant and huge with it so that she had to lean forward to kiss Hannah's cheek.

'You look well, Hannah,' she said. 'At least you're not so skinny as you used to be.'

'Thank you,' said Hannah dryly. 'I can say the same about you.'

The three women talked for an hour while Harry and Walton played in the garden, they had so much to catch up on. Betty was happy in her marriage and look-ing forward to the baby and just about everything she said was prefixed by 'Tucker says' or 'Tucker likes', but Hannah could see there was a shadow of anxiety about her nevertheless. Mam was very happy sitting with her two daughters, discussing how grand it was in Oxford and how nice Alf's girl was. 'Not a bit of side to her,' she said. So Hannah didn't want to ask what it was that was causing the shadow over Betty's happiness, she didn't want to spoil the moment.

'I'll come up and see you during the week,' Hannah said as they were leaving. 'It'll be good to have a proper chat, just like we used to when we shared a bed at home.'

'Oh yes, do that,' said Betty rather quickly, glancing at her mother who was in the garden rounding up the boys for the walk home. Harry and Walton ran on ahead down the dusty road and Hannah and her mother strolled arm in arm in the warm August air. The cokeworks were busy filling the air with the stench of sulphur and coal gas, but to Hannah the smell was not so bad, it was simply the smell of Winton and home. At intervals they stopped and had a word with neighbours and friends who came out to greet Hannah and exclaim over how well she looked, and Nora would glow with pride as she told them how Hannah had a good job in a shop owned by Geordies and how Alf too was doing well in the motor works. All in all, a happy first day home, thought Hannah as she climbed into the bed she was to share with Gloria for the holiday.

'Things are bad, Hannah, they couldn't be worse,' said Betty sadly. It was the following Tuesday and the two sisters were sitting in the garden of Betty's house, drinking home-made lemonade.

'I can see that,' said Hannah, 'the whole place looks poverty-stricken. But the pit's gone through bad times before, it usually gets going again.'

'Yes, but Tucker says the slump is set in this time. He heard Mr Durkin telling the manager that costs have to be cut and that means the wages bill, there's no other way. And you've seen the folk in the rows, they're on starvation wages now and a lot of them are on the dole. Tucker's worried about the future, he thinks the owners have been conniving with the government and stockpiling coal now because they want to have a showdown and break the unions.'

'Do you think there'll be another strike?' asked Hannah. 'Bob thinks that there could be a general strike, he thinks that the workers of the country will support the miners this time.'

'Tucker thinks a strike will come, maybe not yet but soon. Or if not, a lockout to force the men to accept the owners' conditions. Do you think the other unions will support them?'

'I don't know.' Hannah shook her head, thinking of the people she knew in Oxford and Cowley; the mines were so remote from most of the country and she suspected most people knew very little about them as did the people of Oxford. 'Will Tucker be affected if there is a strike?' she asked.

'He will, though not like the men; he'll still get his salary though it may be reduced. But it's Bob and the others like him I worry about.'

'Well, there's nothing you or I can do, Betty, so what's the use of worrying?'

'I don't know, Hannah, but if all the young people think there's no future here and move away like you and Alf did, what will be left? A wasteland, that's all. I don't want my baby to be born into a wasteland.'

Hannah thought about Betty's words as the train carrying them back to Oxford pulled into the station. She followed Alf and Gloria out of the station and looked around her; the contrast between the people here and those at home in Winton or even in the town of Bishop Auckland could not be more marked. The two worlds of Oxford, both town and gown, were indeed so remote from the world of the pit villages of Durham that they might as well be in Timbuktu.

Hannah left Alf and Gloria to go back to Cowley on their own while she went in to see Mr and Mrs Ridley in the newsagent's shop.

'By, am I glad to see you back,' Mrs Ridley said as she went in. 'Now I can put my feet up for an hour, they're killing me.'

Hannah was taken aback. She hadn't expected to begin work immediately – after all, her holiday wasn't over until Monday – but she saw the look of strained tiredness on the older woman's face and decided not to mention that she still had another day's holiday due.

'You've been busy then,' was her only comment.

'Busy? We've been rushed off our feet,' Mr Ridley put in. 'The place is full of visitors, all coming in off the trains and coming in here for a newspaper. Not that I'm complaining, mind, God forbid; the time to complain is when we're not busy.'

'None of the shops at home looked busy,' said Hannah sadly as she went into the back shop to don her overall.

'Aye, we've heard it's bad,' said Mrs Ridley. 'I bless the day we decided to move down here, I do. I thank God every single night.'

Yet even for Hannah the troubles of the distressed mining areas receded into the background as she became immersed in her life in Oxford. The summer turned into autumn and the autumn into winter and her mother wrote that the pit had not, after all, closed down but that Bob was again working a full week. Betty's time came and she had a baby girl, and Hannah knitted a matinee jacket in pink and white and sent it off with her monthly postal order for her mother. But there were days now when she didn't think of Winton at all, she was so busy at the shop during the day, and the evenings were never lonely for Alf was round most of the time to sit on the chesterfield in the lounge with Gloria, holding hands and planning the wedding. And Hannah would willingly wash the dishes and clean up the kitchen while Dan sat at the table reading his *Oxford Chronicle,* exiled from his own lounge. Sometimes Hannah and Reggie made up a foursome with Alf and Gloria to go dancing the one-step and the palais glide or the new American dances they saw at the pictures such as the black bottom or the Charleston.

Hannah liked to go to the Palais, she loved the freedom of the new dances, though sometimes she wondered what Mr Hughes or Mr Hodgson would think if they saw her swinging her legs about in the ultrashort skirts which were the fashion.

But it was almost 1926, these were modern times, she told herself, there was no harm in dancing, how could there be? It was lovely to start the 'gentlemen's excuse me' quickstep with Alf and know that Reggie would tap her brother on the shoulder after they'd done one round of the room and sometimes another boy would tap Reggie's shoulder and he would frown but stand aside nevertheless. And she would feel attractive and popular, like Gloria, who always had three or four partners for this dance and only laughed at Alf's objections.

So she was delighted on Saturday night when she and Reggie were flying about the room to the lively beat of the 'Twelfth Street Rag', to see out of the corner of her eye that someone was tapping Reggie's shoulder and he was slackening his hold on her, though his frown this time was particularly black as he muttered something about 'blooming university blokes'.

She stood looking up into Timothy Durkin's deep-blue eyes, stupid with the shock of seeing him there, while the other dancers wove round them and the mirrored glass ball hanging from the ceiling reflected myriad tiny lights. Then she felt his arms around her and as she automatically put up her own and followed his steps she could feel the steady beat of his heart against hers.

He swirled with her, round and round, saying nothing but smiling faintly down at her, and though she tried to stare straight in front of her at his shirt front she found that her eyes were drawn to his as the music changed. Her step faltered but he held her a little tighter and the singer with the band began to sing through a megaphone.

She saw Reggie approaching through the dancers determinedly but Timothy saw him too and expertly swung her through the double doors of the refreshment room.

'You'd like some lemonade, wouldn't you?' he said as he led her to a table.

Chapter Fourteen

Hannah watched Timothy, feeling slightly dazed, as he caught the waitress's eye with ease and ordered the lemonade. Then he sat back and smiled easily at her across the table.

'How are you, Hannah?' he asked.

'I must get back to the dance floor,' she said instead of answering his question.

'But why? We're not doing anything wrong, sitting here waiting for a nice glass of refreshing lemonade. The dancing has made me thirsty, aren't you thirsty?'

The waitress came with the drinks and Timothy searched in his pocket for change to pay for them, providing a few seconds for her to study him. He was so different from Reggie and Alf, she thought, so self-assured. She glanced around quickly and saw Reggie in the doorway, frowning fiercely at her and jerking his head to one side to indicate he wanted her to come away from the toff. She glared at him, forgetting that a moment before she had been going to leave of her own accord. What right had he to tell her what to do? She picked up her glass and took a sip of lemonade, enjoying the sweet yet tangy taste, and smiled at Timothy.

'Why were you so offhand with me when I saw you in Ridley's shop?' Timothy asked her softly. 'I felt quite hurt, I thought we were friends.'

Friends, she thought, gazing into her glass. She hadn't seen him for years until the day of Betty's wedding and then he had looked at her as though she were dirt; the memory of it was still painful. 'We were never friends,' she said scornfully. 'How could we be? Me a pit lass from the rows and you the agent's son.'

'Oh, now, it was never like that when we sang in the choir at chapel.' He reached out across the table and put his hand over hers. His low, clear voice brought back the remembrance of his baritone mingling with her mezzo-soprano as they sang 'Gethsemane' that Easter, so many years ago. But he had gone, left the chapel without a word, and though she had only been a child at the time, that had hurt too.

She pulled her hand away and started to rise but stopped as she heard Alf's voice, taut with anger.

'Howay, Hannah,' he said, his aggression making him return to the idiom of his native north-east. 'Get back in the dance hall, you promised this dance to Reggie.'

'But it's the interval,' she said, surprised. When she looked up and saw her brother's hard expression and Reggie standing just behind him as though to back him up, she understood and flushed with resentment.

'I don't care if it is the interval, come away with us,' Alf insisted.

'I'm staying here,' she answered evenly. 'I haven't finished my lemonade yet.'

Alf glared at her. 'You'll do what I say,' he snapped. 'I won't have my sister sitting with a university chap, a stranger.'

Timothy had been sitting without saying anything, just looking from Alf to Hannah, but now he intervened. 'I'm no stranger, we're old friends, Hannah and I. Don't you know me?'

Alf stared down at him, his face set. 'Oh aye, I know who you are, mister. But that doesn't mean to say I want to know you, if you see what I mean.'

Timothy got to his feet, keeping his expression pleasant though his eyes were watchful as he replied, 'Well, I'm not all that sure I want to know you. But that has nothing to do with Hannah and me. If she wants to enjoy a drink with me, she has that right. She's not in purdah, you know, this is 1925.'

'Hannah, get out of here when I tell you,' Alf barked, his fists bunched to within six inches of Timothy's nose. Reggie stepped forward just behind him. When Hannah looked into their faces she saw all the enmity there of town for gown which she had heard had existed for centuries but had had no experience of until now.

But Alf wasn't from Oxford. And besides, he knew Timothy Durkin, he had sometimes been in chapel when she and Timothy had sung their duets. Alf had no right, she told herself angrily.

A man was stepping in front of her brother and Reggie. 'We'll have no trouble in here,' he warned, and a murmuring rose from the other tables. Hannah looked round to see that two or three large young men had ranged themselves beside Timothy, standing quietly doing nothing, their eyes as watchful as his. Everyone else in the room was looking at the confrontation too, and the murmuring from the tables grew louder.

'Coming in here after our girls, think they can do what they like –'

'Treat them like dirt, they do –'

She heard the comments and was alarmed. The atmosphere was becoming charged with anger and the bouncer standing between the two groups looked from one to the other.

'I said, we'll have no trouble and I meant it. Mary,' he called to the waitress, 'go and get the manager.'

'No, no, there'll be no trouble,' Hannah stammered. 'I'm coming with you, Alf, let's all go home.' As she spoke she rose to her feet and pushed her way to the door, looking neither to left nor right, her face scarlet with humiliation. She rushed through the dance hall to the cloakroom for her coat, and was buttoning it up with shaky fingers when Gloria came in.

'What was that all about, Hannah?' she asked. 'I missed it, I was powdering my nose and when I came back I saw the boys were crowding into the refreshment room and then you came running out as though the devil was after you.'

'Nothing, it was just Alf making a fuss,' said Hannah. 'We're going home now.'

'But the dance isn't half over,' Gloria started to protest but thought better of it as she saw her friend was struggling to control her emotions. 'All right,' she said, 'I'll just get my coat.'

Nothing was said as the four of them walked to the bus and during the short ride, but the moment they reached the house, Alf turned to Hannah.

'Don't you show me up like that again,' he said. 'All my mates there an' all, and you making up to a student.'

'I wasn't!' Hannah retorted. 'It was an excuse-me dance, wasn't it? Timothy had a perfect right to cut in if he wanted to.'

'They have no right coming to our dances, that lot,' said Reggie. 'They only come round to pick up our girls and the girls are soft enough to let them.'

'But I know him, Reg, he comes from near Winton, he was just being friendly,' Hannah protested. 'What's wrong with having a drink with someone you know?'

'Nothing's wrong with having a drink, but it wouldn't have stopped there, would it? Do you think I couldn't tell what he was after? Grow up, Hannah,' said Alf.

'Alf, leave her alone, there was no harm done,' Gloria tried to intervene. 'She's only a kid, she just doesn't understand.'

'Keep out of it, Gloria,' said Reggie, taking hold of his sister's arm and drawing her away.

'You didn't keep out of it,' Gloria retorted.

'Oh, why can't you all mind your own business?' cried Hannah, thoroughly roused. 'I don't need your help, Gloria, this is between Alf and me, though it's none of his business either, I wasn't doing anything wrong.'

'Don't talk to Gloria like that,' Alf shouted, took hold of Hannah by the arms and shook her. It was so unexpected that Hannah was taken by surprise and her head flicked forwards and backwards painfully.

'Alf!' cried Gloria with a muttered oath. Alf flung Hannah down on the chesterfield couch.

'Now then, what's this all about? You're not fighting, are you?'

Dan Morgan came to the bottom of the stairs dressed only in crumpled, striped pyjamas and stuck the top half of himself round the door. 'What's going on?' he demanded when no one answered him the first time.

There was a moment's silence as Reggie and Alf looked at him, not knowing what to say.

'It's all right, Daddy.' It was Gloria, as usual, who found her voice first and spoke to him quite normally. 'They were just horsing around, I told them they would wake you up. Alf's going home now in any case.'

Dan gazed around uncertainly. 'It sounded like you were having a bust-up,' he said. Fortunately, he couldn't see Hannah properly because Reggie had moved to stand with his back to her, hiding her as she sat with her head hanging down, trying to fight off the sick dizziness which Alf's shaking had brought on.

'Go back to bed, Dad,' said Gloria. 'We're sorry we woke you up. We won't be long, we'll see everything's locked up after Alf goes.'

'Goodnight, then,' said Dan, satisfied, and he closed the door and padded off upstairs.

'Oh!' cried Hannah, jumping up the minute the door was closed and running out to the toilet. Bending over the toilet bowl, she promptly vomited, her head thumping, retching and retching until at last the spasms subsided and she straightened and leaned weakly against the distempered wall. The taste of bile was bitter in her mouth and she searched in the pocket of her dress for her handkerchief but it wasn't there.

'Here, use mine,' said Gloria who had followed her out, full of concern. 'Come on in now and sit down, you'll feel better in a minute or two.'

'Thanks,' said Hannah shakily. 'I think I'll stay outside, though.'

'No, come in, it's too cold. Alf's going now. If you don't want to see him again tonight, go into the bathroom till he's gone.'

Hannah nodded, then winced, even that small movement was painful. She went through the kitchen to the bathroom and locked herself in. Filling the handbasin with water she washed her face and neck, then held the flannel, soaked in cold water, against her forehead.

'Hannah? Are you all right?'

She jumped as Alf called through the door, then stared at her reflection in the glass above the basin. Her dark eyes were wide in her pale face, dull and shadowed, and her hair was all over the place.

'Leave me alone, Alf.'

'I'm not going to hurt you, Hannah, I'm sorry I shook you so hard. But I got so mad, seeing you with that – '

'Go away, Alf. I'll see you tomorrow.'

Hannah opened her tin of tooth powder, picked up her brush and began to clean her teeth. The clean, minty powder took away the sour taste of bile and refreshed her somewhat; the thumping in her head began to fade. As she turned off the tap she heard a whispering outside the bathroom door, then Gloria's anxious voice.

'Are you feeling better, Hannah?'

'I'm all right. Has he gone?'

'He's going now.'

'Goodnight, Hannah, I'll see you tomorrow,' said Alf.

Hannah waited until she heard the back door close behind him before she came out of the bathroom. There was only Gloria in the kitchen; she was sitting at the table pouring cocoa into two cups.

'Come and drink this, it'll make you feel better to have something in your stomach,' she said as Hannah emerged. 'Lordy, Hannah, you look terrible. Will I get you a couple of Aspros?'

'No, just the cocoa, thank you, Gloria.'

'I told Alf he shouldn't have touched you. There is no need for it, if he ever touched me like that I'd leave him, I told him straight.' Gloria picked up her cup in two hands and sipped from it, her face solemn and unhappy.

'Oh, Gloria, he didn't mean to hurt me. He didn't hit me, he just didn't realise how hard he was shaking me, he's a strong man,' said Hannah. This was the first time she had ever heard Gloria criticise Alf and if there was a rift between her brother and his fiancée it would be all her fault.

'He's not a violent man, Gloria,' she tried again. 'He would never hurt you, he adores you.'

Gloria looked across the table at Hannah and smiled, 'Oh, come on, Hannah,' she said. 'You look as though you're dead on your feet. Let's drink our cocoa and go to bed before we wake Dad up again.'

The next day was a Sunday and Hannah decided to go for a walk to clear her head.

'But what about your lunch?' asked Gloria. She was cooking sirloin of beef and Hannah had mixed Yorkshire puddings to go with it. 'Dad and Reg have gone to meet Alf at the Cowley Workers' Club but they'll be back for two o'clock, I thought we'd have a nice family afternoon. After all, we will be a real family after the wedding, it's not long now.'

'I don't feel much like eating a big meal. Don't bother about me, I'd rather walk,' said Hannah.

'But Reggie will expect you to be here.'

'Oh, he won't care if I'm here or not, why should he?'

'Well, because he likes you, I can tell.'

'Gloria, don't talk soft,' Hannah said briskly. 'If he does, he certainly fooled me last night.'

'Oh, it's because you don't want to see them,' Gloria looked relieved. 'Don't worry, they won't say a word to you, I won't let them. You did something foolish but now it's over and done with, we'll all forget about it.'

Hannah opened her mouth to protest that she hadn't done anything but changed her mind, there was no sense in getting into an argument with Gloria.

'Yes, but I think I'll still go for that walk,' she said. 'I need the exercise. I'll see you all later.'

'I'll keep your dinner warm in a low oven then,' Gloria replied as she turned back to her preparations, and Hannah knew she was slightly offended. Shrugging helplessly, she let herself out of the house and set off briskly along Cruel Lane to the junction with Hockmore Street. She turned left and left again into Church Street. The weather was very damp with a low, overcast sky which threatened rain and a cold wind which soon whipped colour into her cheeks, so she decided not to take to the fields but to stick to the streets, for her shoes were thin leather with open fronts and a buttoned cross-bar. She had bought them in the July sales and was trying to make them last until January, when she hoped to find some brogues in the winter sales.

Walking past St James's Church and vicarage, she looked over curiously to try to catch sight of the cows which Gloria had told her the vicar, Georgie Moore, kept. Hannah knew him by sight, he was a large man who drove a pony and trap around Cowley.

'He has been known to marry people with his cow boots on under his surplice,' Gloria had said. 'I hope he remembers to take them off for my wedding.'

The wedding was to be in March, Alf and Gloria had decided. The couple would live in Dan's house at first, just until the new houses being built up the road were finished, then they hoped to rent their own home; they even talked ambitiously of buying, all in good time, of course.

Hannah turned left past the vicarage and left again, to walk up Cruel Lane. But she felt the walk had been too short so she hurried past the house and on to the end of the road, turning right along Hockmore Street. She kept on past the shops, turning corners as the fancy took her, not really caring where she went. She felt restless and unsettled somehow. Her night had been disturbed by bad dreams and long, wakeful periods. She saw the sign, Junction Road, and was thinking of turning back down Temple Road when she noticed the Methodist chapel. The lights were on inside and she could hear the sound of the organ and singing. On impulse she went in and slid into an empty pew near the back.

It was the first time Hannah had been inside a chapel since she came to Cowley. If Alf had kept it up, no doubt she would have gone with him, but he hadn't, and on her own she had not got around to it.

The chapel was very different from the plain, undecorated meeting house in Winton; this one was all polished wood and carvings and bright stained glass in the windows. But the organ music and the singing were the same, even though the minister wore a gown like a vicar. So it made a link with home somehow and Hannah resolved to come more often. The warmth in the church after the cold outside began to make her feel sleepy and during the sermon she dropped off to sleep, awaking with a start as the last hymn began. She got to her feet feeling woolly-headed, thinking at first that she was back in Winton and that Mr Hodgson, who kept an eagle eye on the younger members, must have seen her lapse. But then she remembered where she was and slipped out before the benediction so that she didn't have to talk to anyone.

Outside, the rain had started in earnest so that by the time she got back to the house in Cruel Lane, she was soaked to the skin and her thin shoes were sodden. She went in the back door and Gloria popped her head out of the lounge, exclaiming when she saw the state she was in.

'Hannah! You'll catch your death of cold. Look, I'll run you a bath and you get straight into it and you can have your dinner afterwards, I've kept it hot in the oven.'

'Nothing to eat, please Gloria, I'll have something later,' said Hannah, but she was only too pleased to strip off her clothes and soak in a hot bath, letting the heat seep into her bones. And afterwards she slipped through the hall dressed in Gloria's lounging pyjamas, which her friend had thoughtfully brought down for her. Hearing the drone of men's voices behind the lounge door, she went upstairs to her room, glad of an excuse not to face Alf and Reggie for a while at least. Changing into her nightie, she got into bed, pulling the covers up to her chin. And then, lying watching the raindrops slide down the windowpane, she at last allowed herself to think about Timothy.

'Something up?'

The Honourable Anthony Akers dumped his glass of beer on the table where Timothy was sitting by himself, morosely staring into the middle distance. The bar was full of undergraduates, noisily celebrating or debating.

Timothy shook himself out of his reverie and smiled at his friend. 'Hallo, Tony,' he said. 'No, what could be wrong? I was just sitting here having a quiet drink, that's all.' To illustrate this he took a long swig of his beer before putting his glass down on the table and staring at it as if fascinated.

'You could have fooled me, old son,' said Tony cheerfully. 'If I were asked to diagnose what's wrong with you I'd say woman trouble. Am I right?'

'No, you're not,' Timothy snapped. 'I told you there was nothing wrong. Now, if I'm too quiet for you, why don't you join that lot at the bar? They're noisy enough even for you.'

'Ooh, quite a temper,' observed Tony equably. 'It wouldn't have anything to do with that little girl who almost caused a riot on Saturday night, would it? The one Rupert Rowlands was telling me about? You know, the refugee from the wastes of the industrial north?'

Timothy rose to his feet and, picking up his glass, drained it before replying. 'I can see there's to be no peace in here tonight,' he pronounced, sounding only a little pompous. 'If you don't mind, I'll be off now.'

Tony whistled. 'I say, you really are smitten by this girl, aren't you? Come and sit down and tell your Uncle Tony all about it.'

But Timothy was gone, the door into the street swinging after him. He walked back to his rooms through the gloom of the early December day, then, when he was almost there, he turned round and walked away again. He told himself that he was simply in need of fresh air, even though rain was already falling from a lowering sky. And as he walked, Hannah was in his thoughts, how lovely her face had been as she gazed at him across the table in the supper room of that cheap dance hall, he couldn't remember its name. Her great dark eyes, such eloquent eyes, did she know they mirrored her thoughts so plainly? And the flawlessness of her skin, so fresh and creamy; the entrancing way her dark hair framed her face; the dimple in her chin he had been tempted to put his finger over. He could picture her so well now. But of course he wasn't really smitten by her, as Tony had said he was, Tony was always jumping to the wrong conclusions about everything. It was just that he was interested in her, of course – hadn't he known her years ago when she was a skinny little girl with a large voice? Not that she was skinny now, he mused, oh no. Even in the straight, rather shapeless dress she was wearing he could see how her figure had rounded out, the way the cheap fabric was strained a little over her breasts, and when he had held her to him in the dance he had felt her tiny waist and the voluptuous way her hips swelled beneath. Oh no, she was no longer skinny.

It would be pleasant to talk to her for a while without that loutish brother and his pals interrupting, he thought. He would be interested in finding out what she and her brother were doing in Oxford, so far from their native north-east. He had always thought miners liked to stay in the pits, were born to the work almost, though he had only the vaguest idea of how the girls made their living, before they were married, that is. Of course, some of them became servants, he knew.

With a shock, Timothy came to a halt by the railway station, just across the road from the newsagent's shop, the shop where he had seen Hannah that day, for the first time since she was a child. What on earth had made him walk all the way here? he wondered. Oh, well, he decided, he might as well go in and get an evening paper. Crossing the road he went in.

'Yes, sir?'

It wasn't Hannah behind the counter, but a middle-aged woman with a lilting Geordie accent.

'Umm, the *Standard,* please,' he said, mentioning the first paper which came into his head.

'Twopence, that is, sir,' said the woman and he delved into the pocket of his Oxford bags for the money. He hesitated for a moment and she looked at him, eyebrows raised.

'Anything else, sir?'

'No, thank you. That is, er, there was a young lady in the shop the last time I was in, can you tell me if she still works here? A small girl, about seventeen, I think.'

Mrs Ridley looked him up and down, compressing her lips, her usual merry smile missing. 'I'm sure I don't know who you mean, sir,' she said. 'Now if you don't mind, I am rather busy – '

'A girl from County Durham, perhaps a relation of yours?' Timothy persisted.

'What do you want with this girl?' Mrs Ridley demanded. Timothy had no time to reply for the curtain at the back of the shop was lifted and Hannah came out.

'It's all right, Mrs Ridley,' she said. 'I know Mr Durkin, he's from Bishop Auckland.'

Chapter Fifteen

They sat in a small café near the station, the sort of place which was not quite what Hannah would call scruffy but on the other hand, it didn't pretend to be a genteel tea room either. But the counter and the tables were clean and so were the thick cups and saucers. She had thought of it as a good place to meet for it was tucked away round a corner and so in the unlikely event that Alf or Reggie should come by the station they wouldn't see her.

Timothy had brought cups of muddy brown tea from the counter and now they sat facing each other in the almost empty room. The café was used mainly during the day; at this time of early evening, there were few customers.

'I'm sorry if I caused you any trouble on Saturday evening,' he said softly. She watched him stirring sugar into his tea, two spoons of sugar, she noted abstractedly, he has a sweet tooth. Briefly she thought of Alf's angry reaction when he had found her with Timothy, the way he had shaken her and shouted at her.

'It doesn't matter,' she said.

'The truth is, I was so pleased to see you there I didn't think,' he said. 'I just knew I wanted to dance with you and talk to you, find out what you had been doing during all these years.' He sat back in his seat and smiled at her. Somehow, the smile excluded the people hurrying by on the pavement outside the window and the waitress standing behind the counter wiping pots with a grey tea cloth and watching Timothy and Hannah curiously. It excluded everything; the smile built a world of their own and there were just the two of them in it.

'Look at me, Hannah,' he commanded.

Startled, she looked up into his eyes and a melting sensation crept up from her toes. Beneath it there was a warning voice telling her to be very careful, to hang on to her common sense; he was the agent's son, upper middle class, and as such as far out of her reach as the son of Lord Akers. But all of that was of no account against the way he was looking at her.

'Hannah, why were you so unfriendly that day I found you in Ridley's? I was so pleased to see you and you made me feel like a worm.'

'I don't know,' she mumbled, her face pink as she thought of the reason she had acted that way.

'Did you think I was just trying to pick you up? I know that's what your brother thought at the dance hall that night, though it wasn't that at all. But I was so surprised and pleased to see you after so many years, and in Oxford of all places. Why did you leave home?'

'For the same reason my brother did, to put myself in the way of earning a living,' said Hannah. 'There was no work for either of us at home.'

Timothy was embarrassed, he could have kicked himself. Of course, it was obvious. To cover up he pressed on. 'But why Oxford, of all places?'

'Alf came to work at the motor works, and I followed because he could help me get settled.'

Hannah took a sip of tea and put the cup down hurriedly, it was stewed. She stared out at the rain, wondering what she was doing here with a man like Timothy Durkin who had to have it pointed out to him that girls in her position had to leave home to find work. Sadly, she was becoming more and more aware of the gulf between them, it seemed impossible to cross.

'I'd better be getting off home now, they'll be wondering where I am,' she said, rising to her feet. Timothy automatically stood up too.

'Oh, do you have to? I thought we could go to the pictures or something, maybe have a meal somewhere. We haven't had a chance to talk yet'

'I must go.'

He saw she was determined and shrugged in disappointment. 'Oh, well, if you must. I'll run you home, the motor is parked just around the corner in the station yard, it won't take me a tick to get it.'

'No, I'll get the bus, it drops me at the end of the road,' she said, shaking her head decisively. Alarm showed in her face for a moment as she thought what would happen if she drove up to the house with Timothy and Alf saw her, or even Reggie or Gloria.

Seeing it, Timothy immediately capitulated, half guessing the reason. 'I'll walk with you to the bus, then,' he said. But even though it was only a short distance to the bus stop and the evening was dark and wet, illuminated only by foggy pools of light under the street lamps, she was nervous, looking around all the time, and he could sense it and cursed her lout of a brother for making her so.

'I'll call for you tomorrow evening, same time,' he said softly as they waited at the bus stop.

'Better not,' said Hannah.

'But I want to,' cried Timothy, 'and you like me a little bit, don't you? So why not, we're not hurting anyone?'

The bus was pulling up to the stop and Hannah moved forwards to the step, feeling confused, not knowing what to say. She paused for a moment and the man behind her said, 'For God's sake, girlie, make up your mind, before the bus goes without us.' She climbed up, not looking

behind her at Timothy, and moved down the bus, only
to find that he was with her, taking the seat next to hers.

'What are you doing?' she whispered urgently, glancing around to make sure no one she knew was aboard.

'I'll come all the way with you unless you agree to
meet me tomorrow,' he replied and she knew he meant it.

'All right, all right, but wait outside Ridley's for me,
six o'clock. Don't come in and don't let Mrs Ridley see
you,' she answered and he smiled triumphantly. He
picked up her gloveless hand and kissed the tips of her
cold fingers for anyone to see before getting to his feet
and ringing the bell.

The bus came to a halt just as it turned into the Cowley
Road; he jumped off and waited until it started up again,
to give her a jaunty wave through the window. Blushing,
she glanced round at her fellow passengers. Two girls
sitting opposite were watching her, their eyes alive with
curiosity and something else, was it envy? She looked
away quickly, folding her hands in her lap, still feeling
the touch of his warm lips on her fingers. Dreamily, she
gazed at her reflection in the window until the bus sailed
past her stop and she had to walk all the way back, feeling very foolish.

But she had decided on one thing. Maybe she was a
fool, but she loved being with Timothy, she loved the
way he made her feel special and she was going to stop
letting thoughts of the gulf between them get in the way

of her being with him. She would meet him as often as he wanted to even if that was only until he tired of seeing her. And he would tire of her, her common sense told her he would. But till then, she had this lovely new exciting feeling to cherish and she could pretend it would last for ever and not worry about afterwards. 'Sufficient unto the day is the evil thereof,' as Mr Hodgson had been so fond of quoting.

'Oh, I meant to tell you, I've joined the choral society and there is a practice tonight. Don't bother about any dinner for me, Gloria, I'll get a snack after work. There isn't time for me to come home for anything, the practice starts at seven.'

Hannah rose from her seat on the bus where she had been sitting with Gloria and rang the bell to get off and Gloria followed her.

'But why didn't you tell me?' asked Gloria, looking slightly injured. 'I have a casserole all ready for tonight and Reggie promised to light the oven at three o'clock when he gets up. And Alf is coming round, we were going to have a nice family evening together before Reggie goes to work. He'll be disappointed if you're not there.' Gloria was becoming more domesticated by the day as her wedding approached; she loved to play at happy families.

Hannah turned to her contrite. 'Oh, I'm sorry, I didn't think,' she said. 'I arranged it at lunchtime yesterday and it completely slipped my mind. Still, you don't need me to enjoy yourself, not when Alf will be there.'

'It's Reggie, though; he likes you, Hannah, and he's beginning to think you're avoiding him. You're not, are you?'

'No, of course not,' Hannah said quickly, moving away as she spoke. 'Look, I have to go, Gloria, or I'll be late.' She hurried off to the shop, guiltily thinking of how she was deceiving her friend.

'I'm not doing anything wrong,' she told herself for the umpteenth time as she went into the shop and greeted Mr Ridley. And anyway, she did intend to join the choral society. But not tonight, tonight she was meeting Timothy. The thought of it brought a light to her eyes and a spring to her step. She changed into her overall and began to serve the stream of customers, happiness bubbling up and spilling over into her work so that many a customer went out with a lighter heart than when he came in.

During her lunch hour, Hannah wandered round the shops, wishing she could afford one of the smart outfits she saw in the shop windows, just so that she would look nice for Timothy. But it was only a passing wish, she was level-headed enough to know that her most pressing need was for winter shoes and she had seen just the pair she wanted in a little shop just off Carfax. Dark-brown brogues, stout enough for the winter weather, yet fashionable too. Now she was waiting for January and hoping they would be reduced in the winter sales. Twenty-nine shillings and eleven pence was just too much for her, she reckoned, looking down at the shabby, thin-soled shoes she was wearing. They were beginning to let in water, but she hardly thought they were worth the expense of taking to the cobbler; the last time it had cost her five shillings and she would rather save the money towards a new pair. So she had cut out insoles from a cardboard box, hoping to make them last; it was only a week or two now, she told herself.

Thinking she had just enough time to go and look at the shoes again, she hurried over to the shop where she had seen them. There they were, on a stand in the window. 'Best-quality brogues,' the notice said. 'Snug and warm for the winter.'

'Here's a bonny sight, enough to brighten any winter's day,' said a voice in her ear, and she jumped round with a surge of gladness she couldn't hide.

'Oh!' she cried. 'Hallo, Timothy.' Taken by surprise like that, she forgot that she was guarding against letting him see how she felt about him, and all of her heart was in her eyes. 'I was just window shopping,' she added.

Timothy glanced in the window at the display of shoes, a slightly speculative glance, before he turned back to her.

'I'd offer to walk you back to the shop but I know you would turn me down,' he said, twisting his lips a little discontentedly. He was becoming impatient with all the secrecy, she was aware.

'We'll see each other tonight,' she reminded him. 'Now I must go or I'll be late.' She walked quickly away from him before he could say any more, turning to wave as she came to the corner. But she felt a flutter of dismay as she saw he wasn't watching her till the last possible moment as he usually did. Instead, he was staring moodily into the shop window.

'That friend of your brother has been in to see you,' said Mr Ridley when she got back to the newsagent's. 'He said he'd call back.'

'Reggie?' Hannah was surprised. 'But he's on nights, he should have been in bed.'

'When a man gets out of bed to come and take a girl to lunch, he means business,' said Mrs Ridley, winking at her husband. 'I reckon he's taken a shine to you, lass.'

'He was just being friendly, I expect. He probably had to come into town for something else and thought he might as well eat with me,' said Hannah.

'Right disappointed he looked when you weren't here. Are you sure he's not your sweetheart?' Mrs Ridley grinned knowingly.

'No, he's not, I haven't got a sweetheart,' said Hannah, rather too quickly.

'Nay, lass, for a lass what hasn't got a sweetheart you show all the signs. You're on edge on a night to get off on the dot, then waste time prettying yourself up in front of the mirror in the back. An' when I saw you wearing your good dress underneath your overall, I says to George here, our Hannah's got herself a boy, sure as eggs is eggs. Well, the lad's well enough to look at and seems to have a good job, why keep it a secret?'

'Reggie is not my boyfriend,' Hannah repeated as she went into the back shop to change into her overall, leaving the curtain which usually screened the room from customers half drawn back. Combing her hair, she saw through the mirror Mr and Mrs Ridley looking at each other, Mrs Ridley's usual smile absent. As she put down her comb, the older woman followed her into the back shop and drew the curtain properly.

'Hannah,' she said, 'I hope you don't think I'm an interfering old woman but we neither of us want you to do something you will regret. I mean, about this chap from the university, it's not him you're keen on, is it?'

Hannah didn't answer, she didn't need to; the look of dismay did it for her. Mrs Ridley nodded, her suspicions confirmed.

'I thought as much,' she said. 'Oh, pet, think what you're doing, that sort's not for such as us. It's only in fairy stories that the king marries the beggar maid, you know.'

'I'm not exactly a beggar maid, nor is he a king,' said Hannah.

'But you know what I mean. Oh, I know, he's likely a nice lad an' he mebbe thinks a bit about you, but when it comes down to it, he'll not marry you, pet, bonny though you might be – an' you are, you're pretty as a picture. That's mebbe the trouble, he fancies you, that's all. Aw, lass, don't cheapen yourself, not you, I'd be that sorry to see you hurt.'

All the time Mrs Ridley was speaking, Hannah kept her eyes on her clenched hands; she was quivering with anger and humiliation and at last she could keep quiet no longer. Drawing herself up, her eyes flashing in her pink face, she kept her voice low as she replied.

'Don't worry about me, Mrs Ridley, I'm not doing anything to be ashamed of and neither is Timothy. And he's not like that at all, he likes me for what I am. And as to marriage, well, what makes you think I want to get married yet anyway? I'm too young to get married, for a start.'

Mrs Ridley gazed sadly at her. 'Well, pet, if that's how you want it, all right. I'll say no more.' But as Hannah turned to go into the shop, she couldn't help adding, 'Just be careful, though, hinny, will you? Me and George have none of our own and we're fond of you, you know.'

Hannah smiled, albeit a bit shakily for she felt all churned up emotionally. Mrs Ridley had put into words all her own unspoken doubts and fears. Before she could reply, Mr Ridley called from the shop.

'Is anyone coming out here to give me a hand or do I have to do all the work around the place myself?'

Thankfully, Hannah went into the shop and began serving the usual stream of afternoon customers. Later, when the stream dried up, she took a duster and began the business of cleaning the shelves, keeping herself busy until it was time to leave.

Pulling the wine-red cloche hat over her head, Hannah stood back from the mirror to admire the effect. She felt safe enough doing it in the back shop for Mrs Ridley had gone home to start the evening meal and Mr Ridley never noticed such things. Nevertheless, Hannah drew the curtain that screened off the room before she pulled a tube of lipstick from her bag and applied it rather inexpertly to her lips. But the colour wasn't right with the hat, she saw, and she rubbed it off again, feeling guilty because it had cost a shilling in Timothy White's, the chemists, last payday. And the hat itself had taken five shillings and eleven pence of her savings, but it had looked so pretty she hadn't been able to resist it. In any case, she told herself, it was a good felt and it kept her head warm.

'Goodnight, Hannah,' said Mr Ridley as she went through the shop. 'Have a good time. You know Mother didn't mean to upset you this afternoon. She worries about you, that's what it is.'

'She didn't upset me,' said Hannah. 'Goodnight then, Mr Ridley, I'll see you in the morning.' But as she went out into the cold, damp evening, she acknowledged to herself that Mrs Ridley's plain speaking had touched a raw nerve. She knew it was foolish to hope that anyone like Timothy could possibly be serious about her. She pushed the disagreeable thought away; she was going to meet him because she couldn't help herself, she was desperately in love with him and it didn't matter whether he was serious about her or not, all that mattered was that he was interested enough in her to want to go out with her.

As she opened the door of the café and saw him sitting at their usual table, she couldn't help smiling at him with her heart in her eyes.

She sat down opposite him and he put his hand over hers, slipping his thumb underneath to her palm, caressing gently. It was a gesture he usually made on greeting her and, as always, it sent tiny shivers of excitement up her arm.

'You're not expected at home, are you?' he asked, a small furrow between his eyes. Too often they had met like this and she had said she had to get back after only half an hour of their being together.

Hannah shook her head dreamily, still bemused by the feel of his thumb on her palm. 'I said I was going to choir practice, that I'd joined the choral society,' she admitted, and he laughed out loud.

'You didn't! You little devil,' he cried in mock horror. 'Oh, Hannah, how shocking, telling fibs like that.' They grinned at each other in complete accord.

'Actually, it's not a bad idea, that. It would give us somewhere to meet legitimately, wouldn't it? We'll have to think about it. But for now I have a great idea. There's a hotel I know out on the Banbury Road, we could go there for dinner tonight, what do you say? It's only half an hour's drive.'

'Well, I don't know . . . I'm not dressed for anything grand.' Hannah had never been out to dinner in a hotel in her life. She glanced uncomfortably down at her coat, of a dark-brown wool mixture. Her mother had taken a club out at the co-op store to buy the coat for her first winter away from home and it was definitely showing signs of wear. But the main problem was her shoes.

'Oh, come on, Hannah, you're so pretty no one will notice what you're wearing,' said Timothy. 'But I promise you, we'll find a secluded table away from everyone else if you would rather. Aren't you hungry?'

'Oh, I am,' said Hannah, almost without volition for she was very hungry indeed. All she had eaten at lunchtime was a chocolate bar she'd bought from stock; the walk over to see the shoes had taken up too much of her dinner hour to leave time for a meal.

'Well, come on then,' he said briskly and led the way out to his car. He settled her in the passenger seat, solicitous about wrapping the travelling rug around her and tucking it in carefully, even though the hood was up, and Hannah felt warmly cherished. He went round the car and climbed into the driver's seat and then he turned and kissed her, a gentle, tentative kiss. Hannah lifted her lips to his and kissed him back.

'Sweet little Hannah,' he murmured and put his arms around her and held her close, a little awkwardly in the confined space of the car. Despite this, Hannah's arms found their way around his neck and she breathed in the fragrance of him, masculine and fresh with a faint tinge of something else, something that smelled expensive. His arms tightened around her and he lifted her chin and kissed her again, this time a more demanding kiss, and her mouth opened naturally to his probing tongue.

It was only a few seconds before he let her go, groaning audibly and straightening the rug, which had become disarranged during the embrace.

'Oh, Hannah, you don't know what you do to a man,' he whispered. 'We'd better go before I lose my head altogether.'

Hannah's eyes were still half-closed dreamily and she savoured the taste of him. As he drove out from the shadows of the station yard into the lighted street, she looked up at him wonderingly. At that moment she would have gone anywhere with him, done anything he wanted, no matter what the consequences or what Mrs Ridley or Alf or anyone else thought.

They drove out of the town and along a country road lined with dark, bare hedges. There was very little traffic, just the road, closed in by the hedges, curving and twisting ahead of them, and their tiny enclosed world of the car. For a few minutes, Hannah fantasised that they were truly isolated from everyone and there was no one else to care what they did. Then Timothy was turning into a wide gateway, a gravelled drive, and pulling to a halt by wide stone steps leading to an imposing front door.

'We're here,' said Timothy.

Hannah stayed where she was, reluctant to leave the cosy intimacy of the car, until Timothy got out, walked round the car and opened her door.

'Come on, Hannah,' he said, holding out his hand to her. 'I thought you said you were hungry?'

She got out and waited while he picked up a parcel from the back seat and they walked up the stone steps and into the hotel entrance. Warm air met them as they opened the door and light twinkled from the electric chandelier and bounced off the gilt-framed mirrors on the walls so that Hannah blinked at the brightness. She stood uncertainly but Timothy led her forward and a stately man in evening dress came to meet them.

'Good evening, sir,' he said. 'Mr Durkin, isn't it? We have your reservation,' and he beckoned to a waiting girl to take their coats.

Hannah fumbled with the buttons nervously but Timothy lifted it from her shoulders and the coats disappeared through a door on the left with the girl. Hannah glanced down at her plain dress and was relieved to see it wasn't creased even though she'd had it on under her overall all day at the shop.

'Shall I take your parcel, sir?' asked the man, but Timothy shook his head.

'I'll keep it with me.'

'Very well. This way, Mr Durkin.' And with only a flicker of an eyebrow in Hannah's direction the head waiter – for Hannah had realised that was who he was – led them into the dining room, an old, oak-panelled room with many secluded corners and crannies. Timothy had chosen this hotel well, it was indeed the ideal place for a private meal. Their table was hidden in a corner by the window, the only table there, so that the only indication of other diners was a slight murmuring of voices.

'Do you like it?' asked Timothy and she nodded her head wordlessly. Timothy put the parcel on the floor by his chair and she looked at it curiously. What could be so important about what was in the parcel that he had to keep it with him? But Timothy had noticed her interest and grinned at her.

'You'd like to know what it is, wouldn't you, Hannah?'

'Well, I wondered, that's all,' she replied, blushing.

Timothy waved away the hovering waiter and picked up the parcel and handed it over to Hannah. 'Open it,' he said.

'Oh, no, I'm not that curious,' she answered, blushing even more furiously.

'But it's for you,' he murmured softly and she looked up, startled. 'Go on, open it,' he went on.

Hannah tried to undo the knotted string but the knots were too tight. After a moment watching her, Timothy picked up a knife and sliced through them impatiently. Hannah opened the parcel to reveal a shoebox and straight away guessed what was inside. She looked at the lid, thoughts racing through her head of what her mother, Alf or even Gloria would think of her taking such a gift from a man she was not even engaged to.

'Go on, open it,' Timothy insisted and she looked up at him solemnly so that for a moment he stopped smiling and looked anxious.

She took the lid from the box and there they were, the brogues she had been admiring in the shop window. Tucked in the side of the box was a cellophane packet and through the cellophane she could see a pair of sheer silk stockings. Her toes curled up in her old thin shoes, uncomfortably wrinkling the cardboard insoles. She had never had a pair of silk stockings in her life before; in fact, the only pair she had seen was the ones Betty had had for her wedding. She stared at them for a long moment, the shoes and the stockings, and imagined what it would be like wearing them. Then she looked up at Timothy who was watching her with the indulgent expression she had seen on her mother's face when she had been able to give the children some rare treat. And she remembered how her mother had refused to allow Tucker to give Betty just such a gift as this before they were properly engaged. 'Only loose women take presents like that,' Nora had stated firmly.

'I can't take them,' she said boldly. 'It was nice of you to think of it, but I can't take them.'

Chapter Sixteen

'I'm sorry,' said Hannah as Timothy reached across the table for the shoebox and put it back on the floor at his feet.

He looked at her unhappy face and smiled. 'Don't be,' he said. 'If you can't take them, you can't. Now let's have something to eat before we starve to death altogether.' He picked up the menu and handed it to her. 'What would you like?'

She glanced at the bewildering array of dishes and gave up immediately. 'You choose,' she said and he looked across the room, and magically the waiter was there to take their order. They ate asparagus soup and dainty portions of plaice and the main course was duckling in a delicate orange sauce. Hannah had been sure she would not be able to eat after the misunderstanding about the shoes, but Timothy tucked into his meal so matter-of-factly that she felt less embarrassed about refusing the shoes and her appetite returned and she ate well. But she always waited until he lifted up the correct knife and fork and copied him, just as the advice column in *Woman's Weekly* suggested. And only a few days before she had found a second-hand booklet on etiquette in a box outside a bookstore. It had cost her sixpence but now she knew not to hold her knife like a pen, a piece of advice which had been one of the many little gems she had found in the book.

The white wine Timothy had ordered made her feel a little light-headed after only half a glass so she prudently refused any more. Still, by the time they had eaten their way through several courses and were sipping strong, black coffee, which was so bitter that she hastily added two spoonfuls of sugar, she was intoxicated without the benefit of more alcohol. Simply sitting there with Timothy, talking of nothing in particular and eating good food in such an atmosphere of rich comfort was enough. It was with a sense of loss that she realised that the meal was over and it was time to go.

She slipped out to the ladies' cloakroom and when she came out into the hotel entrance, Timothy had paid the bill and was ready. He was holding her coat for her to put on when the waiter came after them with the shoebox. 'You forgot your parcel, sir.'

Timothy tucked it under his arm with a murmured 'Thank you'. In the car he threw it on the back seat without a word and concentrated on tucking the rug round Hannah. And, still intoxicated by the whole evening, she put her arms around his neck and drew him to her and kissed him.

'Thank you for understanding,' she whispered.

'Oh, Hannah,' he said, lifting his head and looking down at her.

It was a very dark night, there was only the faint light of the lamp which hung over the door of the hotel, and all she could see was just the outline of his head, haloed against the lamp as he bent it to hers. She felt his lips on the nape of her neck and somehow her coat was open and he was cupping her small breasts in his hands. Such shivers of emotion ran through her that she felt she couldn't bear it, the intensity of her feelings taking her completely by surprise.

'I could get a room,' he said, his voice hoarse. 'Not here, they know me, but we could go nearer home, I know just the place.'

And all the warnings and moralising which had been drummed into Hannah at home and in chapel, all the talk of strumpets and whores and the dangers of falling into sin were nothing compared with the compelling necessity of being with Timothy, truly with him. She nodded, wordlessly, and sat quietly under her rug as he turned the car in the drive, drove back along the Oxford Road and pulled into the forecourt of a small inn with a notice in the window, 'ROOMS TO LET', a place much smaller and less grand than the hotel they had just left. She waited quietly as he booked a room, explaining to the sleepy landlord that he and his wife were driving north for Christmas, taking it in easy stages as 'the old bus won't be pushed'. And the landlord didn't appear to notice that they brought no luggage into the inn with them or that she kept her left hand firmly in her coat pocket, just in case he should notice the absence of a wedding ring. He handed over the keys the minute Timothy had signed the book.

'First door on the right at the top of the stairs, bathroom at the end of the upstairs hall,' he told them. 'What time would you like breakfast, sir?'

'Oh, we may sleep late, we're in no hurry,' said Timothy casually, for all the world, thought Hannah, as though he had done this often in the past. Even this thought didn't disturb her; she followed him upstairs and into the tiny room, which was taken up almost in its entirety by an enormous double bed covered in a flowered chintz counterpane. She couldn't take her eyes off the bed as she allowed Timothy to take her coat and hang it in the minute wardrobe alongside his. Then he started to undress her, taking off the brown wool dress and hanging that up too before pulling the ribbon of her camisole so that it dropped from her shoulders and revealed her firm, high breasts. All of her being now focused on him and the intensity of her feelings for him. Feelings which flooded her whole body until she felt she would drown in them.

Hannah woke in the dark winter's morning with a feeling of euphoric contentment. Timothy lay beside her, his head resting on her shoulder, breathing evenly as he slept, one leg bent up over her thighs and an arm flung over her waist. She lay quietly for a while, savouring the closeness of him, the feel of his skin against hers. It must be six o'clock, she thought, twisting her head to try to read the dial of his wristwatch, which was the only thing he was still wearing, but it was too dark to see it properly. Inevitably, the euphoria was seeping away from her as thoughts of the coming day crept into her mind. Sighing, she tried to slip out from under his leg but it lay too firmly across her thigh and as she reached carefully down to lift it, she instead encountered his manhood. Wondering, she left her hand touching it, so flaccid now, so different last night. Cautiously, she moved her hand so that her fingers encircled it and at once it sprang up, almost as though it had a life of its own. Hannah pulled her hand away hastily, but not hastily enough – Timothy was awake, his arm tightening around her, his lips nuzzling her ear.

'Timothy, I must go, I'll be late for work,' she said urgently.

'Not now, you can't do that to a man and just go,' he replied, lifting himself on to his elbow and gazing down at her face, barely outlined on the pillow in the gloom of the dawn. But Hannah was thoroughly awake now and beginning to panic.

'I must, Timothy, please take me back, I have to be in the shop by eight o'clock. Oh, Lord, what am I going to do?'

Timothy sat up in bed. 'All right, don't panic, of course I'll take you back. But I had thought you might take the day off today, ring in and say you're sick or something. Don't you want to stay with me? We have hours yet before we have to get up, then I'll order breakfast – we can't go without breakfast, can we?'

Hannah was reaching into the wardrobe for her coat to cover herself while she went to the bathroom. Her hand stayed for a moment, but then she took out the coat and pulled it on before going to the light switch by the door.

'You don't understand anything, do you?' she said flatly. 'What do you think my brother is going to say if he finds out I've been out all night? He'll likely break my neck, can't you see that? And my job, I can't simply take days off, it's my living, what would I do if I lost my job?'

'Oh, don't be so dramatic, Hannah, I wouldn't let you starve. Now be a good girl and come back to bed.'

Hannah gazed at him as he lay back down on the pillow and lifted the bedclothes invitingly. Without speaking, she opened the door and went out to the bath-room. Locking the door, she gazed at as much of herself as she could see in the mirror over the handbasin. Her breasts felt sore and swollen but as far as she could see they looked no different from how they had looked yes-terday, nor did anything else about her except perhaps her lips, swollen as they certainly were. Still, she didn't look like a fallen woman, though she wasn't sure what they would look like, just that there would be a differ-ence. She thought about running a bath but decided there was no time, it was already getting lighter outside and if she didn't hurry Mrs Ridley would be in the shop and be wanting to know why she was late. So she ran water into the basin, washed herself all over and, shivering, dried on the skimpy towel provided. Still damp, she pulled on her coat and hurried back to the bedroom.

He was sitting on the edge of the bed waiting for her, his trousers on but his chest still bare. 'Sure you want to go back now?' he asked.

'Sure.'

'Righto then.'

She dressed quickly behind the open door of the ward-robe and with her back to him. When she turned round he was still sitting on the edge of the bed, grinning.

'What – ' she began and stopped, blushing, as she noticed that her reflection in the mirror on the inside of the wardrobe door was repeated on the wall mirror opposite so he had had a perfect view of her as she put on her clothes.

'Oh, come on, Hannah, it's a bit late for false modesty, isn't it?' he teased.

'Timothy, please, I have to go,' she pleaded and he jumped to his feet, suddenly businesslike.

'I'm ready, I can bathe and shave when I get back. I'm ready, see, just hand me my coat.' He pulled on his shirt and jacket and flung his overcoat on the top. 'Come along now, don't dawdle, you go out to the car and I'll pay the man.'

They drove along the road to Oxford in a line of morning traffic but just as they reached the outskirts of the city, Timothy pulled into the side and turned to her.

'Timothy, I must get on,' she exclaimed.

'I know, you have to get to work, you told me. But first I want to know – you looked so cross this morning, flying about, desperate to get back – are you sorry it happened?'

Hannah looked away from him, down at her hands, out of the car window at the houses lining the road, anything. She wasn't sure how she felt. Everything was so different in the daytime.

'Hannah? Look at me, Hannah. Don't be sorry, please. It was wonderful and natural and nothing to be ashamed of at all, not when we love each other.'

Something in his voice, something young and vulnerable, made her turn to him. His eyes were very blue and questioning and the faint shadow of stubble on his cheeks and chin paradoxically seemed to accentuate his youth. And she knew, no matter what trouble she had to face during the day, no matter even if she lost her job and Gloria threw her out of the house, she loved him and she wasn't sorry.

'No, I'm not sorry, Timothy, I'm glad,' she said.

'I love you, Hannah,' he whispered and kissed her gently. Restarting the engine, he swung the car out into the morning traffic and headed for Ridley's shop, pulling up a few doors farther on.

'I'll wait for you this evening,' he said.

'Well, I won't be able to stay long, I must go home,' she answered, sounding doubtful.

'I'll wait for you, the usual place,' he repeated, getting out of the car to open the door for her. As she got out, he kissed her again, insistently. Two girls passing by on their way to work blinked at them, startled, before going on their way, giggling.

'Timothy! Suppose someone I know sees us,' she protested.

'Would it be such a disaster?'

'Yes, it would,' she replied, her tone quite sharp with exasperation. But she didn't have time to say any more; already people were pouring out of the station and many of them were going into the shop. With a muttered goodbye she hurried away, leaving him gazing after her.

'And what time do you call this, young lady?'

Her spirits sank as she saw that Mrs Ridley was working behind the counter alongside her husband. As his wife put the question, Mr Ridley paused as he counted out change from the till and stared solemnly at Hannah. She looked away, flushing guiltily.

'I'm sorry I'm late, I won't be a minute getting ready,' she mumbled and hurried to change into her overall. When she came back into the shop, Mrs Ridley finished serving her customer and then went behind the curtain. For perhaps fifteen minutes, the shop was busy, giving Hannah a chance to compose herself, though she still hadn't the faintest idea what she was going to say to them, or rather to Mrs Ridley, for it would be she who demanded an explanation.

'Breakfast, George,' called his wife from the back shop, and Hannah was left on her own for a while. But inexorably the time came when Mr Ridley came back and took her place.

'The wife wants you,' he said, flicking his head towards the curtain and Hannah went through.

Mrs Ridley handed her a cup of tea and picked up her own, and they sat down to drink as they did every morning. But this morning she didn't start chatting about a customer or how the warehouse had let them down or what trouble she was having with her knees.

'Right, lass, out with it,' she said bluntly.

Hannah took a sip of tea and swallowed nervously. 'I'm sorry I was late, I'll make it up tonight,' she began. 'I missed the bus –'

Mrs Ridley snorted and put her elbows on the table. Holding her cup in both hands, she glared at Hannah. 'Don't lie to me, lass,' she said. 'I saw you get out of that car, it was that student's, wasn't it? Eeh, I'm right disappointed in you, that I am, telling me lies an' all. You didn't try to catch the bus, did you?'

Hannah sighed. Mrs Ridley was right, what was the point in telling her lies when it must be obvious to her what was going on?

'No, no, I didn't,' she admitted. 'Timothy brought me. I'm sorry. I'll make sure I'm not late again.' She looked across the table anxiously. 'You're not going to give me the sack, are you?'

'Nay, lass, of course not, you're a blooming good worker, what would we do without you? I just wish you'd mind me when I tell you you're making a mistake about this chap. Stick to your own kind, that's what I think, it's always best in the long run.' Mrs Ridley finished her tea in one gulp and took the cup to the sink and rinsed it out under the cold-water tap. Picking up the tea towel, she dried the cup slowly before putting it down and turning back to Hannah.

'I suppose nothing I say will make any difference to you, though, I might as well save my breath to cool my porridge.

But be careful, lass, that's all. I'll say no more about it. If it's him you want, then you must do what your heart tells you to, that's all. But don't forget, pet, I'm here if you need me, me and George, both of us. We've gotten fond of you and you're a good little worker like I said, we'd do badly without you now, I'll say that. Just try to get in on time and as far as we're concerned that's an end to it. All right?'

Hannah got to her feet and hugged her, feeling close to tears. For a moment, Mrs Ridley was stiff and unbending, then she held the girl to her and patted her shoulder.

'There, pet, it's all right. Now you'd better get back to the shop before George comes looking for you.'

'Thank you,' whispered Hannah. 'I do love him, you know.'

'Aye, pet, I know you do, that's the nub of it,' Mrs Ridley answered.

The morning wore on and a steady stream of customers kept Hannah busy till at last it was one o'clock and she was free for an hour. She had decided that she would seek out Gloria at her work so, pulling on her coat and hat, not bothering to look in the mirror to check if it was on straight, she rushed out of the shop. Walking along in the cold, grey afternoon, Hannah almost bumped into Gloria coming the other way.

'Oh, I was just coming to see you,' she exclaimed, a smile faltering on her lips.

Maggie Hope

'Were you indeed?' said Gloria. Hannah's heart sank as she caught the other girl's tone, which was almost as cold as the day. 'Well, we'd better go in here and have a hot drink. I think you owe me an explanation.'

Meekly, Hannah followed Gloria into a small café and they sat down at a table. 'Two hot chocolates, please,' Gloria said to the waitress. She pulled off her leather gloves with the fur-trimmed cuffs which Alf had bought her for her birthday and loosened the top button of her warm tweed coat. As usual, Hannah thought, Gloria was neat and smart from the crown of her brown velvet cloche with the tiny mink ornament over one ear to her elegantly crossed ankles clad in artificial silk stockings (one and eleven a pair in Marks and Spencer's and too dear for Hannah) and her neat shoes with the decorative tongues over the laces. Hannah could see the shoes peeping out to one side of Gloria's chair and instinctively she pulled her own ill-shod feet out of sight.

'You look terrible,' said Gloria, startling Hannah into glancing up. 'Your hat is on crooked and you look tired to death, you're all eyes. Have you looked in a mirror today?'

Hannah remembered that she hadn't and put her hands to her hat to straighten it.

'Oh, for goodness sake,' snapped Gloria, 'do it in the ladies' after we've had our chocolate.' She fell silent as the waitress served the drinks, waiting until she had

248

gone back behind the counter at the end of the café to take someone's money. Then Gloria launched into her attack.

'Where were you last night? I was worried to death, I laid awake half the night waiting for you and then when I found out you still weren't back this morning I didn't know what to think. It's just as well Reggie's on nights and Daddy never notices anything. I can tell you, they wouldn't like to think you stayed out all night.'

'Er, I stayed with a friend,' said Hannah, not looking at Gloria.

'A friend? What friend? Someone you met at the choral society?' demanded Gloria, and Hannah nodded her head eagerly.

'Yes, it was getting late when the practice finished and it was so cold out, so when my friend offered to let me stay with her –'

'What's her name? I presume it is a her?'

'Er, Jane,' said Hannah, giving the first name which came into her head.

'And I suppose it never occurred to you that I might be worried. I almost went along to see Alf this morning before I came to work, I thought he might know where you were.'

'You didn't, though, did you?'

'No, I didn't, I thought there was no sense in us both worrying about you. He had enough to think about, I wasn't going to upset him when he had a day at the works ahead of him. I've got more consideration for him than that.'

Gloria picked up her spoon and stirred her hot chocolate and Hannah watched her set face, the usually pleasant expression gone.

'He's picking up his new car today, did you remember? It's a big day for him, I didn't want to spoil it. Though naturally, I was worried. Supposing you hadn't gone in to work today? Supposing you'd disappeared for good? He would have blamed me for not telling him straight away, wouldn't he?'

'Picking up his new car?' said Hannah, more to change the course of the conversation than anything.

'Yes, you didn't even remember, did you? You don't take any interest in anything Alf or I do nowadays. I'm that disappointed in you, Hannah, I really am.' Gloria picked up a glove and pulled it on over her carefully manicured and pink-painted nails, then followed suit with the other glove. She sighed heavily.

'Well, I suppose I should be thankful that you're all right. I was imagining all sorts of things had happened to you, you'd been run over and were lying in a hospital bed or taken by white slavers or something,' she said. 'I'd better be getting back now, or I'll be late. Are you coming home tonight? Because if you're not, kindly tell me now, it's only civilised behaviour, you know.'

Hannah rose to her feet, leaving her cup of chocolate untouched. 'Yes, I'm coming home tonight, Gloria. And I'm sorry, I really am, I'm sorry I worried you and everything. Thank you for not telling Alf, I promise I won't stay out again, not unless I've told you beforehand.'

'Oh, come on, walk to the end of the street with me. We won't fall out about it, not this time. I was worried about you, like I said, that's all.' Gloria's expression relented.

Hannah felt miserably guilty as she walked back to the shop. She felt she was entangling herself in a great web of lies, one lie leading to the next and then another and another. If only she had someone to confide in, she thought, someone close she could talk to. Gloria might have been the very person but for her engagement to Alf. Hanging up her coat and hat in the back shop, Hannah remembered her future sister-in-law's comments on her appearance and looked in the mirror. There were dark smudges under her eyes and the only colour in her face was that of her lips, still slightly swollen and bruised. She splashed cold water over her neck and face, dampening the front of her hair, before taking a comb to tidy her short bob. At least she looked a little better now, she thought, studying her reflection before going out into the shop.

'By, I'm pleased to see you back, pet,' said Mr Ridley. 'This has been a long morning, I can tell you. I'm ready for a rest.'

Hannah looked at him, shaken out of her preoccupation with her own troubles, for he sounded even more tired than she was herself. There was a grey look to his face, she saw, and a tiny tic at the corner of his mouth.

'Why don't you take a long dinner hour?' she suggested. 'I can manage fine here, that is until the teatime rush.'

'Aye, I reckon I will,' he answered heavily. 'I feel a bit off colour, mebbe it's the flu coming on. You sure you can manage?' He wrapped a long muffler round and round his neck and pulled his overcoat on over it. Taking a checked cap out of his pocket, he pulled it forward over his face and turned up the collar of his overcoat so that all Hannah could see of him was his nose.

'See you later then, pet,' he said and went out.

The afternoon stretched ahead of Hannah, seemingly endless. As the short December day darkened into evening, there were few customers and she kept herself busy checking the stock and writing a list of things needing to be replenished when the wholesaler's representative called. Four o'clock came, then half past, and still no sign of Mr Ridley, but Hannah wasn't worried. It was half an hour yet before the evening rush began as people dropped in for the evening paper on their way to the trains.

But at half past five, he still hadn't returned and the trickle of customers had increased to a flow and there was an impatient queue forming at the till. And then it was six o'clock, the time Hannah usually finished work, but there was nothing she could do but carry on serving customers and hope one of the Ridleys would turn up to relieve her soon.

'Hallo, Hannah. Got a packet of Park Drive, have you?'

She had been mechanically taking money for papers, cigarettes and matches and hardly seeing faces, only hands, the grubby hands of workmen and the pale hands of academics and businessmen, typists' hands stained with typewriter ink and some with faint traces of oil under the nails and round the cuticles, just like this pair in front of her now. She looked up and saw it was Reggie.

'Oh, hallo, Reggie. Yes, of course.' She handed him the packet of cigarettes and took his sixpence and gave him two pennies in change.

'I've been doing my Christmas shopping,' he said, holding up a brown paper carrier.

'Oh?'

Hannah smiled at him as she took coppers from a customer beside him and dropped them in the till. Desperately, she wished he would go, Mr Ridley would be coming in any minute now and she would be free to run round the corner to the café where Timothy would be waiting for her. But Reggie simply moved to one side so that other customers could take his place at the counter.

'Yes. So I thought I'd call for you, we can go home together.'

The shop was empty of customers for the moment and she started to tidy the piles of papers on the counter; it was something to keep her hands busy while she thought of an excuse. There was the obvious one, of course, she realised.

'I can't leave the shop until Mr Ridley comes back. He's very late, I'm afraid he may be ill.' As if on cue, the door opened and a small boy came in with a note in his hand.

'You Hannah?' he asked, and when she nodded he held out the note. 'Mr Ridley asked me to give you this and I'm to wait for an answer.'

Hannah opened the envelope and read the note and her heart sank.

'Look, Reggie, you might as well go. Mr Ridley's poorly, I have to cash up and lock the shop and take the keys and cash over there.'

'I'll wait for you, we'll go over there together,' Reggie said quickly. 'I'm in no hurry.'

'But Gloria will have a meal ready. If neither of us turn up on time, she'll worry.'

'No, she won't. Don't you remember Alf got his car today? He said he was going to surprise her, pick her up at work and take her for a drive. We'll eat later.'

Hannah couldn't think of any other way of getting rid of Reggie short of telling him the truth. She would just have to stand Timothy up. Surely he would understand when she told him what had happened.

'Well, go and sit in the back, I won't be long cashing up,' she said, giving up.

Slipping the bolt in the door and changing the sign to 'CLOSED', she pulled down the door blind and began counting the money out of the till and putting it in the cloth sack Mr Ridley used to transport it. She had almost finished when there was a knock at the door.

'We're closed,' she called, but the knocking went on, becoming more imperious as she called out again. Sighing, she went to the door and opened it just a little. When she saw who it was, she flung it wide. She was so glad to see Timothy that she forgot all about Reggie, sitting in the back shop.

Chapter Seventeen

'What's wrong? Why didn't you come to meet me?' asked Timothy.

Before she could answer him, Reggie came from behind the curtain, walking out into the body of the shop to where she stood with Timothy.

'The shop's closed, didn't you hear? Hannah called it loudly enough,' he said. 'Now if you don't mind, we'd like to get home.'

'Who are you?' asked Timothy. 'And what has it got to do with you if I want a word with Hannah? Isn't Mr Ridley here?'

'No, he isn't, Hannah's closed the shop and we are going home now so please leave.'

'Oh, yes, I remember you now. You were with Hannah's brother at that dance hall, weren't you?' Timothy became hostile as he recollected where he had seen Reggie before.

'And I remember you too,' retorted Reggie. 'But I didn't think you'd still be pestering my girl. Has he been bothering you, Hannah?'

Hannah stared at him, dumbfounded – what did he mean, *his* girl? For a moment she couldn't think what to say, so there was a tiny silence as Timothy turned to her.

'Tell the man, Hannah, go on, tell him, have I been pestering his girl?' Timothy's face was a mask of jealous rage, yet he spoke softly, almost calmly. 'Whose girl are you, Hannah?'

'Timothy, please don't make a scene. Reggie is my brother's friend, his sister is engaged to Alf. I live with Gloria and Reggie and their father.'

'How convenient that must be for you, so cosy,' he replied with heavy sarcasm.

'And just what do you mean by that?' demanded Reggie stepping between them, his fists bunching. 'Hannah's a good girl, she is, I won't have anyone even hinting such things about her.'

'What do you think I mean?' asked Timothy but he was unprepared for what came next, for the next moment he was on the ground, flattened by a clumsy swing from Reggie, which nevertheless connected with his jaw. Timothy scrambled to his feet with a growl of rage and made to charge at Reggie but Hannah somehow got between them and clung on to him so that he couldn't carry out his obvious intention of returning the blow.

'Timothy, don't. Please go, I'm in enough trouble as it is, please,' she cried, and he looked down at her, the anger dying away from his eyes.

'Oh, I see, you want me out of the way, is that it?'

Hannah looked from Timothy to Reggie and back again, helplessly. Oh, why had Reggie chosen tonight to come to meet her?

'Reggie, please go and wait for me in the back shop,' she said at last.

'I'll do nothing of the sort,' he replied, glaring from her to Timothy. 'I'll not leave you with this rotter, didn't you hear what he was implying about you? I've a good mind to knock him flat again –'

'Reggie! Wait for me in the back shop, I tell you.' Her voice rose as her temper finally snapped. 'You can wait for me in the back shop or get out of here, now.'

Reggie paused, frowning unhappily, then he walked backwards towards the curtain. 'Righto, I will. I'm not leaving you alone with him, though, don't forget, I'm just behind the curtain.'

'Reggie, just go,' she said wearily, and he ducked into the back shop, the curtain swishing behind him. Hannah looked at Timothy, his eyes cold in his set face. He was like a stranger. She couldn't imagine that she had really spent the night with him, it must have been a dream. 'Come to the door,' she said, keeping her voice low, and silently he followed her.

They looked at each other and Hannah could see that he wasn't in any mood to be understanding, but she had to try to explain. 'I'm sorry I couldn't get away to meet you,' she began. 'I was busy.'

'Yes, so I see,' he replied, glancing at the curtain.

'No, you don't. Mr Ridley took ill, I had to take over. That's where I'm going now with the day's takings. Reggie was –'

'Oh, save it, Hannah, you don't have to tell me about Reggie. It's plain to see he's in love with you. It must be quite cosy for you two to live in the same house. You were careful not to tell me about that, weren't you?'

'You never asked me about where I lived,' Hannah pointed out, stung. 'And even if you had, there was nothing wrong, nothing to tell. I don't even know why we're fighting, why you're so different to what you were this morning.'

'Don't you, Hannah? No, perhaps you don't, that's the trouble. I come in here and find you with him and he tells me you're his girl and you don't know why I'm angry. Didn't last night mean anything to you? Well, I congratulate you, you certainly had me fooled with your air of innocence. That was a good move, saying you couldn't take the shoes. What was it, were you hanging out for something more expensive? Well, it's too late now, you've been rumbled. Goodbye, Hannah.' Pulling open the door, he strode away into the gloom, leaving her staring after him in complete disbelief.

'Gone, has he? Not before time,' said Reggie, coming up behind her, and she turned on him furiously.

'What do you mean, acting as though you owned me?' she shouted at him. 'Why did you tell him I was your girl?'

'But Hannah, I thought you were! Haven't we been going out together?'

'No! No, we haven't, except to make up a foursome with Gloria and Alf. That didn't give you any rights over me. I've never given you any reason to think I was your girl, no reason at all.' Hannah lowered her tone as she saw how stricken Reggie looked, his earlier aggressiveness had completely disappeared. 'Oh, Reggie, why did you say it?'

'I don't know, I suppose I just wanted it to be true,' he mumbled. 'I saw red when I saw that university chap hanging round after you again. Hannah, he only wants one thing, can't you see that? They're all the same, these students.'

Hannah stared at him, realising it was a waste of time losing her temper with him. He would never understand how it was between Timothy and her and he would never understand what he had done. She wondered what Reggie would say if he knew she had spent the night with Timothy in a hotel, but her imagination stopped short at that. The thought flashed through her mind that if Reggie was right and Timothy had only been after 'one thing', as he called it, then he had succeeded. But Reggie was wrong, oh yes, he was wrong, Timothy loved her, he did. And when he got over his fit of jealousy he would come back to her, she knew he would.

'Oh, come on, let's get locked up,' she said. 'We have to go over to the Ridleys' place yet. Alf and Gloria will be back from their drive before we get back home at this rate.'

It was only a short walk to the Ridleys' flat, which was a second-floor walk-up above a row of shops. Mrs Ridley opened the door to Hannah's knock.

'Oh, you're here,' she said, looking relieved. It was a measure of her preoccupation that she didn't even cast a speculative glance in Reggie's direction. 'I was beginning to wonder if you'd had a last-minute rush,' she went on.

'Not really,' said Hannah, handing over the cloth sack of coins and reaching into her handbag for the roll of one-pound and ten-shilling notes. 'How is he?'

'The doctor's just been. It's that new flu, he says. He has to stop in bed, though. We'll have to manage the business between us. Do you think you can open up in the mornings for a while? It's six thirty, though, that's the rub, can you get in in time? Is there a bus? We'll pay you extra, like.'

'Of course I can, don't you worry,' said Hannah.

'Keep the keys then, I'll come in when I can to give you a break.' Mrs Ridley glanced behind her as the sound of coughing came from the bedroom. 'Poor George, he sounds badly, doesn't he? I'll have to go and see to him. You know what men are like, proper babies when they have anything the matter with him. I'm grateful, Hannah, I really am; thank God we have someone we can trust to take care of the shop. You won't be the loser, I promise you, pet.'

'Mother? Where are you at?' Mr Ridley called, his words punctuated by a fit of coughing.

'You'd better go. Don't worry, I'll see to everything,' promised Hannah.

'I wanted the telephone put in the shop but George was against it,' Mrs Ridley fretted. 'Now I'll be kept busy going backwards and forwards.' She was already backing towards the bedroom. 'Well, I'll see you tomorrow then.'

It was almost eight o'clock by the time they got back to Cowley, but Gloria and Alf were not back from their drive.

'I don't know, no one seems to care about me getting my dinner on time any more,' grumbled Dan Morgan as soon as they went in. He was sitting in the lounge with the evening paper, looking disgruntled.

Hannah went into the kitchen and checked in the oven. There was a rabbit casserole there just waiting to be warmed up and a pan of potatoes on the ring; Gloria usually left something prepared just to finish off when she came in from work. Hannah lit the gas and went back into the lounge.

'It'll only be twenty minutes, Dan,' she said and he grunted and rustled his paper angrily. Reggie sat down and fiddled with the wireless set, making it whistle and whine before he got it properly on station. American dance music filled the room and Hannah went upstairs to check if the water was hot enough for a quick bath before the meal was ready. Luckily, Dan had lit the geyser and she spent a blissful ten minutes soaking in water as hot as she could bear it before reluctantly drying herself and pulling on an old skirt and jumper. She was combing her hair when she heard the front door open and the excited voice of Gloria over the lower tones of Alf. Bracing herself apprehensively, even though Gloria had said she would say nothing to Alf, she went downstairs. The other girl was in the kitchen.

'Oh, bless you, you've got the dinner on,' she greeted her. 'Dad is moaning on about it, he hates his dinner to be late. We called for a drink and now I'm absolutely starving. Oh, Hannah, the car's lovely, it really is, goes like a dream. You'll have to slip out and see it after we've eaten.'

'It's a bit dark for that,' said Hannah, thinking that Gloria must have kept her word about not saying anything or Alf would have been in the kitchen now 'playing war' with her, as they said back in Winton. And Gloria seemed to have forgotten her earlier annoyance with Hannah.

'Alf parked it under the street light on purpose so that he could show it off,' she said now, laughing. 'You'll be able to see it all right.'

By the time they'd eaten and Hannah, Reggie and Dan had admired the bull-nosed Morris and Hannah had explained about Mr Ridley going down with the flu, it was already ten o'clock.

'You go on up to bed, I'll do the washing-up,' said Gloria. 'You have all my sympathy if you have to get the six-o'clock bus every morning, I think you want well paying for that.'

Hannah was only too pleased to slip away, she felt so weary she could hardly climb the stairs. She'd had nothing to eat all day through worrying about what Alf would say when he found out she'd been out all night and consequently had eaten a little too well of the rabbit casserole and that made her sleepier still. She pulled off her clothes and put on her warm flannelette nightie, shivering in the cold bedroom. Snuggling down under the bedclothes, she lay curled up on her side, listening to the murmur of voices from downstairs. She'd been lucky not to be found out, she thought, very lucky, she would not be so lucky again. But then, with an aching sense of loss, she thought it wouldn't be happening again. She and Timothy were finished, he'd made that very plain to her. Timothy didn't want her any more; he believed Reggie when he said she was his girl.

Chapter Eighteen

'For heaven's sake, Tim, pull yourself together,' Tony
advised. 'What sort of a Christmas are we going to have
with you mooning over a little shop girl the whole time?'

'I'm not mooning over anyone,' said Timothy. 'And if
you don't want my company I can easily go back to Oxford
or even home to Durham. Just say the word and I'll be off.'

Tony sighed. 'Dear me, you are prickly today, aren't
you? Not at all your usual cheerful self. In my experience that means you have woman trouble, deny it as
much as you like. And the antidote to woman trouble is
more women, so get out and enjoy yourself. Now it's the
season of good cheer and here were are in London with
the house to ourselves except for the servants. I for one
intend to have a high old time. Pull yourself together, old
chap, we're partying tonight and tomorrow night after
that. Don't forget it'll be noses to the grindstone in the
new year, with finals looming.'

Timothy gazed out of the window which overlooked Park Lane and the park beyond, only half hearing his friend. He shouldn't have come, he thought, he just wasn't in the mood for jollification. But when Tony had suggested he spend part of Christmas with him in London as Lord and Lady Akers were in New York for a few weeks, he had thought it was just what he needed to take his mind off Hannah. Besides, it was a good excuse not to go home to that increasingly gloomy house in Durham Road to spend a lonely Christmas with his father, who was always preoccupied with business. The only people invited to the house were business friends or members of the Coal Owners' Association and they would have grave discussions over the dinner table about the blind intractability of the miners and their communist leaders.

Besides, Timothy mused, Durham Road was too near Winton and Winton reminded him of Hannah. He would run the risk of meeting her in Auckland if she went home for Christmas. He didn't want to see her again, at least not until he was sure he was properly over her.

'Tim? You're not taking a blind bit of notice of me, are you?' demanded Tony in a tone of outrage. He was normally of a pleasant nature but he was not used to being ignored. Timothy turned from the window.

'Sorry,' he said. 'I was miles away.'

'Yes, I know, that's just what I was talking about,' said Tony crossly. 'Mooning over that girl again, I'll be bound.

Now, come on, we're supposed to be at Lady Cynthia's in half an hour for cocktails before the theatre. Then we're all going on to Rupert's place to dance the night away. That should be enough to take your mind off that girl.'

Trouble is, thought Timothy as he struggled with his bow tie before the mirror in his dressing room, nothing seems to be enough to do that. For the last three or four nights they had followed the same hectic round of cocktail parties and theatre parties, supper parties and dancing parties, where the girls were all pretty and sophisticated and dressed in the latest fashions. Every time he had found himself comparing them with Hannah in her cheap little dresses and worn shoes, and it was always Hannah, with her grave, dark eyes and translucent skin, who had the best of the comparison, though she had never seen the inside of a beauty parlour. He thought of the shoes he had bought for her that day. Having seen the wistful look on her expressive face as she gazed into the shop window he had thought he would surprise and delight her with them and the silk stockings too. But he had been mistaken in that; he just didn't understand Hannah, that was the trouble.

'Ready?' asked Tony through the open door. Timothy wrenched his mind away from thoughts of Hannah and followed his friend out to the waiting car, determined to at least try to enjoy the evening ahead.

*

267

Back in Oxford, Hannah was kept busy from early morning until evening in the shop, every day of the week except Sunday, when she worked until one.

'The doctor says George has to stay away from work for another couple of weeks,' Mrs Ridley reported, a week before Christmas. 'I've tried to get a girl in, temporary like, but you know what it's like at this time of year, all the shops want extra help.'

It was still a novel idea for Hannah that there should be more jobs available than workers, even though she had been in Oxford long enough to realise it for herself. She put her hand in her overall pocket and felt the letter from her mother which had been waiting for her when she got home the evening before. 'Things are bad, Hannah,' Nora had written.

I know they are always bad, but this year they are worse. Half the pits are on short time and that means traders in the town are doing badly too, so there's no work at all for the lasses. Poor Jane, she's talking about taking a job on the coal screens, she's desperate to earn a bit, but I worry she's not strong enough for it. I know she's cured of the consumption, but the screens are lads' work really. We're managing, though, I've got my pension and the bit the shop brings in. Folks are living from day to day, they can't afford to get food in any amount from the big shops, it's all they can do to buy for the next meal and that's where I come in handy. As long as I don't have to ask Tucker to help out and I'm determined not to. It wouldn't be fair, not when they've got baby Simon now, it would be taking advantage.

Betty's baby Simon had been born at the beginning of October and Hannah had knitted a matinee jacket and sent it for him.

Hannah took the money for the *Oxford Times* from a customer and he went out, leaving the shop empty for a few minutes. This was a good time to suggest what she had in mind, she thought, and turned to her employer.

'Mrs Ridley, I've been thinking,' she began.

'Yes, hinny?'

'My sister Jane, she needs work. You know what it's like back home, there's nothing for her at all. But she'd come down here to work like a shot if she was sure of a job.'

Mrs Ridley pursed her lips, considering. 'I don't know, Hannah. The job would only be temporary like, just until George gets on his feet, it wouldn't be fair to bring a lass down for that. And anyroad, where would she stay?'

'She could sleep in my room, that wouldn't be any trouble,' said Hannah. 'And if she was here she would get work after Mr Ridley is better; you said yourself there's plenty of work so folk can pick and choose. It's just that first chance she needs.'

'I don't know, I'd have to speak to George,' Mrs Ridley said doubtfully. 'I don't suppose we could pay much, and then there's the money for her ticket. Would she be able to come straight away?'

Hannah smiled. The battle was won, she could tell by Mrs Ridley's tone. 'She could get the money for her ticket all right,' she assured the older woman. 'And I can ring up my sister, she has the telephone in the house because her husband is the undermanager.'

'Really? Oh, well, I'll speak to George this dinner-time and let you know when I come in at four o'clock. Now, go and get a bite to eat while I'm still here.'

Hannah was pretty sure that George would agree to anything his wife proposed, and in the event she was right. That evening, after closing the shop, she rang Betty from the telephone box in the station.

'Hannah!' cried Betty, immediately apprehensive when she heard her sister's voice. 'Is there something wrong?' It was the first time Hannah had ever telephoned her, for long-distance calls were so expensive.

'No, no, nothing, Betty. How are you? Mam said in her letter that you and the baby are blooming.'

'Oh, we are. Baby Simon's growing fast and do you know, Hannah, he's the image of Tucker. I've just put him down for the night, he's such a contented baby he sleeps all the way through but for his ten-o'clock feed. I wish you could get away for a few days and come up and see him, Hannah. He's quite grown out of that little jacket you sent. But are you ringing for something special?' Betty became businesslike as the operator came on the line, advising that more money should be inserted, and Hannah pushed in another precious sixpence. Quickly, she explained about the job for Jane.

'If she can come the day after tomorrow, there's work here for her at least until the end of January. Then I'm sure she'll get something else. Mam said Jane is desperate for work, and she can sleep with me till she gets a place. Do you think she'll come?'

'Oh, she'll jump at it. And don't worry about the fare, Tucker will see to that. I'll go down to see her now – Tucker's in, he'll keep an eye on Simon. Can you ring tomorrow night, just to make sure?'

'Yes, same time,' said Hannah, just as the operator's voice cut in again with a request for more money. Thankfully, she put the phone down, thinking it gobbled up sixpences at an alarming rate.

Going home to Cowley on the bus, Hannah remembered she had yet to ask Gloria if it was all right for Jane to stay with them, it was a bit cheeky arranging it without asking her nominal landlady. Still, she was fairly sure Gloria would agree.

In the event, Hannah was right about Gloria's consenting to Jane staying, at least in the beginning. And two days later, a Sunday, Hannah stood on the platform waiting for the train bringing Jane. The train was due in at two thirty so Hannah hadn't bothered to go home when she closed the shop at one o'clock; instead she had made herself a cup of tea in the back shop and eaten a sandwich she had brought with her to while away the time until the train from the north came in.

There was a chill wind blowing along the platform but the afternoon was bright and sunny and Hannah was reminded of the day she had come down herself. Of course, she hadn't had to travel on her own, Alf had been with her. But Jane was fifteen now, only a little older than she had been. Jane's sure to be homesick, she thought, remembering the agonies she had suffered herself in the beginning. She would have to help her to feel at home. After all, she and Jane had been very close as children, before Jane had gone away to the sanatorium in Weardale.

The tinny voice announcing the imminent arrival of the train came over the loudspeaker and Hannah watched as it steamed into the station and the doors began to open. She saw Jane at once, clutching the strap of a basket-weave box just like the one which Hannah had brought with her, an age ago, it seemed now.

'Jane! Jane!' she called and ran down the platform to her sister, ready to throw her arms around her, but when she saw Jane's composure she was suddenly shy and simply kissed her on the cheek.

'Hallo, Hannah,' said Jane. 'It was good of you to meet me.' She was small and thin, too thin, Hannah thought, and pale too. Two spots of colour brightened her cheeks, standing out against the white skin like rouge, but Hannah knew they were not artificial.

'Come on, I'll take your box, you must be tired after the journey. It's only a short bus ride to Cowley.' Hannah picked up Jane's box in one hand, took her arm with the other and led the way out of the station and there was Alf, just getting out of his car.

'Oh, good, I've caught you,' he cried, taking the box and heaving it into the back seat before grabbing Jane and hugging her, not at all put off by the way she shrank back, looking stiff with embarrassment. 'Come on, jump in, we'll be home in two ticks and Gloria is making a slap-up tea for us all.'

All the while, Jane had hardly spoken, simply murmuring her greeting. Hannah got into the back seat of the car beside the luggage and Jane climbed sedately into the front seat. She's tired, thought Hannah, and perhaps a little overwhelmed by the suddenness of the change; after all, everything had happened so quickly.

'Look, there's the shop,' she said, leaning forward and pointing out the single-storey lock-up shop with the sign across the top of the window, 'Ridley's Newsagents'. 'I have to come in early tomorrow to open up, six o'clock.

You can come with me for the first day, though usually you'll be starting at eight.'

Jane looked over at the shop, her face expressionless. 'Will I be paid for the extra time?' she asked, and Hannah looked astonished.

'Oh, I don't think you should ask for that. After all, it's just that I can show you the way into town and what to do when you get here,' she replied.

'I just wondered, that's all,' said Jane.

Alf laughed. 'You start as you mean to go on,' he said. 'You should be paid for the hours you put in.' He turned briefly and winked at Hannah, obviously tickled by his young sister's business acumen. Jane said no more, she just stared out of the window at the streets, quiet on a Sunday, especially when the students had gone down for the Christmas break.

'It's a bit different from Bishop Auckland, isn't it?' Hannah tried to keep a conversation going as they turned into Cowley Road but Jane just nodded. Giving up, her sister sat back in her seat. The afternoon was darkening into evening already. Alf switched on his sidelights and began to whistle, cutting through the silence in the car with his rendering of 'Good King Wenceslas'. And then he was pulling up before the house and Gloria came out to welcome them.

'Had a good journey?' she asked. Jane nodded again, but somehow her quietness wasn't quite so noticeable as

Alf was explaining how he had nearly missed them at the station and Gloria was saying they must be starved and she had teacakes under the grill all ready to be toasted and buttered, and wasn't the weather foul? Gloria had set the table in the lounge with the best embroidered tea cloth for Jane's first meal with them and Jane sat, quietly eating, saying nothing unless she was spoken to and then very little. Hannah was thankful to see that Reggie was out for the afternoon; she was getting tired of the way he seemed to take it for granted that they were a couple, even though she had told him again and again that they were not.

Later, when it was time for bed, Hannah took Jane up to the bedroom. It felt as if she was sharing with a stranger.

'It's not very big, is it?' said Jane, eyeing the bed. 'Not much room for us both. I always had a bed to myself at Weardale, and when I came home.'

'But it's only supposed to be until you can get something for yourself,' said Hannah. 'It was the only thing we could think of for now. You and I used to share a bed before, I thought you wouldn't mind.'

'We were children then,' said Jane.

Hannah looked at her, helplessly. 'When you get a permanent job, we'll find you a room somewhere close,' she said.

'But I'll be on my own then, won't I?' Jane pointed out. 'Couldn't *you* get another room? You're older than me.' Before her sister could reply, Jane went out to the bathroom.

Hannah lay awake long after Jane had gone to sleep and the rest of the household was quiet. She was wondering if she had made a mistake in bringing Jane to Oxford. What on earth had changed her little sister into this quiet, self-possessed young woman who was nevertheless so watchful of her own interests? But then she thought of the years Jane had had to spend away from the family in the sanatorium and of the weeks that would go by when Mam would not be able to find the fare to visit her daughter. Jane must have been very lonely and homesick, more so than Hannah had been when she had come to Oxford, she thought. And Jane had been a young child at the time. No wonder the experience had changed her. Hannah resolved to try to be more understanding with her.

Next morning, Jane was ready before Hannah, wearing a dress which Hannah recognised as one of Betty's, taken in at the sides by Nora, she guessed. Straight with a low belt, it fitted nicely round the hips and looked fine but for the neckline, which was slightly baggy. Jane had fastened a little flowered rayon scarf round her neck which partly disguised the badly fitting neckline. She was standing very still, waiting for her sister to finish her tea and toast. Hannah, trying to keep in mind her conclusion she had come to the previous night concerning her sister's attitude, thought Jane was holding her shabby imitation-leather bag a little too tightly and she was very white, apart from the two flags of crimson in her cheeks.

'Aren't you going to have some breakfast, Jane?' she asked. 'At least have a piece of toast.' She held out a slice of buttered toast and after a moment's hesitation Jane took it and ate it daintily.

'There's nothing to be nervous about, you know. The Ridleys come from our part of the country and they are very nice people to work for,' Hannah said but was rebuffed immediately.

'I'm not nervous,' said Jane, finishing her toast and rinsing her fingers under the sink taps. 'Are you ready now?'

A funny girl, thought Hannah later in the day. Jane was quick to learn and listened attentively to everything she was told, and by the late afternoon was serving customers and tidying shelves as though she had been doing it for years. She was like a different person when dealing with other people, especially Mrs Ridley, helpful and bright and smiling. Mrs Ridley was delighted with her.

'I'm so pleased you thought of her, Hannah, she's just what we needed,' the older woman confided as she put on her coat to go home after the evening rush. It was six o'clock and Jane had been sent home already, though she protested she would stay if necessary.

'No, you go, I'm sure it's been a long day for you, your first day an' all,' Mrs Ridley had said kindly. 'Hannah will close up, won't you, Hannah?' Mrs Ridley had got into the habit of taking the day's takings with her when she went, leaving Hannah to hide the small amounts she could take in the last hour somewhere in the back shop.

'I only hope we can get her settled in a permanent job,' said Hannah.

'I wouldn't worry yet. I've been thinking, it might be good for George to have extra help when he comes back, at least at first, give him the chance to ease into the routine again. Anyroad, Hannah, the doctor's coming tomorrow morning, and I might stay at home to see what he says, I never get a proper story from George. You and Jane can manage, can't you? Tell her she needn't come in early with you, eight o'clock will do fine.'

After Mrs Ridley had gone, Hannah sat behind the counter for a while. The shop was empty of customers and the streets outside looked deserted too. Rain pattered on the window and the glass door and she watched it run down, glittering in the electric light. Tiredly, she pushed her fingers through her short, thick hair, lifting it from her scalp and pushing it back from her temples. She rose to her feet and walked to the door, gazing out at the rain. Jane was going to be all right, she thought, she was a good worker. Maybe she was just naturally quiet when relaxing with her family. I'm too fanciful, thought Hannah, absently tracing the trickle of a raindrop down the glass pane with her fingertip, imagining she dislikes me when she is just reserved. She'll be all right when we get to know each other properly again.

She looked at the clock; another half an hour before the London train was due and the usual half-dozen customers came in for their evening papers. When they had gone she could close up for the night. While she waited she went into the back shop and sat down to change her old shoes for the new brogues she had bought with the money she had earned for the extra hours she had worked. They weren't quite like the ones Timothy had bought for her that day, but they were similar.

The sound of the shop bell tinkling made her jump to her feet, her heart pounding – was it him? It was just such a night as this the last time she had seen him, the night when they had that awful row about Reggie.

'Shop!'

The disappointment when she heard the female voice was as sharp as a pain. Fool, she told herself and went out into the shop to serve the customer with a bar of Cadbury's chocolate. The London train came in and with it the small rush of late customers and Hannah was free to lock up the shop.

Without acknowledging to herself what she was doing, she slowed her movements so that she missed the bus home. She decided she might as well go to the little café and have a cup of tea in the warmth while she waited for the next one. At the same table she had shared with Timothy, she sat and drank some of the muddy brew. But no one else came into the café and in the end she had to go for the bus.

After all, she told herself miserably, it was the Christmas break and all the students had gone home for the holiday. Why should Timothy stay in Oxford? It was time she stopped thinking about him and organised her life without him; she was finished with men. As soon as the holidays were over, she would enrol in night school, perhaps do bookkeeping and accounts instead of shorthand and typing. One day, if she worked hard and saved hard, she would have her own business, she vowed, run her own life.

She was so busy planning that brilliant new life that she missed her bus stop and had to walk twice as far as she normally did, and by the time she got home she was soaked to the skin.

It was on Christmas Eve, just as she was closing the shop, that he came. The perpetual rain had swelled the wood of the door and she was having trouble getting it to close properly so that she could turn the key in the lock.

'Here, let me,' he said.

She paused, still glaring at the door, holding the key in the lock. She'd misheard, she thought, it had to be someone else, some passer-by who had seen her difficulty. But then his hand was taking the key from her and he reopened the door, closed it firmly and the key turned easily in the lock. 'Hallo, Hannah,' he said.

Chapter Nineteen

'I give up,' Tony had said when he came down to breakfast and found Timothy moodily stirring cream into his porridge. 'Here you are again with a face like a wet week. The worst of it is, when the girls see you looking all melancholy and forlorn, doing your Lord Byron act, they flock round you, forgetting all about me. And it's not as if you're interested in them at all, you make that pretty plain – I suppose that's half the attraction. No, Timothy my lad, I think it's time you got that girl out of your system. Where is she, still at Oxford?'

'I don't know, I suppose so. Unless she's gone back to Durham for Christmas,' said Timothy. 'Look, I'm sorry, you're right, I'm not much company for you here. I'll clear out if you like.'

'Well, I don't mean to be inhospitable, old chap, but I have to say that's an excellent idea. With you gone, maybe I'll get a look-in with Lady Cynthia. As it is, she's like all the others, eyes for no one but you. Go on, find your little shop girl and turn your charms on her. I'm sure she'll fall into your arms, swooning with delight, and then when you've had enough of her you'll come back to your senses once again.'

'Hmm, I'll have to take the train,' said Timothy, not listening to his friend now as he made his plans, which was just as well for his plans were very different from what Tony thought they were. 'I'll go to Oxford first, I'll have to pick up my car if I'm to go on to Durham.'

They had driven to London in Tony's car, so his own was still in Oxford. But if Hannah wasn't there he would drive home to his father's house and seek her out, he decided, realising it had been in the back of his mind for a while, it had only taken a small push from Tony to decide him. Now his mind was made up he moved briskly and within an hour he was on his way, with Tony acknowledging he was pleased to see the back of him.

There was a feeling of inevitability about it when Timothy came out of the station at Oxford and saw the light go out in the paper shop and Hannah struggling with the door lock. When she turned to face him and he saw the gladness in her eyes, he knew he had done the right thing in coming.

They went first to the little café round the corner but found it had already closed for the Christmas holiday. They stood for a moment in the side street, which was quiet but for the hum of traffic coming from the main thoroughfares close by. A group of late Christmas shoppers went by the end of the street, laughing and talking and then they were gone and it was quiet again. The rain had stopped, but an icy wind sprang up and Timothy drew Hannah close to him protectively as they walked to the car, which he had parked in the station yard.

'What do you want to do?' he asked. 'I can't take you back to my rooms but we could go to a hotel – oh, only to have dinner and a chance to talk,' he added hastily. They sat in the car and as Timothy wrapped the rug around her, Hannah felt the warm remembered intimacy of the tiny enclosed space. She felt her whole body was coming alive after weeks of numbness, and when his hand touched hers her palm tingled in anticipation. But he moved away and sat back in his seat with no attempt to take her in his arms. In the light from the street lamp she saw he was watching her gravely.

'Well, what do you want to do?' he said again.

'I have to go home, Timothy. I can't just go off again, there'll be a terrific bust-up if I do. It's Christmas Eve and I was going to go to the carol service at chapel with my sister Jane, she's here now.'

Timothy nodded. 'Very well, I'll take you home,' he said. 'I've finished with this hole-in-the-corner business, I'll come in and tell them about us. And I'll come to the carol service with you and tomorrow – you're not working tomorrow, are you?'

'No, not on Christmas day, but Timothy, you can't, Alf will go mad if he sees you with me.'

'He'll get over it.'

'No, but –'

Timothy had already got out of the car and was turning the starting handle. The engine burst into life and he got back in and turned the car in the direction of the Cowley Road.

'Please, just drop me off, Timothy, I'll meet you tomorrow,' she begged. Instead, Timothy pulled the car into the side of the road and turned it round and headed back towards the city.

'What are you doing, where are we going?' she asked. 'I want to go home, take me home.' But he didn't answer, driving straight to the high street, where many of the shops were still open to attract last-minute Christmas shoppers and he stopped in front of a jeweller's shop.

'Come on,' he said, jumping out of the car. 'If we don't hurry, the shop will close.'

Hannah stared at him. 'What are you doing? You're not going to buy me a present, are you? I told you I can't accept –'

Timothy took hold of her hand and drew her out of the car; banging the door shut, he marched her into the jeweller's. Hannah felt sick, her mind raced; he was going to try to dazzle her with an expensive gift, she knew it.

'I won't take anything, not even for a Christmas present,' she blurted, her voice wobbling.

'Not even an engagement ring?' he asked.

Timothy and Hannah were married by special licence in the chapel in Junction Road on the first Saturday in January 1926.

'But why so soon?' asked Hannah, when he told her he wanted to marry as soon as it could be arranged. 'I thought, perhaps a summer wedding, back home in Winton.'

Timothy looked alarmed. 'Oh no, we'll get married here in Oxford and this is the perfect time during the vacation. We'll have a few days for a honeymoon before I go back.' He took her in his arms and kissed her, his kiss gentle at first but then more demanding. 'I'd get married tomorrow, wouldn't you? I can't bear to wait; you don't really want to wait, do you, Hannah?' And, of course, she did not.

The only guests at the wedding were Alf, Jane and Gloria. Dan Morgan and Reggie were asked but declined, and Mrs Ridley was helping George in the shop for he still wasn't up to par. The Honourable Anthony Akers was best man. In the chapel beside Timothy he stood looking round with an air of disbelief that he should be participating in this unlikely event.

'I didn't mean for you to marry the girl,' he had said, when Timothy rang him up at his parents' home in Park

Lane. 'Look, you're not yourself, Tim, old boy. I'll come back today and we'll find a way to get you out of this.'

'I don't want to get out of it, Tony. I love her. Now will you be my best man or not? I've got a special licence, it's at the chapel in Cowley on Saturday.'

'The chapel? What chapel?'

'Just come, Tony, I'll show you,' Timothy had said. And Tony had come, though he had protested that he couldn't see what the rush was all about. 'I have my reasons,' Timothy had said and would not be drawn further.

Tony suspected it had something to do with Mr Durkin senior, who had not been invited to the wedding and, as far as Tony knew, didn't even know it was taking place. But Timothy was of age, he didn't need his father's permission; and he had an income of his own from his mother which had come to him when he was twenty-one. Nevertheless, Tony could visualise the almighty row which was likely to erupt as soon as Daniel Durkin found out about the marriage. He had seen and recognised the elder Durkin's snobbery and contempt for the working class, especially the miners and their families, and he was glad he wouldn't be there to see the confrontation between Timothy and his father. Tony couldn't abide any sort of unpleasantness.

Hannah walked down the aisle on the arm of her brother, past rows of empty pews towards the small party at the front but she didn't notice the empty pews or anything

287

else. All she really saw was Timothy, standing there waiting for her, and her heart swelled within her. Her thoughts were a good match for Tony's; if anything, her disbelief of what was happening was greater than his. Ever since Christmas Eve when she and Timothy walked into the house in Cruel Lane and told them they were to be married and she had held out her hand to show them the diamond ring, she had felt as though it was all happening to someone else. It was like watching Greta Garbo at the pictures and pretending it was happening to her. As she saw Alf turn to watch her progress up the aisle, the scene returned to her clearly.

Alf had started up from his seat at the supper table when she went in with Timothy; she had seen the anger rising swiftly in his face and his ugly expression. And then he had frozen, half risen, looking at them with his mouth open. Reggie had pushed his chair back and gone out without a word. Jane had stared at them, her dark eyes, so like Hannah's, wide and unreadable.

'I'm going to marry Hannah so you may as well accept it,' Timothy had said. Hannah would always be grateful to Gloria for the way she had jumped to her feet immediately, rushed over to Hannah and kissed her, and offered her hand to Timothy, congratulating them loudly. Somehow it had relaxed the atmosphere and made it easier for Alf and Jane to follow Gloria's example, and after that everything was fine.

Hannah and her brother reached the end of their walk down the aisle; Alf stepped back as she took her place beside Timothy and the ceremony began. Her dream-like state persisted and she barely heard the minister speak at all, let alone ask her the vital question, though she knew she must have given the correct response for Timothy was slipping the gold band on her finger and they were married.

Afterwards, they drove out to the same hotel where they had had dinner only a few weeks before, though it seemed like an age ago to Hannah. They ate a hastily arranged wedding lunch and drank champagne. Tony talked easily with Alf about the relative merits of various motorcars and was gallant with Gloria and Jane. And then it was time for the newlyweds to head for London, where they were to spend the last few days before the new term at Tony's parents' house in Park Lane.

'Nonsense,' Tony had said heartily when he had offered the house and Timothy had demurred. 'The place will be empty in any case. I'm invited to Cannes for a few days with a party which includes the divine Cynthia – at last she has begun to notice that I'm around, thanks to you disappearing from the scene, so I owe you something for that.'

Hannah accepted everything, as one does in a dream, for it was still a dream and fervently she hoped never to waken. She was even oblivious to the way the servants looked askance at her whenever she opened her mouth and spoke, her northern accent showing through no matter how she tried to cover it up. She went shopping with Timothy during the day and bought day dresses, evening dresses and all the accessories needed to go with them, and pairs of silk stockings by the dozen. Every evening they would dine in, go to bed early and rise late, and fill the hours in between with long, sensual loving. There were times, very occasional though they were, when Hannah would wake in the night with a gasp of fear for she had dreamed that something was threatening their dream, something or somebody was waiting to drag them back to the real world. When she searched her mind frantically for the source of the threat, she would think of Timothy's father, that stern mine agent who had frightened and intimidated her so when she was a child. And though she had not talked about him to Timothy, she guessed he had not been told of their marriage, so in the night she would be beset by fear for the future.

Then she would cling to Timothy and he would waken aroused and they would make love, quickly and urgently as though it was the first time, and then she could sleep once again, her fears smothered under her love.

'We'll rent a flat in Oxford,' said Timothy, on the morning after their wedding. 'Though I must stay in college as soon as the term begins, it's only for a little while, darling, just until the finals are over. Then we'll be together all the time.'

'But –' Hannah started to protest; she was puzzled, she couldn't understand why it had to be like that. Other married students lived out, she knew they did.

'Trust me, Hannah, it will all work out,' he said quickly. 'I just think it's best if no one knows about us for a while.'

Tony knows, thought Hannah, and my family knows. But she didn't say anything, not yet; the questions were there and they would have to be asked but not now, not until they got back to Oxford. In the meantime, the world was filled with Timothy and their love. And Hannah would not have been human if she had not been entranced with other things about her new life, not least of which was the fact that for the first time in her life she did not have to turn every penny over twice before spending it. It seemed to her that her husband was fabulously rich and Timothy, seeing her delight in buying good clothes, could not bear to disillusion her.

When they got back to Oxford and Hannah was installed in a small flat just off the Cowley Road in Princes Street, the dream began to dissolve around her and reality crept in.

Chapter Twenty

'I'll come over as often as I can,' Timothy said as he kissed her in the tiny vestibule of the rented flat he had found for them. 'You understand how it is, don't you, darling?'

Hannah nodded mutely though she didn't understand at all why he couldn't come home to her every evening. What she did understand was that he was determined to keep her and his marriage apart from his life at the university and there was nothing she could do about it, not yet.

'It'll only be for a few months, Hannah, just until I graduate. Come May I'll be free of the university and we'll be together all the time. We'll leave Oxford and go north again if you want to.'

She wanted to ask him about his father then – did his father still not know about her? What would he say if they turned up on his doorstep and announced that they were married? But now was not the time to talk about anything, not when Timothy was rushing off to college. She lifted her face for a second kiss.

'I don't care where we live so long as we're together,' she whispered, and Timothy smiled.

'We'll always be together,' he promised.

After he had gone, she looked round the flat. When she had first come with Timothy the day before, she had been enchanted with the tiny rooms filled with dark furniture and the tiny kitchen and bathroom, complete with water closet. It was to be their own little love nest and she knew they would be ecstatically happy in it. In the light of the shaded electric lamps it had looked warm and inviting. But now, on her own and in the light of day, she saw that the plush of one brown armchair was worn down, showing the coarse weave of the backing, and that the curtains, which had looked a pleasant plum colour the night before, were really a dingy purple. She stood fingering them absently as she looked out into the street, where a pale January sun was shining on the heads of the people scurrying by on their way to work or the shops, and she felt miserably lonely. The long hours stretched out in front of her without even the surety of Timothy coming home in the evening to look forward to. After the excitement of the wedding and honeymoon in London, there was already a flatness about her new life which came over her the moment Timothy left the flat. And it was so unexpected she thought it must be a fault in her – wasn't she married to the man she loved and ecstatically happy about it? Boredom had no place in her life.

'Well, Hannah,' she said briskly to herself, her voice sounding loud in the empty flat, 'best make a list of what to do.' Turning from the window with an air of determination, she looked in her bag for a pencil and something to write on. There was only the envelope which had contained her mother's letter and written consent to the marriage. The sight of her mother's even handwriting with the carefully rounded letters and straight loops, which she had been taught in National School, made Hannah think of Nora and the little house in Winton Colliery and she paused for a minute, forgetting the list she was about to make out. Mam hadn't understood the need for the hasty wedding; after all, Alf and Gloria had been engaged for months now and their wedding was not to be until the spring. Still, Mam had given her consent and Hannah was grateful that she had not asked if the reason was the obvious one.

'I know you are a sensible girl, Hannah,' she had written. 'If you are in love with him then I won't stand in your way.' But Hannah had known that her mother was hurt at not being given the time to arrange to come down to Oxford for the wedding, and she was hurt at being asked not to spread the news of it about. 'I don't know why it is such a secret,' she had written. 'But of course I will do as you say, no doubt you will explain when you come home.'

Hannah sighed, if only she knew what it was all about herself, she would gladly explain to her mother. Her own family were all so open with each other, she had difficulty getting used to having secrets. But her marriage was so new and wondrous to her that when she was with Timothy he was all she could think about, and she still couldn't get over the fearful conviction that it wouldn't last. He would wake up one morning and realise he had made a mistake in marrying a girl like her, a pitman's daughter, and she couldn't bear to do or say anything that might bring that day any nearer. Hannah pushed the thought to the back of her mind and turned over the envelope to make her list, imagining how Mam would scorn the idea that she had nothing to do but wait for her husband to come home and feel the long, empty hours stretching ahead of her endlessly, Mam had no patience with such notions.

'Get going,' she used to say, 'there's always something to be done. Don't tell me you're bored. If you've finished your work, take the bairn out for an airing. The fresh air will do you both good and it'll mebbe brighten your ideas up.'

Hannah smiled as she sat down at the table with her pencil and the envelope and started on a list of things she would do.

First, she would go to see the Ridleys. At this time of day Mrs Ridley was likely to be in the back shop making breakfast for George, and Hannah wanted to make sure they were not offended by the way she had left so hurriedly to get married. And she would see Jane, too. Her brow knitted as she thought of Jane; they were like chance acquaintances rather than sisters, or at least Jane acted as though they were. Hannah licked her pencil and wrote, 'Try to have a talk with Jane.'

Then she would go shopping, buy in some food just in case Timothy came home unexpectedly, something which could be cooked quickly. And she would go to the library and find some good books, books that she could discuss with Timothy and so prove to him she wasn't completely uneducated. Maybe she could even take some classes during the day, when he was in college – that was a good idea. The thought made her jump up and run into the bedroom to comb her hair and take her new camel coat from the wardrobe. As always, she ran her hand down the nap, it was so soft and warm and when she put it on it made her look so smart. So it should, of course, the money it had cost Timothy in Harrods. But he had a private income, she told herself, he could afford it and he liked her to look smart. Smiling as she turned off the gas fire which made the flat so warm and cosy, she went out and ran down the stairs into the street.

Outside, she was glad of the warmth of the coat, for though the sun still shone there was a biting north wind and she stepped out briskly. She had intended to walk to the station but when a bus came along she was glad to board it for the short distance involved. She got off right opposite the newsagent's shop. When she opened the door and went in, she saw it was full of customers and Jane and Mr Ridley were working at full stretch.

'Hallo, Mr Ridley, hallo Jane,' said Hannah, smiling a little uneasily when she saw how busy they were. After all, she thought guiltily, she had left very suddenly and when her sister had barely had time to get to know the work and Mr Ridley wasn't up to par. Jane affected not to hear Hannah at first but she had to acknowledge her sister when Mr Ridley looked up and smiled a welcome.

'What cheor, lass, it's grand to see you,' he cried heartily. Pulling the curtain to the back shop aside briefly, he called to his wife, 'Mother! Come and see who's here. It's our Hannah back from her honeymoon and a grand married lady now.'

Mrs Ridley came out of the back shop with a beaming smile on her face which would have warmed the coldest January day.

'Eeh, lass, it's you,' she said. 'Come away into the back and we'll have a bit of a natter while I make George his breakfast. This rush will soon go and then he'll be demanding his bacon and eggs, as you know.'

Hannah followed the older woman behind the curtain, loosening her coat as she went, for the heat from the gas ring filled the back shop and the smell of frying bacon with it. Mrs Ridley picked up her fork and turned the bacon in the pan, then she looked Hannah up and down.

'Mind, lass, you don't half look smart in that coat – what is it, camel hair? By, it's lovely, it is. Best take it off and hang it up, though, you don't want to get any grease splashed on it, do you?'

Hannah placed the coat on a hanger on the door beside Jane's and then she turned back to Mrs Ridley.

'I've been wanting to tell you I'm sorry I left in such a hurry. I know you were annoyed about it and you had every right to be,' she said. 'I would have waited until Jane had a bit more experience, or at least until Mr Ridley was properly better –'

'Nay, Hannah, think no more of it, it worked out all right,' said Mrs Ridley. 'I must admit I was a bit huffed at first when you went off like that, but your Jane's very good, you know, she's nearly as good as you already. And George has got over his flu so there was no harm done.' Deftly, she lifted the slices of bacon from the pan and broke a couple of eggs into the sizzling fat. Turning the gas down low, she waited for them to set.

'I was wrong, wasn't I, pet?' she said. 'This time the prince did marry the beggar maid, didn't he? And it couldn't have happened to a nicer lass, that's what I said to George, you ask him.' Carefully, she slid the eggs on to the plate beside the bacon and put the kettle on the gas ring.

'I'll tell him it's ready,' said Hannah, going to the curtain. She was relieved and happy now that she knew Mrs Ridley bore her no ill-will, it was something that had been bothering her.

'Breakfast is ready, Mr Ridley,' she called. Then she saw that there were still half a dozen customers waiting to be served.

'Aye, and I'm ready to eat it, only trouble is, I'm too busy for the minute,' said George. 'Tell Mother to keep it hot for me, there's a good girl, Hannah.'

'No, go on, you get your breakfast, I'll help Jane,' she replied, moving in behind the counter.

'If you're sure you don't mind.' He hesitated, but Hannah waved him away.

'Go on, eat it while it's hot.'

The sisters worked steadily away until the shop was clear of customers, about fifteen minutes later. Hannah was alone with Jane in the shop at last and she smiled at her younger sister, noticing that Jane seemed to have put on a little weight and seemed much healthier than she had been when she first came to Oxford.

'How are you liking it here, Jane?' she asked. 'Mrs Ridley says you're doing well. Do you like living with the Morgans?'

'It's all right. At least I have the room to myself now you've gone,' Jane answered.

'I'm glad,' said Hannah. There was a silence between them for a few minutes, then she tried again. 'Have you heard from Mam lately? I haven't had a letter since just before the wedding.'

'There was a letter this morning, I didn't have time to read it before I came out.'

Automatically, Hannah began to straighten out the piles of newspapers which were laid out on the counter, feeling slightly uncomfortable at the lack of response from her sister. She wondered how Jane could bear not to open a letter from home the instant it came. From the back shop they could hear the voices of the Ridleys chatting together. Jane stood behind the counter with her arms folded and a slight smile on her face as Hannah moved from the papers to the rack of magazines and straightened them.

'It must be nice to come in here and play working,' she said suddenly, making Hannah glance across the room at her, startled. Jane hadn't sounded hostile exactly but her tone was not friendly either.

'Oh, I'm not, it's just that I've done it for so long,' said Hannah. 'I wasn't thinking, really.'

'I thought you were checking whether I'd laid them out the way you like them,' said Jane, and there was definitely a sarcastic note in her voice this time.

'Oh, Jane, I don't know why you're annoyed with me,' said Hannah. 'We used to be such friends when we were small, why can't we be friends now? We're family, aren't we?' She kept her voice low so that the Ridleys wouldn't hear.

Jane shrugged. 'What's family? It doesn't mean anything, really. When I was in the sanatorium none of you bothered to come to see me, the nurses were more to me than family.'

'Jane!' gasped Hannah, forgetting all about the Ridleys in the back shop. 'You know we hadn't the money for fares to Weardale. And Mam came to see you whenever she could, you know she did.'

Jane's face twisted in disbelief. 'Do I? Maybe she did. All I can remember are the times I was expecting her and she didn't come. The fact is no one came to see me for weeks at a time and after a while I stopped expecting it.'

Mrs Ridley pulled back the curtain and came into the shop, looking from one girl to the other. 'There's nothing wrong, is there?' she asked.

Jane's whole demeanour changed, and she smiled at the older woman vivaciously. 'No, no, we were just talking of old times back home,' she said. 'Now, shall I have my break now? I thought if we weren't busy I could clean the shelves afterwards.'

'Thanks, pet, you're a good girl.' Mrs Ridley relaxed, obviously thinking she had been mistaken in feeling there was tension between the girls.

'Well, I'll be on my way, then. I have to do the shopping for tonight's meal,' said Hannah awkwardly. She walked to the door, then thought of something and went back to the curtained doorway of the back shop.

'Jane,' she said, 'will you come up to see me at the flat one night next week? For a meal, I mean? Then we could have a proper talk.'

Jane looked at her over her teacup. 'Oh, I don't know. What about Timothy? You don't want me there, really.'

'Yes, I do,' Hannah insisted. 'And Timothy would, too, you're my sister, after all. Anyway, Timothy isn't home every night so there could be just the two of us, we could talk over the old days.'

'Oh, well, if you're lonely and want someone to talk to, I'll come,' said Jane with an air of conferring a favour.

'Tuesday, then, will that be all right?' asked Hannah, hoping Tuesday was indeed an evening when Timothy would not be in. She felt she had to try to get on better terms with her sister; she had to show her that she had not been pushed out of the family when she had had to go into the sanatorium.

Jane put down her cup and stared at Hannah, her expression unreadable. 'If you like,' she said. She picked up a day-old newspaper from the pile ready to go back to the wholesaler and became immersed in something on the front page. Hannah watched her for a moment but Jane did not look up again.

'See you on Tuesday, then,' she said at last and went out through the shop.

'Don't forget to come back and see us,' called Mrs Ridley from behind the counter.

'I won't,' Hannah replied, closing the door after her to the tinkling sound of the bell.

She wandered around the town, her spirits dampened by the insight into her sister's feelings which Jane had revealed. Was Mam aware of Jane's bitterness, she wondered, absently staring at a poster on a telegraph pole; one corner had come unstuck and was flapping in the wind. MFGB it said along the bottom edge, and she read the poster properly. It was the Miners' Federation of Great Britain, how could she not have recognised it straight away? It was something which was talked about almost daily back home in Winton Colliery. But here in Oxford she knew it meant nothing to most folk, why should it? Sighing, she read the rest of it. Arthur Cook, the secretary of the federation, was going to address the Oxford City Labour Party at the Corn Exchange.

'Come and hear the truth about conditions in the coalfields today.'

Hannah looked at the date: Wednesday evening, the day after tomorrow. Oh, well, she thought, Timothy would probably be home on Wednesday evening and she wouldn't be able to go to the talk, but if she was free, she would like to hear what the miners' leader had to say. She went on her way to the butcher's and bought a pound of stewing beef, thinking she would make a beef casserole for supper. She could keep it in the oven on a low gas if Timothy was late in, and it would be fine. At the greengrocer's, she bought carrots, onions and potatoes, and then caught the bus home. It was only when she was getting off the bus that she remembered she had been going to call at the library. Never mind, she told herself, she would start her course of self-education tomorrow.

Back in the flat she made herself a sandwich and a cup of tea and ate it before the gas fire in the tiny sitting room. Arthur J. Cook, she thought, Bob used to talk about him, Bob thought he was a great man. 'A marvellous orator' was what Bob had said. 'If anyone can put across the case for the miners, Arthur J. Cook can.' The last time she had been home, Bob was becoming very involved with the Miners' Federation. She could remember him rushing in from the pit and rushing out to a meeting of the union as soon as he had washed and changed and bolted down his meal. She would have liked to hear this great orator, Arthur J. Cook, she thought, lazily stretching her feet out towards the fire, luxuriating in the warmth, even though it did not have the same cheerfulness of a coal fire.

At eight o'clock she began to give up hope of Timothy coming and went into the kitchen to lift the casserole out of the oven. Might as well eat her own meal, she thought dismally, though her appetite had disappeared under the growing disappointment. Delicious smells filled the room when she lifted the lid of the pot, but they only served to make her feel slightly sick.

Putting the lid back on the dish, she left it on the stove and went back into the sitting room and sat down only to get to her feet almost at once. A brisk walk was what she needed to restore her appetite, she told herself. She had nothing to feel discontented about, nothing at all. Hadn't Timothy told her he might not get home this evening? Nevertheless, she was feeling very down in the mouth.

She changed into her outdoor shoes, grabbed her coat and went to the front door of the flat just as a key turned in the lock. The door opened and there was Timothy.

'You're going out?' he asked, his eyebrows lifted in surprise. She hardly noticed, she was so pleased to see him. Happiness bubbled up in her, her whole being seemed to sparkle as she threw herself into his arms.

'Oh, I thought you weren't coming,' she cried as he stepped into the flat, still holding her, and closed the door with the back of his foot.

'I wasn't going to, I shouldn't be here, really,' he said as he picked her up bodily and carried her to the sofa in the sitting room. 'Truth is, I couldn't stay away, not tonight. Tomorrow night, maybe.' He buried his face in her hair and undid her coat, then the buttons of her dress, stripping them from her and dropping them there on the hearthrug and his own hastily shed clothes on top of them. And Hannah forgot all about her own doubts and worries and everything else in the surge of feeling which engulfed her.

Later, much later, she reheated the casserole and they ate quickly and ravenously at the kitchen table as though they hadn't a moment to spare. She began to gather the dishes to stack in the sink but he took her hand and drew her into the bedroom.

'Do them tomorrow,' he commanded. 'Plenty of time when I've gone.'

A shiver of apprehension ran through her and the light faded from her eyes. When he was gone, when he was gone; the words ran through her head almost prophetically. It was as though he meant he would be gone permanently. But then he was taking her in his arms again and the phrase was blotted out of her consciousness by the feel of his body against hers.

Chapter Twenty-One

Two evenings later, Hannah was on her way to the Corn Exchange to hear Arthur J. Cook. She hadn't told Timothy she was going, she hadn't had the chance, for Timothy had not been home since he went back to college the morning before. She had waited for him yesterday evening, even though he had warned he might not make it but in the end she had put the pork chops she had bought for supper back in the meat safe and gone to bed without bothering to cook one of the chops for herself. She was not expecting him back this Wednesday evening either, for he had said he had an important meeting, and the day had seemed endless to her.

Hannah stared out of the bus window; there seemed to be an awful lot of people on the streets. Although it was half past six, the high street was almost as busy as during the day, with many students, in their short undergraduate gowns, hurrying along in groups, either walking or cycling. She wondered if they were going to the same meeting that Timothy was attending. Maybe she would catch a glimpse of him going along with his friends, she thought hopefully, then smiled to herself at her own naivety. Obviously, in a large university such as Oxford there would be lots of things going on in the evening and it was very unlikely she would see him.

She alighted from the bus as it came to a halt near the Corn Exchange and walked the last few yards, hurrying, for she was late. Once inside, she took a seat near the back and sat quietly to listen to the speeches, which had already begun.

'Is it right that men who have what must be one of the dirtiest and most dangerous jobs in the country should be earning wages at below the subsistence level?' a man was saying. 'Brothers, I appeal to your sense of fair play. The miners need our support.'

There was a burst of applause from the audience and the speaker held up his hand. 'We have with us today someone who can put the case for the miners to you much better than I can, that great champion of the miners' cause, the secretary of the Miners' Federation of Great Britain, Mr A. J. Cook.'

He doesn't look anything special, thought Hannah as the miners' leader stepped forward. He wouldn't have been out of place living in the rows of Winton Colliery. Of course, she reminded herself, he had been a miner from the South Wales coalfield for years before he became the secretary. She gazed at him expectantly, trying to see what Bob saw in him.

He didn't speak at first, simply waited quietly for his audience to settle down and within a minute or two, the hall was quiet.

'Comrades –' At last he began to speak, but the moment was spoiled for Hannah as noise of talking and laughing came from behind her. She looked over her shoulder to see undergraduates filing into the room, quite a large number of them, talking among themselves as they began to walk down the aisles.

'Comrades,' Mr Cook repeated, raising his voice, 'I have come here this evening to appeal to the working men of Oxford.' His next words were unintelligible to Hannah as loud talking broke out close to her and she turned to see that undergraduates were all around her, some with the student magazine *Isis* under their arms.

'Communist!' one shouted. 'Why don't you go to live in Russia?'

Arthur Cook heard the jibe and he began to answer, 'This country belongs to the working people –'

'Come on, men, we'll debag him,' Hannah heard someone shout, and there was a general surge towards the platform. Hannah jumped to her feet, her heart beating painfully as she tried to see over the heads of people in front of her. Arthur Cook was standing his ground and grim-faced men at the front of the hall were turning to face the threat and joining together to form a barrier round the speakers. Then her view was cut off by the crowd.

'Cowards!' she cried, though her voice was lost in the general hubbub. 'Let him speak.' She was jostled and pushed as she struggled to reach the aisle, and frustrated outrage flooded through her. At that moment she hated the students around her with their well-fed faces and strong, healthy bodies more than she had hated anyone in her whole life. If she had had a weapon in her hand she would have lashed out at them regardless of the consequences and felt it as revenge for all the ground-down poverty of the mining folk at home, the men injured in the pits, the children with rickets, her dead father. She hardly felt the weight on her foot as one man stood on it as he went by or the pain in her ribs as an elbow caught her a glancing blow.

'Come with me.'

She heard the voice in her ear but she ignored it until an iron grip took hold of her upper arm and she found herself dragged through the crowd to the back of the hall and the exit, though she fought furiously to free herself.

'Let me go, do you hear me?' she screamed and kicked out at the man's shin. He deftly avoided the blow and then they were outside and he was pulling her away into a side street. As the cold air hit her and cleared the fog of furious hate which had blurred her vision, she glared up at him as he towered over her, ready to fight against whatever he was going to do to her. And it was Anthony Akers.

'You bloody little fool,' he said, still holding on to her arm though she strove to pull herself away. 'What were you doing in there? Where's Timothy? What's he doing, allowing you to go there?'

'Allowing nothing,' Hannah snapped. 'I go where I like. And I haven't seen Timothy since yesterday morning when he went back to college.' Anthony had relaxed his grip and she backed away from him. 'It was a perfectly orderly meeting until your loutish friends came in. I wanted to hear what Mr Cook had to say, I was interested. I thought this was a free country, a man should be allowed to speak without being attacked by a gang of hooligans.'

'We weren't going to attack him, just debag him, teach him a lesson,' said Anthony mildly. 'He won't be hurt.'

'Debag him? Humiliate him like that, a man who is just trying to get a living wage for the men in the pits? Why, you rotten –' Hannah stopped as a thought struck her. 'Timothy's not in there, is he? He's not one of them?' She waited for his answer, dreading what she might hear. Oh God, she thought, Timothy's not like them, he isn't.

311

Anthony stared at her grimly. 'No, he isn't. Which is just as well. What do you think he would have thought if he'd seen you in there at a communist meeting?'

'It's not a communist meeting,' she shouted at him. 'It's a Labour Party meeting, don't you know the difference? Why does anyone who fights for the working man have to be a communist?' She stamped her foot to emphasise her point.

Anthony stared at her in silence, his normally pleasant face grim and baffled-looking. 'Come on, I'll see you home,' he said at last. 'My car's just around the corner. Don't worry, I won't say anything to Tim about your being at that meeting.'

'You can if you want to,' Hannah said sharply. 'I'm not ashamed of going. I come from a mining family, I wanted to hear Mr Cook speak, why wouldn't I? Not that there was much chance of him being heard, not with your university friends there.'

'Timothy is an undergraduate too,' he reminded her as he opened the car door for her, and Hannah was silenced.

It was true, Timothy was a student just like those others, she thought. No, not like them, he was different, he would never try to humiliate a man by trying to take his trousers off in public. Timothy cared about people's feelings. She stole a glance at Anthony as he drove along the road. He had been at the meeting and he was Timothy's friend. Yet he was a pleasant, harmless enough chap.

Would he have joined in with the others if he hadn't seen her and come to get her away from the hall?

'Do you think they will have managed to debag Mr Cook?' she asked.

'Oh yes, I think so,' he replied cheerfully. 'After all, there were two or three rowing blues there, not to mention the rugger players. I don't think they were about to be stopped by those communists.' He glanced at her, seeing her anxious expression. 'Oh, don't worry, they wouldn't hurt him. It's just a lark to most of them, really it is.'

'Let me out. Stop the car and let me out now,' said Hannah, taking hold of the door handle. She was so furious she was spluttering, and if she had managed to get the door open she would have flung herself out of the moving car.

'I say, don't do that, you'll fall and hurt yourself.' Alarm sharpened Anthony's tone and he leaned across her to drag her hand from the handle. 'You're being silly, Hannah. I told you they wouldn't hurt him, what are you making such a fuss about?'

'Let me out, Tony. If you don't, I'll jump.'

Tony hastily pulled into the kerb, but as soon as the car was stationary he grabbed hold of her arm. 'Look, what's the matter with you? Timothy would never forgive me if I let you walk home. Now be a good girl and sit still, you'll be home in a couple of minutes.'

Hannah turned a furious face to him, 'What's the matter with me? What's the *matter*?' She was practically screaming now. 'How would you like it if a gang of young miners tried to take your trousers off in public? How would you like it if they did it to your father? I suppose he will be about the same age as Mr Cook. And you say they weren't going to hurt him?'

'Oh, I say, Hannah, you're taking it all too much to heart,' he said. 'I told you, it was just a bit of a lark. Hannah –'

But Hannah was out of the car and running along the road. He poked his head round the windscreen and called after her but she ignored him. All she wanted to do was get away from him and from anyone who thought like him. An opportune bus came alongside her, slowing down as it came towards a stop, and she raced after it, managing to catch it before it pulled away again. It was half empty and she flung herself down on the nearest seat and stared unseeingly out of the window. Her mind was seething so that even her thoughts were incoherent; her emotions had taken her over completely and she felt physically sick with rage.

The short walk from the bus stop to the flat calmed her down a little. The air was so cold and damp that it penetrated through her clothes and by the time she was home she was shaking more with cold than with temper. Shedding her outdoor clothes, she turned the gas fire up high and made herself a cup of cocoa, then pulling the armchair close to the fire, she sat sipping her drink and mulling over the night's happenings in her mind. She hadn't even heard what Mr Cook had had to say, she thought, remembering the grinning students as they surged forwards in the hall, 'for a lark' as Anthony had said. She felt so alienated from them that they seemed like a different species. How could they be so unfeeling about the suffering of their fellow human beings?

'I'll go and see Alf and Gloria tomorrow,' she said aloud, suddenly feeling the need to be with her own people. 'Alf will understand when I tell him about tonight.' She hadn't seen her brother since her marriage – during the day he was at work and in the evenings she usually waited in, in case Timothy should come home. Except for this evening, she thought and shifted restlessly in her chair at the memory. She yawned suddenly and glanced at the clock on the mantelpiece. Ten o'clock, a bit earlier than her usual bedtime but the emotional stress had tired her. Maybe she would have an early night. Rising to her feet, she stretched luxuriously before carrying her cup into the kitchen and rinsing it under the tap.

The sound of a key turning in the lock made joy shoot through her. She dropped the cup in the sink and flew into the hall.

'Timothy, oh, Timothy, I'm so glad to see you,' she cried. 'I thought you weren't coming tonight. What a lovely surprise.' Flinging her arms around his neck, she hugged him, not noticing at first that he did not hug her back. But her joy faded as he took hold of her by her upper arms and held her away from him, and when he looked up she saw he was very angry, his blue eyes hard and glittering and his mouth drawn into a thin line.

'Timothy?' she faltered.

'Where have you been?'

'I . . . I went to hear Mr Cook at the Corn Exchange. I wanted to hear his speech. Were you here earlier? I thought you weren't coming home tonight, you said you had a meeting, I would have stayed in if I'd known.'

'No, I wasn't here earlier. I had a meeting with my tutor, I told you. Then I was studying in my rooms when Tony came in.'

'Oh. The Honourable Anthony Akers. I suppose he told you what happened? Well, I wasn't in any danger, really, but he forced me to leave.'

Hannah turned and walked into the sitting room before continuing. 'It was disgraceful, Timothy, those undergraduates were acting like hooligans. I thought there was supposed to be freedom of speech in this country. I was so –'

'Hannah!'

She looked up at him quickly, her eyes widening as she saw his expression. 'I told you, I was all right, were you worried about me? Is that why you've come home?'

Timothy strode into the room and faced her. 'You may be all right, that's not the point. You could have been hurt, you could have been trampled on or caught in the crush. What on earth possessed you to go to a Labour Party meeting? You're my wife now, did you not think you might have asked me before attending a meeting of communists? What do you suppose my friends would think?'

'They are not communists. And your friends don't even know you're married,' cried Hannah, her temper rising.

'They would have found out soon enough if you had been caught up in a disturbance and arrested, or even if you had been hurt and taken to hospital.'

Hannah gasped. 'Well, you seem to know which would have been the worst thing from your point of view,' she snapped.

Timothy sighed. 'Oh, don't be a fool, Hannah! Of course I was more worried that you might have been hurt than anything else,' he said. 'But Tony said you were fine, he got you out before there was any trouble. In any case, I found out that it all fizzled out in the end, the stewards got Cook away somehow so nothing happened at all.'

'No thanks to your friends,' she said bitterly. 'I never thought you would side with them, I thought you had some sympathy for the miners and the way the coal owners are trying to force them to accept a cut in wages when they are poor enough as it is.'

'I do, I do, Hannah, but you have to realise it's a question of simple economics. The coal industry is losing money, it can't go on –'

'Oh, no, of course not,' Hannah flared. 'Poor Lord Akers might have to sell one of his estates, or even his house on Park Lane, and we can't allow that to happen, can we?'

Timothy stared at her for a long moment, then he shrugged his shoulders and went back into the hall. 'There's no talking to you when you're in this bitter mood,' he said, taking his coat from the stand where he had flung it when he came in.

'You're not going back tonight, are you?' Hannah asked anxiously. She couldn't believe that that was what he intended to do.

'There's no point in staying here to argue and in any case, I have an early tutorial tomorrow,' he said.

'I'm surprised you found time to come out to see me at all,' said Hannah bitterly.

'Have you sufficient money?' asked Timothy, ignoring her last remark as he pulled out his wallet. 'I may not be back for a day or two, I'd better leave you some.' He put a five-pound note on the hall table.

'But why?' cried Hannah, pain making her voice almost shrill. 'Please don't go now, not now, I'm so upset, you've no idea how what happened tonight affected me, I feel so low.'

'I have to,' he said, 'please understand, Hannah.'

'I *don't* understand, Timothy. There must be other married students, why do we have to be so secretive about it? Is it just your father? Or are you ashamed of me? That's it, isn't it? You're ashamed of me.'

Timothy took a step towards her. 'No, don't think that,' he said. 'Look, I have to go, I don't want the proctors after me. I told you, Hannah, it's only for a short while; come the summer I'll be finished with the university. Now I have to go, I'm sorry.' He opened the door and was gone, leaving Hannah staring at the closed door.

Dully, she went into the bathroom, washed her face and brushed her teeth. She felt icy cold in spite of the gas fire in the sitting room so she filled a hot-water bottle and took it to bed with her. She lay between the cold sheets, hugging the hot-water bottle but still shivering. After a while she got up and went to the sideboard where Timothy kept a bottle of whisky. She poured herself a glassful and drank it down, choking as the unaccustomed spirit burned her throat. But it did bring some warmth into her and she carried the bottle and glass with her back to bed, putting them down on the bedside table. It's not going to work, she thought as she climbed back between the sheets, my marriage is over already. I should have known it wouldn't work. No matter what he says, I know he doesn't want his friends to know about me because he's ashamed of me, what other reason could there be? He's not dependent on his father for money, it can't be that.

Her mind went round and round endlessly and she began to feel dizzy and slightly sick. She was just considering getting up to go to the bathroom when at last she fell into an exhausted sleep, filled with unformed nightmares.

Chapter Twenty-Two

There was a persistent noise of hammering somewhere in the middle distance. Hannah stirred restlessly in her sleep and turned on her back. Then a bell began to ring, buzzing over and over again, and she opened her eyes, puzzled what it might be. Suddenly she sat bolt upright and pushed her hair away from her face. It was the front doorbell – Timothy must have come back.

Jumping out of bed, she pulled on the kimono she had bought a few days before, wincing as her head began to pound painfully. Quickly she looked in the mirror and groaned. She looked awful, her eyes were red-rimmed and puffy and her hair was all over the place – where was her hairbrush? The hammering on the door began again, each blow shooting knives through her head and she gave up the search for her hairbrush and went to answer the door.

'Timothy,' she said shakily as she pulled it open, 'I'm so glad you came back.' Pushing the tangle of hair back from her face, she looked up at the man standing there, though the hall swam around her with the effort. It settled into place with a jolt as she saw it was not Timothy but his father standing there.

'Mr Durkin,' she said faintly, and stood back for him to enter.

Daniel Durkin pushed past her without speaking and strode into the dim sitting room, where he stood with his back to the unlit gas fire.

'You know who I am, then,' he said.

'Yes, of course,' she said as she followed him and hurriedly drew back the curtains at the window. Anyone brought up in Winton knew Daniel Durkin, she thought, and blinked at the light, for even though it was still midwinter, the sun was shining brightly in the street. Confusedly, Hannah wondered why it was so bright so early in the morning. It couldn't possibly be past eight o'clock, she never slept later than that. But when she looked at the clock she saw it was midday.

Mr Durkin was looking her up and down, not even trying to hide his contempt. Flushing, she realised that her kimono was open and her nightie was low-cut over her breast. She pulled it together and tied the belt tightly to keep it in place. Taking the matches from the mantelpiece, she lit the gas fire before turning to face her father-in-law.

'Won't you sit down?' she asked. She was fighting to still the tremor in her voice.

'No, I will not,' he answered. 'I can say what I have to say standing up. It won't take long.'

Hannah's toes curled into the hearthrug as she saw him glance at her bare feet, then bring his gaze slowly up her body to her flushed face and tangled hair.

'Well, do you mind waiting until I get dressed? It won't take me long,' she said stiffly, the tremor gone and a spark of anger taking its place. Still, she strove to keep her tone pleasant even though his manner reminded her vividly of that humiliating day so many years before, when he had looked at her mother and Harry with that same expression. She had been young at the time but she would never forget the scene in the colliery yard on the day she had first met Timothy and his father.

Daniel glanced through the open door of the bedroom to the unmade bed and saw the bottle and glass still standing on the bedside table.

'Go ahead,' he said. 'No doubt you'll need another drink to fortify you before hearing what I have to say to you.'

'Another drink –' Hannah gasped. 'What do you mean? I don't drink.'

Daniel raised his eyebrows sardonically. 'Oh, no? What's in that bottle in there, then? Looks like a pretty famous brand of single malt to me.'

'It's –' she began hotly and then shook her head. No, she told herself, she wasn't going to let him provoke her into losing her temper and her head. She needed all her wits about her if she was going to hold her own against him. 'I won't be a moment,' she said meekly and closed the door of the sitting room behind her. She splashed cold water on her face in the bathroom and cleaned her teeth; her tongue felt as though it was like a lump of soggy cotton wool but at least her head was beginning to settle down and the painful thumping had dulled. Going into the kitchen, she put the kettle on to boil while she was dressing. She refused to let the thought of him waiting in the sitting room make her hurry.

'Of all the days for him to come,' she muttered to her reflection in the dressing-table mirror. Why on earth had she drunk that glass of whisky after Timothy went off last night? It wasn't as if she liked the stuff, it tasted awful and look how it had made her sleep late this morning. She stripped off her nightie and put on her underclothes before looking in the wardrobe for something to wear. She was hesitant, for she was unsure of herself and her judgement and dreading the confrontation awaiting her. Who had told Daniel about her, she wondered, was it Anthony? But surely, if it was Anthony, why had he waited until now? He had known all along about her marriage to Timothy. Unless he had telephoned the evening before, he had been pretty fed up with her then, she thought suddenly. He could have phoned and Mr Durkin could have travelled down overnight. Or even set off early this morning, she admitted to herself wryly, remembering how late in the day it was.

She took out a plain woollen dress in a deep shade of blue, simple but well cut, and pulled it over her head. She had bought it in London and the price had made her gasp in disbelief but Timothy had insisted she have it.

'It looks beautiful on you,' he had said and, remembering, Hannah smiled and took heart. Timothy loved her, didn't he? That was the main thing. There was a narrow leather belt which sat on the hips and she fastened it loosely before sitting down at the dressing table to comb her hair. Her bob was getting a bit long, she saw, it was time she went back to the hairdresser's. A lock of hair kept falling over her eyes so she fastened it back with a plain blue slide over one ear. Pinching her cheeks to bring some colour into them, she stood up and slipped her feet into low-heeled pumps the same colour as her dress. Now she was ready to face him. Timothy's father and now her father-in-law, she reminded herself, squaring her shoulders. It was natural for him to think she wasn't good enough for Timothy. But he couldn't do anything about their marriage, not now, it was too late no matter how enraged he was. Taking a deep breath, Hannah went into the sitting room.

'Would you like a cup of tea?' she asked Daniel pleasantly, as though he were a friend who had just dropped in unexpectedly.

'No, I would not,' he said impatiently. 'I –'

'Well, I'm sure you won't mind if I have one myself, will you? I like to start the day with a cup of tea.' Without waiting for him to answer she went into the kitchen, prepared a tray and carried it back with her. Mr Durkin had sat down in an armchair and she noted it with a tiny feeling of satisfaction. He was saying something about this being a fine time to start the day but she ignored it. Carefully she poured herself a cup of tea and added milk and a spoonful of sugar.

'Sure you won't have one?' she asked and he exploded with wrath.

'Young woman, I haven't come here to drink tea, nor did I expect to be kept waiting all this time by a chit like you,' he roared, getting to his feet once more and towering over her. Hannah picked up her cup with a steady hand and took a sip of tea, though her heart was beginning to pound as painfully as her head had done earlier. Carefully, she replaced the cup in the saucer and looked up at him, aware that her control was dangerously near to breaking.

'Why have you come here, Mr Durkin?' In spite of herself, her voice trembled slightly as she said his name. Abstractedly she noted how Timothy resembled him physically, though Daniel was of a stocky build whereas Timothy was slender. As she looked up at him now, she noticed how his cheeks were mottled with purple and his eyes were lighter than his son's, and harder, much harder.

Daniel glared at her. 'Don't be pert with me, young woman. It won't get you anywhere. I've come to put an end to this ridiculous so-called marriage. How much do you want to leave my son alone?'

'It's not a so-called marriage, it is a true marriage. We were wed in the Methodist chapel in Cowley and I have the certificate to prove it,' she said evenly. 'In any case, it's too late. Timothy is of age, he had a perfect right to marry whoever he wanted to.' Hannah was doggedly hanging on to her temper. 'And he loves me,' she added as an afterthought.

He laughed shortly. 'Wedded in a damn chapel, were you? To think a son of mine should marry in a chapel, it's beyond belief. And you think I can't do anything about it, do you? Well, let me tell you, Hannah Armstrong –'

'Hannah Durkin.'

'Hannah Armstrong, I said, and that's who you are,' he repeated, his tone becoming vehement. 'You'll never hold the right to the Durkin name, believe me, I'm telling you and I mean it. Now stop this pretence, you and I know you're just in this for what you can get out of it. Good God, girl, you didn't think I would agree to my son ruining his life on a damn drunken pitman's brat, did you?'

'Pitman's brat? Pitman's brat? You say that as though you were talking to scum.' Hannah jumped to her feet, upsetting the tea tray so that the cup and saucer fell to the floor and milky tea spilled out over the carpet and hearth-rug. But neither of them appeared to notice. 'Let me tell you, my father was a decent man and a hard worker until he broke his back in the pit. He wasn't a criminal and he was never drunk in his life, he didn't drink hard liquor. What gives you the right to talk about him like that?' Her voice was rising until she was almost screaming at him.

Daniel laughed. 'That's right, my girl, when you forget to play the lady it's easy to see where you come from. And no doubt Timothy will see it too before long, once he's a little less besotted with you. And then where will you be? Now come on, be sensible, let's get this sorry story done with. How does five hundred pounds sound to you? You can have it in your hand once I have your signed statement agreeing to an annulment and your promise not to get in touch with my son ever again.'

Hannah stared at him. He stood before her so arrogantly, sure that the offer of so much money would dazzle her into agreeing to his terms.

'Five hundred or five thousand, I won't take it,' she said at last. 'Can't you understand that Timothy and I love each other? We will not let you separate us.'

Daniel's expression turned ugly. 'I wouldn't be in such a hurry to turn it down if I were you,' he said, 'or you might end up with nothing. For this marriage is finished, Hannah Armstrong. You may depend on it, there is plenty I can do to persuade you of it.' His eyes narrowed

as he glared across the brown stain on the hearthrug.
'I dare say you're as stubborn as that brother of yours,
Robert Armstrong, him and his damn union. But I'll get
the better of both of you, you'll see. Now I'll go and
leave you to think things over. I'll be back tonight.'

'Don't bother,' Hannah replied. 'We Armstrongs are
stubborn, you're right there. I think you'll find I am as
determined to make this marriage work as you are to
break it up.'

He gave her a superior smile, not deigning to answer
her, and she had to grasp one hand with the other to stop
herself slapping him across the face. Instead, she lifted
her chin and stared at him with an arrogance to equal
his own as he walked out. Only then did she crumble
into a heap in the armchair, waves of humiliation washing over her.

After a while she got to her feet and tackled the mess
made by the spilled tea. She fetched soapy water and a
cloth and rubbed away at the stain on the hearthrug until
her arms were tired, but the physical activity didn't stop
her from thinking.

Did Timothy know his father was here, she wondered?
Mr Durkin had seemed so positive that he could have the
marriage annulled – what if he really could? Timothy
had been so angry with her for going to hear Arthur J.
Cook, he had gone off in such a temper that night before.
Perhaps he would be glad to get out of the marriage,

perhaps he saw it as a disaster himself now. Hannah felt sick at the thought. Though she had sipped only a little of the tea, it had left a sour aftertaste in her mouth. What she needed was food, she decided. She went into the kitchen, buttered a slice of bread and forced herself to eat it.

Suddenly the tiny room made her feel claustrophobic and she went back into the sitting room, but that only reminded her of Daniel Durkin for the smell of him hung about, a combination of cigars and some kind of shaving lotion, she supposed. Whatever it was, it made her feel sick again and in desperate need of fresh air. Grabbing her coat from the bedroom, she rushed out into the street and took great gulps of the freezing stuff. Without thinking where she was going, she headed off into the town at a brisk walk.

'Hallo, what are you doing here?'

Hannah looked up, startled, to find she was in the Com Market, the street where Gloria worked. And there was Gloria, just coming away from the shop.

'Oh, Gloria,' she said dully.

'What on earth is the matter with you?' asked Gloria. Her gaze was full of concern. 'No one would take you for a bride, you look more like a deserted woman.'

'Oh!'

Hannah's eyes widened as she realised that that was exactly how she felt; Daniel had done his work well, she thought bitterly.

'Oh, don't look like that, Hannah, it can't be as bad as all that,' said Gloria. 'Look, it's my half-day, let's go somewhere and have lunch. I was just going to have a boiled egg at home, you know how it is, we're saving for the wedding. But it's ages since I had a meal out, we'll splash out on a proper meal, shall we? You look as though you could do with it.'

Hannah felt a surge of gratitude to Gloria; she was a good friend even though they had sometimes had a disagreement. And she was just the tonic she needed. Gloria would never let herself be humiliated by anyone, not even a man like Daniel Durkin. An afternoon with her was just the thing to take her mind off her troubles.

'Oh yes, that'll be great,' she said. 'I'll pay, though. What would Alf say if he knew you were throwing your money away on a restaurant meal?'

'I'll spend my money on what I want to spend it on,' Gloria asserted stoutly. 'Come on, I could just fancy a nice hot dinner I haven't had to cook myself.'

They ate steak-and-kidney pie in a small restaurant in the high street where the food was plain but well cooked and didn't cost the earth. Gloria chatted on lightly about the wedding and Alf. Hannah had only to put in the occasional comment and by the time she had finished her pie she was beginning to feel more herself.

When their coffee came, Gloria sat back in her chair and regarded Hannah seriously. 'Now, tell me all about it,' she said. 'Have you been fighting with Timothy already?'

'No, not really. Well, yes, we did have an argument, but that isn't what's the matter.' Hannah hesitated for a moment before deciding to tell Gloria about her father-in-law's threats. Gloria was the only real friend she had in Oxford, the only one who would understand, and she had to tell someone.

'It's Timothy's father,' she began, and out came the whole story of Daniel's visit. She told it flatly, without embellishment, but even so Gloria gasped with indignation more than once.

'The cheeky sod,' she commented when Hannah had finished. 'Who does he think he is?'

'Well, he *is* Timothy's father.'

'That may be, but he has no right to talk to you like that.'

Gloria spooned sugar into her cooling coffee and stirred it angrily. 'You shouldn't have let him say such things, Hannah, you should have thrown him out, that's what I would have done.' She nodded her head to emphasise the point.

'It's difficult, though, Gloria. After all, he is my father-in-law. And then there's my family back in Winton, he could make things very awkward for them, you've no idea how powerful he is there. You know, if Bob were to lose his job, that would mean Mam would lose the house. He could blacklist Bob and he wouldn't be able to work in the pits if that happened. I don't think you know what it's like in a mining area.'

'No,' said Gloria thoughtfully. 'But surely he couldn't be so vindictive as to put a widow with two young children out of her house? Not when her husband was killed in the pit? This is the twentieth century, people don't stand for that sort of thing.'

'Not in Oxford, they don't,' said Hannah sadly. 'It's different in Winton Colliery.'

'My God, he's like the wicked squire in a pantomime. He didn't really threaten you with that, did he?'

'Well, no, not really. But I think it was implied.'

Gloria shook her head. 'Oh, go on, he was just trying to frighten you. He can't do anything really, not if Timothy loves you. And he does, anyone can see that. Does he know his father's here?'

'I don't think so. I think Mr Durkin came directly to me when he found out, though for the life of me I don't know how he learned about our marriage. We have been so careful to keep it quiet, the only one of Timothy's friends who knows is Anthony Akers and I don't think he would tell, not after being best man and letting us use the house in London for our honeymoon.'

Gloria looked thoughtful. Finishing her coffee, she pulled on her gloves before she said any more and then it was about something completely different.

'Have you seen Jane since you came back?'

Hannah looked surprised. 'I have, as a matter of fact. I went in to see the Ridleys on Monday and she was there. She seems to be doing well, at least they are satisfied with her. I asked her to come over to me for the evening, next Wednesday. Why do you ask?'

'Oh, no reason. She's a funny girl, isn't she? Keeps her thoughts to herself. It's not the same thing having her in the house instead of you, not the same at all. I can't talk to her like I can talk to you.'

Hannah sighed. 'I know she's quiet and shy and it makes her a bit abrupt sometimes, that's all it is. You know, she had to spend such a lot of time in hospital when she was younger, I think that was what made her as she is.'

Gloria nodded. 'Yes. Well, let's go back to my place. We can have a nice long chat on our own before the others come in. You can stay for tea too, Timothy won't be coming in until later, will he?'

If he comes in at all, Hannah thought, but she smiled warmly at Gloria. 'I'd love to. I've been meaning to come to see you all any way. But you won't mention anything about Mr Durkin to Alf, will you? I'd rather he didn't know, not yet anyway. I don't want any of my family to know.'

'I won't say anything,' Gloria assured her.

The family were sitting round the table in the kitchen when Jane came in, all except Reggie who had a date, or so Gloria said.

'She's that plump blonde who works in the baker's in Hockmore Street, do you remember her?'

Hannah did and was pleased. She was cheerful and uncomplicated, probably just the sort of girl for Reggie. Hannah had felt slightly guilty about Reggie even though she hadn't done anything to encourage him. Now she could forget about it.

Jane came into the kitchen. Giving a comprehensive nod of greeting, she sat down at the table, leaving Gloria to jump up and fetch her dinner from the oven.

'Is there any brown sauce?' she asked after the other girl had sat back down.

'Yes, of course.'

Hannah watched as Gloria left her own meal once again and went to the cupboard for the bottle of sauce. Jane must know perfectly well where it was kept, why didn't she fetch it herself? Her sister was not acting like a member of the family as Hannah had done, rather like a paying guest with the emphasis on the paying. She wasn't fitting in as she should have done.

When Alf came in to spend the evening with Gloria, Jane went up to her room without even excusing herself. Her sister's bad manners embarrassed Hannah, but Alf didn't seem to notice. Hannah resolved to speak to Jane about it on the following Wednesday when she came to visit. Maybe she didn't even realise she was being rude. She sighed, Jane was a problem all right. Perhaps it had been a mistake to bring her to Oxford.

Hannah glanced at her wristwatch. 'I've had a lovely time, Gloria, it's been grand. But I'd better be going back now.'

'I should think so an' all. You've got a husband to look after now, my girl,' said Alf, grinning. 'What will he think if he comes in from a hard day's studying and you're not there with his slippers all warmed and his dinner ready? You'd better be running along or he might take a slipper to you. We men have to keep our women in line, you know. That's true, isn't it, Gloria?'

'The first time you take a slipper to me will be the last, my lad,' Gloria warned.

He laughed and put an arm round her waist. 'Oh yes, and what will you do about it?' he asked.

Gloria accompanied Hannah to the door. 'Let me know what happens,' she whispered. 'And don't worry, Hannah, it'll be all right, Timothy won't let you go. I'm sure he's man enough to stand up to that rotten father of his, so don't let the sod intimidate you.'

'I won't,' promised Hannah. 'I would still like to know who told him, though. If he hadn't found out about me until after Timothy left Oxford . . . I think that's what Timothy thought, too; it would have been easier to break it to him if Timothy was working and fully independent.'

She was standing with the door half-open and the night was bitterly cold. A few snowflakes were blowing about in the wind and she watched them against the night sky. 'I'm as miserable as the weather, aren't I?' she asked with an attempt at a grin. 'I'm sorry, Gloria, I didn't mean to dampen your day.'

'Don't be daft,' said her friend.

'Close that blooming door, will you?' Mr Morgan called from the sitting room. 'The draught's enough to freeze us all to death.'

'I'll go. Bye for now,' said Hannah hurriedly and slipped out, closing the door behind her. She was hurrying up the street when she heard her name called and turned to see Gloria running after her.

'I had to tell you, I know I shouldn't really, your sister's post has nothing to do with me and I shouldn't have been reading the envelope . . . '

'What envelope?' asked Hannah. 'Come on, out with it, Gloria. Look at you, you're shivering. Why did you come out without your coat?'

'I . . . Jane had some letters to post, Hannah, and she put them on the sideboard and I saw the name on the top envelope. It caught my eye because it was addressed to a Mr Durkin, the same name as yours, and I read the address and it was somewhere in County Durham. I'm sorry, Hannah, I don't know why she would do such a thing.'

Chapter Twenty-Three

Timothy and his father glared at each other across the table.

'How did you find out? No one knows but Anthony and he wouldn't tell you.'

'Never you mind, I was bound to hear of it some time. And I'm telling you now, do something about that girl or I will see to it that your allowance is stopped.'

'You can't do it. The money's mine, I know I can't touch the capital before I'm twenty-five but in my mother's will she said I was to have full use of the interest when I reached eighteen.'

'With the proviso that it was to be used for your education.' Daniel laughed and the sound was full of derision. 'I have no doubt the pit lass educated you all right, girls of her class –'

'Don't speak about her like that, Father,' warned Timothy.

'I'll speak about her in any damn way I wish,' Daniel snarled, his temper flaring. 'What is she but a lass from those filthy hovels in Winton? What the hell do you see in her, a common miner's daughter? Why you couldn't have had your fun and left it at that I don't know, no one would have blamed you for that. But to actually marry –'

Timothy started to his feet and leaned over the table, taking his father's lapels in his fists and drawing him half out of his chair.

'I said, do not speak of her in that way. In fact, do not speak of her at all. Hannah is my wife.' He did not raise his voice but his father could not mistake the menacing tone. Timothy held the position for a moment or so, his face only six inches from Daniel's. Then he let go abruptly and resumed his seat.

Daniel straightened his coat and tie, giving himself a brief time to compose himself. Timothy watched him coldly.

'You're wasting your time here, Father. Hannah and I are married and we are going to stay that way. I don't believe you can do anything about my inheritance but even if you could, do you think that would make me abandon her? Why, I will graduate this spring, I can work for a living. Hannah will understand if we have to live carefully for a few months.'

'Oh, she will, will she? But will she understand if I cut you off altogether? For not a penny will you get from me if you keep on with this ridiculous marriage, and I'll do my damnedest to see you get no more from the fund set up by your mother. Have you forgotten that Brown-Robinson and I are the executors of the trust? Believe me, Brown-Robinson will do what I say; he's like all solicitors, he knows which side his bread is buttered.'

'Hannah is not interested in money, she loves me. You don't even know her.' A disquieting thought stuck Timothy. 'You don't, do you? You haven't been to see her, upsetting her, have you?'

'No, of course I haven't,' Daniel lied. 'I came to see you, I'm not interested in that trollop.'

'Get out of my rooms, Father, before I throw you out. I swear I will do it if you say any more.'

Daniel stalked to the door, his face grim. His hand was on the doorknob when he decided to try one thing more.

'What do you think Lord Akers will think of this marriage? I tell you this, it will spoil your chances of ever getting a position with him. And good positions are not so plentiful these days. You are jeopardising your whole career, man.'

'I don't think Lord Akers is as class-conscious as you are, Father, but even if he were, I don't expect to have too much trouble gaining a position somewhere. I stand a good chance of a first, you know. And even if I should only achieve an upper second, why, a degree in mathematics is something to base a career on. I'll even teach if I have to.'

Daniel snorted. 'Then to the devil with you!'

He flung the door open and went out, and Timothy could hear him stumping down the stairs. He pulled a textbook towards him and opened it, staring unseeing at the page. In spite of his words, he was rattled by what his father had said. If his allowance was stopped he would have trouble paying the bills he and Hannah had run up on their short honeymoon in London. But Hannah's wardrobe had been almost non-existent before their marriage, he had had to renew it. And she took such a delight in nice things that it had been a pleasure to buy them for her. Only now the bills were piling up at a rate which surprised him and there was the expense of renting a furnished flat to make things even worse.

Hannah thought he was rich and indeed he was by her standards, he mused. He turned over a page in the textbook before realising that though his eyes had followed the words on the previous page, he hadn't actually taken them in, so he had to go back. But it was no good, he couldn't think about his work. He closed the book and flung it across the table. Going to the window, he stared out at the long shadows the afternoon sunshine was making on the grass of the quadrangle and his thoughts went back to the evening before.

It was the first quarrel he had had with Hannah and he could picture the pain on her lovely face as she stood up to him in the poky flat. He had been hard and unfeeling with her, he realised that now. But he had been worried she would be hurt and when she accused him of being more interested in what his friends thought than in what happened to her, he had lost his temper.

I'll go this evening and make it up with her, he thought. It was a waste of time trying to work until he did. Poor Hannah, it was rotten for her having to spend so much time on her own. How could he have blamed her for going to hear that chap Cook at the Corn Exchange? She was a loving, loyal girl, and of course her sympathies were with her own folk. He wouldn't love her so much if she was any different.

At least his father didn't know where she was; Timothy shuddered to think of what it would do to her if she had a visit from Daniel in his present frame of mind.

There was a knock on the door and he turned to face it, subconsciously squaring his shoulders. If his father had thought of something else to try to persuade him to give Hannah up, he really would throw him down the stairs, he thought grimly. But it was Tony who slipped his head round the door.

'Hallo, Tim. Am I mistaken or did I just see your father walking across the quad?' he asked. He pulled a wry face as he saw Timothy's expression. 'I thought he looked a bit thunderous. Found out about the nuptials, did he?'

His friend nodded. 'I'd like to know who told him. It wasn't you, was it?' Tony glared at him, affronted, and Timothy went on, 'No, of course not, sorry.'

'I thought no one else knew.' Tony looked thoughtful. 'There's Hannah's family, of course.'

'I don't think it could have been one of them. Most of them hate my father, they wouldn't give him the time of day. They blame him for everything that has happened in the coalfield since the war.'

Tony nodded. 'Your father and mine, actually.' He sat down before the fire and stretched out his long legs. 'I suppose your dear papa is threatening to cut you out of his will.'

'Worse than that, he says he can stop me using the interest on the money Mother left me. That will leave me in a hole until I graduate and land a job.'

'Well, at least you're pretty sure you'll get through your finals this year, which is more than I am,' Tony commented. 'My tutor reckons I'll be lucky to get a third. But as for money, you can rely on me, old son. I can spare the odd copper to help you out, you know.' He hesitated, looking curiously at Timothy. 'That is if you are absolutely sure about Hannah.'

'I'm sure. How many times do you need to be told? I'm not going to give her up, I'll find a way, just you wait and see.' Timothy's tone rose and took on a note of anger, and his friend lifted his hands in mock surrender.

'All right, all right, I just thought I'd ask. Now come along to my rooms, I've got some muffins, we'll have them toasted for tea. Forget about your father, there's not a lot he can do if you're determined, you'll see. In the end he'll have to give in.'

'Hmm, I hope you're right.'

They went to Tony's rooms and toasted muffins before the fire. Tony laughed at his own jokes and Timothy joined in politely, but it was obvious that his mind was on other things.

'I think I'll spend the evening with Hannah,' he said after a while.

Tony nodded. 'You may as well, your thoughts are with her, they certainly haven't been here with me,' he said. 'But then, I'm used to it by now.' He gazed at the ceiling and said piously, 'Lord save me from becoming entangled by a woman's wiles.'

Timothy didn't hear him. He was already on his way back to his own rooms to collect his overcoat.

I'll have to have a telephone installed in the flat, he thought to himself, his money worries forgotten for the moment. Then I can telephone and let her know when I'm coming. And another time, when I can't make it, I will be able to ring and explain why. Poor Hannah, she must be very lonely there on her own all day. In this contrite mood he went out to the car.

There was a flower seller on the corner and he stopped and bought a bunch of violets to give her as a peace offering. Though they were glass-house flowers, their sweet smell filled the car and brought the promise of spring to the cold winter's evenings, and his spirits lightened. He parked outside the flat, not taking any notice of another car standing in the shadows a little farther up the street. Bounding up the stairs with his key already in his hand, he opened the door and went into the tiny hall.

'Hannah? Hannah, where are you?'

There was a strip of light showing under the sitting-room door. She must be in, he thought, but why wasn't she running to meet him as she always did? Because of last night, that was what it was, she was still upset and annoyed. And rightly so, he thought contritely.

'I've brought you a peace offering,' he began and froze. Hannah was not there; it was his father who was sitting in her chair by the gas fire, a glass of whisky in his hand.

Chapter Twenty-Four

Earlier in the evening, Hannah had been returning to the flat in east Oxford. It was a bitterly cold evening but she hardly noticed it for she was so unhappy. As she came to the entrance, she glanced at her wrist-watch. This time yesterday, she reflected, she had been going to the meeting in the Corn Exchange. How could twenty-four hours make so much difference in her life?

Jane – the sister she had watched and worried over when they were small. How could Jane have changed so much? Hannah had not gone back into the house with Gloria to confront Jane, she couldn't bear to see her, not yet. On Wednesday, perhaps, she could ask her sister about it when Jane came to visit, but now she was filled with a sense of betrayal. She couldn't begin to understand why Jane had done it. Was it envy of her good fortune in marrying someone like Timothy?

The ache inside her intensified at the thought of Timothy, and desperately she wished that she hadn't fought with him the evening before. She thought of his father's words that morning. Would she really hold Timothy back as his father had said? And, would he be so ruthless as to threaten to blacklist her brother, even throw her mother out of her home? Had he done that? Well, even if not in so many words, that was what was implied, she was sure of it. Timothy, Timothy, she pleaded silently, please come tonight, please tell me your father can't hurt us.

A car was parked outside the flat and as she came near the door opened. Her depression deepened as she saw it was Daniel Durkin.

'At last. I've been waiting for you,' he said, not bothering with a greeting.

'What do you want?' Hannah was equally brusque as she walked past him and climbed the stairs. She had intended to go straight in and leave him outside; she really thought she could take no more from him, not tonight. But her fingers were numb with cold for she had forgotten her gloves and she had to fumble about in her bag before she managed to locate her key. By that time he was beside her on the landing.

'I have a message for you from Timothy,' he said.

'Timothy? Then give it to me.'

'It's not written down, he asked me to tell you myself.'

'Go on, then, you can tell me here, there's no need for you to come inside.'

Daniel sighed heavily. 'Oh, come now, Hannah, let's be civilised about this. Let me in and I'll give you the message.'

'I don't want you in my home.'

'I won't be long, just say what I have to say and then I am going. I have to be back in Durham tomorrow morning and it's a long drive, especially at this time of year.'

'Oh, very well.' Hannah capitulated and opened the door. She went into the sitting room, lit the fire and flung her coat on the back of a chair. Then she turned to face him.

'Well? Why would Timothy give you a message for me? I was expecting him to come himself.'

Daniel took out a cigar and lit it without asking her permission. He sat down and blew the pungent smoke out into the room before answering her.

'I don't think Timothy will be coming again, not after what I have told him. He's a soft-hearted boy, but he's not as soft as not to know what he has to do if he wants to go on living a comfortable life. Believe me, my dear Hannah, there was no contest, not when I explained the alternatives to him.'

'What do you mean, the alternatives?' Hannah's scepticism showed plainly on her face.

'You don't believe me?' Daniel laughed. 'I assure you, it's true. When I told him there would be no more money forthcoming unless he agreed to end this disastrous marriage, believe me, he began to listen to reason.'

'He wouldn't! No, he wouldn't, I don't believe you. You're lying.'

'Am I? Well, time will tell, time will tell. Quite soon, too, I should think; in fact, as soon as the rent on this place runs out.'

'But Timothy has his own income, he told me his mother left him money.'

'That's true. But I am the executor and I can stop his income, believe me.'

'But even if he hadn't a penny, Timothy wouldn't do this without telling me himself. He's too good a man to do a thing like that.'

'That's true, he is good, too good sometimes, and, as I said, soft-hearted, else why would he marry a girl like you in the first place? That's why he didn't want to face you. As I told him, a clean break was best and I would see you were taken care of. He wavered a bit, but he's weak, you see.'

'He's not weak! I don't believe –'

'Well, you don't know him as well as I do,' Daniel interrupted smoothly.

Hannah stared at him, longing to contradict, but knowing that in this at least, Daniel was right. She had first met

Timothy long ago but they had been children, and in the intervening years, she had only seen him once or twice. Their meeting in Oxford had been only a few short weeks ago. They had rushed into marriage at Timothy's instigation and she had agreed because she believed he loved her as much as she loved him and was impatient to make her his wife. And that was all that mattered to her at the time. She had believed that they could overcome the difference in their backgrounds; after all, she was young and reasonably intelligent and willing to learn. But now she remembered the times when she had been unsure what Timothy was thinking; in particular, she remembered how angry he had been the evening before because she went to hear Arthur J. Cook. She remembered how he had talked of the economics of the situation and the bitter way she had answered him. Maybe she didn't know him after all, because she hadn't thought they could have disagreed so much on such a subject.

Suddenly her knees felt very weak. She slid down into the chair opposite Daniel and bent her head so that he couldn't see the weary defeat in her face.

'You will be blighting his life if you insist on your rights, Hannah.' Daniel pressed home his advantage; he hadn't spent years negotiating with union men not to know when he had his opponent cornered. 'You don't want to do that, do you?'

'No,' she said, almost inaudibly.

'Well then, be sensible. This is what I propose. You will be out of Oxford tonight, I'll run you to the station.'

'Out of Oxford? How can I do that? There's no need anyway, I can go to my brother in Cowley.' Hannah felt as though she was on a runaway tram like one of those in a Buster Keaton moving picture. Why did it have to be done so soon? 'I want to see him just once more. I want him to tell me himself!' The words burst from her almost of their own volition.

'Now, that wouldn't be very sensible, would it? He's made his decision, he doesn't want to see you again. And you don't want to run the risk of meeting Timothy accidentally, do you? Not when he feels as he does. No, I think you should go now and as far away as possible.' He reached into the inside pocket of his jacket and pulled out a chequebook. 'Now don't be silly about this, you will need money to start again somewhere else. Five hundred pounds, I think I said this morning?'

'I don't want your money.'

'Oh, come now, I said don't be silly.'

Silly, thought Hannah. That just about covered the way she had trusted Timothy. A suspicion came to her; had Timothy insisted on keeping their relationship secret because he was ashamed of her? If so, she had been even sillier than she thought. Lifting her chin, Hannah stared at Daniel.

'You're right, I was being stupid. I do need money and why should I scruple to take it from you? Five hundred pounds, you say. Well, it's not enough, I want seven hundred and fifty at least.'

'Seven hundred and fifty? Very well, but in return I want you to sign for it. Just a simple declaration, that's all.'

'What sort of declaration?'

'Just a receipt, really. I'll make it out for you along with the cheque. In the meantime, why don't you pack your stuff and I'll take you to the station.'

The tram was racing downhill with a vengeance now, she thought, as panic rose in her throat. But she gave no outward sign of it. Numbly, Hannah went into the bedroom and put the suitcase she had bought for her honeymoon on the bed. She threw in her clothes, not bothering to fold them properly. She would have dearly loved to leave everything Timothy had bought her but she didn't, she had very little else to wear. So her new purchases went in higgledy-piggledy, shoes, skirts, hats, everything. Forcing the locks closed, she lugged the suitcase into the hall, went back into the sitting room and picked up her coat.

'Oh, you're ready? That was quick. Well, here you are then, here's the cheque and here's the receipt for you to sign.'

Hannah glanced briefly at Daniel as she took the pieces of paper. He was all geniality now he had got his way, she thought bitterly, so bitterly she couldn't trust herself to speak. She folded the cheque, put it in her purse, took the pen he was holding out to her and signed the receipt.

'Received, a cheque for seven hundred and fifty pounds signed Daniel Durkin in consideration of which I promise not to try to get in touch with Timothy Durkin ever again.'

Well, she thought as she signed it 'Hannah Durkin, nee Armstrong', that's that. She was totally calm, as though this was happening to someone else; she felt no anguish, no pain. She was beyond that.

Daniel looked at his watch as he stowed the paper away in his pocket. 'Right then, I'll take you to the station and then I'll be on my way. It's only seven o'clock, you have plenty of time. Where do you want to go?'

'That is none of your business,' Hannah answered, thinking, only seven o'clock! I have ended my marriage, all but the legalities, in less than an hour. He shrugged indifferently and walked out with her following. She did not even look back as she left the flat which had been her home for so brief a time.

Daniel was back in the flat in under a quarter of an hour, having made sure he got the key from Hannah before she left. He poured himself another whisky and sat down, content with his day's work. It had been a bit of a gamble – well, a hundred-to-one gamble – but he had pulled it off and now he felt as triumphant as he did after besting any of those damn union men. Curse of the nation, they were, trying to tell their betters how to run their business.

He had taken the chance that Timothy would not walk into the flat before he got the chit away, and he had been lucky. Now all he had to do was convince his fool of a son that Hannah had taken the money and gone. He had to admit, he thought as he lit another cigar, he had expected to have more trouble with her. But in the end, breeding had told; like all her kind, she couldn't resist the money when it was waved under her nose.

He leaned back in his seat, willing himself to keep calm as the door opened and Timothy came in. Indeed, it had been a close-run thing; he grinned as he realised how close.

Hannah sat in the overnight Edinburgh express as it clickety-clacked its way north. She was going home, of course, where else would she go? I'll write to Gloria and Alf, she thought, just a note to let them know I'm all right. Maybe it's just as well I haven't time to go to see them, I might run into Jane and if I do there's no knowing what I might do to her.

Restlessly, she gazed out of the window at the dark landscape, lit at intervals by the occasional street lights. She was deathly tired, every bone in her body was aching, but though she had the carriage to herself she couldn't sleep. She looked awful, she saw by her reflection in the window; her hair was unkempt and there were great, dark circles under her eyes. She took out her comb and tidied her hair, then counted the change in her purse. Two pounds, fifteen shillings and threepence halfpenny, that was all. It would be enough for her needs, though, at least until she had the cheque deposited in Barclays Bank in Market Place in Bishop Auckland.

She hadn't said she wouldn't go back to Winton, she thought. And Daniel would never know she was there, he had a contemptuous disregard for anything that went on in the colliery villages. Closing her eyes, she leaned back in her seat. It would be hours before the train reached Darlington, with so many stops in between. She willed herself to relax.

'York. This is York.'

The train chuntered to a halt and Hannah woke up with a start. She couldn't believe she had slept as far as York, surely she had misheard? She peered out at the almost deserted platform – yes, it was York all right. Blinking, she rubbed the sleep from her eyes and glanced at her watch. Three o'clock in the morning, she couldn't believe it. They would be in Darlington in under an hour. Then she would have to wait for the first train to Bishop Auckland, she thought, but what did it matter? Nothing mattered very much, not any more. She had the rest of her life to get through without Timothy.

Opening her purse, she looked at the cheque. Seven hundred and fifty pounds was a lot of money, a fortune, but for the life of her she couldn't remember what it was that had made her agree to take it. Perhaps she should tear it up. Her head ached dully and so did her back and neck, no doubt from sleeping slouched against the side of the seat.

The train started to move slowly out of the station and Hannah rose to her feet and went out into the corridor. One of the windows was slightly open and cold air was blowing in. She stood for a moment, until the draught made her shiver, then went into the toilet and splashed water over her face and neck. Refreshed, she returned to her seat and began to consider what to do.

'Eeh, our Hannah, whatever are you doing here? Look, Harry, see who's here.'

Nora sprang up from the table, where she was spreading dripping on toast for Harry and Walton. Harry, who was squatting down, holding a long-handled toasting fork to the fire, jumped to his feet, forgetting all about the toast, and grinned in delight.

'Mind, you're a sight for sore eyes, all right,' Nora continued as Hannah dumped her case just inside the

356

door and went to hug her mother. The feel of Nora's thin body against her own almost undid her; it took a supreme effort of will to hold her composure.

'But what are you doing here, pet? Eeh, I am pleased to see you, though. Do you know, I was thinking about you all day yesterday, couldn't get you off my mind.' Nora stood back and looked searchingly into Hannah's face. 'You don't look so good, our Hannah, you're not badly, are you? Mebbe a baby on the way?'

'No. No, I'm all right, Mam. It's just that I travelled up on that overnight train, that's all, I'm missing my sleep.'

'And where's that husband of yours? Had to go to his father's place, has he? By, it was nice of you to come to see us before you went there. Howay, take off your coat and we'll have a nice cup of tea, I dare say you could just do with one.'

Nora went to the fire and stirred it with the poker before settling the kettle on the coals, ignoring Harry's protests that she was spoiling it for his toast.

'How long have you got before your man comes for you?' she asked as she returned to the table.

Hannah looked round the kitchen, the familiar kitchen with its faded walls and the black-leaded range with its high mantelpiece surrounded by a cloth she had embroidered herself in sewing class at school. She saw Harry gazing at her, his grin turning to a puzzled frown, and Walton looking at her, his eyes large in his pinched little face as he tried to remember just who she was. She stared at the white-scrubbed boards of the table and the clippie mat on the floor before the fire. A new one, she thought, Mam must have put it down for Christmas. It had a bright red circle in the middle and Hannah recognised the cloth from an old coat of her own. She tried hard to keep her mind on the mat, looking to see if she recognised any other pieces Mam had cut up for it.

'Mam, is it our Hannah?' asked Walton suddenly. 'She looks a bit like our Hannah, I think.'

The question broke something in her and she looked up, caught her mother's eye, and then the tears came.

Chapter Twenty-Five

'Four hundred and fifty pounds, Miss Armstrong, and a bargain at that,' said Mr Eddy. 'And stock at valuation, of course.'

'Offer four hundred and thirty,' said Hannah, 'and we'll talk about the stock.'

She glanced composedly round the walls of the estate agent's office. They were painted a peculiar shade of buff with a brown dado and brown skirting boards. Bills advertising property were pasted to the walls along with a printed notice of terms and a framed certificate which stated that Mr Eddy belonged to a professional body, she couldn't quite make out which.

'I am not empowered –' he began saying. She pulled on her gloves and put her handbag over her arm as though preparing to leave.

'Of course,' she said briskly, 'there are other properties which will do just as well. Quite an interesting one
in Spennymoor and not too far away.'

'Of course, I can always ring and put your offer to
Mr Smith,' said the estate agent. Hannah smiled and
drew off her gloves as he picked up the telephone receiver
and waited for the operator to answer.

Hannah had been home a month. In the beginning,
she had thought every knock at the door was Timothy.
Surely he would seek her out, it must all have been a mistake. She bitterly regretted allowing Daniel to persuade
her to leave so precipitately; if only she had insisted on
seeing Timothy first, she agonised. During the day she
watched for him all the time. When she went up to see
Betty and little Simon, she hurried home just in case
he was waiting for her, parked outside the back gate. If
she went into Auckland she saved her bus ticket, added
up the numbers and divided them by seven, just as she
had when she was a child. The remainder was the important number, 'One for sorrow, two for joy, three for a
letter, four for a boy.' And her heart would beat faster if
the right number came up, a two, or three, or four. But no
matter what the remainder, Timothy did not come.

The nights were the worst. At night, she lay sleep-
less in the double bed she shared with her mother, for
now the family was so much reduced, the boys had the
large bedroom. She ached for Timothy through the long

nights, and after she fell into an exhausted sleep, more often than not when it was almost time to get up, she dreamed of him.

Mam watched her, full of concern. 'You shouldn't have left your man,' she said once. 'No good will come of it. You promised to love and obey him no matter what happened.'

'I had to leave, Mam. He didn't want me. He sent his father to tell me he didn't want me. So you see, I am obeying him.'

'Hmm,' said Nora.

Hannah did not tell her mother everything that had happened, and Nora forbore to question her too closely. Her face had hardened at the mention of Timothy's father and she turned back to her cooking, muttering with impotent rage, 'Come the day, Hannah, come the day. By, if ever a man needed to get his comeuppance it's that one, but God is good, Durkin will come to a bad end, you'll see.'

Hannah watched as her mother pounded the bread dough, lifting it up and flinging it back in the bowl with all the strength in her thin, wiry arms.

A few nights before Hannah went into Bishop Auckland to see the estate agent, she had come to a decision. She would go into business for herself, that way there was no boss to put you down. And the only business she knew anything about was the newsagent business. Consequently, she scoured the *Northern Echo* and *Auckland Chronicle* For Sale columns and found that a number of newsagent's shops were available. The depression in the mining industry affected all the trade in the area and most shops were struggling. She could have picked up a leasehold shop for almost nothing but she was determined to buy and she wanted a shop with living accommodation, in Bishop Auckland for preference.

So here she was, sitting across the desk from Mr Eddy. She knew him well, if only by sight, for she had often seen him about the town or driving his car on the road past Winton Colliery. Of course, he didn't recognise her, she was just a girl from the mining villages which surrounded the town. He finished his conversation and replaced the receiver in its cradle.

'Mr Smith is willing to negotiate with you concerning the stock,' he said, beaming. 'Would you like to make an appointment? Tomorrow afternoon, perhaps – I will be available to go with you at two o'clock, how will that suit you?'

'Thank you, Mr Eddy. I think I would rather go now. After all, it's just up the street and as I'm here, I may as well. Of course, if you're too busy, I can easily go by myself.'

Mr Eddy coughed and glanced at his watch. 'Well, I have an appointment in half an hour, Miss Armstrong. Tomorrow –'

'This is a cash sale, Mr Eddy. I have the money ready and waiting in Barclays Bank.'

'Er, yes, of course, Miss Armstrong. I'll just have a word with my secretary and we'll go. Perhaps I should ring Mr Smith and tell him we're on our way.'

'Don't bother.'

Mr Eddy rose to his feet, looking somewhat put out. This was a very forthright young woman, he thought. As they walked up Newgate Street he stole a glance at her. She had dressed carefully for this interview, and clothes like her smart camel coat and stylish cloche hat were not often seen in Auckland, especially not in these hard days. She walked confidently, her chin up, showing her flawless skin and striking dark eyes. Mr Eddy wondered where she had come from – a young lady obviously well off, suddenly appearing in the town and wishing to buy a newsagent's. Her accent puzzled him: cultured, but with a northern tinge to it.

His speculations ended as they reached the shop and went in. There were a few customers inside, Hannah noted with satisfaction. She had chosen this place because it was the nearest to the station and even in a small market town such as Bishop Auckland, there were some travellers who liked to buy a paper before a journey or as they came to work.

Mr Smith was behind the counter, a small man, coming up to retirement age, she judged. Good, that meant there was a genuine reason for selling. The shop was dingy and, even on this dark late-February day, lit with only one light bulb. There were fewer magazines on the shelves than there had been in the Ridley's shop in Oxford and only one or two national newspapers.

'I'll only be a minute,' the newsagent said, nodding to Mr Eddy, and they waited as he served the customers with local papers and packets of Woodbine cigarettes. It did not take long and then he turned to Hannah.

'Yes, miss?'

'This is Miss Armstrong, the lady I telephoned you about.' Mr Eddy stepped forward and introduced them.

Mr Smith had a firm handshake and held her hand a fraction longer than necessary as he gazed into her face. 'You are very young to be buying a newsagent's,' he remarked.

'That may be, but I assure you I know what I'm doing.'

He nodded, evidently satisfied her offer was a serious one. 'I'll close the shop and we can talk.'

'It need only be for a little while,' said Hannah. 'I know that this can be quite a busy time in a newsagent's. But I would like to see the accommodation if I may.'

There were two bedrooms and a bathroom upstairs and a living room and kitchen at the back of the shop, together with a yard containing a coalhouse and lavatory – a water closet, not an ash closet. Some decorating needed to be done and she would have to furnish the place, but on the whole, Hannah was pleasantly surprised at the condition of the property. By the time she had inspected everything, including the broom cupboard under the stairs, she had decided she would take it.

'Four hundred and fifty including the stock,' she announced.

'But the stock is worth more than twenty pounds,' protested Mr Smith.

'Do you think so?' asked Hannah sceptically. She stared round at the shelves lining the shop walls, some of them covered rather sparsely with boxes of bootlaces and other sundries. There was a stack of cigarettes behind the counter but Hannah had seen no backup stock such as the Ridleys had in their storeroom and she suspected there was none. It looked to her as if Mr Smith had been running down his stock in anticipation of a sale. Apart from the newspapers and periodicals, which would most likely be on a sale-or-return basis, there were only a few novels which appeared to have been on the shelf for quite a time, judging by the dust on them.

'Well . . . ' Mr Smith had followed her glance and realised she knew what she was talking about.

'Perhaps you should wait a while before committing yourselves,' Mr Eddy interjected. He looked somewhat put out, no doubt at having taken so little part in the negotiations.

'My mind is made up,' Hannah replied briskly. 'Now, what do you say, Mr Smith?' She took out her brand-new chequebook and opened it. 'Of course I will give you a deposit, shall we say fifty pounds?'

Mr Smith glanced at Mr Eddy. 'I'll take it,' he said.

'This is all highly irregular,' said Mr Eddy. 'Make the cheque out to me, Miss Armstrong. My customers' account.'

'But where did you get all that money? From the Durkins? Timothy?'

'Yes.'

Nora gazed at her, eyes wide with astonishment. 'By, but it must have cost a fortune to buy a shop in Auckland. Are you sure it's all right spending Timothy's money like this? He will likely come for you yet, you know, then what will he say?'

'He won't come now, Mam.'

Nora bit her lip at the hard note in Hannah's voice. 'Why, man, you're a bit young to give up on your marriage, you've not given it a chance.'

'It's over, Mam. Don't worry, the money is mine to do what I like with.'

'But why didn't you tell me? You kept very quiet about this, didn't you?'

'I wanted to surprise you. I thought you and the two bairns could come to live with me over the shop. Oh, you'll love it, Mam, there's a bathroom upstairs and a water closet in the yard. I might even have a passage built from the back door to the lav, then we won't have to go out in the cold.'

'Me? I'm not leaving here, pet. What about our Bob? He needs me to look after him. And then there's the little 'un, what about school? Eeh, no, pet, there's me shop in the front room an' all, it's building up nicely. But if it's what you want, I'm pleased for you. I hope you make a go of it, I do.'

'Oh, Ma, you can help in the shop in Auckland, it'll be far better than the front room,' Hannah argued. She was disappointed, she'd been so sure her mother would go with her. But Nora was adamant.

'Nay, lass, I think I'll just stay here. Mind, it was nice of you to offer, don't think I don't appreciate it.'

At least there was somewhere for the family to live if Daniel Durkin did evict them, thought Hannah. For Tucker and Betty would not be able to help, Tucker's job would be at risk if they did.

When she told Harry, his reaction was much more positive. 'I can be a paper lad, Hannah. I can, can't I? How much will I earn if I deliver papers?'

'I'm not sure if you can,' she answered. 'After all, you would have to walk into Bishop Auckland and deliver the papers and still be back in time to go to school. I think it would be too much for you.'

Harry was deflated. 'I could do it if I had a bike,' he said wistfully. 'I could be in Auckland in no time at all if I had a bike.'

'That's true,' said Hannah. None of the Armstrongs had ever had a bicycle except Alf. He had had a second-hand one, bought in the days before Da's accident. Since then, there had not been enough money. How much did bicycles cost? When she went into Auckland to see her solicitor, she would see about buying a bicycle.

The following afternoon when Harry came in from school, there was a second-hand bicycle waiting for him in the yard. Though it was full-size, Harry was growing quite tall and Hannah reckoned he would be able to manage it.

'Eeh, ta, Hannah, ta.' Harry touched the bicycle reverently, he could hardly believe it was really there.

'Do you know how to ride it?'

'Aye, oh, aye,' he breathed. 'Well, I had a go on one once, I'm sure it won't take me long to get good at it. Eeh, thank you, Hannah, you're all right.'

'You have a week or two to practise before I get into the shop. Mind, be careful or you'll have to answer to me.'

'I will, Hannah, I will. I'll just take it out now. By, it's grand! My marra's eyes'll pop out when he sees it.'

'Mebbe you shouldn't have let him play with it, not if you want it for the deliveries,' Nora observed as he went out of the yard with the bicycle. She and Hannah walked to the gate and watched him as he climbed on it and wobbled down the row.

'Let the lad have his pleasure, he's had little enough,' said Hannah. 'I can always buy another for the shop, Mam, it was only twelve and sixpence.'

'*Only* twelve and sixpence. That's as much as my pension,' Nora commented as they went back into the house.

February turned into March and March into April; Harry learned to ride the bicycle without wobbling and became quite nonchalant about it. He also learned to ride it downhill with both feet on the seat or sometimes with no hands and his feet on the handlebars, but luckily, his mother and sister never found out about that.

At last the time came to collect the keys to the shop from Mr Eddy. It was a Saturday morning in April, a fine spring morning, and Hannah decided to walk into Bishop Auckland. Harry rode his bicycle by her side, flying past her for a few hundred yards before turning and coming back. She reckoned he must have ridden nine miles instead of three by the time they got to Newgate Street. Nora and Walton were coming in later on the bus, Nora was going to help her clean out the living quarters.

Hannah couldn't describe how she felt as she unlocked the door and entered the shop. For a short while, the perpetual ache for Timothy disappeared in her pleasure at having her very own shop. Even as she was closing the door behind herself and Harry, a customer came and looked in.

'You're not closed, are you?'

'Just for the weekend. I'm the new owner and I'll be open for business on Monday morning.'

'I only wanted a packet of Woodbines,' he grumbled.

'Oh, well, in that case I can let you have them. How many, five or ten?'

'Five.'

She went to the stack behind the counter and brought him the cigarettes, and he handed over three halfpence and went on his way. A good omen, she thought happily as she put the money in the till.

The rest of the day went by in a whirl of activity as she and Nora cleaned, scrubbed and lit fires in all the rooms so they would be dry by the time the furniture arrived. Hannah had bought most of it at the second-hand salerooms, good plain furniture at a fraction of the cost of new. They hung new curtains at the windows and Harry swept the yard and swilled the flags with washing-soda water to get rid of the green mould.

'Can I stay here the night, Hannah?' he asked when the furniture was in place and the curtains drawn, shutting out the sight of the snow which had started to fall at three o'clock.

'It depends on Mam,' said Hannah diplomatically. 'But there are the papers to go out tomorrow, I couldn't risk having them miss a day.'

'It's snowing an' all, I might not be able to come in on my bike,' said Harry. Both of them looked at their mother for her reaction.

'Aye. Mebbe it would be for the best,' she said reluctantly.

'Me an' all, me an' all,' Walton pleaded. He had been dozing in the large leather armchair which Hannah had picked out in the saleroom and which was now drawn up before the fire.

'Eeh, no, pet, you'd better come home with me,' said his mother.

'We could all stay, just for tonight,' Hannah suggested.

'And what about our Bob? Have you forgot he's to see to?'

'No, but –'

'We'll be going, then, me and the bairn.'

Walton snivelled in protest but Nora had her way and Hannah saw them to the bus stop. The snow was melting as it fell, damp and cold. She went back through the shop into the room made cosy by a bright coal fire in the grate.

'I'm famished, our Hannah. What's for supper?' Harry was sitting in the armchair vacated by his brother, reading a comic he had filched from the shop.

'Harry, I didn't say you could have that,' said Hannah sternly.

'But it's last week's, nobody's going to buy last week's *Beano*,' he said reasonably.

'Maybe not. But I'll thank you to ask another time.' She took her purse from the slate mantel shelf and took out a shilling. 'Now, how about slipping down the street for some fish and chips while I boil the kettle?'

There was a letter from Alf, Harry brought it on the Wednesday morning when he came in. It had come to her mother's house the day before. Hannah looked at the envelope with her name written in Alf's firm hand-writing and the Oxford postmark. Oxford, she thought, where Timothy was. A wave of misery swept over her, so intense she leaned back against the counter and closed her eyes.

'Hannah? You're not badly, are you?'

At the sound of Harry's anxious voice she pulled her-self together and managed a smile. 'No, just tired, that's all. Five o'clock is a little early to start the day. No, I'm all right, you go on out with the other boys.' Hannah had kept on the two paperboys, Billy and Dave, who had worked for Mr Smith, and Harry was learning the routes from them. Afterwards, she hoped to build up her business so that she could keep on all three of them.

Satisfied, Harry went out with his bag of papers slung across his chest. There was usually half an hour before customers began to trickle in, so Hannah went into the living room behind the shop and opened her letter. She had written to Alf and Gloria in March and this must be the reply.

Dear Hannah,

I thought I would let you know that Timothy came to see me last night. He wanted to know where you were living. It's not the first time; he came the night after you went away. He was looking for you and mind, he was in a hell of a temper.

Hannah's heart leaped within her. Timothy *had* come looking for her after all, he did want her back! Why hadn't Alf written earlier? Or if not Alf, then Gloria? She read on, eagerly.

I told him that I knew nothing about it, you went away in such a hurry you didn't even let us know. I might tell you, both Gloria and I were pretty upset about that.

She told me what Jane had done and there was a great row and I told Jane she should have minded her own business, not that I hold with keeping secrets in families, mind. In the end, I told the little sneak to find somewhere else to live. You needn't worry about her, though, she's all right, the Ridleys found her a room near them. No doubt she told them a pack of lies and they felt sorry for her.

Hannah looked up from her letter as the bell over the shop door tinkled, and she went to serve the customer. Jane had not written to Mam to tell her she had changed her address, she thought. But then, Jane did not often write home. With the shop once more empty of customers, she went on with her letter.

Anyroad, as I was saying, Timothy came back and demanded to know where you are. I didn't tell him, but it's only a matter of time before he finds out. The thing is, I think he wants a divorce.

Hannah's hopes plummeted. Numbly, she put the letter in her pocket. Gloria had added a postscript, but she hadn't the heart to read it now – later, but not now.

Of course, it was no more than she had expected. She rubbed the fourth finger of her left hand. Her wedding ring had been worn for such a short time that there was not even a mark on the skin. Now it was in the top drawer of her dressing table, she couldn't bear to get rid of it altogether. Hope springs eternal, she thought bitterly.

She would write again to Alf and Gloria and apologise
for the fact that she had left so abruptly. But she would
not mention Timothy. No doubt if he wanted to he could
find out where she was.

It being Wednesday and half-day closing, Hannah
decided to go home to Winton to see her mother. She had
thought she would begin the painting of the shop walls
but the letter had made her restless. She decided to walk;
the snow of the weekend had been the last flurry of the
winter and the wind had veered to the south-west, bringing warmer weather and sunshine. At last it was spring.

Locking up the shop, Hannah took the path past the
iron foundry which led to a wood and the open fields
beyond. The sun shone brightly and there was even some
warmth from it, though under the trees the air was still
cold and dank. But there were crocuses, bright yellow
and purple, under the trees, and the scent of wild garlic
by the stream which ran through the wood. Coming out
on the far side, she could see the old village in the distance with its stone church tower and the winding gear
and engine house of Winton Colliery towering over the
miners' cottages and standing out clearly against the sky.

Too clearly, she realised suddenly – where was the
smoke from the chimney stack, where was the steam
and sulphurous fumes from the coke ovens? Hannah
quickened her pace as she skirted the enormous slag
heap and approached the village. The winding wheel

was still and on the end of the rows, groups of men in their pit clothes, with leather protectors strapped to their knees, were sitting on their hunkers, talking little. An air of despair hung about them; Hannah could practically feel it. Though they were wearing their working clothes, these were not men just up from fore shift and having a natter before they went home, their faces were too clean for that.

'What cheor, Hannah, lass,' and, 'Now then, lass,' one or two greeted her as she went past, but the greeting was automatic, there was no real interest in it. She nodded and hurried on to the end row and home.

Bob was sitting at the table in his shirtsleeves, writing.

'What is it?' she asked him. 'Is something wrong? Why has the pit shut down?'

'Have you been walking round with your eyes shut these last weeks, our Hannah?' Bob demanded. 'What do you think has happened? The same as what happened in '21, that's what!'

'You mean it's a lockout?'

'Aye, that's what I mean exactly. But they won't get the better of us as easily as they did then, I'm telling you that.'

Hannah sat down on the settee, memories of the 1921 lockout filling her mind – the hunger and distress there had been in the rows, the pinched faces of the children. She thought of the time she had smuggled Harry into school so that he could have a free meal and the humiliation they had both felt when the caretaker saw him and told the teacher. What straits they had been driven to!

'No,' Bob was saying. 'This time the country is behind us, the workers won't stand for it. The railway men and the transport workers are on our side, we'll show the bosses what's what.

Why, man, we haven't a living wage now, how can we agree to a cut in our wages again? And then they are insisting on an extra hour on the working day with nowt extra to show for it.'

Hannah stared at him. He had never been out of County Durham in his life, he didn't know any other workers. She remembered the night that Arthur J. Cook was in Oxford, how close he had been to being humiliated. And she knew that the prosperous car workers weren't interested in unions, they were well enough off without.

'It'll be a general strike, that's what,' said Bob. 'The country will support us.'

Maybe it will, thought Hannah. Or maybe it won't.

Chapter Twenty-Six

'GREAT STRIKE BEGUN' said the headlines in the *Daily Journal,* one of the few newspapers that Hannah had for sale. Even that was greatly reduced in size. She stood behind the counter in the deserted shop and considered her position.

Her bank account held just under three hundred pounds and she had no bills outstanding. She suspected that she was in a better position to sit out the strike than most of the other shopkeepers but she wanted to conserve her resources until the strike was over. For she had seen the mood of some of the people in Oxford and was aware that if the rest of the country thought the same way as they did, the general strike would not last long. Then how long would the miners last? Hannah feared a repetition of 1921 and she wanted to be in a position to help the family if need be.

The doorbell tinkled and she looked up to see Bob entering the shop, his face thunderous.

'What the hell are you doing, keeping the shop open? Have you joined the bosses now? You soon jumped from worker to capitalist.' He strode up the counter, glaring at her.

'I'm not . . . I haven't . . . ' She was taken by surprise. For some reason she hadn't looked on opening the shop as breaking the strike.

'What do you think you're doing, then?'

'Don't you think the people will want to know what's happening? How else are they to know if there are no papers?'

'Aw, Hannah, use your brain. The papers that tell the truth will be on strike anyway, there'll only be the Tory press spouting their propaganda for the bosses. The *Daily Herald* is definitely out.'

'Well, I think it's stupid, the papers should have been your best weapon.'

Now that Bob had pointed it out to her, Hannah realised that she should have closed up the shop to show solidarity with her own folk, but his belligerent attitude had put her back up. She would close in her own time, not his, she thought rebelliously.

'Aye, you could be right there,' Bob conceded. 'Anyroad, we've brought out own own news-sheets. The lads are selling them on the streets now.'

'I doubt they'll sell many on Newgate Street,' Hannah said shortly. She walked to the door and looked down the road, straight as an arrow as when the Romans first built it, to the entrance to the marketplace. There were very few people to see and even fewer when she glanced the other way, towards the station. Most of the railwaymen were on strike, not just the station staff, but also those who worked at the railway wagon works at Shildon. Sighing, she closed the door and turned back to Bob.

'Oh, come on through the back for a minute,' she said.

'I haven't the time, it's my job to go round and check who's working and who isn't. And here I find my own sister's a strikebreaker.'

'How can I be on strike against the boss when I'm the boss?' she asked. 'No, never mind, don't answer that, I'm not going to fight with you. But do you want me to refuse to sell cigarettes and chewing baccy?'

'Essential supplies are different,' Bob began, and Hannah laughed.

'Oh, come on, you can spare the time for a cup of tea and a sandwich. I boiled some bacon yesterday, a nice juicy bit.'

Bob wavered and fell. 'All right then, just ten minutes, though.'

While Hannah was preparing the food, her brother talked enthusiastically of the strike. 'By, it's going to be different this time, pet. The country's behind us, I told you it would be. The government will have to give in.

Reports are coming in from all over the place. I tell you, everything's going grand, the strike's a success.'

The shop bell sounded and Hannah put down the knife she had been using to cut the bacon. 'Mash the tea, will you, Bob?' she said over her shoulder as she went to answer it.

The customer was Mr Eddy, immaculate in pin-stripe trousers, black coat and a high stiff collar on a snowy shirt.

'Good morning, Miss Armstrong,' he said, glancing at the few newspapers and periodicals on the counter. 'It's a sad day, a sad day indeed. And such a shame, just as you are starting up. I do hope this emergency won't last long, I do indeed. But you'll see, the working class is all the same, when their beer money runs out and they find the government isn't going to pay them to idle their time away, the workers will come to their senses, I guarantee it.'

Hannah gazed at him and said nothing but he didn't appear to notice her silence.

'I've come for a paper, I thought you would have some in the shop. I suppose your delivery boys are on strike?' He shook his head at the foolishness of boys aping their misguided elders. 'I'll take a *Journal,* I think, as you have no *Times.*'

'I'm sorry, Mr Eddy, I'm afraid I can't sell you a newspaper,' said Hannah.

'What do you mean?' Mr Eddy looked surprised. 'There's one here, why can't you sell it? It's not reserved for anyone, is it?' He picked up the paper and fished in his pocket for coppers to pay for it.

'It's not reserved for anyone, no. But I can't sell it, nevertheless.'

Mr Eddy's eyes widened as he glanced behind her and saw Bob standing in the doorway leading to the sitting room.

'This man is not intimidating you, is he, Miss Armstrong? Just say the word and I'll send for the police.' The colour of his skin above the stiff, white collar had deepened to red and his eyes snapped with indignation.

'Send for the police, would you?' Bob stepped forwards and growled, and Hannah was startled at how dangerous he sounded. Hastily she interposed herself between the two men.

'There's no need for that, Mr Eddy,' she said. 'Of course he isn't threatening me. Bob is my brother.'

Mr Eddy's face hardened. 'Oh, I see, Miss Armstrong, I see,' he said haughtily. 'Your brother, you say. Yes, well, I'll bid you good morning, Miss Armstrong.' He turned and walked smartly out of the shop and Hannah could just imagine him heading straight for his office so that he could telephone his cronies from the Gentleman's Club to tell them that Miss Armstrong was not such a mystery after all. What was a puzzle was how a lass from a pit village who looked hardly eighteen had got the money to buy a freehold business in the town's main shopping street. Oh yes, thought Hannah, she knew well how his mind would be working. Mr Eddy would find out who she was easily enough and soon Daniel Durkin would know where she was and what she was doing.

Not that it was a secret, she thought as she locked the door and went through the shop to the living room. She hadn't promised she wouldn't come home to Auckland.

'I've closed the shop,' she said to Bob. 'I think I'll catch the bus out to Winton to see the family. I can walk up to the farm and see the Burtons, too, I haven't seen them yet.'

'Aye, I'll be on my way an' all. Mind, I think you'll have trouble catching a bus, they're all on strike.' Bob grinned as he pulled his cap down over his head. He was a handsome lad, like all the Armstrongs, Hannah thought as she watched him, with dark eyes and almost black hair, though the colour could be seen only in the short fringe over his forehead for he wore his hair close-cropped like most of the miners. When hair had to be washed every day it was easier that way.

'I'll just have to walk home then, won't I?' she commented as she weighed out a two-ounce packet of black bullets for Harry and one for Walton, to take with her. They went out together, Bob to go to the baking-powder factory to check on the workers and Hannah taking the path for Winton.

A miner stood on the corner of South Church Lane, a bundle of papers in his hands. *'Northern Light,'* he called at intervals. 'A penny for the paper by the workers for the workers.'

Hannah fished a penny out of her purse and handed it over.

'Bless you, miss,' he said and gave her the thin sheet, poorly printed and obviously the work of amateurs. As she walked through the wood, Hannah glanced through the bulletin. There was an air of optimistic determination about it, something like a wartime spirit. There was a job to be done and they were going to do it; the workers of the country had risen and would not be denied. The message was reiterated throughout the paper with accounts of how different groups of workers – railwaymen, transport workers and others – had obeyed the call.

'EVERY MAN BEHIND THE MINERS!' was proclaimed, 'AN INJURY TO ONE IS AN INJURY TO ALL!' And the miners' slogan, the phrase which encapsulated their refusal to take any more cuts in wages or work longer hours for the same pay: 'NOT A PENNY OFF THE PAY! NOT A MINUTE ON THE DAY!'

Hannah sighed, filled with foreboding. Why could the men not see that the government and the bosses were so much better able to stand a long strike than they were themselves? The miners in particular had nothing behind them to sustain their families during a long strike. She folded the paper up and put it in her handbag as she left the wood and fields behind her and headed up the road for Winton Colliery.

'Well, will you just look at her, Miss High and Mighty Armstrong?'

Hannah had been lost in thought but now, as she walked along the road by the bunny banks, where the whinny or gorse bushes were blooming bright yellow against the green broom, she looked up in surprise at the jeering voice. It was Sally Cornish and Kathleen. Sally, as filthy as ever in a bombazine dress which, even in its present ruined state, Hannah could see had once been someone's town dress, stood before her, arms akimbo, grinning widely. The few teeth she had left were black and rotting and her hair was so dirty it was impossible to tell what colour it was.

Beside her was Kathleen, a girl only a year or two older than Hannah, though she gave the appearance of a woman of thirty or forty. She was wearing a lavender gown, much befrilled and ribboned, but in places the frills were coming adrift from the dress and there were food stains on the bodice and worse on the skirt. They must have bought the dresses on one of the second-hand stalls on the market, Hannah decided.

'Hallo, Mrs Cornish, Kathleen,' she said and side-stepped to walk round them, but the Cornish women were having none of it. They moved with her.

'Who does she think she is, Mam?' asked Kathleen, rubbing a hand under her left nostril to remove a drip. 'Walking along with her nose in the air like the Queen of Sheba.' She put out a filthy hand and fingered the material of Hannah's hip-length jacket. 'Dressed to kill an' all, isn't she? Who bought you this, Hannah? A fancy man, was it?'

Hannah stepped back almost without thinking, she couldn't bear either of the two to touch her. 'You know full well who I am, Kathleen Cornish,' she said. 'Now get out of my way.'

'Ooh! Get out of my way, is it?' Sally's jeering tone turned ugly and she caught hold of Hannah's arm roughly and pulled her close so that the stench from her body filled the girl's nostrils and it was all she could do to stop herself from gagging. She pinched in her nose and held her breath and at the same time struggled to pull away, but Sally was surprisingly strong and held on with vice-like fingers. 'I'll get out of your way when I'm ready, my lass. You're just like all the other bloody Armstrongs, think you're too good for the likes of us.'

'She's no different from us, Mam, else where do you think she got her fancy clothes and such? Been on the game, she must have been, that's what, down south where the men have more money to chuck about than the lads round here. Mebbe she's found herself a canny old man to keep her, mebbe she's found more than one, what do you think? Did your fancy man chuck you out, Hannah? Is that why you've come home to your mother?'

'Leave me alone,' said Hannah through clenched teeth. 'Leave me alone or I swear I'll make you pay, see if I don't.' Her anger was rising, lending her strength. With a supreme effort, she wrenched herself away and managed to get past them and fly up the path, only to run straight into Lancelot Cornish as he stepped out from behind a tree.

'Hey, now, not so fast,' he cried and held her fast and the stink of him was even worse than that of his mother and sister.

'Let me go!' she screamed at him in outrage. 'I'll . . . I'll lay you in to the polis! I'll have you up for assault, you hacky, mucky brute!'

Lancelot laughed. 'An' who's going to believe that? Why, lass, everybody knows what you've been doing to come home as flush as you have. It won't hurt you to let me have a bit, now will it? I mean, I'm not exactly going to damage the goods, am I? Not if you're nice to me, that is.'

'Aye, go on, lad, show the bitch what Cornish men are made of,' Sally shouted and Kathleen hooted with laughter. For a moment, Hannah was paralysed with fear. Out of the corner of her eye she could see Sally jumping up and down, laughing and egging Lancelot on. She gazed up at him, at his unshaven chin and wet lips, as his head swayed down towards hers. And even as she watched she saw movement in his dank, greasy hair. Twisting sharply, taking him by surprise, she dragged the heel of her shoe down his shin and he jumped back, releasing her as he grabbed one leg and hopped about on the other, shouting expletives.

But Hannah wasn't there to hear, she was off racing along the road to the village and she neither stopped nor looked back until she got there, though she was panting and she had a painful stitch in her side. There were a few men idling by the end row and they looked at her curiously.

'Is summat the matter, Hannah? There's no one chasing you, is there?'

An older man stepped forward with a look of concern and Hannah saw it was Mr Holmes. She slowed to a walk and struggled to catch her breath.

'No, I'm all right, Mr Holmes,' she managed to say. 'I just thought I needed some exercise so I ran some of the way.' She laughed shakily. 'I suppose I'm not as fit as I thought I was.'

'Hmm,' said Mr Holmes. 'For meself, if I get the feeling I need some exercise I lie down until it wears off.' And he guffawed at his own wit.

Hannah smiled politely and went on to her mother's house. Nora was in the backyard, as she usually was on Mondays when the weather was fine, bent over a tub of soapy water, her sleeves rolled up over her elbows. She was pounding the clothes in the tub with the poss stick, a wooden implement with three short paddles at one end and a crossbar handle at the other. She gave a delighted smile of welcome when she saw Hannah.

'Eeh, lass, I didn't expect you today,' she exclaimed. Leaning the poss stick against the side of the tub, she dried her hands on her apron, pushed a lock of hair back from her forehead and adjusted a hairpin to hold it. Hannah saw with a touch of concern that her mother seemed tired and was breathing quite heavily from the hard work.

'I've closed the shop. There weren't many papers to sell anyway,' she said.

'No, I suppose not. It's a rum business, isn't it?' Nora's face sobered as Hannah's words reminded her of the strike and she sighed. 'Well, go on and put the kettle on, I won't be long finishing this lot.'

'I'll do it, it's ages since I gave a turn to possing. Just lend me a pinny.' Hannah took off her jacket and handed it to her mother before rolling up the sleeves of her blouse. In a minute or two, wrapped in a pinafore which her mother brought for her, she was possing away, up and down, up and down, watching the water swirl round the tub and slap against the sides. It reminded her of schooldays when she would come home at four o'clock and finish off the last of the possing while her mother got the tea. Smiling sadly, she put the clothes through the mangle and dropped them in the blue water in the tin bath.

When the washing was finished, she slung a line across the back row and hung out the clothes, and propped the line up with a wooden clothes prop, out of the way of anyone walking by. The wind caught them and they fluttered like a row of flags in the sunshine.

'They'll be dry by teatime,' said Nora contentedly, watching from the yard where she was emptying the poss tub.

Hannah gazed up at the white shirts and pinafores; there was something satisfying in pinning clean clothes up to dry after all the hard work of washing day. She thought of the encounter she had had with the Cornish family earlier in the day and shuddered as she remembered the filthy state of their clothes and the stink of them too. Turning back to the gate, carrying the tin bath which had held the wet clothes, she saw Mr Hodgson, the Sunday school teacher, watching her covertly as he went by.

'Hallo, Mr Hodgson.' She smiled, prepared to have a few words with him, expecting him to ask how she had got on in Oxford, and was surprised when he mumbled something and went on, almost running down the street.

Shrugging, she went in, thinking he must have been in a tremendous hurry. It just wasn't like him to go off without a word, especially when she had been away for so long. Though she had been back a few weeks now, she hadn't been to chapel and this was the first time she had met him outside. Perhaps his eyes were going, poor man, he was getting on a bit.

The boys came in from school and Bob from his day in Auckland. He was jubilant, the strike was a great success, he reckoned.

'There's nothing to crow about, not with a strike,' said Nora. 'It's my experience that the coal owners always win, no matter what.'

'Aw, Mam, it's different this time. I've told you, we're going to win, it'll only take a week or two. An' it's not just the miners, the country's behind us, we can't lose.'

Nora said no more, but Hannah saw her face was shadowed as she set about frying up a pan of potatoes and onions to eat with the cold meat left over from Sunday.

'I'll walk up to see the Burtons before I go back,' said Hannah when the simple meal was finished. 'I haven't seen them since I got home.' She handed out the packets of sweets to Harry and Walton, enjoying the way their faces lit up with delight at the unexpected treat.

'You spoil those bairns,' said Nora, but it was something she said automatically every time Hannah gave them anything so no one took any notice.

A cool wind had sprung up as Hannah walked up to the farm and she was glad of her jacket. Mr Burton was in the cowshed, she could hear the swish of water as he swilled down the stalls. She would see him after, she thought, best not disturb him when he was busy. Walking up to the kitchen door of the farmhouse, she knocked and opened it. As she had thought she would be, his wife was in the kitchen.

'Hallo, Mrs Burton,' she called and, sure of her welcome, stepped inside and pulled the door to behind her.

The farmer's wife looked up from the table where she was ironing, a newly ironed shirt in her hand. Deliberately, she turned her back on Hannah and hung the shirt carefully on the airer which was strung on a pulley from the ceiling. Only when she was satisfied that it was hanging straight did she give her attention to the girl.

'Now then, Hannah,' she said, her tone neutral.

Taken aback, for a moment Hannah couldn't think what to say. Normally she would have gone farther into the kitchen, maybe even sat down on a chair by the fire, but instead, she hovered by the door, looking uncertain.

'I . . . I thought I would walk up to see you, it's such a long time since,' she said at last.

'Hmm.'

'I hope you are feeling well. And Mr Burton too.'

'We're well enough, thank you.'

Hannah was beginning to feel very uncomfortable and bewildered. What on earth was wrong? Mrs Burton carried on ironing.

'Is there something the matter?' Hannah asked after a lengthy silence.

'Not with us there isn't.'

Mrs Burton licked her finger and touched the flat iron. Dissatisfied with the heat of it, she exchanged it for another, which had been heating up on the bar of the fire. As she turned back to the table, she gave Hannah a level stare.

'That's a nice jacket you're wearing,' she said. 'Not a bad dress neither, I bet it cost you a bob or two.'

Hannah looked down at her dress. It was only of cotton but pretty and well cut.

'You must have had a blooming good job to be able to afford clothes like that.'

'Well, I . . . ' Hannah faltered, realising she couldn't say how she had been able to afford such clothes without telling of her marriage to Timothy. And she wasn't ready for that, oh no, that subject was still too raw.

'Of course, there are other ways young girls get money,' said Mrs Burton.

Hannah stepped back to the door. 'I'm sorry you should think that of me, Mrs Burton, I thought you knew me better. But I can see I'm not welcome here so I'll be saying goodbye.' Walking rapidly out, she did not see the look of uncertainty which flitted across Mrs Burton's face.

'I didn't mean –' the farmer's wife began but she was too late, Hannah had closed the door behind her and was striding off down the track.

She didn't go back into Winton, she felt too full of emotion for that. Instead she cut through the fields and went into Bishop Auckland the other way, a route which led past Durham Road into the marketplace. So that was what everyone thought, even Mrs Burton, was it? she mused bitterly. Well, let them. She hurried on, past Durham Road and up Gib Chare into Newgate Street. She did not lift her head or glance to left or right, all she could think of was closing her own door behind her.

Chapter Twenty-Seven

My Lord,
I beg to acknowledge receipt of your letter of the 2nd
inst. I have to agree that the strike is deplorable. There
is little unrest among the men, they appear to be simply
obeying their leaders. However, by next Saturday, their
last wage packet will be exhausted and they will be
finding it difficult to pay for their beer and then we will
discover how firm is their resolve.

Arrangements have been made this morning for the
bringing-up of the pit ponies and placing them out to
grass. As to the safety men in the pits, contingency plans
have been put into action.

Let us hope the government stands firm and refuses to
give way to the TUC or this country will never recover.

I have the honour to be
Your Lordship's obedient servant,
Daniel Durkin

Daniel stood at the window of his first-floor study as he dictated the letter, looking out over the fields. A girl was walking up the path which led on to Durham Road. She was too far away for him to see properly, but there was something about the way she walked that reminded him of something.

'Fetch my field glasses, Davidson, will you?' he asked. 'They are downstairs by the dining-room window.'

'Yes, sir.'

The secretary left his typing immediately and brought the binoculars. It was Hannah all right, Daniel was just in time to see before she turned the corner for Gib Chare. He frowned heavily. As though he hadn't enough on his mind without that little chit coming back here, he thought angrily. Well, he would just have to find out where she was staying and what she was doing. If she was just playing a waiting game, hoping Timothy would come home before she was discovered, she was to be disappointed. No doubt she thought she would be able to use her wiles to entrap him again. It was a good thing Timothy was still embroiled in his final examinations, he wouldn't be home for another month. And not even then if Hannah was still here, Daniel swore. But she wouldn't be, oh no, not if he had anything to do with it. It hadn't taken him long to get rid of her before and it wouldn't take long now. Turning back to his desk, he picked up the telephone.

Half an hour later, he sat back in his chair, a smile of satisfaction on his face. So she had taken a newsagent's in Newgate Street, had she? Stupid girl, did she really think he was going to let her stay?

'Was there anything else tonight, sir?' Davidson broke into his thoughts.

'What? Oh, no, you can go. Goodnight to you.'

'Goodnight, sir.'

Left on his own, Daniel allowed himself to remember that night in Oxford when Timothy had come into the flat and found him there and Hannah gone. It had taken all his powers of persuasion to convince his son that Hannah's greed had proved stronger than her love.

'I don't believe you,' Timothy had said flatly. 'What lies have you been telling her?'

'None at all, I simply pointed out that your inheritance would be forfeit if you stayed married to her. And she would be much better off taking the money on offer. Girls of her class are easily dazzled by the prospect of a good sum of money.'

Daniel had paused while he lit a cigar; so far the day had gone well and it would be silly to spoil it all by rushing the last hurdle.

'Hannah is not easily dazzled by money,' Timothy said doggedly. 'Why, she would take nothing from me before we were married.'

Daniel laughed. 'No, of course she wouldn't. She was playing for higher stakes. But once I showed her what the alternatives were, she knew where her best interests lay. Though I've got to say I admire her nerve, she wasn't bought cheaply.'

Timothy lunged at his father, taking hold of him by the lapels, and knocking the cigar out of his hand in the process. 'God damn you, Father, I hate you for this. I don't believe that's all that was said, you must have threatened her with something else. Now what was it?'

'Take your hands off me, Timothy, or I will –'

'You'll do what? There's nothing you can do to me now, nothing. You've done it all. I'll never forgive you for this. But I'll find her, mark my words, I will, and then you can go to hell!'

It had been an idle threat, thought Daniel as he left his study and went into his dressing room to dress for dinner. Timothy had stayed at Oxford and by all accounts had thrown himself into his work. No doubt he had come to his senses once the girl had gone and could no longer influence him. Marriage to someone from the inferior classes just did not work. Look at what happened to Ralph Grizedale when he married that girl – what was her name? Hope, that was it, something Hope. He'd taken to drink and the fortune his father had built up had been dissipated. And his son hadn't been any better, he'd run off with a married woman from Winton Colliery with two children.

The younger Grizedale was now a small farmer over by the coast, or so the gossips said. Not that he was so young, must be middle-aged by this time. And no doubt wished he had his time over again now he had to work the farm like a common labourer. Daniel's thoughts returned to his own son.

Better Timothy suffered a little lovesickness now than spend a lifetime regretting a bad marriage, Daniel thought as he strolled downstairs for dinner. Meanwhile, there were more pressing problems to deal with, this strike for one. But it would be dealt with, he had confidence it would, and dealt with successfully. There was a stock-pile of petrol and other necessary goods hidden away for just such an emergency as this; every precaution had been taken to enable the owners to withstand a lengthy strike. These left-wing unionists would find they were no match for Daniel Durkin and his fellows, indeed they would.

Mrs Bates brought in the roast beef and he carved himself a hefty slice and tucked into it with a hearty appetite. He had had a busy day, he deserved his dinner. He began planning the strategy for dealing with the pickets at the gates of the collieries within his jurisdiction.

*

'Will Edwards has been sentenced to three months' hard labour for selling the *Northern Light,*' said Bob gloomily. '"Actions likely to cause dissatisfaction among the civil population," the judge called it.' He rose from his seat by Hannah's fireside and walked to the door of the shop where his sister was standing behind the counter.

'We've been betrayed, Hannah, betrayed by our own class.' He stood in the doorway, his hands in his pockets and his cap pushed to the back of his head.

The general strike was over, it had ended on 12 May. That was it: the railwaymen, transport workers, printers and all the others who had joined in to stand behind the miners were going back to work. It had all happened just as Hannah had feared it would.

'Well, we are determined not to give in, we will carry on the fight for a decent living,' Bob went on. 'The miners will never give in.'

'Oh, Bob, get off your soapbox, you're not giving a speech now,' said Hannah wearily. 'Don't you remember 1921? Why, man, some of our folk haven't paid the Co-op back for the groceries they were advanced then.'

'The union is paying out twelve shillings a week per adult. We will manage,' said Bob stoutly.

'Yes. And for how long do you think the union will be able to carry on paying even that? Don't be so dense, lad.'

Bob stalked to the door. 'Well, if you're going to look on the black side all the time, I'm off home,' he said loftily. From behind his ear, he removed the cigarette butt he had put there earlier, and felt in his pocket for a match.

'Wait a minute, Bob, here, have these,' said Hannah, taking a packet of Woodbines from the shelf and holding them out to him.

'I don't want any charity,' he said, but she could see the hesitation in his eyes.

'Now you're being daft as well as dense. Since when was accepting a packet of cigarettes from your sister taking charity?'

'Aye, thanks, pet.' He smiled wryly and stowed the packet in his pocket. 'I'll be seeing you, then.'

After he had gone, Hannah sat down on the stool she had placed behind the counter for use when the shop was slack. It had been well used in the past ten days and no doubt would be well used in the coming weeks if the miners didn't give in, she mused. But the railwaymen were back at work, at least the ones the management had deigned to take back. People would be coming past the shop on their way to and from the station. Picking up a copy of the *Northern Echo,* she read an account of a train derailment in Northumberland. Some miners had removed a section of rail and then signalled to the train to stop, but instead it continued at a reduced speed. 'The fireman was a medical student, a volunteer,' the article read.

Hannah put down the paper and stared out of the window. She thought of the students she had seen in Oxford, a happy-go-lucky lot on the whole with no idea of how miners lived. Had Timothy driven a train or a bus in Oxford during the strike, she wondered, and the thought of him brought the old familiar ache. How could she have been so mistaken about him? She would have been willing to live with him on a miner's wage if need be. But he had not thought like that, he had preferred life without her if it meant he could keep his comfortable style of living. And how could she blame him? He had been born to comfort and security, unlike her.

She remembered the letter she had had from Alf saying Timothy had been looking for her. Even though Alf had said Timothy mentioned divorce, it had kindled the hope that he would come back, that somehow, magically, everything would come right. Yet at times like this, when she was feeling low, her emotions were so mixed up she didn't even know if she wanted that to happen. She certainly didn't want to be a drag on him, she'd die first. But she loved him, oh yes, and she wanted him. She probed the ache for him in her mind and it grew to unbearable proportions, yet she felt she would be nothing without it, so she nursed it, wallowed in it.

The shop doorbell rang and she glanced up resentfully, not wanting any interruptions to her mourning for her love. The next minute, she was on her feet and facing the man who had just entered the shop, her heart beating painfully in her breast and a slight sweat of fear breaking out on her skin.

Daniel Durkin did not waste time in any preliminary greeting. 'What are you doing here?' he demanded.

'Earning a living, what do you think I'm doing? I put the money to good use and bought a business, as you can see.'

She held out her hands expressively to the counter and loaded shelves.

'I mean, what are you doing in Bishop Auckland?' He twisted his lips impatiently as he spoke.

'I come from here, my family is near. Where else would I go?'

'This was not in the bargain. I expected you to go somewhere else, somewhere away from both Durham County and Oxford. How can Timothy come back here if you are here? No, my girl, you have to go, sell up and get out.'

'You can't make me,' said Hannah. 'The paper I signed promised I would not get in touch with Timothy. It said nothing about keeping away from my home town.'

'You may be from around here but you're not going to stay, believe me. Now why don't you be sensible, put the shop up for sale and go elsewhere? Liverpool, Australia, anywhere as long as it's far enough away.'

'I'm staying here.'

'Right, my girl. We'll see about that, shall we?' Daniel turned for the door but before he opened it he had more to say. 'Timothy won't be home for some time. After his finals, he is going to France with his friend, so you have a month or two to do what I say. And you will do what I say, girl, I'm telling you.'

Hannah stood as stiff as a board with her chin in the air until the door closed behind him. Well, she thought numbly, Timothy is going off on a holiday, probably with the Honourable Anthony Akers. That's how much he cares about me. She did not think about Daniel's threats, they meant next to nothing to her. All she could think of was Timothy and his apparent indifference, and she began to tremble with the pain of it.

She spent a restless night, falling asleep only as the dawn brought streaks of light into the bedroom through the chinks in the curtains. Harry's persistent knocking woke her barely half an hour after she fell asleep.

'By, you take some waking,' he remarked. 'Here's the papers on the step and me and Billy waiting to take them out. What's the matter with you, our Hannah?' He looked critically at her puffy eyes and tousled hair, her kimono tied untidily over her nightgown. 'You're not having a babby, are you?'

'No, I'm not, you cheeky little imp!' she was impelled to cry out with embarrassment as she glanced sideways at the grinning face of Billy. 'What on earth made you say such a thing? I'll tell Mam about you being so brazen, I will!'

'Eeh, Hannah, I was just asking, like,' he said, chastened. 'Only you couldn't wake our Betty up when she was having Simon, I remember it well. She was always dozing.'

'Yes. Well, come on, bring the bundles in and I'll soon have them ready to go out.' She hurried into the living room, combed her hair back and straightened her kimono before going back into the shop to sort the papers. The boys were soon on their way and she went back upstairs to wash and change. While she ate her breakfast, she glanced at the small ads in the local papers.

A small lock-up shop in Winton was to let. She had a mind to expand her business now that the general strike was over. She had hesitated before, thinking that Daniel would find out she was home sooner if she took a shop in the colliery village. But that didn't matter now. The shop was to let at the end of the rows, she had seen the handwritten notice in the window when she had last been in Winton. In these hard times she would probably be able to pick it up at a very reasonable rent, it was privately owned, it did not belong to the colliery. Sure enough, the shop was there in the paper, in the For Rent section. On Wednesday, half-day closing, she would see about taking it. She had known the owner all her life, and didn't anticipate any difficulties. She had to keep busy, that was the thing, she had to stop thinking about Timothy.

'You mean you're setting up in opposition to me, our Hannah?' Nora demanded.

'No, no, Mam, I want you to manage it. You can carry on selling bits and pieces like you do now, but in the shop. And there'll be a newstand there as well.'

'But how can I look after all that and keep the house for the lads an' all? Nay, lass, I'm better off as I am, can you not see it?'

'Mam, think about it. You don't have to do it all yourself, you can give a few hours' work to one of your friends. I'm sure there'll be no shortage of people wanting it, not when the men are on strike.'

'Eeh, I don't know. You know there's the paper shop in Old Winton, is there room for two in the villages? Though, I've got to admit, it'll be nice to have my front room back to myself. I get a bit fed up of folk treading in the muck from the street.'

'There you are then, it's a bargain,' cried Hannah triumphantly.

'What is?' Bob demanded as he stooped to come into the kitchen from the yard.

'Our Hannah's taken the shop on the corner for me,' said Nora, and Hannah could swear she heard a note of pride in her mother's voice.

'We're going to sell papers as well as groceries and sweets,' she told her brother.

Bob laughed shortly. 'Why, Hannah, what sort of trade do you think you'll do in Winton with the men still out on strike? Who can afford a paper to read or a few sweets for the bairns here? It's more than they can do to put a bit of food in their mouths, let alone toffee or black bullets. Before you know it, you'll be bankrupt.'

'No, I won't, you'll see. I've still got a bit behind me and the pit won't be idle for ever. And don't you see, it'll help, it's bringing a bit of enterprise to the place. I intend to sell cheap at first, especially necessities, not much above cost.'

'Can you afford it?' he asked, astonished.

'I can, for a time at least.'

'Oh, well then, lucky for some,' said Bob, but he said it good-naturedly rather than enviously. She was reminded of the time he had hankered to join Uncle Billy in his carrier business. Did he still keep in touch with Uncle Billy? She was about to ask him but he was on his way out. To one of his eternal meetings, no doubt, where they swore solidarity against all the bosses and Daniel Durkin in particular.

Hannah laughed aloud as she thought of Daniel Durkin and what he would think if he knew to what purpose his money was about to be used. The joke was on him, all right. Shoring up the strike, she supposed he would say it was, but she called it relieving distress among her own folk. For now she warmed to the idea, she was determined that even if it took all the money she had left as well as what she could raise on the shop in Auckland, she was going to help her own folk.

'What are you laughing at, Hannah?' asked Walton. She picked him up and waltzed him round the kitchen until he was chuckling with delight.

'Dance to your daddy, my bonny laddie,' she sang and he joined his treble to hers. 'Dance to your daddy, my bonnie lad.'

'Give over, Hannah,' Nora scolded. 'There's no need to act so daft, is there? Folks'll think we've got a loony in the house. What are you laughing at, anyroad?'

'Oh, nothing, Mam, nothing,' said Hannah, subsiding into a chair with Walton on top of her. 'I'm happy, that's all.'

'Well, I'm glad to hear it. I think it's the first time you've said that since you came home from Oxford,' snapped Nora. And the smile faded from Hannah's face as she was reminded of Timothy once again. No matter what she did or whom she was with, the ache for him was always there, waiting to pounce.

Chapter Twenty-Eight

'When the men were at work at least we got our coal allowance,' grumbled Mrs Brown, a miner's wife from the far end of the rows. She stood with her arms folded over a spotless white pinafore, shaking her head and pursing her lips to emphasise her words. There was a small group of women in the corner shop; these last few weeks it had become something of a meeting place. The women would slip out there for a breather after finishing the morning's cleaning and before starting the dinner, under the legitimate excuse of getting the messages.

'You're right there, mind,' agreed one of the other women. 'Though at least the weather is warmer now, we only need a bit of fuel for cooking. It's a grand day the day, isn't it?'

'Oh, aye, the weather's all right,' Mrs Brown allowed as she held out her hand for the two penn'orth of brawn which Nora had been weighing out for her on the new set of scales Hannah had bought for the shop. The brawn had been cooked by Nora on a gas ring at home and it was much in demand. So much, in fact, that Mrs Holmes, who had just entered the shop, watched anxiously as it slowly disappeared into shopping baskets.

'I hope you have some more of that brawn, Nora,' she remarked. 'Our Jack's real fond of a bit of your brawn.'

'You're all right, Mrs Holmes, I have some more coming. Hannah's just gone back to the house for it.'

'That's all right then.'

'You get twice as much for your money here than you do at the butcher's in Old Winton,' asserted Mrs Brown. 'I don't know how you do it and still make a profit, Mrs Armstrong.'

Nora smiled and said nothing. The truth was, the profit they were making was negligible on such items as brawn, even though they saved money by buying pigs' heads at a slaughterhouse in Bishop Auckland and cleaning them and cooking the meat themselves.

Hannah came in carrying the covered tray of meat and the women stood back respectfully for her to pass. Somehow, the gossip about how she came by her money had died down. Knowing she was making a success of the shop in town as well as this one, they assumed she must have been in business in Oxford too. Their understanding of business affairs was hazy in any case, most of them had no experience of anything but life in a pit village.

Even the Cornish family kept quiet on the subject of how Hannah came by her money. They were keeping their heads down altogether lately, for if they had been the scandal of the rows before, they were more so now. Sally and Kathleen had been taken up for soliciting in Auckland and been sentenced by the magistrates to a month's hard labour at the beginning of June. No sooner had they returned to the filthy cottage in Old Winton, both of them somewhat cleaner and thinner after the harsh regime of prison, than Lancelot had been arrested for being drunk and disorderly in the marketplace. He had compounded the offence by pulling a knife and stabbing a policeman. Luckily, he wasn't seeing very straight at the time and merely inflicted a shallow wound in the arm rather than the body of the policeman.

However, this had incensed the mining communities, for the national press had picked up the story and there had been banner headlines. 'STRIKING MINER ATTACKS POLICEMAN WITH A KNIFE' said one and 'ATTEMPTED MURDER OF LAW OFFICER' another. Afterwards, there had been editorials calling for the army to be on call in the coalfields to deal with any disorder. After all, the case had shown that the miners were turning violent and taking up arms to further their claims for more money.

Hannah had read the reports with some disquiet; this was just the sort of thing that would turn the country against the miners, she was sure.

'I'll go now, Mam, if you can manage,' she said now. 'I'd better get back so Betty can come home.'

'Righto, pet, thanks for bringing the supplies,' Nora replied.

Betty and Tucker, though not as badly off as the ordinary pit folk, were feeling the pinch nevertheless, and Betty sometimes looked after the shop in town while Hannah went to the wholesalers or took supplies out to Winton. Her sister insisted on paying her the proper hourly rate.

Hannah had bought a little van, a Morris, and Tucker had taught her to drive on the back lanes around Winton. The van was parked outside the shop and when she went out there was a knot of children standing round it as usual, hoping for a ride round the rows.

'Oh, not today, pets, I have to get back,' she said, but they knew her resolve was easily weakened and set up a clamour of disappointed wails.

'Please, miss, just up the rows, we'll walk back,' entreated one little urchin with great blue eyes in a pinched white face. And of course she capitulated. After all, she told herself, they get few enough treats in these hard times.

'Just up the rows, mind, and you'll have to sit in the back, I can't have you jostling me when I'm driving.'

They crowded in among the boxes and she drove up the row and down the next, going fairly slowly so as to prolong the ride. But she couldn't take too long, Betty would be waiting for her, so as they came to the last row she slowed to a halt and, reluctantly, the passengers got out.

'I'll be coming back at the weekend,' she promised them, and from the brown paper bag which was lying on the passenger seat she gave them each an apple.

'Eeh, ta, miss,' they chorused.

'Stand back now, I don't want to run you over,' she warned, and they retreated to the side as she set off along the road to the town.

Betty was serving a customer when Hannah got back to the shop.

'Oh, good, you're back,' she said as she handed over three halfpence change and a packet of cigarettes to the man, a porter from the station. 'I'm pleased, I want to go down to the store for new shoes for Simon.'

The porter went out and the sisters had the shop to themselves. Betty waited until the door closed after him before turning to Hannah.

'It's lovely to be able to go and get the bairn what he needs without having to ask Tucker for the money. Don't

413

think I don't appreciate it, Hannah. He has enough worries as it is, what with trying to keep the pit right. He goes down every day with the safety men, you know, it's not an easy job, though you'd think it was the way he's had to take less money. And Simon's growing apace now, his clothes don't last him any time at all. But I wanted him to look nice today.'

'He's a big lad all right, he's going to make a big man like his da,' Hannah agreed. 'But don't be grateful to me. If it wasn't for you being willing to step in for me, I'd only have to employ someone else, wouldn't I?'

'And you'd have no trouble finding somebody these days,' said Betty grimly. 'I don't know what's going to happen, I don't. Tucker's worried the men might get violent and stop the safety men going down the pit to keep it right. If that happens there'll be no pit left for anyone to work in when they do go back and Tucker would be out of a job an' all.'

'They won't do that, Betty, they're not violent, you know they're not. It would be against their own interests, anyway.'

'I expect you're right,' her sister replied, sounding none too sure. 'I'll be off then, cheerio. I promised Tucker's mother I would take Simon to Marsden to see them all today, I'll take the teatime train and stop the night at the farm. Father Grizedale hasn't seen Simon for ages, it's time I took him. I'll likely be back tomorrow.' She walked down the sunlit street, a plump, matronly figure in her simple print dress and low-heeled shoes.

Hannah watched her from the doorway of the shop for a moment or two before going in and picking up a copy of the *Journal and North Star* to read in idle moments behind the counter.

'TRAIN WRECKERS SENTENCED' it proclaimed. 'CRAMLINGTON MINERS SENT TO PENAL SERVITUDE. WOMEN FAINT AND SOB.' Hannah sighed. Eight of the men had been sentenced to penal servitude, three for eight years, two for six and the rest for four, though some of the prisoners asserted they were simply walking by the line when the incident occurred. This sort of thing did not help the cause of the miners, she thought sadly. She put the paper down as the door opened and the short dinnertime rush began. This evening she would have to make time to do the books, she decided. Since the end of the general strike the shop had been making a modest profit, which was just as well, because the purchase of the van had made a considerable hole in her small capital.

The shop at Winton wasn't doing so badly either, much to her surprise. Some of it had to do with the shortage of fuel for cooking in the village, especially since Daniel Durkin had decreed that any miner caught riddling the waste heap for small coal would be prosecuted for theft with all the force of the law. It had been a good idea to sell home-cooked food in the shop even at such low prices, it brought in customers. Folk didn't like to use the soup kitchens every single day.

Daniel had not been back in the shop since that time in May, just about when the miners' lockout began. In fact, Hannah had heard nothing from him at all and here it was already August. She did not suppose that he had forgotten about her, though, not for a minute. She could only think he was busy with other things, such as petitioning the government to hold out against the miners. And if Timothy was still away on the continent, well, then, Daniel would think there was plenty of time to deal with her.

There was no way Daniel could force her to leave, Hannah told herself. She owed no one anything, he had no hold over her – except for the family in Winton. The thought niggled. There was Bob, he was a prominent local worker in the Miners' Federation, no further excuse was needed to get rid of him.

The afternoon turned into evening and one or two customers wandered in, but by seven o'clock the street was deserted. Hannah locked the shop door and went through to the living room. The heat was oppressive, and she flung open the window and door to the yard to create a draught. Taking a chair out into the yard, she sat for a while by the covered passageway she had had constructed to connect the outhouses to the main house. It was pleasant sitting there, the only sound the hum of a late bee busy around the flowerpots she had placed around the yard, geraniums and nasturtiums in full bloom. Maybe she would leave the books for another evening.

She was still sitting there, thinking lazily that she ought to get up and prepare something for supper, when there was a thunderous knocking on the shop door. It made her jump to her feet, startled. She glanced at her watch in the gathering twilight; it was nearly ten o'clock. Who could it possibly be at this hour?

The house was almost completely dark and she had to switch on the light before going through the deserted shop. The knocking started up again and she called out as she fumbled with the bolts, 'All right! All right! I'm coming. I can't open up any faster than I am doing.'

At last she got the door open and Harry stumbled in.

'What on earth's the matter? Nothing's happened to Mam, has it?' she cried.

Harry was panting and struggling for breath. He must have run all the way from Winton, she thought, thoroughly alarmed by now. He shook his head and swallowed hard. 'No, no, Mam's all right, but she wants you to come, Hannah, she wants you now.'

'But why? What's happened? Can you not tell me?'

'It's our Bob, she's past herself worried about our Bob, he's ran off. The polis came to our house and Bob ran off!'

'The polis? But why? Bob hasn't done anything wrong. It's not a crime to be in the union now, is it?'

'No – I don't know. Aw, come on, Hannah, I don't know what's happened but something terrible has. And Tucker's down the pit with the safety men and Betty's away so I came for you, Mam's in such a taking, I've never seen her like this before.'

Harry stared in earnest appeal at his sister, his eyes wide with a fear of something, he didn't know what. 'You'll have to come, Hannah, hurry up, will you?' He was desperate to convey the urgency he felt.

'Yes. Yes, of course, I'll come now, I'll just get my coat. I'll only be a minute.'

Harry turned to run back the way he had come and she caught him and pulled him back.

'Wait, it'll only take fifteen minutes in the van. Don't you go running back, you'll make yourself ill. Where's your bike, anyway?'

'Puncture. Eeh, I'm glad you have the van.' His face cleared.

Hannah bit her lip, reminding herself he was barely ten years old. It was easy to forget his age sometimes, he always seemed such a responsible lad, and had proved to be an excellent paperboy. But he must have been in a panic all the time as he ran the three miles or so from Winton to the shop. What on earth was it that had brought the police to the house? Hastily, she went into the living room for her bag with the van keys in it, switched off the light and locked the shop door behind her. Harry was waiting outside by the van, hopping from one foot to the other with impatience.

'Don't worry, Harry, it must be a mistake of some sort. You know Bob isn't one to do anything wrong,' she said, trying to reassure him as she unlocked the vehicle. 'Hop in and we'll soon be on the way.'

Getting into the van herself, she checked it was in neutral and pushed the starter button. The engine flared into life and then died immediately.

'Come on, come on,' she said tensely and tried again with the same result.

'It's not going to start,' said Harry.

'Yes, it is, I'll use the starter handle. It'll only be a jiffy.'

'Maybe I'd better run back, Mam might want me to see to Walton,' said Harry.

'Don't be silly,' snapped Hannah. 'Sit still when I tell you to.' She found the starter handle on the floor by his legs, got out of the car and began cranking the van. It shuddered and burst into life, only to fade yet again. Hannah was almost sobbing with frustration.

'Please, God? Please?' She lifted her eyes to the darkening sky and prayed. And as if in answer, she realised that in her panic she had forgotten to switch on the petrol – of course the blinking thing wouldn't go. Lifting the bonnet, she pushed the switch over and got back into the van.

'Will it go now?' asked Harry.

'Yes!' she said emphatically, and pressed the starter button once again. The engine purred into life and this time it kept on going. Fumbling with the gear lever to find first gear, she forced herself to control her trembling limbs.

'Get a hold of yourself, girl,' she muttered. The gear lever slipped into place and she edged the van away from the kerb. Though it was still dusk, the night was approaching fast. She had never had occasion to drive in the dark before and was surprised at how difficult it was to see.

'Put the headlights on, our Hannah,' said Harry, 'the polis will be after *you* next.'

Heaving a sigh at her own stupidity, she found the right switch on the dashboard and turned on the lights. After that it took only a little more than ten minutes to reach Winton Colliery. As she turned into the row, she saw a police car parked outside the house and a cluster of neighbours around the back gate. She parked the van behind the police car and, without waiting for Harry, ran into the house.

Her mother was standing before the fire, clutching Walton to her and looking strained and anxious. Just inside the door stood a policeman, not the local bobby who lived in Old Winton, but a stranger.

'What is it? What's happened?' she cried, going up to her mother. Nora gazed at her and burst out sobbing.

'It's Mr Durkin. He's been killed. And the polis is saying our Bob had a hand in it. They're after him, Hannah, they're going to take him to Durham Gaol.'

Chapter Twenty-Nine

'Don't, Mam, don't, you're upsetting the boys,' said Hannah. She put an arm round her mother's shoulders and led her to the settee, with Walton still hanging on to her skirts and sobbing as hard as she was. Every few minutes he cast a fearful glance at the policeman standing impassively just inside the back door, and the tears fell even faster.

'You're right, I'm sorry, I am.' Nora made a great effort to pull herself together. 'Harry, bring me a hankie, pet, will you?'

Harry went to the top drawer of the press, took out a large white handkerchief and gave it to his mother. She dried her eyes and blew her nose, then took Walton on her knee to comfort him.

'Whisht, pet, whisht, I'm all right now, I am. Howay, be quiet now,' she whispered in his ear, and he put his arms around her neck and hid his face in her shoulder. She patted his back and after a while he stopped sobbing.

'Come into the sitting room,' Hannah urged. 'We can be on our own in there, you can tell me all about it.'

Nora looked at the police officer standing by the back door. 'No, we can't, there's another one like him just inside the front door.'

Hannah was annoyed. 'Can't you stand outside in the yard?' she asked the policeman.

'Sorry, miss,' he replied, 'my orders are to stand here.' She turned away from him impatiently.

'Listen, Mam, have the bairns had their supper? No? Well then, I'll make them some cocoa and sandwiches and get them to bed. They'll be better off upstairs out of it.'

'Yes, that's right, of course it is. I don't know what I've been thinking of. Fancy me going to pieces like that, I've never done it before. I didn't do wrong to send Harry for you, did I? Only I forgot to give him his bus fare.'

'No, you did the right thing.'

It was true, she couldn't remember her mother in such a state, thought Hannah, as she warmed milk on the gas ring and cut bread for sandwiches. Not even when Da had his accident, not even when Jane had to go away to the sanatorium in Weardale.

But Bob, well, he was different. Hannah was well aware that her mother still felt guilty about letting him go to his grandmother in Consett to be brought up. And even more guilty because she had needed him back home when he was old enough to go down the pit.

Where is Bob? That was the question uppermost in her mind. Why had he run when the police came if he hadn't done anything wrong?

'Our Bob wouldn't do what they say, he wouldn't do anything against the law, you know him, Hannah, he wouldn't.'

Hannah looked up in amazement. It was almost as if she had asked the question aloud and her mother was speaking in answer. But no, Nora was washing Walton's face and hands in an enamel dish she had placed on the cracket by the fire.

'Is the polis going to put our Bob in gaol?' asked Harry. Hannah could have killed him.

'He's not, is he, Mam?' Walton's face began to crumple once more.

'No, he's not, like I said, our Bob hasn't done anything wrong!' Nora snapped, and Harry looked down and flushed. Already washed and dressed in his nightshirt, he was sitting at the table waiting for his supper. Though his eyes were shadowed and his face still strained, he was much calmer now he had his big sister here to help him support his mother. Even her reproof did not upset him really; rather, it reassured him.

'Hurry up and eat your supper, you're going to be very late getting to bed tonight. I'd better call one of the other lads in to do your rounds in the morning.'

'I can do it,' Harry protested.

'No, you can't. Anyway, I want you to stay with Mam, you can run messages for her and mind Walton. I'll go in and get the deliveries under way, then I'll close the shop and come back.'

'Eeh, Hannah, I expect it'll be all straightened out before then,' said Nora.

'It doesn't hurt to plan, just in case,' her daughter insisted.

The boys were soon packed off to bed and Hannah and her mother left alone, apart from the man at the door, that is. She made tea and automatically offered the policeman a cup, but he refused, so she sat down in Bob's rocking chair by the fire opposite her mother, and with her back to the stranger at the door. She had decided the best thing to do was pretend he wasn't there.

'Have you any idea what this is all about, Mam?'

Nora shook her head slowly. She held the cup of tea in both hands, low on her lap, making no attempt to drink it. Gazing into the dead ashes of the fire, she chewed her bottom lip worriedly before answering.

'All I know is Harry came running in saying there were policemen coming up the street and our Bob took off through the front door. I don't know where he went,

I hardly had time to think. But you know they've taken ever so many of the lads to prison – look at that one who was just selling a pamphlet on the street. Three months, he got, and all for selling a bit of paper. And Will Lowther, you know, the Durham miners' leader, they took him to Durham Gaol an' all. So our Bob being active on the committee, he always thought they might take him. But we never imagined they would want him for murder, never. I mean, you know our Bob, he couldn't do a thing like that, he couldn't,' she repeated once again.

'Drink your tea, Mam. I've put plenty of sugar in it, it's good for shock,' Hannah counselled. Somehow in this situation she felt like the mother to Nora rather than the other way round.

Obediently, Nora sipped her tea before continuing. 'I cannot think that it's anybody from the colliery rows as killed Mr Durkin, though mind, he wasn't liked. I well remember that time after your father had his back broke in the pit, how that man spoke to me. You'd think we were dirt, you would. I know he was your Timothy's father –'

Hannah glanced quickly over at the policeman and saw he was listening to her mother, his head cocked on one side and an alert expression on his face. She leaned forward and touched her mother's hand, a warning touch, cutting into Nora's words.

'Don't talk about that here,' she said meaningfully. Nora sat up straight, reminded that they were not alone.

'Anyroad, the polis said that Mr Durkin had been killed in his car. But it could have been an accident, couldn't it? I mean, why should they think he was murdered?'

'I don't know, Mam. We'll have to wait till we find out the whole story. I –'

Hannah stopped as there was the sound of footsteps coming up the yard and both women turned towards the door. Was it another policeman coming to tell them they had caught Bob? The fear and apprehension was plain to see on her mother's face as she was sure it was on her own. But no, the door opened and it was Tucker.

'I'm sorry, I have to know who you are before I can let you come in, sir,' said the man on the door.

'My name is Thomas Cornish, I'm the undermanager and this lady's son-in-law, constable,' said Tucker sharply. 'Now move aside, if you please.'

'Just doing my duty, sir.'

'Yes, well, that's as may be.'

After this short exchange, Tucker, after a brief nod to his sister-in-law, went immediately to Nora.

'How are you, Mother?' he asked. 'Now, don't make too much of this, I'm sure they'll find the man who really did it.'

'Yes, they will, won't they, lad,' whispered Nora. But she was twisting her hands in her lap now, twisting and twisting, wrinkling the material of her dress. Tucker glanced at Hannah.

'I heard what had happened when I came up from the pit, I had to go down this afternoon. The safety men reported some trouble with the supports in one of the seams, and I had to inspect them for myself – the best thing to do, I always think. I came as soon as I heard, I mean, when I came to bank. Betty's over at Marsden, I don't expect her back until tomorrow night.'

'They think Bob's had a hand in murder, Tucker, how could anybody think such a thing?' Nora held out her hand to him and he took it and held it as he hooked a foot round a wooden chair and pulled it over so that he could sit down beside her. He was still in the working overalls he wore when he had to go down the mine and there were streaks of coal dust on his cheeks and darkening his fair hair. Watching him, Hannah thought he looked so strong and dependable, she could hardly believe that he was the son of Wesley Cornish. How could he bear to keep the same name? In his position she would have changed it to Grizedale, that of his stepfather.

'No one who knows him will believe Bob did it, so don't worry any more,' Tucker was saying reassuringly. 'They'll catch the real culprit, you'll see. Now why don't you lie down for a while? You need your rest, you know, the lads will need you tomorrow. Sitting up worrying isn't going to help anything, is it?'

'Eeh, no, I couldn't sleep. No, I'm all right sitting here, Tucker.'

'Can you tell us what happened?' asked Hannah. 'All we know is that Mr Durkin has been killed and Bob's run off.'

Tucker glanced at the policeman by the door and moved his head closer to the two women. 'Well, when I got out of the cage at bank, the pit yard was swarming with police. There's been one on guard since the beginning of the lockout but there must have been a dozen there tonight. It seems that the one who had been on guard went up to the fish shop to get something for his tea; after all, everything has been quiet round here and I suppose he wasn't expecting any trouble. But while he was away, the powder shed was broken into.'

'The powder shed?'

'You know, the locked store we keep the powder in. Well, it's a paste really, the deputies use it to crack up a length of coalface so that the hewers can bring it down more easily. Anyway, some paste was missing and detonators an' all. Mr Hudson thought someone might be going to try to sabotage the mine buildings, or maybe even Lord Aker's place over by Durham, so the special police were called out to guard both places.' Tucker was silent for a moment or two before adding, 'I suppose the powers that be never thought of Mr Durkin being in any danger. With Lord Akers being away in London, the agent was deputising for him at a meeting of the coal owners in Newcastle. He came back this evening. And now there are two men dead.'

'Two?'

Tucker nodded. 'Yes, his chauffeur, a Mr Bates, was driving the car.'

Mr Bates, yes, of course, thought Hannah. Timothy had mentioned the name once, saying how Mr Bates and his wife had been so good to him after the death of his mother.

'But do you know where it happened? Or how?'

'The entrance to his drive, just inside the gates, so the police said. An explosion.' Tucker's brow knitted. 'Though how anyone knew he would be coming home round about the time he did, I don't know. I mean, I didn't even know there was a meeting today in Newcastle. And how did they get the trap laid without anyone seeing them? It isn't so easy to cause an explosion with black powder as all that, you know. Whoever it was knew what he was doing.'

'Like a deputy overman or a shot firer,' said Hannah thoughtfully. 'Our Bob was just a hewer. But you know lots of folk could have read about the meeting, the *Northern Echo* reported it was going to be held.'

'Yes, that's right!' her mother put in, suddenly animated. 'I mean, about our Bob just being a hewer. He couldn't have done it, I told you he couldn't.'

Tucker and Hannah looked at each other and away again. They both realised that Bob must have seen a deputy use the explosive lots of times, he was bound to have some idea of its properties.

'I'll make some more tea,' said Hannah after a moment.

The night wore on: three o'clock, four o'clock. One or two birds began to sing and the cockerel in the henhouse at the bottom of Mr Holmes's garden crowed once or twice. Hannah got up and drew back the kitchen curtains, letting in the dawn light. Mercifully, Nora had fallen asleep on the settee, her head resting against the raised end, and Hannah had covered her with a blanket.

'I must get back to the shop by six to take in the papers,' Hannah whispered to Tucker. 'Why don't you go home and have a bath and change? You'll feel better then.'

Tucker hesitated. 'Betty would never forgive me if I left your mother to face anything alone,' he demurred.

'She won't be alone. If you nip along now, I'll wait until you come back; you're not going to be very long, are you? And I've got the van, it only takes a few minutes to drive to Auckland.'

Tucker got to his feet, stretching himself, and yawned. 'I will then, I won't be long. If I'm clean and dressed and looking like a member of the managerial class, maybe the police will tell me more.'

Hannah stared out of the window after he had gone. The pink streaks which had dyed the sky only a few minutes before were already disappearing, it promised to be a beautiful day. She sagged against the wall. Oh, yes, she thought wearily, a beautiful day, a glorious day. A day which could see the complete downfall of the Armstrong family.

A policeman turned in at the gate and she jumped, her pulse pounding. But it was only the relief for the constable on the door, she had forgotten he was there. The relief came in with a cheery 'Now then' for his colleague. She hushed him with a finger to her lips and a fearsome frown and nodded to the sleeping form of her mother. He muttered something of an apology and took up his friend's former position by the door.

Hannah's mouth tasted vile from too many cups of tea and lack of sleep. Why didn't something happen? This waiting was intolerable. She wished Alf was here, or Betty, both of them older than she. She felt very young and unable to support her mother, should someone come through the gate and tell them that Bob had been charged with murder and taken to prison. She felt she would not be able to bear it.

'Hannah?'

She whirled round to see her mother pushing herself upright on the settee with one hand, the other over her forehead. Nora looked pale and ill with great dark shadows under her eyes.

432

'I must have dropped off for a minute or two. By, my head's fit to bust,' she said. 'Oh, but how could I have slept when our Bob is in so much trouble?'

'You didn't sleep for long, Mam. Anyway, you must have needed it, I reckon it was nature's way of giving you a break.'

'You could be right, I suppose. There's no news, is there? Where's Tucker?'

'He's just gone home for a bath, he's coming straight back. No, there's no news, Mam.'

'I could do with a wash meself,' said Nora wearily.

'Well, I'll put the kettle on the gas ring and you can have one,' said Hannah. Nora glanced at the policeman meaningfully.

'I'll put the basin in the pantry for you,' Hannah suggested. 'You don't want to go upstairs, you might wake the lads and there's nowhere else private.' She caught the officer's eye and he looked away and blushed. Picking up the kettle, she filled it at the tap in the pantry and put it on the ring. That was another inconvenience caused by the lockout, she thought, there wasn't enough coal to heat water in the boiler which formed part of the range, so every drop had to be heated on the gas ring.

By the time Tucker came back, freshly shaven and wearing a clean shirt and smart suit, and with his fair hair still wet from his bath, it was a quarter to six. She just had time to get to the shop before the paperboys if she left immediately.

433

'I won't be long, Mam, just an hour, I think,' she said and rushed out to the van. The police car which had been there the evening before had gone, as had the knot of onlookers, so the row was deserted.

'Come on now, no histrionics,' she muttered as she got into the driver's seat, remembering as she did so that she hadn't turned off the petrol the night before. Were there dire consequences if the petrol was left switched on overnight? She couldn't remember what Tucker had told her about that. Well, she would never know unless she tried it, she thought, and pressed the starter button. The engine burst into life and she sighed with relief. Soon she was driving along the road to Bishop Auckland.

'Can you run and fetch your brother Tom?' she asked Billy, who was waiting for her, propped against the shop door, one leg crossed over the other and his cap pushed to the back of his head. Billy was almost fourteen and would soon be looking for a proper job. He hoped to follow his father into the railway wagon works at Shildon. That left only Dave and Harry, and Harry's round was kept deliberately small because of his age. Tom might be just the lad she needed. If Bob was taken it was more important than ever that she make a success of this business.

Billy's face brightened. 'Aye, I will, miss,' he said. 'Our Tom's a good lad, are you thinking of taking him on regular?'

'I might. We'll see how he goes, shall we?'

Billy nodded eagerly. 'We won't be long, miss, I promise.'

As he ran off, Hannah made a start on sorting the papers, marking them for the houses they were meant for and putting them in the correct piles to go into the boys' bags. By the time she had finished, Billy and Tom were back and Dave had arrived, so she was able to send them on their way.

'Throw the bags over the wall into the backyard when you're finished,' she told them. 'I have to go out.' She hesitated about what to do about the customers who called every morning for their papers, but in the end, she put a pile on a stool in the doorway and a tin beside it with a label stuck to it, MONEY IN HERE. The chance of losing the money was outweighed by that of losing customers because they couldn't get their *Northern Echo*. As an afterthought, she picked up one of the papers and took it with her. Until then, she had avoided looking at the headlines.

She sat in the van and opened up the paper. 'MINING AGENT MURDERED,' she read.

Daniel Durkin, mining agent for Lord Akers, was last night murdered in his car on his way back from a meeting of coal owners in Newcastle. 'An arrest is imminent,' the police inform us.

Daniel Durkin was one of the most respected men in our community.

435

'A dastardly deed,' said Lord Akers when contacted in his London home. He was too shocked to say any more for the time being. Timothy Durkin, Mr Durkin's only son, is believed to be holidaying on the continent with the Honourable Anthony Akers. The police are trying to get in touch with him.

Hannah folded the paper with shaking hands and laid it on the passenger seat. So Timothy was still away in France, she thought numbly as she started the engine and set off to Winton.

It was seven o'clock when she parked the van by her mother's gate in the back row once again. There was no one about: in these long months of lockout, the miners and their wives had got into the habit of sleeping till eight or nine o'clock; after all, there was little to get up for. The sun shone on the paving bricks from a cloudless sky and Mr Holmes's cockerel, newly released from the henhouse after the night, stepped arrogantly about the end of the row, black feathers and bright red comb gleaming. As usual, he was accompanied by his harem of dowdy brown hens.

Hannah pushed open the gate, walked up the yard and went in. There was no policeman standing just inside. No one but her two small brothers, sitting at the table eating bread smeared with treacle, and her mother standing by, her face grey and set.

'Has something happened, Mam?'

Nora looked up at her but didn't answer.

'Mam, has something happened? And where's Tucker?'

Harry answered instead. 'They've caught our Bob, he was hiding up the bunny banks. And Tucker's gone to the police station to see about it.'

Nora gave a shuddering sigh and sat down abruptly. Walton gave her a startled glance and then stared at his plate. Licking his finger, he pressed it on a crumb of bread and treacle and transferred it to his mouth. Hannah moved quickly to her mother's side and put a hand on her shoulder.

'It'll be all right, you'll see.'

'Will it?' Nora put a weary hand to her forehead and rested her elbow on the table. 'I'm not sure of anything any more.'

Chapter Thirty

It was twelve o'clock when Betty walked in. 'I came as soon as I could, Mam,' she said, going straight to Nora's side. 'Tucker rang the farm first thing and told us all about what had happened. Have you heard any more? The paper lads in Sunderland were shouting that someone had been arrested.'

She glanced from her mother's face to Hannah's and slumped into a chair. 'Do you know, I was telling myself all the way here that they must have arrested someone else and Bob would be back here, safe and sound. But it was him, wasn't it?'

'It wasn't Bob that did it!' Nora flared.

'No, no, I didn't mean that. I meant it was him they'd arrested. I know Bob didn't do it, Mam, of course I wouldn't think that.'

'Yes. Sorry, pet, I know you do; I'm tired, that's all.' She tilted her head and looked behind Betty. 'Where's the bairn? Where's Simon?'

'I left him with his grandma. She offered to keep him for a while, just till we get things sorted out here. I thought it was best if he was over there, away from all the trouble. And it leaves Tucker and me with more time to help.'

'Aye. Well, Meg always was a good woman, do anything for anybody, she would.'

'She said to send Harry and Walton an' all, for a week or two at any rate.'

'Eeh, I couldn't do that, our Betty. I wouldn't put on the woman's good nature, no, I couldn't.'

'Well, I'd think about it if I were you,' said Betty. 'After all, the school's on holiday this month and it would be a good thing for them to go somewhere you'll know they'll be properly looked after. And we won't have to worry about seeing to them as well as everything else. It's really a good idea, Mam. I'm sure Walton and Harry would love a holiday by the sea.'

'A holiday? At the seaside?'

The women turned as Walton came through from the sitting room where he had been playing a game of snakes and ladders with Harry. His face was shining and his eyes round with hope as he gazed up at Betty. Harry came up behind him.

'What did you say, Betty?' he asked.

'Mrs Grizedale wants you both to go to her for a holiday. You'd like that, wouldn't you?'

Harry grinned a grin of pure delight which made him seem as young as Walton. But the next minute the grin faded and he looked at his mother.

'Eeh, no, Betty, I'd better not go. Walton can, though, can't he? I'll stay here, Mam might need me.'

This was enough to make Nora's mind up for her. 'No, lad, you go with Walton, you can give an eye to him, help Mrs Grizedale. And Simon an' all, the pair of them will keep you busy.'

'But I want to stay here and help you, Mam,' he protested.

'Yes, well, the best help you can give me is to go with your brother. Go on, lad, you know you like going to the seaside with the Sunday school trips. Well, this time you can go for a whole fortnight and live on a farm, an' all.'

Harry wavered and, in the end, nodded his head.

'I'll pack the clothes for them,' said Hannah. 'It's a good job I have the van, I can take them over there this afternoon.' At least she could help by taking the boys, she thought, as she found the old straw luggage basket and set about filling it with shirts, shorts and the other things they needed. She was glum with a feeling of impotence at having to hang around the house doing just about nothing. Yet she couldn't bear to go back to Bishop Auckland and open the shop as though it was just another day.

Driving back along the coast road after leaving the boys at the farm, Hannah hardly noticed the sun shining on the sea or the gulls swooping about the sky. The sun beat on the roof of the van and the heat penetrated the thin cotton of her dress, making her feel hot and sticky. She was glad of the breeze from the sea as she drove along, past Whitburn, Seaburn and Roker. All she could think of was getting back to Winton to see if there was any more news.

Striking inland through Sunderland, she took the road for Durham, and found the streets of the city were baking hot and stifling. She was glad to get away from them and out on the open road, heading for Spennymoor. Hannah was beginning to feel very tired indeed. She had had little sleep the night before and the drive to Marsden had taken two hours of the hottest part of the day. The afternoon sun was shining on the windscreen, dazzling her and making her head ache. As she came to the end of the houses of Spennymoor, she pulled into the side of the road and stopped the van. Leaning back in her seat, she closed her eyes. Just for a few minutes, she told herself, just until the sun dropped behind the line of trees on the horizon.

She awoke with a start as a loud bang reverberated round her, and fumbled for the door catch of the van. Her stiff fingers wouldn't work at first and another bang made her panic. Someone was trying to blow up the van with her in it, she thought confusedly. Images of black powder and detonators flashed through her mind. At last the door swung open and she practically fell out into the road and ran to the grass verge.

The light was almost gone, only a greenish glow in the sky. How long have I slept? she wondered. It must be late. The next moment, lightning slashed vividly through the sky and a great splash of rain fell on her face. A thunderstorm, that was all it was; she must have been dreaming. Drops of water were coming down fast now and she ran back to the car. Seven o'clock, said the watch on her wrist – where had the last two hours gone? A sudden wind gusted through the open window of the van and she shivered in her thin cotton dress. Best get on, she thought.

The engine had gone cold and the starter button refused to work. Hannah looked out at the pouring rain. There was no help for it but to try the starter handle. She had no jacket; the newspaper she'd left on the passenger seat early that morning was the only protection there was. Picking up the handle and the paper, she got out into the rain and held the paper over her head with one hand as she tried turning the handle with the other, but she wasn't strong enough. Oh, well, she thought, dropping the paper, two hands it is. It seemed to take ages before the engine finally came to life and, thankfully, she climbed back in the van and set off once again.

Of necessity she went along the road at a snail's pace for water was streaming down the windscreen and the wiper was making little impression. But at last she reached Parkhead Bank and there, magically, the rain stopped and the sun appeared, gleaming between the trees on the far horizon. Hannah coasted down the bank into the valley and up the other side to the ridge which marked the beginning of Bishop Auckland. On impulse, instead of turning off for Winton Colliery, she carried on to Durham Road.

She just wanted to see where Daniel had been killed, she told herself. She would just drive past and look in. As she neared the entrance to the drive she slowed to a halt and gazed in horror at the hole blasted in the ground and the shattered glass and gravel in the gutter. One gatepost leaned slightly to one side and the gate, though still attached to the post at the bottom end, leaned the opposite way. Something attracted her gaze to a window on the first floor – a figure of a man, was it? But a drop of water suddenly fell from her hair on to her eyelashes and obscured her vision and when she had rubbed it away, the figure was gone. Probably a trick of the light, she thought.

'Move along there, miss.' A policeman standing by the hedge waved his arms at her and she put the van back in gear and went on her way. Poor Timothy, she thought, how awful it would be for him to be told of his father's death when he was so far away from home. Perhaps he had been told already, perhaps he was on his way back this very minute. She wished she could be with him to comfort him, he had no one now, just the housekeeper, Mrs Bates, and she would be mourning her husband.

'Fool!' she told herself as she went up Gib Chare into the town. He wouldn't want her to comfort him, of course he wouldn't. All he wanted from her was a divorce. She must forget about him for the moment, she had enough to think about with Bob and the trouble at home. And then there was the business. Now she was in Auckland, she might as well go up Newgate Street and check on the shop.

There were two or three newspapers still on the stool with the tin box she had put there for the money on top of them, half full of pennies and halfpennies. Well, she thought as she picked up the papers and the box, people are honest. Lots of folk must have walked past the shop and seen the money but no one had touched it as far as she could see.

Upstairs she took off her wet dress and petticoat and rubbed her skin and hair dry with a towel. She didn't take time for a bath for she was eager to know what Tucker had managed to find out in the police station. Instead she pulled on clean clothes and brushed her hair. Picking up a jacket, for the storm had cooled the air, she ran back down the stairs. In the sitting room, she took her bank books from the bureau drawer and slipped them into her bag. If Bob was going to be charged, he would need a good solicitor and lawyers cost money, a lot of money. She only hoped the family could raise enough.

'You took a long time, did the storm slow you down?' asked Betty when Hannah walked into her mother's house. 'I was just beginning to worry about you.'

'I'm sorry No, I went in to the shop to check everything was all right.' She looked around; there was no sign of her mother or Tucker. 'Is Tucker not back? Where's Mam?'

'I persuaded her to go to bed for an hour or two. She needed the rest and there's nothing she can do here.'

'And Tucker?'

'Yes, Tucker's back. He had to go in to work, though, Mr Hudson sent for him.' Betty looked down at her hands, her face troubled.

'Did he find out anything? What's happening about our Bob?'

'They took him to Durham Gaol, Hannah,' Betty answered, her voice low and full of pain. 'Tucker protested – after all, Bob hasn't even been charged with anything. How can they charge him when they haven't got any proof? And they haven't, I know they haven't, they couldn't have. But the magistrates said they couldn't take the risk of keeping him in the police cells at Auckland, they're frightened there might be a riot.'

'A riot?' Hannah was stupefied.

'Aye. Well, the lads are angry, you know, they think the powers that be are trying to make Bob a scapegoat, him being a union man. But his marras say he was at a meeting last night down at the workingmen's club, there's a host of them ready to swear it, he'd just come in from there when the police came for him. But the bobbies wouldn't take the men's word for it and some of the lads started saying they would get him out themselves if he wasn't set free. It was only wild talk but it was enough for the magistrates to send him to Durham.'

'We'll get him a solicitor. I was thinking about it on my way home. I have some capital left and I could raise a mortgage on the shop.'

'I hope it doesn't come to that, Hannah. But if it does, the Miners' Federation will pay, surely. If they have anything left after this lockout, that is.' Betty sighed and changed the subject. 'Have you thought what all this means for you, pet?' she asked. 'I know no one but the family knows that you're married to Timothy, but if the newspapers find out about it they'll try to make something of it.'

'What do you mean? The marriage is over, you know that. This has nothing to do with my relationship to the Durkins.'

'The police might think it has. While I've been sitting here on my own it went through my mind, they might

446

think our Bob had another motive for murder, apart from the lockout.'

'What do you mean? Oh . . . ' Hannah put her hand up to her mouth in horror as she realised what her sister was saying. 'They wouldn't think that, Betty, no, no, they wouldn't.'

'I hope for our Bob's sake they don't, pet.'

Hannah walked to the window and stared out at the dark yard. Oh, God, she prayed, don't let them find out about me and Timothy, not before they discover who it was killed Daniel. Please, God, what would I do if Bob was convicted because of me?

'Mebbe I shouldn't have said anything, pet.' Betty bit her lip as she saw how her words had affected her sister. 'It's daft speculating, anyway. Like I said, only the family knows you two were wed and we're not going to say anything, are we?'

'There's Anthony Akers,' said Hannah tonelessly. 'There's Jane an' all. What if they go to Oxford and ask questions there?'

'Jane? Jane wouldn't say anything, of course she wouldn't, how could you think such a thing?'

'No, of course not,' Hannah answered. She drew the curtains against the dark and turned back to her sister. 'Well, as you say, it's daft speculating. There's more sense in starting supper, Tucker will be coming here when he's finished work, won't he? He'll be ready for something to eat.'

She went into the pantry, brought out potatoes and onions and began to peel and slice them for a dish of panhackelty – layers of potato, onion and strips of bacon, cooked in meat stock. It was a dish which, once prepared, could be left to itself in the oven. Bob loved his panhackelty, she thought sadly as she worked. And there hadn't been much opportunity to cook it for him since the stock of coal ran so low, most of the miners' coalhouses had been swept bare for months. But Betty had lit a fire with coal Tucker had brought down from their own house earlier in the day, as Nora complained of the cold after the storm. So now it was a good chance to use the already warm oven.

Tucker came in, bringing with him a copy of the *Evening Despatch*.

'Any news?' The sisters asked the question almost in unison as soon as he opened the door.

'Nothing much,' he answered. 'Mr Durkin's son has come home, he and Anthony Akers flew from Le Touquet to London, and then up to Durham with Lord Akers in his private aeroplane. It's marvellous what they can do nowadays, isn't it?'

Betty took the food out of the oven and began dishing it up. 'I suppose it is,' she said, dispiritedly. 'Hannah, should we call Mam or let her sleep?'

'What?' Hannah gazed at her but there was a faraway look in her eyes betraying her inattention.

'Mam, Hannah, should we get her up for supper or let her bide where she is?'

'Oh let her sleep, I think.'

Picking up the paper which Tucker had thrown on the table, Hannah gazed at the front page. There was a picture of Timothy with Lord Akers and Anthony in the background. Timothy's face looked impassive and, stare as she might, she couldn't read anything in his expression. His cheeks were more hollow than she remembered – was he eating properly? Absently, she rubbed her forefinger over the picture.

'It doesn't look like him,' she said.

Betty glanced quickly at Tucker, who raised his eyebrows. 'Newspaper photographs never do,' he remarked. 'Come and get your supper, pet, before it goes cold.' Obediently, Hannah put down the paper and sat at the table. Taking a forkful of potato and bacon, she put it in her mouth and chewed it, then another.

'Poor lad, it must be awful for him to have to rush home like that, his father dead an' all,' said Tucker. 'We've tended to forget about that what with worrying about Bob.'

Hannah put down her fork and glared at him. 'I didn't,' she said flatly. 'I didn't forget him at all, or how he must be feeling.'

Tucker looked embarrassed and suddenly showed an animated interest in his meal. 'This is nice, Betty, a nice surprise. I wasn't expecting anything cooked.'

'Hannah made it.'

The three lapsed into silence until they had finished their meal. Afterwards, Betty and Tucker went back to their own home.

'I have to be near the telephone in case there's any trouble at the pit,' Tucker explained. 'We'll be back first thing so you can go in and see to the papers. Or Betty will be if I can't.'

Hannah smiled at him gratefully. Tucker was such a tower of strength, what would they have done without him? She lay down on the settee when they had gone and pulled the blanket Nora had used earlier over her. It promised to be a long night.

'Howay, Hannah, wake up, pet, it's nearly half past five. Are you going in to the shop?'

Hannah woke with a start to see her mother standing over her, shaking her shoulder gently. She sat up dazedly and glanced at her watch, but she must have forgotten to wind it; it had stopped.

'What time did you say?' she asked Nora.

'Half past five. Look, it's plain enough on the clock.' Satisfied her daughter was awake, Nora turned to the range and picked up the kettle, shaking it to judge how much water it held. Going to the tap in the pantry, she put in more and placed the kettle on the gas ring.

'I'll have to go, the lads will be waiting for me,' said Hannah as she wound her watch.

'Are you not having a cup of tea first?'

'I'll get one there, Mam.' She took a comb out of her bag and dragged it through her hair, looking at Nora as she did so. 'You look better, Mam, did you sleep well?'

'I did,' replied Nora, 'and I am better, I feel more meself. I'm more hopeful an' all, things will come right, you'll see.'

'Course they will.' Hannah gave her mother a swift hug and went to the door. 'Look, I might be a bit late getting back. But Betty's coming down and Tucker as well if he can manage it.'

'Don't worry, I'll be all right now,' said Nora. 'Go on, you have your work to go to.'

Hannah was soon in Newgate Street and seeing to the newspapers for the delivery boys. After they had gone on their rounds, she lit the geyser and when the water was hot she washed her hair and took a bath. She lay in the steaming water, going over her plans for the morning. First of all, she was going to try to see Timothy. And after that, she was going to do something else. She picked up the soap and soaped herself while she tried to think what it was she was going to do next, but it was no use. She simply could not think of anything beyond going to see Timothy.

Chapter Thirty-One

Timothy was not able to sleep at all; his thoughts were whirling around in his head the whole night. Unable to forget the horror of his father's death, he kept going to his bedroom window and staring out at the hole in the drive, trying to make sense of it all. Just as he had been staring out of the first-floor window at the little van parked on the road the previous afternoon, or rather at the face of the woman who was sitting at the driving wheel. He had closed his eyes tightly and opened them again; she was still there and, yes, it was Hannah. The dull ache in his chest which had been there since she left Oxford expanded, rising up into his throat and threatening to choke him.

I'm a fool, he told himself savagely. She doesn't want me, she made that plain when she took the money from my father and ran. He had watched as the van pulled away from the house. Why had she not at least made the effort to come in and see him? She was still his wife, for God's sake! His chaotic thoughts veered endlessly from his father to her and back again to his father's sense-less death.

He thought about Bob, her brother, his father's mur-derer. Somehow he couldn't believe it, not of Bob, not Hannah's brother. They were too gentle a family al-together, surely it could not have been Bob? That he was a union man he knew, but what other evidence did the police have? The inspector at Auckland had seemed so sure, though.

'Bob Armstrong is a deputy, he's well used to explo-sives. And whoever broke into the powder shed knew what he was after, all right. He knew exactly how much paste he needed and where the detonators were kept and how to do it. I understand from the manager that it's a low-grade explosive and needs an enclosed space and someone who knows what he's doing to get it to blow a hole like the one in your drive, Mr Durkin. Oh yes, I think we have the right man.'

But Timothy wasn't so sure. After all, a lot of men would know how to cause such an explosion, he thought. The fact that Bob was active in the Miners' Federation didn't automatically mean he was a violent man, though some of the owners thought it did.

The night shadows were beginning to give way to a grey, misty dawn. Timothy pulled on his clothes and went down into the garden. There was still a policeman stationed at the entrance to the drive.

'Morning, sir,' he said as Timothy came up to him. 'A fine morning too.'

'It is,' said Timothy. 'Look, why don't you go into the kitchen? I'm sure Mrs Bates will find you a cup of tea. She's up, I heard her as I came through the hall.'

'I don't know, sir. My orders were to stay here, just in case there was any trouble,' said the policeman doubtfully.

'Oh, go on, no one will know. I'll stay here until you get back. I'm sure you could do with a cup of tea,' Timothy said persuasively. The officer nodded and headed for the back of the house.

Left to himself, Timothy walked to the edge of the hole in the drive. It was quite a sizeable hole, he thought, not for the first time. Leading away from it, the line could be seen where the wires had been uncovered by the police. Whoever did it must have been hiding behind the mock-orange bush over by the hedge. He crossed over the grass towards the bush, feeling the dew soaking through the thin soles of his house shoes. Surely there must be some sign of who had been hiding there?

The police must have been over the ground more than once, he told himself; it was stupid, really, expecting to find anything. Still, he searched the ground, looking at every blade of grass, every little patch of soil under the bushes. There was nothing to be seen. Timothy went as far as the boundary wall of the garden and turned and walked back, still staring at the ground. Nothing, there was nothing. Doggedly, Timothy went back over the same ground once again. He was standing by the boundary wall when the constable came back from the kitchen.

'Everything all right, sir?'

'Yes . . . yes, everything's fine, officer.' Timothy glanced up to see the policeman regarding him curiously. 'I was just looking at the garden,' he added lamely.

'It's all been checked, sir. You'd best go in now, your feet are wet through. Been a heavy dew overnight, sir. Thank you for keeping an eye out for me, sir.'

Timothy walked down by the boundary wall towards the house, feeling dispirited. His shoes were squelching, so instead of going in the front he decided to carry on round the side of the house to the back door. He was surprised to find his way blocked by a large black retriever dog, lying across the back entrance with something in his mouth, a tin of some sort. Mrs Bates was there, too, a bone in her hand.

'I didn't know you had a dog, Mrs Bates,' said Timothy, and she blushed.

'He belongs to next door, sir. I hope you don't mind me feeding him? He comes through the hole in the hedge yonder. He's company, like.'

'No, of course I don't mind, why should I?'

Mrs Bates relaxed. 'His name's Black Boy, you know, after the pit near Eldon. Come on, Black Boy, here's your bone. Shoo now, go home and take it with you.'

Dropping the tin, the dog got clumsily to his feet, his tail wagging slowly. He looked over at Timothy and evidently decided he was a friend, for his tail carried on moving from side to side. Licking Mrs Bates's hand in thanks, he gently took the bone from her and sat down again, slavering.

'I said go home, Black Boy,' said Mrs Bates.

The dog paused and looked up at her before rising once again. He tried to pick up the tin to take with him but only succeeded in dropping the bone; he tried again but dropped the tin. Mournfully, he regarded it.

'Come on, boy, I'll throw that over the hedge for you,' said Timothy and picked up the tin. It was an oblong box, much marked now with Black Boy's teeth. There was some lettering on the side – what was it? It looked like 'R.C.' though the short leg of the R was barely decipherable. Timothy turned it over in his hand. 'Winton Colliery' was stamped on the undersurface.

The tin had to have something to do with the explosion.

'Sorry, Black Boy,' he said to the dog. 'I'm afraid I need to keep this myself.'

'What is it, sir?' asked Mrs Bates, her face alive with curiosity. 'I noticed he had an old tin, but I thought he must have dug it up somewhere.'

'He very likely did, Mrs Bates,' said Timothy. 'As to what it is, that's something I mean to find out. Will you have a look at it for me, see the lettering on the tin?'

Mrs Bates took the tin in her hands and turned it over, examining it carefully 'I think that's an R,' she said after a moment. 'It's definitely a C, anyway. And something to do with the colliery, isn't it?'

'It is,' replied Timothy. 'Do you think you would remember it if you saw it again?'

'Oh yes, of course, sir. With those teeth marks on it an' all.'

'Thank you, Mrs Bates. I have to go out now, I'll just go up and change my shoes.'

'But what about breakfast? You can't go out with nothing on your stomach,' the housekeeper objected.

'Don't worry, I'll get something in town if I'm hungry.' Already on his way through the kitchen to the stairs, he called back to her over his shoulder.

Mrs Bates stared after him, mystified. But she wasn't really that interested in what Timothy was doing just now, with the weight of misery lying across her chest since her husband was killed in the car along with Mr Durkin. Sitting down at the kitchen table, she poured herself a cup of tea and spooned sugar into it, stirring the spoon round and round, hardly knowing she was doing it.

'Can you tell me anything about this tin, Mr Holmes?'

Mr Holmes, the overman who lived in the end house of Winton Colliery, blinked as he opened the door and saw young Mr Durkin standing there, holding out the battered, oblong tin. Behind him, the clock on the kitchen wall was just striking eight. Why, he hadn't even finished his breakfast! His braces were still dangling round his waist and his face unshaven. What was the young fellow doing, banging on his door at this time of a morning and then not even greeting him properly but rushing straight into stupid questions.

'Eh?' he said.

Timothy looked impatient for a moment, then he remembered his manners and began again. 'Good morning, Mr Holmes,' he said. 'I wonder if I could come in for a minute.'

Mr Holmes stood back in automatic courtesy and at the same time fumbled for his braces and pulled them over his shoulders. Too late now to do anything about his bristles or his lack of a collar.

'Aye, lad, of course, come in and have a bite of breakfast.'

'Thank you, Mr Holmes, very kind of you. But I won't have anything to eat, just a cup of tea if that's all right.'

'Sit yourself down and I'll get one for you. Mother's having a lie-in the day. She's not been feeling over grand lately.'

'Oh, I'm sorry to hear that,' said Timothy. He cradled the tin in one hand and accepted tea in a china cup which Mr Holmes took out of a glass-fronted press. He contained his impatience until the older man had sat down himself and picked up the pint pot which held his own tea.

'Now then, lad – Mr Durkin, I mean, no disrespect, like. What is it you're after?'

Timothy held out the tin. 'Do you know what this is, Mr Holmes? It's a bit battered, I know, a dog's had hold of it.'

Mr Holmes took the tin but needed only a cursory glance to recognise it for what it was. 'Why, it's a powder tin from the colliery,' he said positively. 'Where did you find it? It's the sort the men have to keep the black powder in in the pit. They have their own, you know, the initials is on them. See here, I can't read it properly, what do you make of it?'

'I think it says R.C.,' said Timothy.

'Oh aye, I think you're right. Now who could that be? There's Robert Clary, but I doubt it would be his, he's too careful, he wouldn't lose his tin. An' then there's Ralph Cornish –'

'Ralph Cornish?'

Timothy remembered Ralph Cornish, everybody knew the Cornish family, they were notorious for miles around. Mr Holmes was nodding his head.

'Where did you say it was?'

'I didn't but as a matter of fact, I found it in the garden at home. I reckon whoever set the bomb must have dropped it'

'I wouldn't put nowt past that Ralph Cornish, him nor his dad. So-called dad, like, he was born six months after his mother came back from service at Grizedale Hall. Funny that, he's more like Wesley Cornish than the rest of the brood. But I say, I've just tumbled, if we can prove that tin belongs to Ralph Cornish and it was found in your garden, that means Bob Armstrong –' Mr Holmes stopped abruptly and his eyes gleamed.

'Exactly, Mr Holmes. Now I'm going to see this Ralph Cornish and confront him with it.'

Mr Holmes jumped to his feet and reached for his jacket, which was hanging on the back of the chair. 'Wait on, lad,' he said, his voice full of determination. 'I'm coming with you. You'll likely need somebody to back you up at that place.'

Filthy and ragged curtains were still drawn across the grimy windows of the Cornish cottage when the two men arrived in Old Winton village. If anyone was in they were either drunk or dead, for no matter how hard Timothy banged on the door, no one came to answer. Frustrated, he stepped back and glared at the house.

'They'll be in there all right,' Mr Holmes observed grimly. Cupping his mouth in his hand, he yelled up at the front bedroom window, the bellow issuing from his mouth astonishingly loud. 'Wake up, you lot in there! Ralph Cornish! Wesley! You're wanted down here.'

A couple of doors down the street, the landlord came out of the Pit Laddie and strolled over to them. Two or three other cottage doors opened and curious neighbours began to gather.

'They'll still be pallatic drunk, them two,' the landlord said grimly. 'The lasses now, they went off on the early bus for Bishop Auckland, I saw them get on it. I don't know about Lancelot, though. I used to think he was a canny lad but he's getting just like his dad an' all.'

'Have you seen Ralph lately?' asked Timothy.

'I have that,' said the landlord. 'I had him to throw out of the bar last night, causing a ruckus, he was, him and Wesley. Shouting something about getting the old bastard at last, no other bugger had the guts to do it.' He glanced quickly at Timothy. 'Begging your pardon, sir.'

'Was he now?' said Timothy, pursing his lips.

'I was going to mention it to the polis when he comes round this morning. I would have sent for him last night but I thought mebbe Ralph was just bragging in his cups.'

Behind them, the door of the Cornish cottage was pulled open at last.

'What's all this bloody noise about?'

Timothy whirled to face Ralph and almost gagged at the blast of fetid air which came out of the open door of the cottage. Ralph himself smelled strongly of stale sweat and vomit, traces of which could be seen down the front of his clothes. When he saw Timothy he grinned and, putting a hand inside his shirt, lazily scratched himself.

'Well, look at the young gaffer,' he drawled. Clearing his throat noisily, he spat at Timothy's feet.

Timothy saw red. Stepping forwards he lunged for Ralph's throat.

'Leave my lad alone!' Wesley yelled and flung himself into the fray, but he was easily felled by a blow from Mr Holmes. Howling, he tried to get to his feet, but the overman promptly sat on him. Murmurs of appreciation came from the couple of locked-out miners and their wives who were looking on.

'Gan on there, Holmsey,' one called. 'It's time the old bully-boy got what's coming to him. Land him one for me!'

Ralph's fists were flailing wildly at Timothy but to no avail, Timothy easily evaded them and knocked him to the dirt alongside his father. In doing so, the powder tin fell out of his pocket and one of the miners picked it up.

'Hey, look 'ere,' he said, showing it to his fellows. 'What's this?'

Before anyone could answer him, the village policeman arrived. Whether someone had called him or he had seen the scuffle from his window, Timothy didn't know.

'Righto, righto, now, break it up. I'll have no fighting 'ere!' he said importantly. Then he noticed Timothy. 'Oh, it's you, sir, is it? I didn't see you there. What's this all about?' As he spoke he was hauling Ralph to his feet and securing his hands behind his back with handcuffs.

'What are you doing?' yelled Ralph. 'I didn't do nothing, I was minding my own business when he set on me! Isn't that right, lads?' he appealed to the bystanders but no one backed him up. He turned vicious. 'By, it's one law for the rich and one for the bloody poor, that's what it is!' His eyes grew wilder as the policeman began to drag him along the street to the police station, and he began to scream out curses at the crowd. 'I'll make you pay, see if I don't! You canna back your own against a bloody gaffer – cowards, the lot of ye! None of you would have the guts to get rid of the old bastard, it took a real man to do that! An' I'll get the better of the young 'un an' all, see if I don't!'

His voice faded as he was hustled into the station and after a few minutes the policeman reappeared and came back to them.

'Right, then, I'll take the old 'un,' he said calmly. Mr Holmes rose from his sitting position on Wesley's chest.

'You'll likely have to fumigate the cells after you've had them two in,' he commented, and the policeman grimaced with distaste as the full odour of Wesley's body reached his nostrils.

'Aye, well, it won't be the first time I've had it to do after this lot,' he remarked. 'Let's hope it's the last, that's all.' He looked round at Timothy and Mr Holmes. 'I dare say the inspector will be wanting a word with you about this.'

'Certainly, officer. I'll just go home and change first. I'll come back for you and run you in if you like, Mr Holmes.'

'Aye, well, I'd best go back to Winton Colliery and let the missus know what's happening, then,' said the overman.

Timothy nodded and was about to go for his car when he remembered the powder tin. 'Oh, I forgot,' he said to the policeman. 'I think your inspector will be interested in that tin, it's evidence. You'd better take it for him. I'll explain when I get there, tell him.'

Chapter Thirty-Two

Hannah parked the van at the bottom of Gib Chare and walked up the hill to the Durkin house. The morning was much fresher than the previous day; the rain had cooled the air besides washing away the dust. She wore a long white cardigan over her simply cut white dress. Her shoes were low-heeled, brown with a bar over her instep and fastened with a button, and she carried a brown handbag to match. She had decided against wearing a hat, simply combing out her bob and clipping it back at the side with a brown and white clip. She had put a lot of thought into what she should wear to meet Timothy, changing her mind more than once before finally deciding. Should I have worn a more sombre dress? she wondered now. But no, Timothy had liked her dressed in white.

Approaching the gate which still leaned drunkenly away from its post, her heart began to thud uncontrollably and her breath quickened.

'Take a hold of yourself!' she muttered, standing still and forcing herself to take great mouthfuls of air into her lungs, holding it for a few seconds before releasing it. Slowly her heartbeat quietened and she resumed walking. The policeman standing guard on the gate had been watching her approach and he stepped forwards as she made to turn into the drive.

'Sorry, miss,' he said. 'No one is to go in.'

Hannah gazed at him levelly. 'I am a relative,' she said firmly. 'I wish to see Mr Timothy Durkin, is he at home?'

'I'm sorry, miss, I was told no one was to be allowed in, no one at all.'

'But I told you, I am a relative! Now, if Mr Timothy Durkin is at home I wish to see him,' she snapped imperiously in the best accent she could manage.

'He's not at home, miss,' he answered uncomfortably. 'But you understand, I couldn't let you in anyway, this is a very bad time. My orders are –'

'Constable, let her through, it's all right.'

Both Hannah and the policeman turned in the direction of the aristocratic voice, the policeman jumping to attention. Anthony Akers was standing before the open front door, his face grim.

'Yes, sir.'

Hannah walked up the edge of the drive, avoiding the shallow hole in the middle, trying not to look at it. 'Hallo, Anthony,' she said, and he nodded gravely.

'Come in. We can talk in here.' He indicated a door to the side of the hall and she went into a room furnished as a sitting room.

'Do sit down,' he said formally and as she sat, he took the chair opposite and leaned forwards with his elbows on his knees and his hands clasped together. 'This is a bad business, a very bad business.'

'My brother had nothing to do with it, Anthony, you must believe me. He was at a meeting, he couldn't have done it.'

Anthony gazed at her. 'I understand he ran from the police, though,' he said.

'Only because there have been trumped-up charges against the Miners' Federation men. You must know a lot of innocent men have been imprisoned.'

Anthony jumped to his feet and walked to the window. 'Let's not go into that, Hannah. Communists have to be dealt with harshly, we want no revolution here,' he said, his voice cold and remote.

'My brother is not a communist'

Anthony shrugged his shoulders and Hannah looked down at her hands, twisting them on her lap, trying to summon up the courage to ask after Timothy. She felt she was choking, and swallowed hard. After a moment she gained control of her voice enough to put the question, the all-important question.

'Is Timothy here?'

Anthony answered without turning round. 'No. He's gone with my father to examine new evidence the police have about the murder.'

'How is he?' The anticlimax was almost unbearable for her.

Anthony whirled abruptly and stalked up to her, stopping only a yard away with his hands clasped behind his neck. Suddenly he looked very much like his father; the same imperious lift to his chin, the same arrogant gaze.

'How do you expect him to be? Don't you know what you have done to him? These last few months, since you walked out on him, he has been in a terrible state. How he got through his finals I'll never know. Timothy is my friend, he has been my friend ever since we went up to Oxford, but I tell you, he's not the man he was, not by any manner of means. It's been like trailing a nobody around after me. No sense of humour, no bright ideas, no nothing. Just a face like a wet week, he had no interest in anything. And then this had to happen. How do you think he is?'

'I didn't leave him, he sent me away! He sent his father to tell me he was finished with me, he couldn't even tell me to my face.'

Anthony stared at her. 'Well, it's easy enough to blame his father now, isn't it? Now Daniel Durkin can't answer back, can he? He was my father's agent and a damn good one at that. Come on, Hannah, you'd better go. I think you've said enough.'

'I'm not going, I want to see Timothy. I don't care what you think about me, I'm telling the truth. And our Bob is telling the truth an' all, he is, I tell you,' she cried, slipping back into the local idiom. She hung on to the arms of the chair as though she thought Anthony might eject her physically, and gazed up at him in desperation.

He stared back at her and gradually his expression softened and he sat down abruptly. 'I don't know, Hannah, maybe I shouldn't have said what I did. I have to admit I was against Timothy marrying you in the first place, but when he did he seemed so happy. I always thought you were a nice girl, I couldn't believe it at first when he told me you'd taken the money and run.'

'I thought I was a drag on him, Daniel said I was. He said Timothy would never get a position worthy of him while he was married to me, a pitman's daughter. I understood that he would lose his inheritance if he stayed with me, even that from his mother. And so he decided to send me away. That's what I was told. You can believe me or not.'

Anthony's eyes opened wide and he whistled soundlessly. 'His father said that?' he asked. 'Oh, surely you must have misunderstood.'

'Well, I don't think so, that's the gist of what he said.'

They sat a few minutes in silence. Suddenly the telephone bell rang in the hall, making them both look up expectantly. Hannah waited for him to answer it but it didn't seem to occur to him. After a moment it rang again, stopping abruptly as a girl's voice answered it. Of course, she thought, Anthony was used to having telephones answered for him. There was a soft knock at the door.

'Come!' called Anthony.

'A telephone call for you, Mr Anthony,' said the girl's voice.

He made his excuses and went out into the hall. Hannah rose to her feet and walked to the window, gazing out over the fields towards the village and winding gear of Winton Colliery. What was happening there? she fretted. She should have tried to engage a solicitor for Bob before she came here, that was what she should have done. But was the Miners' Federation doing that? Perhaps they were; surely they had enough money left in the funds to provide legal aid for their own officials, especially those wrongly accused of a crime.

Hannah felt very tired and confused and guilty. She had given way to her impulse to see Timothy and attempt to put things right with him, when her first priority should have been her brother. When Anthony came back she would tell him she had changed her mind, she wouldn't wait to see Timothy, not now. Now she had to see if Tucker was home and talk to him about hiring a lawyer for Bob.

'That was my father,' said Anthony, coming back into the room and interrupting her thoughts. 'He wants me to go down to the police station in Bishop Auckland.' He paused and bit his lip. 'He says further evidence has come to light, the police are ready to prefer charges. He wants me to be there to give my support to Timothy if he needs it. We don't know how the miners will take it.'

'Oh! Oh, I must go home, I must find Tucker,' she cried and ran past him into the hall and out by the front door.

'Hannah! Come back, it's not . . . ' But Hannah was gone, racing over the fields towards Winton, forgetting all about the van parked in the road. Anthony reached the front door just in time to see her disappearing behind the hedge. He hesitated; should he go after her? But his father had said it was imperative he come immediately. Sighing, he went back inside.

'Was there some news, sir?'

Mrs Bates was standing by the door which led to the kitchen, her face wan and pale. She had lost her husband in the explosion, he reminded himself, of course she should be told the news. She had a right.

'Yes, Mrs Bates, I'm glad to say the police have caught the men who murdered your husband and Mr Durkin.'

'Yes, sir, but I believe they caught him yesterday, sir,' she said. 'Do you mean they now have the evidence to secure a conviction?'

'They have; my father says the man has actually confessed. But it's not the man they took into custody yesterday, Mrs Bates. No, it's someone else entirely, in fact, there are two of them, father and son, so I was told. Now I'm going to the police station. They are sending an extra policeman out to guard the house, so please don't worry about anything.'

Chapter Thirty-Three

Hannah burst into the kitchen, flinging the door open so violently it swung on its hinges. 'Have you heard?' she cried.

Betty and her mother were standing by the dresser, Betty with her arms around Nora's shoulders. Nora was sobbing as though her heart would break and as Betty was comforting her, neither answered Hannah at first.

So they have heard the bad news, she thought wearily. The stitch in her side, which had been nagging at her for the last half-mile, spread across her chest and she bent over double, panting for breath. She could hear muffled sounds of distress from her mother and Betty. What could she say to them to give them hope? Tucker, I need to speak to Tucker, she thought, we need to see a lawyer. The stitch eased a little and she straightened up.

Mam and Betty were watching her, and though there were still signs of tears on Nora's face, they were laughing, actually laughing. Had they gone mad?

'Haven't you heard the news?' she demanded.

'Yes, isn't it grand? Tucker just came in and told us,' said Betty. 'He's been down to the police station and knows all about it.' She glanced round for her husband. 'Where's he gone? Oh, there you are. Come and tell Hannah all about it, she looks a bit flummoxed.'

Tucker came out of the pantry carrying the kettle he had been filling. He looked pensive but when he saw the girls were watching him, he too grinned.

'I'll just put the kettle on. If a man wants a cup of tea and a bite round here, he has to get it himself.'

A wild hope was stirring in Hannah; perhaps Anthony had got it wrong, perhaps Bob hadn't been charged. 'Tell me!' she demanded. 'Pull yourselves together and tell me what's happened. I think I must have it wrong, I thought it was bad news.'

'Eeh, no, it's not. I'm sorry, pet,' said Nora, 'we thought you would know. It's our Bob, he's coming home. I told you he couldn't have done it, didn't I? I knew all along everything would be all right.'

Betty caught Hannah's eye and they burst out laughing and Nora joined in. Bob was coming home, he wasn't going to be charged with murder. Hannah repeated it to herself; after all the worry it wouldn't sink in properly.

'Tell me, Tucker,' she repeated.

'Yes, of course I will, pet.' Tucker sobered and his tone took on a hard note. 'We might have known who actually did it. I mean, who is it causes all the trouble round here?'

Wesley Cornish, thought Hannah. She sat down on a chair by the table and leaned on it with one arm. Oh, dear God, how awful for Tucker! Even though there was nothing between them now and Wesley had never been a true father to him, hadn't he brought enough shame on Tucker without this?

'How did they find out?' she asked.

'Well, I can see I don't have to spell out the name,' said Tucker bitterly. 'They found out easily enough. If they hadn't come looking for Bob soon after it happened and if Bob hadn't tried to get away, they would have found out sooner.' Tucker sighed and Betty put a sympathetic hand on his shoulder.

'I'm sorry I laughed, lad,' she whispered. 'It was the relief, you know, I didn't think.' He patted her hand and held it there for a moment. 'No, I know, it's all right, Wesley's nothing to me,' he reassured her before turning back to Hannah.

'Yes, it was Wesley Cornish and Ralph, they planned it between them, no one else was in on it, they've said so. In fact, I heard it on the quiet from the manager that they were actually boasting about getting rid of the agent themselves and landing the blame on Bob. "Nobody else had the guts to do it," Ralph told the landlord in the Pit Laddie last night. But it was Timothy Durkin who went looking for them, he'd found something belonging to Ralph in the garden. There was a fight in the old village about it, Timothy waded into them.' He watched Hannah carefully and when she went white he led her to the settee.

'Sit down, lass, it's all over now,' he said.

'He's all right? He's not hurt?' Hannah remembered all the bullying and fighting the Cornish men had been involved in over the years; they were hard men. She began to tremble.

'Eeh, lass, of course he's all right,' Nora put in quickly. 'He made short work of that Ralph, I'm telling you. By, I'll never forget what he's done for us.'

Nor me, nor me, thought Hannah and her heart yearned for Timothy. She felt utterly confused.

The kettle began to sing and Nora moved automatically to set the table. 'There's nothing much in the house to eat,' she said. 'I've not thought of getting any messages in.'

'I'll go to the corner shop,' suggested Hannah, standing up. She was anxious to get a few minutes on her own, she had to straighten out her thoughts. 'We'll just have to have sandwiches, that's all. What do you fancy, corned beef or sardines?' She heard herself saying the mundane words but she felt detached from them somehow. She walked out of the house and up the street to the corner, not seeing anything about her at all, not even hearing when a neighbour said how glad he was Bob had been cleared. The neighbour stared after her until she turned the corner and then went in to his wife.

'That Armstrong lass is suffering from shock,' he commented to her.

Hannah was remembering what Anthony had said about Timothy's bitterness towards her. Maybe he was finished with her altogether, she thought dismally as she picked up a tin of corned beef and one of sardines for good measure. Could she bear to return to the house on Durham Road and try to see him again? What would she do if he refused to see her? No, no, she couldn't bear that to happen, she couldn't. If Timothy did want to see her he would seek her out, wouldn't he? And if he didn't come, well, then . . . She didn't want to think about how she would feel if he didn't come. But he had cared enough to find out the true murderers and clear Bob's name, hadn't he? Had he done it for her? Or was it just a coincidence that the man he cleared was her brother? During the afternoon, one person after another came in to congratulate the family on the news of Bob's innocence. Mr Holmes and his wife came in about three o'clock.

'Bear up, Nora, it won't be long before the lad's home,' said Mr Holmes. 'I'm right glad an' all, it makes you think there's some justice in the world, doesn't it?'

'They're still keeping him, though, aren't they?' said Nora. 'I can't understand why, not now, he's done nothing. Why don't they let him come home?'

'He'll come, you'll see. It'll just be the formalities,' said Tucker.

'Aye, well, we all knew he hadn't done it,' said Mr Holmes. 'That's why the lads were up in arms, they were all for marching to Durham and setting him free themselves. But it's quiet now. I was talking to Tommy Hutchinson a minute or two ago, he was getting off the bus from Auckland. He said the crowd outside the police station this morning had dispersed. I could see myself when I went in with young Mr Durkin they were pretty angry, all sorts of rumours were going round. But then Tucker came out and told them Bob was to be let go free, it was Wesley and Ralph Cornish that blew up Durkin's car. I tried to tell them myself but they were not in the mood to listen to me. They listened to Tucker, though, and Tucker told the lads to go home, Bob would be released. So that's what happened, they all came away soon after I left. By, Nora, Mr Timothy stood up to Ralph Cornish all right, he did well for your Bob.'

'I wonder why they did kill Mr Durkin. After all, Wesley's not even active in the union,' Nora mused aloud.

'Brooding about Lancelot getting put in gaol, I should think,' said Mrs Holmes. She tossed her head. 'By,

I always said those Cornishes were a disgrace to the community.'

'Whisht, woman!' said her husband and she blushed.

'Eeh, I didn't mean you, Tucker, you know I didn't.'

'No. Don't worry, Mrs Holmes, I know,' he answered.

Hannah walked up to Durham Road after tea to collect her van. At least, that was the reason she told herself she was going. After all, she needed it and she couldn't leave it on the main road for long. But she knew that was partly an excuse, she really wanted to see Timothy. She couldn't bear to think of him only a mile or two away and not seeing him. She had forgotten all about her resolve to wait and see if he sought her out.

A workman was filling up the hole in the drive when she arrived.

'Now then, Miss Armstrong,' he greeted her and she looked up in surprise. Her head was so full of Timothy, she hadn't realised she knew him. It was the colliery mason from Winton. Of course, this would be a company house, she thought. Timothy would have to leave it in due time to make way for the new agent. It was a strange thing, almost equating him with the families of pitmen who had to leave their houses when their man was killed, or died naturally.

'I was pleased to hear the good news about Bob.' The mason leaned on his shovel and pushed his cap on to the back of his head, smiling. 'Has he got home yet?'

'Not yet, but he will,' she replied. Nodding, she passed on up the drive and knocked on the front door, half expecting to see Anthony. Instead, it was the maid, Mary, who opened it.

'May I see Mr Timothy?' she asked.

'Can I take your name, miss?'

'Just say it's Hannah. He'll see me, I think.' Hannah stepped firmly into the hall, though Mary looked uncertain. The house was very quiet; of course, it was a house of mourning.

'Wait here, please, miss.'

Hannah waited in the silence, and from nowhere there flashed into her mind a memory of years ago, when she was a child and had come here with the chapel choir, carol singing. She remembered how she had gazed around in wonder at the furnishings, which had seemed opulent to her eyes. And she remembered the tall young boy who had gazed at her as though she was a real person, not a thing, as his father had done that day in the pit yard. And he had listened attentively when she sang and even joined in one of the carols. 'Still the Night', was it? She could almost see him now, in the doorway of the sitting room, the room she had sat in only that morning.

'Hannah.'

He was at the top of the stairs looking down at her and she tried to read his expression but his face was in shadow and she couldn't see it properly.

'Hallo, Timothy,' she said and he walked down the stairs, not rushing but taking each step deliberately. And then he was there beside her, looking down at her, and she still couldn't see what he was thinking.

'Come into the drawing room,' he said quietly, his voice neutral, and led her into the same room she had been in earlier. Of course it was a drawing room, she thought abstractedly, what else would it be? She walked in and sat in the chair he indicated.

'How are you, Timothy?' she asked politely. 'I was very sorry to hear about your father.' For all the world as though she were paying a courtesy visit on someone in the village who had been bereaved.

'Were you?'

She glanced up at him and away again. 'Yes, of course,' she said. 'And I am so grateful for what you did for Bob.' She wished he would sit down, she wished he would put out his hand and touch her, say something human. But he merely nodded. His hands were clenched at his side; she gazed at his right hand, it was clenched so tightly the knuckles were white. He's just lost his father, she thought and remembered how she had felt when Jake died. A wave of sympathy washed over her; poor Timothy, poor lad! Almost without thinking she put out a hand and touched the white knuckles with her finger-tips. He jumped back violently as though her touch had burned him.

481

'Don't do that!'

Hannah pulled her hand back into her lap, clasping it tightly with the other. He couldn't bear to feel my touch, she thought miserably.

'Why have you come here? And don't say it was to offer your commiserations for I won't believe you.'

'I . . . I wanted to see you, thank you for what you did for Bob and offer my sympathy for your father . . . '

Her words trailed off as she realised how ridiculous they sounded. I'm a fool, she thought, I shouldn't have come. I should get up and go, say I made a mistake, I shouldn't have come. She rose to her feet and moved towards the door and still he didn't speak. When she got there, she turned to face him.

'Alf said you wanted a divorce. Do you?'

Timothy shrugged. 'Do you?'

It was like walking on eggshells, thought Hannah and reached for the door handle. With it in her hand, she paused. If she went out now, she would never have the courage to come back. And she had to hear him say it himself.

'If you don't want me any more I will divorce you. Or you can divorce me, I don't know how these things work. But you just have to say so, Timothy.'

'Hannah, don't go yet. I'm sorry I was so abrupt, I can't seem to say the right things.'

She whirled to face him, hope flaring for a brief instant. He took a step towards her and stopped. 'This isn't the time to talk about anything. There's the inquest and the funeral and a thousand other things to see to. Later perhaps, but not now. Let's not rush into anything, we learned our lesson last time,' he went on.

'No, it isn't. You're right,' she replied. Of course this wasn't the time to discuss divorce; she squirmed at her own insensitivity. 'I'll go.'

Timothy walked with her to the door. 'I'll be in touch,' he said.

She walked to the van, not even noticing the mason filling up the hole. Well, she thought. I knew he didn't want me before I went, so nothing has changed. Taking out the starting handle, she started the engine and drove into the town, up Gib Chare and into Newgate Street and the shop. On a sheet of foolscap, she wrote out a notice and stuck it in the window.

Open for business, it read. *We apologise for any inconvenience to our customers while the shop was closed. The closure was unavoidable, due to pressing family business.*

Then she went inside and stood behind the counter, ready to serve the men who would be coming on the train from Shildon wagon works.

Hannah was standing on a stool, dusting the top shelf in the shop, when the bell rang. It was September and as the door opened, it let in a cold draught which ruffled the

483

papers on the counter and turned over the cover of the *Beano* on the shelf nearest the door.

'I won't be a minute,' she said without turning round, 'there's just this last bit to finish. Close the door, will you? There, I'm finished.' Jumping down from the chair, she went behind the counter. 'What can I do for you?' she asked and looked up.

It was Timothy.

'That depends on you,' he said.

Hannah stared at him dumbly. His face was pale and tired-looking and the blue of his eyes seemed deeper, almost a navy blue, and set in dark shadows. He has come to see about the divorce, she thought. Well, she had known he would, now that the funeral was over and a new agent was installed in the house on Durham Road. She'd read all about it in the *Auckland Chronicle* and *Northern Echo,* and she had been expecting him to come. But even so, it still came as a shock and her heart began thudding against her ribs. She couldn't speak, all her being was concentrated on making herself act normally and not throwing herself at him and begging him to take her back.

'Can we go somewhere we can talk?' he asked, his voice neutral.

'What? Oh, yes.'

She looked at her watch; it was almost closing time. 'I'll just shut the shop,' she replied. 'We can go into the sitting room.' As she walked to the door and locked it and turned the notice in the window to CLOSED, Hannah was intensely aware of him watching her, and her hands trembled. She didn't look at him, she dared not, for she still felt unsure of her self-control. Timothy held open the door to the living room for her and she was very careful not to brush against him as she passed.

'Would you like a cup of tea?' she found herself asking.

He shook his head impatiently.

'You've come to see about the divorce?'

There, she'd said it. Well, it was over now, all she could do was try to hold on to her dignity.

'No. Well, not exactly.'

Abruptly, Hannah sat down on the settee. Timothy hesitated a moment, then turned the armchair towards her and sat in that. He leaned forwards so that he was barely a foot from her and clasped his hands together. She gazed at his hands, so clean and well cared for, not at all like her brothers' hands. She thought of the feel of Timothy's hands on her body and looked quickly away. She wasn't hearing him correctly, she decided, she'd misunderstood, that was it.

'Sorry, what did you say?'

'I . . . oh, Hannah, what did my father tell you? Anthony told me something of it, but how could you go off without a word like that?'

485

'I had to. He said I would ruin your future; he said when it came to a choice between your inheritance and me, I came a bad second.'

'And you believed him?'

Timothy's voice rose in anger and he jumped to his feet and caught hold of her by the shoulders, pulling her up too. She looked up at him, her eyes wide, feeling his fingers digging into her flesh, hurting.

'I didn't, not at first, but then he repeated that your life would be ruined if I stayed. And I thought how angry you were when I went to hear Mr Cook at the Corn Exchange, how you didn't understand how I felt when the students tried to humiliate him. You were like a stranger. All that secrecy about our marriage an' all, I didn't understand that, I thought you were ashamed of me.' Hannah bit her lip, trying not to cry. 'I wanted to see you, I wanted you to tell me to my face that you didn't want me. But he said . . . he said . . . ' Her head dropped and she found herself staring at the lapels of his linen jacket.

'Hannah, look at me.'

His fingers relaxed their hold on her shoulders and he spoke quietly and calmly. He drew her close, so close that her head went back automatically. He bent his head to hers and his arms tightened as he lifted her off her feet and sat down on the settee with her on his lap. At least, that was the position she found herself in when he moved his lips from hers. Her body began to clamour for him, insistently,

486

her mouth was full of the taste of him, all she could see or smell was him for she had been denied him too long.

'Oh, Hannah, I've missed you so much,' he whispered thickly and the surge of her body's responses rose high and overwhelmed them both. They forgot about explanations for a while, they didn't matter, all that mattered was that they loved and the sensuous delight they took in their love.

Some time later he bought fish and chips from the shop down the street and they ate them in the yard in the September twilight, shielded from the eyes of neighbours by the high stone walls.

'I needed to keep our marriage quiet, Hannah,' he said, pausing in the middle of his meal and gazing at her soberly.

'Shush,' said Hannah, 'it's over now.'

'But you have to know. I couldn't let Father spoil it for us, I knew he would if he found out. And when he did, I just wasn't prepared for the way he went about separating us. I shouldn't have believed him, I'm sorry.'

'Oh, love, can't we forget about it now?'

Hannah moved round the table and bent her head to his. The meal was left unfinished as their need to make love again became so imperative that they forgot their hunger and hurried upstairs and fell on the bed clasped in each other's arms.

*

Insistent banging on the shop door woke Hannah. Carefully, so as not to wake him, she moved from under Timothy's arm and picked up her watch from the table by the bed. Six o'clock. She looked dreamily at Timothy's sleeping face on the pillow, closed her eyes tight and opened them again. He was still there, though she couldn't rid herself of the feeling of unreality. Tentatively, she touched his cheek with the tip of her finger and he moved a little.

'Hannah?'

The way her name was bawled out made her jump. It was Harry calling up to the bedroom window. She'd better let him in, she thought lazily. Slipping out of bed, she pulled on the nightgown she had discarded some time the night before and covered it with her kimono before going downstairs to let her brother in.

'By, our Hannah, I don't know what's the matter with you,' Harry grumbled as he picked up a bundle of papers and brought them into the shop. 'We're going to be late now and I wanted to go down the dam head with Dave and Billy for a swim after. It's a good job they aren't here yet an' all, when you haven't got their bags ready for them.'

'Well, you can still go for a swim, can't you?' she pointed out. 'The school's still on holiday, isn't it? Come on, we'll soon have the papers ready if you give me a hand.'

Harry looked at her disapprovingly. 'Are you not going to comb your hair even? You're not going to serve in the shop without getting dressed properly, are you?'

'I will soon get dressed, in a minute, after we've got the papers ready,' she replied, pushing her hair back with her fingers.

'Well, you'd better hurry up –' Harry broke off and his mouth fell open as Timothy appeared in the doorway from the back shop, his feet bare and his hair even more tousled than Hannah's. Hannah forgot her brother as Timothy slid his arms around her waist and drew her to him.

'Good morning, my love,' he murmured and kissed her earlobe, and Hannah's eyes closed as she leaned against him.

'Our Hannah! I'll tell me mam of you carrying on an' in the shop an' all. Why, man, anybody could come in and see you!'

Hannah opened her eyes and there was Harry, his hands on his hips and his chin thrust forward. His frown was that of an outraged father.

'Has that man been here all night?' he demanded. ''Cos if he has, I'm telling you, me mam'll have a fit!'

Chapter Thirty-Four

'Lord Akers has offered me a position,' said Timothy. He placed the letter he had been reading back in its envelope and gazed at Hannah across the breakfast table, concerned how she would take the news.

'Not here, not in charge over Winton –' she began, panicking, but he interrupted her quickly.

'No, not here, in the head office in Durham. There's a period of training, of course, and some of that will be in the field but it will be north of here. His estates cover a large area, as you know.'

Hannah glanced down at the piece of toast in her hand and placed it carefully back on her plate. She looked about the small room; they had been so happy here. Oh, she had known that Timothy would not be content to live in the cramped accommodation behind the shop for ever, how could he be? It was just not what he was used to. But these last few weeks it had been their own private heaven, a refuge from the sadness and despair which pervaded the very air in Winton Colliery and spilled over into the town. And how could she leave the family now, just as the miners were defeated? She shivered slightly, and Timothy noticed immediately.

'Are you cold, my love? I'll build the fire up, these November days can be so dark and damp and the cold so penetrating. I don't want you catching a cold.' He half rose in his chair but she shook her head.

'No, I'm all right, not cold at all, just sad. I don't know why. Well, I do really, I was thinking how happy we've been here.

And about my mother and Bob and the boys, it will be hard to leave them. How are they going to manage?'

'We're only going to Durham, love,' he pointed out. 'And they have Tucker and Betty, and Bob is a grown man, after all. Oh, I've been happy here too, but we have to move on.'

Hannah looked into his eyes, so full of concern and understanding. 'I am a fool, aren't I?' she said. 'I can visit Winton from Durham easily, it's only half an hour's drive. But this shop will always be special to me, it's hard for me to let go.'

'It doesn't have to be sold,' said Timothy. 'Why can't Bob run it? Didn't you say he's always hankered after a little business?'

'But that was when he was a boy. Bob's a miner, not a shopkeeper!'

'Oh, Hannah, my love, you know as well as I do it will be a miracle if he ever gets work in the mines again. None of the union men will be taken on, not while any miner who took no active part in the strike is out of work. The Owners' Association are agreed on that.'

'It was a lockout, not a strike,' she reminded him flatly.

'Sorry, I meant lockout,' Timothy said quickly. He looked uneasy. Usually he was very careful not to comment on the troubles of the last few months for Hannah felt so deeply about them. Naturally so, he mused, remembering the shock and horror he had felt when he first saw for himself the extent of the poverty and distress in Winton. And Winton was just one of many pit villages in the same position.

The long months of the stoppage had devastated them and he could hardly believe it was the same world as the one he and his friends inhabited. It was as though the coalfield had taken a step back in time to the early nineteenth century and the social conditions of the Industrial Revolution. Still, the miners were back at work now and surely conditions would improve as the coal trade picked up. And it would pick up, he was certain.

Hannah had a faraway look in her eyes as she thought of her brother and how he had looked when he was released from Durham gaol. He had been imprisoned for only a few days but those days had changed him so much. He seemed to have lost his belief that the men would win in the end because their cause was just. He was quieter and began staying away from the meetings of the Miners' Federation; instead he spent hours sitting in the kitchen and staring into the cold grate. And when the men capitulated and went back to work, forced at last to accept the conditions laid down by the owners, he did not even comment on it. He put on his pit clothes and went with the rest to the colliery office, only to be turned away and told there was no work for him.

Timothy came round the table and lifted Hannah into his arms, holding her close. 'Please, my love, don't look so sad. If it's going to make you unhappy, I won't take the position.'

Hannah snuggled into his shoulder, feeling the steady beat of his heart against hers. The clean scent of his skin filled her nostrils and the now familiar feelings of love and contentment rose in her and overwhelmed her, cutting out everything else from her thoughts and mind. She put up a hand and felt the crisp hair on the back of his neck, and his arms tightened around her.

'Hannah?' he asked, his voice husky. She lifted her head from his shoulder and looked up into his face, her mind made up. He was ready and eager to start on his career and she had no right to hold him back, he had to come first with her.

'No, Timothy. You must take the position,' she said softly and offered her lips for his kiss.

Author's Note

The May 1926 General Strike in support of the miners lasted for ten days. The miners struggled on alone for seven months, but by November they had to admit defeat. The long months of stoppage availed them nothing; rather, it brought a great deal of distress and suffering, often the mothers and children suffering most. The Poor Relief and soup kitchens organised by the Miners' Federation and other philanthropic bodies prevented outright starvation in the pit villages and there were few instances of physical violence by the men. Labour Party members and other miners' leaders were often branded as communists and some imprisoned.

In the end, Durham County branch of the Miners' Federation of Great Britain, along with most other districts, recommended a return to work though a majority of the men wanted to struggle on. Some of these men, especially those who were considered to have been leaders, were not to obtain work again until the advent of the Second World War.

The miners who returned had to accept conditions that were worse than those they had had to endure before the lockout.

Also by Maggie Hope:

ELIZA'S CHILD

Torn between love and duty...

After the birth of their son, Eliza naively hopes her
husband Jack will put his gambling habit behind him
and become more responsible. But then he loses their
home and abandons her, leaving Eliza with no choice
but to return to her parents' house.

She inadvertently attracts the attention of the ruthless
mine owner Jonathan Moore. But can she sacrifice her
reputation to protect her son?

EBURY
PRESS

Also by Maggie Hope:

AN ORPHAN'S SECRET

Life is a long, tough struggle for Meg Maddison...

Growing up caring for her brothers after the death of
their mother, it is only her indomitable spirit that gets her
through the hard times. And when she marries and starts
a family of her own, it seems as if the hardships are over.

But the return of a darkly menacing figure from her
past threatens to destroy all she has fought for...

EBURY
PRESS

Also by Maggie Hope:

THE MINER'S GIRL

**A terrible choice between her sweetheart and
her reputation...**

Orphaned from birth, Mary Trent has always dreamed
of the day she can escape from poverty, and when she
meets the dashing young doctor Tom Gallagher, it
seems her prayers have been answered.

But an untimely pregnancy spells disaster and the threat
of returning to a life of destitution. Is a marriage of
convenience the only thing that can save her?

EBURY
PRESS

Also available from Ebury Press:

A MOTHER'S DUTY

by June Francis

A family at war...

Raising three boys and running the Arcadia Hotel
almost single-handed are enough to keep widow Kitty
Ryan busy. She has no time for romance – unless it's in
the form of a rare evening out at the local picture house.

Then along comes John Mcleod, bringing with him a second chance at happiness. However, Kitty finds her sons
unwilling to accept another man into their household.

Unless she can reunite her menfolk, the future looks set
to be that of a family in conflict, in a world on the eve
of war...

EBURY
PRESS

Also available from Ebury Press:

A DAUGHTER'S CHOICE

by June Francis

**Seventeen-year-old Katie is about to discover a
devastating family secret...**

Katie is the apple of her mother's eye and is being
groomed to take over the family business. But when
Celia, her natural mother, re-enters her life, her world is
turned completely upside down.

Tormented by her divided loyalties, Katie is plagued
by a question Celia refuses to answer – just who is her
real father?

EBURY
PRESS

Also available from Ebury Press:

A SISTER'S DUTY

by June Francis

She will do what it takes, for the sake of the children…

Rosie Kilshaw is only fifteen when her mother Violet is killed in a tragic accident, but as the oldest of her siblings, she vows to keep her family together, no matter what the sacrifice.

But as distant family members begin to resurface into their lives, Rosie quickly realizes that there is a lot more to parenting than she first thought. And when her estranged aunt Amelia decides to take them in, she will have a difficult choice to make…

EBURY
PRESS

Also available from Ebury Press:

WORKHOUSE ORPHANS

by Holly Green

All they have left is each other...

Life has always been tough for May and Gus Stirzaker.
Their father went away to sea never to return, and then
their mother falls victim to the typhus sweeping through
Liverpool. Regarded as orphans by the authorities, May
and Gus are sent to the Brownlow Hill Workhouse.

Like all workhouses, Brownlow is the last resort for the
poor and the destitute. May and Gus will have to rely
on each other more than ever if they are to survive the
hardships to come...

EBURY
PRESS

Also available from Ebury Press:

AMBULANCE GIRLS

by Deborah Burrows

On duty during London's Blitz...

As death and destruction fall from the skies day after day in the London Blitz, Australian ambulance driver Lily Brennan confronts the horror with bravery, intelligence, common sense and humour.

Although she must rely upon her colleagues to carry out her dangerous duties, Lily begins to suspect that someone at her Ambulance Station may be giving assistance to the enemy by disclosing secret information. Then her best friend, Jewish ambulance attendant David Levy, disappears in suspicious circumstances. Aided – and sometimes hindered – by David's school friend, a mysterious and attractive RAF pilot, Lily has to draw on all of her resources to find David, and negotiate the dangers that come from falling in love in a country far from home in a time of war…

EBURY
PRESS

Also available from Ebury Press:

WAR ORPHANS

by Lizzie Lane

"If at all possible, send or take your household animals into the country in advance of an emergency. If you cannot place them in the care of neighbours, it really is kindest to have them destroyed."

Joanna Ryan's father has gone off to war, leaving her in the care of her step-mother, a woman more concerned with having a good time than being any sort of parent to her.

But then she finds a puppy, left for dead, and Joanna's becomes determined to save him, sharing her meagre rations with him. But, in a time of war, pets are only seen as an unnecesary burden and she is forced to hide her new friend, Harry from her step-mother and the authorities. With bombs falling over Bristol and with the prospect of evacuation on the horizon can they keep stay together and keep each other safe?

EBURY
PRESS